MW01128510

# Prologue

Hearing his name being called, Mr Thomas Bennet marked his place in his book before laying it aside, fixing his eyes upon the door to the library as he patiently awaited the arrival of his wife. She appeared not a moment later, a determined and triumphant look in her eye which caused her husband to sigh inwardly.

"Yes, my dear?" he asked before she had a chance to speak. He noticed then that she held a letter in her hand.

"I have heard from my brother," she stated before adding a trifle impatiently, "At last. He is an abysmal correspondent," she complained as she came to sit in the chair beside his. "Six weeks I have been waiting - six weeks!"

"Shocking," Mr Bennet replied with more than a hint of sarcasm; when his wife's eyes narrowed dangerously he quickly asked, "What does he have to say for himself?"

"He has granted permission for Elizabeth to come and stay with us," Mrs Bennet revealed, looking very pleased with herself.

"I was not aware we had invited her," Mr Bennet replied slowly.

"*We* didn't," was the pointed reply. "*I* did. For the Season."

Mr Bennet could not suppress a groan upon hearing this.

"Not again Fanny," he complained. "You promised me after Jane that there would be no more matchmaking."

"Who said anything about matchmaking?" Mrs Bennet asked with all the appearance of innocence; her husband was not fooled and looked piercingly at her.

"You have invited our nineteen year old unmarried niece to spend the Season with us," he reminded her. "How can you claim to be anything but matchmaking?"

"Perhaps I simply wish for her to enjoy all the delights a Season in town has to offer," Mrs Bennet countered, as she made a show of rearranging her skirts. "And if she happens to meet an eligible man, well then I..." she trailed off as her husband's head fell back against his chair and he looked up at the ceiling, appealing to the Lord for strength. "I do not see why it is such a terrible thing," she stated, sounding quite hurt. "All I want is to see my nieces and nephews well married; is that so very awful?"

Feeling a little guilty, Mr Bennet reached out and took her hand.

"No, no, it isn't at all awful. I know you mean well, my dear."

Mrs Bennet dabbed at her eyes with her handkerchief.

"I only want them to be happy, as I would have our own children, had we been blessed."

"I know," Mr Bennet sighed, squeezing her hand. He smiled comfortingly when she met his eyes. "I understand, I really do. I did not mean to upset you."

"I know," Mrs Bennet patted his hand in an affectionate manner and returned his smile.

"So," Mr Bennet pronounced after a moment. "When are we to expect our niece?"

Mrs Bennet beamed at her husband in response, which did somewhat mollify him and lessened the feeling that he had given way far too easily. But then again, he thought with resignation, he always did where his wife was concerned.

"She travels here in January," Mrs Bennet replied, after briefly consulting her brother's letter. "And we shall leave for town soon afterwards; there will be much to do if we are to be ready in time."

"This *much to do* will involve a lot of shopping and a good deal of money, I presume," Mr Bennet noted dryly.

"Naturally," Mrs Bennet quipped in response. "Though not your money, I'm sure you'll be pleased to know. Edward shall be paying for everything," she added.

Mr Bennet nodded approvingly; he did not appreciate many of his brother-in-law's character traits, but at least the man seemed generous when it came to his daughters and the necessary funds. He would happily have footed the bill himself, for despite his protestations about the upcoming Season, he was very fond of his niece, but he was nevertheless pleased it would not be necessary.

"I must send my reply before Edward has a chance to change his mind," Mrs Bennet was saying as she rose from her seat. "And then I must write to Mrs Long and Mrs Philips. Oh, and Lady Lucas of course. Though perhaps Elizabeth will have written to Charlotte already." She seemed to realise that her husband was only half listening and, with an indulgent smile, kissed him on the forehead. "Thank you my dear."

"For what?" Mr Bennet asked, a little perplexed.

"Well, for granting your permission for Elizabeth to spend the Season with us, of course," his wife replied.

"It is nice of you to pretend I had any say in it at all, my dear," Mr Bennet teased. "But you are welcome."

ॐ☙☯

"Father, are you hiding?"

Eight year old Catherine Darcy regarded her father curiously as a number of expressions passed over his face before he replied.

"Whatever gave you that idea, Cathy?"

Catherine shrugged her shoulders and pointed out the obvious.

"You're sitting in the corner in the dark."

"I suppose I am," Fitzwilliam Darcy, the Duke of Farleigh replied - in truth, he had been hoping to avoid detection but he wasn't about to admit that to his daughter. She would want to know why. "I hadn't realised."

"But Mrs Hughes is always telling us that it's bad to read in the dark." Catherine frowned delicately as she said this. "It hurts your eyes, she says, though mine have never hurt before."

"Mrs Hughes is quite correct," Darcy stood up and went to his daughter. "And you must be a good girl and listen to her."

"I do listen to her," Catherine replied; she looked up at her very tall father and asked, "Does that mean I am a good girl?"

When you choose to be, Darcy thought wryly as he bent down to be at Catherine's level. He tapped her nose and smiled lovingly.

"You are a very good girl, my petite princess."

Catherine beamed and blushed prettily at the endearment.

"Where is your brother?" Darcy asked and was amused by the scowl which abruptly appeared on his daughter's face.

"I don't care," she replied petulantly and then began squirming when Darcy looked at her disapprovingly. "He was mean to me," she defended herself in a small voice.

Darcy sighed.

"What did he do this time?"

"He laughed at me," Catherine replied with a pout; when Darcy realised that was all she was going to say he asked her to explain a little more. "When I said I wanted to be as pretty as Lady Jane when I grow up he said I was silly thinking of such things because I'm still a baby. I'm not a baby, am I Papa? I'm a lady!"

"Yes you are," Darcy placated her, making a mental note to talk with his son. "And you are already as pretty as Lady Jane," he added, smiling when she looked delighted.

"Do you think so?" she asked and Darcy nodded.

"I know so," he stated confidently, chuckling to himself when Catherine threw her arms around him and kissed his cheek.

"I love you Papa," she whispered.

"I love you too," Darcy replied before pulling away and patting her on the back. "Now run along, back to Mrs Hughes. I will see you later."

He watched as his daughter hurried from the room, his smile lingering long after she had left. It was in this position that his friend, Sir Charles Bingley, found him.

"Ah ha!" He declared when he spotted Darcy. "Found you! You've been hiding again, haven't you," he accused playfully as he shut the door behind him and then advanced further into the room.

"I don't know what you mean," Darcy replied haughtily. "I have been here all morning."

"Then why didn't I see you when I checked here earlier?" Sir Charles challenged, still grinning.

"You obviously weren't paying attention," Darcy lied straight-faced; Sir Charles simply laughed again and Darcy rolled his eyes. "Very well, now that you have found me, what do you want?"

"I was simply wondering if you'd given any thought to what I'd said," Sir Charles replied lightly and Darcy shifted uneasily from one foot to the other.

"Charles," he began, but his friend cut him off.

"You know I won't let up until you say you'll join us," Sir Charles pointed out with a grin.

"Yes," Darcy sighed. "Hence why I was hiding," he added in an undertone - his words set his friend laughing again. "It's not that I don't want to join you," he began.

Sir Charles interrupted him again.

"It's been years since you've been to town, longer still since you've come for the Season. You never know, you might actually enjoy yourself this time. And everyone will be there - Jane and I, your sister and your cousin and their children, your aunt..."

"Yes, yes," Darcy held his hands up. "You've made your point."

"So you'll come?" Sir Charles asked, almost excitedly.

"What about the children?" Darcy made one last attempt to avoid what was beginning to feel like the inevitable. "You can't expect me to leave them for such a long..."

"I don't expect you to leave them at all," Sir Charles countered. "Bring them with you. Plenty of people do these days, you know. And we shall be taking Daniel so they shall have plenty of company."

Darcy sighed. He really did not relish the prospect of a Season in town, but he knew that Charles would not take no for an answer, and he also felt that he owed it to his friend. He had always been a quiet man, reserved and more inclined towards solitude than socialising; these tendencies had only increased since the death of his wife and were it not for Charles and a handful of other friends, Darcy probably would have retreated from society altogether. He knew he was a hard man to know, to be friends with, and if Charles really wanted him to go to London for the Season, it was perhaps the least that he could do.

"Very well," he said at last. "I'll go."

6

# Chapter 1

Elizabeth glanced to her left and right at her challengers, smiling to herself as she paused for a moment.

"*Onetwothree*, go!"

She took off at a run, taking full advantage of her head start. The three boys she was racing soon caught up with her though and, by the time they all sprinted across the finish line, she had been pushed into a (very respectable, she thought) second place. Bending over with her hands braced against her legs, Elizabeth smiled as she heard the cheers of the other children as they hurried over.

"A very impressive performance, Miss Gardiner," the children's teacher, Miss Lewis, congratulated her.

"I'm not as quick as I used to be," Elizabeth admitted as she straightened, still breathing heavily. She noted with some satisfaction that the three boys she'd raced were in much the same condition.

"Nevertheless," Miss Lewis replied. "You did very well to come second; I doubt I would have managed to run so far without falling!"

"I very nearly did so at one point!" Elizabeth laughed as she admitted. "I believe the only thing that kept me on my feet was the prospect of such mortification!"

Harry, one of the boys she had raced, came over to her and congratulated her.

"Well done, Miss Gardiner."

"Thank you, Harry," Elizabeth replied graciously. "And well done to you as well. I expected John to win," she confessed as the eldest boy and victor came over to join them, "but you very nearly bested me as well! Give it time and I daresay you will be fastest of all," she added and, as she had intended, the other boys, John included, began good-naturedly arguing over her prediction.

"Children, children!" Miss Lewis clapped her hands together and waited until she had everyone's attention. "We only have time for one more game. What would you suggest?"

After a good deal of deliberation the children decided they would play hide and seek and eagerly tried to coax Elizabeth into playing with them again; she laughed and shook her head.

"I am much too worn out! I shall sit with Miss Lewis and watch you play though."

Accepting her decision, the children set about electing who was to be the seeker whilst Elizabeth and Miss Lewis went to take a seat on a nearby bench.

"I shall miss this when I am in London," Elizabeth admitted after several moments of comfortable silence; she had always gotten along very well with Miss Lewis, and considered them friends of sorts. Friends as much as a school teacher and the daughter of a Viscount could be, at least. "I have enjoyed helping you so very much."

"I daresay the children will miss you as well," Miss Lewis replied kindly. "But it is only for a few months; you will return when the Season ends, after all," she pointed out lightly.

Not if my aunt has her way, Elizabeth thought with an eye roll. She was well aware of the purpose behind the invitation her aunt had extended - Mrs Bennet meant to find her a husband, and if Jane's experience was anything to go by, Elizabeth was going to have to keep her wits about her, else she would find herself engaged before she could say "I would like a husband". And she would, like a husband that is. She just worried that her ideas about who would make her a good husband didn't necessarily correspond with her aunt's. She loved Mrs Bennet dearly, and she and Mr Bennet had been very good to her, but her aunt was a firmly established member of the ton and as such shared their views on marriage and men. And whilst they all concerned themselves with things like wealth, family and titles, Elizabeth cared about only one thing - she wanted to marry for love.

Her elder sister Jane had married for love, as had their parents and Elizabeth wanted that for herself. She wanted a happy marriage. She wanted to love her husband and for him to love her in return. She wanted them to be friends, to share their secrets and worries, to make each other laugh. She wanted to have children with a man who would be a good father, who would love and cherish each and every child she gave him. Was that too much to ask? Elizabeth let out a breathy laugh at her fanciful musings, fully aware that yes, it probably was too much to ask.

"Miss Gardiner?"

Elizabeth blinked a few times and looked at Miss Lewis.

"Forgive me, I was lost in my thoughts."

"That's quite alright," Miss Lewis assured her. "I was just saying that it is close to three o'clock."

"Already?" Elizabeth asked, glancing up at the sky. "Then I had best head home."

She stood up and Miss Lewis called the children over to say goodbye. Several of the younger ones hugged her and protested that they did not want her to go, and by the time she was finally able to leave she knew she was going to be late home. Not overly concerned, Elizabeth decided to tarry a little longer and spent another hour calling in on the wives and families of some of her father's tenants, as well as the elderly Reverend Baker.

"I do hope you enjoy yourself," he told her as he saw her to the door after they had shared a cup of tea. "And give my best to your sister when you see her."

"I will," Elizabeth promised and with a final wave began the short walk from the rectory to her home.

Evening was fast descending and there was a decided chill in the air as she walked briskly through the park, pulling her light coat tighter around herself. She glimpsed the tower through a break in the trees, smiling at the way the setting sun cast a glow upon the stonework and each of its windows. Longbourn had been the home of the Viscount Darwen for many generations, and the house was beginning to show its age. The tower in particular, as the oldest part of the structure, was in need of repair, as was a worryingly large portion of the roof of the main house, and several of the windows needed replacing. It was a draughty place, cold and damp in places, and falling apart at the seams. It was home, though, and Elizabeth loved it even if she was aware of its many shortcomings. There were times, however, when she wished that her father was not such an impractical man, that he would see to the necessary repairs *before* the roof collapsed down on all their heads. There was no guarantee, though, that the Viscount would act even then, as long as his precious study remained intact.

Pushing such disloyal thoughts from her mind Elizabeth picked up her pace and hurried to the house, entering through the kitchens and exchanging a few words on her way through with Mrs Braddock, their cook, and the other servants busily preparing dinner. She was rushing now because she had not returned when she said she would, and because her father would become agitated if she failed to appear on time for dinner. He was an interesting man, her father. Eccentric, certainly, but a little odd as well. Elizabeth was quite used to his many quirks and adjusted her behaviour accordingly, but she could not claim to understand him. Indeed, the only person who could have claimed with any degree of certainty to have understood Edward Gardiner, Viscount Darwen, was his wife and Elizabeth and Jane's mother, Madeline. She had sadly passed away though, and Jane had married, leaving Elizabeth to cope with their father alone. They muddled along together quite well, happy in their way, though Elizabeth would admit to feeling a little lonely at times if she was pressed. She remembered fondly the days when the four of them had lived as a family, not quite normal but as close to it as Elizabeth had ever known. She missed those times more than she liked to admit, and did her best to keep herself occupied whilst her father hid himself away from the rest of the world in his study or in his greenhouse.

Elizabeth entered her room to find her dress already laid out for her and her maid, Wilson, waiting impatiently for her arrival.

"What time do you call this, missy?"

"Forgive me," Elizabeth replied with a smile, already shrugging out of her coat. "I lost track of time with the children, and then I paid a call to Reverend Baker on my way home."

"Hmm," was the only reply and Elizabeth suppressed another smile.

Wilson had worked at Longbourn for nearly thirty years, beginning as a maid and working her way up until she eventually became lady's maid to Elizabeth's mother. Elizabeth had still only been a child when her mother had died, too young for a maid of her own, but her father had kept Wilson on, seemingly realising that his daughter would be comforted by her continued presence. It was because Wilson had known her since the day she was born and she had been such a faithful servant, that Elizabeth allowed such apparently disrespectful behaviour to go unpunished. She was in truth rather fond of Wilson who, despite her tendency to scold her mistress, was fiercely loyal and had a heart of gold - though she would never admit it. And her crotchetiness made Elizabeth laugh.

Proving her value yet again, Wilson had Elizabeth dressed and ready for dinner with time to spare, so that when she breezed into the drawing room to join her father she was the picture of composure.

"You didn't come home when you said you would," were the words her father greeted her with.

"I know, I'm sorry," she soothed. "I was with Reverend Baker and decided to stay another hour."

Her father looked mollified.

"How is he? Well? I must invite him here, I have found a passage in Pickard which I require help translating. Tomorrow, I will invite him tomorrow. Or perhaps Tuesday. Or perhaps...what day is it today?"

"It is Thursday, Papa," Elizabeth replied patiently.

Yet another of her father's quirks - he could speak four languages, had read more books than Elizabeth had even heard of and was an amateur scientist and yet he often struggled to keep track of what day it was, where he had left his glasses and occasionally, where he was. Elizabeth reasoned that these difficulties were one of the reasons her father put such stock in good time keeping. Time was the one thing he had no trouble with and he had always been most insistent that his family and household run according to a carefully regimented system. Elizabeth and Jane had both resented the restrictions when they were growing up but as she had gotten older, Elizabeth had found ways to circumvent some of the rules. The servants aided her in this because as far as they were concerned, as long as their master was happy, what he didn't know couldn't hurt him.

"Tomorrow then," her father decided before offering Elizabeth a glass of sherry to enjoy before dinner - another tradition they strictly adhered to.

"You remember, don't you, that I leave tomorrow?" Elizabeth questioned as she sat down.

"Of course I remember," her father replied a trifle sharply. "Not likely to forget a thing like that, am I?"

"No, of course not," Elizabeth agreed at once, just to placate him.

"You are all ready to leave, I presume?"

"Not quite," Elizabeth replied. "I have more packing to do yet, though there is still time."

Her father hummed his agreement and they sat across from one another in silence, sipping their drinks and listening to the ticking of the clock on the mantelpiece.

"Damned nuisance, this trip of yours you know," her father pronounced suddenly, surprising Elizabeth. "The timing could not be worse."

"In what way, Father?" Elizabeth asked, restraining the urge to remind her father that he had been the one to grant his permission for her to go.

"You are away all spring," her father replied. "I don't know what I was thinking, I have need of you."

Elizabeth bit back a sigh. It would have been nice for her father to be sorry to see her go because he would miss her; his first thought, as always, was for the inconvenience her leaving would cause him.

"I'm sure you will manage very well without me, Father," she told him firmly. "And I will return in June."

Her father did not seem pleased with this reply and frowned.

"Perhaps I should simply find someone else to help me."

"Perhaps you should," Elizabeth granted evenly, refusing to rise to the bait. The days when she confused being useful with being loved had long since passed, and she was not worried about being replaced. "I'm sure it will not be difficult."

Fortunately, before the discussion could escalate further, a footman arrived to announce dinner.

With a deftness borne of many years of practice, Elizabeth steered the conversation away from her upcoming trip and towards subjects much more agreeable to herself and her father, so that dinner passed by quite pleasantly. The desire for more stimulating company and conversation was one of the main reasons Elizabeth was looking forward to her trip so very much, besides the obvious delight she anticipated at seeing her aunt and uncle, and sister and brother-in-law again. A part of her felt that she should be sorry to leave her father for so long, but she was honest enough to admit to herself that she did not feel that way at all. And if that made her a bad daughter, then so be it; she had never been one to pretend to feelings she did not have.

As soon as dinner was over, her father stood up and announced, "I have work I must get on with. I shall say goodnight."

"Good night Father," Elizabeth replied and watched as he left the room and she was left to her own devices for the rest of the evening.

Desirous of company, she left the dining room and went to the front hall, donning her coat and stepping outside regardless of the frigidly cold night. With a quick step she went to the stables, still dimly lit by a single torch, and entered through the side door. She smiled when she found Greg, one of the stable hands, waiting patiently for her. They were only a year apart in age and he had lived on the estate for as long as Elizabeth could remember. Growing up together they had had many adventures and Elizabeth thought of him more as a friend than a servant.

Moving to one of the stalls, Elizabeth slipped inside and was immediately nuzzled by the horse within, a beautiful mare with a dappled grey coat, most aptly named Dot.

"Hello, my sweet," Elizabeth greeted her horse with an affectionate pat and a treat which Greg handed to her. "I've come to say goodnight, and to see that you are wrapped up warm."

"You take better care of her than you do of yourself, Miss Lizzy," Greg observed with a smile at the thin coat Elizabeth had on, standing next to Dot with her thick blanket.

Elizabeth simply smiled in response before turning back to her horse, speaking to her in low tones as Greg found something to busy himself with.

"I will miss you, sweet," Elizabeth breathed as Dot sniffed and then tried to eat some of her hair. "I would take you with me, but I fear I won't have time to ride you. I would not wish to leave you languishing in the stables for weeks on end."

She spent a few minutes with her horse before stepping out of the stall, making sure to firmly shut the door behind her as Dot tried to follow her.

"I'll take good care of her," Greg assured Elizabeth as he came back over to join her.

"I know," Elizabeth replied with a smile, stroking Dot's nose. "I'll just miss her."

"And we'll all miss you," Greg pointed out with a grin when Elizabeth looked a little shy.

Greg knew that he was not exaggerating, as almost all of her father's tenants and servants were extremely fond of Elizabeth and would genuinely miss her. She had taken on the role of mistress since the elder Miss Gardiner's marriage and had done a fine job of it, seeing to the wellbeing and happiness of the tenants and their families, and generally being a pleasure to work for. She was perhaps fighting a losing battle against the Viscount's negligence, who was as lackadaisical a landlord as ever there was, but her diligence and commitment were noted and appreciated by all.

"I expect you to have some happy news for me when I return, Greg," Elizabeth told him after a moment, eager to move the subject away from herself and smiling playfully at him.

Greg narrowly avoided blushing as he mumbled, "I'll do my best."

Elizabeth smiled to herself but resisted making any comment, taking pity on her friend. He had been waiting patiently to offer for a local girl, his sweetheart from childhood, and had just recently been made head stable hand. He hoped one day to be master and finally felt himself in a position to offer marriage - all he had to do was actually ask Lucy, something which he had been putting off for the last few weeks.

"Perhaps you will have some news of your own," he pointed out boldly, laughing when Elizabeth glared playfully at him.

"I will have you know I intend to resist my aunt's matchmaking efforts to the utmost of my ability," she informed him confidently. "I have no intention of finding myself engaged to some ageing lord, or pompous dandy. Any form of dandy, really," she amended with a smile.

They chatted for a few minutes more before the cold finally got the better of Elizabeth and she said goodnight and goodbye to Greg before heading back to the house. She went up to her room, entering to find Wilson putting a few more items of clothing into a case and her cat, Deirdre, lounging on her bed. They were both watching one another with matching expressions of distaste.

"Wretched creature."

Deirdre, her hackles raised, hissed in response to Wilson's muttered comment and Elizabeth felt compelled to intervene before war broke out. She walked over to her bed and sat down, letting her cat climb onto her lap as she asked Wilson, indicating the open case.

"Is that the last one?

"It is," Wilson replied. "Though you still have to decide whatever else you wish to take with you," she reminded her mistress lightly. "Books and the like. Are you taking any art supplies with you?"

"Of course," Elizabeth replied with a definite nod.

"Do you think you will have much opportunity for drawing?" Wilson asked dubiously.

Elizabeth smiled.

"I shall make time."

"I'm sure you shall," Wilson replied with an amused smile before going back to her work. "I expect it will be nice for you to be able to sketch something besides plants," she commented after a moment.

"Yes," Elizabeth admitted, though she said no more, not wishing to pursue that line of conversation any further. She preferred to keep her problems with her father as private as possible, though Wilson sometimes became the outlet for her frustrations. Taking the hint, Wilson asked her about her day and Elizabeth spent the next half an hour chatting quite happily about the children and the tenants' families she had seen. Once the packing was complete, Wilson helped her prepare for bed and said goodnight, for though it was still only early they had an even earlier start in the morning.

ಶೃಶ

Mrs Bennet sprang from her chair and hurried to the window upon hearing the approach of a carriage.

"At last, she is here! I thought they would never arrive!"

Mr Bennet rose to his feet as well and followed his wife out into the hallway at a much more sedate pace, smiling to himself at her excitable behaviour. They descended the steps and stood waiting for the carriage to pull up.

"She is early," he could not resist pointing out after consulting his pocket watch. "They have made very good time; it should have been another hour at least."

Mrs Bennet gave no sign of having heard him and her husband smiled at her stubborn refusal to show any outward reaction to his teasing. He lightly put his arm around her waist and pressed an affectionate kiss to her temple before turning to smile at his niece as she was assisted down from the carriage by a footman.

"Lizzy!" Mrs Bennet greeted her effusively, rushing forward as soon as Elizabeth had safely stepped down, wrapping her up in an enthusiastic embrace. "My darling, how good it is to see you! It has been far, far too long."

"Hello, Aunt," Elizabeth replied with a laugh as she returned the gesture. "It is lovely to see you too."

"Fanny, do not crush the poor girl," Mr Bennet joked as he observed the pair. He stepped forward when his wife released their niece and pressed a kiss to her cheek. "Welcome, child. It is lovely to see you again."

"Thank you," Elizabeth replied with a bright smile as she looked between her uncle and aunt; she had always been very fond of the Bennets.

"Are you hungry Lizzy? Shall I have something prepared for you now? Or would you like to rest?"

"I should like to change my gown," Elizabeth interrupted gently. "But I am not at all hungry, or tired. I slept in the carriage and we had a fine luncheon at one of the inns where we changed horses. Thank you, though, for offering."

"You're perfectly welcome darling," Mrs Bennet replied. "But come along, let me show you to your room. You can change and refresh yourself and then come and join us in the drawing room when you are ready."

Whilst his wife and Elizabeth climbed the stairs, Mr Bennet returned to the drawing room to await their return. He was sat perusing the paper when his wife appeared and returned her happy smile.

"She has grown since we last saw her," Mrs Bennet pronounced as she came to sit with him.

"I thought so too," Mr Bennet replied with a nod. "And she looks more like her mother than ever."

Mrs Bennet nodded and then sighed lightly.

"She is a beautiful girl, isn't she?"

"Yes," Mr Bennet agreed with a slight laugh. "Though in truth no longer just a 'girl'. She has become a young woman."

"I cannot wait to introduce her," Mrs Bennet admitted, her expression full of anticipation. "I am determined she shall be a success."

"Not too determined, I hope, my dear," Mr Bennet cautioned; he wished his niece to enjoy her first real Season in town and suspected she would not do so if his wife was too heavy-handed.

Mrs Bennet ignored the comment.

"It is long overdue; she made her bow two years ago and showed such promise then. If only my brother hadn't fallen ill, she might even be married now, or at the very least engaged."

Mr Bennet sighed and pointedly returned to his paper, ignoring the indignant noise his wife made at such rude behaviour. When Elizabeth joined them she found them sitting in stony silence and her brows rose slightly; at her appearance, however, both her aunt and uncle smiled broadly and warmly invited her to take a seat and speak with them.

"How was your journey?" Her aunt asked first after Elizabeth had sat down across from them.

"Quite pleasant," Elizabeth assured her. "It was an early start, to be sure, but the weather was fine and the roads were good. I feel very well, having come so far."

"Oh good, I'm glad to hear it," Mrs Bennet replied positively, but she still added, "though I suggest you retire early tonight anyway."

"And how is your father? Well, I hope."

"He is very well," Elizabeth replied evenly. "Occupied with his work."

"He will miss you, I am sure," Mrs Bennet put in, unwittingly sounding a tad defensive. She knew her husband did not think much of her brother.

"Yes," Elizabeth agreed with a smile that hid her true feelings on the matter. "And I him."

"I must admit I was a little surprised he gave his permission for you to come to town with us," Mr Bennet confessed, ignoring the sharp look his wife sent him.

"So was I," Elizabeth admitted with a light laugh. "But I did not question my good fortune! I am so looking forward to the coming months."

"As are we," Mrs Bennet replied, looking much happier with the new topic. "We shall have a marvellous time. We received our first invitation of the Season but two days ago."

"So soon?" Elizabeth exclaimed, sharing a look with her uncle who simply rolled his eyes.

"It is for the Llewellyn-Jones ball," Mrs Bennet informed her. "It is *the* event of the start of the Season, and anyone who is anyone will be there. It is the perfect occasion for your re-introduction into society."

"And with that, any chance of your looking forward to it is effectively destroyed," Mr Bennet commented wryly and Elizabeth laughed.

"I am sure it will be delightful," she stated confidently. "I have every faith in your ability to prepare me for the occasion, Aunt," she told Mrs Bennet fondly.

The lady shot her husband a triumphant look before turning back to her niece.

"I have already begun making plans for when we arrive in town. Our first concern is your wardrobe, of course, but there is so much more for us to see to before the Season starts."

"For my sake," Mr Bennet put in, "I hope you will leave further discussion of the details until I am not present."

"Well, we could save our discussion for the carriage ride to town..." Mrs Bennet suggested lightly, trailing off when her husband huffed and, taking his paper with him, hurriedly quit the room. She turned to Elizabeth with a wicked smile and her niece laughed.

"Now, where were we?" she asked, and Elizabeth thought to herself that she was truly going to enjoy the next few months staying with the Bennets.

ℰℭ

Stepping out of the carriage in front of the Bennet's townhouse, Elizabeth looked up at the imposing façade and smiled to herself; she remembered when she had come for her debut two years ago, and how nervous she had felt stepping out of the carriage then. Today she felt nothing but a pleasing sense of anticipation and entered the house with a confident step.

True to her word, Mrs Bennet had arranged a number of appointments in town for her niece and Elizabeth was left with little choice but to trail in her aunt's wake as Mrs Bennet bustled from shop to shop, leading her niece through what felt like the whole of London in her quest to see Elizabeth properly fitted out for the Season.

By the end of their third week in town Elizabeth was exhausted, suitably impressed and awed by her aunt's superior fortitude and possessed of a new appreciation for Mr Bennet and his patience with his wife. Fortunately, with the most pressing task of Elizabeth's new wardrobe behind them, Mrs Bennet relaxed somewhat and allowed Elizabeth some rest in between excursions, and even went so far as to allow her niece to have a say in where they would travel to next. A shop on Lincoln Street, which specialised in art supplies, was one of their first ports of call, followed by Flannery's for music and McCarthy's for books. With these purchases, Mrs Bennet at last deemed their shopping complete, and her niece ready for the Season, and not a day too soon, for the very next morning they had a most welcome visit.

ℰℭ

"Jane!"

Lady Jane Bingley laughed as her younger sister practically launched herself at her, embracing Elizabeth with equal enthusiasm as her husband and their son watched with matching smiles.

"Good morning, Lizzy," Jane greeted her sister calmly, once she had been released, pulling back a little to see the changes the past six months had wrought in Elizabeth's appearance.

"It is *so good* to see you," Elizabeth told her sister earnestly, as she squeezed her a little tighter. "It has been too long."

Jane expressed her agreement and Elizabeth turned to smile at her brother-in-law and nephew.

"And it is wonderful to see you both again, gentlemen."

Sir Charles and Daniel both smiled, as the former replied.

"I shan't demand such an enthusiastic greeting as the one you gave my wife, but I should like at the very least to be able to embrace my sister."

Elizabeth was happy to oblige him and gave him a quick peck on the cheek for good measure before turning to her nephew, Daniel, who executed a perfectly respectable bow for a seven year old. Elizabeth responded with a very ladylike curtsey before catching Daniel in her arms and pulling him in for a hug. Both Jane and Sir Charles laughed as their son blushed, but nevertheless returned the gesture. Mr and Mrs Bennet by this time had appeared at the front door and Elizabeth followed the Bingleys inside, chatting happily with her nephew as he told her about his latest adventures. Once in the morning room and after the usual pleasantries had been exchanged, Mr Bennet offered to take Daniel with him to the library, giving the ladies a chance to talk undisturbed. Sir Charles also went with them and Jane, Elizabeth and Mrs Bennet found themselves alone.

"I suppose you have completed all the necessary preparations for the Season," Jane began, looking between her sister and their aunt.

"Yes, though the last item was only purchased yesterday," Mrs Bennet revealed, sharing a smile with Elizabeth.

"Indeed!" Jane replied. "But I thought you had been in town for some time?"

"We arrived more than three weeks ago," Mrs Bennet admitted, "but there was much we had to purchase. There was little - please don't take this personally, Lizzy - but there was little of Elizabeth's wardrobe that would have been suitable to wear here in town; we had to start almost from scratch."

Jane frowned delicately as she turned to her sister.

"Father does set aside an allowance for your needs, surely?"

"Of course," Elizabeth assured her sister lightly. "I was well provided for, and were I still at home my existing wardrobe would easily have sufficed. Meryton is a long way from London, however," she concluded playfully, "and my gowns, whilst perfectly serviceable, were not quite fashionable enough. At least our aunt did not deem them so," she added with a smile at Mrs Bennet, "and in such matters she has my complete trust."

"I would not say *complete* trust," Mrs Bennet pointed out, smiling as well. "You refused to oblige me on a number of points as I remember, my dear."

Elizabeth laughed and Jane looked between them.

"On which points?"

"Oh, usually to do with the choice of colour for my gowns," Elizabeth replied lightly. "I do not care what anyone says, orange is a hideous colour and nothing and no-one will ever convince me to wear it."

Jane regarded her sister thoughtfully for a moment.

"Actually, with your colouring it might suit."

"Never!" Elizabeth declared with temerity, and then dissolved into playful laughter.

Jane and Mrs Bennet shared a smile before the latter chose to move the conversation along.

"You and Sir Charles shall be at the Llewellyn-Jones ball, won't you?" she asked Jane.

"Of course," her niece replied. "We would never miss Lizzy's official re-introduction into society."

Elizabeth rolled her eyes.

"I wish people would stop calling it that; you can hardly *reintroduce* someone whom no-one remembers being introduced to in the first place. I likely faded into the background along with all the other debutantes when I made my bow."

"I promise you, my dear," Mrs Bennet stated, "that that will not be the case this time. I shall see to it that you are a success."

*I am not entirely sure that that is a good thing*, Elizabeth thought to herself as she imagined the lengths her aunt would go to to ensure her "success".

"In fact," Mrs Bennet went on. "I have been meaning to ask you something, Jane."

"Oh yes?" Jane replied evenly, though Elizabeth thought she could detect a note of caution and smiled inwardly; obviously she was not the only one wary of Mrs Bennet's plans.

"Yes. I heard a rumour," Mrs Bennet began, "that a certain friend of your husbands is coming to town for the Season. Is it true?"

"It is," Jane confirmed reluctantly. "Though I am curious as to how you came to know this."

Mrs Bennet waved her hand carelessly.

"I simply knew who to ask."

"I shall never cease to marvel, Aunt," Elizabeth stated dryly, "at your talent for knowing everyone else's business whilst remaining perfectly charming and inoffensive. It really is a gift."

"Oh, thank you, dear," Mrs Bennet replied and Elizabeth bowed her head to hide her smile. "Anyway, I was hoping it would be possible for us, with the Duke's help, to arrange for Elizabeth to dance the first set at the Llewellyn-Jones ball with his cousin, Mr Wickham."

"Mr Wickham?" Jane repeated with surprise. She glanced at her sister and then back at her aunt. "I am not entirely sure that is a good idea."

Watching her sister closely and observing her reaction to the gentleman's name, Elizabeth was suddenly wildly curious about this Mr Wickham.

"Why ever not?" Mrs Bennet asked. "How better to announce your sister's arrival in town than to have her stand up with one of the best catches of the last few Seasons? Her reputation would be established in an instant."

"I'm quite certain the reputation she would gain from spending any time with Mr Wickham is not at all what I would want for my little sister," Jane stated with surprising bluntness for her.

"But Jane," Mrs Bennet pointed out with a smile. "You know what they say - reformed rakes make the best husbands."

"I'm not entirely sure I would like to find myself married to a rake," Elizabeth spoke up. "Reformed or otherwise."

"Well, no," Mrs Bennet hesitated. "And I'm not really suggesting that Mr Wickham is a rake or that you *marry* him, only," she realised she'd approached the issue all wrong and began again. "I only thought that it would be advantageous to make an immediate impression upon everyone."

"I think we should simply trust that Lizzy will make an impression all by herself," Jane responded. "She does not need a man, and certainly not a man like Mr Wickham, to help her do that."

# Chapter 2

By the time the day of the Llewellyn-Jones ball finally rolled around, Elizabeth had already been introduced to more people than she had ever cared to meet, and the Season had barely even begun! That being said, she had met some perfectly charming people over the last few weeks, and without a doubt her most pleasant encounter had been with the Duke of Farleigh and his two children. She had met Sir Charles's friend before, though many years earlier when she was still just a child, and she had vaguely remembered him as a tall, quiet man. He and his children had called on Sir Charles and Jane when Elizabeth herself had been visiting her sister.

೫ംവ

As the two sisters sat together in the parlour, Jane laughing as Elizabeth related to her some amusing story from the past week, the butler entered and announced, "His Grace, the Duke of Farleigh has arrived, Ma'am, and has requested a moment of your time. Shall I show him in?"

"Yes, please do so," Jane replied and Elizabeth shot her sister a curious look as the butler departed. "He has an appointment with Charles; I suspect he has brought his son and daughter along with him. Daniel so enjoys playing with them," Jane explained just before they were joined by the Duke himself, accompanied by his two children, just as Jane had predicted.

"Good afternoon, Your Grace," Jane greeted her husband's friend with a kind smile. "And good afternoon, children. I hope you are all well?"

"We are very well, thank you," the Duke replied as his son and daughter responded in kind, their eyes on Elizabeth. "And yourself?"

"I am well also," Jane replied; she looked at Elizabeth with a smile and added, "And happy too, now that I have seen Elizabeth again. Do you remember my sister, Sir?"

Elizabeth smiled as the Duke turned to look at her; he studied her for a moment before frowning slightly.

"I'm afraid I do not recall."

"I am not at all surprised," Elizabeth replied playfully before Jane had a chance. "The last time we met was at Jane and Sir Charles' wedding, and even were your memory that good I was still only 11 at the time and undoubtedly looked somewhat different!"

The Duke's frown cleared and he nodded.

"I do remember you, now that I think about it."

"Oh dear," Elizabeth teased. "I had hoped you would not. I have reached an age, you see, when I like not to think of myself as I once was as a child. It is rather embarrassing," she concluded with a light laugh, smiling brightly at the Duke and his two children, both of whom smiled in response.

"Speaking of children," Jane interrupted. "Daniel is upstairs and will have finished his lessons; if you wish to join him, I'm sure he would be more than happy to see you," she said to the children, who both looked up at their father for permission.

"Very well, off you trot. I shall fetch you when it is time to go home."

His son and daughter excused themselves with a polite bow and a slightly wobbly curtsey and left the adults to themselves. As soon as they were gone Elizabeth smiled at the Duke.

"Your children seem delightful, Your Grace."

"Thank you," he replied quietly, though Elizabeth could tell he was pleased with the compliment. "They are very fond of your nephew."

"And he of them, I assure you," Jane replied before asking, "Will you sit with us, or do you wish to join my husband? He is unoccupied at present, I believe."

"Then I had best keep my appointment with him," the Duke replied. He bowed and then straightened, looking at Elizabeth as he said, "It was a pleasure meeting you again, Miss Gardiner."

"And you as well, Your Grace," Elizabeth responded. "Perhaps you and Sir Charles will join us once you have completed your business?" she suggested lightly and, though he seemed a little surprised, the Duke nodded and then took his leave.

The sisters resumed their seats and Elizabeth turned to Jane.

"He seems a pleasant gentleman, if perhaps a little reticent. Not at all who I would have chosen for your husband's friend," she admitted playfully and Jane nodded her agreement.

"They have always gotten on remarkably well, given their differences."

"How old are his children?" Elizabeth asked.

"James is thirteen and Catherine is eight," Jane replied.

"And their mother?" Elizabeth enquired delicately.

"She passed away soon after Catherine was born," Jane revealed quietly, and Elizabeth was silent for a moment with sympathy for the Duke and his two young children.

"How sad," she said eventually, and once again Jane nodded.

"I only met her on a few occasions, but the Duchess was a delicate woman and her health was never good," Jane revealed after a moment. "I do not think it came as a surprise when she passed away, though it was, as you say, very sad for the Duke and his children. They are a delightful pair though," she concluded with a smile, "and His Grace positively dotes on them."

"I am glad to hear it," Elizabeth replied in a playful tone, though her smile did not reach her eyes. "I do so like a man who loves his children. I think I will go and look in on them," she went on before Jane could comment. "It would be nice, I think, to be properly introduced. Do send someone to fetch me if Sir Charles and His Grace decide to join you."

Elizabeth stood up and, after a slight hesitation, Jane smiled and nodded. Quickly leaving the room, Elizabeth climbed the stairs up to where she could hear the children. She stood at the door to the playroom, leaning against the frame with her arms crossed, quietly observing the scene with a smile on her face, as yet unnoticed by any within. Daniel and Catherine were sat together on the floor, playing with blocks and figures, absorbed in the fairy tale world of their own creation. Elizabeth was certain she heard the names Arthur and Galahad and stifled a chuckle; Sir Charles had obviously been delighting his son with yet more tales of the Knights of the Round Table. Noticing James sat off to one side, not participating in the other's game, Elizabeth's smile faded slightly and she wondered why he did not join in. Did he feel too old? Thirteen was perhaps a little old for such things. Just as she was pondering this, Daniel happened to look up and see her.

"Aunt Lizzy!"

"Hello Dan," Elizabeth straightened and entered the room. "I thought I'd come and say hello. Won't you introduce me to your friends?"

"This is Catherine," Daniel obliged her with a careless flap of his hand in the girl's direction. "And this is her brother, James. This is my Aunt," he told his two friends.

"Everyone calls me Lizzy," Elizabeth told the two children. "And you can too, if you like."

"Yes, please," Catherine replied happily. "Papa and James and everyone call me Cathy."

Elizabeth smiled and gave a playful little curtsey before turning to Catherine's brother.

"And what shall I call you, young man?" she asked James with her friendliest smile, having noted that the elder boy had yet to say a word.

"He always insists that everyone call him James," Cathy replied before her brother could. "He's so boring."

James glared at his little sister as Elizabeth suppressed a smile.

"Then James it is. It's a pleasure to meet you. You may call me Elizabeth, or Miss Gardiner if you prefer."

"Pleased to meet you, Miss Gardiner," James replied and Elizabeth was charmed by the impression of how like his father he was, and how grown up he seemed for his age.

"Would you like to play a game?" she asked, as she came and sat beside him at the little table. "I'm sure there are some cards around here somewhere. We could play bridge, or loo? I'm not very good at either I'm afraid," she admitted with a light laugh. "But we could give it a try."

"Do you know piquet?" James asked a little shyly. "My father is teaching it to me."

"Of course," Elizabeth replied with a smile; she stood up and searched out a pack of cards before returning to her seat. "Let us see how well I remember the rules."

They sat down to their game and Elizabeth did her best to get to know James, keeping up a steady stream of chatter throughout their game, asking him a variety of questions and encouraging him to do the same.

"Have you been in town for very long?" she asked at one point.

"No," James replied, his eyes on his cards. "Not very long. We came with Sir Charles and Lady Bingley."

"Oh, of course," James looked up with a puzzled frown and Elizabeth explained, "I remember my sister telling me that you all were guests at Netherfield. It had slipped my mind; not surprising really, when one considers the sheer volume of information I have been bombarded with in the last few weeks."

"What information?" James asked curiously as Elizabeth thought about her turn.

"I am here for the Season," she explained. "And my aunt has been drilling me in all the necessary things a lady must know before being let loose on society. I could tell you the names of all the principle performers at the theatre, the stars of the opera, the programme of performances and shows for the upcoming Season, where it is best to attend said performances and why, the balls and dinner parties already planned for the next month or so, who is hosting them, their connections, whether they have any single, eligible young men in their immediate family, the character and tastes of said gentlemen. I could go on, but I see you have understood my predicament," Elizabeth concluded merrily as James continued to laugh at her teasing.

"And I thought that geometry and mathematics were a trial!" he joked when he had caught his breath. "I believe that your lot is worse even than mine."

"Oh, undoubtedly," Elizabeth replied, "for at least what you are obliged to learn has some practical application. My lessons have no value whatsoever."

"Besides helping you find a husband," James pointed out wryly and Elizabeth, after a moment of stunned silence, burst out laughing.

"I think you and I are going to be great friends," she predicted happily and James smiled shyly and looked quite pleased.

"What are you laughing about, Lizzy?" Daniel asked as he and Cathy took a break from their game.

"Silly things," Elizabeth replied. "Have you managed to rescue the princess from the dragon?"

"Of course," Daniel grinned. "King Arthur is always triump...triumpham..."

"Triumphant," Elizabeth supplied kindly. "As he should be - for good always triumphs over evil. Especially when the outcome rests in your hands," she added playfully and James chuckled lightly - the comment went over the heads of the other two, however.

"Shall we go down now?" Catherine asked. "We could find Lady Jane."

"Father has told you about bothering Lady Bingley, Cathy," James pointed out with a slight frown. He looked at Elizabeth and explained, "She knows she is not supposed go to Lady Bingley unless she is called for."

"I can't imagine my sister would mind a little company," Elizabeth replied diplomatically. "And I shall take you all down, so Cathy will simply be doing as she is told."

Catherine beamed at this response before shooting her brother a smug look; James was old enough not to rise to the bait, however, and simply set about clearing the cards he and Elizabeth had been using. Elizabeth helped Daniel and Catherine pack away the things they had been playing with before shepherding the two of them from the room.

"Cathy is fond of my sister, then?" Elizabeth surmised as the four of them walked down the stairs.

James smiled ruefully as he replied.

"She thinks Lady Bingley is 'as beautiful as a princess' and likes nothing more than to sit beside her and pretend to be a lady herself."

"How sweet," Elizabeth responded with an affectionate smile at the little girl in front of her, watching as she and Daniel held hands and carefully descended the stairs. "And who can blame her? My sister is rather beautiful."

"No more so than you," James replied with a nonchalant shrug and Elizabeth smiled to herself at his frank, if erroneous, assessment of her appearance. She predicted that it would not be very many years before he was unable to look at a woman in such a rational, objective way.

"Well it is very kind of you to say so," she replied eventually just as they reached the ground floor and turned to go to the parlour where Elizabeth had left her sister.

"James."

Elizabeth turned to find the Duke striding towards them. Looking between father and son she smiled at the resemblance between them - James was, in almost every respect, simply a younger version of his father.

"Hello, Father," James replied formally, though his tone was warm.

"Hello again, Miss Gardiner," the Duke greeted Elizabeth before turning back to his son. "Where is your sister? I'm afraid it is time we were leaving."

"She is with Daniel," Elizabeth replied before James could. "We were about to go and sit with my sister."

"Shall I fetch her, Father?" James asked and when the Duke nodded he left to do just that, leaving Elizabeth alone with his father.

"Your son and I have been playing piquet," she revealed, for want of anything better to say. "Well, attempting to," she amended with a smile. "Daniel and your daughter were playing quite boisterously at our feet and our concentration was subsequently disturbed rather frequently."

"I shall not ask how well James did then," the Duke replied with a slight smile. "For I doubt the game was an accurate reflection of your skills."

"He still beat me quite soundly," Elizabeth joked. "Which does say very little for my skills at least!"

The Duke allowed himself a smile before hesitating a moment.

"I hope you did not feel obliged to entertain him. I know he is much too old for the childish games which Catherine prefers."

"On the contrary, Your Grace," Elizabeth assured him honestly. "I enjoyed his company very much. He is a lovely young man."

"If you wish to spare his blushes," the Duke surprised Elizabeth by joking. "I would not let him hear you say that."

Elizabeth laughed lightly in response and this was how Jane and the three children found them. Elizabeth noted with amusement that Catherine was walking besides Jane, her face a picture of adoration as she gazed up at the woman beside her, and shared a knowing smile with James.

"Are you sure you cannot stay longer?" Jane asked the Duke once she had reached them.

"I am afraid not," he replied. "My meeting with your husband has regrettably left me with much to do. We look forward to your visit on Wednesday though, don't we children?"

James and Catherine both replied in the affirmative before their father shepherded them towards the door and the servants waiting with their coats. Sir Charles came to see his friend off and he, Jane, Elizabeth and Daniel all stood on the steps and waved as the Duke's carriage rolled away.

ഇൽൽ

Elizabeth had not seen the Duke since that day, though she had been fortunate enough to see both his son and daughter on another of their visits to the Bingleys' house, this time in the company of their governess, Mrs Hughes. From what Elizabeth understood, the lady and her husband were both engaged by the Duke for the care and education of his children and their charges were certainly of credit to them - and the Duke, of course. Cathy was a bright, lively girl, quite precocious though utterly charming too; James was quieter, a little shy at times but possessed of a quick wit and wry sense of humour which belied his years and which Elizabeth thought likely to have been inherited from his father. Elizabeth had learned from Mrs Bennet that this was the Duke's first Season in town since the death of his wife, and though his appearance was interesting, *he* was not to be considered of interest. As though

Elizabeth needed to be told that a man twenty years her senior was not to be considered! Her aunt really did make her laugh sometimes.

Speaking of her aunt…

"Ah, darling, there you are!"

Elizabeth smiled as her aunt finally discovered her hiding place in one of the window alcoves in the upper hallway.

"I have been looking everywhere for you. It is time you lay down; you must get some sleep now if you wish to look your best tonight."

Elizabeth did as she was told and went to her room, but she did not try to sleep. Instead she sat and finished a drawing she had started the evening before, and then read her book until it was time. When Wilson came to wake her she frowned upon finding her mistress wide awake and the bed still made.

"Don't come crying to me if your aunt berates you for being tired."

"I wouldn't dream of it," Elizabeth replied flippantly, smiling impishly when Wilson grumbled to herself.

"You had best go join your aunt and uncle," Wilson told her after a glance at the clock.

"Oh there is no rush," Elizabeth carelessly replied. "I shall simply say I overslept," she teased as she got up and walked over to where her gown for the evening was hanging. She fingered the exquisite material and sighed.

"It really is a beautiful gown," she breathed.

"That it is," Wilson agreed as she came to stand beside Elizabeth.

"I fear I shan't do it justice at all," Elizabeth lamented with a rueful smile. "I'm not nearly beautiful enough. It should be worn by someone like Jane or,"

"Oh, ridiculous!" Wilson interjected gruffly. "You'll look wonderful wearing it. And if anyone says otherwise, they're blind."

"Oh Wilson," Elizabeth replied affectionately. "You really are a dear sometimes."

"Only sometimes?" Wilson teased in a rare moment of levity.

Elizabeth grinned.

"Only sometimes," she asserted, and Wilson very nearly smiled.

෨෬

Following behind her aunt and uncle, who had already found some friends to speak with, Elizabeth could not quite contain her curious excitement and looked about herself with avid interest as they waited in the receiving line at the Llewellyn-Jones ball. It seemed so long since she had attended so large and grand an event - it was almost daunting!

They finally made it to the front of the queue and stood for a moment looking down into the ballroom below as the couple in front of them were announced; suddenly it was their turn and Elizabeth felt a little thrill at hearing her name called in the resounding, clear voice of the Llewellyn-Jones' butler. She descended the stairs behind her aunt and uncle, her eyes searching the crowd for any of their friends and family. Smiling happily to herself, Elizabeth was unaware that she was a subject of interest to several people present. At last she caught sight of Jane and Sir Charles and steered Mr and Mrs Bennet in their direction. It took them a long time to reach her sister, for they were frequently waylaid by friends and acquaintances of her aunt and uncle, all of whom Elizabeth had to be introduced to. She found she could countenance the delay quite well, however, for she was asked to dance by three gentlemen, and was feeling more than a little pleased by the evening so far when they finally reached Jane's side.

"Oh Lizzy," Jane exclaimed upon seeing her sister. "Your hair! I love it. It suits you so well!"

"Do you think so?" Elizabeth asked, self-consciously fingering her recently cut hair - it was a lot shorter than it had been, and the shortest she could remember ever having it.

"Absolutely," Jane replied positively. "And this style complements your features beautifully."

"I'm so glad you think so," Elizabeth admitted with a relieved laugh. "Aunt wasn't at all sure about it you see, but I like it and...well, it's nice to hear that you like it too."

Jane smiled and turned to speak with her aunt and uncle, leaving Elizabeth to look about herself for the moment, admiring the ladies in their beautiful gowns and the men in their immaculately tailored evening wear. She spotted the Duke of Farleigh walking in their direction and smiled in recognition; once again she seemed to catch him by surprise but he eventually smiled in response and came towards her.

"Good evening, Your Grace," Elizabeth greeted him after curtseying gracefully, her smile still in place.

"Good evening, Miss Gardiner."

"Darcy!" Sir Charles turned and saw his friend. "There you are. I looked but couldn't find you earlier. How are you?"

"Quite well," the Duke assured her brother-in-law with a slightly wry twist of his lips and Elizabeth wondered what had been left unsaid.

"Surviving?" Sir Charles joked and the Duke did smile this time when he replied.

"As you see."

"My friend dislikes dancing," Sir Charles said to Elizabeth, sensing her interest. "And balls in general, really. He is here under duress."

"Really?" Elizabeth was intrigued. "And how did you compel him to attend?"

"Blackmail," Sir Charles joked with a laugh as the Duke rolled his eyes.

"Blackmail? Of which sort?" Elizabeth asked smilingly.

"Oh, purely emotional," Sir Charles replied easily.

"The very worst kind," Elizabeth asserted with teasing gravity, her eyes dancing with playfulness as she looked between the two men. "I had thought better of you, brother."

Sir Charles shrugged and was utterly impenitent.

"How else was I to get him to come to town?"

Elizabeth laughed before turning to the Duke.

"And how exactly *did* he manage it?"

"He repeatedly stressed to me that it was the sincerest wish of himself, his wife, my sister and her husband, as well as all of our children that we all spend the Season in town together," the Duke replied, smiling slightly.

Elizabeth laughed again and looked at her brother-in-law.

"Oh, shameful behaviour! I cannot believe you would manipulate your friend like that!"

"And yet," the Duke spoke up before Sir Charles could, "I confess I do not mind."

"Really?" Elizabeth asked.

"Really," the Duke replied, smiling at his friend. "For he is unfailingly charming, and even though he always gets his way I've always found it hard to hold it against him, even when I know I probably should. I've often thought he would make a brilliant politician," he added as Sir Charles laughed.

"I've never thought of him that way before," Elizabeth admitted as she regarded her brother-in-law with mock-thoughtfulness.

"I don't doubt it," the Duke replied. "He is very clever. Were we not such close friends, and if I did not trust him completely, I daresay I would be quite wary of him."

"You make me sound quite devious and conniving, Darcy!" Sir Charles laughingly objected.

"That is not my intention, I assure you," the Duke replied, saying to Elizabeth, "for whilst he does possess a certain skill for getting me to do what I would rather not, I trust that he always has my best interests at heart, and I let that thought console me when he manages to get his way, which I must admit is shamefully often."

"Then I had best stay on his good side as well," Elizabeth joked in response.

"I daresay you are safe," the Duke replied, with a nod in Jane's direction. "For he would be in trouble with his wife if he ever led you astray, and it has been my observation that Lady Bingley seems the only person immune to his powers of persuasion."

"It is true," Sir Charles lamented with a sigh as Elizabeth stifled a laugh at the Duke's teasing. "Jane *never* lets me have my way."

"I am glad to hear it," Elizabeth replied primly and smiled up at the Duke when she heard him chuckle in response.

Any further conversation was forestalled by her partner for the first dance, Mr Heston, the son of one of Mr Bennet's cousins, coming to claim her hand just as the musicians struck up the call for all the couples to assemble. He was a gentleman of only two and twenty and as she curtsied to him, Elizabeth could not help reflecting how young he looked when standing beside Sir Charles and the Duke. She smiled at them both before allowing herself to be led away, noticing that whilst Sir Charles moved to claim her sister for the dance, the Duke remained standing where he was. She wondered why he did not have a partner for the first dance when he seemed like such a nice man.

Elizabeth thoroughly enjoyed her first dance. Mr Wallace Heston was the ideal partner, cheerful and enthusiastic and ready to enjoy himself. He and Elizabeth kept up a lively conversation all throughout the set, comparing their impressions of the evening so far and just generally enjoying themselves as two such young people could be expected to do. Mr and Mrs Bennet, particularly the latter, watched with satisfaction as their niece showcased herself to the best possible advantage, her dancing light and graceful. Her age seemed to make her stand out when compared to the much younger debutantes, as did her obvious enthusiasm when compared to the girls of her own age who were by now experiencing the Season for the second or third time.

Three more equally enjoyable dances followed the first, one with Sir Charles and the other two with gentlemen she had met before the ball who had requested her hand for a set. They were both rather likeable men, not at all handsome but genial and perfectly acceptable partners; indeed, her mood was so buoyant that her partner would have had to have been particularly unpleasant for her not to enjoy herself!

Her tendency to throw herself into the dance with such enthusiasm left Elizabeth, by the conclusion of her fourth dance, rather breathless and feeling that a slight rest would be advisable before she danced again. She said goodbye to her latest partner and then made her way to one of the doors which led out onto the large terrace which stretched around the back of the house. She did not exit through the main door and so found herself quite alone in a more secluded area, a happy circumstance which suited her needs perfectly.

As she was standing at the balustrade, letting the cool breeze wash over her, she heard another door being opened not far away and turned to look to her left; though this part of the terrace was mostly in shadow, she thought she could recognise the figure of the man who walked up to the balustrade and assumed a pose similar to her own. Before she could make up her mind whether to approach the gentleman or not, however, he was joined by another man. She could make out the ensuing conversation quite well from where she was stood.

"Good evening, Your Grace," the second man greeted the first, and Elizabeth's suspicions as to the identity of the first man were confirmed. "I had heard you were in town, and when I saw you come out here I thought I'd come and greet you."

"Good evening, Swanley" the Duke replied evenly, though Elizabeth noticed his tone was not encouraging.

"What a charming amusement dancing is. I think it a sign of a truly polished society," the second man observed, with somewhat forced cheerfulness.

"Do you?" the Duke asked mildly. "I believe it is equally in vogue among less polished societies as well."

There was a pause during which Elizabeth saw the second man look at the Duke with confusion and she had to stifle a laugh.

"I saw your sister and her husband dancing," the second man went on. "They performed delightfully; I do not doubt that you are as adept yourself, Your Grace."

"You have seen me dance, I'm sure," the Duke replied repressively.

"Yes indeed, though not for some years!" His companion joked. "Do you intend to dance tonight?'" he asked, and Elizabeth detected more than curiosity in his tone; the man probably had an unmarried daughter somewhere inside.

"It is unlikely," the Duke responded bluntly.

"Would it not be a proper compliment to the place?" The second man pressed.

"It would, but it is a compliment I do not pay to any place, if it can be avoided."

At this reply Elizabeth could not quite keep her laughter contained and both men looked swiftly in her direction; thankful for the cover of the shadows she stole away from the terrace and back into the ballroom before her identity could be discovered. Blushing furiously at being caught eaves-dropping, she dove into the sea of people and hurried back to her aunt and uncle, though by the time she reached them she was smiling again as she remembered the Duke's droll reply.

"What's tickled you, Lizzy?" Mr Bennet asked when he noticed her expression.

"Oh, nothing," Elizabeth replied, a little flustered at being caught. She quickly changed the subject. "Is it our dance next?"

"It certainly is," Mr Bennet confirmed and taking her proffered hand led her to where the other couples were assembling.

As they were waiting for the music to begin, Elizabeth saw that the Duke had returned from the terrace and was stood speaking with a tall, slender lady and a shorter, plain looking man in military uniform; from their mannerisms and the slight physical similarities between the Duke and the lady, Elizabeth suspected a familial relationship.

"Is that the Duke's sister and her husband?"

Mr Bennet looked over his shoulder in the direction Elizabeth indicated and then turned back to her, nodding.

"Yes, Lady Georgiana Fitzwilliam and her husband, Colonel Richard Fitzwilliam. A lovely couple. I would be happy to introduce them to you after this dance, if you would like?"

"I would," Elizabeth replied positively just before the music and the dance began.

ജ∞ങ

"Who is that?"

Darcy startled inwardly at the unexpected question, pulling his eyes away from Miss Gardiner to look instead at his sister.

"Who?" he dissembled - he knew perfectly well who Georgiana meant.

"The girl dancing with Mr Bennet," his sister replied.

"Miss Gardiner," Darcy supplied. "His niece."

"Lady Bingley's sister?" Georgiana clarified; her brother nodded. "They do not look at all alike. Have you been introduced? What is she like?"

*Lovely.*

Darcy scowled at the inappropriate thought.

"Will?" Georgiana questioned upon seeing his expression. "Do you not like her?"

"No, I mean of course I...she seems a very pleasant young lady," he said at last in what he felt was suitable language. "Catherine and James are rather fond of her already."

"Then I am sure I will like her very much," Georgiana predicted happily and her husband smiled affectionately at her from his place at her side. "You shall have to introduce us to her."

"I think he will be spared the task," Richard spoke up suddenly. "They are coming over."

Darcy turned and saw that his cousin was indeed correct and that Miss Gardiner was approaching on the arm of her uncle.

Mr Bennet bowed slightly and greeted the Fitzwilliams.

"My niece expressed a desire to meet you both, and I could do nought but oblige her."

"I am glad you did," Georgiana replied with a warm smile. "For I was just enlisting my brother's aid in securing an introduction to *you*, Miss Gardiner. I am very glad to meet you at last."

"At last?" Elizabeth repeated.

"Indeed, for your sister and I are rather good friends, and she always speaks so highly of you. I was rather eager to meet you after hearing so much about you."

"I fear I shall not live up to your expectations, my Lady," Elizabeth playfully replied. "For my sister no doubt greatly exaggerated my good qualities and painted a not entirely accurate, albeit decidedly flattering, portrait of my character. I only hope that I do not disappoint you *too* much," she concluded with an impertinent grin.

"I assure you, Miss Gardiner," Georgiana replied smiling, as Richard chuckled at Elizabeth's teasing, "that there is very little chance of that! I like you so much already. We shall have to sit together at supper so that we may get to know each other more. That is if you have not already made other arrangements?"

Elizabeth assured her that that was not the case and happily consented to the plan. As the supper set was next and she had yet to locate her partner for it, Elizabeth reluctantly departed with her uncle to return to Mrs Bennet.

Once she and Mr Bennet were out of earshot, Richard turned to his cousin with a grin.

"I predict she and my wife shall be fast friends by the end of the week."

"The end of the night, I'd say," Darcy replied and Richard laughed his agreement.

"You are probably right," Georgiana admitted cheerfully. "I am inclined to like her simply by virtue of her being Jane's sister, but she seems rather delightful in her own right. How old is she, do you know?"

"She cannot be above twenty," Darcy replied - he had worked this out for himself based on how old she had been at Sir Charles and Lady Jane's wedding.

"And yet she is clearly older than the other girls here for their first Season," Richard noted. "Why has she only just come to town?"

"I gather from Bingley that she made her bow two years ago but had to return home prematurely when her father was taken ill. He has only now given his consent for her to return."

"Her father being?" Georgiana asked.

"Viscount Darwen," Darcy responded, frowning when Richard choked on a laugh.

"Forgive me," he said, looking a little contrite. "I did not mean, it is just that I remember Father telling me tales of the Viscount. He is somewhat eccentric, I believe."

"I have never heard of him," Georgiana admitted. "Have you met him, Will?" she asked her brother.

"Once, at Bingleys' wedding," Darcy replied.

"And?" Richard prodded when his cousin failed to elaborate.

"And what?"

"Is he as mad as they say?" Richard asked jokingly.

"He had recently lost his wife," Darcy responded a trifle brusquely. "If his behaviour seemed at all strange, I daresay I attributed it to his grief."

The two cousins glared at one another and it fell to Georgiana to keep the peace.

"Well," she stated lightly. "I am sure he is perfectly agreeable, if his daughters are of any indication. And if he is a bit eccentric; well, aren't we all, in our own way?"

"Yes dear," Richard agreed, recognising the effort she was making. "I am sure you are right."

"Of course I am," Georgiana replied primly and both men smiled, happy to let the moment pass. In truth, Darcy was unsure as to why he had responded so strongly to Richard's jest, though he eventually put it down to his respect for the Bingleys.

"Have you seen George yet tonight?" Georgiana asked him, breaking into his thoughts. "I have heard he is here."

"Not yet, no," Darcy replied, before admitting in an undertone. "I have not exactly been looking for him."

"I'll wager he's in the card room," Richard put in darkly. "Earning his money for the week."

"Shush, not so loud," Georgiana cautioned him with a quick glance around them.

"I do not see why we have to help him maintain the fiction," her husband argued, though he did lower his voice. "It's downright deceitful."

"No it isn't," Georgiana argued back. "We've never lied about anything."

"No, we've just withheld the truth," Richard responded sarcastically and Georgiana frowned at his tone.

"It is not for us to reveal the truth of his circumstances," Darcy spoke up at last; his tone did not encourage argument. "He is family, and to expose him would be an embarrassment to us as well as him. It would also not be right - he is not doing any harm." Richard looked about to protest and Darcy firmly went on. "I am not saying that I approve of his lax morals, but as long as he wishes for his lack of wealth to remain a secret, he will not risk having his honour engaged."

Richard scoffed.

"I think you give him too much credit! He is simply a cad, and avoiding exposure is his perfect excuse for dallying with so many women. Even were his pockets full, he would still behave the same way - one woman would never be enough for him."

"Perhaps he has yet to meet the right woman," Georgiana suggested lightly.

"Or perhaps," her husband replied, "he has yet to completely run out of money. The day he does is the day we will see him suddenly eager to find himself a bride - though the truth of his situation will no doubt present some difficulties for him!"

Darcy was inclined to agree with Richard's cynical assessment of their cousin's motives, though that being said he knew that George was no fool. He was something of a rake, but he always knew when to retreat, deftly avoiding compromise and never having his honour engaged. Darcy did not approve of his behaviour, but as long as George only continued to deceive society at large and did not hurt anyone (or their family's good name), he was resolved to keep his silence.

"Speak of the devil," Richard muttered and the trio looked up to see their cousin passing close by them, a beautiful woman on his arm. He nodded his head and Darcy and Richard both returned the gesture.

"Who is that with him?" Darcy asked quietly.

"Lady Palmer," Georgiana replied, equally as quiet. "Her husband is at home with a broken foot; a riding accident, I believe."

Darcy decided they had spent enough time talking about George.

"Shall we make our way to the dining room? Before the rush?"

Both agreed it was a good idea and they began to skirt their way around the edge of the ballroom, Darcy following behind the couple, nodding occasionally to a passing acquaintance and watching the dancers progressing through the set. He could see Miss Gardiner with her partner at the opposite end of the ballroom, and felt a smile appear as he watched her skip through the steps and saw her laugh at something that was said to her. He felt almost inexorably drawn to her, to her lightness and the joy which seemed to surround her.

He accidentally bumped into another man and, apologising for his blunder, continued on his way, his thoughts effectively distracted from Miss Gardiner. It was just as well, he thought with a shake of his head and one final look in her direction. He well knew that such thoughts were beyond inappropriate.

ഇന്ദ

Once the supper set had concluded, Elizabeth's partner returned her to her aunt and uncle, bowing and somewhat reluctantly departing - he had been hoping that they would sit together, but alas, the lady had other plans. She went with her aunt and uncle into the dining room and squeezed through the crowd, hoping that Mr Bennet, who seemed to be leading them, knew where he was going. They eventually came to a stop and Elizabeth was delighted to find the Duke, Lady Georgiana and Colonel Fitzwilliam already seated - she happily took the seat between the lady and her brother.

"I did not think we would make it! What an awful crush."

"It is rather," Lady Georgiana agreed. "Here, have some water - you look a little flush."

"Oh, thank you," Elizabeth replied pressing a hand to her cheek a little self-consciously. She took a sip of her drink and fell quiet.

Colonel Fitzwilliam leant around his wife.

"I see you danced the last with Mr Henry Jefferson. How is he? His elder brother and I were at Cambridge together and I've not spoken to either of them for months."

"He is very well," Elizabeth replied softly. She brightened when she added, "Do you know that his brother's wife is expecting?"

"I had no idea!" the Colonel exclaimed, looking and sounding very pleased. "Nicholas will be delighted. I shall have to write to him."

"Mr Jefferson is very happy for them," Elizabeth went on. "He is looking forward to becoming an uncle for the first time."

"I must say I am surprised he confided in you, Lizzy, about so private a matter," Jane observed from her place across the table.

Elizabeth frowned slightly.

"I did not...I was simply telling him about Daniel and Catherine and James, and how much fun we all have together, when he told me his happy news."

She was surprised when the Duke spoke up.

"No doubt he felt Miss Gardiner would understand his excitement at the prospect of a young niece or nephew."

"Oh, undoubtedly," Mrs Bennet laughed. "I swear she spends more time with those children than she does with us!"

Everyone laughed as Elizabeth blushed slightly, though she laughed a little as well. As everyone began to fall into conversation, Elizabeth felt the Duke's eyes upon her and looked up at him.

"Catherine and James speak very highly of you," he told her with a kind smile. "You have quite won them over."

"I did nothing special," Elizabeth demurred.

"Perhaps you do not think so," the Duke replied. "But it usually takes them much longer to warm to strangers, particularly Cathy."

"But she is so outgoing!" Elizabeth responded, greatly surprised.

"If she is comfortable, yes," the Duke agreed. "She can be quite shy around people she does not like or know very well. But she took an instant liking to you."

"Well, I am flattered," Elizabeth teased in reply and the Duke smiled. "And you may tell Catherine and James that I am equally as fond of them, though of course when you tell James you may want to use less sentimental language," she added with a playful grin.

"What would you suggest?" The Duke asked, still smiling.

"Oh, something along the lines of 'Miss Gardiner wishes you to know how much she enjoys your company and looks forward to future occasions when you can be in company together' ought to suffice," Elizabeth replied. "Wouldn't you say?"

"Quite," the Duke agreed, chuckling.

Their conversation was interrupted when Lady Georgiana asked Elizabeth a question, and Sir Charles took the opportunity to talk to his friend. Elizabeth and the Duke did not speak again directly for the rest of the meal, and before long the latter had left with his sister and cousin to return to the ballroom. Left alone with her family, Elizabeth was chatting quite happily with her uncle when they were interrupted by Mrs Bennet.

"Look, Mr Wickham is coming over," she whispered, grasping Elizabeth's arm.

Elizabeth looked in the direction her aunt was indicating and saw a tall gentleman approaching them. As he drew nearer she could see he was rather handsome, with sandy brown hair and brown eyes and a generally pleasing countenance. His smile when he reached them rendered him even more handsome, and when his eyes alighted on her as her uncle introduced them, Elizabeth very nearly blushed.

"It is a pleasure to meet you, Miss Gardiner," he intoned as he bowed over her hand. He spoke with the easy charm of a wealthy, well-bred gentleman.

"And you, Mr Wickham," Elizabeth replied.

"If you are not otherwise engaged," Mr Wickham went on. "I would be honoured to dance the next with you."

"I am afraid all of my dances are taken," Elizabeth informed him.

Mr Wickham smiled slowly.

"Of course they are," he responded charmingly. "I should have known your card would be full and asked earlier. I am sorry to have missed my opportunity - for tonight at least, for I hope you will permit me to claim a dance for when we next meet."

"I would be happy to reserve a set for you," Elizabeth replied; she smiled as she teasingly added, "though I shall not do so indefinitely."

"Then I hope we meet again soon," Mr Wickham responded. "For I should not wish to be deprived the pleasure of standing up with you."

Elizabeth laughed lightly at this reply.

"You are very charming," she noted with a smile.

Mr Wickham grinned.

"I try my best."

"So I hear," Elizabeth quipped with an arched brow.

"My reputation precedes me, I see," her companion noted, sounding amused.

"It would not be much of a reputation if it did not," Elizabeth pointed out and Mr Wickham laughed at her reply before regarding her with an appreciative look for a long moment.

Just as she was beginning to feel a little self-conscious, Mr Bennet asked the gentleman a question and he pulled his eyes away. Mr Wickham remained with them a few minutes more before eventually taking his leave, though not before reminding Elizabeth of her promise and vowing to claim his dance at the first opportunity.

"You did that very well, my dear," Mrs Bennet complimented Elizabeth as soon as they were alone. "Very well indeed."

"I was not aware that I *did* anything," Elizabeth contradicted.

Mrs Bennet shot her an amused look.

"You are many things, Lizzy, but naïve is not one of them. You will have seen the way he looked at you."

Elizabeth did not attempt to deny it.

"I was simply making conversation."

"If you say so, dear," Mrs Bennet responded knowingly. She went on before Elizabeth could. "He is rather handsome, isn't he?"

"Undoubtedly," Elizabeth agreed.

"And so very charming! I shall have to manage it so we have him to dinner soon," Mrs Bennet mused.

"I have the utmost faith in your abilities, Aunt," Elizabeth somewhat sarcastically replied. "But if you will excuse me, I see my partner for this dance approaching."

Mrs Bennet watched as her niece departed on the arm of yet another young man, her head full of plans for the coming weeks. She was delighted with how well the evening had gone and all the attention her niece had received - Elizabeth had danced every dance and had had to turn down a number of offers, and they had been approached on a number of occasions during dinner by people seeking introductions. Yes, she was very pleased. And now Mr Wickham appeared to be showing an interest.

"I hope you do not plan to encourage him," Mr Bennet broke into her chain of thought. "Or to encourage Lizzy to encourage him," he added firmly. "I do not like the man."

"What is there not to like?" Mrs Bennet argued. "He is rich, handsome, well-mannered and popular and has good connections. The daughter of an obscure Viscount could do a lot worse."

"And our niece," Mr Bennet contradicted, "could do a lot *better.* He is a complete rake and I will not have him dallying with her!"

"But what if he develops real feelings for her?" Mrs Bennet argued.

Her husband rolled his eyes.

"There is more chance of his falling in love with *you*, my dear. I doubt he knows how to appreciate a woman outside of the bedroom."

"Mr Bennet!" His wife objected. "Please; there is no need to be vulgar."

"Then open your eyes, Fanny," Mr Bennet responded lowly. "Make no mistake - any interest Mr Wickham shows in Elizabeth will have nothing to do with love, and *everything* to do with lust. I will not have her hurt or humiliated - or worse - by him."

"Oh very well," Mrs Bennet conceded at last. "I shall not encourage him. That is not to say I will discourage him though, because I think you are being very harsh on the poor man."

Mr Bennet groaned inwardly and abandoned the argument, knowing it was a pointless exercise; he knew also that he would most likely be proved right in the end.

৪০০৪

Elizabeth had just danced her final set of the night and was being escorted by her partner back to her aunt and uncle when she heard her name being called. She turned and saw her long-time friend, Charlotte Lucas, coming towards her.

"Charlotte!" She greeted her happily and the pair embraced before Elizabeth introduced her partner to her friend. Seeming to sense he was no longer required and his company no longer desired, her partner excused himself and left the two friends alone.

"Mr Lyall?" Charlotte mused as she watched him walk away. "Is he?"

"The younger son of the Earl of Barlow; yes," Elizabeth supplied, guessing the question. "I have almost lost count of the number of sons and younger sons that I have met tonight; I shall never be able to keep track of them all."

"Poor you," Charlotte teased. "It must be such a hardship to be so in demand."

Elizabeth laughed.

"It was gratifying at first, I will admit, but now I find myself wishing for a moment to myself! I am tired of the performance."

"Then let us disappear for a while," Charlotte suggested and taking Elizabeth's hand led her to a small alcove which was partially covered by a curtain.

"There, is that better?" she asked, when they were safely ensconced in their hiding place.

"Much!" Elizabeth laughingly replied. She embraced her friend once more. "It is so good to see you! I have kept an eye out for you all night but did not see you."

"We only arrived just before supper," Charlotte replied. "You know what my father is like - his time keeping is appalling. We were on the verge of leaving him at home."

"When did you arrive in town?" Elizabeth asked.

"Yesterday." Charlotte laughed at Elizabeth's expression. "I know - father again. And he always insists we travel together."

"How is your family?"

"Very well. Robert is likely to become engaged in the next few weeks," Charlotte confided.

"To Miss Hamilton?" Elizabeth clarified; her friend nodded. "Your parents must be pleased," she stated neutrally.

"They are. It is a very good match for him," Charlotte added, in the manner of one reciting their lines.

Elizabeth simply looked at her friend until Charlotte grimaced.

"Fine! She is perfectly horrible and will make him utterly miserable. There, happy now?"

"Not particularly," Elizabeth replied soberly. "I've always liked your brother - he deserves so much better than Delia Hamilton."

"And yet were she not so awful," Charlotte pointed out sagely. "She would not be marrying my brother. I gather from what I have heard that Lord Hamilton had quite despaired of finding any vaguely suitable man willing to take her. Even with her twenty thousand."

"But she is only two and twenty!" Elizabeth objected.

"A veritable antique," Charlotte jokingly declared before laughing and adding, "though what that makes *me*."

Elizabeth laughed as well, not worried about injuring her friend because she knew that Charlotte was not overly concerned to be still unmarried at five and twenty. Her parents loved her and were happy and able to support her, and Charlotte was content to wait for the right man.

"Where is Lord Hamilton's estate?" Elizabeth asked after a moment. "I cannot recall."

"Dorset," Charlotte replied.

"Delia will be very far from home when she marries your brother," Elizabeth observed.

"Yet another advantage to the match from Lord Hamilton's point of view," Charlotte muttered quietly and Elizabeth laughed again.

"Oh I've missed you, Charlotte," she stated affectionately. "You must come to tea tomorrow so that we can talk more."

"I certainly shall try my best," Charlotte promised with a smile. "Though I'm sure mother and I will call in a few days anyway. She has *so* much to tell your aunt."

"I'm sure she does," Elizabeth replied. "They are terrible, aren't they?"

"Yes," Charlotte agreed smiling.

Realising that they had likely been gone too long, the two friends said goodbye and went their separate ways. When Elizabeth found her aunt and uncle, stood together with Jane, Sir Charles and the Duke, she smiled apologetically at them all.

"I'm sorry I disappeared - I was with Charlotte."

"How is she?" Jane asked.

"Is Robert engaged?" Mrs Bennet asked before Elizabeth could reply. "I have not heard anything from Lady Lucas but..."

"Then let us assume there is nothing to announce as of yet," Mr Bennet broke in gently. He turned to Elizabeth and reiterated Jane's question.

"She is very well," Elizabeth replied. "As are the rest of her family."

Mr Bennet nodded and then consulted his watch.

"I think it is time we were leaving," he announced. "The sun will be up before we reach home otherwise!"

Jane, Sir Charles and the Duke expressed their desire to leave as well and they all left the ballroom together. They had to wait in the hall whilst a servant fetched their things and Elizabeth decided to approach the Duke.

"Did you have a nice evening?" she asked, as she reached his side.

"I did," he admitted.

"Your faith in Sir Charles has paid off then," Elizabeth surmised playfully.

"So it would seem," the Duke replied. "Though please do not tell him that - he does not need any further encouragement."

"If asked I shall say you had a horrid time," Elizabeth avowed and the Duke smiled.

"Did you enjoy yourself?" he asked.

"Very much so," Elizabeth replied positively. "Particularly meeting your sister and her husband - they are a lovely couple."

"You are very kind to say so," the Duke replied.

"It also happens to be the truth," Elizabeth responded playfully before going on. "I also met your cousin, briefly."

"Which one?" The Duke questioned.

"Mr Wickham," Elizabeth supplied. She studied her companion thoughtfully and noted, "I can see the resemblance between you now."

The Duke nodded but did not venture any further comment. When a footman appeared with Elizabeth's cape he took the garment from him.

"Please, allow me," he said as he placed it over her shoulders.

Elizabeth smiled up at him.

"Thank you."

"You are welcome," he replied just as Mrs Bennet called for Elizabeth to come along and, after a hasty curtsey to the Duke, she obligingly followed her aunt and uncle from the house.

# Chapter 3

Darcy rolled over in bed, still mostly asleep but vaguely aware of a noise which had disturbed him. He lay on his front, clasping a pillow in his arms and listening for anything unusual. He heard the approach of small footsteps and smiled to himself.

"Is that you, Catherine Darcy?" he mumbled, his voice thick with sleep still.

He heard the footsteps hesitate before rushing towards the bed; the mattress dipped slightly under her weight and he felt his daughter lie down beside him on the bed. Darcy turned his head and opened his eyes - he was almost nose to nose with Catherine.

"How did you know it was me?" she asked.

"No-one else would dare disturb me," Darcy replied, only half joking.

"I missed you," Cathy told him as she leant forward and pressed a sweet kiss to his cheek. "Good afternoon, Papa."

"Afternoon?" Darcy repeated, surprised.

Cathy giggled and nodded.

"It is one o'clock."

"Papa was very late to bed," Darcy replied in explanation. "And was very tired."

"But now you have slept all day so you are not tired anymore?" Cathy guessed.

In truth Darcy was still very tired - he was not as young as he used to be, and had not stayed out so late in many a year.

"No, not anymore."

Cathy looked excited.

"Tell me about the ball," she implored. "Tell me about all the ladies in their dresses."

"There were plenty of those," Darcy agreed straight-faced.

"Was Lady Jane the beautifulest?" Cathy asked and Darcy smiled at her obvious bias.

"Most beautiful," he corrected lightly before saying, "And yes, Lady Bingley did look beautiful, but so did many of the other ladies. Aunt Georgiana, for instance."

"And Miss Gardiner?" Cathy asked, surprising him.

"Yes, she was beautiful too," Darcy replied, remembering how becoming she had looked in her gown and with her hair cut in a new style.

"James thinks she is just as pretty as Lady Jane," Cathy surprised him again by saying. "But I am not sure. What do you think?" she asked.

Darcy, who had seen the question coming, still needed a moment before he replied.

"I think they are both beautiful in different ways."

Fortunately this answer seemed to satisfy his daughter.

"Did you dance?" Cathy asked him next.

"Once or twice," Darcy responded.

"Not enough!" Cathy scolded him and he almost laughed at her impertinence. "You must dance all the dances, Papa!"

"Must I?" Darcy questioned.

"Yes, because then all the ladies will think you are charming," Cathy replied primly and Darcy laughed, pulling her into his arms and kissing the top of her head affectionately.

"I promise I will dance more next time," he said after a moment, looking down at his daughter. "But in truth there is only one lady whose opinion I care for."

"Who?" Cathy demanded.

"My petite princess," Darcy replied and Cathy smiled delightedly. "As long as you think I am charming, I am quite content."

Cathy kissed his cheek again.

"You are even more charming than Sir Charles."

Darcy laughed heartily.

"Thank you, my dear, that is good to know."

He enjoyed a few more minutes of holding his daughter as she chatted aimlessly to him about her morning, before he finally sent her on her way and got out of bed. When he was washed and dressed he ventured down to his study.

"Aha! He lives!"

Darcy frowned slightly when he walked into his study and found his cousin sat comfortably ensconced in one of the arm chairs. He appeared to have been there for some time.

"What are you doing here?" he asked.

"Nice to see you too," Richard joked. "My wife sent me to ask if the children can come tomorrow to spend the day with the boys. The Bingley's boy is invited as well."

"We have no plans," Darcy replied.

"Excellent!" Richard declared. "You have to come too, by the way. I shall be vastly outnumbered otherwise."

"Why, who else shall be there?" Darcy asked.

"Lady Bingley and her sister, and probably their aunt as well," Richard replied. "Then there will be the governesses too. I shall definitely need you to bolster my numbers; else it will just be me."

"It isn't a war," Darcy pointed out with a chuckle.

"You say that now." Richard joked. He stood up out of his chair. "I take it I can assure my wife you will all be there."

"Of course," Darcy assured him.

"Then I'd best be on my way. I've lots to do today and I've wasted time waiting for you to get out of bed, you lazy dog."

"You could have just left a note," Darcy pointed out.

"And missed the opportunity to rib you? Hardly!" Richard joked and Darcy laughed in spite of himself as his cousin took his leave.

ଊଓ

Whilst the Duke had been catching up on his sleep, Elizabeth had spent her day meeting all the callers who had come to visit. Several of the gentlemen she had danced with came to the house, as did many of those she had had to turn down. Mrs Bennet was naturally delighted, and was in her element playing chaperone and exerting all her skills as a consummate hostess. Though she was tired, Elizabeth still managed to have a pleasant time and genuinely enjoyed the company of several of her callers, though some, such as the ridiculous Mr William Collins, were a trial on her nerves. She persevered with the task at hand, though, and would have been pleased to know that the majority of the people who called left with a favourable impression of her. Who does not like to know they are liked, after all? Just as the clock was about to signal the end of calling hours and Elizabeth was about to breathe a sigh of relief, the butler appeared and announced another visitor.

"Mr Wickham to see you, Ma'am."

"Oh!" Mrs Bennet appeared flustered for the first time that day and Elizabeth's eyes danced with laughter - if she did not know better she would have suspected her aunt of having a fancy for the gentleman.

"Show him in, show him in," her aunt instructed the butler before turning to Elizabeth. "Sit up straight dear, shoulders back."

Elizabeth ignored the instruction and remained just as she was as Mr Wickham strode into the room. He appeared every bit as handsome as she remembered him, and looked not at all worse for wear for having been up until the early hours of the morning. He bowed and then looked up with a grin at the clock as it began to chime.

"Just in time."

"Somewhat apropos, wouldn't you say?" Elizabeth observed with a wry smile.

"What do you mean, dear?" Mrs Bennet asked her, not understanding.

Mr Wickham, though, smiled and looked at Elizabeth with the same appreciative speculation of the night before.

"That I should appear only just within the bounds of propriety."

"Something like that," Elizabeth replied boldly and Mr Wickham laughed deeply.

"I see I shall have to watch myself around you, Miss Gardiner," he noted.

Elizabeth smiled sweetly.

"I am sure the exercise will do you good."

"You are planning to keep me on my toes, then?" he surmised, and Elizabeth nodded.

"I shall certainly do my best."

"I look forward to it," he replied with a slight bow and Elizabeth blushed at his tone and the look he sent her.

Seeming to recall that Mrs Bennet was still present, Mr Wickham took the seat beside her.

"I do apologise for my tardiness. I was visiting with my mother and lost track of time."

"How is Lady Wickham?" Mrs Bennet asked as Elizabeth studied the gentleman and wondered whether his choice of subject - perfect if he was looking to win Mrs Bennet over - had been intentionally manipulative. She was pulled from her thoughts when she heard her aunt say her name.

"Yes, Lizzy is invited there tomorrow with Lady Bingley and her son. Lovely couple, the Fitzwilliams. Do you know if the Duke and his children will be there tomorrow as well, Lizzy?"

"The children, certainly," Elizabeth replied. "But I am not certain if the Duke shall be there too."

"How do you like Catherine and James?" Mr Wickham asked with a smile. "They are rather quiet little things, aren't they?"

Elizabeth hesitated. In her experience the Duke's children were not overly quiet at all and she did not wish to openly contradict the gentleman. Unfortunately, her aunt was not so circumspect.

"Quiet!" Mrs Bennet exclaimed. "I'm certain you are not serious, Mr Wickham. We had them here just last week and the whole house was in uproar! Quiet indeed," she concluded with a laugh. "You shall not fool us, Mr Wickham!"

Mr Wickham laughed and the moment passed, though it made an impression on Elizabeth and it remained in her mind for the rest of his visit. She could not help thinking of what the Duke had said about his children, about how they were only shy around people they did not like or know well, and wondered which category Mr Wickham fell into? Either way, it did not speak well for him. She was still considering the question when Mr Bennet surprised them all by making an appearance, perhaps expecting all their visitors to be gone. He did not seem particularly delighted to find Mr Wickham sitting in his parlour, though he did his best to hide it. He took a seat beside Elizabeth and encouraged them all to continue with their conversation.

"We were just speaking of the theatre," Elizabeth told him.

"Indeed?" Mr Bennet replied with a look at Mr Wickham. "I gather you are quite a patron of the arts, Mr Wickham."

An odd look passed over his face before Mr Wickham replied.

"I do enjoy the theatre, yes."

"I had thought your tastes ran more towards the opera," Mr Bennet responded and Elizabeth looked between the two men, sensing that they were not really talking about what they appeared to be talking about.

Mrs Bennet knew exactly what her husband was intimating - everyone knew that Mr Wickham's former mistress was an opera singer - and sent him a fulminating glare as Mr Wickham smoothly replied.

"In the past, perhaps, but I have moved on."

"Yes," Mr Bennet responded. "You do not strike me as a man with *committed* preferences."

"Perhaps I have simply yet to find something to commit to," Mr Wickham replied and his tone certainly sounded a little colder to Elizabeth.

She was quite fascinated by the exchange and was almost disappointed when her uncle seemed to withdraw from it with his next reply.

"Perhaps. Have you been to any performances yet this Season?"

"Not yet, no," Mr Wickham replied and Elizabeth noticed that his smile was back in place. "Though I gather the programme this year is particularly good."

The discussion moved on and eventually Mr Wickham regretfully stated that he had to leave.

"Thank you for your visit, Mr Wickham," Mrs Bennet told him as they all rose.

"It was my pleasure, Madam," he replied gallantly. He turned to Elizabeth and surprised her by asking, "If the weather continues to improve, Miss Gardiner, would you honour me by accompanying me on a walk in the park? Perhaps on Wednesday?"

"I would be delighted," Elizabeth replied, knowing without needing to look that her uncle was frowning.

Mr Wickham smiled.

"Excellent. Is eleven o'clock convenient for you?"

"Eleven will be fine."

"Then I shall see you then," he declared before taking his leave and departing.

Feeling Mr Bennet's eyes upon her, Elizabeth turned to him with a smile and reassured him.

"There is no harm in walking, uncle."

"Did I say anything?" Mr Bennet replied and Elizabeth laughed.

"You did not have to," she replied before leaving him and her aunt to themselves. She could tell an argument was brewing and had no wish to bear witness to it.

೮ಉ೪

The following day Jane and Daniel collected Elizabeth from the Bennet's townhouse on their way to the Fitzwilliams', Mrs Bennet deciding not to accompany them as she was expecting a call from a friend. Daniel was rather excited at the prospect of spending the day with so many of his friends and could hardly sit still in his seat, which made both Elizabeth and Jane smile.

"Won't you tell me about your friends, Dan? What are their names?"

"Bradley, Clara and Joseph," Daniel replied.

"And what are their ages?"

"Joseph is eight, Bradley is five, and Clara is a baby," Daniel responded and Elizabeth chuckled.

"Clara is three," Jane supplied, smiling as well.

"Will the Colonel be there, mother?" Daniel asked eagerly and Elizabeth could see the Colonel was evidently a favourite of her nephew's.

"Perhaps," Jane replied. "We shall have to wait and see."

"Does he have a limp, Jane?" Elizabeth asked curiously - she had wondered this since the ball when she had seen him dancing with Lady Georgiana.

"Yes," her sister affirmed. "He was injured on the continent. He most probably should have retired from the army, but he found other ways to make himself useful."

"What do you mean?" Elizabeth asked.

"I believe he works in intelligence," Jane responded and Elizabeth was somewhat surprised - she could not imagine the friendly, jovial man she had met working as some sort of spy.

Conscious of the fact that her son was still listening, Jane changed the subject.

"Clara is such a sweet little girl - she is the very picture of her mother."

"I have no doubt she is utterly charming, then," Elizabeth replied. "For Lady Georgiana is quite stunning."

"They are a striking family, the Darcys," Jane noted and Elizabeth expressed her agreement.

"I saw that you met Mr Wickham at the ball," Jane went on after a moment. "What did you think of him?"

"He seems pleasant enough," Elizabeth replied evenly. "He called yesterday and we have arranged to walk in the park on Wednesday."

"I shall refrain from cautioning you to be careful," Jane teased lightly. "I daresay you are old enough now to know how to take care of yourself."

"Yes," Elizabeth laughed lightly. "And with uncle on guard there is little chance of anything happening to me! He does not approve of Mr Wickham."

"Quite rightly, in my opinion," Jane replied.

"I gather he is not close with the rest of the family," Elizabeth ventured slowly. "I can't imagine they approve of him either."

"No, not particularly close," Jane agreed. "They are perfectly cordial with one another, but beyond keeping up appearances they have little to do with him."

Elizabeth nodded and fell silent, thinking to herself about whether or not *she* should have little to do with Mr Wickham as well. She trusted the opinion of her uncle and sister, but at the same time had nothing to hold against the gentleman herself - he had been all that is charming and polite to her, after all. Perhaps she would just have to see how he behaved when they next met and go from there, bearing in mind what she had been told about him. The carriage pulled up outside the Fitzwilliams' townhouse and Jane turned her attention to her son, cautioning him to wait to be assisted down. Elizabeth followed after them and smiled as she looked up and saw Daniel run up the steps to meet the two Fitzwilliam boys, who were almost hopping from one foot to the other in their excitement.

Lady Fitzwilliam and the Colonel, the former with her daughter in her arms, greeted Jane and Elizabeth as they entered the house and were divested of their things.

"Come along then boys," Colonel Fitzwilliam declared in a carrying tone. "To the parlour, on the double!"

The ladies followed at a more sedate pace as the boys went on ahead under the watchful eye of the Colonel.

"This must be Clara," Elizabeth noted with a soft smile as she looked at the little girl in Lady Georgiana's arms. "Jane told me she was the picture of you," she admitted, "but the likeness is really quite striking."

"Yes," Lady Georgiana agreed, stroking back her daughter's blonde hair. "My husband likes to joke that he had no part in her creation, so little of his appearance there is in her."

"Perhaps she will have more of his character," Elizabeth suggested.

"It is that way with Daniel," Jane put in.

"I confess that the boys take after him so much," Lady Georgiana confided with a smile, "that I should not mind if Clara were to take mostly after me."

"I cannot imagine your husband would object, either," Elizabeth teased - when Lady Georgiana looked at her for an explanation she added, "You seem to hold one another in some affection, if you do not mind my saying so."

"Not at all," Lady Georgiana replied with a warm smile, accepting the truth of Elizabeth's words.

"My brother and his children should be here soon," she told them as they reached the parlour and found the boys already tucking into the few cakes and sweets that had been prepared.

"Joseph!" She scolded her eldest son as the little boy turned to her with his cheeks full of food. "What have I told you about over-filling your mouth?"

"Sorry Mama," he mumbled through his mouthful and Elizabeth had to turn away as she stifled a smile.

"And no talking with your mouth full," Lady Georgiana added, then looked at her husband and said, "He gets his awful manners from you, you know."

"I don't know what you mean," the Colonel replied blithely before popping a whole piece of cake into his mouth at once, grinning at his wife.

"Is your husband like this?" Lady Georgiana asked Jane as they took their seats.

"Sometimes," she admitted with a smile as she watched her own son devour the treats. "You would think we did not feed them!"

They sat chatting quite happily between themselves for some time before the door was opened and the Duke entered with his two children. Cathy immediately ran over to her aunt and cousin, kissing Clara on the cheek and curtseying to Lady Georgiana who responded with an affectionate smile. James meanwhile followed his father's example and bowed to the ladies, though he did smile at Elizabeth as he straightened.

"Have you grown again James?" Colonel Fitzwilliam joked as he came to stand beside him. "Why, you're as tall as I am!"

"A not so remarkable feat," the Duke responded with a smile, "for you are so remarkably short."

"Beast!" Colonel Fitzwilliam cheerfully replied. "I shall get you for that one!"

"I should like to see you try," the Duke retorted, grinning.

"Oh ho, fighting talk!" The Colonel exclaimed and his wife rolled her eyes and turned to her guests.

"Please excuse my husband. *And* my brother," she added with a pointed look at the Duke who did look a little embarrassed.

By this point Cathy had managed to squeeze herself between her aunt and Jane on the settee, and was sat busily arranging her skirts and trying to appear as grown up and ladylike as possible.

"Would you like some cake, Catherine?" Elizabeth asked her as the Duke and James found themselves seats.

"Yes please," Cathy replied very politely - though she could not quite contain her delight when Elizabeth prepared her a small plate complete with a napkin and fork just like the ones she and Jane and Lady Georgiana had. Cathy accepted the plate and sat with it very carefully in her lap, watching Jane and eating very dainty bites whenever she did.

Elizabeth caught her sister's eye and they a shared a smile before she looked over at the Duke; he was watching his daughter with a very loving look and she was touched by his obvious affection.

"Well, now that you and James are here," the Colonel surprised them all by announcing, looking at the Duke, "and have partaken of tea and sustenance, I think it is time we began. Come along gentlemen, to the garden!"

"Richard, what?" Lady Georgiana began but seeing that the boys were already up and out of the room simply sighed and said, "Please be careful."

"Don't worry," her husband assured her. "Darcy here will keep an eye on us."

He clapped the Duke on the shoulder, who looked at him dubiously.

"You'd think you were old enough by now to not require adult supervision."

Elizabeth suppressed a laugh but her smile still gave her away as both men looked in her direction.

"Would you like to join us, Miss Gardiner?" Colonel Fitzwilliam offered gamely.

"Actually, I think I would," Elizabeth surprised him by replying. "As long as you do not mind?" she asked her hostess.

"Not at all," Lady Georgiana assured her. "I should feel better knowing there are two sensible adults present," she added with a playful look at her husband.

"I would not be so sure about that," Jane commented with a smile as she watched her sister leave the room with the two gentlemen.

The trio headed to the back of the house, Colonel Fitzwilliam in front with the Duke and Elizabeth following. He exited the house first and the Duke held the door open for Elizabeth to precede him into the garden. She turned and thanked him but before he could reply the Colonel's voice drowned out all other noise.

"ALRIGHT! In a line, quick now, no dilly-dallying. Don't push your brother Joe, good lad. In age order please, hands at your sides, backs straight, feet together. Good work men!"

Elizabeth covered her mouth with her hand so that none of the boys would see her smile as they stood smartly to attention and the Colonel paced up and down in front of them. She could feel the Duke silently laughing from his place next to her and chanced a look up at him; he caught her eye and grinned.

"You can take the man out of the army," he murmured quietly and Elizabeth's eyes danced with amusement.

"Now," Colonel Fitzwilliam went on once he was satisfied with the state of his troops. "I have a special treat for you boys today, but you must first promise to listen to what you are told and that you will do everything that I say. Do you promise?"

"Yes, Sir!" The boys all chorused and the Colonel nodded.

"Very good. Now stay here and choose a partner whilst I go and get everything set up."

Joseph and Daniel immediately chose each other, as they were close in age and fast friends, whilst James paired up with Bradley and Elizabeth looked up at the Duke.

"Partners?" she proposed.

"Gladly," he replied cordially.

"Do you know what we are doing?" Elizabeth asked him.

"No, I," the Duke began before his attention was caught by something over her shoulder. Elizabeth turned and saw several men carrying three targets and putting them into place whilst Colonel Fitzwilliam strode back over to them carrying bows and several quivers of arrows.

"Oh, archery!" Elizabeth exclaimed happily. "I do so enjoy it."

"You do not require instruction then?" the Colonel asked, having heard her.

"Oh, no, I shall manage quite well," Elizabeth assured him.

She could see now why he had been so insistent that the boys promised to do as they were told and watched as he showed them how to hold the bow and fit the arrow. James appeared to know what he was doing but Joseph and Daniel both listened and watched with rapt attention.

"Shall we?" The Duke proposed, indicating the third target and drawing Elizabeth's attention away from the others.

They selected their bows from those on offer (they were a little too small but would be sufficient for the task at hand) and the Duke stepped aside so that Elizabeth could go first.

"It has been quite a while since I last did this," she admitted as she fitted her arrow.

"Just as long as your shot does not go over the wall," the Colonel joked, pausing in the process of helping Daniel take his shot to watch her.

The boys all laughed and Elizabeth smiled as she pulled back her arm, took aim and released the arrow. It struck the target just off centre but close enough to earn her cheers of congratulations from her little audience. The two men also looked impressed.

"My mother enjoyed the pastime," Elizabeth stated with a little shrug. "And I kept it up after she passed away."

"I doubt I shall be able to match you for skill," the Duke openly admitted as he stepped forward for his turn and Elizabeth thought well of him for being able to do so.

As she waited for the Duke to prepare his shot, she watched Daniel have his go (his shot went hopelessly wide) then turned to watch James and Bradley. The elder boy knelt on the ground with Bradley stood in front of him, his arms either side of the younger boy as he helped him hold the bow and arrow steady. More than once whilst she watched they lost their grip or the arrow slipped and they had to begin again, and Elizabeth admired James for his patience which showed no signs of abating. Finally, they were ready and Bradley stood with his lip between his teeth in concentration, preparing to take his shot. All the others had noticed and stopped to watch as well and they all cheered uproariously when Bradley fired his arrow and it hit the very edge of the target, though it did not have enough force behind it to embed it in the canvas.

"That's my boy!" The Colonel declared, sweeping his laughing son up into his arms before setting him back down amongst his brother and friends.

"Well done, Son," the Duke said quietly to James who blushed a little at the praise. "It was good of you to take the time to help him."

He patted his son on the shoulder and James smiled, looking pleased.

"Why don't you partner with Miss Gardiner?" The Duke suggested. "And I will help Bradley. Go on," he added when James looked about to protest. "Enjoy yourself. I am no match for the lady anyway," he added with a smile at Elizabeth who was perfectly happy to partner with either the father or the son.

"Your father was about to take his shot," she told James when he finally capitulated. "So please, have your turn."

"I am not very good," James told her, sounding embarrassed. "I much prefer actual shooting, or fencing."

"You fence?" Elizabeth replied.

"Yes," James responded, though he kept his eyes on the target. "I practice with father. *He* is a brilliant swordsman," he added with quiet pride and Elizabeth smiled.

"Better even than the Colonel?" she teased.

"Yes," James averred seriously.

"Well, I'm impressed," Elizabeth replied with a teasing note in her voice; the Duke had glanced over at hearing himself mentioned and looked a little shy at his son's boasting. She smiled playfully at him and then turned back to watch James take his shot. They passed a very enjoyable hour out in the garden, the adults as pleased with the company as the children were with the pursuit. Colonel Fitzwilliam was declared the resounding champion, and Elizabeth accepted second place with a laugh.

"It seems my lot, of late," she noted and then explained the outcome of the footrace back at home when the boys asked her what she meant.

"Let's race now!" Joseph exclaimed excitedly and his father chuckled.

"Not right now, Joe - it's time for luncheon."

As the boys ran on ahead back into the house, Elizabeth waited for the Duke and the Colonel before heading inside as well. She liked both men exceedingly, for they were both good company and their conversation was engaging and intelligent - as befitted their age, she supposed. She put both men in their late thirties, and guessed that the Duke was the younger of the two, even though his children were older. She liked how, despite her being much younger than them, and younger than their wives as well, they spoke to her like a lady and made her feel older than her years.

They joined Lady Georgiana and Jane in the parlour and once the boys had entertained them with tales of their successes, the whole party (with the exception of Clara who had gone for her nap) went into luncheon. All the children, besides making a little noise, behaved themselves admirably and Elizabeth could tell that their parents were pleased with them. Elizabeth, Jane and Daniel only stayed another hour after luncheon before deciding that it was time to return home.

"Are you available on Wednesday, Miss Gardiner?" Lady Georgiana asked Elizabeth as she prepared to leave.

"I have made plans with your cousin, Mr Wickham, in the morning," Elizabeth informed her, "but I am free in the afternoon."

"Oh, well, never mind," Lady Georgiana replied. "I'm sure we shall see one another again soon, at any rate."

"I hope so," Elizabeth replied positively. "It was lovely to meet you, boys," she added, smiling at Joseph and Bradley.

"Will you come with Dan next time he comes to our house to play?" Cathy asked, her tone beseeching. "*Please?*"

"I should be delighted," Elizabeth told her, "though we must check with your papa first."

"You are more than welcome, Miss Gardiner," the Duke assured her.

Cathy clapped her hands and smiled delightedly.

"Tomorrow! You must all come tomorrow!" She declared.

"We shall see, princess," the Duke replied affectionately as everyone else smiled at his daughter.

Saying a final goodbye to everyone, Elizabeth followed Jane and Daniel out to the hall where they gathered their things before going out to the carriage.

"What a lovely day!" She declared once they were underway. "I like the Fitzwilliams very much."

"As do I," Jane agreed.

"When can I go to Cathy and James' house, Mama?" Daniel interrupted them.

"When it is convenient for the Duke, Daniel," Jane responded-seeing her son's disappointment she smiled and added, "Perhaps sometime this week."

"Are you sure you want to go too, Lizzy?" she asked her sister after a moment. "I hope you don't feel as though you have to."

Elizabeth smiled ruefully.

"Perhaps a small outing would be better?" she suggested. "To the park, maybe? Though I'm sure I would be happy enough with Mrs Hughes and Miss Watts for company were I to accompany Dan to the house."

"I will see what can be arranged," Jane decided. "Else I shall simply invite James and Cathy to the house and you can join us all there."

Elizabeth nodded and Dan, seeing that the sisters had concluded their discussion, eagerly engaged Elizabeth in a conversation about archery, pressing her for tips as to how he could improve.

಑ಀಃ

"So, George has an engagement with Miss Gardiner."

The children had all been sent upstairs under the care of the Fitzwilliams' governess, and Darcy remained in the parlour with his sister and cousin. He made no response to the latter's comment.

"What do you suppose he means by it?" Colonel Fitzwilliam asked the room in general.

"Does he have to mean anything by it?" Georgiana responded with amusement. "You make him sound quite the villain."

"Well," her husband hesitated. "How would you describe him?"

"Me?" Georgiana paused for a moment to consider. "Well, I daresay I would think him quite the loveable rogue, were I not aware of how shallow and self-centred he is. But I do not think him a villain at all. And he can be very charming when he wants to be," she added.

"Yes, as evidenced by the number of women who welcome him into their..." the Colonel began to say.

"Please, Richard!" His wife interjected.

"Parlours! I was going to say parlours!" Colonel Fitzwilliam protested and Darcy chuckled at his expression.

"Jane tells me that George is not the only gentleman with whom her sister has engagements," Georgiana began, moving the conversation along. "She has made quite an impression, by all accounts."

"Is her father looking to marry her off?" Colonel Fitzwilliam asked; he was surprised when his wife laughed. "What?"

"I have no idea as to her father's intentions," Georgiana replied, "but if I know Mrs Bennet at all then I daresay *she* will be exerting considerable effort to secure a good match for her niece. I remember what she was like when Jane was first out, and she had set her sights on Sir Charles as the perfect choice," she concluded with a smile. "I have no doubt she shall be just as determined this time around."

"I hope Miss Gardiner does not make an unhappy match, just to please her aunt," Darcy noted, breaking his silence for the first time.

His cousin chuckled.

"The young lady did not strike me as one to simply acquiesce to her aunt's wishes. I think she can handle herself."

"Let us hope so," Georgiana stated and the subject was dropped, though it played on Darcy's mind for some time.

# Chapter 4

The weather on Wednesday was perfect for walking and when Mr Wickham arrived promptly at eleven o'clock, Elizabeth was ready and waiting for him. They spent a few moments with her aunt and uncle before setting off on foot for the park, Wilson following behind at a respectable distance.

"So, have you been enjoying yourself since I last saw you?" Mr Wickham asked as they walked arm in arm.

"I have, yes," Elizabeth responded. "I spent the day with the Fitzwilliams, as you know, and have visited some friends, been to the theatre and last night dined with some friends of my aunt and uncle - the Phillips?"

"Oh, yes, I know them. And are you enjoying your first Season?" Mr Wickham asked her.

"In truth it is really my second," Elizabeth replied. "Though it shall be my first full Season. I made my debut two years ago," she explained when her companion looked intrigued, "but my father was taken ill and I returned home to him. I was only in town for a month."

"Alas that we were not introduced in that time," Mr Wickham lamented charmingly. "For I may have enjoyed your acquaintance for so much longer."

"I am flattered that you think so," Elizabeth replied with an amused smile. "Though I cannot help but wonder whether your regard would have been strong enough to last two whole years - I rather think you would have gotten bored of me after a month," she accused with playful impertinence, though, in truth, it was her honest opinion.

"You do yourself an injustice, Miss Gardiner," Mr Wickham answered with a smile, "in thinking yourself so easily set aside; and you do me an injustice," he added, "in thinking that I would be foolish enough to take for granted so charming a lady."

Elizabeth laughed at this flattering response, which nevertheless rang false with her.

"I see you are determined to live up to your reputation, Mr Wickham."

"My reputation is apparently undeserved," he noted dryly, "given my obvious lack of success in charming you, Miss Gardiner. Laughter was *not* the response I was hoping for."

"Surely you cannot expect *every* woman to fall under you spell?" Elizabeth replied. "And I would not say that I am not charmed - only that I am charmed for, I suspect, all the wrong reasons," she added, laughing lightly again.

Mr Wickham seemed to smile in spite of himself as he replied.

"You will forgive me if I do not ask what reasons they are - I am not sure my ego could stand it."

"Might I suggest, then, in the interest of preserving your ego, that you try to refrain from any attempt to charm me and simply talk to me instead," Elizabeth proposed lightly. "I am much less likely to laugh at you that way, and I am sure we shall get along famously."

"I suppose I could try," Mr Wickham granted with a sigh, followed by a grin. "Though I cannot promise anything."

"As long as you try, that is all I can ask," Elizabeth replied and they lapsed into a brief silence before her companion asked her what she had seen at the theatre and they fell into a discussion of the performance.

When they reached the park they found it to be rather busy with people out enjoying the nice weather and Elizabeth couldn't help noticing the attention she and her companion were garnering. Mr Wickham noticed it too and laughed unexpectedly.

"They would not be half so interested if they knew that you had placed an embargo on flirtation," he noted and Elizabeth laughed at the notion.

"Do you usually create so much interest?" she asked him quietly, not wishing to be overheard.

"Usually," Mr Wickham replied casually, with a slight shrug.

"How flattering for you," Elizabeth noted sarcastically.

"Should I have said that it was your lovely, stunning self that was drawing the attention?" Her companion asked with amusement. "Were I allowed, I daresay I would have, but I am almost certain that would count as flirting," he teased with his usual charming grin.

"It would also be utter nonsense," Elizabeth pointed out. She smiled when Mr Wickham seemed surprised and went on, "I think we both know that they could not care less about me or whether I am lovely or stunning - they are interested only in the fact that we are *together*, and all the possible implications of that fact."

"You really do not mince your words, do you Miss Gardiner?" Mr Wickham asked rhetorically. "You are quite correct, of course, but I am not sure I know of many other young ladies who would have been quite so frank about it."

"Why should we pretend?" Elizabeth responded lightly. "If we are to be friends we should have no illusions about each other."

"Being friends with me could cause you a lot of trouble - not least with your uncle," Mr Wickham replied and grinned when Elizabeth laughed.

"He is not particularly fond of you," she agreed.

"I would say he positively hates me!" Mr Wickham asserted, still smiling.

"I can manage my uncle," Elizabeth assured him, "just so long as you behave yourself."

"Cross my heart," her new friend teased and she smiled in spite of herself at his cheeky, irrepressible grin.

"This shall be a first for me," he noted after a moment. "I have never been simply friends with a woman before. What does it entail, precisely? Apart from no flirting," he teased. "Are we allowed to dance?"

"Of course," Elizabeth replied. "We may do all manner of things - though for now why don't we just enjoy the lovely day and each other's company?" she suggested lightly and her companion deemed it a good plan.

"Will you tell me about yourself?" Mr Wickham asked some time later as they ambled around the park. "I should like to know more about you."

"I shall answer whatever questions you put to me - within reason," Elizabeth qualified with a warning look.

"Very well; let us start with the basics. Where are you from?" Mr Wickham asked first and Elizabeth smiled at his teasing.

"Hertfordshire. My father's estate is called Longbourn and I have lived there my whole life."

"And how long is that?"

"I shall be twenty this year."

"And your sister, Lady Bingley," Mr Wickham went on, "she is your senior by ten years?"

"Nine," Elizabeth corrected.

"And is it just the two of you? You have no other siblings?"

Elizabeth shook her head and then smiled when Mr Wickham told her he was an only child.

"Why am I not surprised to hear that?" she teased.

Her companion chuckled and then asked her to tell him more about her home. She was happy enough to oblige him but kept her answers brief - for all his apparent interest Elizabeth could tell he was only asking her these questions because he thought it was what she wanted to talk about. She suspected that he would forget all about what she had said before the day was out. She told him a little about Longbourn and some of her neighbours before turning the tables and asking about his home.

"I reside here in town for most of the year," he replied.

"With your mother?"

Elizabeth blushed as soon as the words passed her lips and Mr Wickham smiled roguishly before he eventually replied.

"No - I have rooms in Belgrave Street. My mother stays with a friend whenever she comes to town - which is rather rarely - but otherwise lives in Nottinghamshire."

"You cannot see her often, then," Elizabeth observed.

"I see her whenever I can," Mr Wickham replied lightly, but Elizabeth thought the way he quickly moved the conversation along quite telling. "Have you ever been to Nottinghamshire?"

"Yes, many times. Sir Charles and my sister live there."

"Of course, forgive me. How do you like it?"

"Very much," Elizabeth replied. "Though I hear it is nothing compared to Yorkshire, or Derbyshire."

"You have not been to Pemberley, then," her companion surmised. "My cousin's estate in Derbyshire," he explained when Elizabeth looked at him, confused.

"No, I have never had the pleasure," she replied before asking, "Are you cousins through marriage?"

"My mother was the old Duke's sister," Mr Wickham responded before going on to say, "Our family tree is rather complicated."

"How so?"

"Well, Uncle George married Lady Anne Fitzwilliam, the eldest daughter of the then Earl of Matlock, whose youngest daughter, Catherine, married Sir Lewis de Bourg. Lady Catherine's daughter Anne married her cousin, the current Duke, whilst the youngest son of the old Earl, Colonel Fitzwilliam, married his cousin Georgiana, the Duke's sister."

"That is rather complex!" Elizabeth laughingly agreed. "I had no idea that the Duke and his wife were cousins," she admitted.

"Yes - it was one of those pre-arranged things that old families like the Darcys and the Fitzwilliams are so fond of," Mr Wickham teased, though Elizabeth thought his voice held a note of derision.

"Families like yours, you mean," she pointed out.

"*I*," her companion informed her proudly, "am a Wickham. Our ideas are a little more modern."

"That is one word for it, I suppose," Elizabeth quipped and Mr Wickham laughed.

They had reached a large pond around which a number of other people were walking and several children were feeding the ducks. Elizabeth smiled as she observed them.

"You seem fond of children, Miss Gardiner."

"Oh, I am," Elizabeth replied. A little way away from them two boys began arguing ill-temperedly and she smiled and qualified, "Nice children, at least!"

"I cannot claim to have any fondness for them, myself," Mr Wickham surprised her by saying. "I should be happy not to have any, though I suppose I must."

"You would be happy to see all your worldly goods pass to some obscure relation, then?" Elizabeth teasingly inquired.

Mr Wickham shrugged.

"Perhaps. Rather that than bring a child into the world that would not be properly cared for." Elizabeth must have looked a little appalled for he hastened to add, "I do not mean to say that I would wilfully neglect any child of mine, but even my best efforts must fall short. I am a hopeless creature, and not at all cut out for parenthood," he concluded with what Elizabeth supposed was meant to be an endearing smile.

"I suppose you expect me to compliment you for having the wherewithal to recognise your own shortcomings," she replied. "But to be honest I think you are just making excuses."

"For what?" Mr Wickham questioned.

"For your self-centredness," Elizabeth replied lightly, not at all critically.

Her companion nevertheless frowned.

"I am not sure we have been friends long enough for you to say so, Miss Gardiner."

"Perhaps not," Elizabeth granted. "But did you not note earlier that I do not mince my words? And did I not say that there was no need for pretence? Why don't you just admit that you do not want children because you do not wish to spend your time raising them? I daresay most people share the same sentiment," she concluded.

"But you do not," her companion pointed out.

Elizabeth smiled.

"No, I do not. But I hope that honesty would take precedence over any desire to pander to me, Mr Wickham," she added. "We shall never be friends otherwise."

Mr Wickham looked at her for a long moment of indecision before finally smiling ruefully and shaking his head.

"I cannot recall anyone ever speaking to me in this way - let alone a girl who is not even twenty!"

"Trust me," Elizabeth teased him irrepressibly. "It will do you the world of good!"

"My reputation would be ruined if anyone heard you," he noted with a reluctant smile as he looked about them.

"Shall I make a show of simpering and gazing at you adoringly when we leave?" Elizabeth asked. "Would that make you feel better?"

"I daresay it would," Mr Wickham joked with a self-deprecating grin.

"Then why don't we begin our journey back now," Elizabeth suggested. "For Wilson is looking a little frightening. No doubt she is suspicious of our having tarried here for so long."

"All you need do is tell her of our conversation," Mr Wickham replied as they began to retrace their steps through the park. "And she will think me as harmless as a lamb."

Elizabeth laughed.

"That would make me the wolf, I suppose."

"In sheep's clothing," Mr Wickham averred with a grin. "And I should know, for that is usually *my* role!"

ം‌‌ღ‌‌ഓ

The door had barely closed behind her before Charlotte had eagerly approached her friend and sat down beside her.

"Well?"

"Well what?" Elizabeth asked, confused.

"Your walk with Mr Wickham this morning," Charlotte elaborated. "How was it? What was he like? Mother has sent me with detailed instructions of all that I must find out from you!"

"All teasing aside, Lizzy - how was it?" Charlotte asked after the two of them had shared a laugh.

"It was just a walk," Elizabeth replied with a smile.

"No one goes on just a walk with Mr Wickham," Charlotte pointed out, smiling also.

Elizabeth rolled her eyes.

"It was fine."

"Just fine?"

"Quite enjoyable, I suppose," Elizabeth admitted. "He is an entertaining companion, if a little lacking in substance."

"Really?" Charlotte looked surprised. "But everyone speaks so highly of him, or of his charms, at least," she amended and Elizabeth chuckled.

"Oh, of those he has plenty! Though rather misapplied in my case. He *is* rather amusing," she felt compelled to admit before adding, "but I think his company would become rather tiresome very quickly. I shouldn't like to be stuck with him for any length of time."

"That seems a little harsh," Charlotte objected softly.

"Perhaps it is," Elizabeth granted easily. "But I am sure you would agree with me. He is so...he just has no substance! I cannot think of a better way to describe him. He smiles and laughs and seems utterly charming, but as soon as he departed I was left with the impression of," she gestured vaguely with her hands as she searched for the right words. "Nothingness? We really spoke of nothing of any importance, and he did not say anything which did not seem intended to please me, unless I had goaded him into it."

"What do you mean?" Charlotte asked and Elizabeth proceeded to relate to her friend some of the pertinent particulars of her conversation with Mr Wickham.

"Lizzy!" Charlotte giggled even as she tried to chastise her friend. "You did not really say those things!"

"I am afraid I did," Elizabeth averred with a slight blush. "Which I think goes to show how little I thought of him - I would never have spoken to another gentleman that way."

"I *am* surprised he allowed it," Charlotte admitted thoughtfully.

"So was I," Elizabeth replied before confessing worriedly, "though now I fear that he thought I was flirting with him all along."

"He could easily have taken your words in that way," Charlotte felt compelled to agree and Elizabeth sighed.

"Do you think my manner is often mistaken for flirtatious?" she asked her friend after a moment, trusting that Charlotte would be honest with her.

"Sometimes," Charlotte replied after a slight hesitation before adding, "Although I have to say that though your teasing can sometimes create the wrong impression, the fact that you tease *everyone* in the same manner soon sets things right again. Don't let it trouble you," she advised, "your behaviour is not at all improper."

"Nevertheless, I think I shall try to be a little more circumspect in future. And certainly with regards to Mr Wickham!"

"Do you plan on seeing him again?" Charlotte asked.

"I doubt I shall be able to avoid it," Elizabeth pointed out dryly. "My aunt seems to have set her sights on him. And I did tell him I thought we could be friends," she admitted, "though time will tell what he thought I meant by *that!*"

Charlotte laughed.

"I should like to be there if you have to rebuff his advances - his surprise would no doubt be rather amusing to see!"

"Thank you for laughing at my predicament," Elizabeth retorted, smiling.

"You are perfectly welcome," Charlotte replied and the two friends shared a laugh.

"Oh, I meant to ask you," Charlotte exclaimed some time later, interrupting their discussion of an upcoming party they had both been invited to. "Father and I are going to view the Elgin Marbles tomorrow, if you wish to join us?"

"Oh, yes, I would like that," Elizabeth replied.

She and Charlotte made arrangements for her friend and Sir William to collect her the following day before Charlotte realised the time and had to return home. The two friends said brief farewells, knowing that they would see one another again soon.

&#8359;&#8360;

The following morning Elizabeth found herself part of a larger party than originally planned as they travelled to the British Museum, as Mr Bennet and Charlotte's younger sister, Maria, had both decided to join Charlotte, Sir William and herself. They all bundled into the Lucas's carriage and carried on several enthusiastic conversations as they made the short trip across town. The recently acquired marbles were housed in a temporary gallery whilst the aptly named "Elgin Room" was being built and Elizabeth and her party went directly there, joining the throngs of people eagerly examining the much talked of exhibition.

Mr Bennet and Sir William soon paired off, leaving the girls to their own devices as they wandered around the gallery. Charlotte, Maria and Elizabeth remained together for some time as they examined various figures, but the latter's tendency to linger over the exhibits soon resulted in her being left by herself as the sisters went on ahead. Elizabeth did not mind this at all and was quite happy to move from piece to piece at her leisure, reading the information provided and wishing that there was more. She was amazed by the sheer scale of some of the statues, and the workmanship they displayed, her hand itching to reach out and touch the marble, to see if it felt as smooth and cool as it looked. The whole Elgin collection consisted of more than just the famous marbles, and Elizabeth eventually found herself in a smaller gallery which housed vases, bronzes, jewellery and drawings - as well as the most curious part of the collection (in Elizabeth's opinion), a colossal stone carving of some sort of beetle. As she was staring at it in confused amazement, she felt someone come to stand beside her.

"It is a scarab beetle."

Elizabeth looked up with surprise and then smiled.

"Your Grace!"

The Duke returned her smile and gave a slight bow.

"Good day, Miss Gardiner."

"What a pleasant surprise to see you," Elizabeth noted after she had wished him a good day as well.

"Yes," the Duke agreed. "I saw you standing here and could not help coming over. You are not here alone?" he asked.

"Oh, no," Elizabeth assured him. "I came with my uncle and Sir William Lucas and his two daughters. They will be here somewhere," she concluded before teasingly adding, "unless they have left without me! I shall have to rely on your goodness to see me home, if that is the case."

"I should be happy to help," the Duke responded, "though I sincerely doubt you have been abandoned."

"Certainly not completely," Elizabeth replied, "though as you see I have been left to peruse the exhibition all alone. Charlotte and Maria's interest only goes so far, I'm afraid," she lamented with a smile. "I think they will simply be happy to say that they have seen the collection. Not that there is anything wrong with that," she added quickly, lest it seem she were insulting her friends.

The Duke nodded.

"It is what the exhibition is for, after all."

"Exactly," Elizabeth concurred with a bright smile. She looked back at the massive carving and admitted, "Though for myself I cannot help but wish there was a little more information. This is a scarab beetle, you say?"

"Yes," the Duke replied, coming closer so they could examine the piece together. "An Egyptian creature. Elgin acquired this piece in Istanbul."

Elizabeth looked up at the Duke with interest.

"Do you know anything more about it?"

"Only that it is carved in granite," the Duke replied apologetically. "There is, as you say, limited information available about the collection, particularly these pieces which were not taken from the Acropolis. I have tried my best to find out more, though, for I find the history of the Greek civilisation quite fascinating."

He looked a little embarrassed after saying this, as though he were worried about boring her.

Elizabeth hastened to reassure him.

"So do I! I should love to go to Athens one day to see it for myself, though I doubt it shall be for many years, if I manage to go at all. I suppose for now I shall have to content myself with viewing collections such as this," she concluded cheerfully.

"I have mixed feelings as to whether Elgin was right to take these pieces from the Acropolis," the Duke confessed, "but I must admit it is a pleasure to be able to see them."

"Will you be my guide?" Elizabeth asked on impulse. "As you seem to know so much about the collection."

"I am no expert," the Duke hesitated.

"Please?" Elizabeth asked. "I really would like to know more."

After a slight pause, the Duke finally smiled.

"Very well. Where would you like to begin?"

"I will leave that up to you," Elizabeth replied.

"It would take us too long to go through the entire collection in detail," the Duke mused.

"How large is it?" Elizabeth interrupted curiously.

"There are over thirty pieces of architecture from the Parthenon alone," the Duke replied. "And over two hundred feet of frieze."

"Do you know much about the frieze?" Elizabeth asked and when the Duke nodded she suggested, "Then why don't we begin there?"

They went back into the main gallery and made their way to the first piece of the frieze. They began making their way along it, the Duke describing what was depicted, the figures and what they symbolised. At first he was a little hesitant and kept glancing at Elizabeth with uncertainty, as though he were trying to judge whether she were bored and losing interest, but she was honestly fascinated by all he had to tell her and the glances soon stopped and he proceeded with more enthusiasm, getting caught up in his subject. His intelligence was easily apparent, and he was an engaging companion, easily maintaining her interest and entertaining her with the occasional flash of humour.

"Oh, I wish I had my drawing things with me," Elizabeth sighed as they stood in front of one of the frieze panels, speaking almost to herself.

"I did not know you draw," the Duke commented and she startled inwardly before smiling up at him.

"Oh, yes."

"And you enjoy drawing things like this?" The Duke asked, gesturing to the piece in front of them.

"I would, very much," Elizabeth replied. "I also draw people and landscapes when I have the time. When I am at home I help my father with his studies," she revealed, and then wondered why she had done so.

"His studies?" The Duke queried with a look of interest.

"His is a horticulturalist, I suppose you could say. He is fascinated by plants and flowers, and often conducts experiments with them. I help him by illustrating the studies he conducts."

"You must be very talented, to draw with the necessary detail," the Duke noted and Elizabeth was grateful to him for avoiding commenting on her father's rather unusual hobby.

"I confess it took many years to reach the level of skill required," Elizabeth admitted - she fell silent for a moment as she remembered her efforts as a young girl, trying her hardest to please her father, to gain just a little of his attention.

"So do you paint as well as draw?" The Duke gently pulled her from her melancholy thoughts.

"A little," Elizabeth replied. "Though only with watercolours. I really prefer drawing."

"I should very much like to see some of your work," the Duke said. "If you would not mind showing me, that is."

"Not at all," Elizabeth assured him. "And if I have the chance to make a study of these," she gestured to the carvings beside them, "I most assuredly will show them to you."

"I would like that very much, thank you," the Duke responded with a smile and they continued on their way along the frieze.

Happy as she was in the Duke's company, Elizabeth was oblivious to the passage of time and would happily have remained with him for even longer had not Charlotte and Maria interrupted them.

"Lizzy! There you are! We have been looking everywhere for you!"

Charlotte and her sister made their way to Elizabeth's side, only then realising she was with someone. Maria blushed with sudden shyness whilst Charlotte managed to hide her surprise and curiosity quite well.

"I'm sorry Charlotte," Elizabeth apologised lightly. "I lost track of time. Have you been introduced?" she asked, indicating her companion who stood silently beside her.

"I have not had the pleasure of being introduced to either of your friends," the Duke replied before Charlotte could and so Elizabeth happily did the honours.

"This is my good friend, Miss Lucas, and her sister, Miss Maria Lucas. Charlotte, Maria, this is His Grace, the Duke of Farleigh."

"It is a pleasure to meet you, Your Grace," Charlotte intoned as she and Maria both curtseyed politely and the Duke bowed slightly in response.

"His Grace has been acting as my guide through the exhibit," Elizabeth explained to her friends. "And has played his part admirably - you had me quite enthralled!" She concluded with a smile up at the Duke who returned it shyly.

Charlotte nodded and looked between the two of them before she turned to her friend.

"Well, I'm sorry to interrupt you, but my father and your uncle both wish to leave."

Elizabeth's disappointment was obvious.

"Oh, well, I had best come along. Thank you so much for indulging me," she said to the Duke. "I know it was an imposition, but I have had a lovely time."

"On the contrary, Miss Gardiner," the Duke assured her sincerely. "It was my pleasure."

"Perhaps when our paths next cross we can resume our discussion," Elizabeth suggested hopefully and was pleased when the Duke replied in the affirmative.

"I would be happy to. Until then, Miss Gardiner," he bowed slightly and Elizabeth smiled as she curtseyed to him and then followed after Charlotte and Maria.

"Were you with him the whole time?" Charlotte asked once they were out of earshot.

"Not the whole time, no," Elizabeth replied, a little surprised by the question. "Why?"

"I just, you seemed quite familiar with one another. I did not realise you knew him at all well," Charlotte explained.

"In truth I have only begun to know him since coming to town," Elizabeth replied. "But we have been in one another's company a number of times. He is a very nice man."

Charlotte regarded her friend for a moment before dismissing her suspicions - Elizabeth's tone and expression gave no indication that she thought anything more of the Duke than what she had already stated. Remembering the way *his* eyes had lingered on her friend, however, Charlotte was not sure she could say the same for the Duke.

಄಄಄

Darcy remained at the museum for some time after Miss Gardiner had departed before he made his way to his club, where he had arranged to meet a friend for luncheon. He was a little early and sat down to wait, smiling when he finally saw his friend, the Duke of Bellamy, striding towards his table.

"Darcy!"

"Ellerslie," Darcy returned the greeting, clapping his friend on the shoulder and shaking the proffered hand.

Matthew Walker Ellerslie, the fifth Duke of Bellamy, was a short, stout man with black hair and blue eyes. He and Darcy had known each other since school, but had not seen each other for almost two years.

"How are you?" Ellerslie asked as they both sat down. "You are looking well."

"I am very well," Darcy replied - he grinned as he noted, "You are looking old."

Ellerslie gave a sharp bark of laughter.

"Thank you very much! You are quite right though," he admitted ruefully after a moment, running a hand through his hair which was heavily threaded through with grey. He eyed Darcy's deep brown locks with something akin to envy. "You look as young as ever, damn you."

"My existence is a good deal more peaceful than yours, I imagine," Darcy responded and his friend sighed and rolled his eyes. "How are things with your family these days?"

"Jacqueline and I still fight like cat and dog, and my eldest is more trouble than he's worth. He is determined to send me to an early grave, I swear it," Ellerslie lamented, only half joking.

Darcy looked at his friend with sympathy, though he knew there was nothing he could really do or say to help.

"Why my parents had to choose me such a shrew for a wife?" Ellerslie muttered, shaking his head. He gestured to Darcy, "You have always had all the luck. Anne was a good woman."

"Yes," Darcy agreed quietly. He had not loved his wife, or held her in very much affection, but they had gotten along quite well, in their own way, for the duration of their brief marriage and as his friend's experience showed it could have been a lot worse.

"But enough of my complaints," Ellerslie shook himself up and smiled over at his friend. "Tell me what you've been doing with yourself. And your family, the children, how are they? How old are they now?"

"James is thirteen, and Catherine is eight," Darcy replied with a soft smile. "And they are both well - enjoying spending time in town, I think."

"James must be starting school soon, no?"

"In the autumn," Darcy confirmed and it was obvious from his expression how little he liked the prospect.

"They grow up fast, don't they," Ellerslie noted with a smile - he and his eldest son had their problems, but he got on very well with his second son and daughter.

"They do,' Darcy concurred. "James is as tall as Richard now."

"No!" Ellerslie laughed. "He must tower over me!"

Darcy laughed and admitted that his son was indeed quite a bit taller than his friend.

"The lad obviously takes after you, then," Ellerslie noted. "And all the other Darcys."

"It certainly seems that way," Darcy agreed. "Speaking of which, my niece, Clara, is the very image of Georgiana. You shall have to meet her and see for yourself - it is like looking at Georgiana at that age."

Ellerslie smiled with remembrance.

"She was a sweet little thing when she was a child. And utterly smitten with you," he added with a chuckle when Darcy looked a little embarrassed. "What about Catherine? She doesn't take after her namesake, I hope."

Darcy looked a little disapproving - he did not like to be disrespectful of the dead - but nevertheless replied.

"No, not at all, she is very much her own person," he paused and then grinned, "although saying that, she does enjoy getting her own way, and can issue demands like a queen."

"That sounds like Lady Catherine," Ellerslie noted and Darcy chuckled in spite of himself.

The two friends enjoyed a leisurely luncheon as they continued to catch up on one another's lives, having not seen each other for so long. They made plans for their families to spend time together, knowing that James and Lawrence, Ellerslie's second son, would be particularly pleased to see one another again.

"Are you going to the Harding's affair tonight?" Ellerslie asked after they'd finished luncheon and were about to go their separate ways.

"I believe so," Darcy responded. "I can't keep track of all these damned engagements."

Ellerslie clapped him on the shoulder.

"You haven't played the social game for a while. But I shall see you there. It is good to see you again, Darcy."

"You too," Darcy responded warmly and the two friends shook hands and then left for their respective homes. When Darcy got back to his townhouse he immediately sought out his son, who was upstairs at his lessons with Mr Hughes.

"Could I interrupt for a moment?" he asked, when he reached the school room. James looked up from his work and then rose to his feet.

"Hello Father."

"Good afternoon," Darcy replied. "I've just got back from luncheon with Ellerslie. You remember my friend, don't you?"

"Of course," James assured him. "How is he?"

"Very well," Darcy replied. "We have made plans next week for us to visit with his family. Lawrence is home from school at the moment - I thought you'd like to spend some time with him."

"I would like that very much, thank you Father," James responded politely, though Darcy could tell how pleased he was by the prospect. Lawrence was only a year older than James and one of the few boys of his own age that James counted as a good friend.

"I shall leave you to your lessons," Darcy said, nodding at Mr Hughes who stood patiently waiting to resume teaching. "Come and find me when you are done and we shall have a game of something," he told his son.

"Could we practice fencing?" James asked hopefully instead.

"Perhaps," Darcy replied neutrally, though his smile gave him away.

"I shall be as quick as possible," James promised and, true to his word, promptly sat down and went back to his work.

Darcy smiled with affection and pride before leaving his son to his lessons and going in search of his daughter. He found her in her room, sat on the floor surrounded by an elaborate scene.

"What do we have here?" he asked, eyeing the dolls and chairs and tables as he came forward and crouched down beside his daughter.

"Hello Papa," Catherine greeted him, holding her face up expectantly. Only when Darcy had pressed a kiss to her cheek did she reply, "It is a dinner party."

"I see," Darcy responded. "And who are the guests?"

"This is you," Catherine indicated the doll at the top of the table. "And this is Uncle Richard. And this," she held up her favourite doll and stroked the hair, "is Lizzy."

"Lizzy?" Darcy repeated with confusion - he had been expecting her to say Lady Jane.

"Miss Gardiner," Catherine explained patiently.

"I see," Darcy replied calmly. "And what are we having?"

"Shortbread with jam and cream," Catherine stated decisively and Darcy chuckled.

"For dinner?" he asked.

"It is Lizzy's favourite," Catherine replied. "I asked her."

"Well, in that case," Darcy responded, hiding his amusement. He bent and kissed the top of his daughter's head as he said, "I shall leave you to your party."

"Are you going out tonight?" Catherine asked as he straightened. When he nodded she asked, "You will come and say goodnight, won't you?"

"Of course I will," Darcy promised. "And tomorrow we shall read some more of our story."

James appeared in the doorway.

"I have finished, Father."

Darcy smiled and shook his head with amusement.

"That was quick. I shall see you later, princess," he said to his daughter but she was already busy playing with her dolls. He and James shared a smile before he pretended to sigh and said, "Come along then, let's see if you can best me yet."

"There is very little chance of that, father," James replied as they walked together to the stairs.

"The day you manage it I shall feel very old indeed," Darcy joked.

"You're already old," James pointed out with a grin, laughing when his father cuffed him on the arm.

"Cheeky bugger!"

# Chapter 5

When Darcy walked into the ballroom at the Harding's home, he searched the crowd for any of his friends and family. He spotted Mr Bennet off to one side and immediately headed towards him.

"Good evening, Your Grace," Mr Bennet greeted him when he saw him approach.

"Good evening, Mr Bennet," Darcy replied. "You are well, I hope?"

"Oh, perfectly fine," Mr Bennet replied in his careless way - Darcy had always had the impression that Mr Bennet could not be bothered to feel anything besides fine.

"You are not here alone?" Darcy asked and the elder man chuckled.

"As if I would be here were the choice left to me," he responded. "My wife is over there with a friend, and Lizzy, as you see, is dancing."

Darcy looked where he had indicated and saw Miss Gardiner looking as lovely as ever as she danced with yet another young man. She certainly seemed to be as popular as Georgiana had stated.

"She told me of her meeting with you this morning, at the museum," Mr Bennet went on. "I was sorry to have missed you myself. It was very good of you to show Lizzy around."

"It was my pleasure," Darcy assured Mr Bennet politely, just as he was expected to. Mr Bennet would never know that Darcy was not just being polite.

"Did you follow the proceedings of the Committee, when the issue was debated in Parliament?" Mr Bennet asked him.

Darcy nodded.

"I did."

"The government certainly drove a hard bargain when they purchased the marbles from him, eh?" Mr Bennet chuckled and Darcy expressed his agreement. "I expect he was happy to see the back of them - more trouble than they're worth, I'd say."

"Did you not enjoy the exhibit?" Darcy asked just as Miss Gardiner appeared on the arm of her dancing partner. She smiled up at him as she curtsied.

"Hello again, Your Grace."

Darcy returned her smile and then Mr Bennet introduced her partner to him - a Mr Jacob Long - who bowed deeply to Darcy before excusing himself to return to his family. As Miss Gardiner watched him go, Darcy noticed that she seemed to be suppressing a laugh and wondered what was so amusing - her uncle noticed it too and was less circumspect.

"What's so funny, Lizzy?"

Miss Gardiner glanced at Darcy and seemed to hesitate for a moment before she replied.

"Mr Long and I were playing a little game whilst we were dancing, and I won, so now he has gone to receive his punishment."

"You are speaking in riddles, my dear," Mr Bennet told her dryly. "Please explain."

Miss Gardiner sighed dramatically and rolled her eyes.

"Fine. Though it is rather embarrassing, and I shall blush terribly, especially with His Grace here as well."

"I can go..." Darcy was about to offer to absent himself when Miss Gardiner laughed lightly and laid her hand on his arm.

"I was only teasing," she assured him with sparkling eyes. "Please don't go."

Reassured, Darcy remained where he was and listened to her explanation.

"Mr Long has returned to his mother to report that our dance was not at all a success, and that he fears he has lost all favour with me - he is no doubt suffering her ire whilst Mrs Bennet silently rejoices. Had *I* lost our game I would have had to report to Mrs Bennet that I was very pleased with my partner and thought him delightful, pleasing Mrs Long and greatly vexing my aunt."

"Why would Mrs Bennet be displeased that you enjoyed your dance with Mr Long?" Darcy asked as Mr Bennet chuckled quietly beside him.

"She believes that *I can do better*," Miss Gardiner replied in a perfect imitation of her aunt and Mr Bennet laughed outright. She looked a little embarrassed as she admitted to Darcy, "I know it was cruel of us, but Mr Long and I both find their competitive behaviour rather amusing. And their matchmaking," she added with an eye roll.

Darcy smiled in spite of himself and was reassured that Miss Gardiner would not let herself fall victim to any of her aunt's machinations.

"But I interrupted your conversation," Miss Gardiner reminded them suddenly. "You were speaking of Elgin and his marbles."

"So we were," Mr Bennet said. "And to answer your question, Your Grace, I share Lord Byron's view that such artefacts should be left in the hands of history, to decay with time, as is natural. Lizzy disagrees with me though," he added with a smile at his niece. "Don't you my dear?"

"Yes, and certainly after today," Miss Gardiner replied. "Lord Byron may wish it, but I should be sorry to see the Acropolis fall into ruin and fade away into history. I think such important artefacts should be preserved."

"If not only for our own enjoyment," Darcy put in, "but for the enjoyment and education of future generations. I plan to take my children to see the exhibit, and it pleases me to think of them doing the same with their own."

Miss Gardiner nodded and smiled but was then distracted by something over Darcy's shoulder.

"Oh, look, I believe your sister is trying to catch your attention, Your Grace."

Darcy turned and saw that Georgiana was indeed waving to him from across the room. He turned back to his two companions.

"I shall go and speak with her. It was a pleasure speaking to you both."

"Thank you again for today, Your Grace," Miss Gardiner told him with a smile and Darcy nodded. And then he had said the next words before he even had a chance to think about it.

"Would you do me the honour of dancing with me this evening, Miss Gardiner?"

"I should be delighted," she replied. "I am engaged for the next two sets, but I shall reserve the next for you."

Darcy bowed and departed, inwardly berating himself. What on earth had possessed him? *You know exactly what possessed you*, his mind whispered at him and Darcy shook his head and went in search of his sister. He needed to find some other ladies to dance with, and quickly.

&#8270;&#8270;&#8270;

Elizabeth watched the Duke go for a moment before turning back to her uncle, intending to ask him if he had seen Jane or Sir Charles at all yet. She was prevented from doing so by the arrival of Mr Wickham.

"Good evening, Mr Bennet, Miss Gardiner."

He took her hand and bowed over it as Elizabeth, a little surprised by his sudden appearance, finally remembered to curtsey and did so with not as much grace as usual.

"Good evening, Mr Wickham," she greeted him at last.

"It is a pleasure to see you again," Mr Wickham told her with a broad smile. "I thoroughly enjoyed our walk the other day and have been waiting for the opportunity to enjoy more of your delightful company."

"And storing up compliments in the meantime, I see," Elizabeth quipped and Mr Bennet choked on a laugh.

Mr Wickham was undeterred - indeed, he seemed pleased with her teasing.

"I am ready to do battle this evening, Miss Gardiner. I have sharpened my wit in preparation, you could say," he joked and Elizabeth smiled reluctantly.

"If you have need to prepare, you are obviously no match for my niece," Mr Bennet pointed out.

"Don't be so hard on him, Uncle," Elizabeth replied before Mr Wickham could. "He is new to this game."

Mr Bennet's brows rose and Elizabeth's eyes sparkled mischievously - Mr Wickham remained oblivious to the slight and forged ahead.

"Ah, but I am an eager player."

"Of that we are well aware, Mr Wickham" Elizabeth responded dryly and then she smiled sweetly. "You have come to claim your dance, I suppose?"

"I have," Mr Wickham confirmed. "I would be delighted to dance the supper set with you, so that we may..."

"I'm afraid I have already granted that set to someone else," Elizabeth interrupted him, and wishing to bring him down a step or two she added, "Indeed, all my dances bar the sixth are taken."

Elizabeth had intentionally left the last but one dance free, knowing that it was perhaps the least important and wishing to send Mr Wickham a clear message - she was not waiting for him to sweep her off her feet.

"And there is no chance that you could swap partners for the supper set?" Mr Wickham suggested cheekily, his grin boyish and charming.

Elizabeth was unmoved.

"I'm afraid not."

"Then I shall content myself with the set you have given me," Mr Wickham recovered quickly. "And look forward to it with pleasure."

"Until then, Mr Wickham," Elizabeth replied, effectively dismissing him. She noticed as he bowed and walked away that several people turned away when she looked at them and realised that they must have been watching.

"I don't know what I was worried about," Mr Bennet commented with a chuckle once they were alone. "You were running rings around him!"

"It is rather easy to do," Elizabeth replied. "Which takes some of the enjoyment out of it."

"Only some, though, eh?" Mr Bennet teased and Elizabeth grinned.

 හ෴ෆ

Darcy, with the help of his sister, managed to find two partners for the sets preceding his dance with Miss Gardiner. If Georgiana was surprised by his sudden desire to dance, she didn't show it, and helped him find suitable partners. Both were pleasant ladies and he enjoyed his dances as well as he was able, enduring them as a necessity now that he had asked Miss Gardiner to dance. He still didn't know what had possessed him, though he tried to tell himself it was perfectly acceptable for him to dance with Miss Gardiner. Indeed, her reaction - or even lack of reaction - should have been reassurance enough that there was nothing unusual in his requesting a set and eventually he realised that he was worrying over nothing. What would people think, after all? That there was a match in the making? That he, who was known for his lack of interest in socialising, was pursuing the young, beautiful and vivacious Miss Gardiner? The idea was preposterous, ridiculous even, and Darcy was quite consoled. No one would suspect a thing and his inclinations (he would not call them *feelings*) would remain a private matter.

"You had best locate your partner, Darcy, else you will miss your set," Ellerslie, who Darcy had been speaking with, prompted him and Darcy heeded his advice and went in search of Miss Gardiner.

He found her with her sister and Sir Charles and the couple both greeted him warmly.

"We shall see you at our table," Sir Charles said to him as he led his wife away to join the other couples, leaving Darcy and Miss Gardiner alone.

Darcy turned to her and she smiled sweetly up at him as he bowed slightly.

"Miss Gardiner."

He took her hand and led her to the dance floor, noticing as he did so how small her hand seemed enclosed in his own much larger one, though she was not what he would call petite as the top of her head easily reached his chin. She just had very small, delicate hands.

"Your Grace?"

"Forgive me," Darcy startled back to attention. "I was miles away."

As they progressed through the first few movements of the dance he racked his brain for something to say, but his mind had gone frustratingly blank.

"You must be in a complimentary mood tonight, Your Grace," Miss Gardiner surprised him by saying as they passed one another, and he noticed that her eyes were dancing again.

"Must I?" he replied, a little confused.

"Indeed, for you are dancing," she replied. "And I know it is a compliment you rarely pay to a place, if you can avoid it."

Darcy must have looked as surprised as he felt as Miss Gardiner skipped away, laughing lightly.

"It was you, in the shadows," he said when the dance brought them back together.

"Indeed it was!" Miss Gardiner admitted merrily, blushing rather becomingly, Darcy thought. "I had no intention of eavesdropping, but I'm rather glad I did. You have a fabulous sense of humour, Your Grace."

"Thank you," Darcy responded with a grin. "I must say, surprised though I was, I was glad *someone* understood the joke."

"I know exactly what you mean," Miss Gardiner emphasised and they shared another smile.

"I must say, though," she complimented him a moment later: "you dance wonderfully, for someone who professes to dislike the pastime so much."

"Thank you," Darcy responded again, gratified that she should think so when she had danced with so many other - and younger - men.

They did not speak again for several minutes after this as Miss Gardiner was distracted by the woman dancing next to her, falling into what appeared to be a very absorbing conversation. Darcy watched with interest, waiting for a return of her attention.

"Forgive me," she said at last, turning back to him. "I was neglecting you."

"I could see you were quite captivated by your partner to your left," Darcy responded, simultaneously expressing his curiosity and indicating that he had taken no offence.

"Apparently," Miss Gardiner surprised him by saying, "there has been a burglary."

Darcy frowned at the unwelcome news.

"Where?"

"At the home of Lord and Lady Blendiscoe," she replied. "Apparently a group of men were interrupted in the act of stealing some of the silver. A footman raised the alarm - earning himself a knock over the head for his trouble - but they made their escape before anyone could stop them. Lord and Lady Blendiscoe have just left the ball to meet with the authorities."

"I hope the footman was not badly injured," Darcy commented - he was not overly concerned about what or how much had been stolen - and Miss Gardiner nodded.

They were interrupted again when the man to Darcy's left asked him what had happened and he was obliged to share the story.

"Oh dear," Miss Gardiner commented, looking like she was trying not to laugh. "I fear this may begin to resemble a game of Whisper Down the Lane."

Darcy looked up and down the line of dancers and grinned.

"I fear you are correct."

"By the time it reaches the last couple," Miss Gardiner teased, "the poor footman will have been murdered and all the valuables in the house stolen."

Darcy chuckled in spite of himself.

"It really isn't a laughing matter. Let us hope it is not the beginning of a spate of such incidents."

"Don't say that!" Miss Gardiner hushed him dramatically. "You will start a panic!"

Darcy laughed and Miss Gardiner grinned at him.

"Are you not afraid, Miss Gardiner?" he asked her teasingly. "The Blendiscoes do not live far from your aunt and uncle."

"Not in the slightest," she confidently asserted. "Wilson will protect me - she is as fierce as a tiger."

"Wilson being?" Darcy queried.

"My maid," she replied and Darcy laughed at the unexpected reply.

"Well," he said once he had his breath back. "I have no tiger, but I do have a very old, very affectionate dog who is likely to try to lick any would-be burglars, rather than maul them," he admitted with a lopsided smile.

Miss Gardiner seemed delighted at the thought.

"What is her name? And what breed is she?"

"She is called Agatha," Darcy responded. "And she is a Great Dane. She is a little older than James and I have had her since she was born. She spends most of her time in front of the fire in my study these days."

Under usual circumstances Darcy would not have confided these details, would have focused instead on what a great hunter Agatha was, or shared the story of the time she caught a poacher in the act, but something told him that Miss Gardiner would appreciate hearing what he chose to tell her instead. From the smile she gave him, he guessed he was right.

"I should love to meet her," she told him. "I always wanted a dog, but my father...I have a cat, though, called Deirdre. Wilson hates her," she confided with a grin.

Darcy laughed and was very sorry a moment later when their dance finally came to an end. As all the other couples rushed away, no doubt to discuss the news of the burglary, he stepped closer to Miss Gardiner and offered his hand. She smiled up at him as she took it, and the people swarming around them went unnoticed as Darcy bent and pressed a kiss to the back of her hand.

"Thank you for reminding me why I persist in dancing, Miss Gardiner." She looked a little confused before he added, "With the right partner, it can be a delightful experience."

Elizabeth felt herself blushing and was relieved when the Duke offered her his arm and they began making their way through the crowd towards the dining room- at least from his position by her side he could not see her face. She was a little embarrassed by her reaction. She knew he was just paying a compliment and being the nice, gentlemanly man she knew him to be - but still, it was a lovely thing to say.

They joined Jane and Sir Charles, Mr and Mrs Bennet, Lady Fitzwilliam and Colonel Fitzwilliam at the same table and the Duke held her chair out for her before seating himself beside his cousin. Somewhat predictably the conversation at the table was dominated by the story of the burglary and, as Elizabeth had predicted, the facts had already been distorted and exaggerated in the multiple retellings. She caught the Duke's eye at one point and he grinned at her, the same thought obviously occurring to him - she responded with a smile and then turned her attention to her sister and aunt for the rest of the meal.

She danced the first set after dinner with the son of one of Mr and Mrs Bennet's neighbours before she was finally approached by Mr Wickham for their dance. He was smiling, as always, and spent some moments charming Mrs Bennet before he led Elizabeth away to join the other dancers.

"I suppose you have heard about Lord and Lady Blendiscoe," he said once the dance was underway.

"Of course," Elizabeth responded. "I'm not sure I could have avoided hearing about it."

"It does get a little tedious," Mr Wickham agreed. "How a whole room can be discussing the same thing. No doubt by tomorrow it will be some other story that occupies them."

"I'm not so sure that this story will be easily forgotten about," Elizabeth contradicted him lightly. "It is rather shocking."

"You are not worried, I hope, Miss Gardiner?" Mr Wickham asked with all the appearance of concern.

Elizabeth laughed.

"And if I was?"

"I would happily volunteer to stand guard," Mr Wickham replied with a rakish smile.

"Outside in the cold? How sweet," Elizabeth teased just as the dance required them to pass in front of one another, her back to her partner.

Mr Wickham bent his head and spoke softly into her ear.

"Or just outside your chamber door."

Elizabeth administered a swift, sharp kick to his shin and then affected innocence and dismay as he stumbled and muttered a curse.

"Oh, Mr Wickham, I am sorry! How clumsy of me!"

"No harm done, Miss Gardiner," Mr Wickham assured her easily, mindful of their audience. Several couples dancing near them were watching, as were many people not dancing and he kept his smile firmly in place. Elizabeth continued to affect concern, though her eyes were mocking her partner as they continued to dance.

"I did warn you to behave yourself," she said at last and Mr Wickham's composure slipped slightly before he smiled ruefully.

"Yes, you did. I do not know what came over me. I claim momentary insanity. Please forgive me."

"Just don't do it again, else I will be forced to kick you again," Elizabeth told him, and then smiled to show there were no hard feelings.

He was hopeless, a complete rascal, and she did not know why she did not give him the cut direct, except that he amused her and she enjoyed "running rings around him", as her uncle had so succinctly put it. It flattered her ego.

"Consider the lesson learnt, Miss Gardiner," Mr Wickham responded. "And the bruise on my shin shall serve as a reminder if I begin to forget it."

"I hope I did not hurt you too much," Elizabeth expressed insincerely.

"Not at all," he assured her, adding almost to himself, "I am just glad you did not take your anger out on another piece of my anatomy."

Elizabeth laughed.

"Rest assured, had the infraction merited it, I would have done."

"Then I really *had* best be on my best behaviour from now on," Mr Wickham replied and then grinned boyishly, looking utterly unrepentant.

"I couldn't help but notice who partnered you for the supper set," he commented some time later as they danced past one another. "I see now why you were so anxious to adhere to propriety – I wouldn't want to offend my cousin!"

"I assure you, Mr Wickham," Elizabeth responded with unmistakable bluntness, amazed at his conceit, "propriety had nothing to do it - I was exercising my *preference*."

"But everyone loves dancing with me," Mr Wickham replied and Elizabeth saw he was making fun of himself and smiled reluctantly. "I am a delightful partner."

"You are a conceited ass," Elizabeth accused, laughing, "that's what you are."

"That too," Mr Wickham granted with a shrug and a grin.

"Does that usually work?" Elizabeth asked him suddenly, elaborating when he looked confused, "Saying things like that into lady's ears? Does it make them fall into your arms?"

"That and other things," Mr Wickham replied carefully. He smiled and pointed out, "We really shouldn't be discussing this."

"Come now, Mr Wickham, no need to be shy," Elizabeth teased him.

"Do you really want to hear about my conquests?" he asked, looking both intrigued and confused by the prospect.

"Not particularly, though at the same time I must admit I am a little curious about you," Elizabeth confessed. "You are not quite what I was expecting after everyone warned me."

"Did they tell you I was a terrible rake and womaniser?" Mr Wickham asked. Elizabeth nodded. "And you were expecting someone tall, dark and dangerous? Who ravishes women in the dark corners of rooms?"

"Something like that," Elizabeth admitted.

"I know some men like that," Mr Wickham replied, "I could introduce you to them if you like?"

"I think not," Elizabeth replied dryly - she could handle Mr Wickham, but she did not doubt she would be out of her depth with the true libertines she had heard about. "My uncle would have a heart attack."

Mr Wickham laughed.

"In truth," he said after a moment of thought, "I think the chief difference between men like that and myself is that I love women. I simply *adore* them," he added with a warm look as he casually perused Elizabeth's figure and she blushed scarlet.

"As opposed to?" she asked.

"Men like Lord Waltham," he nodded to a tall man in the far corner, obviously in the middle of seducing the brunette with him, "dislike women. Certainly, they enjoy them, but that's all. They use women for their own pleasure and then toss them away when they're finished, regardless of feelings or reputations, because they think so little of them. They have no respect for them at all."

"That's awful," Elizabeth was appalled by the picture Mr Wickham painted.

"And yet I would wager a quarter of the women here would love to be *mistreated* by Waltham and his like," Mr Wickham responded knowingly.

"But why?" Elizabeth asked and she glared at her partner when he laughed.

"*That* is something I utterly refuse to discuss on the dance floor, with a girl of nineteen. I do have some standards, you know," he added as though offended.

"You could have fooled me," Elizabeth replied, but she knew what he was referring to.

"This has to be one of the most bizarre dances I have ever shared with anyone," Mr Wickham mused with an amused smile. "An assault, a flirtation gone awry, and a discussion of rakes and libertines."

"I would hardly call my kicking your shin an assault," Elizabeth objected, smiling as well. "And you deserved it."

"No doubt," Mr Wickham conceded.

"I can tell you aren't like those other men," Elizabeth told him after a moment. "Waltham, and the others."

"I like to think so," Mr Wickham responded neutrally before surprising her completely by adding, "Please don't make the mistake of thinking too well of me, though, Miss Gardiner."

"There is absolutely no chance of that, I assure you," Elizabeth asserted with a slight laugh, though beneath the teasing she was quite serious. And she appreciated the warning, though it was not necessary.

# Chapter 6

Following the Harding's ball, London enjoyed a spell of lovely, sunny days and taking advantage of the fine weather, Jane arranged for her son to spend the day in the park with the two Darcy children, the two Fitzwilliam boys and the son and daughter of another friend of hers. Jane, Elizabeth and Daniel arrived mid-morning to find Catherine and James feeding the ducks with Mrs Hughes.

"Good morning," Elizabeth greeted them happily - she had not seen either of them for a few days. "And good morning to you too, Mrs Hughes."

"Good morning, Miss Gardiner," Mrs Hughes responded quietly, smiling - she liked Lady Bingley's lively younger sister.

"How are you both?" she asked the children and they both assured her that they were very well and looking forward to the rest of the day. "As am I! We shall have marvellous fun."

"Father said he may join us," James told her, "and bring Agatha with him."

"Oh, that dog," Jane remarked with affection. "Wait until you see her Lizzy - her head comes up to here on me," and she indicated a point well above her waist.

"I can't wait," Elizabeth enthused quite honestly, for she had always loved dogs.

"Papa used to let us ride her when we were little," Cathy told her and Elizabeth smiled at the thought. "She is too old now, though."

"And you are far too grown up," Elizabeth pointed out, earning herself a smile from the little girl.

"Why don't you three finish feeding the ducks," Jane suggested, looking between her son and his two friends. "And Elizabeth and I will see to the chairs and blankets. I'm sure the others will be here soon to join us and I shall have to introduce you to Martha and Nathaniel."

Cathy looked up at Elizabeth.

"Who are they?"

"They are the children of one of my sister's friends - Mrs Patmore. I am sure you will like them very much. Martha is eight too," she added and Cathy beamed.

"We can play dolls!" She shot the two boys a look. "The boys can run around."

Considering Elizabeth was intending to join the boys in running around, it was with some effort that she suppressed a smile. Leaving the children to the care of Mrs Hughes, she joined Jane as her sister directed the servants in setting out the chairs for the adults, and the blankets for the children. She had brought her drawing things with her and fetched her bag from the coach, placing it under her chair for the moment.

"Look, there's Joe and Bradley!"

Daniel's shout prompted her to look up and she saw Lady Fitzwilliam and her two sons approaching their little area of the park.

"Good morning," Lady Fitzwilliam greeted them both cheerily. "My, doesn't this all look lovely! You would think it were a summer day."

Joe and Bradley were quick to join the others with the ducks, leaving the three ladies to take their seats and spend a few minutes chatting amicably between themselves. The friendship between Elizabeth and Lady Fitzwilliam which had begun at their initial meeting had continued to flourish over the past week or so, and Elizabeth hoped that they would remain friends in future.

"What is that under your chair, Miss Gardiner?" Lady Fitzwilliam asked Elizabeth curiously at one point.

"Oh, my bag - it has my pencils and sketchbook in it. I thought I might do a little drawing later."

"I had no idea you were artistic," Lady Fitzwilliam responded. "I have a friend, Lady Andrews, who is the most wonderful painter. I have one of her paintings hanging in my sitting room at home and it is my favourite piece in the house. I shall have to introduce you to her."

"I would like that very much," Elizabeth replied before adding, "though I cannot claim to be quite so talented."

"Have you sat with the children yet?" Jane asked Lady Fitzwilliam. "Charles keeps saying we should commission a picture of the three of us, but I honestly cannot imagine Daniel sitting still long enough to accomplish it!"

"We have one with the boys," Lady Fitzwilliam, "and another of just Clara and I. With the right person it can be accomplished quite easily."

"Which artist did you commission?" Jane asked and Elizabeth let her attention wander as the other two ladies began discussing artists and the possibility of engaging them.

She sat watching the children, the four boys and little Catherine, feeding the ducks, smiling as Bradley and Joe jostled each other and James stepped in before Mrs Hughes even had a chance to say anything.

"Lizzy? Elizabeth!"

"Yes?" she startled and both Lady Fitzwilliam and Jane laughed lightly.

"You can go and join them if you like," Jane told her. "Please don't feel like you have to sit here with us."

"I shall wait for the others first," Elizabeth replied. "What were you saying?"

"I asked whether you had heard the latest about the Blendiscoe burglary," Lady Fitzwilliam supplied helpfully.

"No, I have not," Elizabeth responded. "Have they apprehended anyone yet?"

"Yes - one of the footmen," Lady Fitzwilliam replied.

"Not the one who was knocked over the head?!" Elizabeth guessed and Lady Fitzwilliam nodded.

"The very same. It appears *he* was in cahoots with the burglars and having them knock him unconscious was meant to remove him from suspicion."

"That's rather ingenious," Elizabeth noted admiringly and her sister scolded her. "What? It is! How did they discover the truth?" she asked Lady Fitzwilliam, who was trying not to smile.

"Apparently he had been seen a few days earlier by another member of staff speaking with a man who matched the description of one of the burglars. He had a large, bushy beard which made him quite memorable."

"Ah, well, *that* was not so smart," Elizabeth noted and ignored Jane's huff. "Has the footman given up his accomplices?"

"Not that I have heard," Lady Fitzwilliam replied before predicting, "It shall only be a matter of time before he does though, I'm sure."

"Well, it has certainly been an exciting episode," Elizabeth teased. "Well timed, too, as I was just getting tired of hearing the latest gossip about who danced with whom, and who wore what."

Lady Fitzwilliam smiled and then announced,

"Oh, look, there is my brother."

Elizabeth turned in her seat and saw the Duke walking towards them with Agatha trotting obediently beside him, her lead held loosely in his hand. The dog barked when she saw James and Catherine but didn't attempt to pull away, and only when the Duke released her did she bound over to the children. Elizabeth stood up and went over to be introduced, laughing when the huge dog licked her hand and then made appreciative noises and wagged her tail as Elizabeth rubbed behind her ears.

"Oh, aren't you beautiful!" Elizabeth enthused as she stroked her new friend, utterly smitten already.

Agatha had a grey coat and clear blue eyes and it was immediately evident that she was very sweet natured and affectionate. It was also obvious that she was enjoying all the attention!

"Good morning, Miss Gardiner," the Duke greeted her, a smile in his voice as he watched her with Agatha.

"Good morning, Your Grace," Elizabeth replied. She looked up at him as she playfully asked, "Do you think my father would notice if I returned from town with a Great Dane?"

"I'm afraid he would notice, yes," the Duke responded with a chuckle.

"And Agatha lives with us!" Cathy interjected and Elizabeth laughed.

"I did not mean that I would take Agatha," she assured the little girl. "Only that I would love a dog just like her for myself."

"Perhaps a smaller dog would be better," James suggested with a grin. "You could hide it in one of your trunks."

"Oh, don't tempt me!" Elizabeth teased and they all shared a laugh, causing Agatha to bark and bounce around a little, excited by their behaviour.

"Oh, calm down you silly baggage," the Duke said to his dog as he ruffled her ears and patted her back when she went to him for attention. "Come and say hello to the ladies with me. Miss Gardiner?"

He offered Elizabeth his arm and she went with him back to where Jane and Lady Fitzwilliam were still sitting, Agatha trotting along beside them. Elizabeth kept glancing down at her and was surprised when she heard the Duke chuckle.

"I see she has won you over already, Miss Gardiner," he noted when she looked up at him.

"Entirely," Elizabeth readily admitted. "I do so love dogs, and she is quite beautiful."

"Most ladies we meet are intimidated by her," the Duke admitted, looking down at Agatha who was a typical size for her breed. "They are afraid because she is so big."

"I have no doubt that were she to jump up at me I would be flat on the ground in a second," Elizabeth replied with a laugh, "but the thought of it does not scare me. And it is clear she has a good nature, and is well trained. Look how she walks so calmly beside you," she indicated with her free hand. "Even though there are so many people around to distract her."

"She is a good girl," the Duke admitted, before he smiled and added, "though we have to watch her around the ducks. She likes to chase them," he confessed with a grin.

"Good morning, William," Lady Fitzwilliam greeted her brother when they were close enough. "It is lovely to see you - I'm glad you could join us."

"It seemed a shame to waste such a lovely day," the Duke replied before turning to greet Jane. "Good morning, Lady Bingley, Master Daniel."

As soon as the Duke and Agatha had appeared, Daniel had run to his mother and was stood behind Jane's chair, looking a little frightened. Elizabeth was surprised by his behaviour, doubting that there was any reason for him to be afraid of Agatha.

"Good morning, Your Grace," Jane replied with a smile - she turned to her son. "Say good morning to the Duke, Daniel."

"Morning," he mumbled, keeping his eyes on the dog.

"I'm so sorry," the Duke replied, looking regretfully at the little boy. "I forgot that your son does not like dogs. I shall take her home again."

"No, please, there's no need for that," Jane assured him. "Is there Daniel? You know that Agatha won't hurt you, don't you?"

Daniel nodded and bravely edged around so he was standing beside Jane's chair, rather than behind it. Agatha, bless her, with very good timing, chose that moment to flop down on the blanket and close her eyes, looking about as threatening as a big, grey pillow. All the adults smiled to themselves when they saw Daniel let out a relieved breath.

"Have you fed all the bread I gave you to the ducks?" Jane asked her son - when he shook his head she kissed his cheek and suggested, "Then why don't you go and help the others finish the bag. Hopefully Martha and Nathaniel will be here soon and Lizzy will have some games for you to play."

Daniel nodded and proceeded to walk an exaggerated circle around Agatha on his way back to the pond.

"I had no idea he was afraid of dogs," Elizabeth said once he was out of earshot. She demonstrated her own feelings very eloquently when she settled down right next to Agatha on the blanket and proceeded to stroke the dozing dog.

"I'm not sure where the fear came from," Jane admitted. "But he has always been uneasy around them."

"I am sorry for bringing Agatha," the Duke said again from the seat he had taken beside his sister. "I did not think."

"There is no harm done," Jane assured him kindly and then turned to her sister. "I knew *you* would be delighted with her, Lizzy."

"I want one," Elizabeth joked and Jane laughed. "I can just imagine a dog just like this, loping around Longbourn."

"And I can just imagine Father's reaction," Jane teased.

"I shall just have to content myself with having you for a friend, shan't I?" Elizabeth said to the dog beside her.

Almost in response, Agatha rolled over onto her back, her paws in the air, and the Duke laughed.

"She loves having her belly rubbed - do that, and she will be your friend for life."

"That sounds like a fair trade," Elizabeth teased and she set about rubbing Agatha's belly as Agatha growled her appreciation.

"Oh, look, here's Mrs Patmore and the children," Jane pointed out suddenly. She stood up and called her son over to her. "Come here for a moment, please, Daniel - let's introduce Martha and Nathaniel to the other children."

Jane handled the introductions between Mrs Patmore and everyone else as the children came over to welcome the new arrivals. Catherine in particular was noticeably eager to meet the other little girl, and Jane did the honours.

"Martha, this is Lady Catherine Darcy. Cathy, this is Miss Martha Patmore."

Catherine curtsied just like she had seen Jane and other ladies do.

"Everyone calls me Cathy, specially my friends, so you can too if you like."

"Thank you," Martha replied shyly, clutching her doll and looking rather uncomfortable at all the attention.

"Come sit with me," Cathy offered her hand and led Martha to the blanket. "I have my dolls with me too. This one is Clarissa, and this one is Betty."

"Well, I think we can leave them to entertain themselves," Elizabeth noted with a smile.

"Daniel, why don't you introduce Nathaniel to your friends," Jane suggested lightly and her son did as he was asked, in his usual careless manner.

"James, Joe, Bradley, this is Nathaniel. Nathaniel, this is James, Joe and Bradley. Joe and Bradley are brothers," he indicated the two younger boys. "And James is their cousin. Can we go play now, Mother?"

"Yes, dear, off you go," Jane replied and all of the boys bar James scampered off without another word.

The Duke knew what James was waiting for and properly introduced him and Mrs Patmore to each other before his son finally ran off to join the other boys.

As the boys ran off to play, Jane and Mrs Patmore fell into conversation and took their seats as Lady Fitzwilliam sat by Cathy and Martha, smiling as they each showed her their dolls. This left Elizabeth and the Duke who moved his seat to sit beside her, Agatha getting up and moving to lie down at his feet. Realising that Agatha was partially lying on her bag, Elizabeth bent down to move it out of her way.

"What is that?" The Duke asked, his attention drawn by her action.

"I brought my sketchbook with me," Elizabeth replied. She propped her bag up against the side of her chair and then patted Agatha. "There, that must be more comfortable for you."

"May I?" The Duke asked, indicating the bag.

"Of course," Elizabeth granted. She withdrew the book and passed it over to him. "There are not many drawings, I'm afraid. I only began that book when I left for town."

"Is this Deirdre?" The Duke asked, tilting the book and indicating the first drawing.

"Yes," Elizabeth replied with a nod. She shifted her chair a little closer to his so she wouldn't have to lean so far to see.

"I must admit, I am not very fond of cats," the Duke confessed and Elizabeth laughed softly.

"Don't worry," she assured him. "No one likes Deirdre - besides me, that is. She is a little demon and terrorises the whole house."

"She sounds delightful," the Duke responded dryly.

"She is a complete darling with me," Elizabeth explained. "She just enjoys tormenting everyone else. I appreciate her loyalty," she teased and the Duke smiled before turning the page to the next drawing.

Though most of the drawings were self-explanatory, the Duke asked her several questions and he and Elizabeth spent almost half an hour sat together over the book of drawings. When he reached a charcoal sketch of one of the pieces of the Elgin collection, the Duke paused and smiled.

"You went back after all."

"No," Elizabeth replied, obviously surprising him. "I haven't had the chance to yet. I began this before leaving for the Harding's ball and finished it the next day."

"All from memory?" The Duke looked at her, impressed. "That is remarkable. I even recognise which piece it is."

"You do?" Elizabeth was pleased. "I wasn't sure if I hadn't conjured it from my imagination."

"Not at all," the Duke assured her. "It is clearly recognisable. You are truly very talented, Miss Gardiner."

"Thank you," Elizabeth could feel herself blushing at the praise. She startled when Daniel, who had run over to the blanket, loudly said her name. "Yes, Dan?"

"Can we play baseball now, please?" he asked, in a tone of appeal. "Please?"

"I think it would be best to wait until after luncheon," Elizabeth replied - before he could protest she added, "I have some other games we can play before then, though."

Daniel was mollified and as he ran back to tell the other boys, Elizabeth stood up and looked down at the Duke.

"You don't mind if I leave you to look through them on your own, do you? Duty calls, I'm afraid."

"Not at all," he assured her with a smile.

"Then I had best be on my way," Elizabeth said and, leaving him to his occupation, she went to the carriage to retrieve the hoop she had brought with her and then joined Daniel and the other boys.

"I warn you now, gentlemen," she told them with a smile as she held the hoop aloft. "I am the undisputed champion at this game."

Joe and Daniel immediately asserted that they would be the winners whilst James, Bradley and Nathaniel looked variously amused, bemused and confused.

"But how do you fit?" Bradley asked, looking between her and the hoop whilst James choked on a laugh.

"I may be tall," Elizabeth replied, her eyes dancing with amusement as she smiled down at the youngest boy. "But I can make myself very small when I want to be."

"I don't understand the game," Nathaniel admitted and Joe was quick to explain it to him.

"You roll the hoop along the floor and you have to jump through it without knocking it down or touching it."

"Won't I get dirty?" Nathaniel looked down at his clothes and up again, clearly worried about the possibility.

"I wouldn't worry too much," Elizabeth assured him. "The ground is nice and dry today and not too muddy. No-one will mind," she added when he didn't look convinced, "I promise, Nathaniel, it will be fine. And trust me; once we get started you'll enjoy yourself so much that it won't matter about your clothes."

"Can I go first?" Daniel asked impatiently and Elizabeth chided him.

"You should let your friends go before you, Dan - it's only fair. Joe, why don't you show Nathaniel how it's done," she suggested lightly, and Joe was only too happy to oblige.

He took the hoop from her and ran a little distance away, lining himself up with a clear, even piece of grass. Setting the hoop rolling, he ran after it and made to dive through it, almost making it clear but catching his foot and bringing the hoop down with him. Bradley thought it all great fun and laughed and cheered excitedly.

"My go! Can I have a go! Please, me now!"

"Yes, alright Bradley, you can have a turn now," Elizabeth granted and before she even had to ask, James took hold of his young cousin's hand and led him to his brother and the hoop.

Because Bradley was so small, James held the hoop and rolled it along slowly so that Bradley could keep up with it and so that it would not fall.

"Come on Bradley, you can do it!" Elizabeth called, sensing he needed a little encouragement to make the jump. Joe, Daniel and Nathaniel all added their own encouragement.

Gathering his courage, Bradley made a sort of hopping jump through the hoop, hitting the top of his head on the top of it (James managed to keep it steady) but otherwise making it through. He turned and watched the hoop roll on and then turned his delighted face back to his audience.

"I did it!" He declared triumphantly. He ran as fast as he legs would carry him over to his mother, who had been watching all along. "Mama! Mama! Did you see? I did it, I made it!"

As Lady Fitzwilliam listened to her son's exultations and tried to calm him down, Elizabeth turned back to the other boys.

"Nathaniel, would you like to try?"

"Can someone else roll it for me?" he asked shyly. "I think it would be easier that way, just for my first go."

"Of course," Elizabeth granted easily. "James, would you mind?"

James was happy to help, and even offered Nathaniel a few helpful hints as to when was best to jump, and how. He obviously listened carefully, for he very nearly made it through and it was an admirable effort for his first go. Everyone said as much, and Nathaniel looked shyly pleased with himself.

"James, your turn," Daniel told the older boy who shook his head and smiled over at Elizabeth.

"I think we should let Miss Gardiner go next."

"I'd be happy to," Elizabeth stated and walked over to retrieve the hoop from James.

"I can't imagine how you'll manage it in a dress," he admitted and Elizabeth smiled.

"I shall either manage it with grace and flair, or get in a terrible tangle and make a complete fool of myself. Something tells me you'd rather see the latter," she added playfully.

James laughed and didn't bother to deny it as he moved aside so that Elizabeth could line up her run. She could feel the eyes of the adults as well as the children on her and could just imagine Jane shaking her head at her antics - and in a public park, no less! Gathering up her skirts so she would not tread on them, but leaving her enough freedom to run, Elizabeth steeled herself and then gave the hoop a push, setting it into a smooth, straight roll. She ran alongside it and, keeping her fingers crossed, darted sideways, crouching low and skipping through, managing to not only avoid touching the hoop but staying on her feet as well. She gave a little whoop and threw her hands up in the air, delighted with her success and bowing to her audience.

"That was amazing!" Joe declared, very impressed. "I've never managed to stay on my feet."

"It takes a lot of practice," Elizabeth replied. Her nephew had run after the hoop and she called out to him, "Your turn now, Dan."

Daniel took his turn and gave them all a good laugh when he made an exaggerated dive through the hoop, not touching it at all but sliding along on his front and covering his clothes in grass. James then had a go, also managing to clear the hoop but tripping over his feet on the other side and dirtying his knees, and the game soon descended into nothing more than the boys running and diving through the rolling hoop, sliding on their fronts and getting muddier by the minute. Even Nathaniel joined in and by the time Jane called them all over for luncheon, all five boys were a fine state.

"Oh, would you look at you all," Lady Fitzwilliam looked like she was trying not to laugh as she wiped a smear of mud from Bradley's face. "How did you get so dirty?"

"It's entirely my fault," Elizabeth stated with complete unconcern as she flopped into her chair next to the Duke, who was watching her with a smile. "I'm sorry."

"You seem to have escaped unscathed," the Duke noted and Elizabeth was quite clean in comparison.

"Almost," she replied, looking down at a grass stain near her knee. "Wilson shall be most seriously displeased with me, nonetheless."

"I daresay she should be used to it by now," Jane remarked and Elizabeth chuckled.

"You'd think so."

Sometime later, having finished her luncheon and feeling a little restless, Elizabeth turned to the Duke.

"I think I shall take a turn around the pond - could I take Agatha with me?"

"Of course," he replied before saying, "Actually, I think I will join you, if you do not object to some company?"

"Your company would be most welcome, Your Grace," she assured him and, standing up, she told the others of their intention.

"May I come too, Father?" Catherine asked politely and the Duke easily granted permission.

The others were all either still eating or quite comfortable on the blanket and chairs and so Elizabeth set off with father and daughter and dog for company. She accepted the arm the Duke offered her, offering her hand to Catherine whilst Agatha trotted along on the Duke's other side.

"So, Cathy," Elizabeth asked the little girl as they slowly wandered around the pond. "Do you like Martha?"

"Very much," Catherine replied with a bob of her head. "She is my new friend."

"Oh good," Elizabeth smiled and then asked, "And did you have fun playing with your dolls?"

"Oh yes," Catherine enthused. "Martha's doll is called Lillian, and she is so pretty. Her hair is so soft and her dress is very fine. It was Martha's birthday and Lillian was her present," she explained knowledgably, and Elizabeth nodded along. "She also got a Little

Fanny from her grandma, she said, though she is not allowed to bring it out with her in case bits go missing."

"What is a Little Fanny?" Elizabeth asked curiously.

"It is a book," Catherine replied, "with lots of different costumes in it. You move Fanny's head and the book tells you a story. I should like one very much, but Papa says I must wait until my birthday," she admitted with a little pout.

"And when is your birthday?" Elizabeth asked - she could see the Duke smiling out of the corner of her eye.

"June 13th," Catherine replied succinctly. "I shall be nine years old."

"Then you do not have long to wait at all," Elizabeth consoled her, "it will be June before you know it, I'm sure."

"I hope so," Catherine admitted - she sighed wistfully, "I so wish to be nine."

Elizabeth bit her lip to hide her smile, and caught the Duke looking like he was doing the same thing.

"When is your birthday, Lizzy?" Catherine asked her.

"July," Elizabeth responded.

"Do you know what you would like?"

Elizabeth looked down at Agatha.

"A puppy."

"I'm sure if you ask very nicely, and stay on your best behaviour, your Papa will get one for you," Catherine asserted with childish innocence as the Duke chuckled to himself.

"I hope so," Elizabeth replied and then turning to the Duke asked him, "And what would you like for your birthday, Your Grace?"

"I have my eye on a fine Thoroughbred which will soon be up for sale," he replied and Elizabeth laughed lightly.

"A little expensive for the children, don't you think?"

"I was thinking I would treat myself," he replied with a grin.

"Ah, but have you been on your best behaviour?" Elizabeth teased him.

"I would say so," he replied gamely; he looked down at his daughter, "What say you, princess? Have I been a good papa this year?"

"Yes," Catherine replied sweetly. "You are the best Papa in the whole world."

Elizabeth was sure her heart gave a little sigh as she looked between father and daughter, feeling the warmth of their affection and finding it quite touching.

"Would you mind, Miss Gardiner?" The Duke asked her, holding Agatha's lead out for her to take.

They swapped places and the Duke walked with his daughter, holding her hand in his as Elizabeth walked with Agatha. By this time they had walked almost completely around the pond and were not far from where the rest of their party still sat. They followed the path beside the water where the pavestones covered the bank and slopped down into the pond, for it was large enough to hold a few small row boats in the warmer months. Agatha, who had up until this point behaved wonderfully, decided that she would like a swim and suddenly, without warning, made a dash for the water.

Elizabeth was tugged sideways with an exclamation of surprise, but realising that there was no way she could hold Agatha back, let go of the lead. Unfortunately she had been pulled from the path to the bank and on the wet, slippy stones she lost her footing and fell backwards, landing quite heavily and sliding into the water well above her knees. All of this had happened in only a few seconds, too quickly for the Duke to do more than save her from slipping any further.

"Miss Gardiner!" He seemed quite alarmed as he pulled her from the water and assisted her to her feet. "My God, are you alright?"

Elizabeth, from a combination of embarrassment and genuine hilarity, just laughed and attempted to shake off some of the water.

"I'm fine," she assured him at last, still laughing. "Oh, I can't believe that just happened! I hadn't at all planned on swimming today."

Catherine began giggling but the Duke looked stern as he called to his dog in an angry voice.

"Agatha! Come here, now."

"Oh, please, don't be too angry with her," Elizabeth appealed to him, smiling irrepressibly. Yes, she was wet and muddy, and yes people were watching and it was embarrassing, but it was also terribly funny.

Agatha came back to the bank, climbing out and proceeding to shake herself, flinging water all over the place. Elizabeth and Catherine laughed again and even the Duke smiled in spite of himself.

"I am so sorry," he apologised to her but Elizabeth just waved her hand.

"There's no harm done," she assured him before adding merrily, "and it shall make for a funny story in years to come!"

"Here, you must be cold," the Duke said as he moved to strip off his coat.

"Oh, no, please," Elizabeth protested but he had already removed it and placed it over her shoulders.

"Please, I insist. I do not want you to catch cold."

"Oh, very well," Elizabeth held the sides of the coat closed around her with one hand. "Thank you."

"I daresay it is the least I could do," he responded and then taking Catherine's hand again suggested that they return to the others.

"Jane is going to tell me off," Elizabeth predicted with certainty, though she was still smiling. "And when my aunt sees me...I shall have to tell them it is all your fault," she teased playfully and the Duke looked a little chagrined.

"I should never have asked you to hold her," he said, looking back at Agatha who seemed to sense she had done wrong, and was walking with her head down. "She is far too strong for you to handle."

"Please don't berate yourself on my account," Elizabeth told him kindly. "I am perfectly fine, and not at all perturbed. I will soon dry off."

The Duke smiled down at her.

"I believe you are the only lady of my acquaintance who could say, with all honesty, that they are "not at all perturbed" about having just fallen into a pond."

Elizabeth smiled brightly.

"It is a dubious mark of distinction, to be sure, but I am proud of it all the same."

"Lizzy!" Jane exclaimed as soon as she saw her sister - everyone else turned and began asking what had happened.

"Agatha pulled me into the pond," Elizabeth explained succinctly, before amending herself, "well, almost. She pulled me in the direction of the pond and then I slipped over and slid into the water."

"Look at your dress," Jane lamented as she began to fuss over her. "You must be freezing. We shall return home at once and..."

"Oh Jane, there is no need for that," Elizabeth interrupted her. "I shall simply sit in the sun for a while to dry off. Or better yet, have a run around with the boys. I promised them a game of baseball, after all."

"You cannot mean to remain in public in such a state, Miss Gardiner," Mrs Patmore put in sternly and Elizabeth immediately resented her words.

"I believe Mrs Pattmore and your sister are right, Miss Gardiner," Lady Fitzwilliam put in kindly. "It is becoming quite cloudy, and you will be very cold sat in a damp dress. Better to go home and postpone your game for another day."

"Oh very well," Elizabeth sighed. "You have convinced me to be sensible. But you should stay, Jane," she told her sister. "I can return home and send the carriage back for you - there is no need to cut short Daniel's day."

After a little more persuasion, Jane was convinced to remain in the park whilst Elizabeth, accompanied by Daniel's governess, took the carriage home to their aunt and uncle's house.

"Did you really fall in the pond?" Joe asked her as Elizabeth bent to retrieve her bag with her sketchbook and charcoals in.

"Yes, I really did," Elizabeth confirmed with a smile. "Fortunately, your uncle was good enough to rescue me, though, before I sank completely."

"Can't you swim?" Nathaniel asked.

"No, I cannot," Elizabeth responded. "Though thankfully the pond was not deep. I should have really needed rescuing otherwise," she added playfully.

"Papa would have rescued you, wouldn't you Papa?" Catherine said, looking up at the Duke.

"Of course," the Duke affirmed, and though he was smiling Elizabeth could tell he was also quite serious. Having gathered up her things, Elizabeth said goodbye to everyone in turn, promising the boys that they would have their game of baseball in future and returning his coat to the Duke with a thank you. She said goodbye to James and then looked down at Agatha, who was sat meekly by his side, looking up at her with beseeching eyes.

Elizabeth caved in a moment.

"Oh, come here. I could not be angry with you even if I wanted to - not when you look at me like that!" She said as she bent and gave the dog an affectionate cuddle and quick pat.

James laughed.

"She has perfected that look - only Father is impervious to it, and not always."

"I am glad it is not just me," Elizabeth responded as she straightened.

With a final farewell she left them all to enjoy the rest of the day, walking to the carriage and settling inside, feeling herself shiver slightly as soon as she was out of the warmth of the sun.

"A warm bath when I get home is in order, I believe," she said to her companion who smiled knowingly. The carriage had just begun to move when there was a call and it stopped again.

The Duke appeared at the window, still in just his shirtsleeves and waistcoat, and apologised for delaying them.

"I just wanted to apologise again, Miss Gardiner, for the whole episode. And I thought I might call upon you in the morning, to see how you are and to accept whatever punishment your aunt deems necessary," he joked lightly and Elizabeth smiled.

"That is very kind of you, Your Grace," she replied warmly. "I shall expect you tomorrow."

He nodded and stepped back.

"Good day, Miss Gardiner."

"Good day, Your Grace," Elizabeth replied and at the Duke's nod the driver spurred the horses and the carriage rolled away.

ൟൟ

When Darcy arrived at the Bennet's townhouse the following day, he was shown into a small but finely appointed morning room with a distinctly feminine feel. Mrs Bennet and Miss Gardiner both stood on his arrival and curtsied to him before the former expressed her welcome.

"It is so good of you to call, Your Grace," Mrs Bennet said to him in a tone perfectly pitched somewhere between friendliness and deference.

"I said I would," Darcy replied, looking at Miss Gardiner. "To ascertain that your niece did not suffer any after-effects of yesterday's mishap."

Mrs Bennet pursed her lips in obvious displeasure but her reaction was ignored by the other two.

"I am perfectly well, Your Grace" Miss Gardiner assured him and Darcy smiled.

"Yes, I can see that - I am glad of it."

"I am not one to fall ill at the drop of a hat," she said with her usual playfulness. "Or let such a silly incident faze me. Though I suspect you have gathered that already," she added and Darcy bit back a grin.

"The children were all sad to see you go," he told her. "I am sorry your day with them was curtailed."

"As am I," Miss Gardiner replied, "though the weather improves with each day - we shall be able to enjoy many more days in the park together, I'm sure."

"I hope so," Darcy expressed honestly before teasing, "Though perhaps next time we should give the pond a wide berth."

"A capital idea," Miss Gardiner responded playfully. They had all taken their seats during this conversation and she gestured to the table where the tea things were. "Shall I pour you a cup?"

"Please," Darcy replied. "Not too much sugar, though, please."

"And some carrot cake?" she asked him and then smiled at his expression. "Catherine told me it was your favourite."

Darcy hesitated and then grinned.

"Perhaps just a little piece."

Miss Gardiner fixed him his cup and cake and passed both to her aunt, who passed them to Darcy.

"Will we see you at the opera tonight, Your Grace?"

"I will not have that pleasure, sadly," Darcy replied. "I dine with a friend this evening."

"A pity for us," Mrs Bennet stated with a smile. "Though I am sure we shall all enjoy ourselves in our various pursuits."

"I hope so," Darcy responded politely and then sipped his tea, for lack of anything else to do. He felt a little stymied by Mrs Bennet's presence, and could not think of what to say.

"You have heard, of course, that Don Giovanni by Mr Mozart is to premiere at the King's Theatre soon," Miss Gardiner said to him after a moment - at his nod she asked, "Shall you attend, do you think?"

"I would like to," he admitted. "I have heard many people praise it."

"My aunt does not think it suitable for us to go," Miss Gardiner revealed, looking amused. "My young, innocent sensibilities need to be protected, apparently."

"I gather it is rather..." Darcy struggled for the right, and polite, word but Miss Gardiner eventually took pity on him.

"Shocking?" she suggested lightly. "Yes, I have heard as much. I should still like to see it, though."

"I am quite decided about the matter, Lizzy," Mrs Bennet told her. "And you shall not be going."

Miss Gardiner looked at Darcy with laughter in her eyes.

"Suddenly I understand your daughter's desire to be a little older."

"It wouldn't matter how old you are, my dear," Mrs Bennet told her, smiling. "I still wouldn't take you."

"Does that mean if I find someone else to take me?" Miss Gardiner hinted and Darcy grinned at her persistence.

"Oh, by all means," Mrs Bennet granted, sounding a little irritated but too well-mannered to show it. "Though I know your sister has no intention of going, and neither do the Lucases."

Miss Gardiner just smiled and Darcy got the impression that she already had a plan to get what she wanted.

"Mr Bennet and I are hosting a card party on Friday evening," Mrs Bennet said to Darcy, distracting him from her niece. "I hope you will join us, Your Grace."

"I would be delighted," he assured her. "And I have no prior engagements."

"Wonderful," Mrs Bennet enthused. "Your cousin shall be joining us, and I will be sure to invite Lady Fitzwilliam and the Colonel."

"My aunt is to come to town that day, I believe," Darcy informed her. "So they may be unable to attend."

"Well I shall extend the invitation to include your aunt, just in case - though I suspect Lady Matlock will be tired from her journey."

Darcy was about to reply, but was surprised when Miss Gardiner suddenly rose from her chair.

"Oh, I have something for you - I almost forgot. I will be back in a moment," and she hurried from the room, leaving Mrs Bennet and Darcy to keep each other company.

"I am sorry for what happened yesterday," he said to the lady after a moment of silence. "To Miss Gardiner."

"Please don't trouble yourself, Your Grace. Lizzy is always getting herself into mischief - I doubt it was your fault at all."

Darcy felt compelled to defend Miss Gardiner.

"Well, had I not asked her to hold Agatha's lead, she would not have been pulled near to the water."

"And yet, would you have asked any other young lady to do the same?" Mrs Bennet asked him in response and Darcy frowned slightly. Before he could reply though, Mrs Bennet answered her own question, "Of course you wouldn't have. It is just because my niece is so," she sighed and rolled her eyes, "*Lizzy*-like. I quite despair of her sometimes, I really do."

"You shouldn't," Darcy told her before he could convince himself to remain quiet. "She is a lovely young woman."

Mrs Bennet looked at him with some surprise, but Miss Gardiner returned before she could say anything.

"I did this for you," Miss Gardiner said to Darcy as she held out a sheet of paper, "and the children."

He took the offering and looked down at the beautiful drawing she had done of Agatha, an impressive likeness. Darcy was delighted.

"Thank you so much," he said to her, smiling his appreciation. "I shall find a place for it at home."

Miss Gardiner blushed prettily in response and looked pleased, but her aunt was the first to reply.

"That is very good of you, Your Grace. We are honoured, aren't we Lizzy?"

"Yes," Miss Gardiner agreed, dutifully expressing her thanks, and though Darcy smiled, he was beginning to feel a little irritated by Mrs Bennet's presence.

The feeling increased a moment later when Mr Bennet joined them.

"Ah, good morning, Your Grace," he greeted Darcy cordially. "Come to enquire about Lizzy's welfare I suppose? You've had a wasted journey I'm afraid - my niece is made of sterner stuff than most of her counterparts. Though I daresay my wife would prefer it had she taken to her bed," Mr Bennet concluded dryly, and took a seat beside his, now frowning, lady.

There was a brief silence following this little speech by Mr Bennet, and Darcy sought for something suitable to say. Fortunately, Mr Bennet himself rescued the situation.

"It's not long now until the racing season begins. Will you be entering many horses this year?"

"A few," Darcy responded vaguely - the other man smiled knowingly.

"I saw your colt run the Derby last year," Mr Bennet said. "And heard about his showing in the two thousand Guineas. A fine piece of horseflesh you have there, Your Grace."

Darcy dipped his head in acknowledgement, but he was not inclined to discuss the matter. He was pleased when Miss Gardiner addressed him again a moment later.

"Are you particularly fond of horses, Your Grace?"

"Yes, I would say so," he admitted.

"I had to leave my horse at home - there is so little opportunity to ride here in town, and I couldn't bear the thought of her trapped in a stall for so long. I miss her terribly, but at least I know she is being well-looked after and enjoying plenty of exercise."

Darcy smiled, pleased by Miss Gardiner's obvious care and sincere affection for her horse. As far as he was concerned, horses were beautiful creatures and he always appreciated meeting someone who shared his love for them. He asked her more about her horse, and they fell into a lengthy discussion on the subject, Darcy sensing her genuine interest and revealing more about his extensive stables than was usually his want. He could tell that Mr Bennet was listening attentively as well, but paid him no heed - whilst her uncle was obviously interested in the horseracing, Miss Gardiner was clearly interested by the horses themselves and Darcy felt he could have talked to her for hours about what was something of a passion for him. Unfortunately, politeness, and another appointment, prevented him from staying as long as he wished and at the acceptable time he announced it was time he was leaving. As his carriage was sent for he turned to his hosts and thanked them for their hospitality.

"I hope you enjoy your evening, Your Grace," Mrs Bennet said. "And we shall see you on Friday."

Darcy bowed and then turned to Miss Gardiner, who surprised him by offering to see him out.

"You need not trouble yourself." Darcy demurred but she smiled and made to accompany him anyway.

"It's no trouble at all," she assured him easily. They left the Bennets behind and walked out to the front hall where Darcy accepted his things from the butler.

"Thank you for coming to call," Miss Gardiner said to him as he was pulling on his gloves. "It was very kind of you."

"It is the least I could do," Darcy responded. "I am glad you are well."

"I am perfectly fine," she replied with dancing eyes; she smiled and teased, "And even were I not, I would not let you see it. Neither would my maid," she added with a slight eye roll.

Darcy looked at her with a quizzical smile.

"Wilson was determined to have me looking my best," Miss Gardiner confessed, "so 'that poor man won't feel guilty when it is all your own fault anyway'. I swear everyone has decided that I leapt into the pond of my own freewill," she concluded dryly and then smiled when Darcy chuckled.

"I hold you completely blameless," he assured her.

"That is some consolation, I suppose," she replied and they shared another smile.

"I was wondering," Darcy began just as Miss Gardiner said, "Do you think?"

"Please, after you," Darcy stated politely, sorry to have interrupted her.

"I was just going to ask if Agatha could accompany James and Catherine when they next visit Daniel," Miss Gardiner admitted with a smile. "I can easily contrive to be there as well, and I would love to be able to do some more sketches of Agatha. I promise I'll look after her," she added with a beseeching look when Darcy hesitated.

"I have no doubt of that," Darcy replied warmly. "I am more worried about *you*."

"Fortunately there are no large bodies of water at my sister's house," she teased and Darcy smiled in spite of himself.

"Very well," he granted and was rewarded with a brilliant smile.

"Oh, thank you! I shall make a gift to you of my best drawing of her in return."

Darcy smiled at her enthusiasm, inordinately pleased to have pleased her.

"What were you going to ask me?" she reminded him after a moment.

"I am taking James and Catherine to the Mechanical Museum next week," Darcy responded, "and was wondering if you would like to join us? And your nephew, naturally," he added quickly.

"The Mechanical Museum?" she repeated, sounding curious. "How intriguing. I should be delighted to join you - as I'm sure will Dan."

"Would Monday be agreeable?" Darcy asked.

"I believe so - I shall speak with Jane and let you know on Friday," Miss Gardiner replied and Darcy nodded.

"I had best be on my way," he said and bowed slightly. "Until Friday, Miss Gardiner."

"Good day, Your Grace," she replied and Darcy turned and descended the steps to where his carriage was waiting. He climbed in and looked back at the house, returning Miss Gardiner's small wave just as the carriage pulled away and she disappeared from view.

☙❧

Elizabeth leant closer to her friend.

"Remind me again, which is which?"

Charlotte smiled and, in an undertone, replied.

"The one on the left is Alistair, the one on the right Julian."

"And which is the elder?" Elizabeth asked as she and her friend studied the two identical men stood across the room from them. They were the sons of the Earl of Maxwell and as the title could not be split in two, one of the twins had lost out.

"Julian," Charlotte responded. "By ten minutes, as gossip would have it."

"That will teach a person to be punctual," Elizabeth teased and they shared a light laugh.

"I must say I'm impressed that your aunt managed to get them both to come," Charlotte confided after a moment. "They don't tend to attend small events like this together."

"It must be a little frustrating, being constantly confused for your brother," Elizabeth noted before smiling and saying, "And you know my aunt, Charlotte - she has a talent for this sort of thing."

"I suppose their joint attendance might have something to do with *their* attendance," Charlotte guessed, looking over at the Drake sisters who were both very beautiful and very rich.

"You have hit the nail on the head, my dear," Elizabeth teased her friend. "I heard my aunt planning her strategy," she revealed with a grin. "She would have made a fabulous general."

Charlotte smiled and then the two friends turned their attention back to the rest of the room - it was an interesting study. Besides the Lords and Ladies and Misters and Misses, there was also a surgeon, a writer, a notable liberal MP and an artist, invited to encourage conversation and to diversify the company. There was a nice balance of married couples and single ladies and gentlemen, of old and young, and Elizabeth had to admire Mrs Bennet's skill as a hostess. The only people missing, as far as Elizabeth was aware, were the Duke of Farleigh and Mr Wickham, though for her own part, Elizabeth cared not whether the latter chose to attend.

"Speak of the devil," she muttered to herself just as Mr Wickham entered the room.

"Pardon?" Charlotte looked over at her.

"Nothing," Elizabeth sighed. "Promise to stay by my side Charlotte – I do not have the energy to fend off his attentions tonight," she indicated Mr Wickham as he greeted Mr and Mrs Bennet.

"If you wish. Is he so tiresome?"

"Repetitive," Elizabeth replied under her breath as the gentleman in question was walking directly towards her.

"Good evening, Mr Wickham," she greeted him with a polite smile. "Do you know my friend?"

"I have not had the pleasure," he replied charmingly and Elizabeth handled the introductions, noticing as she did so that Charlotte appeared torn between laughter and affront.

"I was sorry to miss you after the performance on Tuesday," Mr Wickham addressed himself to Elizabeth. "I got caught up in the rush to leave - you know how it is."

"Oh, yes," Elizabeth agreed, though her brows rose at his blatant falsehood.

When she had attended the opera with her aunt and uncle, they had met Mr Wickham there and he had spent some time with them before the performance. He had also come to their box in the interval, sitting in the chair next to Elizabeth's and engaging her in a teasing (and admittedly very amusing) discussion of several other people present for the performance. He had said he would return at the conclusion of the night but Elizabeth had seen him with her own eyes as he departed during the final act, leaving long before anyone else. At least, anyone *respectable.*

"Did you enjoy yourself?" he asked, pulling Elizabeth from her thoughts.

"I did, very much," Elizabeth replied. She turned to Charlotte. "Have you been?"

"I have," Charlotte affirmed and Elizabeth engaged her in an in-depth and involved discussion of the performance, the composition and its interpretation of the original.

Mr Wickham stood beside them, contributing very little but nodding and smiling as though he understood everything they were saying.

"What do you think, Mr Wickham?" Elizabeth purposely surprised him by asking as they debated the characterisation of the female lead.

"Err..." He faltered for a moment before recovering admirably; he smiled and stated, "I must say I agree with you, Miss Gardiner. But if you will excuse me, I have been meaning to speak with Brennan."

He departed with a smile and a brief bow, leaving Elizabeth and Charlotte to wait until he was out of earshot to begin laughing quietly.

"Lizzy! You are wicked!" Charlotte hid her laughter behind her hand.

"Did you see his face when I asked him what he thought?" Elizabeth giggled. "Utterly startled."

"I suppose you noticed *my* face when he said he had not had the pleasure of meeting me before," Charlotte commented dryly, still smiling. At Elizabeth's nod she revealed, "We have been introduced at least three times, the latest time not even three weeks ago."

Elizabeth rolled her eyes and shook her head.

"He lied when he said he was caught up in the rush at the opera. I saw him leave earlier."

"Alone?" Charlotte asked, one brow raised knowingly.

"Yes - though I suspect he did not remain so for long," Elizabeth replied.

It was well known that gentlemen and their paramours tended to slip away during the performances for more intimate entertainment. Elizabeth had noted a few women leaving early as well and had no doubt that Mr Wickham had arranged an assignation with one of them.

"Shall we sit down?" Charlotte asked - there were already a few groups sat playing at the tables spotted about the room.

"I think I will wait a little longer," Elizabeth replied, thinking she would wait to greet the Duke when he arrived, if he came at all. "But by all means, go ahead."

After ascertaining that Elizabeth was sure, Charlotte went to sit with her brother and his fiancée, Miss Hamilton, and Mrs Long and joined them in their game. Left to her own devices, Elizabeth wandered over to her uncle, who was stood speaking to the artist, a young man by the name of Stephenson, along with Lord Hamilton and Mrs Drake. She listened with interest to Mr Stephenson's plans for an exhibition at the Royal Institute, and made a mental note to go along. Eventually, just as she had given up hope of seeing him that night, the Duke of Farleigh was announced. He came straight over to his host.

"Please forgive me for arriving so late - my daughter was feeling unwell, and it took some time to see her settled."

Elizabeth couldn't help noticing the varying reactions to this statement. Her uncle merely smiled and nodded whilst Mrs Drake smiled somewhat derisively, and Lord Hamilton looked overtly unimpressed and mocking. The Duke showed no reaction to their expressions, and either did not notice, or simply did not care. For herself, Elizabeth was once again touched by his attentiveness to his children, and showed him with her smile how it pleased her to see how much he cared. She didn't care that it wasn't *fashionable* to love and look after ones children.

"I hope she is well now," she expressed sincerely, drawing the Duke's attention to her.

"She seemed much improved," the Duke replied and Elizabeth understood what he had left unsaid - that he would not have left her had that not been the case.

"I cannot imagine Catherine would make a very good patient," Elizabeth teased impertinently, smiling. "She would not countenance being ill well, I think."

"You are unfortunately quite correct," the Duke responded with a grin. "She is quite the little madam when she feels poorly."

Elizabeth smiled with genuine affection at the thought.

"I hope she will be well enough for our outing on Monday."

"I am sure she will be right as rain," the Duke assured her before the rest of their company decided they had been ignored long enough and Lord Hamilton re-started the conversation with Mr Stephenson.

"I had best go and greet your aunt," the Duke said quietly to Elizabeth, obviously about to excuse himself.

"I shall come with you," she said, "I have a new game for us to play, and was going to ask if she would like to join in."

"A new game?" The Duke asked as they crossed the room together.

"Yes. It does not involve cards, but I played it last week and found it rather fun. It's called Grandmother's Trunk."

The Duke looked a little bemused and Elizabeth smiled and assured him.

"Trust me, it is not quite as boring as it sounds. It is a memory game. Will you join us?"

"Thank you, but once I have greeted your aunt I should like to speak with Sir Charles for a moment," the Duke responded evenly and Elizabeth smiled.

"Very well - until later on, then."

He nodded and they parted for the moment with a smile. Elizabeth did not notice that the Duke's gaze lingered on her for several moments as she walked away from him – but from across the room, her friend Charlotte certainly did.

❧❦

"...he certainly seems to be paying her a lot of attention."

"...I heard they were together at the Mendalls' party."

"...saw them together at the opera."

"...he'd never marry her - she's not exactly a beauty, and Wickham only goes for the best."

Darcy was trying to listen to what Bingley and Sir William were saying, but he kept catching snatches of the conversation going on behind him at the table where the Drake sisters and the Brennan brothers were all seated. It was obvious they were discussing Miss Gardiner and George Wickham and he frowned slightly at what they were implying; when the youngest Brennan insulted Miss Gardiner, his slight frown became a pronounced glower and his friend noticed.

"Darcy? What's wrong? I thought we'd agreed to meet with Donald next week," Bingley asked and Darcy was momentarily embarrassed at being caught out.

"Nothing," he shook his head. "Forgive me, my thoughts were elsewhere. I agree completely with the arrangements," he assured his friend and after a moment Bingley picked up where he'd left off.

Darcy nodded and pretended to listen whilst actually trying to listen to what the group behind him were now saying; it became obvious that their conversation had moved along and Darcy relaxed, feeling relieved. He wasn't sure why it bothered him so much to hear them gossiping about Miss Gardiner and George, but it certainly did. Perhaps it was the thought of them being gossiped about collectively, *together*.

He heard a burst of laughter and looked over to see Miss Gardiner and George laughing over something, obviously enjoying themselves. For a moment, as he watched Miss Gardiner, he forgot about everything else and just watched her as she laughed and smiled, her whole face lighting up and her entire being radiating happiness. How could Brennan not think her beautiful? She was the most beautiful thing he had ever seen.

"Darcy!!"

Bingley laughed when Darcy jumped and looked at him sharply. "What?!"

"What has got in to you tonight?" Bingley asked laughingly, clapping Darcy on the shoulder. "You are away with the fairies."

"Hardly," Darcy retorted sarcastically and made a point of focusing his whole attention on his friend, trying to dismiss Miss Gardiner from his mind.

"I am so looking forward to our outing on Monday."

Elizabeth could see she had surprised the Duke by suddenly appearing beside him, but she had noticed him standing alone, brooding in the corner, and had felt compelled to join him.

"As am I," he responded and his expression immediately lightened. Elizabeth wondered what had been on his mind to make him look so sombre and forbidding. Perhaps he was worried about Catherine?

"Have you enjoyed yourself this evening?" she asked him lightly and he assured her that he had. "Thank you for coming - I'm sure you would rather have stayed at home with Cathy."

The Duke looked about to deny it, but at the last moment his expression changed and he smiled ruefully.

"I am sorry if I have been poor company," he apologised and Elizabeth was quick to correct him.

"Not at all, Your Grace! Your company has been as delightful as always. I am always happy to spend time with you - unlike some people," she confided with an eye roll and a glance in Mr Wickham's direction.

The Duke looked where she indicated and seemed surprised by who she meant.

"You dislike him?"

"Well, I wouldn't say that." Elizabeth teased. "Dislike is such a strong word. I suppose I find him rather amusing, though only in small doses. *Very* small doses," she added playfully and the Duke grinned.

"I am the same," he admitted and Elizabeth smiled.

"Really? Oh, I'm so glad it's not just me. Everyone else seems half in love with him," she noted dryly, "I thought I was at fault in some way."

"I assure you," the Duke responded playfully, "I am not at all in love with him."

"That is good to know," Elizabeth half-whispered and then chuckled lightly, "I cannot believe I am having this conversation with you of all people - he is your cousin!"

"You started it," the Duke pointed out and Elizabeth laughed.

"A fair point!"

They shared another laugh before Elizabeth asked him to tell her more about his stables at Pemberley and they spent the next twenty minutes enjoying their discussion, and each other's company, in relative privacy as the other guests all played cards or chatted in small groups. When she noticed that Mrs Drake and her two daughters were taking their leave, Elizabeth pointed it out to the Duke.

"Now you can make your escape."

"That would imply that the evening has been unpleasant," he responded in a warm tone, "and I assure you that is not the case. I have enjoyed your company very much, Miss Gardiner. As always."

"Thank you," Elizabeth replied with a slight blush. "I am glad you came. And I look forward to seeing you again on Monday."

"As do I," the Duke averred and surprised her by taking her hand and bowing over it. "Good night, Miss Gardiner."

"Good night, Your Grace," Elizabeth responded and watched as he walked away to say goodbye to his friends and her aunt and uncle.

Charlotte quietly strolled over to stand beside Elizabeth, watching the Duke as well.

"You two seem to be getting along well," she noted and something in her tone made Elizabeth turn to look at her.

"Yes," she agreed slowly, studying Charlotte's expression. "I suppose we are. What of it?"

"Oh, nothing," Charlotte responded lightly and effectively changed the subject by saying, "I hate Delia."

Elizabeth laughed at her friend's bluntness and the two fell into a laughing discussion of why it was that Charlotte disliked her future sister-in-law so much.

# Chapter 7

Darcy smiled at Miss Gardiner as she climbed into his carriage behind her nephew. James, Catherine and Mrs Hughes were all seated on one side of the carriage and so she and Daniel settled themselves besides him, with the small boy between them.

"Good morning, everyone!" she greeted them all chirpily.

"Good morning, Lizzy," Catherine and James both responded.

"Good morning, Miss Gardiner. And good morning to you too, Master Bingley," Darcy added, smiling down at the boy next to him.

"Morning," he cheerfully replied. "I am so excited!"

"Oh good," Darcy responded - he looked across at his children. "I think we all are, aren't we?"

"Oh yes," Catherine stated, her little feet kicking in the air as she spoke.

"What are you most looking forward to seeing?" Miss Gardiner asked them all - she must have caught Darcy's surprised look for she smiled and admitted, "I did a little research after you invited us along. It sounds fascinating!"

"I wish to see the animals first," Daniel replied. "There are birds and mice and others."

"And the tarantula," Miss Gardiner added, her eyes lighting up.

"What's a tranchula?" Catherine asked.

"A tar-an-tula," Miss Gardiner corrected smilingly. "It is a *spider*."

"A very large spider," Darcy qualified and his daughter recoiled.

"I don't like spiders," she cried and Mrs Hughes was quick to soothe her.

"It won't be a real spider, dear. And you don't have to see it if you do not wish to."

"Have you seen one in real life, Your Grace?" Miss Gardiner asked Darcy, leaning around Daniel.

"Unfortunately, yes," Darcy replied with a slight grimace. "I had the dubious pleasure of coming across one whilst travelling in the Mediterranean."

Miss Gardiner looked utterly fascinated and Darcy couldn't help smiling.

"I thought young ladies were supposed to be afraid of spiders."

Miss Gardiner shrugged and carelessly replied.

"I rarely do what I'm supposed to."

Darcy silently agreed with her, and was glad of it.

"What would you most like to see?" Daniel asked, looking up at him.

"It will sound boring," Darcy responded. "But the clocks interest me the most."

"And the perpetual motion machine," James added, nodding along with his father.

"Do you understand such creations?" Miss Gardiner asked. "I confess the science behind it confounds me."

"It is rather complex," Darcy responded. "Though the primary idea is for a machine or mechanism to maintain motion with no outside input."

"So it is self-perpetuating," James added again. "And, theoretically, should therefore run indefinitely."

"I see," Miss Gardiner replied slowly. "Well, almost. I shall leave such complicated matters to you both, I think," she added, smiling between Darcy and his son.

The group spent a few minutes more discussing what they hoped to see before the carriage finally pulled to a stop at the museum. The two boys both hopped out first, followed by Darcy who assisted the three ladies down. They entered the museum, Darcy paying the admission for the entire group, and went directly to the main room which was over one hundred feet long and housed the majority of the pieces. The children were quickly distracted by certain attractions and, after promising they would stay together, James and Daniel were allowed to go off on their own. Catherine was immediately enthralled by a dancing ballerina and Mrs Hughes was promptly tugged in that direction. Darcy and Miss Gardiner looked in both directions and then at each other.

"You want to go and see the tarantula, don't you?"

"Is it so obvious?" she teased and Darcy chuckled, shaking his head.

"Go - we shall catch up with you."

"Only if you're sure," she hesitated and Darcy assured her it was fine. "Very well, I shall see you soon."

She headed off in the direction James and Daniel had gone and Darcy walked over to join his daughter and Mrs Hughes.

"Isn't it beautiful, Papa?" Catherine said to him when he joined them. She was looking up at the silver figure which appeared to dance and pirouette across a small stage. She was a little too small to see over the top of the display counter and, noticing this, Darcy bent down and picked her up.

"There, is that better?"

Catherine smiled and kissed his cheek.

"Thank you, Papa."

"You are perfectly welcome, princess," he replied and stood holding her in his arms and watching the figure.

"Lizzy!!"

Elizabeth startled when Dan tugged on her dress, pulling her eyes from the Duke and his daughter.

"What is it?"

"Look, they even make noises!" Daniel indicated the cage before them, which housed several mechanical birds that did indeed move and tweet.

"So they do," Elizabeth noted. She looked around them and noticed a small crowd of people. "Do you suppose that is where the tarantula is?"

"Probably," James agreed before suggesting, "Shall we see the perpetual motion machine first and let the crowd go down a bit?"

"By all means," Elizabeth granted happily. "I shall rely on you to educate me some more about it, James."

"I will try my best," he replied modestly, though Elizabeth sensed he knew more about it than he was letting on.

"Are you interested in engineering, James?" she asked him in an encouraging tone.

"Yes, I suppose so," he admitted. "Though perpetual motion is primarily a question of physics. People have been trying to create a perpetual motion machine for over five hundred years."

"Really, that long? Has anyone ever accomplished it?"

"Some people think so," James replied. He indicated the clock they had just come to. "Mr Cox's clock. It runs without needing to be wound."

"How long has it been running?" Elizabeth asked curiously, examining the beautifully ornate gold clock before her.

"Over fifty years," James replied and Elizabeth was suitably impressed.

"Isn't that amazing, Dan?" she said to her nephew who stood next to her, looking a little bored. "This clock has been going for fifty years and has never needed winding."

"Can we go see the birds again now?" he asked in response and Elizabeth rolled her eyes and ruffled his hair, sharing an amused look with James.

"If you wish," she responded and left James to look over the rest of the timepieces alone.

"Look, Dan, there's no one near the tarantula now," Elizabeth said to her nephew some time later. "Let's find James and go have a look."

The trio made their way over to the eagerly anticipated display, where a small box was sat atop the counter.

"Where is it?" Daniel asked.

"Just wait," Elizabeth shushed him.

As soon as she had done so the box opened and the steel tarantula came out and made them all jump. As they watched it began running backwards and forwards on the table and then stopped and stretched out and drew in its legs, the motions seeming almost lifelike. It then returned to its box.

"That was amazing!" Daniel exclaimed loudly and Elizabeth could only agree.

"Did you see its legs?!" James was just as amazed and they stayed to watch the whole sequence once more.

"Ah, I see you have found what you came for."

Elizabeth turned to find the Duke with Catherine and Mrs Hughes standing behind them.

"We have indeed - it really is amazing, though only you can judge how true to life it is."

The Duke moved to stand beside her as Mrs Hughes and Catherine stood on her other side, the latter doing her best to hide behind the two ladies skirts. They waited for a moment and then the spider performed its show once more.

"Isn't it clever, Father," James said, looking up at the Duke.

"It certainly is," the Duke agreed, seeming impressed. "And very life like. Though I remember the fangs being longer."

"Perhaps that was your fear playing tricks on you," Elizabeth teased and he laughed.

"You are probably right."

"I don't like it," Catherine caught their attention by saying quietly, looking quite upset. "It is scary."

"Oh, sweetie," Elizabeth cooed. "There's nothing to be afraid of - it's only metal. But come with me, I have something to show you."

She offered her hand to the little girl and together they walked over to an exhibit Elizabeth had glimpsed earlier and that she thought Catherine would appreciate.

"Oh, a swan!" Catherine exclaimed when she saw it.

It was a very large creation, mounted on a table and easily reaching above Elizabeth's head. The swan was silver and seemingly swam on moving water, with little fish leaping from the water that it bent down to catch. The whole thing shimmered and danced in the light and the inventor had perfectly captured the elegance of the real bird, the regal curve of its neck and body.

"It's so beautiful," Catherine breathed, watching the swan move gracefully.

"Can you see the fish?" Elizabeth asked her, noticing that the table was a little high for her.

Catherine shook her head.

"I am too small. Can you pick me up, please?"

"I'm not sure I could manage it," Elizabeth responded apologetically.

"Papa can," Catherine told her and before Elizabeth could stop her, the little girl had run back to her father and patted him on the leg.

Elizabeth watched as the two spoke, smiling when Catherine indicated her and the Duke looked her way. He nodded and allowed Catherine to lead him back to the swan.

"Please, Papa," she added prettily and the Duke smiled as he bent down to pick her up.

"You will be too big for me to do this, soon," he noted and Catherine shook her head.

"Never."

Elizabeth smiled softly but quickly looked back at the swan when the Duke looked her way.

"Do you see the fish now, Cathy?" she asked the little girl and Catherine nodded.

"This is my favourite one of all," Catherine declared and Elizabeth agreed with her.

"Not the tarantula?" The Duke asked and Elizabeth smiled and shook her head. "Have you seen the figurines?"

"No, not yet," Elizabeth replied.

"Shall we show them to her, princess?" he asked his daughter and Catherine nodded. "Then let me put you down."

"Oh, but, Papa!"

"No buts please, Catherine," he interrupted firmly, though his tone was still warm. "We are both too old for me to carry you everywhere."

Elizabeth laughed lightly.

"I would hardly say you are old, Your Grace."

"Papa is very old," Catherine put in knowledgably, and both adults looked at her, surprised and vastly amused. "I am only eight, and he is..." she hesitated and they could see her counting on her fingers, "Oh, I lost count. Let me try again."

"I am thirty years older than you, princess," the Duke provided helpfully.

"Yes! See, he is very old," Catherine said to Elizabeth who was struggling valiantly not to laugh.

"I see what you mean," she managed to say and the Duke, seeing her dilemma, distracted his daughter by offering her his hand.

Elizabeth allowed herself a light laugh and then caught up with them.

"How old are you, Lizzy?" Catherine asked her when she did so.

"I am nineteen," Elizabeth replied. "Which is eleven years older than you."

"Then you aren't that old," Catherine stated and the Duke chuckled.

"Thank you," Elizabeth teased. "I'm glad you think so."

"It is Papa's birthday soon," Catherine said next and Elizabeth nodded.

"Yes, I know - we spoke about it in the park. Do you remember?"

"Yes, just before you fell in the pond," Catherine replied and then giggled.

"Precisely," Elizabeth shared a laughing look with the Duke.

Fortunately they had reached the display of figurines and Catherine spent the next ten minutes or so showing them all to Elizabeth. Eventually the boys and Mrs Hughes joined them and they remained as a group as they perused more of the pieces.

"Miss Gardiner?"

Elizabeth looked up from the mechanical mice.

"Yes, James?"

"Would you like to come and see the mechanical umbrella with me?" he asked, and Elizabeth detected something in his tone which made her curious.

"Of course," she agreed and they moved away from the others.

As the umbrella opened and closed next to them, Elizabeth looked at James with one brow arched in enquiry. He smiled ruefully.

"I'm sorry, that wasn't a very good excuse to draw you away. I have a favour to ask of you. Both me and Cathy do, actually."

"What is it?" Elizabeth asked curiously.

"We saw the drawing you did of Agatha," James replied. "And I thought that for Father's birthday you could do a drawing of us. As a surprise for him."

"What a lovely idea," Elizabeth complimented before hesitating, "though I'm not sure that I..."

"Please," James interrupted. "You are the only one who could do it - there is no way for us to find someone else. And I know you are talented enough, so don't say that you aren't," he added and then grinned sheepishly at his boldness.

Elizabeth hesitated for a moment before finally smiling.

"Very well, I would be happy to help you."

"Thank you so much," James thanked her sincerely and smiled happily.

"You are perfectly welcome," Elizabeth replied. "But come, let us go back to the others."

The Duke looked up when they rejoined the group, glancing between the pair of them.

"I was just showing Miss Gardiner the umbrella," James answered the silent question.

"Yes - a silly contraption," Elizabeth noted and the Duke smiled before turning his attention back to Daniel as the little boy chatted happily up at him about the mechanical parrot.

"Look, Lizzy," Catherine caught her attention and Elizabeth went to her side, silently reflecting that she really had had a lovely morning so far.

"Have you had a good time?" she asked the little girl and Catherine nodded. "I'm happy you were able to come - your father told me you were a bit poorly last week."

Catherine nodded again.

"My head hurt, and I was hot and couldn't sleep. Papa made me all better though."

"And how did he do that?" Elizabeth asked - she glanced over at the Duke and could see he was listening.

"He held me in his lap and sang to me," Catherine replied guilelessly. "I think I fell asleep, because I woke up in my bed the next day and felt much better."

"I think you are very lucky to have such a wonderful papa," Elizabeth told the little girl sincerely, utterly touched. She was not usually the sentimental type, but there was something about the Duke and his children that warmed her heart.

"I am," Catherine agreed with a decisive nod. "I love him very much."

Elizabeth could see the Duke blushing slightly and looking both gratified and embarrassed, and was a little taken aback when a voice inside her said, *I can see why.*

# Chapter 8

The next few weeks passed by in a whirl of social activity for Elizabeth. She accompanied her aunt and uncle to a different event almost every night, and spent her days making and receiving calls, shopping and generally enjoying the delights of the Season. She was proving to be something of a success (to Mrs Bennet's immense pleasure). Whereas other girls were demure models of ladylike and feminine behaviour, Elizabeth seemed to delight everyone by being impulsive and lively. She was also clever and direct, and the combination of her wit, beauty and personality had gained her the attention of several eligible men.

Attracted to her gaiety and the easy playfulness of her manners, these men paid her many compliments and competed amongst themselves for her attention; Elizabeth was never without a partner for a set, and it was a rare morning indeed when no one called upon her. She had a smile for everyone, and received their attentions with a mixture of surprise and gratitude, but though she was often impertinent and teasing, the uniformity of her manner towards her erstwhile suitors should have given them little encouragement. If she teased one she teased them all, and had no intention or inclination to form a closer attachment to any of them.

Mrs Bennet was unfortunately blind to these nuances of her niece's behaviour and entertained serious hopes that Elizabeth would be engaged by the end of the Season. She was confident it would be the case, and was also quite certain which of her suitors her niece would choose, as it seemed to her that Elizabeth had developed a decided partiality for Mr Wickham.

She wasn't alone in thinking that a match was in the making between Elizabeth and Mr Wickham. Society had long ago taken note of their acquaintance, and every dance they had shared, every dinner they had attended, every encounter they had had with one another had been tallied and gossiped about. What Society and Mrs Bennet couldn't know, however, was that Elizabeth thought of Mr Wickham as nothing more than an amusing distraction and that more often than not she was simply putting up with his company, rather than actually enjoying it.

For his part, Mr Wickham would have been happy had Elizabeth entertained hopes of that nature regarding himself. What had begun as an amusing and invigorating flirtation had, for him, become something much more and he cursed himself for allowing Elizabeth to get under his skin when he knew- *knew*- that he had to stay away. She was rich, but her dowry wasn't nearly large enough to suit his needs, and her family would never allow the match - not with his reputation and total lack of funds. He needed to find himself a rich wife with a less discerning family and the task would have been a whole lot easier without the distraction of being half in love with Miss Gardiner.

For her part, Elizabeth was totally ignorant of the nature of Mr Wickham's feelings and was unaware that appearances had led to such speculation about their relationship - amongst Society at large, but also between members of her own family. She would have been distressed had she known it, most especially if one person - one man - in particular believed the rumours to be true. She knew what was in her heart with regards to him, though she had yet to fully admit it to herself and scarcely dared to hope that he felt the same.

&#8284;&#8285;

Darcy stepped down from the carriage and turned and offered his hand to his sister; when she had stepped down he turned back and smiled as he offered his hand to Miss Gardiner.

"Thank you," she said softly and went to his sister's side; he watched her for a moment before being distracted by his cousin.

"I think I can manage quite well by myself," Richard joked when he saw Darcy stood beside the carriage, looking as though he were offering his assistance. "Though I am flattered by your gallantry."

Darcy rolled his eyes.

"I hope you fall on your face."

"Now that would be ironic," Richard quipped as he - quite safely - stepped down and stood beside his cousin. "So, this is it, is it?"

"It" was the Dulwich College Picture Gallery, Britain's first ever purpose-built public art gallery and just recently opened.

"Yes, this is it," Darcy responded. He glanced at his cousin. "I'm still not entirely sure why you're here."

"My mother has been living with us for almost a month," Richard replied. "I was hoping for a little time away from her with my wife."

"I see," Darcy chuckled and smiled. "Does my sister know this?"

"I doubt it," Richard admitted with a grin. "I'm counting on your support."

"I rather thought you might be," Darcy noted wryly and Richard nodded.

"I need you to distract Miss Gardiner whilst I spirit Georgiana away. Won't be too much trouble for you, will it?" he asked hopefully.

"Not at all," Darcy assured him neutrally. He would be more than happy to spend the time alone - relatively - with Miss Gardiner.

"Capital!" Richard patted him on the back.

"Did you engineer this whole outing yourself?" Darcy asked curiously, suspecting it was the case.

"Not entirely," Richard replied. "Georgiana had already issued the invitation to Miss Gardiner - I just invited the pair of us along too."

Darcy simply rolled his eyes and shook his head.

"Shall we head inside?" Georgiana called from a little way away where she stood with Miss Gardiner.

"By all means, my dear," Richard responded and stepped over to her, offering his arm and smiling down at his wife. He shot his cousin a quick look over his shoulder and Darcy suppressed a grin.

He joined Miss Gardiner and offered her his arm.

"Miss Gardiner?"

"Thank you," she replied again and took his offered arm. Darcy saw her look between him and Richard a few times, and then begin to ask him something before hesitating and remaining silent.

Darcy grinned - he wasn't at all surprised she had noticed something - and confided in her.

"My cousin wishes to use this opportunity to enjoy some quality time with his wife."

"Oh?"

"Yes - I gather his mother's continued presence in their home is not agreeable to him," he teased and Miss Gardiner bit her lip and suppressed a smile, though her eyes betrayed her.

"Lady Matlock is quite a presence," she stated diplomatically and Darcy laughed lightly.

"That is certainly one way of putting it."

"So are you here to entertain me, whilst your cousin distracts his wife?" Miss Gardiner asked him after a moment and Darcy nodded.

"Yes, apparently. I had no idea until Richard told me just now."

"I hope you don't feel as though you have to." Miss Gardiner began but Darcy reached up and pressed her hand before she could go on.

"On the contrary, Miss Gardiner. It is my pleasure."

She held his gaze for a few beats before looking away, a slight blush tingeing her cheeks. Darcy knew he was playing with fire, but over the past few weeks their friendship had blossomed and with every increase of intimacy he felt himself falling further under her spell. It was with a mixture of disbelief and joy that he perceived that she seemed to receive his attentions with pleasure, and despite his better judgement he had started to entertain hopes for what may be in the future. He was distracted from his thoughts when they entered the gallery and Miss Gardiner gasped.

"Oh my!"

Darcy had known that the design of the gallery was special, but even he was taken aback by the dimensions of the gallery and the sheer amount of light which streamed into each of the rooms from the overhead skylights. It was so different from what he had seen before, but so ideally suited to its purpose - the paintings were truly displayed to their best advantage in such a setting.

"Isn't it marvellous?" Miss Gardiner asked him, looking up at him with a bright smile.

"Yes," Darcy agreed warmly. "The amount of light is astounding."

They moved further into the gallery, exploring each of its rooms and examining the skylights and, for the moment at least, taking very little note of the paintings. Eventually, when they had satisfied their curiosity with regards to the design of the gallery, they turned their attention to the pieces on exhibit.

"Farleigh!"

Darcy turned and saw an old friend, Lord Hallam, approaching with another man whom he did not know in tow. The two friends shook hands and Darcy introduced Miss Gardiner.

"Pleased to meet you, Miss Gardiner," Lord Hallam responded politely before turning to the gentleman at his side and introducing him as Mr Danvers.

"Mr Danvers works with the Royal Academy," Lord Hallam explained. "And when I saw you he expressed a desire to be introduced."

"Yes," Mr Danvers nodded and Darcy could see he was nervous. "I wanted to thank you for your latest donation, Your Grace."

"Please, there is no need to thank me," Darcy replied sincerely. "I applaud the work the Academy does - and I am looking forward to the Summer Exhibition very much indeed."

Mr Danvers smiled and bobbed his head again.

"The preparations are very nearly complete. I hope you will honour us by attending the opening dinner," he stated hopefully and Darcy smiled.

"I would not miss it for the world," he assured him. He glanced at Miss Gardiner, who was listening to the conversation with obvious interest, and had a sudden thought. "I thought this year I would bring some guests - if it is not too much trouble."

"Not at all, Your Grace!" Mr Danvers eagerly assured him. "How many?"

"I am not certain as of yet," Darcy responded before Mr Danvers could go on. "But I shall send a note when I know."

"Yes, of course, whatever you wish, Your Grace," Mr Danvers nodded - *again* - and Darcy almost smiled.

"Well," Lord Hallam deftly concluded the conversation. "That's settled then. It was good to see you again Farleigh - I suspect I shall see you at the club."

"Yes," Darcy agreed. "Good day."

"Good day, Miss Gardiner," Lord Hallam said, bowing slightly and then steering Mr Danvers away.

"What a nervous little man!" Miss Gardiner smiled and noted.

"Yes, he was rather," he agreed lightly.

"I cannot imagine how you could make anyone so nervous," she surprised him by saying. "You are not at all intimidating."

"Thank you," Darcy replied dryly, and then pretended to look wounded.

Miss Gardiner smiled and shook her head.

"I did not mean it like *that*. Only that you are, well, you are so approachable, so open."

Darcy laughed.

"What?" Miss Gardiner asked, frowning delicately.

"Those are not adjectives which people usually apply to me," Darcy responded, still smiling.

"Then how would people usually describe you?" Miss Gardiner asked.

"Quiet," Darcy replied. "Shy, reserved. Taciturn, reticent, and dare I say it," he teased, "aloof."

"But you aren't any of those things!" Miss Gardiner protested. "Well not really. You're certainly not aloof! Just because you don't rattle away like other men. Honestly!"

Darcy chuckled deeply and smiled affectionately down at Miss Gardiner, touched by her spirited defence of his character. In truth he knew that as a younger man he *had* been aloof and reticent, and though he had mellowed over the years he still had a tendency to be rather reserved. That Miss Gardiner seemed unable to give credence to the idea was proof of the positive influence she had had on him.

"It is gratifying to know you think so well of me, Miss Gardiner," he stated at last, still smiling down at her, and saw her blush slightly at his words.

"Yes, well, I like to give credit where credit is due," she replied primly; a smile tugged at her lips and she glanced up at him as she admitted, "And I simply cannot stand it when other people fail to appreciate the things that I appreciate."

"Like shortbread with jam and cream?" Darcy teased. "And over-sized dogs?"

"Exactly," Miss Gardiner replied with a smile. "And you, of course," she added and Darcy returned her smile, feeling exceeding pleased.

"My aunt will be quite envious of you," Miss Gardiner said after a moment as they were stood admiring a large landscape painting. "I gather that invitations to the Royal Academy dinner are rather exclusive - she will no doubt covet yours."

"Would you like to go?" Darcy asked and saw that she was surprised before she smiled brilliantly.

"I would love nothing more!" She enthused and Darcy smiled at her delight.

"I thought you would like to go," he admitted. "I shall invite my sister and Richard along - you can come as Georgiana's guest."

"Thank you so much," Miss Gardiner thanked him sincerely, laying her hand on his arm.

Darcy was conscious of how close together they were standing, but allowed himself to enjoy it for a moment before stepping back slightly.

"You are perfectly welcome," he replied with a smile. "I cannot think of anyone who would appreciate the evening more; and I would be honoured to escort you," he added with a burst of courage and was rewarded when Miss Gardiner held his gaze and smiled shyly up at him.

"Ah, there you are!"

Darcy was glad he had already put some distance between himself and Miss Gardiner before his cousin and sister appeared.

"We have been looking for you," Georgiana told them. "Isn't it remarkable?" she stated, referring to the gallery.

They spent a few moments discussing the gallery and its collection before Darcy informed his sister and cousin about the Royal Academy dinner, and his plans for their party to attend.

"How wonderful!" Georgiana enthused. "My friends shall all be quite envious of me getting to view the Summer Exhibition before any of them - though I suspect Lady Andrews will also be there."

"Mother will want to come," Richard put in, not sounding at all pleased by the thought.

"I didn't think she enjoyed art particularly much," Darcy replied.

"She doesn't," Richard averred. "But she wouldn't miss an event like this for anything."

"I told you the invitations are coveted," Miss Gardiner pointed out teasingly and Darcy sighed and nodded.

"I shall simply have to secure another place."

"No doubt another generous donation will do the trick," Richard joked and his wife lightly chastised him.

"You know that is not why William supports the Academy."

"I know, I know," Richard soothed and spoke a few quiet words with his wife.

"Is it time we were leaving, do you think?" Darcy asked his trio of companions. "Miss Gardiner? Have you seen enough?"

"Yes, I think so," she replied and when Georgiana invited her to join them all for luncheon she readily agreed.

"I should be delighted - thank you."

"Then let us be on our way," Darcy stated and followed his sister and cousin outside to their carriage, Miss Gardiner still on his arm.

৪০৫৪

Elizabeth was a little nervous as she entered Colonel and Lady Fitzwilliam's townhouse, knowing who was no doubt waiting inside. She was not particularly fond of Lady Matlock, and got the distinct impression that the Dowager Countess did not approve of her. They had met on a handful of occasions, and each time Lady Matlock had peppered Elizabeth with intrusive questions and seemed greatly dissatisfied with the answers. As far as Lady Matlock was concerned, she was just the daughter of some obscure, countrified member of the lower aristocracy who was shockingly impertinent.

"Ah, Richard, darling."

Elizabeth heard Lady Matlock greet her son as he entered the room ahead of her. She put on a brave face and followed Lady Fitzwilliam into the room, the Duke following after her.

"Oh." Lady Matlock spotted her and all her prior warmth disappeared. "Good day, Miss?"

"Gardiner, Mother," the Colonel supplied with a smile, though there was a slight tightening around his lips.

"Oh, yes." Lady Matlock turned to the Duke, effectively dismissing Elizabeth. "Fitzwilliam, dear, did you have a nice time?"

"Yes, I did," the Duke replied. He turned to Elizabeth. "I think we all did - wouldn't you say, Miss Gardiner?"

"Yes," Elizabeth agreed, smiling her gratitude. The Duke's eyes were warm and understanding. "I had a lovely time."

"Yes, well," Lady Matlock looked put out. "I daresay you'll be returning home now, Miss Gardiner."

"Actually Elizabeth is to join us for luncheon," Lady Fitzwilliam piped up and Elizabeth was beginning to feel quite awkward - should she invent some excuse to slip away?

"In fact," Lady Fitzwilliam went on. "It should be ready shortly - shall we go through now?"

"Why not?" Her brother responded cheerfully and offered his arm to Elizabeth, completely ignoring all the rules which dictated that his aunt go ahead of her. "Shall we, Miss Gardiner?"

Elizabeth took his offered arm and tried not to smile too much. When they had all seated themselves and their luncheon had been served, there was little to be done but listen to Lady Matlock talk, which she did almost without any intermission until the conclusion of the meal. She enquired into her son and Lady Fitzwilliam's domestic concerns and gave a great deal of unsolicited advice; Elizabeth was a little consoled by the thought that she was not the only one Lady Matlock quizzed in such an intrusive manner. She felt sorry for Lady Fitzwilliam having a mother-in-law who so enjoyed dictating to others.

"Do you play and sing, Miss Gardiner?" Lady Matlock surprised her by asking at one point.

"Very little," Elizabeth replied honesty. She had no illusions as to the extent of her musical talents.

"Then some time or other we shall be happy to hear you, though I doubt you could match the skill of my daughter-in-law," Lady Matlock looked proudly at Lady Fitzwilliam, who in turn seemed embarrassed by her mother-in-law. "Your sister, Lady Bingley, plays, presumably."

"No, she does not, I'm afraid," Elizabeth responded lightly.

Lady Matlock looked disapproving.

"Why did you not both learn? You ought both to have learned. Does she draw? Your sister?"

"No, not at all."

"Well, that is very strange," Lady Matlock declared and Elizabeth's lips twitched. "Your mother should have brought you to town for the benefit of masters."

"My mother would have, but my father hates London," Elizabeth replied before adding quietly, "And my mother passed away when I was just a child and too young for such an undertaking."

"You are never too young to learn," Lady Matlock decreed authoritatively. "I daresay you and your sister would have benefited from having begun your education earlier."

"Perhaps," Elizabeth conceded quietly, inwardly adding *lack of accomplishment and education* to her list of faults, as Lady Matlock perceived them. She caught the eye of the Duke who sat across from her and saw that his eyes were dancing with suppressed laughter; they shared a smile before going back to their meal.

ꕥ

"Really, Georgiana, I don't understand why you keep up an acquaintance with that girl."

Miss Gardiner was barely out of the room, finally on her way home, before Lady Matlock expressed this opinion and all three members of her family frowned at her.

"I could understand your taking her under your wing to see her well suited - as a project of sorts, one might say - but from what I hear she doesn't lack for suitors, and she has that awful Mrs Bennet to help her anyway."

"Mother!" Richard said sharply. "Mr and Mrs Bennet are both friends of ours - as is Miss Gardiner. If you cannot think of anything nice to say, kindly keep your opinions to yourself."

Lady Matlock pursed her lips and stared at her son coldly for a few moments before turning to Georgiana with a smile on her face.

"Georgiana, my dear, where are my grandchildren? I have not seen them yet today."

"I shall fetch them now," Georgiana replied, rising reluctantly.

She knew her children would have liked to have seen Miss Gardiner, but she had kept them above stairs so that they could avoid their grandmother for as long as possible. They did not particularly like her.

"There is no need for you to go," Lady Matlock told her. "Have their governess bring them."

Georgiana merely smiled and passed out of the room, effectively ignoring her mother-in-law's decree.

"Well," Lady Matlock paused for a moment and then focused on Darcy. "Tell me, Fitzwilliam - surely you agree that Miss Gardiner is not appropriate company for your sister to keep. Or my grandchildren, for that matter."

"I could not disagree more," Darcy stated resolutely. "And even if I did agree with you," he added firmly. "I should never presume to dictate who my sister can and cannot associate with."

"Neither should I," Richard concurred decisively. "And I happen to like Miss Gardiner. As do our children."

Lady Matlock looked between the two of them with obvious irritation - she did not like to be contradicted, but was not fool enough to challenge them both.

"Well, if you insist. I only hope she is married soon - she needs a husband to curb her behaviour."

Darcy opened his mouth to protest but was forestalled by the appearance of his sister and his niece and nephews, all looking somewhat afraid. Clara clung to her mother as Joe and Bradley performed the requisite bows before their grandmother, and then retreated by several steps. The children's visit did not last long - Lady Matlock firmly believed that children should remain above stairs and be neither seen or heard for the majority of the day - and it was not long after Joe, Bradley and Clara had left that Darcy rose to leave as well.

"So soon, Fitzwilliam!" Lady Matlock complained. "But you have only just arrived."

"I have an appointment at my club which I must get to," Darcy lied. He wished his aunt a perfunctory good day before kissing his sister's cheek and shaking his cousin's hand, promising to see them again soon.

It was only once he was seated in his carriage that Darcy breathed a sigh of relief at having made his escape. His aunt had always been overbearing and dictatorial, but she had grown worse over the years as the control she had over her family had waned. Fortunately she had learned very early on that Darcy was not to be ordered about, though that did not stop her from trying on the odd occasion. Darcy was vastly relieved that she was not his problem to deal with, though he did pity his sister and cousin.

As his carriage rolled through the streets of London, Darcy replayed the rest of the morning in his mind and a pleased smile graced his features as he recalled the time he had spent with Miss Gardiner at the gallery. He made a mental note to secure their places at the Royal Academy dinner at the earliest opportunity, and looked forward to the evening with much anticipation. The presence of his aunt was not something he had anticipated, and he had no doubt that she would spoil what would otherwise have been a perfect evening, but he was still excited at the prospect of escorting Miss Gardiner to the dinner and witnessing her delight. She was so beautiful when she was captivated by something, so honest in her expressions. She did not try to hide her emotions, and even had she tried her eyes, so expressive, would have given her away.

Darcy looked down at his hands and smiled to himself - shyly, hopefully. He was surprised by his feelings. He was a grown man who had seen much of life and bore many responsibilities; he was father to two wonderful children whom he cared for and adored. He had been a faithful husband and was a loving brother and cousin.

He was also in love with Miss Elizabeth Gardiner, a young woman half his age, who made him feel happier than he could remember being in a very long time.

Was it not ridiculous? Was he not old enough – practically - to be her father? Was he not greying at the temples and beginning to creak in the joints? Was she not beautiful, vivacious and impertinent, meant for a man ten years his junior?

Yes - yes to all those things - yes!

But he still loved her, and that was what mattered most. What mattered was how she made him feel, and how they felt about each other. He was in love with her, but he also knew that he could make her happy, as happy as any man - happier even, because he loved her. Lord, how he loved her. She was wonderful, so beautiful, and full to the brim with life. Meeting her had been like sunshine breaking through the clouds - he hadn't known what was missing until she had come along. He hadn't known he had needed her happiness and joy, but now he didn't know how he could go without.

And they complimented each other perfectly. Her intelligence and curiosity matched his own, and he knew they would never grow bored with one another. She was mature beyond her years, but at the same time made him feel younger and more alive. And she adored children, and with her loving and affectionate nature Darcy knew she would be a wonderful mother to James and Catherine. As well as any other children they might have.

Darcy laughed aloud at this last thought.

"Slow down, man. You have to marry her first."

*More children would be nice though*, his mind whispered at him and Darcy grinned.

# Chapter 9

Darcy crouched down in front of his daughter and son as they stood on the front steps, bidding him farewell. At Easter every year he travelled down to Rosings, the estate in Kent he had inherited through marriage to his wife, and this year he had decided that the children were old enough to remain in town. He would only be gone a week at most, and though he would miss them Darcy felt they were well settled and happy where they were.

"Now be good, and look after each other for me."

"We will," James promised him. "Take care, Father."

"I'll miss you," Catherine said, throwing her arms around him. "Come back soon."

"I will," Darcy assured her, kissing her cheek and slowly standing up.

James moved closer and put his arm around his sister's shoulders and Darcy smiled with affection and pride. He climbed into the carriage and waved from the window as it pulled away.

James and Catherine watched for a moment, the latter sniffing and trying very bravely not to cry.

"Don't worry Cathy," James told her. "He'll be back soon. And when he comes back we'll have a surprise for him."

Catherine smiled at the reminder of what they had planned.

"Is Lizzy coming today?"

"Tomorrow," James replied as they walked inside together. "And she will have plenty of time to finish Father's present before he returns."

"I shall wear my best dress," Catherine declared. "And ask Mrs Hughes if I can have a ribbon for my hair."

"You will look very pretty, I'm sure," James complimented his little sister, knowing that with their father gone it was up to him to take care of her.

Catherine smiled and squeezed her brother's hand in thanks.

Agatha was trotting along behind them, keeping careful watch over her two charges, and James turned to look at her.

"I think it would be nice if Agatha were with us in the picture," he said, then looked at his sister. "Don't you think?"

Catherine scrunched up her nose.

"She is too scruffy."

James laughed lightly.

"Don't say that- she'll hear you. And we can smarten her up a little," he pointed out reasonably.

"We could give her a bath," Catherine suggested lightly, looking up at her brother for approval.

Agatha, hearing the dreaded "b" word, immediately stopped, turned tail and lopped off in the other direction.

"We'll have to catch her first!" James laughed and set off after Agatha.

"Wait for me!" Catherine called and, picking up her skirts, hurried after her brother.

ꙮ

"Oh, you are such a sweetheart! Yes you are!"

Elizabeth was sat on the floor of the Duke's library, showering Agatha with attention. The Great Dane was stretched out on her side with her head in Elizabeth's lap, her tail wagging and thumping the floor. She was making a sound that was somewhere between a growl and a snore and Elizabeth found it utterly endearing.

"Are you purring Agatha, is that what you're doing?" Elizabeth asked as she rubbed Agatha's tummy.

She looked up as Mrs Hughes and the children entered the room, smiling at their amusement at finding her in her current position.

"You are spoiling her rotten, Miss Gardiner," Mrs Hughes remarked, not unkindly.

"I know - I can't help it," Elizabeth replied as she gave Agatha one final cuddle before getting to her feet.

"I'm sorry we kept you waiting," Mrs Hughes went on. "Miss Catherine was not happy with her hair."

"Well I think you look absolutely beautiful sweetheart," Elizabeth told the young girl who did look very pretty in a blue dress with matching ribbons in her hair.

"Thank you," Catherine replied shyly. "I want to look my best for Papa's picture."

"And James, you look very smart too."

"Thank you," James replied with a wry smile. "*I* was ready ages ago," he pointed out and Elizabeth smiled.

"I'm sure you were."

"Where shall we sit?" Catherine asked Elizabeth, looking around.

"Well, that really depends on what sort of picture you would like," Elizabeth responded. "Would you like a formal portrait, or something more natural?"

"Is there time for you to do both?" James asked. "We could display the formal one in the hallway, but I'm sure Father would like one for his study."

Elizabeth smiled and assured him that they had plenty of time for more than one drawing.

"May I suggest then, as Miss Catherine is wearing her best dress, that we do the formal portrait first?" Mrs Hughes spoke up and Elizabeth agreed it would be the most sensible thing to do.

"Why don't you sit here?" she said to the children, indicating a small settee. "Side by side. And if we can get Agatha to sit at your feet."

James produced a biscuit from one of his pockets and Agatha was immediately there, sitting very still and straight and watching him patiently.

"Turnaround, turn, that's a good girl," James got Agatha to sit facing where Elizabeth would sit. "Now down, lie down. Good girl Agatha, good girl. Now stay."

Agatha woofed down her biscuit and stayed where she had been put, proving yet again how well trained she was.

"Perfect," Elizabeth complimented as she gathered up her things and took the seat she had placed opposite the children. "Now don't move," she teased with a playful smile as she quickly sketched a rough outline of their positions.

Catherine wriggled in her seat and Elizabeth caught the movement.

"Ah! I saw that! And again!"

Catherine giggled at Elizabeth's teasing and James made her laugh outright when he mumbled without moving his lips.

"Ooo ill 'ave a urry ace if oo oo at Athy."

"What was that James?" Elizabeth joked, laughing lightly.

"Ei aid, ooo ill 'ave," James began to reply; he grinned when the others all laughed.

Once their laughter had died down, Elizabeth took a deep breath and tried to be serious, though every time she caught James' eye he smiled and laughter threatened again.

"I'll never get this done if we spend the whole time being silly," she pointed out, trying to sound stern; she was fighting back a smile though and the two children could see it.

"Orry," James mumbled and Catherine let out a peal of laughter.

Elizabeth hung her head and laughed; she looked over at Mrs Hughes and was glad to see that the other woman was also struggling with her amusement.

Eventually they all regained their equilibrium and the children sat for almost an hour without any significant movement, Agatha asleep at their feet. Elizabeth kept up a steady stream of conversation so they wouldn't be bored, and the children seemed to be having a pleasant enough time of it.

"There," she declared at last, sitting back in her chair.

"Is it finished?" Catherine asked excitedly, hopping down from the settee and rushing over to look.

"No, not yet," Elizabeth replied with a smile - a drawing like this would take her at least six hours to finish. "But I have the outline done - you won't have to sit still from now on."

"Oh," Catherine seemed disappointed but she quickly rallied. "Well least we can move now."

"Yes," Elizabeth replied - she looked at Agatha and smiled. "Not moving didn't seem to bother Agatha."

"She was a treasure," James agreed, crouching down and patting the old dog. She opened one eye and rolled lazily over onto her side.

"Thank you Aggy," Catherine cooed, kneeling down beside her and stroking one of her huge floppy ears.

Elizabeth watched for a moment and then, hit by a sudden idea, picked up a fresh sheet of paper and quickly began sketching. It was very rough, but she wanted to capture the moment before it was gone.

"Are you hungry, Miss Gardiner? I can have the tea things brought if you are," Mrs Hughes asked.

"A little tea would be nice, I think," Elizabeth agreed. "And I'm sure we will all appreciate the break."

Once the tea things had been brought in and the two ladies had served themselves cups, Catherine turned to Elizabeth.

"Where do you come from, Lizzy?"

"I was born in Hertfordshire," Elizabeth replied, smiling at Catherine's wording. "My father's estate is called Longbourn."

"Is your papa a Duke like mine?" Catherine asked.

Elizabeth shook her head.

"No, my father is a Viscount."

"And you have no mama either," Catherine said seriously.

"Miss Catherine." Mrs Hughes cautioned quietly but Elizabeth assured her it was alright.

"No, I have no mama. She died when I was eleven."

"I never knew my mama," Catherine replied frankly - Elizabeth supposed the little girl could hardly be expected to mourn someone she had never known. "But Papa and James tell me she was very nice."

"She was," James put in quietly, staring down at his hands. Elizabeth's throat tightened at the sight.

"What was your mother like?" Catherine asked her and it was a moment before Elizabeth could reply.

"She was lovely. Lady Jane looks just like her. I don't remember much about her, less and less as I get older, but I remember that she always seemed happy. And that her favourite colour was yellow," she added quietly, lost in the memory.

"What was Mama's favourite colour, James?" Catherine asked her brother, not realising how hard this conversation was for either he or Elizabeth.

"I don't..." James began to reply before he paused and thought for a moment. "Lavender," he said at last, and then smiled to himself, obviously recalling some memory.

"What?" Catherine began but Mrs Hughes gently interrupted her.

"That's enough questions for now, dear. Please finish your cake."

Elizabeth sipped her tea and used the moment to compose herself, caught off guard by the sombre conversation. She looked over at James and saw that he was similarly affected and resolved to rally her spirits in an effort to lift his.

"Do you play spillikins?" she asked, looking between James and his sister. When he nodded she proposed, "Would you like to play? I am hopeless at it, but I can draw whilst you play."

"James always beats me," Catherine pouted and Mrs Hughes assured her that she would help her play. "Oh, in that case - alright then."

As the children were playing their game and Elizabeth was drawing quietly, Catherine looked up and addressed Elizabeth.

"What is your papa like, Lizzy? Is he like ours?"

Elizabeth hesitated for a moment before replying. The obvious, honest answer was a resounding "no", but if she admitted that to Catherine she knew what inevitable question would follow.

"He is much quieter than your papa," she responded at last. "He is very busy most of the time with his studies and I do not see very much of him."

"Oh," Catherine replied with a delicate frown. "That is sad."

"What does he study?" James asked curiously.

"Plants mostly," Elizabeth replied. "And some insects as well. He has a wonderful collection of butterflies."

James nodded and then turned back to their game, obviously realising that it was not a subject Elizabeth wanted them to pursue. She was sorry she couldn't be more open, but her relationship with her father was complicated, and it would have been hard to explain it. She also doubted whether James and Catherine, with such a loving father as the Duke, would understand how her own father could be so absent and remote.

༄༅

Mrs Bennet, hearing the front door open, laid aside her sewing and bustled from the room, meeting her niece in the front hall as she was divested of her things by a footman.

"Where have you been?" she demanded without preamble.

Elizabeth looked up, surprised.

"I was with James and Catherine - I told you this morning that I was going."

"You said you were spending the morning with them," Mrs Bennet corrected irritably - the servants all discreetly absented themselves. "It is almost four o'clock!"

"I lost track of time," Elizabeth responded lightly, refusing to respond to her aunt's anger. "I didn't think it would matter."

"Not matter!" Mrs Bennet repeated loudly - by this point Mr Bennet had also appeared, disturbed from the library by the sound of his wife's raised voice. "You missed several calls whilst you were gone - and what excuse did I have for your absence? That you were off spending the day with some children! I was so embarrassed!"

"I don't see why," Elizabeth replied stubbornly. "There's no shame in it - I happen to like spending time with Catherine and James. And whoever called can simply call again," she pointed out nonchalantly, further irritating her aunt.

"For your information, it was Mr Wickham who called. *And* Mr Collins, who was particularly disappointed to find you out *when he had expressly told you he was going to call!!*"

"It slipped my mind," Elizabeth lied and Mr Bennet chose that moment to intervene.

"Might I suggest we move this discussion from the hallway into the library? Lest the entire household overhear - though I daresay they've heard enough already."

Mrs Bennet glared at her husband before turning and marching into the library, her skirts sweeping behind her. Elizabeth followed reluctantly.

"Now," Mr Bennet began, looking between them. "What seems to be the problem?"

"I am simply trying to impress upon our niece the importance of keeping appointments," Mrs Bennet stated impatiently. "Especially those made with gentlemen who offer the prospect of marriage."

"Marriage!" Elizabeth exclaimed. "I wouldn't marry Mr Collins if he were the last man on earth! And Mr Wickham would sooner marry *you* than he would me!"

"Ooh," Mrs Bennet fumed. "Why do you have to be so difficult?"

"Fanny, dear," Mr Bennet attempted to sooth his wife but she ignored him.

"I would have you know, Miss Lizzy, that you could do a lot worse than Mr Collins. He is rich, handsome, well-connected, sensible - though why he favours you I do not know!"

"Sensible!" Elizabeth protested, ignoring the insult to herself. "He is a complete fool!"

"Fine," Mrs Bennet quickly changed tack. "Not Mr Collins then. But what of Mr Wickham? I know you like him, and though you stubbornly refuse to see it, he most certainly likes you. All he needs is a little encouragement."

"I don't want to encourage him!" Elizabeth argued, thoroughly exasperated. "Why on earth would you think that I want to marry him?"

Elizabeth noticed that her uncle seemed surprised by this announcement and looked at him with disbelief.

"You didn't honestly think I was in love with him, did you? Oh my God," she exclaimed when she saw him exchange a look with his wife, "you did! Why?"

"You seem to enjoy his company, Lizzy," Mr Bennet defended himself. "And you're always laughing together. We thought that, well, that you certainly had some affection for him. Don't you?" he questioned.

"No!" Elizabeth denied. She sat down heavily into the nearest chair, trying to make sense of this revelation and what it might mean. "Does everyone else think like you do?"

"Yes, I'm afraid so," Mr Bennet admitted. "Though obviously, with Mr Collins showing interest as well the thing isn't seen as being quite settled."

Elizabeth groaned and covered her face with her hands.

"Are you saying that neither of them are acceptable?" Mrs Bennet asked and Elizabeth raised her head.

"Yes; is that so hard to understand?"

"I think it would be a mistake to refuse two such attractive offers," Mrs Bennet replied.

"I am only nineteen," Elizabeth pointed out. "This is my first season. Why must I marry so quickly?"

"You are beautiful, rich and sought after," Mrs Bennet responded. "But who can say how long that will last?"

Elizabeth shook her head.

"So I should consign myself to a life of misery just in case my luck changes in future? No."

"There's no need to be so dramatic," Mrs Bennet scolded and Elizabeth felt like crying.

"I thought you cared about my happiness," she said quietly, looking at her aunt with new eyes. "I thought you cared about *me.*"

"We do," Mr Bennet put in, uncomfortable with the turn of the conversation. "Of course we do. We just thought; well, never mind what we thought, we were obviously mistaken."

"May I be excused now, please?" Elizabeth eventually asked, unaccountably upset by the conversation.

"Yes, of course," Mr Bennet granted quickly, before his wife could protest.

Elizabeth stood up and left the room with her chin up, walking with as much dignity as she could muster; when she reached the second floor she hastened to her room, tears beginning to fall. She crossed her room and fell on to her bed, crying into the pillow.

"Now what time do you call this Missy?"

Wilson appeared from the dressing room, her usual greeting when Elizabeth was tardy on her lips - it faded away to a stunned silence as she looked at the prostrate figure on the bed.

"Why, petal, whatever is the matter?"

She bustled over and immediately began to mother her young charge, sitting next to Elizabeth on the bed and encouraging her to sit up so she could put her arms around her.

"What is it? What's happened?"

Elizabeth tried to reply but couldn't manage it. The last few weeks she had been so happy, so sure even that the Duke returned her feelings; now she felt a fool, wondering if he like everyone else thought her in love with Mr Wickham. All her hopes seemed so silly now, and she couldn't bear to think that she had been so wrong.

"Shh, shh, that's enough now, come on petal, calm down. That's it - that's my girl. Shh, everything will be fine."

Wilson rocked her and soothed her like a child, and eventually Elizabeth's tears subsided.

"Now, tell me what the matter is," Wilson gently instructed her and Elizabeth, who had kept her own confidences for so long, couldn't help confiding in Wilson now. The truth came spilling out.

"I'm in love with the Duke of Farleigh, and I thought that he loved me, but my aunt and uncle tell me that everyone believes me about to marry Mr Wickham, or Mr Collins, and it seems as though I have been fooling myself all along."

"Elizabeth," Wilson instructed calmly, overcoming her initial surprise at Elizabeth's confession. "I want you to start from the beginning. You say that you are in love with the Duke?"

Elizabeth nodded mutely.

"And how long have you felt this way?"

"I think, almost from the first moment I met him, I knew there was something special about him."

"And you are sure?" Wilson asked gently. "You don't think it is just..."

"A silly infatuation?" Elizabeth provided when her maid hesitated. "No. I love him Wilson. He is so very dear to me."

"Oh, my darling girl," Wilson cupped her cheek and smiled tearfully, touched by Elizabeth's emotion. "If that is the case, I am happy for you, and I will do everything I can to have you married to him before the year is out!"

Elizabeth managed a tearful smile at Wilson's teasing.

"Now, don't you worry what your aunt and uncle think," Wilson went on, her usual business-like manner returning. "The only two people who truly know what is happening are you and the Duke. If you think he shares your feelings, you have to trust yourself."

"I did think," Elizabeth admitted slowly but stopped, doubts crowding in again.

"That he cared for you too?" Wilson prodded and Elizabeth eventually nodded. "Well, that is good. And I have to say if he has the good sense to love you, I like him more than ever."

Elizabeth smiled again and wiped away some tears.

"I can see why your aunt and uncle – well, everyone, really – have overlooked the attachment." Wilson went on thoughtfully.

"The Duke is significantly older than you, and already has children of his own - he is not the type of man one would expect a girl like you to marry."

"Why?" Elizabeth questioned. "If one were to discount his age, why would I not wish to marry him? He is loving and kind and good; truly, he is the best man I have ever known."

"I am glad to hear you say so, petal," Wilson replied, smiling as she added, "Though I shall have to decide for myself whether I think he is good enough for you."

Elizabeth laughed, her mood much improved.

"Well, imagine what your aunt will say when she finds out; she will be beside herself! You, a Duchess, and not even twenty years old."

"I don't care about that," Elizabeth stated vehemently. "I would marry him were he a penniless sailor - and all I would ask is for my family to be happy for me."

"I think you would be asking too much, my darling, in that situation," Wilson replied gently. "Though fortunately the Duke isn't a penniless sailor, so we need never find out."

Elizabeth smiled, but it quickly faded as she sighed heavily and then looked at Wilson.

"What should I do? If he doesn't realise how I feel, I mean."

"Do?" Wilson repeated with a smile. "Just be yourself and let the Duke fall in love with you; if he is meant to, he will. He seems a sensible man, though," Wilson added, "and he would have to be a fool not to appreciate the gift of your love."

Elizabeth blushed and smiled, leaning her head against Wilson's shoulder.

"Thank you, Wilson."

"You are perfectly welcome, petal," Wilson replied quietly.

# Chapter 10

Mr Wickham smiled slightly and leant close so that he wouldn't be overheard.

"I'm trying not to take your lack of attention personally, but my ego can only withstand so much, you know."

"Pardon?" Elizabeth asked absently, not listening to her companion at all. She was too occupied with her own thoughts.

Mr Wickham laughed and shook his head.

"Oh! How you wound me, Miss Gardiner."

Elizabeth realised she was being very rude, and managed a slight smile.

"I'm sorry, I was lost in my thoughts. What were you saying?"

"Nothing of great import," Mr Wickham responded lightly; he studied her closely for a moment. "Are you well, Miss Gardiner? You do not seem quite yourself."

Elizabeth hesitated for a long moment before replying.

"Did you know that everyone considers us to be on the verge of becoming engaged?"

Mr Wickham looked surprised, and then a little chagrined.

"I had heard gossip of that sort, yes."

"And you let it continue?" Elizabeth demanded, partly in anger but also partly in surprise. Surely he was as uninterested in the prospect as she? "Why did you not refute the rumours?"

"That isn't how one usually goes about these things," he replied slowly and Elizabeth rolled her eyes.

"And how does one usually go about these things?" she asked sarcastically.

Mr Wickham glanced around before replying, lest their conversation be overheard. They were at yet another soiree thrown by yet another Lady and though they were in a corner a little separate from the rest of the company, they were hardly in private.

"Well, for a start had I denied any intention of marrying you, everyone would have immediately wanted to know why - especially given our apparent friendship and the length of our acquaintance. We have been linked together for so long, if I had cried off people would have assumed that there was something wrong with you, that I had found you lacking in some way."

Elizabeth was immediately incensed.

"Why must I be the one who is lacking? Why not you?"

Mr Wickham shrugged.

"It is simply what people would think if I denied any interest. If you or your family were the ones to end our relationship, people would look to me for the answer."

"Then perhaps I should ask my aunt to refrain from issuing you any more invitations," Elizabeth commented and almost smiled at the slim chance of *that* happening.

"Have I fallen out of favour with you then?" Mr Wickham teased and Elizabeth rolled her eyes at him.

"You were never in favour with me," she replied bluntly. "At least never in that way. I do not care for you at all and it pains me to know that everyone thinks that we are in love, of all things! Honestly, is not the whole idea ridiculous?"

Mr Wickham grinned, but not before Elizabeth glimpsed a flash of regret pass across his face. She started slightly, stunned by the thought that he had feelings for her after all. Had they not, *both* of them, made it clear from the start that marriage was never an option or a desire?

"It is, rather," her companion agreed at last, his voice strained. "I'm sure you are the last person I would want to marry!"

"I am glad to hear it," Elizabeth played along, pretending she had not noticed anything unusual in his manner.

"I hope you aren't considering that fool Collins, though," Mr Wickham commented after a moment. "That would be an atrocious waste of your considerable charms."

"My aunt does not seem to think so," Elizabeth muttered under her breath and then remembered with whom she was speaking. "Please forget that I said that."

"And I always thought Mrs Bennet favoured my suit," Mr Wickham teased and Elizabeth smiled in spite of herself.

"Oh, don't worry, you have her quite fooled," Elizabeth assured him lightly. "And it seems even my uncle is willing to overlook your less than perfect character."

"I have been very well behaved this Season, I'll have you know," Mr Wickham replied primly and Elizabeth patted his arm.

"Well done you - there may be a chance for you yet."

"But not with you," he commented and Elizabeth looked at him sharply. "Don't fret, I didn't mean it like that. The fact is," he admitted after a moment, "however well I behave there are still things which would prevent me from ever being able to offer for you."

"Besides our lack of affection for one another?" Elizabeth pointed out lightly, smiling to take away the sting. "Or the fact that we would drive each other mad within a month?"

"Two months," Mr Wickham countered and Elizabeth chuckled lightly.

"I think you are being a tad over optimistic."

Whilst Elizabeth continued to talk with Mr Wickham, Mrs Bennet was surreptitiously watching them from across the room. Despite what her niece might say about it, she was convinced that Elizabeth was partial to Mr Wickham, and he to her; that being said, however, Mrs Bennet had long ago conceded that her husband was probably right, and that it was not wise to place all of their eggs in that particular basket. Partiality was one thing, it would take much more, she knew, to induce Mr Wickham to propose. No, as far as Mrs Bennet was concerned it was best to cultivate as many options for Elizabeth as possible.

With that in mind, Mrs Bennet silently resolved to speak with her niece again about Mr Collins and to write him a note arranging a time for a private interview on his return to town. There was still hope yet, in that quarter, though if nothing came of it there were still other avenues to be explored.

ෂ෮ଓ

Darcy woke to the sound of barking and his children's voices as James, Catherine and Agatha all piled onto his bed. He had only returned from Kent late last night and grinned as he sat up, hugging his daughter as Agatha tried to lick his face.

"Argh, Agatha, get out of it! Good morning, sweetheart."

"Morning, Papa," Catherine replied, kissing his cheek. "I missed you! Happy Birthday!"

"Thank you," Darcy responded. "I missed you too, princess." He looked over at his son who sat smiling and stroking Agatha. "Good morning son."

"Good morning, Father," James replied. He held out a large, flat package. "Happy Birthday."

"What's this?" Darcy asked curiously, taking the package. He turned it over a few times, considering. "A painting?"

"No," Catherine shook her head and bit her lip, obviously excited for him to open his present.

"No? Hmmm, I wonder what it could be then." Darcy teased, intentionally stalling.

"You have to open it!" Catherine burst out at last and both James and Darcy chuckled at her.

"Very well, then," Darcy carefully ripped off the wrapping, revealing two sheets of thick paper separated by a thin piece of board. "Err?"

"The other side, Father," James provided helpfully and Darcy smiled ruefully as he separated the two sheets, revealing the drawings on each piece.

Darcy turned the drawings the right way up and gasped as he realised what he was looking at. His throat tightened as he stared at the two beautiful drawings of his family, especially loving the candid one of the children stroking Agatha.

"Do you like them?" Catherine asked excitedly. "Lizzy did them for you."

"Elizabeth?" Darcy repeated - he cleared his throat and corrected himself. "Miss Gardiner?"

"Yes," James replied with a nod. "Whilst you were at Rosings."

Relief briefly registered in Darcy's mind - relief that he had been in Elizabeth's thoughts at least a little whilst he had been away. She had hardly left *his* thoughts, day or night, even for a moment.

"They are wonderful," Darcy stated, still struggling with his emotions. "I shall treasure them. Come here," he motioned to his daughter who eagerly climbed into his lap. "You too, James."

After a slight hesitation James moved closer and Darcy pulled him the rest of the way, wrapping him tightly in his spare arm.

"I love you both so much," he said thickly, kissing the tops of their heads. "I hope you know that. And thank you so much for my present."

"We love you too, Papa," Catherine replied sweetly, squeezing him tightly. "Don't we, James?" she prodded her brother.

"Yes." James nodded and shyly said, "I love you too, Father."

"You will never be too old to say that to me, Son."

James smiled ruefully, silently admitting that he had been a little embarrassed and feeling reassured by his father's words.

Darcy looked down at the two drawings.

"So Miss Gardiner did these? I shall have to pay her a visit to say thank you."

"Can we come?" Catherine asked him. "I want to see if she is better."

"Has she been unwell?" Darcy asked, looking at his son for an answer.

"No," James hesitated for a moment before admitting, "but when she was last here she seemed upset. We have not seen her at all since then- she sent these here with a servant," he concluded, indicating the drawings.

"I see," Darcy responded thoughtfully, hoping that nothing unpleasant had occurred. He was sure if anything serious had happened he would have heard of it from Charles. "Well, perhaps we shouldn't."

"Oh please Papa!" Catherine implored. "Please?! I want to see Lizzy. I miss her."

Darcy hesitated for a moment before finally giving in.

"Oh, very well. We shall go after breakfast."

ᏠᏅᏟᎶ

Elizabeth was sat reading in the library when a servant appeared with a request from Mrs Bennet for her to come to the morning room. Expecting yet another argument about Mr Collins and the idea of her marrying him (they had had three so far); Elizabeth reluctantly put aside her book and answered the summons, unprepared to find the gentleman himself sat with her aunt and obviously waiting for her.

"Lizzy, please sit down. Mr Collins has something to say to you," her aunt told her and rose with the obvious intention of leaving.

"Aunt, don't go. Mr Collins can have nothing to say that anyone could not hear."

Mrs Bennet simply ignored her niece, and smiled at the gentleman before taking her leave.

"I shall return shortly."

The door closed behind Mrs Bennet and Elizabeth found herself alone with Mr Collins. She looked at him and he took that as an invitation to begin.

"My dear Miss Gardiner, I will come straight to the point. From the very first I singled you out as the woman I desire as the companion of my future life!"

"Mr Collins," Elizabeth tried to protest but he continued on unperturbed.

"I hope I do not alarm you with the violence of my affections, but I know you can be in no doubt as to the power you have over me. Your beauty has overwhelmed me; I am undone!"

"Mr Collins, please!" Elizabeth protested in an agony of embarrassment, getting to her feet. "I have no wish to listen to such sentiments from you."

Mr Collins blinked, stunned, and Elizabeth seized her chance for escape. She dipped a hasty curtsey and scurried from the room, heading straight for the front door and the promise of freedom. Imagine her surprise when found the Duke and his two children just come to call - she could have jumped for joy!

"Oh, I am so glad to see you!" She greeted them delightedly and hurried over.

James and the Duke both seemed surprised by her enthusiasm but Catherine simply responded to it and threw her arms around Elizabeth.

"Lizzy! I missed you! Why did you not come to our house?"

"I'm sorry sweetheart," Elizabeth apologised sincerely. "I missed you too."

"We came to say thank you for Papa's present," Catherine explained and Elizabeth looked up at the Duke with a smile. She felt almost light-headed; she was so glad to see him. The week he had been away had felt like a lifetime and she had missed him so much.

"Oh, yes, today is the day. Happy Birthday, Your Grace."

"Thank you," he responded warmly before adding, "And thank you for your part in my wonderful gift."

"I hope you liked it," Elizabeth expressed.

"I love it - I cannot imagine a better gift. I shall treasure it always."

Elizabeth smiled shyly, pleased with his response and glad to have been able to do something special for him. In the next moment, however, she remembered Mr Collins' presence in the parlour and her aunt's likely return and she hastily concocted a plan to escape.

"It is such a lovely day," she stated, looking between the Darcy trio. "Shall we go for a walk? Do you have time?"

Catherine agreed at once to the proposal and her father, after looking at Elizabeth for a long moment, eventually agreed as well. She couldn't quite hide her relief as she requested her coat and other things from a nearby servant and asked that Wilson be sent for to act as chaperone.

"How was your trip to Kent?" she asked the Duke, glancing nervously over her shoulder and listening for any sounds of her aunt.

"Quite productive, thank you," he responded, looking quizzically at her, smiling slightly at what must have seemed quite odd behaviour.

"And you completed all your business to your satisfaction?" Elizabeth asked distractedly and this time the Duke smiled openly.

"Yes," he replied. "Is everything well, Miss Gardiner? You seem distracted."

"Oh! Yes, I'm quite well." Elizabeth blushed with embarrassment and tried to pull herself together; she finally saw Wilson bustling towards them and sighed audibly before hastily pulling on her gloves. "Ah, here she is! Off we go then; here, Cathy, hold my hand."

She led the way from the house, just in time to hear her aunt shout.

*"ELIZABETH GARDINER!"*

"I think your aunt..." James began to say but Wilson slammed the door.

"No, no, it's nothing! Come along."

Elizabeth missed the look the Duke and his son exchanged behind her as she was too busy trying to put as much distance as possible between herself and the house.

ᚽᚽ

"Are you going to tell me what that was about?"

Elizabeth looked up with a blush as the Duke smiled down at her expectantly. The children were with Wilson, feeding the ducks with the bread that she had thought to bring, whilst she and the Duke stood a little way away from them.

"I don't suppose you would believe me if I said that I don't know what you're talking about?" she replied resignedly, sighing slightly when the Duke merely quirked a brow in response.

"Do you know Mr William Collins?" she asked him to begin with and he thought for a moment.

"Short man, red hair?" Elizabeth nodded and the Duke asked, "Yes - what about him?"

"He was attempting to propose to me just before you arrived," she confessed and it seemed as though the Duke wasn't entirely sure how to react.

"Oh."

"Yes," Elizabeth sighed again; then she rolled her eyes and smiled. "It was *ridiculous!* I had just run from the room when I came across you and the children."

"I did wonder why you seemed so very pleased to see us," the Duke admitted with a slight chuckle. "Is it safe for me to assume, from the fact that you ran from the room and then felt the need to escape the house as well, that I need not wish you joy?"

Elizabeth closed her eyes and laughed at both his teasing and herself.

"Oh, the entire episode is worthy of the stage!" She laughingly exclaimed before sobering abruptly as she remembered her aunt's shout and the likely reception she would get when she returned home. Perhaps she needed to ask Jane if she could stay with her and Charles for a while?

"I'm sorry, I shouldn't joke about such things," the Duke apologised, obviously noticing her change in mood.

"No, it's not your fault. And I must laugh," Elizabeth pointed out with a grim smile, "else I'm sure I would cry."

"I am sure your aunt and uncle will understand your refusing Mr Collins' proposal," the Duke stated reasonably but Elizabeth shook her head.

"I am not at all sure of that."

"But surely - if they know that you dislike him..." he began and then stopped. "Forgive me, I have no business speaking of such things - they are your private affairs."

"I don't mind," Elizabeth boldly admitted, looking up at him. "I feel as though I can talk to you about anything."

Before he could reply, Catherine came running over to join them and Elizabeth reluctantly gave the little girl her attention - she had seen how the Duke had responded to her words, the look that appeared in his eyes and wished that Catherine had not interrupted them. What might he have said?

The Duke seemed thoughtful after their conversation and was quiet for the rest of their stay in the park. When they finally left to return to the Bennet's townhouse, Elizabeth took his silently offered arm and walked with the Duke whilst the children and Wilson walked in front.

"Miss Gardiner?"

Elizabeth looked up from her study of the pavement to look at the Duke - she was surprised to find he looked a little uncertain, almost nervous.

"Yes?"

"Forgive me, but I was wondering…I mean…Why did you refuse Mr Collins?" he finally asked before hastily adding, "I am not blaming you, I only wish to understand, I suppose, though I know that I really have no right."

Elizabeth took pity on him.

"He is a silly man. Pompous, self-important, obtuse. Not a man I would wish to have as my husband."

The Duke nodded and looked ahead of him; Elizabeth wondered what he was thinking.

"I also do not love him," she added softly after a moment of silently warring with herself as to whether or not to stay quiet. The Duke looked at her quickly and she went on, "Indeed, I doubt I ever could, but I also, that is to say I…" she faltered nervously.

"Yes?" The Duke prompted eagerly, a light springing into his eyes.

Neither noticed that they had slowed almost to a stop, the other three going on ahead as they focused intently on one another.

"I…" Elizabeth swallowed past the lump in her throat and held his gaze, drawing strength from his look. "I could not marry Mr Collins because I wish to marry someone else."

The Duke stopped their progress entirely and turned to face her, taking her hands in his, his movements agitated and excitable.

"You do?" he asked hopefully - he was smiling and Elizabeth felt a bubble of joy swelling up within her.

"Yes," she nodded and hardly noticed how his hold on her hands tightened in response - she was watching his expression too closely to notice anything else.

"And am I wrong to think that that person is me?" he asked a tad breathlessly and Elizabeth shook her head, her voice choked with sudden tears, her smile brilliant.

"You love me?" he asked with a combination of disbelief and joy.

Elizabeth could only smile and nod.

"Elizabeth!" The Duke declared joyously, and heedless of their very public location swept her up into his arms. "Say it! I must hear you say the words."

"I love you," Elizabeth was laughing and crying at the same time as she held the Duke's shoulders and he span her in a circle.

He set her back on her feet and leant down to press a sweet kiss to her lips.

"How I love you, my darling Elizabeth," he whispered.

She was about to reply in kind when their moment was interrupted by a scandalised Wilson, who had finally noticed what was happening and rushed back down the street. James and Catherine stood together in the distance, the latter excitedly tugging at her brother's sleeve and pointing at her father and Elizabeth.

"Elizabeth Hyacinth Gardiner! What do you think you are doing?"

Elizabeth looked adoringly up at the Duke as he replied without taking his eyes away from her.

"She is about to make me the happiest of men, Miss Wilson, by accepting my hand in marriage."

Darcy waited with baited breath as Miss Gardiner, *Elizabeth*, smiled tearfully up at him and then finally replied.

"There is nothing I would love more, than to be your wife."

He was hardly able to savour the joy of the moment before Miss Wilson firmly interfered.

"Yes, well, that's all very nice - may I remind you, though, that you are on a public street and are causing a scene."

Darcy looked around, saw that they did indeed have an audience, and awkwardly cleared his throat, removing his arms from around Elizabeth's waist; she caught hold of his hand and he looked at her, responding to her reassuring look with a shy smile. His heart was still soaring, but his mind was rather quickly coming back to reality.

"Papa!" Catherine ran towards them, dragging her brother along behind her. When she reached them she was breathless with excitement, her small hands grasping at her father's coat. "Papa! Papa!"

"What is it?" Darcy teased, smiling down at his daughter.

Catherine smacked his leg and Darcy chuckled as he bent down and swept her up into his arms.

"Why are you hitting your old papa, hmmm?"

"What is happening?" Catherine demanded, looking between him and Elizabeth. "I saw you pick up Lizzy. And kiss her," she added in a hushed voice, blushing.

Elizabeth smiled shyly and returned the Duke's warm look.

"Yes, you did see that. The truth is, princess, I have just asked Miss Gardiner, Elizabeth," he corrected in a caressing tone which gave her goose bumps, "to marry me."

"Did she say yes?" Catherine asked; she looked at Elizabeth. "Did you say yes?"

"I would have thought that was obvious," James pointed out with a grin, breaking his silence. He simply laughed when his father lightly cuffed him round the head.

"Did she say yes?" Catherine asked again, getting impatient.

"Yes, sweetheart, I did," Elizabeth replied before Darcy could, and then smiled happily as Catherine squealed and hugged her father tight.

"Oh, I'm so happy!" The little girl enthused. "I shall have a mama at last."

Elizabeth saw the Duke's smile wobble slightly when his daughter said this, and her heart went out to him. Catherine asked to be put down and hurried over to embrace Elizabeth, who bent down and kissed the top of her head.

"You will be a wonderful mama, I know it!" Catherine told her and Elizabeth smiled.

"I'm glad you think so," she replied, straightening up and noticing that Wilson was watching the scene with a tear in her eye. She smiled slightly and then looked at the Duke, taking his proffered hand and squeezing it tightly.

"Well, this has certainly been a very good birthday so far for you, Father," James noted lightly, smiling and looking between the two adults. "I wonder what the rest of the day shall bring."

"Nothing could better this," his father responded intently, his eyes on Elizabeth, and James sighed and admitted to himself that perhaps they required a little more time to savour the moment.

"Come on, Cathy," he held out his hand to his sister. "Let's carry on."

As James went ahead with Catherine, Darcy offered Elizabeth his arm, surprised by Wilson's stern warning.

"I shall be watching you, Your Grace. You had better behave yourself from now on."

Elizabeth bit her lip at the Duke's expression - he obviously was not used to being spoken to in such a manner.

"I think I may just have been scolded," Darcy quietly said after a moment as they walked with Wilson closely behind them.

"I assure you, Your Grace," Elizabeth teased in response, "as someone who has been on the receiving end of many lectures from my dear Wilson, that you got off rather lightly."

Darcy grinned and leant closer.

"I don't doubt it."

Wilson pointedly cleared her throat and he retreated to a more acceptable distance as Elizabeth stifled a laugh.

"I think I may have been remiss," Darcy commented after a moment. "If I recall our conversation correctly, I don't believe I actually asked you to marry me."

"One would have thought that were rather important," Elizabeth teased, her eyes dancing with laughter as she looked up at him.

"One would," Darcy agreed with a smile. "Though considering the unusual nature of our conversation, I don't know why I am surprised to have skipped a somewhat important step."

"I believe, if you consider what was said, I very nearly proposed to *you*," Elizabeth observed with a playful smile. "So at least one of us almost managed it."

Darcy chuckled and they smiled brightly at one another.

"Are you as surprised as I?" he asked quietly and Elizabeth knew exactly what he meant.

"Yes," she admitted. "Delight, shocked, surprised, overjoyed. All of these things."

"And happy?" Darcy checked.

"More so than ever before," Elizabeth replied and Darcy felt himself leaning down before he caught himself just in time.

"I had best get you home, before I give your maid an excuse to do me physical harm," he quietly joked.

"Don't worry - her bark is worse than her bite."

As if on cue, Wilson sharply reminded them to maintain a respectable distance from one another and Darcy and Elizabeth shared a light laugh.

Whilst their father walked with Elizabeth, James and Catherine walked a little further ahead of them, the latter alternately peppering her brother with questions and turning to look back at the couple behind them.

"Is Papa in love with Lizzy then, James?" she asked at one point and her brother smiled.

"So it would seem," he replied, glancing back over his shoulder and seeing his father smile at something Miss Gardiner said to him.

"Did you know?"

"I knew he was her friend," James replied. "But I did not know he loved her. But then there is much about Father that we do not know."

"And Lizzy loves Papa too?"

"Of course," James stated confidently. "She would not have said yes otherwise."

He firmly believed this to be the case, and the thought that Elizabeth did not share their father's feelings had never even occurred to him.

"Does this mean we will have brothers and sisters?" Catherine then asked and James chuckled.

"Perhaps," he replied. "I certainly hope so - I think it would be nice, don't you?"

"I suppose," Catherine mumbled and James put his arm around her, having an idea as to what was bothering her.

"You mustn't worry that Papa will love us any less if we have brothers and sisters," he told his little sister comfortingly. "He will love us just as much as he does now - and Elizabeth will love us just the same, too."

"How do you know?" Catherine asked, looking up at him with complete trust.

"Because the more children there are to love, the bigger their parent's hearts grow," James told her, remembering the words their father had once said to him when he had been feeling jealous of his baby sister.

"So there is room for enough love for everyone?" Catherine guessed and James smiled.

"Exactly."

Catherine nodded thoughtfully and then after a moment smiled, obviously satisfied with this answer.

"You're so clever James," she told her brother and James grinned.

"I'm going to remember you said that," he teased and taking her hand once more they walked on together, happily discussing the prospect of Elizabeth becoming a part of their family.

As he walked with Elizabeth, Darcy couldn't help noticing that the closer they got to the Bennet's townhouse the quieter she became, until it was obvious that something was troubling her.

"What's wrong?" he asked finally, pressing the hand that rested on his arm. She looked up and he said, "I can see that something is bothering you - what is it?"

"It is just that I'm not entirely sure how my aunt will react to our news," Elizabeth confessed with a heavy sigh.

"I suspect she will be rather surprised..." Darcy began, but something in Elizabeth's expression made him ask, "Do you think she will disapprove?"

"On the contrary," Elizabeth replied with a wry grimace. "I believe she will be delighted, though I doubt for the reasons I'd prefer."

"I see," Darcy breathed, suddenly remembering how pleased Mrs Bennet had been with the match between Sir Charles and Lady Jane; an unexceptional match, in comparison to he and Elizabeth.

"I am not at all sure what she is going to say when we return and announce we are engaged."

"Not very much, I imagine," Darcy commented dryly. "For the first few minutes at least. Perhaps I should simply appeal directly to your uncle - or is it to your father that I must apply?"

"My uncle is authorised to act in my father's place," Elizabeth replied. "You need not speak to my father at all."

"Well, I should like to eventually," Darcy teased but when Elizabeth only smiled tightly in response he set aside that subject for the time being.

They were in view of the house, James and Catherine were already climbing the steps when Elizabeth stopped and turned to face him.

"Will you promise me something?" she asked; at his nod she went on. "Please promise me that no matter what my aunt and uncle's reaction, you won't change your mind."

"Elizabeth," Darcy solemnly assured her, stroking her cheek with his gloved fingers. "*Nothing* could sway me from my purpose. I love you, and I mean to make you my wife."

Elizabeth smiled, effectively reassured.

"Come," Darcy turned and led her the rest of the way. "Let us see how this scene plays out."

ಬಂಡ

Wilson was a godsend.

As soon as they entered the house she effectively took control of the situation, ascertaining the whereabouts of Mrs Bennet (upstairs, taken to her bed in a fit of pique), Mr Bennet (in his library, hiding) and Mr Collins (long gone, thank goodness). She then saw to it that the children were comfortably installed in one of the front rooms with warm milk and some sweet treats, leaving Elizabeth and the Duke free to seek out Mr Bennet.

"Perhaps I should speak to him alone?" Darcy proposed quietly but Elizabeth shook her head.

"I think it best if I join you - I am certain he shall send for me anyway, as this will require some explanation."

"He will not immediately jump to accept my suit then?" Darcy teased. "And I thought a Dukedom guaranteed success in these matters."

"I'm sure it would," Elizabeth quipped in response, "were you ten years younger."

Darcy laughed.

"Touché."

They went together to the library and Elizabeth knocked on the door.

"Elizabeth, at last, I..." Mr Bennet began; he spotted Darcy and bowed slightly. "Your Grace. Thank you for seeing my niece safely home. I cannot apologise enough for this embarrassing situation - I am sorry you were dragged into the matter."

Elizabeth blushed scarlet and looked down at her feet and Darcy frowned.

"I am afraid you have misunderstood, Sir. The children and I were happy to walk with Miss Gardiner, and on no account did I feel 'dragged' into anything."

"Be that as it may," Mr Bennet replied, "I hope that in future we can manage to keep the affairs of our family private."

"Uncle..." Elizabeth began but Mr Bennet cut her off.

"I will speak to you later, Elizabeth."

"Mr Bennet..." Darcy began, reaching over and taking Elizabeth's hand and squeezing it tightly. She looked up at him and then back at her uncle, seeing that he was looking at them with an expression of complete and utter surprise. "Let us start again, and forget about what happened earlier today. I returned here with your niece with a purpose, Mr Bennet. I have, for some time now, harboured feelings of a tender nature towards your niece, and whilst out walking today was delighted to discover that those feelings are reciprocated. I come to you now seeking your consent for our marriage."

"You are engaged?" Mr Bennet asked in a stunned tone.

"With your blessing," Darcy replied, "yes."

"Well, it is good of you to say so, Your Grace," her uncle surprised Elizabeth by stating dryly. "Though I'm sure we both know that I can hardly refuse you anything."

"Uncle!" Elizabeth interjected.

"I appreciate this must be unexpected," Darcy began but Mr Bennet interrupted him.

"Indeed; so unexpected in fact that I would like to have a few words alone with my niece, if you would not mind, Your Grace?" Mr Bennet requested, though his tone implied he would brook no argument.

"I shall wait outside," Darcy replied firmly, setting aside his pride; he parted from Elizabeth with an earnest, heartfelt look before leaving the room.

"Oh, Uncle!" Elizabeth exclaimed as soon as they were alone.

"Are you mad, Elizabeth?" Mr Bennet demanded at the same time. "What are you thinking, accepting him?"

"Would you rather I had said yes to Mr Collins?" Elizabeth retorted bitterly, surprised when her uncle scoffed.

"Hardly! Despite what your aunt might think, I have no intention of seeing you married to such a fool as he. Indeed, I have no desire to see you married against your wishes or inclinations, which is why I was willing to accept Mr Wickham, given that we all thought that you liked him. But this...!" He gestured towards the door. "Elizabeth, think about what you are doing!"

"What is wrong with the Duke?" Elizabeth demanded indignantly.

"He is twice your age!" Mr Bennet responded loudly. "Marrying a man old enough to be your father is a heavy price to pay to become a Duchess, Elizabeth."

"I would never...!" Elizabeth spluttered, highly offended. "I would never be so mercenary!"

"I would certainly hope not," Mr Bennet responded. "But how else am I to explain your accepting him?"

"I love him!" Elizabeth burst out, her chest heaving with suppressed anger, shocking her uncle into silence. "The Duke loves me, Uncle, and *I love him.* I have loved him for weeks, months even; not Mr Wickham!"

"But...what?" Mr Bennet floundered, flabbergasted by Elizabeth's unexpected outburst. "*The Duke?*"

"Yes," Elizabeth sighed with exasperation. "Not Mr Wickham, nor Mr Collins or any of my other 'suitors'. I love the Duke and wish, with my whole heart, to marry him."

"Then we had best fetch him back in," Mr Bennet responded after a long moment, this time surprising Elizabeth. "So that we can settle the matter and I may apologise to him for my rudeness."

"Really?" Elizabeth asked, convinced it could not be that easy.

"Indeed," Mr Bennet replied - he smiled as he teased, "I am quite convinced of your sincerity, my dear. Your aunt would have been proud of that outburst."

Elizabeth blushed and smiled in spite of herself.

"I'm sorry I shouted at you."

"I daresay I deserved it," Mr Bennet commented before crossing to the door and opening it himself. "Please come in, Your Grace."

Darcy immediately looked to Elizabeth and sighed with relief when she smiled at him; standing outside the room he couldn't help hearing their raised voices.

"I owe you an apology, Your Grace," Mr Bennet stated once Darcy had taken his place beside Elizabeth. "I misunderstood the situation and jumped to an erroneous conclusion; I'm sorry for my earlier words."

"They are forgotten," Darcy replied. "I understand that you were only trying to protect your niece."

Mr Bennet inclined his head and then cleared his throat; he smiled between the pair.

"Shall we try again? I believe you have something you wish to ask me, Your Grace?"

"May I marry your niece?" Darcy asked simply and Elizabeth laughed quietly.

"You may," Mr Bennet granted lightly and smiled patiently when Darcy and Elizabeth looked lovingly at one another, grasping each other's hands.

"Well..." he gently broke into the moment. "I must say again what a surprise this is. You both kept your feelings very well hidden!"

"Yes," Darcy agreed quietly, looking down at Elizabeth and silently adding, *though not from each other, thank God.*

"This certainly calls for a celebration," Mr Bennet went on before pausing to consider his wife and adding, "Though perhaps at a later date..."

"I have several business appointments this afternoon, and the children need to return home for their lessons; perhaps it would be best if I return tomorrow, to discuss more of the details?" Darcy proposed, pleased when Elizabeth nodded and expressed her agreement.

"That would be for the best, I think," Mr Bennet concurred. "And I shall have time to come to terms with this latest development," he joked and Elizabeth discreetly rolled her eyes.

"I shall come and say goodbye to the children," she said to Darcy and they left her uncle to his thoughts.

"Well," she sighed once they were alone. "That was both better and worse than I feared. How much did you hear?" she asked, blushing when Darcy replied.

"I couldn't really help overhearing."

"I honestly did not mean to shout," Elizabeth began - she paused when Darcy reached out and lightly rested his hand on the small of her back.

"Don't apologise on my account - I was rather pleased to hear you declaring your feelings for me so...vocally."

Elizabeth smiled, shyly pleased with his teasing words, and was still blushing slightly when they entered the room where James and Catherine were being kept company by Wilson.

"Well?" The latter asked when they appeared.

"My uncle gave his consent," Elizabeth replied and whilst the children expressed their delight and embraced their father and then Elizabeth in turn, Wilson simply nodded.

"I don't suppose you mentioned your little...display on the street to your uncle, did you?" Wilson commented a tad sternly when Elizabeth approached her.

"I did not have to," Elizabeth replied evasively. "The truth of my feelings was enough to convince him."

"Let us hope the same can be said when you request a short engagement," Wilson dryly noted but Elizabeth saw the twinkle in her eye which gave her away.

"I can tell you are trying not to smile, you know."

"I don't know what you mean," Wilson denied - then she smiled and pressed a motherly kiss to Elizabeth's cheek.

"I'm so happy," Elizabeth whispered and looked over at Darcy who was watching her as Catherine chatted excitedly up at him.

Wilson smiled; a little wistfully in must be said.

"And you deserve to be, petal."

❧❧

That night as he was tucking Catherine into bed, Darcy smiled lovingly as she yawned widely and mumbled a thank you.

"What for, princess?" Darcy asked quietly, stroking her hair.

"I have always wished for a mama," Catherine replied candidly and Darcy felt his throat tighten at the admission. "And now I shall have the loveliest mama in the whole world."

Darcy leant down and drew his sleepy daughter into his arms, holding her close, feeling tears pricking the backs of his eyes. After a moment Catherine released a soft sigh and he looked down and saw that her eyes were closed; he softly laid her back against her pillows and kissed her forehead.

"I love you, princess," he whispered before rising and leaving her to her dreams.

He walked a little way along the hallway and lightly knocked on the door of his son's room.

"James?"

James looked up as his father opened the door and smiled - a happy, contented smile.

"Come in, Father. I was just reading before going to bed."

"What are you reading?" Darcy asked, coming to sit in the chair beside James' bed.

James showed him the title and they spent a few moments discussing the merits of the story before falling silent, the son watching the father expectantly.

"I wanted to say," Darcy began at last, "that I'm sorry if you feel that I should have spoken to you about Miss Gardiner and my intentions towards her."

"Why should you have?" James replied sensibly.

"Well, I..." Darcy paused. "I suppose because my marrying Elizabeth will greatly affect you and Catherine, and proposing to her was not a step I intended on making without speaking to you both about it first."

James grinned.

"I rather thought it all happened a little...unexpectedly."

Darcy grinned ruefully.

"You are far too astute for your age, son. But you are correct - I did get caught up in the moment somewhat."

"I am happy for you father. For myself as well - I think Miss Gardiner will be a wonderful addition to our family - but most especially for you."

"Thank you James," Darcy replied, touched. He wished his son goodnight before leaving him to his book and making his way downstairs. His butler was waiting for him and informed him that his cousin had come to call.

"He is waiting for you in your study, Your Grace."

"Thank you, Parks," Darcy responded and then proceeded to his study, where he found Richard making himself comfortable with a glass of Darcy's finest brandy.

"You have a singular talent for making yourself very quickly at home in other people's houses, Richard," he noted as he shut the door and then went to pour himself a drink.

"Good evening to you too, Darcy," Richard replied good-humouredly. "I daresay my feelings are almost hurt."

"I must be losing my touch, if that is the case," Darcy commented dryly and his cousin grinned.

"Happy Birthday," Richard tossed Darcy a small package as he took his seat. "From all of us."

"I take it from your cavalier attitude that it is not breakable," Darcy noted with a smile as he unwrapped the offering. It was a new gold watch chain to replace the one which had recently broken.

"Please thank Georgiana and the children for me," he said as he set aside his gift.

"I will," Richard replied before asking, "What did James and Catherine get you this year?"

"I will show you," Darcy stood up and went to his desk, picking up the two drawings and handing them to his cousin.

Richard whistled his appreciation.

"These are remarkable! How on earth did they accomplish this?"

"Miss Gardiner," Darcy replied simply, unable to suppress his smile as he pronounced her name. "They sat for her whilst I was at Rosings."

"She is an extremely talented young woman," Richard complimented sincerely and Darcy expressed his agreement.

"You must be delighted with these," Richard noted as he handed the drawings back to his cousin.

"I am," Darcy replied. "It was a wonderful surprise." He paused and then added, "Indeed, today has been full of surprises."

"Oh?" Richard lightly inquired as Darcy returned to his seat and faced his cousin. He was bursting with the need to share his news and ended up blurting it out.

"Yes. The children and I paid a visit to Miss Gardiner today, to say thank you for the drawings, and, well, the long and short of it is, we're engaged."

Richard choked on his drink.

"Excuse me?!"

A part of Darcy knew that he should probably explain a little more, but he couldn't stop himself from babbling on.

"Miss Gardiner and I are engaged to be married; I've already spoken with her uncle and tomorrow I shall go over and begin sorting out all the details. The children are thrilled, and I'm delighted, obviously. We shall have to have a short engagement - quite a few people saw me kiss her, unfortunately - and I'm sure people will talk, but that can't be helped. Hopefully we can be married before the Season is over, and I can take her to Pemberley in the summer. She will love Pemberley, I think."

"William." Richard interrupted his ramblings and Darcy looked up to find his cousin watching him with a dumbfounded expression.

"You are engaged to Miss Gardiner?" Richard repeated, just to be sure. When Darcy nodded he rubbed his forehead and asked, "Why?"

"Why do you think?" Darcy replied with a smile. "I love her."

"But Darcy," Richard countered gently. "She's so young."

"Does that matter?" Darcy responded evenly. "I confess, I thought it did at first, but now I've come to realise what matters is how we feel."

"We," Richard picked up on this important point. "Miss Gardiner shares your feelings, then?"

"Yes - amazingly," Darcy replied. He smiled and shook his head, looking down at his hands as he quietly admitted, "I had not dared to hope that she would ever...but she loves me, Richard," he looked up at his cousin, "as much as I love her."

The two men lapsed into silence as Darcy pleased himself with thoughts of Elizabeth and Richard tried to make sense of this unexpected news. He could see plainly enough that Darcy was sure of his own feelings and was surprised that he had not noticed them before. What of Miss Gardiner, though? Richard had always liked her, and knew that Georgiana considered her a good friend, but doubts now began to intrude as to her motives for accepting his cousin.

In the past he had always trusted Darcy's judgement, and was aware in the back of his mind that it was rather foolish of him to worry, given that Darcy was a grown man, but it was all too quick and unexpected for him to be easy about it. When he finally offered his cousin his congratulations, Richard could see that Darcy knew he wasn't completely sincere.

"It's alright," Darcy said to him, quite resigned to this reaction. What more could he expect, having hidden his feelings from everyone, and given the unusual nature of the match? "I know it will take time for you to accept this - though when you do, I reserve the right to say I told you so," he joked and Richard smiled in spite of himself.

"So, tell me, how did it happen?" he asked expectantly after a moment, reaching for his glass, thinking that he should make up for his lack of enthusiasm.

"Well, that Collins fellow had just tried to propose to Elizabeth when..." Darcy began and Richard choked on his drink for the second time that night.

"What?!" he spluttered and Darcy chuckled deeply.

℘℃℅

Once his cousin had gone home for the night (swearing that Georgiana was never going to believe the story he had to tell), Darcy retired to his room, smiling to himself over Richard's reaction. Indeed, when he thought about the whole episode Darcy was a little shocked at himself. He did not regret his rash actions, indeed how could he when they had had such a happy outcome, but he was somewhat surprised by his impulsiveness. He had always adhered to the rules of propriety, and if anyone had told him that he would one day embrace and kiss a lady in the street he would have laughed and thought them well in their cups!

As he lay in bed with his hands folded behind his head, Darcy knew he would not be able to sleep for many hours yet, not when feeling such a lightness of spirit and profound sense of joy. Despite his euphoric state, however, he was still a practical man and his thoughts turned to the task of informing their relations and friends. As his experience with Richard showed, he had hidden his feelings well, and had no doubt Elizabeth had been equally as circumspect. Everyone would be shocked at the news and Darcy wondered, once that initial feeling had passed, how their friends and family would react - he hoped they would be happy for them.

Darcy knew, rationally, that he had gone about it all wrong - the timing indeed could certainly have been better - but what did that really matter? He knew now how Elizabeth felt, and this knowledge had done away with his doubts and any reasons he had for waiting to propose - why wait when they loved one another, and there was no impediment to their marriage?

Marriage, he thought with a sigh, letting the word sink in. He was going to be married. How strange a thought, when six months ago he had been convinced he would spend the rest of his life alone. He was not inclined to question his good fortune, however, and offered up a silent prayer of thanks to whoever had seen fit to bring

Elizabeth into his life. He vowed to cherish and protect her, and to do everything in his power to make her happy.

ℰℭ

When Mrs Bennet declined to join her husband and niece for dinner that night, Mr Bennet and Elizabeth decided between them that it would be best if she were left to rest, and that they share the news of Elizabeth's engagement with her the following day. Mrs Bennet's absence proved advantageous, for it allowed Mr Bennet and Elizabeth time to talk and by the time he retired for the night Mr Bennet was utterly convinced of Elizabeth's feelings, and was of a mind to regard the match rather favourably. Indeed, he was quite happy with the turn of events, however unexpected.

Rising at her usual time the next day after quite a sleepless night, Elizabeth went down to breakfast and found her uncle already sat at the table, reading the paper.

"Good morning Lizzy," he greeted her cheerfully and his good mood bolstered Elizabeth's confidence.

"Good morning, Uncle," she replied and helped herself to some tea and muffins.

"I am told your aunt does plan on joining us this morning," her uncle informed her and Elizabeth nodded. "I have come prepared; the smelling salts are in my pocket."

Before Elizabeth could reply the door opened and Mrs Bennet, looking quite her usual self, entered and took her place.

There was a brief silence before Elizabeth asked if her aunt would like some tea.

"That would be lovely, thank you Lizzy," Mrs Bennet replied and Elizabeth quickly prepared a cup and presented it to her aunt.

"I hope you are feeling better this morning," she tentatively ventured.

"Oh, much better," Mrs Bennet assured her, patting her hand affectionately. "Thank you for your concern, dear."

Elizabeth resumed her seat and shared a glance with her uncle; Mr Bennet laid aside his paper, sat slightly forward in his chair and, taking a deep breath, began.

"My dear, there is something Elizabeth and I must tell you."

"Oh?" Mrs Bennet queried, looking between her husband and niece. "And what is that?"

"This will no doubt come as a surprise to you," Mr Bennet forged on, "Indeed, I was quite surprised myself, though now I must say I am quite reconciled to the idea."

"You are rambling, my dear," Mrs Bennet interrupted with a gentle smile. "What is your news?"

"The Duke and I are engaged to be married," Elizabeth blurted out before Mr Bennet had a chance; she flushed scarlet and waited for her aunt's reaction.

"I beg your pardon?" Mrs Bennet responded, bewildered. "The Duke? Which Duke? What do you mean, engaged?"

"The Duke of Farleigh, my dear," Mr Bennet replied, his lips twitching. "The only Duke with whom Elizabeth is acquainted."

"The Duke of Farleigh..." Mrs Bennet breathed, a dazed expression appearing on her face; her tea cup wobbled precariously in her grip and Elizabeth quickly rescued it. "Well I never..."

"Now, now," Mr Bennet cautioned, recognising the signs his wife was exhibiting. "Please do not swoon, my dear."

"I wasn't going to swoon!" Mrs Bennet objected, coming back to herself sharply. She looked at Elizabeth and demanded, "How did this happen? Why did you not tell me? Oh, please do not say that you have done anything foolish!"

"Fanny!" Mr Bennet barked as Elizabeth flushed with mortification. "I shall pretend you did not say that."

Mrs Bennet bristled at the rebuke but chose to let it pass; she focused once more on Elizabeth.

"Well? Aren't you going to explain yourself?"

"We are in love, Aunt," Elizabeth replied quietly. "That is all there is to explain."

"He is far too old for you, you cannot possibly..." Mrs Bennet began but Elizabeth firmly cut her off.

"I assure you, Aunt, I am sure of my feelings, and of his. We are in love and we are to be married."

"I know this is a shock, my dear," Mr Bennet put in. "But just think of it; Elizabeth is going to be a Duchess!"

Elizabeth shot her uncle an annoyed look.

"I am well aware of that, Mr Bennet," Mrs Bennet responded briskly. "And I am equally aware that, Duke or not, this match is an embarrassment."

"How kind of you to say so, Aunt," Elizabeth retorted, stung. She placed her napkin on the table and stood. "Excuse me."

"Fanny," Mr Bennet sighed when their niece had departed. "I thought you would be pleased."

"Pleased? *Pleased?*" Mrs Bennet repeated irritably. "We are going to be a laughingstock! Don't you remember what it was like when Lord Craske married Miss Davies? It took weeks for the gossip to abate, and Mrs Davies couldn't show her face again for the rest of the Season without someone mentioning it!"

"Please, Lord Craske was a horrible old lecher who bought himself a pretty young wife. The circumstances couldn't be more different."

"Well we know that," Mrs Bennet retorted. "But no one else is going to. He's old enough to be her father! I tell you this match is going to embarrass me."

"Yes, so you've said," Mr Bennet interrupted sharply. "And I don't care to hear it again. If you had any sense, you'd give Elizabeth your blessing; I think an estrangement between us and the newly married couple would be more embarrassing in the long run, don't you?"

Mrs Bennet had no reply to that, and Mr Bennet finished his breakfast in silence.

৪৩

"Well, congratulations! Our dear Lizzy - engaged to be married. And to a Duke no less! I am very proud - and I am sure you will be very happy together."

"Thank you, Ma'am," Darcy replied graciously, glancing quickly at Elizabeth who mentally rolled her eyes.

"You must tell us how it happened," Mrs Bennet went on eagerly. "We were both so surprised!"

As Darcy related a somewhat abridged version of the events of the day before, Mrs Bennet listened and nodded and smiled at all the right moments, playing her part with perfect aplomb. She had very quickly realised her mistake at breakfast and was determined that the Duke would find nothing lacking in her manner. She would have to make amends with her niece as soon as possible, before Elizabeth had a chance to make the Duke aware of her initial reaction to the news; it would not do to displease him. As Mr Bennet had so rightly pointed out, being shunned by the Duke and Duchess would be far more embarrassing than the unexpected suddenness of the match.

"Well, how lovely," Mrs Bennet stated warmly when Darcy had concluded the tale, smiling between the couple. "And do you have any idea when the happy event shall take place?" she asked.

"We do not know, yet" Elizabeth replied, looking at her uncle briefly. "That has yet to be discussed."

"Well there is plenty of time for that," Mr Bennet stated, smiling reassuringly at his niece.

"It would be nice, I think," Elizabeth went on slowly, looking up at Darcy, "to be married before the Season finishes. Then we could spend the summer at Pemberley."

Darcy smiled down at her before Mrs Bennet interrupted the moment.

"Do you wish to be married from here? Or would you prefer to marry at home?"

"Here," Elizabeth answered without hesitation and blushed a little self-consciously.

"I must write to your father, I suppose," Mr Bennet put in, predicting with a slight frown, "He will not be happy at the prospect of having to travel to town."

"He need not trouble himself," Elizabeth responded lightly, though Darcy noticed that her eyes were cold. "I would be happy for you to give me away."

Mr Bennet smiled and patted her hand affectionately as Mrs Bennet, as always, was quick to defend her brother.

"I am certain my brother will think nothing of the inconvenience of a trip to town when he comes here to see his youngest daughter married. He will be delighted, I'm sure of it."

You give him more credit than I do, Aunt, Elizabeth thought cynically but chose to keep such reflections to herself. She felt Darcy looking at her and managed a smile, but he was still somewhat concerned by her reaction to the mention of her father. He would have to ask her about it in future.

# Chapter 11

Jane smiled and greeted her sister warmly as Elizabeth came and sat with her.

"Good morning, Lizzy. How are you?"

"Never mind how I am, how are *you?*" Elizabeth asked pointedly - they had not seen each other recently because Jane had been feeling a little under the weather.

"Oh, I am fine," Jane assured her; she blushed a little and smiled happily as she confided, "Better than fine, really. We have found out the reason for my feeling unwell."

"The reason?" Elizabeth repeated, confused. Then her face cleared and she grasped her sister's hands delightedly. "Do you mean...? Are you with child, Jane?"

"I am," Jane confirmed, laughing when her sister threw her arms around her.

"Oh, Jane! Congratulations! I know how long you have waited for this! Charles must be thrilled."

"He is quite pleased," Jane replied, which was a gross understatement - they were both utterly delighted.

Elizabeth peppered her sister with questions and Jane assured her that she was feeling fine, that the doctor had seen her and declared her perfectly healthy. She had yet to feel the quickening but the doctor did not think it would be far off - Jane was farther along than she had expected.

"I do not know why I did not realise sooner," she admitted. "Though I did not experience the same sickness as I did with Daniel. They do say it is different with each child, I suppose."

"And when is the baby due?"

"Some time in the autumn," Jane replied, smiling and seeming pleased to be sharing her news.

"I am truly happy for you, Jane," Elizabeth told her sister quietly and they sat for a moment simply holding hands.

The moment was interrupted when Jane heard a carriage pulling up outside.

"Whoever it is must be here to see Charles," Jane noted when nobody was brought to them and they heard the sound of footsteps moving in the opposite direction.

"So," Jane turned back to her sister and began a new subject, "Tell me what you have been doing since we last saw one another. Is

Mr Collins still paying court to you?" she asked teasingly. "And Mr Wickham? And all the others whose names I cannot recall?"

"There are not that many, Jane," Elizabeth protested.

"Our aunt will be keeping a very accurate count, I'm sure," Jane noted dryly and Elizabeth laughed.

"It matters not now," she replied before she could stop herself and could have kicked herself for the mistake.

"Why?" Jane asked, immediately curious. "Has something happened? Has one of them proposed?" she asked and Elizabeth grimaced and sighed.

"Yes, but I..."

"Oh, really?" Jane asked, her expression sharpening for a moment before she smiled. "Of course you didn't say yes - you would have told me right away. But who was it, if you refused him?"

Elizabeth looked at the door, hoping to be rescued from her predicament, but when no one appeared she was forced to confess.

"Mr Collins."

Jane struggled to keep her opinion from showing in her expression and Elizabeth laughed lightly at her struggle.

"I know, I know," she chuckled. "*Not* who I hoped to receive my first proposal of marriage from."

"How did he take your refusal?" Jane asked, choosing to move the conversation away from Mr Collins' desirability as a husband.

Elizabeth's lips twitched.

"I'm not entirely certain."

Jane shot her sister a curious look and was about to ask that she explain when they were joined by her husband and, to her surprised pleasure, the Duke of Farleigh.

"Good morning, Your Grace," she greeted her husband's friend with a welcoming smile. "How lovely to see you. Lizzy and I were wondering who had come to call."

Darcy caught Elizabeth's eye and they shared a knowing look before he replied.

"It is lovely to see you as well, Lady Bingley. And may I offer you my heartfelt congratulations - Charles has just told me the happy news."

"Thank you," Jane replied with a blushing smile as her husband came over to her side and kissed her cheek. "Please, won't you sit down?"

She had gestured to one of the vacant armchairs but Darcy surprised both of the Bingleys by seating himself beside Elizabeth on the settee and taking her hand.

"We have news, as well," he stated and smiled as Sir Charles and Jane exchanged a look of confusion.

"What sort of news, Darcy?" Sir Charles asked his friend.

"This will come as a surprise to you," Darcy began, "but I assure you Elizabeth and I are both very happy. We are engaged to be married, and would very much like it if you would both stand up with us at our wedding."

Darcy squeezed Elizabeth's hand in reassurance when silence met his announcement.

"Well…" Sir Charles breathed eventually; he cleared his throat and tried again. "Well I must say, this is, umm, yes, well …congratulations!" His sudden exclamation surprised them all and Elizabeth smothered a light laugh.

"Forgive me," he apologised, grinning. "This is very unexpected, but, well, if you are really happy then I suppose congratulations are indeed in order."

Sir Charles crossed the room and offered his friend his hand.

"Congratulations Darcy!"

"Thank you, Charles," Darcy replied, heartened by the genuine congratulations his friend offered. He couldn't help noticing that Lady Jane took a moment to follow her husband's lead, though her congratulations seemed genuine as she embraced her sister.

"I hope you know what a treasure you have found in my sister, Your Grace," Jane said to him after she had offered her congratulations and he had kissed her cheek in thanks.

"I assure you, Lady Bingley," Darcy replied intently, "that no one is more conscious of my good fortune than I."

"And here am I," Elizabeth teased, overhearing their conversation, "convinced that all the benefit is on my side!"

"I see my friend has you effectively fooled," Sir Charles joked, pretending to draw her away. "I shall enlighten you now, before any more permanent steps are taken."

"You are too late," Darcy responded whilst he gently but inexorably drew Elizabeth back to his side, causing them all to laugh. "The announcement will appear in The Times today."

"You called just in time, then," Sir Charles noted and then laughed heartily. "It was intentional! You called here separately but at the same time so that you could tell us together!"

Elizabeth and Darcy shared a smile and admitted that had been the case. Elizabeth noticed what seemed to be a flash of irritation cross her sister's face, but was distracted by her brother-in-law before she could consider it any further.

"Come, we must have a toast!" Sir Charles instructed a footman that champagne be brought.

"Charles," Jane protested. "It is not even twelve o'clock."

"I don't care," Sir Charles replied jovially. "We have much to celebrate!"

When everyone had a glass, he raised his glass and toasted the couple with a happy smile.

"To Elizabeth and Darcy - may you be very happy together."

"And to you and your lovely wife," Darcy surprised his friend by putting in, smiling as well. "May your child be healthy, and as wonderful and kind-hearted as his parents."

"Or her," Elizabeth added playfully and Darcy chuckled.

"Or her parents," he amended. "Cheers!"

&#x245E;&#x2463;

After spending a very enjoyable hour with Elizabeth and the Bingleys, Darcy returned to his townhouse for a meeting with his solicitor. He had spent the entire afternoon of the day before shut away with Mr Bennet, hashing out the details of the marriage contract, and today he was to meet with Mr Hayles to have it all put down in writing. They had yet to decide on a date for the wedding, though everyone seemed to agree that before the end of the Season would be best.

Arriving home, Darcy stepped down from his carriage and smiled to see his sister and cousin waiting outside. He had been surprised to receive no visit from Georgiana yesterday, though he had stayed to dine with Elizabeth and the Bennets and so had been away from home for most of the day. With a spring in his step, Darcy took the front steps two at a time and cheerfully greeted his butler when he opened the door for him.

"I see that I have visitors, Parks," he observed with a smile and the butler nodded.

"Indeed, Your Grace. Lady Matlock and Colonel and Lady Fitzwilliam await you in the blue drawing room."

Darcy stifled a groan.

"And Mr Hayles?"

"He has arrived, Sir, and is available at your convenience."

"Thank you, Parks," Darcy replied and steeled himself for an unpleasant encounter before proceeding to the drawing room where his relations were waiting.

A footman opened the door and Darcy was instantly hit by a barrage of noise.

"You might have told me, William!"

"Sorry, Darcy - I tried to hide the paper!"

"This is not to be borne!!"

Darcy turned to look over his shoulder at the footman who still held open the door; the man jumped and quickly gave them some privacy.

Choosing to address his aunt first, Darcy turned to her.

"What is not to be borne, Aunt?"

"You cannot be serious in your intention to marry this girl, Fitzwilliam?" Lady Matlock demanded. "It is unthinkable!"

"I hardly see why," Darcy responded coldly, his face hardening. "And I hardly see what business it is of yours."

"Anything which concerns this family is my business," Lady Matlock stated imperiously. "And in case you have forgotten, Anne was my niece and her children are of paramount concern to me. You can hardly expect me to stand by and watch as you marry someone so woefully unfit to be responsible for their welfare!"

"You insult me by supposing that I would ever marry a woman I thought incapable of properly caring for *my children*," Darcy bit out angrily. "Elizabeth will be a wonderful mother."

"She is young enough to be your daughter!" Lady Matlock burst out and Darcy knew they had gotten to the truth of the matter. "It is indecent - obscene!"

"Mother that is enough!" Richard barked and the force of his command compelled his mother to obey.

There was a heavy silence and Darcy endeavoured to master his anger; when he spoke, it was in a tone of rigid control.

"I refuse to justify my actions to you, Aunt. I will only say that my children and I are happy - very happy - that I am to marry Elizabeth and I hope that you are able to be happy for us, also."

"And if not?" Lady Matlock asked and Richard glared at her.

"If not," Darcy responded. "You will no longer be welcome in any of my homes."

"So you choose this girl over your family," Lady Matlock surmised.

"I choose Elizabeth over *you*, Aunt," Darcy countered firmly. "That is all."

In the silence that followed Darcy glanced at his cousin and sister and found them both looking at him with matching smiles of admiration. He grinned a little sheepishly and Georgiana hurried across to him.

"Well I am happy for you," she whispered in his ear as they embraced. "Though you still might have told me yourself," she added as she pulled back.

"I'm sorry Georgie," Darcy apologised. "I meant to call yesterday, but there was much I had to discuss with Mr Bennet, and then they invited me to stay for dinner."

"It's alright William," Georgiana assured him lightly. "I am only teasing you. And I am truly happy for you," she added again, just in case he needed further convincing. "It was a surprise, I cannot deny it, but when Richard and I spoke about it more I think we both realised that it is a fine match."

Richard nodded.

"Yes. I am sorry for my initial reaction Darcy - I was caught off guard, I think. You may say I told you so, now," he added with a grin and Darcy laughed lightly.

"Thank you, both of you," he replied. "I am glad you are both happy."

"As long as you are, Brother," Georgiana responded and Darcy kissed her cheek affectionately.

"I am," he assured her quietly, leaving Lady Matlock to sit and stew in silent resentment as his sister and cousin pressed him for more details about his engagement.

ࠐࠇ

Elizabeth was sat at her vanity table as Wilson arranged her hair for the evening when they were interrupted by a knock at the door, followed by the appearance of Mrs Bennet.

"Hello dear," she greeted her niece. She came in and looked around the dressing room until her eyes fell upon the gown hanging in the far corner, waiting for Elizabeth to put it on. "Oh, is this the dress you were thinking of wearing tonight?"

"Yes," Elizabeth replied, turning in her seat. Wilson was watching her aunt closely. "I think it is lovely, don't you?"

"Of course - all your dresses are, dear," Mrs Bennet replied carelessly, studying the dress. She seemed to come to a decision and whirled around to face her niece. "But I am not sure this one will quite do for tonight. I shall choose a better one for you."

Elizabeth saw Wilson bristle at the slight and braced herself.

"And your hair," Mrs Bennet went on heedlessly. "We can do something better with it, I think. I shall have someone fetch Hannah - she has a talent for it."

She made to leave the room but Elizabeth stopped her.

"I appreciate your help, Aunt, but I am quite happy for Wilson to do my hair. And I am perfectly content with the gown she has already selected for me to wear to dinner."

Mrs Bennet pursed her lips and looked at Wilson; she quickly looked back at her niece.

"Lizzy, darling, I only want you to look your best. Tonight you shall be introduced to everyone as the Duke's betrothed - you must look the part."

"And I am sure I shall," Elizabeth patiently replied. "I have every faith in Wilson."

Mrs Bennet looked displeased for a brief moment before she replied.

"Very well. I shall see you downstairs when you are dressed."

Once her aunt had gone, Elizabeth turned in her seat and faced the mirror once more, smiling as she caught Wilson's reflection - her maid did not say anything, but the slight blush on her cheeks and the smile playing about her lips spoke volumes.

"You are welcome," Elizabeth said quietly and Wilson nodded, obviously deciding to keep her thoughts to herself for once. Elizabeth was quite surprised; that was until a moment later when Wilson couldn't help herself.

"Fancy thinking that I would send you out looking anything but your best; silly woman."

Elizabeth bit her lip to keep from laughing.

☙☕

Slapping his gloves against his knee with increasing impatience, Darcy resisted the impulse to urge his coachman to go faster, feeling both nervous and excited about the dinner he was soon to attend. Finally arriving, he quickly hopped out and ascended the steps, sparing a quick smile of thanks for the Bennet's butler as the man held open the door for him. He was shown to the parlour where Elizabeth and her family were waiting and he immediately smiled upon seeing her; she came towards him and he took both of her hands in his own.

"Hello, my love," he greeted her warmly, quite ignoring Mr and Mrs Bennet.

"Hello, Your Grace," Elizabeth replied, blushing slightly at the endearment.

Since their engagement two days ago it seemed as though they had had very little time to themselves, and she had hopes that tonight they would be able to spend some time together.

"William, please," Darcy reminded her and Elizabeth nodded.

"I will try to remember," she promised, adding quietly, "William."

Finally remembering his manners, Darcy greeted Mr and Mrs Bennet with both courtesy and politeness, but neither warmth nor particular pleasure. Their reaction to his and Elizabeth's engagement he found lacking, and he was tired of being the subject of the former's supposed witticisms, and the latter's fawning manners.

"Are we ready to leave?" he asked the room in general, though looking particularly at Elizabeth. On receiving a positive response he said, "Then let us be on our way."

He escorted Elizabeth to the front hall, accepting her things from the waiting servant and assisting her himself.

"Thank you," Elizabeth quietly stated as he placed her cloak over her shoulders; she glanced back at him and was reminded of the first time he had performed this office for her, after the Llewellyn-Jones Ball. Their thoughts had obviously followed the same path, judging by Darcy's reply.

"I never thought then that this would be the happy outcome of meeting you."

"Nor I," Elizabeth admitted, returning his smile and turning so she could take his arm.

The carriage ride to Lord and Lady Fairfax's home was uneventful, passed in idle small talk between Darcy and Mr and Mrs Bennet as Elizabeth sat in silent observation, watching three rather disparate people trying their best to get along. It had not escaped her notice in the past that between the Bennets and her betrothed there was no particular intimacy, and she did not foresee that changing very much once she and the Duke were married. The thought cost her some pangs of conscience, but she could not pretend that compared to the company of the Darcys, Fitzwilliams and Bingleys, she did find the company of her aunt and uncle a little lacking. And that was to say nothing of her father, whom she anticipated seeing even less than the Bennets.

Their arrival at the Fairfax's home was well timed - they were neither the first to appear, nor the last, and so avoided having to endure all of the dinner guests whispering and observing their entrance with eager interest. With the Duke by her side, and her sister and brother and the Fitzwilliams already in attendance, Elizabeth felt quite secure and met the curious stares of their audience with confidence and composure. Their hosts were warm in their congratulations, and though Mrs Bennet threatened to embarrass them all with her insistence on being included, the first few moments after their arrival passed by with no real threat to their enjoyment.

Joining their friends and family, Darcy smiled as his sister warmly embraced Elizabeth.

"I am so happy for you both. I shall love having you as a sister, I am quite certain of it. And I look forward to more nieces and nephews," Lady Georgiana added and Elizabeth blushed and smiled and expressed her own delight with the engagement.

After Richard had added his own congratulations to those of his wife, Darcy stood with Elizabeth on his arm, chatting amiably with their friends and family and frequently smiling down at his lovely betrothed, whose spirits seemed livelier than ever this evening. They were continually approached by other couples and individuals offering their congratulations, evidently eager to learn more of their shock engagement; Darcy deftly handled their enquiries whilst Elizabeth was unfailingly cheerful and friendly to them all, even those who dared to venture an impertinent comment about the speed and secrecy surrounding the match.

"Imagine if they knew the truth," Elizabeth whispered up at Darcy at one point, following a few insinuating questions from Lady Barlow and her daughter about the circumstances of their engagement. She was smiling mischievously and Darcy grinned in spite of himself.

"I doubt they would believe it," he responded and Elizabeth laughed lightly.

"I daresay it is easier for them to imagine that I somehow compromised you," she teased. "It is always easier to imagine the woman in the wrong."

"Especially given that I am regarded as such a paragon of virtue," Darcy replied playfully. "Undoubtedly it was all your doing."

"Fortunately I have a healthy sense of duty and am willing to do the right thing by you," Elizabeth teased, continuing in the same vein. "I would not wish to see you ruined, after all."

"I am glad you have such a regard for my reputation," Darcy replied straight-faced.

"It is only natural," Elizabeth informed him pertly. "You are to be my husband, and I cannot have my honour besmirched by any aspersions cast against you."

"Though you were perfectly willing to besmirch my honour," Darcy pointed out and Elizabeth smiled.

"Ironic, is it not?"

"Whatever are you two speaking of?" Sir Charles enquired with a laugh, "I keep overhearing the oddest things."

"Nothing of consequence," Darcy replied as he and Elizabeth shared a smile. He distracted his friend by asking, "Did you see whether Ellerslie has arrived yet?"

"Yes, I think..." Sir Charles looked over to the other side of the room, "Yes, I see him there."

"Come," Darcy said to Elizabeth, drawing her away from their small party. "There is someone I particularly would like you to meet. Ellerslie and I were at school together." As they drew nearer to the couple, Darcy thought to add, "His wife is somewhat..."

He was unable to finish his sentence, but Elizabeth was nevertheless forewarned and prepared herself for the introduction.

"Darcy!" Ellerslie smiled widely on seeing his friend. "There you are! And this must be Miss Gardiner. You're a sly dog, Darcy - though you always did play your cards close to your chest!"

Elizabeth smiled, taking an immediate liking to the man as Darcy replied to the teasing.

"Perhaps that is because I play to win, my friend."

Ellerslie laughed.

"And what a prize you have won for yourself this time."

Elizabeth blushed slightly at the praise, more so when Darcy looked down at her with open affection before properly introducing her to his friend.

"I am delighted to meet you," Ellerslie intoned with a genuine smile.

"And I you, Your Grace. William tells me you were at school together - I look forward to hearing stories of those days," she added playfully.

Ellerslie chuckled and promised to satisfy her curiosity before turning to the woman at his side and very formally introducing her as his wife, the Duchess of Bellamy.

Elizabeth sank into a deep curtsey as the other woman barely returned the courtesy before addressing her husband.

"I see Lady Stayne - I must speak with her."

She left without another word, leaving Elizabeth, Darcy and Ellerslie to enjoy a somewhat awkward silence.

"Please forgive me," Ellerslie said at last, looking angry and ashamed at his wife's rudeness.

"There is nothing to forgive," Elizabeth easily assured him. After a moment she asked, "Is it your son whom James is such good friends with?"

"Yes," Ellerslie replied, glad for the change of subject. He could not help thinking that his friend had chosen extremely well for himself - but given he had no need to marry again, why should Darcy not exercise his preference?

"I thought so," Elizabeth nodded. "James was telling me of some of their latest antics."

"Oh really?" Darcy questioned, one brow arched in inquiry. "And what have they been getting up to? I assume neither of us knows about it," he added, indicating himself and his friend.

"My lips are sealed," Elizabeth playfully informed him.

"You are supposed to be on my side, you know," Darcy replied and Elizabeth laughed.

"We are not married yet, Your Grace," she reminded him teasingly. "And even then I am afraid I cannot promise to always take your side."

"You would have me compel you to tell me the truth?" Darcy questioned lightly, not for the first time that night forgetting the rest of the company.

"I am not at all sure how you would accomplish *that*," Elizabeth replied naively and Darcy smiled slowly.

"Wait until we are married, my love - then you will see."

His words had the character of a promise, and coupled with his tone of voice and the warm look in his eyes had the effect of causing Elizabeth to blush without completely knowing why.

Ellerslie knew exactly what his friend was implying and barely managed to suppress a laugh; he looked knowingly at Darcy when his friend looked at him, appearing surprised to still see Ellerslie standing there.

"Did you forget about me?" he questioned lightly and chuckled when Darcy replied.

"Something like that."

Further comment was prevented by the announcement that dinner was served and everyone began to filter through to the dining room. Elizabeth found that she was seated quite near to Darcy, though across the table from him, and close as well to the

Duke of Bellamy. The latter, never one to stand on ceremony, asked to switch places with the lady who was to sit beside Elizabeth.

"I shall regale you with tales of your future husband's misadventures whilst he is too far away to do anything about it!"

"Is that what prevented you earlier?" Elizabeth teased him - she looked across at Darcy. "I had not thought him so intimidating."

"Not at all," Ellerslie replied. "My earlier silence was selfishly motivated - for he has as many stories to tell about me!"

Elizabeth laughed and fell into an easy conversation with the Duke as Darcy, pleased to see them getting along and happy Elizabeth was enjoying herself, finally turned his attention to his dinner companions and patiently answered their questions regarding his engagement.

"And so Agatha pulled you into the lake?"

Elizabeth nodded, smiling merrily and Ellerslie laughed heartily.

"It was really just a pond, though, not a lake," Elizabeth pointed out, still smiling and the Duke shook his head.

"And you did not mind a bit, I can tell. I am beginning to see why Darcy kept all of this so secret - obviously he was afraid someone else would come along and snap you up before he could. He wanted to keep such a treasure all to himself."

"I am flattered you think so," Elizabeth replied lightly, though in truth she felt the compliment.

"When you get to our age," Ellerslie confided with a glance across at Darcy, "you learn to appreciate the finer things in life."

Elizabeth laughed in spite of herself and then felt compelled to explain.

"Forgive me - it amused me to think of myself in the same class as a well-aged whisky, or a good cigar."

Ellerslie smiled soberly.

"I assure you, Miss Gardiner, that whilst such things may indeed be very fine, when compared to the value of a good woman they are worthless. Take it from someone who knows of these things," he concluded with an obvious allusion to his wife.

"You drink a lot of whisky, then, Your Grace?" was Elizabeth's response, but each knew that they were understood by the other.

"So you hope to marry in a few weeks?" Ellerslie asked a moment later and Elizabeth nodded.

"Yes - well, before the Season is over, at least."

"Pemberley is beautiful in the summer," Ellerslie told her. "It is beautiful all year round, in fact, but most particularly in the summer. I take it you have never been there?"

"No, never," Elizabeth replied. "I have had the opportunity in the past, on account of my sister and Sir Charles being friends with His Grace, but for some reason have never taken it. From the accounts I have heard of it, I am certain I shall love it. I am sure we shall be very happy there," she concluded, looking across the table at Darcy who just happened to look up and offered a warm smile.

"I shall drink to that," Ellerslie stated with a smile, picking up his wine glass; Elizabeth picked up hers and he offered a toast, "To your happiness."

"Thank you, Your Grace," Elizabeth replied.

"You are welcome," he responded before adding, "And call me Ellerslie - all my friends do."

"Very well - thank you Ellerslie."

"And thank you, Miss Gardiner," Ellerslie responded meaningfully, "for making my friend a very happy man."

"It was my pleasure," Elizabeth teased and her new friend laughed.

When dinner was over and it became time for the separation of the sexes, Lady Fitzwilliam was quick to approach Elizabeth and immediately linked arms with her.

"We shall sit together and talk - I am still in the dark as to how this has all come about, and I must insist you enlighten me. I should never have guessed that you had such feelings for my brother. When did it all start?"

Elizabeth laughed lightly.

"Oh, I hardly know. I always felt that he would make someone a good husband - after all he is kind, considerate, good humoured."

"Handsome?" Lady Fitzwilliam put in and Elizabeth blushed.

"...and yes, handsome, of course. Any woman would be very lucky to have him, and I thought so very early on. I cannot remember the exact point, however, when I started to feel that I wished to be that woman."

"William liked you from early on," Lady Fitzwilliam confided. "I remember some of the things he said about you - little compliments which at the time I merely put down to an appreciation of you as a lovely young woman, an appreciation I shared. It is only now when I look back that his words take on a different meaning, and I wonder that I did not notice the change in him sooner."

"The change?" Elizabeth queried curiously.

"He is happy," Lady Fitzwilliam replied with a contented smile on her brother's behalf. "That is not to say that he was unhappy before he met you, but over the last few months I have seen the brother I used to know gradually reappear. It all makes sense now that I know his feelings, but as I said, I wonder that I did not see it before."

"It is not that we acted together, or wished to keep you all in ignorance," Elizabeth stated. "Rather, that we were neither sure of the others feelings, and so kept them to ourselves."

"Oh, do not think that I blame you for acting as you did," Lady Fitzwilliam assured her, laying a hand on her arm. "Nothing could be farther from the truth. It is just a little strange - now that you have declared yourselves it is so very obvious that you are in love, and I think to myself - how did I not notice?"

The two ladies shared a light laugh before Lady Fitzwilliam went on.

"You must tell me more about the proposal. Richard told me some garbled nonsense involving Mr Collins, but I'm certain he was only teasing me."

Elizabeth's blush was quite telling and Lady Fitzwilliam was all curiosity – she pressed Elizabeth for the truth and Elizabeth was obliged to give in, relating the story of that day to her in full. When the gentlemen finally rejoined the ladies, Darcy and Colonel Fitzwilliam found Lady Fitzwilliam laughing merrily with a blushing Elizabeth sat beside her, looking like she was struggling not to laugh as well.

"What amuses you so much?" the Colonel asked his wife who was for the moment unable to reply because she was still laughing.

"Mr Collins," Elizabeth supplied helpfully.

"I told you I was telling the truth!" he stated with a grin and his wife found her voice long enough to apologise for doubting him.

"Not that I can really blame you," the Colonel added with a laughing look in his cousin's direction. "It does defy belief."

Darcy decided to make his escape before his cousin could tease him any further and offered Elizabeth his hand.

"Shall we circulate, my dear?"

"Certainly."

They left the Fitzwilliams to enjoy themselves at their expense, Darcy smiling ruefully when he heard his cousin's laughter. He looked down at Elizabeth who was laughing quietly to herself.

"Mr Collins, or Wilson?"

"Oh Wilson, always. Do you remember how she scolded you?"

"I doubt I shall ever forget it," Darcy responded dryly. "Or the way she bustled along the street towards us, in high dudgeon. *Elizabeth Hyacinth Gardiner!*"

Elizabeth stifled a laugh at his impression.

"She has perfected that tone over the years; not even my father could match it, though of course he rarely had the opportunity to try."

Once again Darcy couldn't help noticing how Elizabeth's tone changed whenever she referred to her father and he looked down at her.

"This is hardly the time or the place for this conversation, Elizabeth, but I cannot help but wonder whether your relationship with your father is a happy one?"

Elizabeth looked up at him, opened her mouth to reply, paused and looked down at her hands.

"How long have I been in town, William?" she asked at last, looking back up at him. "Four months? I have had one letter from my father in that time, berating me for not returning sooner and informing me that I needn't bother as he has found an adequate replacement. If I seem cold when I speak of him, I daresay that helps you to see why."

"A replacement?" Darcy repeated, confused. "What do you mean?"

"I told you, I believe, that I used to help my father with his studies by doing illustrations for him," Elizabeth replied. "Well, he has found someone else to do it now and subsequently has no further need for me."

"But you are his daughter, of course he..."

"William," Elizabeth interrupted him, not unkindly but firmly. "You do not know my father. You do not know what he is like and cannot possibly understand our relationship."

"Then help me understand," Darcy replied. "I want to understand."

Elizabeth was about to reply when they were interrupted by yet another couple coming to offer them their congratulations.

"It was certainly a surprise," Lord Perry remarked in his jovial manner. "We all thought your cousin was the man...but I suppose Mr Wickham was in on it all along, eh?"

"Mr Wickham and I are simply friends," Elizabeth replied composedly as she felt Darcy stiffen slightly beside her. "And I will be happy to count him as family once His Grace and I marry."

"Any idea when the happy event will take place?"

"We have no fixed plans as of yet," Darcy responded. "Though we hope before the end of the season."

They made idle chit chat with Lord and Lady Perry for a few more minutes before the couple moved away; seeing an empty window seat set a little apart from the rest of the company, Darcy steered Elizabeth in that direction and they both sat down.

"William," Elizabeth began, thinking to tell him that they really could not have this conversation here. Darcy interrupted, apparently having read her thoughts.

"No one will interrupt us, Elizabeth," he said. "They will assume we are having an intimate tête-à-tête and will not wish to intrude."

"You credit them with greater discretion than I do," Elizabeth commented as she looked into the room and several people quickly pulled their eyes away. "They are watching us."

"But they cannot hear us, which is the important point," Darcy replied. He reached over and took her hand. "Now speak to me."

Elizabeth sighed.

"I do not know what you want me to say."

"Tell me about your father," Darcy requested. "What is he like? What are his habits, his interests?"

Elizabeth could manage this with not much difficultly and described her father's passion for his studies and experiments, unaware that she was providing Darcy with several insights into her father's character and her relationship with him. When she mentioned the amount of time the Viscount spent on his work it signalled to Darcy how little time he spent with her; when she mentioned how completely absorbed the Viscount was by his studies, how little attention he paid to anything else.

The overall picture she painted was not a happy one - it was clear to Darcy that Elizabeth had grown up with a difficult man who, amongst other things, was incapable of engaging with his daughter or showing her any true affection.

"What was it like when your mother was still alive?" Darcy asked gently when Elizabeth had finished explaining to him her father's insistence on living by a strict routine. He wondered whether the Viscount's odd behaviour had come after his wife's death, or if he had always been...not quite right.

"Better," Elizabeth replied quietly. "I was only a child and my memories are those of a child, but I remember we were all very happy together, and my father was more present. That is not to say he was at all like you are with James and Catherine," she added with a smile. "But we did things as a family, and he was not always working as he is now."

"And after your mother died…" Darcy prodded.

Elizabeth sighed again.

"After Mama died…we did not see him for almost a month; he refused to quit his room except for the funeral. And then when he did come out, it was only to resume his work. It was as though we had lost both parents, not just one. I do not blame Jane for wishing to escape and marrying Sir Charles so quickly after Mama's death - I daresay I would have done the same."

*Would you, though*? Darcy thought silently, glancing over at Lady Bingley. He had always admired her, and thought her a lovely woman, and yet couldn't help thinking it had been selfish of her to abandon her eleven year old sister to cope with their father all alone. He did not think Elizabeth would have done it, were their situations reversed.

Elizabeth was speaking again and he focused his attention back on her.

"I know I should not hold it against him - my father cannot help who he is - but it is hard not to feel a little resentful. When I was a child I was so desperate for his attention - I learnt to draw so I could help him - and because I was young I mistook the attention he gave me as love. When I realised my mistake, that he did not care for me as a daughter, that my value was only in being of use to him, I confess it hurt me. But it is the way it is, and there is no use dwelling on it now."

"It still hurts you though, doesn't it," Darcy said and after a moment Elizabeth nodded.

"Yes, I suppose it does."

Darcy stroked the back of her hand with his fingers.

"I'm sorry."

"Please don't be," Elizabeth replied. "I plan to spend the rest of my life deliriously happy with you and not to waste my time dwelling on things I cannot change."

Darcy smiled briefly.

"I hope you know that I would never neglect any child of ours."

Elizabeth placed her hand on his arm.

"I know. Of course I know - it is one of the many things I love about you, William."

Darcy was forced to content himself with a kiss to the back of her hand, but silently promised himself that at the nearest opportunity he would express his feelings properly.

# Chapter 12

The following morning Elizabeth and Darcy joined the Fitzwilliams for a walk in the park, and whilst the children ran around them and the other couple trailed some distance behind, they were able to walk and talk together in relative privacy. Their conversation after dinner last night had given Darcy much to think about, and as he lay awake in bed, he had come to realise something - there was much he still did not know about Elizabeth, and she about him. That was not to say they did not know each other enough for marriage - with each other's characters they were well acquainted, and he was confident they knew enough to make each other happy - but there was still much, particularly pertaining to the past, that they had yet to share.

"William?"

"Hmmm?"

"Was Ellerslie's wife always so...?" she trailed off discretely, but Darcy caught her meaning.

"Yes," he replied with a sigh. "Unfortunately."

"Then why did he marry her?" Elizabeth asked with a slight frown.

"His parents," Darcy responded. "They arranged the match for him."

"I see- as your parents did for you," Elizabeth replied and, though it was not the opening Darcy had been looking for, he was glad that the subject of his previous marriage was begun.

"Yes - who told you that?" he asked lightly.

"Mr Wickham," Elizabeth informed him. "We were speaking of family and he was explaining your family tree to me - it is rather complex, as I remember!"

Darcy admitted that was indeed the case.

"I was more fortunate than my friend, however. His parents, his father in particular, cared not for his son's happiness in marriage - my parents at least gave it some consideration."

"Were you happy?" Elizabeth tentatively ventured and Darcy pressed her hand to indicate he did not resent the question.

"In my way, I suppose I was," he replied thoughtfully. "Or perhaps it would be better to say I was not *unhappy*. Ellerslie and his wife - they have been at sixes and sevens since the day they were married and I know have made each other miserable over the years.

Anne and I, we were not like that. We never argued, and there was always harmony between us."

"What was your wife like?" Elizabeth asked.

"She was a very delicate woman. Her health was always poor, and she lacked the necessary emotional strength to prevail against her body's deficiencies. She had a weak spirit, further undermined by her poor health, and she possessed little or no will of her own; I daresay she would have done whatever I demanded of her, had I been the type to tyrannise so pitiful a creature. I preferred rather to leave her to spend her days in the solitary, sedentary pursuits which she seemed to enjoy, and our lives were so separate that at times it was almost as though I did not have a wife."

"I am sorry," Elizabeth quietly said, saddened by the picture he painted. "You must have been quite lonely."

"Yes, I think I was," Darcy admitted; then he smiled and said, "But then James was born, and Catherine a few years later."

"It must have put a great strain on her health, to have children," Elizabeth observed with a delicate frown.

Darcy sighed.

"Yes, it did. When she had James the doctor recommended that he should be her only child, but Anne was desperate to do her duty, as she saw it. Her mother, my aunt, had very firmly pressed upon her the need for her to produce heirs, and Anne was anxious that I should have my "spare" to go along with James. I was reluctant to put her in any danger and for many years put off any thought of another child, but she was finally able to convince me, and the doctor, that she was strong enough to try again. Sadly she was mistaken, and she died but three weeks after Catherine was born."

"Did you...do you...miss her?" Elizabeth asked and then immediately regretted doing so. "Forgive me, I shouldn't have -"

Darcy smiled tenderly and once again pressed her hand.

"No," he replied honestly. "I did not. I was saddened that she had died, of course, and sad that the children would be without a mother, but our lives were so separate that I hardly felt her absence. My feelings caused me some pain, I will admit - I felt guilty that I did not care more - but I no longer blame myself for feelings which I think were natural for a man in my situation. I also think that it was only a matter of time before Anne's health failed her, and at least I did my best to make her happy whilst she was still alive."

"William!" Elizabeth turned to him and wrapped her arms around his waist, pressing her cheek into his chest as she said, "You truly are the best of men."

Darcy returned the spontaneous embrace and rested his chin atop her head for a brief moment before he espied his sister and cousin coming closer.

"Come, love," he quietly said, "This is not the place for this."

They detangled themselves and resumed their previous positions just as Georgiana and Richard joined them.

"Is it time to be going, do you think?" Richard asked them lightly.

"Yes, I am afraid you may be right," Darcy replied reluctantly, glancing at the sky and judging the hour.

"Will you come back with us?" Georgiana asked Elizabeth who was forced to decline.

"I expect a visit from my friend, Miss Lucas, this afternoon."

"Then we shall take you home," Georgiana replied. She offered Elizabeth her arm, saying as she did so, "Tell me about your gown for the Pearton ball. The one you wore to dinner last night was quite lovely. Who is your modiste?"

Richard and Darcy watched the two of them go on ahead for a few moments before Richard called to the three boys still running around.

"Bradley, Joseph, James - we're leaving!"

The two cousins walked together behind the two ladies as the boys followed behind them.

"So, what is it that you were discussing which led to such a public display of affection?" Richard asked lightly after a moment, smiling to himself.

"Anne," Darcy replied, somewhat surprising his cousin.

"Really? I thought you were going to say the wedding date, or plans for the wedding trip, not...well, it had the same effect, I suppose."

Darcy rolled his eyes, but otherwise remained silent.

"Have you spoken any more about a date?" Richard asked, moving the conversation along.

Darcy shook his head.

"Not yet. We are waiting to hear from the Viscount before making any further plans - though if he has no objections, I think four weeks will suffice."

"Four weeks!" Richard repeated, laughing lightly.

"Can you blame me?" Darcy responded calmly. "It is not as though time is on my side."

"You should not think like that," Richard cautioned him and Darcy sighed.

"I know, I know. And usually I do not - I suppose speaking of Anne has reminded me of all those years...well, it is in the past now. And I have the rest of my life to enjoy."

"May it be very long, and very happy," Richard put in and Darcy smiled his thanks.

ഇരുന്നു

That afternoon as Elizabeth was waiting for Charlotte to arrive, she was surprised when the butler appeared.

"Mr Wickham to see you, Miss Gardiner."

Quickly hiding her surprise, Elizabeth stood to welcome her unexpected guest.

"How do you do?" she greeted him; Mr Wickham grinned and shook his head.

"Don't act the innocent with me. How could you not tell me? Quite the fool do I feel now, let me tell you."

Elizabeth smiled playfully.

"I don't know what you mean."

Mr Wickham chuckled and took a seat as Elizabeth resumed her own.

"Has it been very bad?" she asked.

"Terrible. I shall never live it down. I cannot go within ten feet of my club."

"Well, it is entirely your own fault," Elizabeth responded with no attempt at sympathy; her companion smiled. "But I have the perfect solution."

"I should find someone to marry - and quickly?" Mr Wickham guessed and Elizabeth nodded. "The thought had occurred to me."

"It would be for the best," Elizabeth teased - she was not seriously suggesting that he find a woman to marry simply to avoid further ridicule. "That way we could pretend that we have been in each other's confidence all along."

"I wish I had been more in your confidence," Mr Wickham said quietly. "I would have left off immediately had I known you were in love with another man."

"I rather thought that would simply add to the challenge," Elizabeth replied pertly but he shook his head.

"Not if I had known my cousin was the man in question - Darcy is a good man, and you deserve one another."

"Thank you," Elizabeth responded, touched. She softened considerably to say, "I am sure you will find someone else."

Mr Wickham offered a sincere smile - then he grinned and flippantly replied.

"Oh, as to that, I have a number of other options."

"Of course," Elizabeth fell easily back into the usual tone of their conversations. "How foolish of me to assume that I was the only one to benefit from your attentions."

"I daresay in your case it was a dubious benefit," Mr Wickham commented knowingly. "I can't imagine my cousin was particularly happy about it."

"I doubt he would have been," Elizabeth granted, "had I not taken the trouble of informing him at the outset that I had not the slightest interest in you."

Mr Wickham dramatically put a hand to his heart.

"Oh, how I have struggled, and all in vain."

Elizabeth tried not to, but smiled in spite of herself.

"Oh well," her companion sighed, adding philosophically, "these things happen, I suppose. And as I recall, you did warn me."

"I certainly did," Elizabeth agreed.

"I hope we can still be friends," Mr Wickham expressed and Elizabeth smiled softly.

"I should like that - though I think William would prefer it were you to attempt to mend your ways, shall we say?"

"Oh, but then knowing me would not be half so much fun," Mr Wickham teased and Elizabeth laughed.

"No, you are probably right," she admitted and they shared a smile.

"Well, I had best be on my way," Mr Wickham stated after a moment. "Wouldn't want anyone to get the wrong impression."

"Again?" Elizabeth quipped, but she rose to say farewell.

"Congratulations, Miss Gardiner," Mr Wickham said as he bowed to her. "I hope you and my cousin are very happy together."

"Thank you," Elizabeth replied. "And I hope you find a woman who makes you happy, Mr Wickham."

He smiled weakly but still managed to a teasing reply.

"I shall not have to look hard - London is so very full of utterly enchanting women."

Elizabeth rolled her eyes and shook her head and with one last bow and roguish grin, Mr Wickham was gone.

ಬೋಡ

Mr Wickham was not to be Elizabeth's only surprise visitor that day. She was sat with Charlotte, laughing as she listened to her friend declare that she had known all along that she and William were in love, when they were interrupted by the appearance of Mr Bennet, looking particularly grave.

"What is it, Uncle?" Elizabeth asked him, at the same time becoming aware of much noise and bustle at the back of the house.

"I have heard from your father, Lizzy," Mr Bennet replied - Elizabeth noticed he was holding a letter. "I have just received this letter, along with..."

He paused and seemed reluctant to go on.

"What does my father say?" Elizabeth asked with admirable calmness, for her mind had immediately leapt to the conclusion that her father had refused his consent.

"He gives his consent," Mr Bennet began, and Elizabeth let out the breath she had been holding, "and reiterates his desire for me to act in his stead with regards to the settlements and contracts."

"And will he be coming to the wedding?" Elizabeth asked, knowing what the answer would be.

"No," Mr Bennet shook his head and heaved a sigh. "And Lizzy...I have to tell you..."

There was a loud bang from the courtyard and Elizabeth smiled quizzically and looked at her uncle.

"What is all that noise?"

"It is your father's carriage," Mr Bennet replied with obvious reluctance. "He sent this letter along with some of your things...I daresay he thought you might need them."

At first Elizabeth was confused, but finally her uncle's awkwardness of manner made sense and she stood up, leaving Charlotte and Mr Bennet to follow her to the back of her house. She stepped out into the courtyard to find the carriage half unloaded, a pile of trunks waiting to be taken inside as two grooms went about untying the rest from the equipage. Elizabeth knew, from the sheer number of trunks, that her suspicions had been correct and her uncle had lied when he had said that her father had only sent "some" of her things. This was *everything.*

Amidst all the noise and bustle Elizabeth became aware of a distinctive sound and after concentrating on it for a moment, went to the carriage. She opened the door to find a wicker basket sat on the floor between the benches; pulling off the fastenings, she opened the basket and Deirdre immediately sprang out, digging her claws into Elizabeth's dress and arms and clinging on for dear life.

"Oh, poppet," Elizabeth soothed her traumatised cat. "Shh, it's alright, you're safe now."

"What is all this?" Mrs Bennet had been disturbed from her afternoon nap by all the noise and appeared at the back door.

"My father has disowned me, it seems," Elizabeth replied before Mr Bennet could.

"Lizzy..." he protested.

"Is Dot here too? If not, I want her - Mama gave her to me. She belongs to me."

"She's here," Mr Bennet replied quietly, seeing that despite her bravado his niece was close to tears.

Elizabeth nodded and turned and walked in the direction of the stable block, cradling Deirdre in her arms.

"Mr Bennet, what has happened? What did Lizzy mean that Edward has disowned her?" Mrs Bennet asked her husband, apparently forgetting Charlotte's presence.

"I received his reply to my letter," Mr Bennet replied, brandishing the offending missive. "He spends most of it extolling the virtues of his new 'assistant', a Mr Hounsell who is, and I quote, 'of more help to me than my daughter ever was'. Indeed, were it not for Mr Hounsell he says he would refuse his consent to the marriage altogether for the inconvenience to himself would be too great - as it is he no longer has need of Elizabeth and is happy for her to marry. As his work is at this time at its peak, he declines coming to town for the wedding and has decided to send the letter along with all of his daughter's things so that she need not disturb him from his work by returning home. Perhaps in the autumn she and her new husband may visit. That is the sum of his letter," Mr Bennet concluded disgustedly, "and a more selfish missive was never written."

"Oh dear," Mrs Bennet replied weakly; she was surprised when Charlotte spoke up.

"I would suggest Elizabeth not be allowed to see that letter."

"I intend to burn it," Mr Bennet replied soberly and then asked, "Will you go and speak to her?"

Charlotte nodded and picked her way through the courtyard. She found her friend stood inside Dot's stall, stroking her horse's neck and speaking quietly to her as Deirdre chased mice in the hay at their feet.

"Lizzy?" she ventured quietly.

Elizabeth raised her head and Charlotte could see she had been crying.

"She looks well," she noted, indicating Dot.

"She is," Elizabeth agreed, running her hand over Dot's shoulder. "Greg takes good care of her for me."

"You must have missed her," Charlotte said and Elizabeth nodded.

"I will take her for a ride in the park tomorrow, if the weather is fine."

"Perhaps the Duke would like to join you," Charlotte suggested. "I hear he is fond of horses."

"Yes," Elizabeth replied quietly before lapsing into thought once more.

Charlotte sighed.

"I'm sorry Lizzy. That was very thoughtless of your father. Even for him."

Elizabeth nodded but remained silent and after a moment Charlotte sighed again.

"I shall go back inside. When you are ready perhaps..."

"No, Charlotte, wait," Elizabeth interrupted her. She took a deep breath and spoke a few more quiet words to Dot before turning away. "I'm coming."

She bent to gather up Deirdre in her arms and smiled.

"Wilson is not going to be happy to see you."

"Whoever is, besides you?" Charlotte asked with a smile as she reached out to stroke Deirdre and was rewarded with a low growl of warning.

Elizabeth laughed lightly and kissed Deidre's head, who purred loudly in response. Charlotte threw up her hands.

"I rest my case!"

They walked together back into the house and found Mr and Mrs Bennet sat in the former's study - both looked a little anxious but upon seeing Elizabeth's smile relaxed somewhat.

"Well," Mrs Bennet began once Elizabeth and Charlotte had sat down. "We must try to see the best in things, and with all of your things here we can be wonderfully thorough with your trousseau."

"Yes dear," Mr Bennet replied with an eye roll as Elizabeth and Charlotte both stifled smiles - how typical that Mrs Bennet's mind had immediately thought of shopping.

"Well there is nothing worse than arriving at your new home and realising that you are missing something essential," Mrs Bennet defended herself. "Or worse, that you have accidentally bought too much of one thing. I remember a friend of mine was left with *four* blue coats because she forgot she already had two at home."

"Disastrous," Mr Bennet sympathised and Elizabeth choked on a laugh.

"And as Lizzy will be living in Derbyshire, which is so much colder than the rest of the country, she will have to take extra care to have everything she needs," Mrs Bennet went on, determinedly ignoring her husband. "I shall have to ask Lady Fitzwilliam for her advice - she will know what is required."

"There is something I would like to buy before I leave town," Elizabeth spoke up. "It is Catherine's birthday in June, and I should like to have her present ready for her before we all leave for Pemberley."

"Of course," Mr Bennet replied, "and I'm sure your aunt will happily assist you."

"Oh, indeed," Mrs Bennet assured her. "How old will she be?"

"Nine."

"Hmm, a little young for jewellery perhaps." Mrs Bennet mused and then clapped her hands. "Oh, I know just the thing! Yes, quite ideal."

"That's settled then," Mr Bennet teased and his wife smacked his arm.

"Would you stop making jokes at my expense? I would have to be quite the simpleton not to notice, you know."

"I'm sorry, dear," Mr Bennet replied, chastened - Charlotte and Elizabeth shared a smile.

"Now, isn't this exciting," Mrs Bennet went on after a moment. "Lizzy is to be married, Jane is going to be a mother again."

"Is she?" Charlotte smiled, "I didn't know - how wonderful!"

"Yes, isn't it?" Mrs Bennet enthused. "This has been a happy season for our family, indeed!"

"Yes, so it would seem," Mr Bennet agreed and Elizabeth smiled as well, determined that the heartache occasioned by her father's actions would never spoil her happiness.

# Chapter 13

Greg smiled upon hearing Elizabeth's approach and straightened from his task of fastening Dot's saddle.

"Good morning, Miss Lizzy," he greeted her and she returned his smile.

"Good morning Greg - how is my favourite girl today?"

"Ready to go," Greg replied. "And fairly chomping at the bit!"

"It is a pity it is such a distance to the park," Elizabeth lamented as she checked all the fastenings herself, simply out of habit. "I should love to give her her head straight off."

"Well I have made sure to ride her most every day you've been away," Greg began and Elizabeth patted his arm.

"Oh, I don't mean to doubt you. I am sure she has had plenty of exercise. I would just like it, is what I meant. It would do me good to have a gallop, I think."

"Then shall we be on our way?" Greg proposed, turning to his own mount and gaining the saddle.

Elizabeth grinned and, with the aid of a mounting block, hopped up into her side saddle.

"By all means. After you."

"Oh, no, after you," Greg replied with a bow. "I am expected to keep an eye on you - and I can hardly do that if you are behind me."

"Has my uncle been speaking to you?" Elizabeth asked as she led the way from the courtyard.

"No," Greg replied. "Wilson has."

Elizabeth laughed.

"Of course, I should have known," she said, still chuckling. "Did she task you with guarding my honour?"

"Something like that," Greg replied with a slight blush, which fortunately went unnoticed. "Though I don't know how I am supposed to tell a Duke his business."

Elizabeth chuckled.

"Wilson has no problem with it whatsoever."

"Wilson could take the King to task," Greg muttered and Elizabeth had to tell him to stop making her laugh, else she would be in serious danger of losing her seat.

"You needn't worry about William," she told him as they rode together down the street. "The Duke," she added when Greg looked confused, "is the perfect gentleman."

"Oh, good," Greg replied, sounding quite relieved - he had been quite worried about getting himself into trouble.

"So, Gregory," Elizabeth began with a teasing lilt in her voice, "do you have anything to tell me?"

Greg flushed and his shy smile was all the answer Elizabeth needed.

"You did it! Oh, well done - though it took you long enough. But at least it is done - and you shall finally be married."

"I asked her last month," Greg admitted, still blushing. "And we hope to marry when I get back home again."

"Well I shall send you home tomorrow then, if that is the case," Elizabeth teased and Greg chuckled. She sobered somewhat when she added, "I shall have to find someone else to look after Dot for me, I suppose."

"I heard that the Duke has very fine stables," Greg commented. "His people will know how to care for a horse."

"Yes, of course," Elizabeth replied, though an idea was taking shape in her mind.

As they rode to the park Elizabeth peppered Greg with questions about Longbourn and the surrounding area which he did his best to answer to her satisfaction; regardless of her father's wishes and actions, Elizabeth was almost resolved on paying one final visit to her home, if only to ensure that everything was in hand and would be well managed without her. She meant to speak with William about it that day during their ride.

They arrived at their destination to find Darcy patiently waiting for them; when he saw them he dismounted and came towards her, smiling his greeting. As he reached her side Elizabeth held her hands out and he helped her slide down from the saddle.

"Good morning, my dear," he greeted her warmly.

As Dot was shielding them from view, Elizabeth leant up on her tiptoes and spontaneously kissed him on the lips.

"Good morning, William."

Darcy only had time to look surprised before she drew back and Greg stepped into view.

"This is Gregory Foster - you remember my telling you about him?"

Darcy cleared his throat.

"Umm, yes. I do remember."

He gave a brief nod and Greg bowed deeply, obviously feeling a little bit flustered, having never met a Duke before. Darcy then turned to look at Dot and after a moment observed.

"You obviously know you're business, Mr Foster. She is looking very fine."

He had heard a lot about Dot from Elizabeth and wasn't disappointed; he stroked her neck and shoulders, admiring her shining coat and muscled but sleek frame.

"Thank you, Milord," Greg mumbled, blushing with pride. Elizabeth shot him a laughing look and he recovered himself a little to say, "Her dam was an Epsom Oaks winner, and her sire was Lord Egmont's prized hunter, Ashton."

Darcy was suitably impressed.

"Ashton was a fine horse - I have two fillies in my stables at Pemberley who are part of his line. One of them will be running in the Oaks this year."

"You've yet to introduce us to your mount, William," Elizabeth prompted him before Greg could respond - she knew that if they got started they could both talk about horse breeding for hours on end.

"This is Fletcher," Darcy stated, calmly holding out his hand and waiting as his horse ambled over to him. "He is my old friend."

"He is very handsome," Elizabeth complimented, stroking the stallion's long neck. "I have never seen a horse such a pure white before. And very calm, especially for a stallion."

"His spirit took a few knocks when he was young," Darcy revealed just as Elizabeth noticed that both of Fletcher's front knees were scarred. "I will not name names, but the son of his former owner was a reckless beast who very nearly ruined him - I was lucky enough to come across him when I did, else he was destined for life as a work horse."

"Because of his knees?" Elizabeth asked, already knowing the answer. She deplored the fashions which dictated that a horse with even the slightest blemish was not fit to be seen in a gentleman's stables and admired her betrothed all the more for ignoring conventional wisdom.

"Yes," Darcy replied. "And because they had not taken the time to properly break him in."

"What was he like when you found him?"

"In a very sorry state indeed," Darcy responded, stroking Fletcher's nose. "I won't lie, it required a lot of time and patience to overcome his bad start, but the rewards...He is the best horse I have ever known; the best a man could wish for."

He glanced down at Elizabeth and was surprised by the loving look she was bestowing upon him.

"You have such a kind heart, William. You are the most loving and compassionate man I have ever known."

Darcy reached up to stroke her cheek before instructing Greg, who was hovering in the background, to leave them.

"But..."

"Now, please, Mr Foster."

Greg sighed and stepped around to the other side of Dot, occupying himself with the straps of his saddle.

Elizabeth's eyes danced with amusement.

"I cannot imagine that working on Wilson."

"Not a chance," Darcy agreed with a chuckle. "Now, what were you saying?"

Elizabeth smiled.

"Only that I love you, so very much."

"As I love you, my darling Elizabeth," Darcy responded as he curled his hand around to the small of her back and drew her closer. "You know, it has been far too long since I last kissed you."

"It was but a few moments ago," Elizabeth reminded him a tad breathlessly, as their lips were only inches apart and the heat of his body seemed to be wrapping itself around her.

"That," Darcy whispered, "was not a kiss."

"Then what...?" Elizabeth began but was cut off when Darcy captured her lips with his own and proceeded to show her what a kiss between lovers felt like.

"Urhhmmm," Greg discreetly cleared his throat and when this garnered no response he did it again, louder.

"What is it, Foster?" Darcy asked with his hands still tangled in Elizabeth's hair, his lips barely parted from hers.

"I'm sorry, Sir, but umm...well, there's some people coming this way, is all."

Elizabeth smiled at his obvious embarrassment, which saved her from feeling too much herself; she and Darcy shared one final, slow kiss before they separated and he helped her set her clothing and hair to rights.

When she stepped out from behind Dot she looked quite presentable and sounded tolerably composed.

"Thank you, Greg. Will you help me mount, please?"

"Of course," Greg responded at once, hoisting her up into her saddle whilst avoiding her eye.

"Thank you," Elizabeth said, then added quietly, "And I hope you won't tell Wilson about this little episode."

"I think I would be even more trouble than you Miss Lizzy," Greg replied candidly, "if she found out."

Elizabeth laughed and Darcy, who had by this time mounted as well, asked her what caused her such amusement.

"I think Wilson has put the fear of God into poor Greg," she replied as they urged their mounts to walk side by side, Greg following a little way behind, out of earshot.

"I must say I like him as a chaperone," Darcy remarked with a grin and Elizabeth smiled.

"Yes, I'm sure you do." She was quiet for a moment before saying, "He is soon to be married."

"Really?" Darcy did his best to appear interested in the life of a servant he had only just met.

"Yes. And he is very hard working. And takes very good care of Dot," Elizabeth went on, and Darcy picked up on her tone and thought he could guess the idea behind it. "He is sure to be master at Longbourn stables eventually, though Mr Nelson will probably live for many years yet. But he is a very hardworking, good sort of man. And his future wife is lovely, too."

"Indeed? And what does all that have to do with me?" Darcy asked teasingly.

"If there is space for him, and if he wants to, can he come with us to Pemberley?" Elizabeth asked. "Please?"

"Are you asking because you think it will be best for him?" Darcy asked her lightly, though the question itself was a serious one. "Or because you want him to look after Dot for you? Because I assure you my staff at Pemberley are more than capable."

"It is partly due to selfish reasons, I own," Elizabeth admitted, "but I also think it will be good for him. Longbourn stables are very small, and I fear will only diminish further with time - my father has no interest in them at all. I worry that the horses will all be sold and Greg and the others will be let go, to make savings and spare the trouble of maintaining the stables."

Darcy nodded thoughtfully.

"So you think it would be better if Greg and his wife were to come and settle at Pemberley instead?"

"I do," Elizabeth replied and Darcy nodded again, though his mind was focused on something else she had said.

"Is there a reason that savings have to be made at Longbourn?" he asked eventually. "Is the estate in any difficulties?"

"Not yet," Elizabeth admitted, "but I think it is only a matter of time. My father is an indifferent landowner at best, and has entrusted his affairs to a number of incompetent individuals in the past, who have further mismanaged things. Fortunately the current steward is a good man, and he knows his business well - I worked quite closely with him whilst I was living at home and between us we managed things fairly well. But now that I am leaving; I hope Mr Nichols will continue on, but I would not blame him for seeking a better situation. He is underpaid, overworked and under-appreciated by my father, and I do not think it will be long before he decides to leave. And then what will happen, I do not know."

"I do not understand why these are your concerns," Darcy stated, "though I admire you for taking them on regardless."

"I know it is odd," Elizabeth replied. "My mother was always quite heavily involved in the estate and growing up I carried on that tradition, though always keeping to the usual occupations of a gentleman's daughter - I took baskets to the poor, helped those in ill health, and gave my time to the school. It was only two or three years ago when I became aware, through my uncle, that my father was such a poor manager. It was Mr Bennet who found Mr Nichols for us, and perhaps once I marry he may be persuaded to take more of an interest in the affairs of Longbourn, though he has his own estate to manage and it is not at all his responsibility."

"But what of the heir?" Darcy asked. "I have never heard him mentioned. Surely it is his responsibility."

"Mr Gardiner," Elizabeth replied, "lives in America, and has made it very clear that he has no intention of returning to England at any time. He is apparently extremely wealthy in his own right and does not care for the title. His father and mine quarrelled when they were young men, and did not speak again before the latter's death. Mr Gardiner senior apparently passed on his grievance to his son, who is quite the stranger to us."

"Then what will become of the estate when your father passes away?"

Elizabeth gave a small shrug.

"I do not know."

They lapsed into silence as Darcy considered this sad state of affairs; his thoughts were interrupted by Elizabeth.

"My uncle received a letter from my father yesterday - he will not be coming to the wedding."

"Did he say anything else?"

"Only that I need not bother returning home again before or after the wedding as he will be too busy to receive me," Elizabeth replied lightly, though her eyes were sad. "And to ensure I did not come, he sent along all of my things with the letter. Hence why my darling Dot is here," she added, patting her horse's neck as Darcy bristled with indignation.

"How...what...the beast!" He managed to exclaim at last and Elizabeth couldn't help laughing lightly at his expression.

"It was a little callous," she commented, having had time to think about it and overcome the initial hurt. "But then normal standards do not apply to my father. He probably did not even realise his actions would hurt me. He thinks only of himself and his convenience."

"Please do not tell me anymore," Darcy implored, "else I shall not be able to meet him with any semblance of respect or composure."

"You still want to meet him, then?" Elizabeth teased and Darcy reluctantly smiled.

"No," he replied. "I would gladly forego that pleasure."

Elizabeth thoughtfully worried her bottom lip.

"I was thinking I would like to go to Longbourn, perhaps on our way to Pemberley. Just for the one night," she hastened to add when Darcy looked at her like she had lost her senses. "To say goodbye. It was my home for almost twenty years and I had many happy moments there. And there are people too, whom I should be sorry to leave behind without a proper farewell."

"What about your father?" Darcy asked. "I should be happy to take you there, if you really wish to go, but won't he object?"

"He does not have to know," Elizabeth replied primly. "I shall write directly to the housekeeper - Mrs Carey will be quite happy to accommodate us."

Darcy's brows rose at this scheme.

"If that is what you wish, then that is what we shall do."

Elizabeth smiled and thanked him.

"And Greg?"

"I will write to my steward when I get home," Darcy promised. "There is always a place for a good man in my stables, but I shall need to check that there is a suitable cottage available for him and his wife before I engage him. When I hear back from Benson, I will speak to Mr Foster."

"Thank you," Elizabeth said again, pleased with the outcome of their discussion. She liked that they could talk things over together in this way.

"I do have one request."

"Yes?"

"Could you please call him Foster in future?" Darcy asked calmly; he smiled as he admitted, "I should like to be the only man you address by his given name."

"Of course," Elizabeth easily agreed. "It is only a childhood habit; he shall henceforth be Mr Foster to me."

"Thank you," Darcy replied.

"You are perfectly welcome - may all your requests be so easily granted!" Elizabeth teased.

"I have another," Darcy replied in kind, "as you are in so generous a mood."

"Ask away," Elizabeth instructed airily, with a wave of her hand.

"Reserve the first two and the supper set for me tonight?" Darcy requested and Elizabeth smiled.

"My love, it would be my pleasure."

They shared a smile and continued on with their ride.

"Now that we have your father's reply, we can set a date for the wedding. Do you have a preference?" Darcy asked.

"Next week?" Elizabeth replied at first and then she laughed lightly, "No, my aunt would never forgive us. Perhaps four weeks?"

"Three?" Darcy countered hopefully and Elizabeth thought for a moment.

"We could have some things ordered and sent to Pemberley...yes, I think three weeks will be plenty of time."

Darcy smiled delightedly and reached over to press her hand before they then spent some minutes in discussion of where they wished to marry; they decided on the church Elizabeth frequented with the Bennets and the Bingleys.

"I trust your aunt to handle the arrangements for the wedding breakfast," Darcy stated confidently once they had settled that point. "But what do you wish for afterwards? We can leave town immediately, if you like, or stay a little longer - we could host a ball, or...?"

"What I would like," Elizabeth interrupted him quietly, "is to find some quiet place, perhaps on the coast, where we would know nobody, and nobody would know us, to spend our first day and night together as man and wife. And then I would like to go to Pemberley, so that the final piece of the puzzle may fall into place and I can understand you utterly and completely."

"It is done," Darcy promised with a kiss to the back of her hand, though in the next moment Dot danced away from Fletcher and he was forced to let go. "Though I cannot pretend to understand what you mean about my being a puzzle. Surely you know me well by now."

"Of course," Elizabeth assured him softly, "but Pemberley is your home, the home of your family, and where you spent your formative years. It is part of your legacy and the history of the Darcy family - I know you are proud of it, how seriously you take all of your responsibilities, and I cannot wait to see you at home there."

Darcy nodded, though inwardly he was wondering whether seeing Elizabeth at Longbourn would help him to better understand her.

𝔢𝔬𝔠𝔤

When his daughter's squirming in her seat finally got the better of him, Darcy was forced to intervene.

"Cathy, princess, please stop fidgeting. You will crease your dress."

"I'm sorry Papa," Catherine replied as she stopped moving and sat very still - Darcy suspected it was the comment about her dress rather than his request that had persuaded her.

"Would you prefer it if we waited until later to see Elizabeth, Father?" James asked and his sister immediately protested.

"No, no, of course not," Darcy assured him. "Elizabeth has been looking forward to seeing you both."

"As long as we are not in the way..." James ventured, anxious that his father and his future wife not feel as though he and Catherine were intruding on their time together.

"You could never be that," Darcy replied with a soft smile. "We are soon to be a family. But I appreciate your asking, Son - it was very thoughtful," he added and James nodded and gave a small smile.

"It is a good thing we had not made any plans to go outside today," Darcy observed after a moment, watching the heavy rain which beat against the windows.

"Yes," Mrs Hughes, who had been sat quietly beside Catherine, spoke up, "though perhaps this poor weather will help the children focus on their lessons a little more."

Both children looked a little sheepish at this reflection.

"Yes, else I will have to rethink some of the outings we have planned."

Whilst Darcy couldn't really blame Catherine or James - the weather for the past two weeks had been glorious and he well remembered how difficult it was to study when sunshine beckoned - he could not excuse their recent misbehaviour and was firm in his conviction that their education came before all else.

"I am sure you shall have no more trouble," Darcy commented to Mrs Hughes, looking between his son and daughter. "Isn't that right, children?"

"Yes Papa," they both chorused and Darcy was satisfied; he shared a look with Mrs Hughes but before he could say more they all heard the sound of a carriage pulling up outside.

"Ah, this must be them."

Agatha, who had been dozing by the fire, also heard the sound and leapt up, racing to the door and moaning impatiently for Darcy to open it for her. When he did so she ran on ahead and he called after her.

"Agatha, no jumping up!"

Elizabeth turned from handing her things to a footman on hearing Darcy's voice and just had time to brace herself as Agatha barrelled into her.

"Ooof! Hello Agatha!"

Whilst Agatha licked Elizabeth's hands and wagged her tail madly, Georgiana laughed.

"Well, she is certainly pleased to see you!"

"I'm sorry Elizabeth," Darcy said when he reached her, pulling Agatha away. "Calm down, you silly girl."

"It is alright," Elizabeth assured him happily, "I am pleased to see her too."

"The children and Mrs Hughes are waiting in the morning room," Darcy informed Elizabeth and his sister after he had properly greeted them. He offered each of them an arm and said to Agatha, "Go on, run along."

Agatha didn't need to be told twice and ran back to the drawing room, greeting their arrival there with two of her toys in her mouth which she eagerly presented to Elizabeth.

"Oh, are these for me?" Elizabeth accepted the offering and tickled Agatha behind the ears.

"Here, let me," Darcy took the toys and tossed them out into the hall; Agatha chased after them and he promptly shut the door behind her.

Elizabeth laughingly scolded him.

"Oh, that was mean."

"Perhaps," Darcy replied with an unconcerned shrug. "But she would plague us mercilessly to play with her otherwise."

"I suppose you are right," Elizabeth admitted and then turned her attention to the children. She and Catherine shared an affectionate embrace before Elizabeth turned to James and offered her hand.

"Hello James," she smiled warmly. "How have you been?"

"Very well, thank you, Miss Gardiner," James replied and Elizabeth chuckled.

"You really must call me Elizabeth now, James," she told him lightly. "We shall be family soon enough, after all."

"You must call her mama like I will, James," his sister piped up and Elizabeth saw an uncomfortable look pass across James' face as he hesitated.

"I think Elizabeth will be just fine," she said, sparing him the necessity of a reply.

She was not surprised at his reluctance to address her in such a way, and had thought about how best to approach the issue many a time. She knew that he still remembered his own mother, and coupled with the fact that she was only six years his senior she could understand why he was uncomfortable with the idea of calling *her* "mother". From his slightly relieved expression, Elizabeth guessed that she had done right and smiled softly. She suspected that the relationship between herself and James would resemble that of siblings and thought that they would get along very well together once she and William were married.

"And have you been well, Elizabeth?"

"I have," Elizabeth responded before playfully adding, "though my aunt seems determined that I visit every shop in London before the wedding."

"Did you go to Cutlack's in the end?" Georgiana asked, joining their conversation. "I really do think they are the best for winter clothing."

"We did," Elizabeth confirmed, then with a smile she took pity on James and said, "Don't worry, James, you needn't pretend to be interested. I know my uncle cannot stand to hear of our shopping excursions, and from your expression, and your father's, I would say you are both the same."

James looked at his father with a grin.

"I thought I had managed to look perfectly interested."

"We both need a little more practice, it seems," Darcy replied and they all shared a laugh.

Catherine, who was impatient to begin, tugged on Elizabeth's dress.

"Can we start now, please? There is so much I have to show you."

Elizabeth was a little surprised at first but she quickly recovered.

"Of course, I am ready. Please lead the way, poppet."

Catherine took hold of Elizabeth's hand and began pulling her towards the door; Elizabeth glanced back with a laughing look at Darcy and his sister, both of whom just smiled helplessly.

"I think I shall return to my studies whilst you view the house," James said to his father. "I shall join you all for luncheon, though."

"Very well, James," Darcy replied, pleased with his initiative. "We shall see you later then."

James nodded just as they all heard Catherine call out from the hallway.

"Come along Papa, you must keep up!"

"I swear she grows bossier with each new day," Darcy muttered, shaking his head; Georgiana laughed lightly.

"And whose fault is that?" she asked, and Darcy glared playfully at her.

"Oh, be quiet."

They soon caught up with Catherine and Elizabeth and joined them in viewing the first and second floors of the house, pausing so Elizabeth could admire the vast library - which she was informed by her little guide was nothing to the one at Pemberley - and lingering for some time in the gallery which housed portraits of the Dukes and Duchesses of old.

"Is there a painting of James and Catherine's mother here?" Elizabeth asked Georgiana quietly at one point, and her soon to be sister-in-law shook her head.

"No, it is at Pemberley," she replied softly. "Along with most of the family portraits - this is just a very small part of the whole collection."

"Your family must stretch back many generations," Elizabeth observed and noticed that Georgiana's smile was proud as she replied.

"Yes, the Darcys are one of the oldest families in England. And I am so pleased you shall soon be one of us," she added fondly, and Elizabeth knew she meant it.

"Is there a painting of Pemberley anywhere in the house?" she asked after a moment, curious to see what her new home would look like.

"There are several," Darcy joined their conversation, "though perhaps the best is hanging upstairs. In my bedchamber," he concluded with a warm look in his eyes.

"I shall have to wait until after we are married to see it then, I suppose," Elizabeth replied with a slight blush.

"I see no harm in viewing it today," Darcy stated innocently, "as long as we are adequately chaperoned."

Georgiana cleared her throat.

"Yes, and your chaperone is still standing right here, in case you have forgotten."

"How could I ever forget my dear sister?" Darcy responded with a smile.

Georgiana rolled her eyes.

"Flattery will get you nowhere with me, William."

"I see you have taken a leaf out of Wilson's book," her brother quipped, not bothering to deny that a moment alone with Elizabeth had been his aim. Elizabeth stifled a laugh.

"Who is Wilson?" Catherine asked curiously.

"She is my ladies maid," Elizabeth replied just as Darcy muttered, "Elizabeth's guard dog."

Both Georgiana and Elizabeth heard him, but fortunately his daughter did not; when both women looked at him with matching expressions of shock he grinned boyishly and shrugged his shoulders.

"Oh," Catherine was uninterested. "Can we carry on now, please?"

"Of course," Elizabeth granted easily. "You have been a very good guide so far, I must say."

"Thank you," Catherine replied with a look at her father, as if to say I told you so.

"We will need to spend some time with Mrs Dawson once we reach the bedchambers," Georgiana thought to inform her niece. "There are details we must discuss."

"Perhaps whilst they do that you could do some study before luncheon," Darcy suggested lightly and after a slight protest his daughter acquiesced to his wishes.

Before they reached what would be Elizabeth's chambers, Catherine insisted on showing her her own room and the rooms they used for their lessons and play time. James, who was busy studying, rose to his feet on their arrival.

"Oh, I'm sorry if we disturbed you," Elizabeth told him. "I can see you are working hard."

"To little effect, unfortunately," James admitted with a slight frown.

"Can I help?" Darcy offered.

"If it isn't too much trouble."

"Not at all," Darcy replied.

"I daresay he is happy for an excuse to get away; you don't really want to stand about discussing furnishings and colour schemes with your sister and I, do you?" Elizabeth teased.

"Once again I have been found out," Darcy quipped with a smile and Elizabeth and Georgiana left him to help James whilst Catherine reluctantly took up her own work as well.

"I gather Mr and Mrs Hughes have been having trouble this week with getting Catherine and James to concentrate," Georgiana confided to Elizabeth once they were alone. "They are rather excited by your engagement to their father."

"Oh dear," Elizabeth smiled. "Let us hope then that after the wedding they return to their more studious habits."

"Richard and I will make sure they do not neglect their studies whilst they are with us," Georgiana assured her, missing Elizabeth's surprised expression as she went on. "Especially James, as he is to start school in the autumn."

"James and Catherine are to stay with you?" Elizabeth asked and it was Georgiana's turn to look surprised.

"Yes - did William not tell you?" she grimaced regretfully. "Oh, he must have wanted it to be a surprise. They are to stay with us for the fortnight after the wedding," she revealed.

"Oh," Elizabeth was touched that William had arranged for them to spend some time alone.

They had just reached the rooms they were to look over, and found Mrs Dawson waiting patiently within, preventing Georgiana from saying more on the subject of Catherine and James' visit.

"Good morning, Mrs Dawson," Georgiana greeted the housekeeper. "I do not think you have met Miss Gardiner?"

"I have not had the pleasure, My Lady," Mrs Dawson replied before turning to Elizabeth. "May I say how pleased we all are for His Grace, Miss Gardiner. This house has been without a mistress for too long, if you don't mind my saying so."

"Thank you," Elizabeth replied with a demure smile, feeling the weight of expectation pressing down upon her all of a sudden.

"Well, these are to be your rooms," Georgiana stated with a gesture. "The dressing room is through that door, and that door connects with my brother's chambers."

"And that door?" Elizabeth asked, indicating one on the far wall.

"A sitting room," Mrs Dawson supplied. "Her Grace would often spend her mornings there."

"I see," Elizabeth nodded and looked around the room. It looked almost newly decorated to her and she asked when it was last done.

"Last year?" Georgiana looked to Mrs Dawson for help. "Or the year before that? I hardly remember."

"The year before," Mrs Dawson replied.

"And you chose the colours," Elizabeth surmised, looking at Georgiana.

"Yes," she admitted. "My brother decided it needed doing, but as you so astutely pointed out, such things do not interest him. He left the task to me."

"I like the colour," Elizabeth confessed. "And this fabric is beautiful," she added, gently tracing her fingers over one of the armchairs.

"But...?" Georgiana encouraged her to speak her mind.

"I am not sure that the style...it is not quite what I like," she admitted. "It is too..." she trailed off, for fear of insulting either Georgiana or Mrs Dawson.

"Ostentatious?" Georgiana surprised her by saying, a knowing smile on her face. "Gaudy? Lacking any real elegance?"

"Yes - how did you know?" Elizabeth asked.

"Most of the furnishings in this room were brought here from Anne's chambers at Rosings," Georgiana revealed. "The estate where Anne grew up. My Aunt Catherine's tastes were...well, as you see."

Elizabeth nodded, feeling quite relieved and Georgiana went on.

"I decided not to go to the expense of ordering new things made for these rooms when I redecorated - it is one thing to refresh the papers and upholstery, but new furnishings seemed unnecessary. I did not anticipate these rooms being used again for many, many years, after all."

Elizabeth smiled.

"You mean by James' wife."

"Yes," Georgiana replied, also smiling. "Though I am happy to have been mistaken in that belief."

Returning to the task at hand, the three ladies spent the next half an hour discussing what Elizabeth would like to change and whether the new furnishings had to be ordered, or if they could be brought in from elsewhere.

"There are some things at Longbourn which I would like to take with me to Pemberley," Elizabeth admitted some way into their discussion. "Though it is such a long way."

"You needn't worry about that," Georgiana assured her. "Transportation can easily be arranged. What did you have in mind?"

"My mother's writing desk," Elizabeth replied quietly. "And a cabinet from my bedroom - it was a gift from my parents many years ago."

Georgiana nodded.

"I can see they mean a lot to you - we will have them brought to Pemberley. Is there anything else?"

Elizabeth shook her head and they returned to the discussion of when and where to order the new furnishings.

"Fortunately the rooms at Pemberley are much nicer," Georgiana commented with a smile. "I think, based on what I have heard today, that you will like them very much."

"I am sure I shall," Elizabeth replied just as Darcy stepped into the room.

"How are things here?" he asked, "Is it safe for me to come in?"

"It is safe," Georgiana stated with a smile. "For now."

"Have you arranged all to your satisfaction?" he asked, directing his question to Elizabeth.

"Yes, I think so. Have we covered everything, Mrs Dawson?"

"I believe so, Miss Gardiner," Mrs Dawson affirmed. "I will see that your wishes are carried out."

"Thank you," Elizabeth replied. "I am quite content to leave everything in your capable hands."

Mrs Dawson bowed her head at the compliment.

"Shall we return to the drawing room? Luncheon should be ready very soon."

"You have yet to show Elizabeth the painting of Pemberley, brother," Georgiana reminded him and she returned her brother's curious look with an impassive one of her own.

"Indeed, how remiss of me," Darcy stated, offering Elizabeth his arm. "It is just through here."

He and Elizabeth went on ahead with Georgiana following behind them - instead of proceeding into his chamber; however, she paused just outside the door and turned to speak once more to Mrs Dawson. Darcy and Elizabeth both looked back over their shoulders and then at each other; Darcy smiled.

"Apparently flattery does work."

Elizabeth smiled but she was distracted by the fact that she was in his chamber.

"I have never been in a man's room before," she commented almost without thought, advancing slowly towards the centre of it.

"Not even your father's?" Darcy queried and she shook her head. "What do you think?"

"It is very you," Elizabeth replied shyly, running her hand over the back of a large wingback chair. "Do you often sit here?"

"Yes, at the end of the day. Usually with a book."

Elizabeth smiled.

"That is just how I imagined you."

"It has a twin," Darcy stated, drawing her attention. "That chair, it is one of a set. I will have the other brought in for you."

"I would like that," Elizabeth replied with a becoming blush.

"I rather hoped you would," Darcy responded intently; he stepped forward and was about to reach for her when his sister interrupted the moment.

"What do you think, Elizabeth? It is a very fine likeness of the house, I have to say."

Elizabeth turned to look at the painting with an embarrassed blush as Darcy shot his sister a look; Georgiana judged that she had chosen the wrong moment to intrude and smiled apologetically at her brother.

"It looks beautiful," Elizabeth commented after a moment during which she had composed herself.

"I am glad you like it," Darcy responded and they shared a smile. He glanced at his watch and observed, "We had best go down - luncheon will surely be waiting for us by now."

He offered Elizabeth his arm.

"I believe that when we are finished Mrs Dawson wishes to introduce you to Mrs Procter, our cook here in town."

"Indeed, Your Grace," Mrs Dawson, who had been hovering in the background, concurred. "If Miss Gardiner has the time, that is. Mrs Procter has some questions regarding her preferences, and Mrs Reynolds has written to me from Pemberley with similar enquiries from Mrs Maddison."

"Oh dear," Elizabeth laughed lightly, "I am not at all sure I shall be able to keep track of all these names. Mrs Reynolds is Pemberley's housekeeper, I presume."

"Indeed she is," Darcy replied, adding, "And do not worry Elizabeth - there is plenty of time for you to learn everything you need to know."

"I know," Elizabeth assured him. "I was only teasing. And I have every faith in Mrs Dawson and Mrs Reynolds to help me," she added with a smile at the housekeeper, who nodded approvingly, liking the young lady His Grace had so unexpectedly chosen to marry.

"And I have every faith in *you*," Darcy asserted and Elizabeth had not known how much she had needed to hear those words until they had been said.

"Thank you," she replied with a soft smile and once again Darcy was left to curse their lack of privacy and to content himself with a kiss to the back of her hand.

# Chapter 14

On the morning of her wedding, Elizabeth was already awake when Wilson quietly entered her room and approached the bed.

"Could you not sleep?" Wilson asked and Elizabeth shook her head.

"I am too excited," she confessed.

"And a little nervous, I'll wager," Wilson replied as she perched on the edge of the bed and Elizabeth sat up.

"Perhaps a little," Elizabeth admitted with a smile, rubbing her eyes. "Can you believe that before the day is out I shall be married?"

"Believe that my little petal is going to be a married woman?" Wilson responded, smiling tenderly at the young woman she had watched grow up. "It is a strange thought indeed - a happy one, though."

"I am so glad you are here Wilson. Since Mama died, you have been..."

"Now, now, petal," Wilson soothed, also getting rather emotional against her will. "You do not want to have red, blotchy cheeks when you marry your handsome Duke."

Elizabeth nodded, knowing she was understood, and took a moment to compose herself.

"Is everything packed and ready?"

"Of course," Wilson assured her, sounding much her usual self once more.

"And Deirdre?" Elizabeth asked and Wilson scowled.

"She is in my room, and I have instructed young Foster that if he lets her out of his sight on the journey to Pemberley I will have his hide."

Elizabeth laughed lightly.

"Oh, poor Greg. I do hope nothing happens to her, though," she added worriedly.

"She will be fine," Wilson assured her patiently. "As long as she is kept inside for the first few weeks - Pemberley will soon become home to her."

"I am so pleased that Greg and his wife are coming to Pemberley with us."

Wilson expressed her agreement.

"It is a good place for him; a firm footing on which to start a family."

Elizabeth felt herself blushing and prayed Wilson would not notice; her ever perceptive maid, however, straight away saw her reddened cheeks.

"I daresay your aunt has had a talk with you."

"Must we discuss it?" Was Elizabeth's slightly pleading response and Wilson took pity on her.

"Of course not," she replied. "Though I hope you know that if there is anything you want to ask me."

Elizabeth looked at her with obvious surprise and Wilson almost grinned.

"There is very little one cannot learn from servants gossip, my dear."

"Then you...you have not..." Elizabeth could not make herself ask the question.

"I am a good Christian," Wilson responded evenly, but there was something in her eyes which left Elizabeth still wondering.

Wishing to avoid any further questions, Wilson stood up and became business-like.

"Shall I have some breakfast sent up to you? Do you think you could manage something?"

"Just some tea, I think," Elizabeth replied as she pushed aside the covers and slipped out of bed.

"Very well. Your bath is ready for you. I shall return in a moment," Wilson told her and she left to see that a tea tray was brought up.

As she bathed, Elizabeth's mind was preoccupied with thoughts of the coming day, and of the wedding trip she was to take with William. Before that, however, was the ceremony itself, followed by the wedding breakfast which Mrs Bennet had meticulously planned. The guests had been carefully chosen and included, amongst all the family and true friends, a number of illustrious personages whom Mrs Bennet deemed necessary for the celebration of a Duke's marriage. Elizabeth had no doubt that her aunt would have planned a much larger event, along with a ball in the evening, had she had the time, and she was pleased with the way things had turned out. It would not be long before she and William could slip away, and they would finally have the privacy they both craved.

Wilson interrupted Elizabeth's thoughts when she appeared in the doorway.

"Are you not done yet?"

"Yes, I have finished," she replied quickly and Wilson helped her dry off and, once wrapped in her dressing gown, led her over to the dressing table.

"Did you find my mother's comb?" She asked with not much hope.

Wilson smiled as she leant over Elizabeth's shoulder and placed the aforementioned comb on the dressing table.

"I did."

"Oh," Elizabeth took it up and smiled delightedly at Wilson's reflection in the mirror. "You found it! Where was it? I thought for certain that it was lost."

"It was in amongst the things which were sent from Longbourn," Wilson replied, though it was obvious that Elizabeth was too absorbed with looking at the precious comb to pay her much attention.

"Thank you for finding it for me," Elizabeth quietly said as she looked up once more.

"You are welcome, petal," Wilson replied softly and began brushing Elizabeth's hair in preparation.

The tea tray soon arrived and Elizabeth sat quietly sipping from her cup as Wilson worked quickly and expertly, arranging her hair into a simple but elegant style and added her mother's comb as the final touch.

"There, all done," Wilson pronounced at last and then asked, "What do you think? Are you happy with it?"

"Yes," Elizabeth assured her, turning her head from side to side. "You have arranged it to perfection, as always."

"Something tells me your aunt will not be of that opinion," Wilson commented knowingly and Elizabeth smiled in spite of herself.

"Wilson," she began thoughtfully after a moment as her maid was tidying away the brushes and spare pins. "Things will be different for us, once I am married, won't they?"

Wilson paused in what she was doing and looked at Elizabeth.

"Yes, they will. By necessity, but I suspect by choice as well. Your husband will be your confidant now, and the first person you turn to with your concerns."

"Even if my concerns are about him?" Elizabeth queried dubiously and Wilson smiled.

"Well, perhaps not then," she admitted, "but at other times…and I daresay I will have to learn to hold my tongue. It is all very well expressing my opinion of your aunt and uncle but...well, I shall have to keep my thoughts to myself in future, that is all."

She turned away and resumed her task, leaving Elizabeth frowning slightly as she watched her work. She had become so used to the relationship she shared with Wilson that she found the prospect of change difficult to grasp; at the same time, however, she was aware of her shifting loyalties and knew, as Wilson had hinted, that she would not like to hear her husband criticised by anyone - except perhaps herself.

"I think," she stated quietly, causing Wilson to turn back to her, "that things will be different, but I hope you will stay with me for as long as you are happy to. I am sure I could not face the prospect of being a wife, and a Duchess, quite so bravely if I thought I would not have you with me."

"I shall stay as long as you will have me," Wilson promised her, pressing her hand in a rare display of affection. "But you must promise me one thing."

"Anything," Elizabeth vowed and Wilson smiled tenderly.

"Try to forget about me, about what I have been to you. It has been just the two of us for so long, but today you will be married. You will have a husband who loves you and will take care of you - you do not need me anymore. Oh, you will need me to do your hair and press your dresses," she added when Elizabeth looked about to protest, "but you will not need me to love you and look after you. You will have him for that," she concluded with a soft smile, "and he deserves the devotion of your whole heart."

"But I..." Elizabeth blinked back tears. "I can't. You are too dear to me, I couldn't just..."

"Yes, you can," Wilson interrupted firmly. "You can, and you will. Trust me Lizzy - your marriage will be the better for it. Please, don't misunderstand me," she continued when Elizabeth continued to look upset, "I will always be here for you, and you shall always be my dear petal, but from today we can never be quite what we were to one another."

Elizabeth was silent for some minutes before she finally replied.

"I think you will always be as dear to me as you are now, but I know that you speak the truth and I will try to do as you say."

"You think it will be hard now," Wilson told her reassuringly, "but trust me - once you have settled into your marriage, you will see that I am right."

Elizabeth nodded but before they could say more they were interrupted by the voice of Mrs Bennet coming from the bedroom.

"In here, Aunt," Elizabeth called lightly and Mrs Bennet appeared in the doorway.

"Oh, thank goodness, you are up. And your hair is done already I see - very good. Though perhaps...What?" she demanded when Elizabeth laughed and Wilson turned away to hide her smile.

"Nothing, Aunt," Elizabeth replied, controlling herself. "Did you see that Wilson found my mother's comb?"

"Oh, wonderful," Mrs Bennet noted, pleased. "I had thought that if it could not be found that I would lend you my mother's instead, but I am glad there is no need for that now."

"Thank you, Aunt," Elizabeth replied, touched by the thought. She looked at Wilson and asked, "Is it time for me to dress?"

Wilson agreed that it was and Elizabeth stepped behind a screen to change her undergarments whilst Wilson went and retrieved her wedding dress.

"Do you have everything packed which you wish to take with you today?" Mrs Bennet asked as she took a seat.

"Yes - well, almost everything. Wilson knows what else there is to pack," Elizabeth replied as she dressed, careful not to disturb her hair.

"Do you know where you are going?" Mrs Bennet asked curiously.

Elizabeth smiled to herself.

"No - only that it is a modest house on the coast somewhere."

That her future husband had arranged things so perfectly to suit her wishes was yet more proof of his goodness, and Elizabeth hoped that the time they spent there would reward his efforts.

She stepped out from behind the screen.

"I must admit I am excited to see where we are going - I cannot remember the last time I saw the sea."

"And you are to spend one night here in town before going on to Longbourn and then Pemberley?" Mrs Bennet asked, reiterating the plans her husband had explained to her.

Elizabeth nodded.

"I gather it is too far to travel from where we are staying to Longbourn in one day."

"Hmmm. I wonder where you are going..." Mrs Bennet mused thoughtfully and with a smile Elizabeth left her to her cogitations.

She went to the mirror and checked that her hair was all still in place before picking up the necklace she wore every day and fastening it about her neck. It was a simple gold and ruby cross on a light chain which her mother had gifted her - the last present

Elizabeth had ever received from her. The pain of losing her, which usually resided somewhere deep inside Elizabeth, had that morning come to the fore and left her with a dull ache in her heart. She wondered for a moment what her mother would have said to her, what words of wisdom she would have imparted, but her thoughts were interrupted by the reappearance of Wilson.

"Are you ready, Elizabeth?" Mrs Bennet asked and after a moment during which she studied her reflection in the mirror, Elizabeth turned to them with a smile.

"Yes, I am."

ༀ

"Those whom God has joined together, let no man put asunder."

Elizabeth raised her sparkling eyes to those of her husband, smiling brilliantly, and Darcy could not help himself; he leant down and captured her lips in a sweet kiss, full of happiness and promise.

"Steady on, Farleigh!" Someone called good-naturedly and Elizabeth giggled and blushed as Darcy reluctantly straightened, a joyous smile on his face. He laughed when Catherine rushed over from where she had been sitting beside Georgiana and leapt into his open arms.

"Congratulations Papa," she told him with a kiss to his cheek; she held out her arms for Elizabeth and bestowed a kiss on her cheek as well. "Congratulations Lizzy."

"Thank you, poppet," Elizabeth responded before turning to accept the congratulations of her sister as Sir Charles congratulated his friend.

James approached the newly married couple as well and, with a smile that almost matched his father's, bowed to Elizabeth

"Welcome to the family, Elizabeth."

Elizabeth smiled mischievously and pulled a startled James into her arms for a warm embrace. After a moment of awkwardness he smiled once more and returned the gesture, blushing slightly when she kissed his cheek.

"I shall conquer all your formality, James. Give me a week, and we shall be as close as siblings."

They shared a smile as Elizabeth released him and others came forward to offer their congratulations; it was some time before Darcy could lead Elizabeth over to sign their names in the register, and those that had been present for the ceremony gradually departed for the wedding breakfast. Georgiana and Richard took

James and Catherine with them in their carriage, leaving Darcy and Elizabeth alone for the short journey to the Bennet's home.

"You look wonderful, my love," Darcy told his blushing bride as their carriage set off, sitting beside her and taking her hand.

"Thank you," Elizabeth replied with a shy smile; she rallied enough to say, "And you look very handsome in your blue coat."

"Did I look nervous?" Darcy surprised her by asking. "When you first entered the church?"

"Not nervous exactly," Elizabeth replied. "A little stern, perhaps. Forbidding almost. But then you smiled," she concluded, smiling herself. "And the impression vanished."

"I was terrified," Darcy admitted with a lopsided grin. "I cannot have slept more than an hour last night, I couldn't eat a thing this morning, my hands were shaking...until I saw you, my nerves were in a fine state, let me tell you!"

Elizabeth laughed lightly at the picture he painted.

"But why? What did you have to be nervous about?"

"I may have been married before, Elizabeth," Darcy replied warmly, "but today I married the woman I love, who I would move Heaven and Earth to make happy - it was as new an experience for me as it was for you."

"Oh William," Elizabeth sighed, reaching out to lovingly stroke his smooth cheek. "That should not make you nervous - simply being with you makes me happy."

"That is fortunate," Darcy quietly replied, leaning towards her, "for you are quite stuck with me now, my lady."

"And you with me," Elizabeth breathed, "*my* lord."

Darcy was still chuckling as he kissed his wife for the second time that morning.

ॐ

"A toast, to the Duke and Duchess of Farleigh!"

Everyone raised their glasses and drank heartily to the health of the happy couple, who shared a smile and then thanked their host. Mr Bennet waved away their thanks.

"It is my pleasure, I assure you. I cannot tell you how much it pleases me to see my niece so happily married to such a fine man," he told Darcy, who bowed his head in recognition of the compliment. "And I cannot tell *you*," he teased his niece, "how much it pleases me that you made a match my wife heartily approves of. I am not sure I could have lived with her complaints."

Elizabeth rolled her eyes.

"Jane and I have both been very obliging in that respect, haven't we?"

"Extremely," Mr Bennet concurred, his eyes dancing playfully. "You always were good girls."

Elizabeth laughed in spite of herself, glancing up at her husband and seeing that he was also trying not to smile, before being distracted by yet another guest calling her name.

"Elizabeth!"

She looked over at Mr Wickham who was approaching her with a wide smile.

"You look positively radiant," he complimented, bending and kissing her cheek; Elizabeth felt her husband stiffen beside her and looked at Mr Wickham with amusement.

"Thank you, Mr Wickham," she replied.

"Oh, please, you must call me George. We are family now, you know, and we must take advantage of the familiarity that allows us."

"That is quite enough familiarity for the present," Darcy stated lowly and Elizabeth was quick to diffuse the situation.

Laughing lightly, she patted her husband's arm.

"Oh, Mr Wickham is only teasing. It is just his way."

"She is correct, of course," Mr Wickham informed his cousin, who seemed a little mollified. "I cannot help myself. I see a beautiful woman and I...Ah, but I can see my presence is no longer desired, if it ever was, so I shall take myself off. Until we meet again, sweet Elizabeth."

He disappeared as quickly as he came, leaving Darcy frowning after him as Elizabeth laughed quietly to herself.

"Oh, he is a scoundrel! I cannot help liking him, though - I see no harm in him really."

For a split second Darcy thought about sharing with her the truth of his cousin's circumstances but in the next moment he realised that there was no reason to spoil her impression of her friend. It was stupid and irrational to feel any degree of jealously towards George, after all, when Elizabeth had expressly told him that she felt nothing more than friendship towards his cousin.

"What he needs is to fall in love with a woman who has the wherewithal to make him work to earn her heart, rather than simply presenting it to him on a plate."

"And who happens not to already be in love with someone else?" Darcy added with a knowing look, and Elizabeth's slight blush told him that he had been correct in his suspicions of his cousin's feelings.

"You should feel sorry for him, really," she told him quietly after a moment. "He never knew his opponent, and how little chance of success he had. I would think you the best of men if you found it in your heart to be kind to him."

"My darling," Darcy replied magnanimously, "I do pity him, and you have my word I will be kind to him. That being said, however," he added, smiling slightly, "I can tell you here and now that I will *never* look with a friendly eye on any man who presumes to treat my beloved, dearest wife with such open familiarity. Think of me what you will, I reserve the right to feel as possessive towards you as I like."

"I should punish you for that speech," Elizabeth responded with a flirtatious smile, "but I find I have no inclination for it. I find your possessiveness very...appealing," she confessed with a charming blush.

Darcy leant down, his lips almost touching her ear.

"I will show you tonight how possessive I can be, Elizabeth." His wife looked positively overheated as he straightened and, with a perfectly straight face he asked, "Would you like something to drink, my love? You look a little flush."

"You are wicked!" Elizabeth scolded him as she gratefully accepted the glass of champagne he had plucked from the tray of a passing footman.

"You started it," Darcy reminded her with a grin.

"Yes, but *I* hardly know what I am getting in to, do I?" Elizabeth retorted, smiling in spite of herself as she tried to discreetly fan her face.

"You won't have that excuse in the morning," Darcy quipped and laughed when his wife blushed anew.

"What has happened to you?" she demanded playfully. "Where is the quiet, reserved man I met not six months ago?"

Darcy took her glass from her, set it on a nearby table and gathered his wife up in his arms as he replied.

"He is gone; he is no more. He was lonely and sad; I am happy and in love. I hope you will not miss him, for he is never coming back."

Elizabeth smiled and cupped his face in her hands.

"Oh, you silly man. You dear, dear, silly man. Of course I will not miss him, for I have you, and I love you so much."

With a full heart Darcy leant down and kissed his wife, caring not at all for their audience, knowing that he could finally do as he wished and no one could tell him otherwise.

ೞೞ

"Oh, princess, please don't cry. We shall see you again in two weeks, and then it will be your birthday."

"You promise you will be home before then," Catherine replied, her big brown eyes swimming with tears as she looked at her father.

"I swear it," Darcy promised and then, looking at Elizabeth, added, "We both do."

"Yes, indeed," Elizabeth put in kindly, laying her hand on Catherine's back and patting it soothingly. "For we would not miss such an important day for the world. And I have a special present for you," she confided with a smile. "Which I cannot wait to give to you."

"You do?" Catherine asked, effectively distracted; Darcy shot Elizabeth an amused look as she replied, "Of course. But it is a secret, and you must wait until your birthday to find out what it is."

"Did you buy it here in town?" Catherine asked, searching for clues.

Elizabeth smiled and shook her head.

"My lips are sealed." Catherine pouted adorably but Elizabeth remained firm, simply kissing the little girl's cheek. "Patience, poppet."

"I so wish it were my birthday already." Catherine lamented, not for the first time.

Whilst Darcy assured his daughter that the next few weeks would pass before she knew it, Elizabeth turned to James.

"Well, James. I hope you have a nice time staying with your aunt and uncle and cousins."

"I am sure I shall," James replied. "And I hope you and Father enjoy your trip to the coast."

Elizabeth nodded and then smiled.

"Now, how shall we part? With a handshake or...?"

She was pleasantly surprised when James stepped forward and pressed a kiss to her cheek and then offered his hand.

"I look forward to seeing you again at Pemberley, Lizzy."

Elizabeth laughed delightedly.

"Such progress already! I knew how it would be," she teased before taking his hand and saying more seriously, "I shall see you soon, James. We will have a lovely summer all together, I think."

James expressed his heartfelt agreement and they parted at last with good feelings on each side.

"Well, I daresay it is time we were on our way," Darcy announced and Elizabeth returned to his side as Catherine and James joined their aunt and uncle on the steps. Darcy and Elizabeth had already taken leave of the rest of the guests, who all remained inside.

"I hope you have a pleasant journey," Georgiana expressed with a smile at the couple before her. "And do not worry, we shall take good care of these two," she added, stroking Catherine's hair as the little girl stood cuddled up beside her.

"Of that I have no doubt," Darcy responded before assisting Elizabeth up into the waiting carriage and climbing in behind her. They both waved goodbye from the open window.

"Goodbye Papa!" Catherine called, waving energetically. "Goodbye Lizzy!"

"Have fun!" Was Richard's parting call as Georgiana and James simply smiled and waved.

"Goodbye," both Elizabeth and Darcy returned as the carriage pulled away, quickly leaving the house and their family behind.

Darcy sat back in his seat and regarded his wife with a soft smile.

"Well, that went better than I expected."

"Yes," Elizabeth agreed. "Though perhaps the mention of presents helped," she added teasingly.

"Undoubtedly - that was a master stroke," Darcy complimented. "I see you shall have no trouble with motherhood."

"I hope not," Elizabeth stated and beneath her smile Darcy sensed a small measure of doubt; he switched seats, taking the one beside her.

"You will be a wonderful mother, Elizabeth. Catherine and James already love you - you simply have to be yourself and all will be well. You are a natural, my love."

"So are you," Elizabeth replied, smiling when her husband looked a little embarrassed at the praise. "I wish every man were as good a father as you are."

"I am glad you think me a good father," Darcy responded, "but for the next two weeks I am most concerned that you find me a good husband."

"If the experience of this morning is any indication," Elizabeth replied playfully, "I can see myself being perfectly content with you."

Darcy smiled and drew his new wife into his arms.

"Content? I will have you deliriously happy, and nothing less."

"Well you have made a very good beginning," Elizabeth responded quietly as Darcy gently caressed the soft, flushed skin of her cheek.

"Oh, but I have barely begun," he muttered deeply, focused on her parted lips which he finally captured with his own.

ଚ୦୯ଃ

Just as their carriage was pulling into the driveway at their destination, Darcy turned to his wife.

"Shut your eyes."

Elizabeth laughed lightly and looked at her husband.

"I'm sorry?"

"Shut your eyes," Darcy reiterated with a grin. "We are almost there - I want it to be a surprise."

Elizabeth hesitated for a brief moment but eventually shut her eyes.

"Thank you. I promise I won't let you fall."

"I should hope not!" Elizabeth joked and Darcy chuckled as he took her hand.

Their carriage came to a smart stop in front of the house and a footman hurried forward to let down the steps. Climbing out first, Darcy turned and assisted his wife, who faithfully kept her eyes shut as she slowly took the steps, relieved when she felt solid ground beneath her feet. Darcy's coachman, John, smiled from his seat as he watched his master and new mistress together, though he quickly hid his amusement when Darcy looked up at him.

"Please see to everything here, John."

"Yes, Your Grace," John replied and Darcy took his wife by the waist and led her away from the house.

"Where are we going?" Elizabeth asked, wild with curiosity - a light breeze blew their way and she suddenly exclaimed, "I can smell the sea!"

She went still for a moment and Darcy waited expectantly.

"And I can hear it! It must be very close."

*Just wait and see*, Darcy thought with a sense of anticipation, eager to see her reaction. He led her to the end of the garden and turned her back to face the house. Then he stood behind her and bent down to whisper softly in her ear.

"You can open your eyes now."

Elizabeth smiled and did as she was instructed, pleasantly surprised by the sight before her. When Darcy had said they would be staying at a "modest house" she had formed a certain picture in her mind, but the building in front of her far exceeded her expectations. It was a large, square building, well-proportioned with tall windows and ivy growing in marvellous abundance all over the façade.

"William..." she began, twisting her head to look up at him. "What a lovely house."

"With a charming view," Darcy replied as he stepped to the side and turned Elizabeth so that she could look out over the bay which the house, stood atop a hill, overlooked. The sun was just setting and the sky was a vivid shade of pink, the sea a deep blue as the waves rolled onto the sandy beach not three hundred metres away.

Elizabeth gasped with delight, arrested by the beauty of the scene. She spun around and threw her arms about her husband's neck.

"Oh, William! It is so beautiful! However did you manage to find this place?"

"I have stayed here before," Darcy revealed with a smile, still holding Elizabeth in his arms. "Many, many years ago, when I was at university. It belongs to a friend who was happy for us to stay here for a few days."

"Thank you," Elizabeth said, rewarding him with a kiss before turning to admire the view once more. "It is wonderful."

'I hoped you would be pleased," Darcy replied quietly, drawing his wife closer so that her back was pressed against him, the top of her head reaching to just below his chin. She had long ago abandoned her bonnet and Darcy allowed himself a moment to appreciate the feel and smell of her hair before saying, "There is a path which leads from here down to the beach."

"I suppose it is too late for us to take it now," Elizabeth noted regretfully and Darcy smiled.

"Yes, I am afraid so - it will be dark soon. But there is always tomorrow," he promised and Elizabeth nodded.

They stood in companionable silence, watching the sun go down together.

"Come, we should go inside. I do not want you to catch cold."

Elizabeth knew that she was made of sterner stuff than that, but she was happy to return to the house with her husband; they walked slowly, admiring the gardens in the deepening twilight, speaking quietly with their heads close together.

When they reached the house they found the housekeeper patiently waiting for them, a welcoming smile on her face.

"Ah, good evening Mrs Walsh," Darcy greeted her directly. "I hope you had no trouble arranging things in our absence."

"None at all, Your Grace," the lady replied. "Your trunks have been taken to your rooms and dinner can be ready whenever you desire it."

"An hour, I think, shall suffice," Darcy replied after glancing at Elizabeth to gain her opinion. "We shall wash and dress before we dine."

"Very good, Sir," Mrs Walsh bowed; she smiled and added, "And may I offer my congratulations on your marriage, Sir."

"Thank you," Darcy responded kindly and then turned to Elizabeth, effectively dismissing Mrs Walsh who quietly left them to see to the arrangements.

"Shall we?" Darcy offered his arm and led her upstairs to their chambers.

"How old were you when you were last here?" Elizabeth asked as they climbed the stairs.

"Well, let me see." Darcy thought for a moment. "It was twenty years ago. I must have only been eighteen or nineteen," he replied at last.

Elizabeth regarded her husband with her head tilted to one side.

"I cannot imagine you as such a young man."

"I doubt you would have liked me, had you met me then," Darcy predicted with a grin. "I was a little too proud, and had a tendency to disdain those not of my circle."

Elizabeth's brows rose.

"Really?"

"Oh, yes," Darcy admitted. "I was taught, you see, to think of myself as above others. It was only as I got older and experienced more of the world that I realised how mistaken that idea was, how wrongly I had been treating others."

"I suppose it is hard to know you are wrong, when everyone about you tells you you are right," Elizabeth commented and Darcy nodded.

"Yes, precisely. My entire family - my parents included - were all of the same opinion and I was fortunate, I think, to have met more open-minded people towards the end of my time at university, when their influence could still do me good."

"Is that when you met Sir Charles?" Elizabeth asked and Darcy admitted that it was.

"I was also spending more time with Richard," he added with a grin, "who had just joined the army, and he took great pleasure in ridiculing my more snobbish behaviour."

"Well I am glad I did not meet you then," Elizabeth commented lightly just as they reached their chambers. "I think you are quite right - I would not have liked you at all - and there would have been no hope of our falling in love."

"It is strange to think what could have been, isn't it?" Darcy asked and Elizabeth smiled.

"Indeed," she replied coyly, "though personally I prefer to think of what is to come. Shall I see you in an hour?" she asked, turning and leaning with her back against the door to her room, facing her husband with an intentionally provocative smile.

"You shall," Darcy replied, capturing her hand which was poised to open the door and trapping her body with his. "Minx," he whispered, his warm breath tingling across her lips.

A noise from a passing servant startled them and Darcy abruptly straightened as Elizabeth flushed with awareness. They shared a secret smile before Darcy cleared his throat.

"I shall see you in an hour, then."

"Yes," Elizabeth nodded and with a final look Darcy turned and walked to his own room.

Letting out the breath she had been holding, Elizabeth stepped into her designated room and smiled upon seeing Wilson waiting for her. She immediately hurried over and embraced her dear friend.

Wilson smiled and patted her back.

"How was your journey? Not too long?"

"No, it was quite pleasant," Elizabeth replied as she pulled away. "And yours? Have you been here long?"

"We arrived an hour or so before you," Wilson responded as she turned Elizabeth and began to undo the buttons at the back of her dress. "I have everything ready for you - how long do you have before dinner?"

"An hour," Elizabeth replied before suddenly grasping Wilson's hand, saying, "I am so glad you are here."

Wilson smiled affectionately at this glimpse of nervousness from Elizabeth.

"And where else would I be, hmm? Isn't this a beautiful place, though? So close to the sea - you must be delighted."

"Yes," Elizabeth admitted with a smile. She related the particulars of how William had arranged their stay to Wilson as her maid quickly had her out of her travelling clothes and into a light dressing gown.

"If you wash first I will redo your hair and then you can chose which dress you would like to wear - I have a few choices for you," Wilson said, busying herself with another task and therefore sparing Elizabeth's blushes about her hair being in such a state.

Elizabeth did as she was bid, gratefully washing away the traces of the road and the long journey. When she was done she took a seat at the dressing table and, in a repeat of the scene from that morning, sat in comfortable silence as Wilson brushed and arranged her hair. *What a difference a few hours have made,* she thought to herself, looking at the ring which now adorned her finger. *This morning I was just Miss Elizabeth Gardiner, and now I am Elizabeth Darcy, Duchess of Farleigh.*

Wilson quietly broke into her thoughts.

"Shall you go down to the beach tomorrow, do you think?"

"I expect so," Elizabeth responded. "As long as the day is fine. William says there is also a castle nearby which we may visit if we wish."

"That sounds nice," Wilson commented, and Elizabeth nodded; she smiled when Wilson tutted and scolded her to keep still.

*Some things are still the same, though,* she thought with amusement, and found the idea strangely comforting.

ஐ ௸

Whilst Elizabeth continued to get ready, Darcy was in his room, standing and quietly contemplating the view as a cooling breeze from the open window gently washed over him. His man, Pattinson, was busying himself with Darcy's evening clothes.

"There, it is ready when you are, Sir."

Darcy turned from the window and strode over to the wardrobe, where Pattinson assisted him into a fresh shirt and the waistcoat and coat he had selected to wear that night. When his cravat was tied and Pattinson had brushed any specks of lint from his coat, Darcy turned to look at himself in the mirror.

"Well, Pattinson, what do you think? Will I do?"

"I would say so, Sir," Pattinson replied evenly, though his Scottish brogue was tinged with amusement.

Darcy ran his hand over his chin to check the closeness of his shave.

"Is it close enough for you Sir? Shall I...?"

"No, no," Darcy quickly assured his man. "It is fine as it is. I don't quite know why we are fussing this way," he added with a wry smile.

"It is not every day you get married, Sir," Pattinson pointed out in their defence and Darcy chuckled.

"True - but my wife is not a lady who places too much importance on such things."

"Perhaps not, Sir," Pattinson replied as he set about clearing away his things. "But there is no harm in a newly married man wanting to look his best."

"Well said," Darcy commented quietly and Pattinson bowed his head slightly before continuing on with his task.

Glancing at his watch and seeing that he still had over twenty minutes left, Darcy went to a small writing desk tucked away in the corner of the room and sat down. Gathering paper and ink, he began a letter to his son and daughter with the intention of finishing it the following evening and then sending it to them.

Pattinson broke into his concentration about ten minutes later.

"I have finished now, Sir. Do you require my help with anything else?"

"No, no," Darcy replied, laying down his pen. "And I can manage by myself later. I shall ring for you in the morning."

"Very good, Sir," Pattinson bowed and departed.

Once he was alone, Darcy spent a few more minutes on his letter before setting it aside and rising. He checked his appearance in the mirror one final time and then went to the connecting door to Elizabeth's room, knocking gently. On hearing her voice bid him to come in, he opened the door and stepped into her room.

"I am not too early?" he asked, as he shut the door behind him.

"Not at all," Elizabeth assured him, rising from her seat where she had been waiting in readiness for his arrival. "Wilson is very efficient."

"Has she gone?" Darcy asked, looking around and not seeing Elizabeth's maid anywhere.

Elizabeth nodded.

"Yes, I sent her down."

Darcy smiled and walked over to her, gently putting his arms around her and drawing her close to his chest.

"You look lovely," he commented quietly, brushing a wayward curl back behind her ear. "Almost as lovely as you looked this morning in the church."

Elizabeth sighed contentedly.

"It was a lovely ceremony, wasn't it?"

"I own I did not pay that much attention to it," Darcy surprised her by replying, and she laughed lightly. "Just enough to know when it was my turn to speak."

"I hope you weren't bored," Elizabeth teased.

"Enraptured, rather," Darcy replied and Elizabeth blushed prettily at the praise.

"I think we had best go down to dinner," Darcy said after a moment of indecision during which sense battled against desire. "Before I completely lose all inclination for it."

"I am not at all hungry," Elizabeth admitted boldly, her blush deepening.

"Neither am I," Darcy replied honestly, "but we really should eat."

"Yes, I suppose we should," Elizabeth conceded and when Darcy released her she looped her arm through his. "To dinner then; let us hope that the cook has not laid on too many courses."

"With a Duke and Duchess to serve," Darcy teased as they left her room and walked down the hallway together. "I fear that an elaborate meal is inevitable."

"Oh dear," Elizabeth frowned delicately. "All joking aside, I really am not hungry at all. I hope we won't offend the poor woman."

"Just be sure to heartily praise whatever you do partake of, my love, and all will be well. One compliment from you will be enough," he asserted with the confidence of experience and Elizabeth smiled at him.

"You are quite used to this, aren't you," she commented lightly. "Wielding such influence."

"It has been my lot for almost twenty years," Darcy replied with a light shrug before assuring her, "You will get used to it in time."

"Do you always get your own way?" Elizabeth inquired teasingly and Darcy grinned.

"Not always - and I suspect I shall be getting my way a lot less from now on," he added playfully and Elizabeth patted his arm.

"I am glad you realised that by yourself."

Darcy laughed heartily at her cheek.

"You seem confident of your ability to carry your own point with me."

"That is because I am fully prepared to utilise every weapon in my arsenal," Elizabeth replied saucily and, as they had just arrived at the drawing room, she sauntered in ahead of him, swaying her hips as she walked.

"Then let battle commence," Darcy quietly stated, following in his wife's wake and admiring the tempting view.

⧫⧫⧫

True to Darcy's prediction, the cook had laid on a fine meal and he and Elizabeth struggled to do justice to it. Elizabeth offered utterly sincere compliments on what she did try, however, and as he had earlier predicted, Darcy was confident that that would do away with any potential offence. They enjoyed their first dinner together as a married couple very much; the novelty of being able to speak without an audience or interruption, of whatever took their fancy had still not worn off, and Darcy suspected it would not do so for a long time. He had already known that his bride was a bright, intelligent and lively woman, but released from the restraints of propriety and an audience she became that much more of a delight to him. Sat by her side Darcy felt alive with possibilities - for that night, for the next day, the coming weeks and months and years - and his soul, which had started to feel old within him, now felt as though it had been given a new lease of life. He wondered whether Elizabeth knew the extent of his feelings, and smiled to himself when he thought that she believed all the good fortune to be on *her* side.

"What is that smile for?" Elizabeth gently broke into his thoughts, resting her head on her hand and regarding him with a soft, inquisitive smile.

"Was I smiling?" Darcy responded lightly.

"Most assuredly. I cannot quite describe it - you seemed amused, but perhaps a little dubious as well. And satisfied - definitely satisfied."

"You can read me so well?" Darcy replied, somewhat surprised. "You can read so much in a smile?"

"But of course," Elizabeth quietly said. "Can you not read me equally as well? Can you not tell what I am thinking now?" she questioned, looking steadily at her husband with a look he well recognised.

"That you love me," Darcy stated confidently, taking up one of her hands. "It is all in your eyes," he added when his wife nodded.

"And what do my eyes tell you now?" Elizabeth asked quietly as Darcy proceeded to press soft, lingering kisses to the back of her hand.

Darcy turned her hand over and kissed the delicate skin of her wrist before softly replying, his eyes locked with hers.

"That it is time we retire to our chambers."

He was confirmed in his opinion when his wife blushed slightly but held his gaze; still retaining her hand, Darcy rose from his seat and then assisted his wife to her feet.

"Come."

They left the dining room and slowly climbed the stairs together; when they reached the door to Elizabeth's room, Darcy, seeing that the hallway was deserted, drew her into his arms and slowly kissed his wife, who responded with shy enthusiasm.

"How much time do you need?" Darcy asked huskily as his fingers tangled in her hair.

"Twenty minutes?" Elizabeth shakily replied.

"So long?" Darcy teased. This made Elizabeth smile and relieved some of the tension between them. "I shall see you again in twenty minutes, then," he stated before kissing her a final time and pulling himself away, turning and going to his own room.

Once again Elizabeth, when she entered her room, found Wilson waiting patiently for her. Her maid smiled on her appearance and straightaway began to chatter about her dinner, and the other servants she had met, and the conversation she had had with Pattinson, the Duke's valet - all the while helping Elizabeth undress and letting down her hair. It kept Elizabeth occupied and distracted and stopped her dwelling too much on what was to come - which would only have made her nervous. Once again she was very thankful that Wilson was with her, and said as much when she was finished and the twenty minutes were almost up. Wilson just smiled affectionately and patted her arm.

"I will see you in the morning - just ring for me when you are ready," she instructed Elizabeth when they had both moved from the dressing room into the bedroom, and she was about to take her leave.

Elizabeth blushed and nodded.

"Oh, yes, of course. I did not...I shall see you tomorrow. Good night."

"Good night, petal," Wilson quietly replied and disappeared through the door to the servant's hall.

Elizabeth was left alone and had just sat down when there was a knock at the connecting door.

"Come in," she called and was pleased her voice did not shake so much.

Her husband appeared in the doorway, looking handsome and virile with his shirt sleeves rolled up and his throat exposed to her gaze, having abandoned his coat, cravat and waistcoat. Elizabeth had no doubt that her voice would surely shake *now*, and cleared her throat before she tried to speak.

"Has it been twenty minutes already?"

"Just," Darcy admitted as he quietly shut the door and came forward, trying not to stare.

Elizabeth was sat on the bench at the end of the bed, her dark hair cascading in smooth waves down her back and contrasting with the pristine whiteness of her silk nightgown and the creamy skin of her neck and shoulders, exposed to his eager gaze by the thin straps of her gown. Though the night was balmy and warm there was still a small fire burning in the grate and by its light Darcy stood and was transfixed by the beauty of his wife, his heart pounding in his chest.

"William?" Elizabeth's voice was shy and tentative and it drew Darcy from his reverie.

"Forgive me," he murmured quietly, coming forward and offering her his hand, drawing her body against his own when she stood and gently wrapping her in his arms. "You are so beautiful, Elizabeth."

Elizabeth was about to reply but was distracted when her bare feet brushed against his and she looked down.

"You have no shoes on."

Darcy chuckled at the unexpected direction of their conversation.

"No. And neither, may I point out, do you."

"I have hardly anything on," Elizabeth muttered before she was even aware of what she was saying, and then flushed scarlet with embarrassment.

She felt her husband's deep chuckle rumble in his chest as he softly replied.

"Yes, I had noticed that."

Elizabeth shyly looked up into her husband's face, half illuminated by the firelight.

"Do I please you, William?"

"Did I not just say you are beautiful?" Darcy replied quietly, cupping her cheek in his hand, stroking his thumb across the smooth skin which he could see was still flushed.

"Yes, but..." Elizabeth began but was cut off when Darcy softly kissed her.

"Elizabeth," he stated in a half-whisper, his lips hovering barely a centimetre from hers.

"Uhhmmm?"

"No more talking," he breathed. "Let me show you how beautiful I think you are."

Elizabeth had no objections to this; and even if she had, her husband was quick to capture her lips in a thorough kiss and it was much, *much* later before anything like meaningful conversation passed between them.

ℰℴℭℬ

When Elizabeth awoke the next morning it was still very early and, conscious of her husband lying asleep beside her, she tried to remain still and quiet so as not to disturb him. They had spent the night in blissful, loving communion, and though she was tired, nothing could ever possibly taint the memory of their first night together as man and wife. Sighing contentedly and feeling herself a very happy and fortunate woman, hopelessly in love with her wonderful, tender and passionate husband, Elizabeth rolled over to face him and received quite a surprise.

"Good morning," Darcy greeted his wife, chuckling at her look. "Did you think I was asleep?"

"Yes," Elizabeth admitted, curling up against his chest, already accustomed to the warmth of his body beside hers. "It is early still."

"I know," Darcy replied as he drew her closer for a lingering kiss. "How do you feel?" he asked quietly as he pulled back to better see her face. He had done all he could to be gentle, and though she had found pleasure in their union he was still concerned for her welfare.

"I am well," Elizabeth assured him and then she remembered their conversation from the night before. "I feel beautiful," she added quietly and Darcy smiled lovingly.

"I am glad to hear it," he replied, punctuating his words with soft kisses. "My darling...wonderful...*beautiful* wife."

"William?" Elizabeth stated, looking at her husband with dancing eyes.

"Yes Elizabeth?"

"No more talking," she whispered and Darcy chuckled before accepting her advice and wordlessly expressing all that was in his heart.

# Chapter 15

The weather that day continued very fine and after rather a late breakfast, Darcy and Elizabeth took the path from the garden down to the beach. The way was steep and in places the ground quite loose but Elizabeth, used to walking, was surefooted as she followed behind her husband, who frequently stopped and turned to check on her progress.

"William!" Elizabeth laughed at one point, after he had stopped for at least the fifth time in ten minutes. "I am fine - please stop worrying."

Just as she said this her foot slid on some loose earth and she nearly slipped over; with her husband's aid she righted herself, blushing as Darcy looked at her with an arched brow.

"You were saying?"

"Oh, be quiet," she admonished him lightly, going on undeterred.

Darcy chuckled and shook his head, following behind and keeping a careful eye on her.

"If you are like this now," Elizabeth commented over her shoulder. "I dare to think what you will be like once we are at Pemberley and I begin to explore. I warn you now that if your park is as fine as I have been told, I will be gone for whole days."

"I hope you will not object to my accompanying you," Darcy responded in kind. "At least on your initial forays."

"As long as you can keep up," Elizabeth cheekily replied just as they reached the foot of the hill and the beach stretched out before them.

"Is that a challenge?" Darcy asked with a chuckle as he came to stand beside her.

"Yes!"

Darcy was caught off guard and left standing alone as his wife gripped her skirts and darted away, running towards the water with surprising speed. Elizabeth's laughter reached him and Darcy grinned as he took off after her, catching up just as she reached the waves.

"Married for one day and already you are running away from me!" Darcy joked as he caught her up in his arms. "This does not bode well."

"But that you caught up with me with such ease surely does," Elizabeth replied breathlessly, her cheeks flushed from her run and the invigorating sea air.

A wave rushed up the beach and washed over their feet before Darcy could reply or act upon the desire to kiss her.

"Oh no!" Elizabeth exclaimed, laughing and dashing further up the beach and away from danger. Darcy followed at a slower pace, knowing that his boots would do a better job of keeping his feet dry than hers.

"Oh, it has been so long since I have been to the beach," Elizabeth enthused as she looped her arm through her husband's when he joined her. "I had almost forgotten what it was like."

Darcy smiled at her obvious delight.

"I am glad the weather is so good - it would not be so pleasant here were it raining."

"I would love it even then," Elizabeth averred. "Because I am here with you and we are married and these are the first days of the rest of our lives together."

Of course, she was right, and Darcy could do nought but bend down and kiss her in heartfelt agreement. They turned and strolled arm in arm along the beach, seeing no one but the occasional fisherman and a man walking his dog. The sight of the latter made Darcy smile.

"Agatha would love it here."

"Where is she?" Elizabeth asked, wondering how she could have forgotten such a presence.

"She has gone with the children to stay with my sister," Darcy revealed, smiling wider. "Georgiana was not at all happy about it, but Catherine and James were rather insistent."

Elizabeth smiled in spite of herself.

"She and Richard will certainly be busy, with five children and a very large dog to look after."

"Georgie said it was their wedding gift to us," Darcy confessed and Elizabeth laughed lightly.

"Shall we head back?" Darcy asked a few minutes later, looking how far they had come. "It will be time for luncheon soon."

"Breakfast does not seem that long ago," Elizabeth replied but she nevertheless turned around and they began to retrace their steps. "We were very late risers this morning."

"I daresay it was expected," Darcy commented and Elizabeth nodded.

"Yes, Wilson mentioned that she had enjoyed the extra sleep," she admitted and Darcy laughed and shook his head.

"Why am I not surprised? She is a funny one, that maid of yours. I think I will have to watch myself around her."

"I thought she was very respectful towards you," Elizabeth countered, thinking of earlier that day when her husband had entered her room whilst Wilson had been doing her hair.

"Oh, she was - or she certainly appeared to be," Darcy replied, "but I think I ruffled her feathers a little when I told her to leave us be."

"Yes, I daresay she is not used to that," Elizabeth admitted with a reluctant smile.

"Well she will have to get used to it," Darcy stated warmly, "for I intend to kiss you whenever I wish, and without an audience."

"Do the same rules apply to your valet?" Elizabeth asked impertinently. "Can I enter your room and dismiss him as I wish?"

"With the express purpose of kissing me?" Darcy teased. "But of course. In all seriousness, though," he went on after a moment, "I consider our chambers to be our shared space, and I hope we will come and go freely between the rooms, with no awkwardness or formality."

"I can see myself being quite happy with that arrangement," Elizabeth replied positively. "And Wilson will simply have to adjust."

"As will Pattinson," Darcy agreed and they continued on their walk back to the house.

&#8200;&#8723;&#8723;

"Goodness, it looks as though it is about to rain."

Darcy looked out of the window and saw that, if the dark clouds were anything to go by, his wife was correct.

"I thought it felt a little close during luncheon," he observed and then turned to Elizabeth, "We may have to postpone our outing."

They had planned on going to the nearest town to visit the shops and walk along the waterfront.

Elizabeth expressed her agreement.

"Let us hope that the rain will have passed by tomorrow so that we still may go to the castle. And I'm sure we will have no trouble entertaining ourselves for the rest of the day," she concluded with a smile which Darcy returned.

"In fact," Elizabeth said after a moment, struck by an idea. "I have just the thing. I will return in a moment," and she left the room before Darcy had a chance to utter one word.

He smiled to himself and patiently awaited her return, wondering what she had in mind. Elizabeth soon reappeared, carrying all of her drawing equipment. Darcy looked at her questioningly.

"I have captured everyone's likeness but yours, Sir," she cheerily informed him, "and I think this the perfect opportunity to do just that."

Darcy grimaced slightly, his natural modesty rising to the fore.

"Must you?"

"Well, I shan't if you really do not want me to," Elizabeth replied fairly, "but I would like to. I promise you won't even know I'm doing it, I can talk whilst I draw," she cajoled and with a sigh Darcy relented.

"Oh, very well. Where would you like me to sit?"

"You are fine where you are," Elizabeth assured him and she took the seat at the opposite end of the settee, drawing up her knees and resting her board and paper against them. Once she was settled she asked, "Did you finish your letter to Catherine and James?"

Darcy smiled at the choice of subject but nevertheless replied.

"Yes - I have not yet sent it, though. I thought you might like to add something to it."

"I would," Elizabeth agreed with a smile, busily sketching. "I will do so after dinner. Have you ever brought them here?" she asked curiously and Darcy felt himself beginning to relax into the conversation.

"No - though I took them both to the seaside once, when Catherine was about six, I think."

"Can they swim?"

"James can, quite well," Darcy replied. "But Catherine cannot. I attempted to teach her last summer," he confessed, "but she was rather adamant in her refusal to enter the water."

"Perhaps she will be more willing now she is a little older," Elizabeth commented thoughtfully. "Where do you take them to learn?"

"Just the lake at Pemberley. It is very large and there are a number of places where it is safe to swim, though it is also very deep in places. When we were boys, Richard and I used to build rafts and no doubt made our parents extremely nervous," Darcy admitted with a rueful grin. "When I think of it now, I am amazed at our daring. We so easily could have drowned."

"And I suppose it was only when Richard was visiting that you got up to such mischief," Elizabeth teased him, taking her eyes from her drawing and looking at him with a smile. "He was always the one leading you astray, and never the other way around?"

"But of course," Darcy replied with a grin. "I was the epitome of good behaviour when Richard was not there to corrupt me."

Elizabeth smiled and they chatted happily for the next hour or so, surprised when the clock struck the hour at which they were expected to dress for dinner, the afternoon having flown by almost unnoticed.

"We shall have to finish this another day," Elizabeth stated as she tucked the half completed drawing away and uncurled herself from her position on the settee.

"But I thought you could complete your drawings from memory," Darcy replied as he stood up and offered his hand. Elizabeth accepted his aid and rose to her feet.

"I can. But with your picture I much prefer to do it this way."

Darcy smiled and wrapped his arm lightly around her waist.

"I hope you intend to reward me for my sacrifice."

Elizabeth arched her brow at his teasing.

"You cannot simply grant me this small favour, out of the goodness of your heart?"

Darcy grinned.

"And establish such a precedent so early in our marriage? I think not."

Elizabeth slapped his arm with mock indignation and Darcy laughed heartily as she smilingly accused him.

"You are incorrigible!"

"So I've heard," Darcy responded, still chuckling, and Elizabeth could only roll her eyes and laugh at his good humour.

ɛ⌀ʒ

With the exception of the rain they had that first afternoon, the weather for their stay on the coast was very fine, and together Elizabeth and Darcy enjoyed many a walk on the beach and outings to explore the surrounding area. They would happily have prolonged their stay at the house, and would always look back with fond memories of their first few days together as husband and wife. Plans had been made, however, and promises which had to be kept, so they departed for London on the pre-appointed day, arriving at the Darcy townhouse in the late afternoon.

"Would you like to go out this evening?" Elizabeth asked her husband as he assisted her down from their carriage.

"Actually, I have a surprise planned for you."

Elizabeth was immediately curious and playfully pressed him for more details; beyond a smile, however, Darcy did not respond and she was forced to admit defeat.

"You must at least give me some clue," she commented as they entered the house together. "I must have some idea so I know what to wear."

"I have already informed Wilson of my plans," Darcy surprised her by replying. "She will see to it that you are properly attired for the evening."

"And have you sworn her to secrecy too?" Elizabeth asked playfully. "Because she will tell me if I ask her."

"Oh, I know," Darcy responded. "I also know that she would tell you even if I *had* sworn her to secrecy - hence why I did not bother. I leave it up to you whether or not you wish to spoil your surprise."

"You are far too clever some times," Elizabeth complained with a slight pout but before Darcy could reply they were greeted by Mrs Dawson, the housekeeper.

"Welcome back, Sir, Ma'am. I hope your journey was pleasant?"

"Quite uneventful, Mrs Dawson," Darcy replied before asking, "Has everything been arranged as I requested?"

"It has, Sir," Mrs Dawson affirmed and Elizabeth felt that she did not like being so totally in the dark as to her husband's plan.

Perhaps seeing this, Darcy leant down to her.

"Shall I give you a clue? Your aunt would not approve."

"But that could mean anything," Elizabeth replied without thinking and Darcy laughed.

"I suppose so," he admitted. "But that is all I shall say for now."

"I'm not entirely sure I like surprises," Elizabeth commented as they entered the parlour where the tea things awaited them.

"Well I promise this shall be the last one I arrange for you," Darcy replied with teasing gravity. "Though I assure you, you will enjoy this one."

"I hope so," Elizabeth responded as she prepared his tea and then passed it to him.

Darcy took the cup and then pressed her hand.

"You can trust me, you know. And I will tell you what I have planned, if you really wish to know."

"No, no, there is no need for that," Elizabeth assured him. "I am just being foolish. But I hope you know I do not need for you to be constantly arranging all these things for me."

"I know," Darcy replied softly. "That being said, I hope you will indulge me from time to time when I have the urge to spoil you. It brings me pleasure to do so."

"As long as I am allowed the same privilege," Elizabeth stated with a smile. "I can have no objection."

"We are in agreement then," Darcy commented and grinned when Elizabeth offered him her hand and they playfully shook.

"We are quite good at this, I think," she commented lightly, sipping her tea.

"At what?" Darcy queried.

"Being married," Elizabeth replied and Darcy smiled.

"Early indications would suggest as much, yes," he agreed and chuckled when Elizabeth touched her tea cup to his in a mock toast.

"To us."

�`Ꮖ

Elizabeth refrained from asking Wilson about what her husband had planned for them that night, but when they sat down to an early supper she thought she had some idea of where they would be going. She hazarded a guess at the conclusion of their meal.

"Are we going to the theatre? Or the opera?"

"We are," Darcy confirmed, waiting to see whether or not she could fathom the rest of the surprise.

"And my aunt would not approve." Elizabeth mused thoughtfully; realisation dawned, "Oh! Don Giovanni!"

"Yes, precisely. I remembered you expressing a desire to see it - and now you are a Duchess, you may do as you please, regardless of your aunt's opinion," he teased and Elizabeth smiled in response.

"I wondered why Wilson was so particular about my toilette tonight," she commented after a moment. "But now I understand - this shall be my first public appearance as your wife. And as a Duchess," she added almost as an afterthought.

"And I have every faith in you," Darcy stated sincerely, whilst inwardly he smiled at how she obviously put being his wife before being a Duchess.

"Thank you," Elizabeth replied with a slight blush before asking, "Do you know if anyone else we know will be there? My sister? Or Ellerslie, maybe?"

"I'm afraid I do not know," Darcy replied apologetically. "I'm sorry, I should have thought about it and extended an invitation to your sister and Charles."

"Oh, do not trouble yourself," Elizabeth easily assured him. "I am more than happy to simply enjoy your company for the evening. And I shall see Jane again soon enough, I'm sure - we shall be living within thirty miles of each other after all."

"Yes, though with your sister expecting another child I doubt she will make the journey often," Darcy pointed out.

"I will simply have to go to her," Elizabeth stated before adding worriedly, "I hope everything goes well for her this time. She and Charles have waited so long."

"I am sure she will be fine," Darcy assured her gently and after a moment of quiet thought Elizabeth set her worries aside.

"Is it time we were leaving?" she asked her husband who, after consulting his watch decided that though it was a little early there was no reason they could not leave now.

"In case I forget to tell you later, my love," Darcy spoke quietly into his wife's ear as he helped her on with her light cloak, "You look absolutely stunning this evening. I fear I shall have trouble keeping my pride in check with you by my side tonight."

"Perhaps the thought that my beauty has nothing whatsoever to do with you shall help you with that," Elizabeth quipped dryly and Darcy laughed.

"You would think so," he replied, turning her to face him. "But I take credit for this," he touched her glowing cheek, "and most especially this," he concluded, delicately stroking the corner of her eye and smiling at the happiness he saw shining there.

"I had no idea I had married such a proud man."

"If you could see what I see, my dearest Elizabeth," Darcy replied earnestly, "you would think I had no improper pride."

Elizabeth smiled tenderly and forgot herself so much as to almost lean up and kiss her husband in full view of all the servants. Darcy saw her abandoned action, however, and swept her away into the carriage where they could enjoy some privacy, and she could express her feelings freely.

They arrived at the opera house in good time, and rather than mill about with the rest of the crowd decided to proceed directly to Darcy's box. They were met by friends, acquaintances and many others along the way, wishing to offer their congratulations or seeking an introduction, but with consummate skill they navigated their way through the crowd and were not long in reaching the safety of their private box. Once there they entertained a number of couples and individuals whom Darcy was happy to introduce to his wife, and true to his earlier prediction he felt immensely proud of Elizabeth as he stood watching her as she conversed and laughed with the various people who approached them. His behaviour did not go unnoticed, nor did his obvious admiration for his wife, and though many remarked it with amusement, those of a softer hearted nature smiled and thought it nice to see a man so clearly in love with his wife. That Elizabeth conducted herself admirably was almost universally agreed upon, and though some thought her liveliness unbecoming a Duchess, most thought her as charming as ever - more so, in fact, for what was seen as impertinence in an unmarried girl of nineteen was admired as a quick wit in a married Duchess.

The opera itself was of secondary interest to most of those present, compared to the study of the rest of the audience, but Elizabeth watched with rapt attention, shocked by the subject matter but able to admire the composition and the staging and the performance of the principal characters. Darcy spent most of the performance watching *her*, charmed by the reactions which she made no attempt to conceal, and it was with difficulty that he held up his end of the conversation when Elizabeth turned to him with eagerness at the start of the interval. He was saved by the most welcome appearance of Ellerslie.

"I didn't expect to see you again for many weeks yet," he said by way of greeting as he entered their box. "You should be off enjoying your wedding trip. I thought you were destined for the coast somewhere?"

"We have been and come back again," Elizabeth replied, rising to her feet to welcome their friend. Ellerslie bowed over her hand as she added, "We leave town again tomorrow."

"And you thought you would catch a show whilst here," Ellerslie surmised. "What do you think of it? Rather daring, eh?"

"I can certainly appreciate why it has caused such a fuss," Darcy admitted. "Elizabeth's aunt would not allow her to see it when she was unmarried."

"And now you are taking advantage of your new status? What else do you plan to do now that you are free to do as you wish?" he asked Elizabeth playfully and she smiled and teased, "Oh, I have a long list of things. I have always wanted to try riding astride, which of course would also entail wearing trousers, which I've always wanted to try as well..." Elizabeth grinned when both men looked at her with matching expressions of disbelief and then assumed an innocent expression, "What?"

"You cannot be serious," Darcy was the first to recover his voice. "It would be far too dangerous."

"I don't see why," Elizabeth pretended to argue. "It is much more precarious to sit sideways on a horse, you know. I have always wondered why they make women do it, when we are supposedly more likely to fall off anyway. It would make much more sense if we were allowed to ride astride."

Ellerslie, seeing that his friend was at a loss for words, smacked Darcy on the back.

"Don't worry, man, she is only teasing you."

"Mercilessly," Elizabeth agreed and laughed when her husband heaved a sigh of relief, "Don't worry, William, I have no intention of doing anything quite so...wild."

"Thank goodness for that!" Ellerslie laughed. "I think poor Darcy here was about to have an apoplexy at the thought!"

"Yet another reason I would never attempt it," Elizabeth replied, smiling at her husband who finally recovered his voice.

"Should I be concerned that my concern for your welfare outweighs your own?" he asked and Elizabeth laughed lightly.

"Not at all - for your feelings carry so much weight with me that I shall never forget to take care of myself."

"There is some consolation in that, I suppose," Darcy replied quietly with a soft smile and Ellerslie rolled his eyes.

"I am feeling superfluous, yet again," he pointedly stated. "So I shall take me leave. Elizabeth, it was lovely seeing you. Marriage obviously agrees with you. I hope it is not too long before I have the pleasure of your company once more. And Darcy - you lucky sod. Try not to look quite so smug, please."

"I can't help it," Darcy joked and the two friends shared a laugh before Ellerslie departed.

After Ellerslie had gone a few more friends stopped by to share a few words but the interval was soon at an end. Once again Elizabeth was lost in the music and the story, and Darcy sat back and watched her, feeling exactly as Ellerslie had said - rather pleased with himself. Soon though, as he gazed at his wife, his eyes slowly taking in each of her features, with the powerful music and lyrics washing over him, his thoughts began to turn in another direction. He watched her now as a man watches his lover, seeing the rise and fall of her chest with each delicate breath, watching her wet her full lips with the tip of her tongue, staring at the blush appearing on her cheek as, perhaps, she felt the heat of his gaze. He had never felt such passion for a woman as he did for Elizabeth, and the nights they had shared since their marriage had only served to increase his desire for her. He wished they were away from this place, at home in his bed, loving one another until the early hours of the morning.

Elizabeth happened to look over at him just as this thought was passing through his mind, and the way he was looking at her brought a further blush to her cheeks; less than a week of marriage had taught her much about her husband's looks, and she recognised this one well. Taking advantage of the low lighting, Darcy leant forward and captured her lips in a slow, sensuous kiss, hot and open-mouthed.

"Come away with me," he coaxed when he pulled away and Elizabeth's eyes slowly opened.

"But, the opera..." she protested weakly.

"Please," Darcy pressed inexorably, "Let me take you home and make love to you."

Elizabeth did not reply, she simply stood up and allowed her husband to quietly lead her from their box, so focused on him that she did not notice the whispers and stares which accompanied their departure. As they quickly descended the stairs to the main lobby she did her best to ignore the few attendants they passed, though she only felt comfortable when she was safely inside the carriage. And then her husband wrapped her in his arms and she cared for nothing and no one else.

Atop the carriage, John the coachman glared as his counterpart elbowed him in the ribs and chuckled suggestively.

"Me thinks His Grace prefers more intimate forms of entertainment."

John shook his head, muttering angrily under his breath at the other man's disrespect and whipping the horses with a little more force than he'd intended. The carriage pulled off with a sudden jolt, almost upsetting the other coachman and earning John a sharp reprimand from inside the carriage.

"Sorry, Sir," John called and then hissed angrily at the man next to him, "Now see what you made me do!"

"Don't seem to have bothered 'em too much," his companion observed with a grin as the sound of feminine laughter reached them.

"Idiot," John muttered and hunkered down for the journey home.

೮つび

Darcy woke with a start, instantly alert. Elizabeth was still sleeping peacefully beside him and their chamber, cloaked in darkness, was still and silent; something, though, had woken him and Darcy gently extracted himself from his wife's arms. He sat up, listening intently, and heard a faint but unmistakable knock at the hallway door. Slipping out of bed and throwing on the robe he had earlier discarded, Darcy crossed quietly to the door and stepped out into the hallway where he was met by a footman holding a candlestick aloft.

"What is it?" Darcy asked in a whisper, conscious of his still sleeping wife.

"Forgive me for disturbing you, Sir," the footman replied, "But the Duke of Bellamy is here and urgently requests your help."

"Ellerslie is here?" Darcy repeated with a frown and a sense of foreboding - he knew that his friend would not have appeared at such an hour without a very good reason. "Tell him I will be down in five minutes."

The footman nodded and hurried away as Darcy turned and re-entered the bedroom; Elizabeth was sat up in bed, clutching the sheet in one hand to cover her nakedness.

"What is it?"

"Ellerslie is here," Darcy replied, "I do not know why, but he needs my help. I will return when I can," he promised as he bent to swiftly kiss her before striding away and disappearing through the connecting door.

Elizabeth wanted to call him back, but she did not wish to needlessly delay him when the situation seemed so serious. Instead she climbed out of bed, wrapped herself in a dressing gown and went to the window to look down into the street; a carriage was waiting in front of the house, the horses pawing the ground impatiently, steam rising off their backs in the cold night air. Feeling a shiver run through her as the cold from outside seeped into the room, Elizabeth stepped back, allowing the curtain to fall back into place and plunging the room into darkness once more. She jumped when her husband, appearing once more obviously hurriedly dressed, addressed her.

"You should try and go back to sleep Elizabeth - it is not even dawn yet."

Elizabeth shook her head.

"I will wait for you. Please be careful," she added, unable to help herself; she was unaccountably anxious. Darcy quickly crossed to her and gathered her up in his arms.

"I will be fine," he promised and with one final kiss was gone.

Darcy found his friend anxiously waiting in the front hall, pacing up and down. He looked up when he heard Darcy on the stairs.

"Thank God!"

"Matthew," Darcy addressed his friend without preamble, "What has happened?"

"It is my son," Ellerslie admitted shakily. "My damned son."

"Is he hurt?" Darcy demanded. "What of him?"

"No, he is not hurt, but he will be dead before the morning if you do not help me William. There is not a moment to be lost," Ellerslie replied urgently and Darcy grasped his arm.

"Then tell me the rest on the way."

The two friends quickly left the house and climbed into Ellerslie's waiting carriage, which sped away as soon as the door was closed behind them. Ellerslie began his explanation as they streaked through the darkened streets of London.

"There is to be a duel. Frank - he was drunk as always - and he attempted...he tried to force himself on a married woman."

Even in the dark of the carriage Darcy's thoughts must have shown because Ellerslie groaned and covered his face with one hand.

"I know, I know. I cannot believe it either. Drunkenness and gambling and whoring are one thing - but to impose himself on a respectable woman? A gentlewoman...I can hardly bear to think of it."

"Who was the woman?" Darcy asked quietly and Ellerslie reluctantly looked at him.

"You know her," he admitted. "It was Hadlee's wife."

"Hadlee!" Darcy exclaimed with a combination of dismay and anger. "John Hadlee? Then your son attempted to...to...he attacked Claire Hadlee?"

Ellerslie could only nod and there were several moments of tense silence; Darcy had known John Hadlee since the younger man had been born and their estates bordered one another at home in Derbyshire. He knew Claire quite well also, and could not believe that Frank Ellerslie had attempted to do something so awful to such a woman.

"What happened?" he asked at last, trying to master his anger. "And how can I help?"

"I do not know the full story of what occurred," Ellerslie confessed. "It was not witnessed, and I only learnt that there was to be a duel when one of Frank's friends found me at the club. From what I have gathered, though, Hadlee was the one to rescue his wife, he issued the challenge and I have no doubt he intends to kill Frank in this duel."

*It would serve him right*, was Darcy's initial dark thought but reason quickly returned.

"Have you spoken to Frank? And to Hadlee? Or his second?"

"Only his second," Ellerslie replied. "And he made it very clear that Hadlee had no desire to speak to me and was not to be persuaded to abandon the duel. I haven't been able to find Frank," he concluded with a heavy sigh. "He is hiding somewhere in one of his haunts, no doubt drinking even more to bolster his courage."

Darcy shook his head.

"Matthew."

"I know, I know," his friend replied brokenly. "I cannot, I am so ashamed that my son, *my heir*, could do such a thing. I am of half a mind to let Hadlee kill him," Ellerslie admitted quietly. "But he is still my son. I can't sit by and let my boy be killed."

"Do you want me to try and talk to Hadlee?" Darcy asked, having guessed his friend's intentions; when Ellerslie nodded he said, "I will do my best to convince him not to kill Frank - though I stand by his right to shoot Frank for what he did to Claire."

Ellerslie nodded again.

"I know, it is the least that Frank deserves."

Darcy sighed heavily and turned to look out of the window, away from his friend. He prayed that he could convince John Hadlee to spare Frank, though he knew that were he in John's place and someone had attacked Elizabeth, he would not be inclined to show mercy.

When their carriage eventually reached the appointed place of the duel, the sun lightening the early morning sky, they found both parties already assembled and Dr Marshall, Ellerslie's personal physician, hovering away to the side, there in case he was needed.

Whilst Ellerslie went straight over to his son (whom he found to be as drunk as he had expected), Darcy jogged to his other friend.

"Hadlee!" He called as he neared him; Hadlee looked up with surprise.

"Farleigh! What the devil are you doing here?!"

"Bellamy," Darcy replied, "He asked me to come."

"And what does he expect you to do?" Hadlee asked angrily. "Here to persuade me to not to kill his worthless son?"

"Yes," Darcy replied quietly, calmly, hoping not to further fuel his friend's justifiable anger.

"He would deserve it," Hadlee spat. "Did Bellamy tell you what his son did to my wife? What he tried to do to Claire?"

"Yes," Darcy replied again, in the same tone. "I am sorry."

"I don't want your sympathy," Hadlee burst out. "Your sympathy won't console my wife! It won't blot out the memory of what he tried to do, or heal the bruises on her face." Seeing Darcy's shocked expression Hadlee smiled darkly. "Oh, did Bellamy not mention that his son struck Claire as well? She resisted him, and when I found them he was just raising his hand to strike her again..."

Darcy closed his eyes with sincere remorse.

"How is she?"

His obvious concern seemed to penetrate through Hadlee's anger and Darcy watched as the younger man's shoulders slumped.

"She is hurt, Farleigh. She, I..."

"I am so sorry John," Darcy said, reaching out and laying a hand on Hadlee's shoulder. "I wish to God none of this had happened."

Hadlee nodded and took a few moments to compose himself; when he spoke again his tone was cold and determined, but he was no longer quite as angry.

"He deserves to suffer for what he did, Farleigh."

"I know," Darcy replied. "And I do not dispute your right to punish him, John - God knows I would do the same were I in your position - but you mustn't kill him."

Hadlee opened his mouth to protest but Darcy was too quick for him.

"Think about it, John. Duelling is illegal, and you could not murder the Marquess and expect to go unpunished. You could go to prison, John, or be hanged, and what would become of Claire and your daughter then? You need to think about them, rather than just your desire for revenge."

Hadlee sighed and looked across at Frank, who was arguing loudly with his father, and then down at the gun in his hand. He was quiet for a long time, obviously thinking hard, and when he finally spoke Darcy let out a relieved sigh.

"I won't kill him, I give you my word."

"It is the right thing to do," Darcy said, pressing the younger man's shoulder once more and then looking across the field to where the others stood.

The next few moments seemed to pass by in a blur. Darcy saw Frank arguing with his father and carelessly waving his gun around; then he heard the loud report and saw the accompanying puff of smoke. He felt the impact of the bullet and the ensuing pain it caused; then he was on the floor, the dampness from the grass soaking into his back as his warm blood seeped into his clothes. And then Hadlee was leaning over him, calling for help.

∞CB

Knowing she would be unable to sleep even if she tried, and determined to wait for her husband's return, Elizabeth did not go back to bed and instead sat beside the fire in her room, wrapped up in a warm dressing gown. Disturbed by all the commotion in the house Wilson soon appeared, fully dressed and looking alert.

"What is going on?" she asked, when she found Elizabeth sat alone. "What is all the noise? Where is the Duke?"

Elizabeth explained the situation as best as she was able, but this did not satisfy her maid.

"But where has he gone, and why? What reason has he for dashing off in the middle of the night?"

"It is not the middle of the night," Elizabeth, for some reason, pointed out. "It is dawn already."

She and Wilson shared a look as comprehension dawned.

"No, surely," Elizabeth breathed. "Ellerslie would never fight a duel, surely?"

"Men are often fools," Wilson replied unhelpfully. "And I daresay the Duke - your Duke - would be a good choice of second."

Elizabeth paled at the thought and then shook her head.

"No, there has to be another explanation."

"Well *someone* is duelling," Wilson stated. "And somehow your husband is involved. Let us hope he has sense enough to stay out of the firing line."

"Wilson, stop, please," Elizabeth pleaded and seeing that she was really distressed Wilson hurried over to her.

"Oh, petal, don't you worry. Your husband knows how to look after himself, I'll wager. He'll be home again before you know it, tired and wondering why you aren't keeping his bed warm for him."

Elizabeth managed a small smile at this.

"I couldn't try to sleep."

"Then can I get you anything?" Wilson asked kindly. "Some tea, maybe?"

When Elizabeth nodded Wilson went herself to prepare it and when she returned they sat down together to wait for William's return. When she finally heard the sound of a carriage Elizabeth leapt to her feet and rushed to the window.

She saw a carriage and horses and watched as a tall man with blonde hair jumped down, another man just behind him. They both turned back to the carriage and reached inside, assisting a third man with dark hair and skin as white as his shirt once was, now stained red with blood. Elizabeth had recognised her husband at once, but it took her mind a moment to register what she was seeing and she remained at the window, fixed with shock.

And then there was a bang from the front hall, the sounds of raised voices and running feet and Elizabeth had flown from the room before Wilson had a chance to stop her. Darcy, leaning heavily upon Hadlee and accompanied by Dr Marshall, looked up in time to see his wife fly along the corridor and rush down the stairs at a fearful pace.

"Lizzy be careful!" He called in a panicked voice, the thought of her falling frightening him. She checked her pace, barely, and was soon with him.

"You shouldn't take those stairs so quickly," he scolded her unthinkingly. "You could have fallen and broken your neck!"

"Well you shouldn't come home covered in blood and looking half dead!" His wife retorted tearfully and there was a stunned silence.

"Lizzy," Darcy softly spoke when he had recovered his voice. "I'm not, I'm fine."

"William," Elizabeth contradicted him, "you have been shot. You are not fine."

"Perhaps not at this very moment," Dr Marshall interrupted gently, "but he will be soon enough. Truly, Madam, there is no need to worry - your husband is in no danger. Though he is in a certain amount of pain," he added with a glance at his patient, "and has lost a fair bit of blood, so the sooner we get him upstairs to bed, the better."

Elizabeth immediately sprang out of the way as though she had been burnt and Darcy's heart clenched when he saw her expression; reaching out for her, ignoring her attempts to resist, he pulled her towards him with his good arm and kissed her in front of everyone.

"I am alright," he whispered so that only she could hear and was pleased when she nodded, looking calmer. She stepped aside and Hadlee and Dr Marshall helped him up the stairs, Elizabeth following behind them. Word of Darcy's injury had already spread throughout the house and Pattinson was waiting in his master's room, ready to assist as several maids appeared with towels and bowls of hot water and coals for the fire. Feeling useless and in the way, Elizabeth kept her distance, anxiously wringing her hands as she stood silently in one corner, watching the proceedings.

Hadlee helped Darcy onto the bed and Dr Marshall stepped forwards.

"Now, let's take a look at this wound. The bleeding should have lessened by now, so I will be able to stitch you up without too much trouble."

Darcy nodded and then caught sight of his wife hovering in the background; he looked at Hadlee.

"Would you look after Lizzy for me? I don't want her to see this - take her to her maid, she will know what to do."

Hadlee nodded and left Darcy in the doctor's capable hands; he walked over to Elizabeth and addressed her.

"Come, Your Grace, there is no need for you to watch."

"I am staying here," Elizabeth stated, quietly implacable. "I am not leaving my husband."

Hadlee hesitated and then agreed.

"Very well. Though please warn me if you are about to swoon so that I may catch you," he requested and Elizabeth quickly looked at him, amazed by his levity at such a time. "Your husband would be most displeased if I let you fall."

"I do not swoon," Elizabeth informed him, though her tone was friendlier than before. "So you needn't worry."

Hadlee nodded and then decided to introduce himself, for lack of anything else to say.

"My name is John, John Hadlee."

"Hello," Elizabeth replied distractedly. "My name is Elizabeth."

"Yes," Hadlee smiled. "Darcy told me. I'm so sorry about all this," he added suddenly, feeling guilty that his friend had been hurt trying to help him.

Elizabeth shook her head, her eyes on her husband.

"I'm sure it wasn't your fault."

"Actually, I think it was," Hadlee replied unthinkingly. "I can't be certain, but I think your husband saved my life. I think he pushed me out of the way, and took the bullet instead..."

Elizabeth suddenly burst into tears and hurried from the room, leaving a dismayed Hadlee staring after her. Hearing his wife's distress, Darcy attempted to rise from the bed but Dr Marshall restrained him with a sharp reminder that he needed to keep still.

"John!" Darcy barked angrily. "What did you do?"

Hadlee looked askance at him.

"Nothing! I don't know what I said that upset her so much!"

Darcy huffed in frustration just as Dr Marshall pronounced that he was almost done.

"Then get on with it," Darcy grumbled ill-temperedly, "So that I can see to my wife."

Hadlee and Dr Marshall shared a look before the latter went back to his work.

"What exactly did you say to my wife, John?" Darcy asked the younger man through gritted teeth, trying to ignore the pain in his shoulder.

Hadlee related the extent of his and Elizabeth's conversation and Darcy groaned.

"You realise you made it sound as though I dove in front of this bullet. How do you think my wife feels about that, considering we have been married less than a week?"

"Ah," Hadlee grimaced. "I see what you mean. Shall I go and explain?"

"I think you've done enough," Darcy stated wryly, shaking his head. "Perhaps you should go home to your own wife John, and leave me to worry about mine."

Hadlee did not need much persuasion to return home, but before he could leave Darcy called out to him.

"What are you going to do about Frank?"

Hadlee sighed.

"I think almost killing his father's best friend is punishment enough for what he did. I will let his father deal with him."

Darcy nodded.

"He is, I think, a very troubled young man."

Hadlee laughed unexpectedly, shaking his head.

"Farleigh, you are the only man I know who would feel sympathy for a man who had just shot you."

"It was an accident," Darcy asserted and though Hadlee looked sceptical he let it pass.

"I will call again this afternoon, to see how you fare," he promised but Darcy shook his head.

"Please don't - I just want to be with my wife."

"Very well," Hadlee agreed easily. "I am loathe to leave mine for long, if I am completely honest."

"I hope she is well again soon," Darcy expressed and the two friends shook hands before Hadlee finally took his leave.

Finishing his work a few minutes later, Dr Marshall straightened.

"There, done. Now you need to stay in bed..."

Darcy was already attempting to get to his feet and rather than argue the doctor helped him up.

"Will you at least lie down somewhere? Please" he asked and Darcy almost smiled.

"Yes, I will. Thank you for your help, Doctor."

"It was the least that I could do," Dr Marshall demurred before returning to business and giving Darcy his instructions for the next few days and weeks. When he was finished he quickly took his leave, sensing Darcy's desire to go and find his wife.

Darcy watched him go and then allowed Pattinson to help him wash away any traces of blood and change into a fresh set of clothes. This done, he went directly to the connecting door and entered Elizabeth's room. His wife was sat upon the bed, her maid speaking to her in soothing tones. Wilson looked up upon his arrival and with a face like a thunder cloud stood up and marched over to him, obviously intent on giving him a piece of her mind, Duke or not. Darcy, however, was in no mood to listen and abruptly dismissed her.

"That will be all, Wilson. *My wife* will call when she needs you."

The added emphasis did not go unnoticed and after a second of hesitation Wilson backed down, stepping aside and leaving the couple alone. Darcy approached the bed and gingerly sat down, gently laying a hand on his wife's shoulder. Her face was turned away from him but he could see that she had been crying and it pained him to know that he was the cause of her tears.

"Elizabeth?"

Elizabeth turned to look at him, at his heavily bandaged shoulder and his pale face and felt the onset of yet more tears.

"Please, Lizzy, don't cry," Darcy pleaded. "I am fine."

"You could have been killed," Elizabeth tearfully pointed out. "You could have died. How could you have been so foolish? What about James and Catherine? What would have happened to them if you had been killed? Did you consider them at all?"

Resenting the implication that he had been reckless and at fault, Darcy very nearly said something he would quickly come to regret. Reminding himself that she was just upset and afraid, that it was her love and concern for him that was making her react this way he took hold of Elizabeth's hand and gently requested that she let him explain what had happened that morning.

"But I don't understand," Elizabeth breathed when her husband had finished his explanation. "Did Frank mean to shoot or...?"

"I have no doubt in my mind that it was just an accident," Darcy asserted. "I remember him waving his gun around - he must have inadvertently pressed the trigger."

"And you did not push your friend out of the way," Elizabeth clarified and Darcy shook his head.

"Not that I remember. And I certainly did not intentionally put myself in harm's way," he added earnestly. "I would never do that, to you or the children."

"I know," Elizabeth replied quietly, biting her lip. She looked up at him and said, "I am sorry for what I said. You aren't at all foolish."

"It's alright," Darcy assured her tenderly. "I know why you said it. I'm sure I would have reacted in much the same way, had I thought that you had willingly placed yourself in danger. I am no hero, though, whatever John might think," he concluded with a wry smile.

"I am glad of it," Elizabeth asserted, tears springing once more to her eyes. "It would be of little comfort, had you been killed, to know you had died courageously. I would rather still have a husband, than only the memory of a brave one."

Darcy gathered her up in his good arm.

"Do not think of it. I am fine. I am so sorry for frightening you, but there is no danger now."

Elizabeth nodded and studied her husband's face; even in the dim light she could see how pale and tired he looked and gently pulled away.

"You should lie down - you need to rest."

"Only if you stay with me," Darcy replied as he nevertheless moved to lie down upon the bed, a heavy sigh escaping him.

"Of course I will stay," Elizabeth promised and she began helping him off with his boots.

"You don't have to," Darcy began but Elizabeth shushed him.

"I know. Now let me look after you."

She carelessly tossed aside each of his boots and then pulled the coverlet up and over him, climbing into bed and settling down on his good side.

"Are you comfortable?"

"Mmmmhmm," Darcy mumbled, his eyes already closed. A moment later he began to snore softly and Elizabeth smiled, watching him sleep. She was comforted by his deep, steady breathing and the strong beating of his heart beneath her palm, but it was still a long time before she was able to finally drift off to sleep.

# Chapter 16

The pain in his shoulder eventually woke Darcy, and he stifled a groan when he tried to move his arm. Elizabeth was asleep beside him and he took his mind off the pain by focusing on her, smiling weakly at the hold she had on him, which was at the same time both gentle and firm. Obviously she was conscious of hurting him even in her sleep, but unwilling to completely let go.

Sighing heavily, Darcy admitted to himself that though he had played down her fears for his life, in the first few moments after he had been shot he had entertained the same thoughts. Lying on the damp grass, confronted with his own mortality, he had felt frightened and vulnerable - hardly the hero Hadlee had made him out to be. He shuddered at the thought of what his death would have meant for Elizabeth and his children and was not aware of how tightly he was clutching his wife until she suddenly woke.

"What is it, what's wrong?"

Relaxing his hold, Darcy forced a smile onto his face as Elizabeth looked up at him.

"Nothing - everything is fine. Go back to sleep."

"How do you feel?" Elizabeth asked, ignoring his instructions.

"Sore," he admitted. "But stronger."

"You should have something to eat," Elizabeth began, sitting up. "What time is it? I suppose it is still early but I can easily have,"

"Elizabeth," Darcy quietly interrupted her and she looked down at him. "I want - can we not just lie here together for a little longer? I want to hold you."

Elizabeth, whether he wanted her to or not, saw the vulnerability in his eyes and lay back down beside her husband.

"Of course, there is plenty of time for breakfast yet."

"All the time in the world," Darcy sighed and even though the events of that morning suggested otherwise, he still found comfort in the thought.

⊱⊰

Glancing up at her husband and seeing that he was still asleep, Elizabeth gently slipped out of his hold and climbed out of bed, successfully managing to extricate herself without waking him. It was still only late morning and Elizabeth knew that rest would help her husband regain his strength - she left him to sleep in peace, promising herself that she would return to him soon. Quietly going to her dressing room, she found Wilson silently working on one of her dresses, which she laid aside on Elizabeth's appearance.

"How is he?" she asked quietly.

"He is still sleeping. I will leave him for another hour or so, and then I will see that he has something to eat."

"You look tired," Wilson observed, noting the dark circles under Elizabeth's eyes. "Perhaps you should,"

Elizabeth quickly dismissed her concerns.

"I am fine. I need to speak with Mrs Dawson and Pattinson too. And I shall have to write to Mrs Carey as well. We will not be travelling to Longbourn today."

"Why don't you have some breakfast first, and then," Wilson began but once again Elizabeth cut her off.

"No, I will eat with William. I shall not bathe now, but if you could have some water fetched I will have a quick wash. And I think the blue muslin with the long sleeves will do for today."

Wilson quickly did as she was bid and Elizabeth went through to her husband's room. The bed had been changed and all sights of the earlier commotion cleared away; she found Pattinson quietly occupying himself with some piece of his master's wardrobe, though he quickly set it aside when he saw Elizabeth.

"Is His Grace awake? Does he require my assistance?"

"No, he is still sleeping. I only came to ask if the doctor left you with any instructions for my husband's care. Any medications for him to take?"

"Only laudanum,' Pattinson replied. "Should the pain become too much. And I believe Dr Marshall gave His Grace instructions for his own care."

Elizabeth sighed.

"Of course. Let us hope my husband is sensible enough to follow them, then."

Pattinson refrained from commenting, but inwardly he thought that his new mistress already knew her husband well.

"I am relying on you to help me with this, Pattinson," Elizabeth went on. "I am sure my husband will try to play down his injury, and I do not want him to hinder his recovery by attempting to do too much too soon."

"Of course, Ma'am," Pattinson assured her. "I will do all I can to aid my master."

"I never doubted it," Elizabeth replied confidently and left Pattinson to appreciate the compliment as she returned to her dressing room.

When she had washed and dressed and Wilson had secured her hair in a tidy, sensible chignon, Elizabeth went in search of the housekeeper, leaving her maid quietly impressed by her poise and composure. She did not blame Elizabeth for her earlier tears - how else was a new bride to react in such a situation? Still, she was pleased to see how well Elizabeth was handling her role as mistress of the household, and wife of an injured man.

Elizabeth found Mrs Dawson in her room and the elder lady quickly got to her feet.

"Madam! How is His Grace?"

"He is still sleeping," Elizabeth replied. "Though I plan to wake him soon. When I do, I would like some breakfast to be served in the sitting room adjoining my chambers. Nothing too fancy, just something to help him build up his strength. And the morning paper, if that could be sent up too, I'm sure he would like to read it."

"Of course," Mrs Dawson readily replied. "I will inform the kitchen at once."

"Thank you. We shall require meals for this afternoon and evening as well," Elizabeth went on. "We shall not be travelling to Longbourn today."

"And tomorrow?" Mrs Dawson asked and Elizabeth hesitated for a moment before replying.

"I will consult with my husband first before deciding, though I think it advisable for us to spend another day here before attempting such a journey. Perhaps you could tell the kitchen to be prepared for us to continue our stay here for at least another day."

Mrs Dawson nodded and Elizabeth smiled.

"I knew I could rely on your efficiency, Mrs Dawson. Now if you excuse me, I must write to Longbourn and inform them of our change of plans. Oh," she added, remembering one final detail, "And if anyone comes to call, please tell them we are not at home. Unless it is family," she amended, "or a particular friend."

"Of course," Mrs Dawson replied again and watched Elizabeth go, quite favourably impressed by her new mistress.

Once Elizabeth had written her letter to Mrs Carey and seen it sent, she returned upstairs to her husband, entering her bedroom to find him awake and propped up against the pillows.

"Where have you been?"

"Seeing to your breakfast," Elizabeth replied as she sat down beside him. She leant closer and pressed a brief kiss to his lips, smiling as she pulled away and commented, "You need a shave, my darling."

"I must look a state," Darcy agreed, rubbing his jaw and running a hand through his hair. "A bath is in order as well, I think."

"Hmm," Elizabeth hummed her agreement and Darcy chuckled.

"Is that your delicate way of saying that I smell?"

"You do not smell quite as charming as usual, no," Elizabeth teased lightly.

"Oh, and how do I usually smell?"

"Manly," Elizabeth replied with playful exaggeration. "Like leather and horse and tobacco - very manly."

"You are not allowed to mock me," Darcy informed her with a grin. "I am hurt."

"You also smell and look awful," Elizabeth quipped, "So I shall mock you if I like."

"Humph, some wife you are," Darcy complained playfully and Elizabeth just laughed, pleased that the colour had returned to his face and that he no longer had that weakened look about him.

"You mentioned breakfast, I think," Darcy said as his stomach reminded him that it was many hours since he'd last eaten.

"Yes, I will ring for it now," Elizabeth said, rising. "And I will speak to Pattinson about getting your bath ready."

She turned when Darcy called her back, smiling when he grasped her wrist and tugged her back down next to him, cupping the back of her head with his hand and pulling her close for a deep kiss.

"I love you, wife," he told her when they finally separated.

"And I love you, husband," Elizabeth replied fondly, adding when she stood up, "But if you ever get yourself shot again I will not be happy with you."

"I will keep that in mind," Darcy promised, chuckling.

"Please do," his wife replied over her shoulder before disappearing through the connecting door.

℘℘℘

Elizabeth looked up when her husband entered the small sitting room where they had eaten breakfast, freshly shaven, bathed and dressing in his usual clothes. The only indication of his injury was the sling which supported his arm, and Elizabeth was delighted to see him looking so much his normal self. Tears sprang to her eyes as she got up to meet him and her husband saw them.

"What, surely I do not look so bad?"

Elizabeth smiled and wiped her eyes.

"No, I am just so pleased to see you looking well again."

"I shall be back to my normal self in a few days," Darcy assured her, surprised when she frowned in response.

"Please don't overdo," she worried.

"I won't. I must say I like having you look after me this way," he added lightly and Elizabeth smiled in spite of herself.

"I have been thinking, William, and unless you have any objections I think we should travel directly to Pemberley and leave our visit to Longbourn for another time."

Darcy was surprised by her decision and it showed.

"But I thought you wished to say goodbye, and to check that everything is in order there?"

"I did," Elizabeth replied. "I still do, but I can wait, and a letter to Mr Nichols I am sure will satisfy me as to the running of the place. I just think it would be better if we went straight to Pemberley," she concluded, reaching across and taking his hand. "For you."

Darcy shook his head.

"There is no need to alter our plans - I am fine. Visiting Longbourn will hardly tax my strength, after all, and I know how much you wished to go there."

"And I know," Elizabeth quietly replied, "that after what happened this morning you must wish to be at home with your children."

Darcy opened his mouth to argue, but slowly closed it again, unable to deny that the desire to see James and Catherine - to hold them - had been at the forefront of his mind since he had woken up. He looked at his wife, who was watching him with a tender look, and wondered how she had learnt to understand him so completely.

"Longbourn can wait," Elizabeth softly stated. "Let us go home."

"Thank you," he replied but Elizabeth waved away his words.

"There is no need to thank me - you always try to do what is best and right for everyone else; I am simply returning the favour."

Her husband looked a little self-conscious at this reflection and Elizabeth smiled inwardly before moving their conversation along.

"Well, now that that is decided I must write to Mrs Carey again to tell her we will not be coming after all. I am only glad my father was not aware of our intention to visit - this last minute change of plans would have unsettled him tremendously."

"When you wrote to Mrs Carey earlier," Darcy queried, "what did you tell her had happened?"

"Only that you had had an accident," Elizabeth replied and Darcy nodded approvingly. "I know that it is best to keep this entire episode quiet."

"Best for all parties involved," Darcy agreed thoughtfully, wondering what had become of Ellerslie and Frank. His friend, after ascertaining that Darcy was not badly wounded, had been quick to collar his son and whisk him away from the place, though what had been said and done after they had departed still remained a mystery.

Elizabeth broke into his musings.

"I told Mrs Dawson that I would discuss our travel plans with you first, but that I did think it probable we would still be here tomorrow."

"It should not be a problem to have everything packed and ready to leave in the morning; I will write ahead to the inns I had arranged for us to stay at, informing them of the change of plans."

"Tomorrow?" Elizabeth repeated. "Are you sure? Shouldn't we wait at least a day so that you have time to recover a little more before attempting such a journey?"

"Sitting in a carriage does not require much energy, my dear," Darcy pointed out. "And if we take it slowly my shoulder will not be jolted over much."

"Well, if you are sure..." It was obvious Elizabeth was not convinced and, smiling tenderly, Darcy pressed her hand and suggested a compromise.

"But I can see you are not happy with that arrangement; perhaps if we stayed another night on the road, would that satisfy you?"

Elizabeth thought for a moment and then nodded.

"Yes, I think that would be best."

"Very well," Darcy replied. "I will make the arrangements. It will mean three nights spent at inns, though," he thought to point out, thinking of his wife's comfort.

Elizabeth's mind, however, was on *other* things when she replied with a slight blush.

"I do not mind - until your shoulder is better we cannot be intimate together, anyway."

Darcy chuckled.

"Whether you would be comfortable spending so many nights in such a way was more my concern, darling."

"Oh." Elizabeth blushed and distractedly picked up her tea. She took a sip, not realising that it was cold until too late.

Her husband smiled at her expression of distaste.

"Is something wrong, dear?"

"Nothing at all," Elizabeth lied, determined not to let him fluster her any more than he already had. "Now if you will excuse me, I have some letters I need to write. I will be in my study if you need me."

Darcy turned in his seat and watched his wife sweep from the room with a dignified air, chuckling to himself. He so enjoyed ruffling her feathers.

ᏭᏅᏓ

Later that afternoon, Darcy was not wholly surprised when a footman appeared and announced that he and Elizabeth had a visitor.

"His Grace, the Duke of Bellamy requests to see you, Sir, and Madam."

The couple looked at each other and after a moment Darcy responded.

"Please see him to the library and tell him we will join him in a moment."

The footman nodded and disappeared and Elizabeth addressed her husband, "He is here to ascertain your welfare, I suppose."

"I daresay he already knows I am fine," Darcy replied. "Dr Marshall is his personal physician."

Something in his tone made Elizabeth question him.

"Do you not wish to see him?"

Darcy sighed and passed a hand over his brow, looking tired.

"I do not know. I did not think I felt any ill will towards him, but as soon as I heard his name announced I felt angry, and resentful."

"Perhaps it would be best if you did not see him," Elizabeth suggested but Darcy shook his head.

"No, no, I must. He is my oldest friend, and I cannot imagine how *he* is feeling at this moment. He will blame himself."

"I will come with you," Elizabeth stated and at his nod she and her husband went to the library together.

They found Ellerslie stood at one of the windows, looking almost physically oppressed by all of his worries and cares. He turned when they entered and his expression was one of mingled relief and shame.

"Can you ever forgive me, William?" he asked, and Darcy approached him with no anger.

"It was an accident Matthew," he stated. "There is nothing to forgive. You were trying to save your son - there is no shame in that."

"I should never have involved you," Ellerslie countered, shaking his head. "Not with two young children and a new wife at home. I should have let you be, and none of this would have happened."

"No, but Frank would likely be dead and Hadlee on his way to prison," Darcy pointed out bluntly. "The lives of two men would have needlessly been ruined - I think this is the much better outcome, don't you?"

Ellerslie sighed heavily as Darcy's arguments began to sink in; Elizabeth stepped forward and gently laid a hand on his arm.

"It was not your fault. And no one was seriously hurt."

Ellerslie looked at his friend.

"Your shoulder, Marshall said it was not bad?"

"No, not bad," Darcy assured him and Ellerslie sighed yet again.

"What of Frank?" Darcy asked quietly after a moment and Ellerslie's face hardened.

"I have made my decision regarding his fate, and only time will tell if I can correct the mistakes I have made with him."

"What are you going to do?" Darcy asked with a sense of alarm.

"I have holdings in Antigua which have long been in need of my attention; Frank and I sail in six weeks."

"Antigua!" Darcy exclaimed. "Surely you go too far. The journey alone will take you several months."

"Yes, I know. I do not intend for us to return for at least a year, perhaps two."

"But what of your other children?" Darcy asked. "What of Lawrence and Sarah? Who will take care of them?"

"Lawrence is at school and Sarah has a good governess - they do not need me," Ellerslie replied and Darcy shook his head.

"And your estates? Who are you leaving to manage them?"

"I have good stewards in place at all of my estates - I trust them to continue to work well in my absence."

"I cannot believe you would abandon all your responsibilities - your family, your property - to the care of strangers, Matthew!" Darcy objected strongly.

"Frank is my responsibility too," Ellerslie retorted heatedly and Elizabeth had the impression that he had already had this argument with someone else. "And I have failed him terribly. He attacked an innocent woman, Darcy, and he could have killed you! What does it matter if a few of my estates suffer whilst I am gone, if it means I can right what is wrong with my son?"

"Is there anything we can do?" Elizabeth asked firmly before her husband could reply and likely say something he would later regret. Both men looked surprised at the interruption. "Lawrence and James are friends; perhaps we could have him to stay during his breaks from school? And Catherine and Sarah, are they not of similar ages?"

Ellerslie pressed her hand in thanks as Darcy looked at his wife with open admiration, impressed with her handling of the situation. He turned to look at his friend and realised that Ellerslie had made his decision, and needed his support.

"Elizabeth is right. Ask anything," Darcy told his friend. "We will do whatever we can to help you."

"Thank you," Ellerslie sighed, almost overcome with emotion. They discreetly looked away as he composed himself. "I am leaving the care of Lawrence and Sarah in my wife's hands, but I am sure that having them to stay with you can easily be arranged. And I am confident that my stewards will manage well without me, but it would ease my mind to know that, if they needed to, they could come to you for help and advice Darcy."

"Of course," Darcy gave his assurance. "I will keep half an eye on things for you whilst you are gone."

Ellerslie offered his thanks, and seemed to want to say more but glanced at Elizabeth before falling silent; sensing his desire to speak to her husband without her present, Elizabeth excused herself on some pretext and left the two men alone.

"What is it?" Darcy asked when it was just the two of them.

"I do not know what to do about Jacqueline," Ellerslie admitted with a heavy sigh. "I can hardly take her with me, but then I hardly trust her to remain here alone. I highly doubt she would remain faithful to me once I am gone, and I do not wish to return home a laughingstock, or worse, to find her in difficulties."

"I do not know what I can do..." Darcy began uncomfortably, aware that despite their many years of friendship his generosity only stretched so far; and certainly not far enough to accept the burden of Ellerslie's wife.

"I am only looking for suggestions," Ellerslie assured him and Darcy breathed a sigh of relief.

"Why do you not just invite her mother to live at Collerton for the duration of your absence?" Darcy asked and Ellerslie smacked him on the shoulder.

"That's it! Darcy, you are a genius. She can help look after the children *and* keep her daughter in check - why did I not think of that?"

"Likely because you have not slept since the night before last," Darcy pointed out calmly and Ellerslie sobered instantly.

"I am very tired," he admitted and Darcy thought he looked it.

"Go home. Sleep. And then be with your family - if you are truly set upon this plan then these six weeks will be the last you have with them for some time."

Ellerslie nodded and then, after a moment of indecision, looked up at Darcy.

"If I die..."

"I will take care of everything, you have my word," Darcy vowed before adding, "But you had better *not* die; I have a lovely new wife to occupy myself with, in case you'd forgotten."

Ellerslie chuckled.

"Forgive me. I must be interrupting your honeymoon."

"You are," Darcy flatly replied and Ellerslie laughed outright.

"I take it it is safe for me to return now," Elizabeth said from the doorway, stepping into the room when her husband beckoned to her. "What amuses you so much?"

"We were discussing why my death would be of great inconvenience to your husband," Ellerslie flippantly replied before Darcy could and Elizabeth's eyes widened.

"Indeed? And that is funny?"

"He is extremely sleep deprived, my love," Darcy responded, rolling his eyes at Ellerslie. "Anything is funny to him in such a state."

"Yes, I was just about to go home and go to bed," Ellerslie stated, turning and bowing to Elizabeth. All trace of amusement was gone as he said to her, "I am so sorry for leading your husband into harm's way."

"Apology accepted," Elizabeth softly replied. "On one condition."

"Oh?" Ellerslie queried with a slight smile.

"You mustn't leave before seeing us again," Elizabeth told him. "I will never forgive you otherwise."

"Well, I cannot have that," Ellerslie quietly stated and then turned to look at his friend. "I quite envy you, you know."

"I do," Darcy averred and Ellerslie smiled enigmatically before taking his leave of them both and following a footman from the room.

"Do you think we *will* see him again?" Elizabeth asked worriedly when he was gone and Darcy was quick to assure her.

"Of course, if only because I know he would not break a promise to you."

"What did he mean, when he said he envied you, William?" Elizabeth asked, looking up at him, and Darcy smiled sadly.

"I am happily, very happily married, to a wonderful woman. He is not. That is what he meant."

"I hope nothing happens to him, or his son," Elizabeth expressed quietly. "I think he is such a nice man."

"He certainly deserves a better hand than has been dealt him," Darcy agreed and just because he felt like he needed to, he drew his wife into his arms. "He always said that I had all the luck."

Elizabeth wondered what was lucky about having to endure years of loveless marriage and then being widowed with two young children to raise, but she kept that thought to herself.

ℰℭ

Elizabeth reached out a hand and gently stilled the nervous bouncing of her husband's leg as they sat beside one another on their way to the Fitzwilliams' estate to collect James and Catherine. Smiling ruefully, Darcy sighed and adjusted his position, relaxing further into the cushions of the carriage.

"I'm worried," he admitted quietly. "They will be upset - Catherine especially, when she sees the sling, but James will notice that I am in pain and trying not to show it."

"Perhaps you should tell him what really happened," Elizabeth suggested lightly. "He is old enough to know, I think."

Her husband had written to his sister to inform her of his injury before they left town, but had requested that James and Catherine be told only that he had taken a fall and hurt his shoulder.

Darcy hesitated a moment before shaking his head.

"No, I don't think so. I do agree that he is old enough to know," he explained, lest Elizabeth think he had not given her suggestion any thought. "But I do not want him to think about what could have happened; I would spare him that, at least."

"Very well," Elizabeth agreed and they lapsed into a thoughtful silence.

"I hope Georgiana was careful when she told them what I asked," Darcy expressed after a few moments, his brow creased with worry. "I wish I knew how they reacted. I do not like to lie to them, but it is surely better this way."

"Of course it is," Elizabeth assured him kindly - she had very quickly recognised that her husband was not going to be at ease until he had seen his children and was doing everything she could to support him and alleviate his worry. "And I am sure Georgiana would have been very careful, if only to avoid upsetting them."

"But if *she* were upset about it, then perhaps they would have been able to tell."

"William," Elizabeth interrupted him patiently. "All will be well - trust me."

"I'm sorry," Darcy sighed again, shaking his head. "I am being ridiculous. You must think me a fool. I *am* a fool."

"No you are not," Elizabeth contradicted him a trifle sharply; Darcy looked at her with surprise as she went on, "You are demonstrating, yet again, how much you love your children. I think that is admirable, not foolish, and if you imagine otherwise, even for a moment - well, then, you *are* a fool."

"I stand corrected," Darcy quietly responded and Elizabeth flushed slightly at her outburst.

"I'm sorry," she apologised after a moment. "I just, I do not see how loving your children can be wrong. I have lived with the alternative, and it is horrible."

"*I* am sorry," Darcy stated as he put his arm around her shoulders and drew her to his side. "I did not mean to upset you."

"I upset myself," Elizabeth sighed, but she was still happy to lean into his good side and rest her head on his shoulder.

"After today," Darcy confidently asserted, "things will start to go back to normal. James and Catherine will be home, my shoulder will heal and - what?"

Elizabeth looked up, chuckling softly.

"Normal? Have you forgotten you have a wife now, my love? Personally, I foresee life from today continuing very different."

"Good point," Darcy responded with a grin and Elizabeth was pleased to see him smile.

When they reached the Fitzwilliams' estate, Darcy flung open the carriage door and jumped down before the equipage had even come to a stop. He caught his daughter as she flew down the steps and launched herself into his arms, ignoring her aunt's sharp call to be careful of his arm.

"Oh Papa, I missed you so much, I was so worried about you," Catherine said into his neck as Darcy held her with his good arm.

"It's alright princess, Papa is fine, just a little bruised," Darcy assured her calmly, looking down over his daughter's shoulder at his son.

James hovered worriedly at a slight distance and Darcy nodded and sent him a reassuring smile, disappointed when his son did not return it. Fortunately at that moment Elizabeth appeared at his side and added her own easy reassurances.

"Indeed, it was just a silly tumble - and entirely my fault. I slipped you see, and your father lost his footing whilst trying to help me keep mine. Wasn't that very gallant of him?" she concluded with a bright smile, looking at Catherine.

"Yes it was," Catherine agreed and kissed her father's cheek. "Well done you, Papa."

"Thank you, dear," Darcy replied with a grin and even James cracked a smile at his tone.

"Princess, I'm sorry," Darcy noted regretfully a moment later, "but I'm going to have to put you down."

"That's alright," Catherine replied lightly as he set her on the ground. "I am a little too old, I suppose, now that I am very nearly nine."

"Very, very nearly," Elizabeth put in playfully. "Only a few days left now!"

Catherine smiled and then moved to wrap her arms around Elizabeth's waist.

"I didn't say hello to you, Lizzy, I'm sorry."

"That's perfectly alright, princess," Elizabeth replied and bent to kiss the top of the little girl's head.

As Elizabeth and Catherine spoke to one another, Darcy approached his son, surprised when James suddenly hugged him fiercely. Feeling his heart clench painfully, Darcy returned the gesture.

"I am well, Son, truly."

"I know what really happened," James admitted in a quiet voice and Darcy couldn't help tensing in reaction. "I saw your letter. Aunt Georgiana was upset, and I knew she and Uncle Richard weren't telling us something, so, so I found the letter and read it. I know I shouldn't have, Father, but I had to know. I'm sorry."

Georgiana and Richard and their children were all approaching now and Darcy knew it was hardly the time for such a discussion; he gave his son a reassuring squeeze.

"It is alright. We will talk more later."

James nodded and they separated, Darcy pinning a smile on his face as he turned to be welcomed by the rest of their family and James taking a moment to compose himself. He looked up when Elizabeth quietly spoke from beside him.

"I promise he is quite well, James."

"I know," James nodded. "I can see that."

"I'm sorry we were not entirely honest with you," Elizabeth said seriously but James shook his head.

"It is alright, I understand. I am just glad he is well, and that you were with him."

Elizabeth smiled unexpectedly.

"I do not think I was much help at first, to be truthful - I was too busy shouting at him. I was not, impressed."

James' eyes widened and then he smiled; his smile became a laugh and soon the rest of the family were looking at him and Elizabeth and wondering what was so funny.

"Come, let us go inside," Georgiana said, taking her brother's good arm and leading him in, prepared to fuss over him for the duration of his stay.

If anyone was surprised by her failure to properly greet her new sister, no one said anything and Elizabeth was quite happy to accept Richard's arm and have him escort her into the house. Once settled into the parlour with cups of tea and cake, they all spent a happy hour listening to Elizabeth and Darcy speak of their time on the coast and all the things they had done there, before pressing Elizabeth to reveal her opinion of Pemberley, now that she had finally seen it.

"It is a truly beautiful place," she said with a smile of recollection. "The sun was just setting when we arrived, and the colours on the water were wonderful."

"Darcy took you on a tour of the house, I suppose," Richard commented but Elizabeth shook her head, sharing a smile with her husband.

"No, not yet. We thought we'd save that for when the children were home and they could join us."

"Speaking of," Darcy began, looking between James and Catherine. "Are you ready to go home?"

"Oh yes!" Catherine enthused and Richard laughed good-naturedly.

"And I thought you'd enjoyed yourself here with us, Miss Catherine."

"I have, Uncle Richard," Catherine replied, her eyes wide and innocent. "But I would still very much like to go home with Papa and Elizabeth and James."

"And Agatha," Elizabeth added and Richard guffawed.

"Oh yes, please! You must take her with you!"

"I hope she has not given you too much trouble," Darcy expressed with a slight frown but his cousin waved away his words with a grin.

"Oh no, not *too* much."

"Where is she?" Elizabeth asked.

"In the stables - it seemed the safest place for her."

"I see," Elizabeth noted, trying very hard not to smile.

"Well, if you are keen to be off, perhaps James and Catherine should go up and ensure that all their things have been packed," Georgiana suggested lightly. "Just in case - we wouldn't want you to leave anything behind, after all."

*Because it is such a distance between here and Pemberley*, Darcy thought with silent amusement but decided to bow to his sister's wishes, suspecting that she was only sending the children away so that she could speak properly to him.

James and Catherine promptly did as they were bid and left the room accompanied by their two cousins; as soon as the door closed behind them, Georgiana rounded on her brother.

"Oh William!"

"Now Georgie," Darcy placated her with patient amusement. "There is no need to fuss."

"No need!" Georgiana exclaimed.

"That's exactly what I told her," Richard put in.

"As you see, I am quite well," Darcy said, opening his arms with an easy gesture.

"You were shot," Georgiana argued. "And could easily have been killed. And what were you thinking, travelling all this way so soon afterwards? I must say I am surprised you allowed it, Elizabeth," she added, glancing at her new sister.

All three of the other occupants of the room stiffened at her tone and the barely veiled reprimand contained in her words; Darcy placed one of his hands over Elizabeth's.

"Not that I feel any need to justify my wife's actions to you, Georgiana, but Elizabeth made every attempt to dissuade me from making the journey so soon. And I daresay she only agreed when she realised how much I wished to be at home with my children."

"I did try and tell her that Elizabeth had little chance of making you change your mind; stubborn fool that you are," Richard commented and brother and sister both glared at him.

There was silence for a moment before Elizabeth spoke up.

"I hope you weren't too distressed when you received William's letter. I thought about sending my own, to reassure you that he really was alright, but I realised that you would likely only be happy once you had seen him and judged for yourself."

Georgiana nodded and after a moment quietly apologised.

"I am sorry Elizabeth, I did not mean to chastise you. I hope you will accept my apology."

"Of course," Elizabeth assured her warmly. "You were worried about your brother - I can hardly hold that against you. I *do* look after him, though," she added quietly and Darcy squeezed her hand.

"Yes, you certainly do," he agreed as Richard shot Georgiana an 'I told you so' look, which she pointedly ignored.

ຽСຽ

"Ow, Catherine, that was my foot!"

"Agatha, you're on my dress!"

"Sit still, you silly dog!"

Chuckling at the minor uproar coming from the carriage, Darcy thanked his sister and cousin once again for taking care of the children whilst he and Elizabeth were away.

"You know it was our pleasure," Georgiana replied, leaning up to kiss his cheek. "Take care, brother - no doubt we shall see you again soon."

"Very soon, I hope," Elizabeth put in, smiling to show that she bore her new sister no ill-will. "We must make the most of this beautiful weather we are having."

"Yes," Darcy agreed. "And as this will be James' last summer at home before he goes off to school, we must ensure it is a good one."

"We will expect to hear from you soon, then," Richard replied, adding playfully, "*Very* soon."

Elizabeth and Darcy said their final farewells to the other couple and their children before joining Catherine, James and Agatha in the carriage. James had finally gotten Agatha to settle down on the floor between the seats and Darcy and Elizabeth managed to arrange themselves around her.

"How we shall manage this when the two of you have grown I'm sure I don't know."

James and Catherine looked at one another and shared a smile at the thought as the coachman secured the door and climbed up to his seat.

"Goodbye," Joseph and Bradley called as Georgiana and Richard waved them off. Agatha barked loudly in response and the Fitzwilliams all laughed as the Darcy's carriage pulled away.

Relaxing back into the cushions of the carriage, Darcy put his arm around his wife and smiled across at his children.

"So, here we are, all together at last - a family."

"A happy family," Elizabeth agreed, smiling as well.

"If a little squashed," James couldn't resist adding with a cheeky grin, laughingly protesting when Catherine smacked his arm and his father and Elizabeth only smiled.

"When we reach Pemberley, what do you say to showing Elizabeth around the gardens?" Darcy proposed to his children before turning to his wife, "Would you like that?"

"That sounds lovely," Elizabeth replied quietly and both James and Catherine agreed that they were more than happy to act as guides.

"And perhaps this evening, as Mr and Mrs Hughes are still visiting with their relatives - perhaps you two would like to dine with Elizabeth and me?" Darcy asked James and Catherine lightly and then smiled at their enthusiastic reaction.

"Could I wear my blue dress, Papa?" Catherine asked prettily, "If I am very careful?"

"Yes, I think so," Darcy granted. "It is a special occasion, after all," he added, looking down at Elizabeth who smiled softly with understanding.

"What occasion?" Catherine asked, looking at her brother for enlightenment when their father did not reply. "James?"

"It will be our first meal together as a family, Cathy," James replied quietly.

"Indeed," Darcy finally tore himself away from his preoccupation with Elizabeth's dancing eyes and smiling lips. "The first of many."

"Oh, I see," Catherine replied, though it was clear that she did not *quite* grasp the importance of the occasion when she added, "I shall definitely wear the blue then."

As Darcy and Elizabeth both regarded her with amused affection, James put his arm around his sister's shoulders.

"You will make a very fine lady one day, Cathy."

"Really?" Catherine looked pleased at the compliment. "That's very nice of you to say so James. I think you will be a very nice man, too."

"Thank you," James responded with a grin, avoiding looking at either his father or Elizabeth, for fear of laughing.

"You're welcome," Catherine replied innocently, oblivious to the amusement of the other three as she launched into a discussion of what else they could do once they reached Pemberley.

Elizabeth sat and listened with a feeling of utter contentment, wondering how she could feel so at home already; she smiled when Darcy pressed a soft kiss to her forehead, somehow knowing that he was experiencing the same feelings, and took a second to savour the moment before giving Catherine her full attention.

ಐಲ

After dinner, Darcy knocked gently on the door to his son's room.

"James?"

"Come in, Father."

James offered a small smile as he watched his father shut the door behind himself and walk over to join him by the fire.

"I was just reading."

"Again," Darcy noted with a smile of his own. "What this time?"

"Robinson Crusoe," James replied and Darcy resisted the urge to fall into a discussion of the story.

Taking a seat next to his son, Darcy turned to him and quietly began.

"I thought it time we talked, about what you told me earlier."

James nodded mutely.

"I am not angry with you, Son," Darcy assured him. "I think you know it was wrong to read your aunt's private correspondence, and I don't expect you to do anything like that again; that being said, however, I can understand why you did what you did."

"I tried to ask Uncle Richard, but he wouldn't tell me what had happened to you," James admitted quietly. "Reading the letter - it really was my last resort. I do know it was wrong, though, like you said."

"I am sorry you had to find out the truth in such a way," Darcy noted with an unhappy frown. "I would have kept it from you entirely if I could - I did not want you to worry about me - but to discover it in such a way, and to have to keep your knowledge to yourself. It must have been hard for you, Son, and I am sorry I could not spare you such pain."

"It was horrid, but I brought it on myself, Father," James pointed out wisely. "I should have trusted my aunt and uncle, and you to know what is best for me."

"I find myself less sure of that these days," Darcy admitted with a rueful smile, looking down at his son who appeared so like himself in so many ways. "You are growing up very fast."

"I feel like I have aged a year this past week," James confessed tiredly, sounding far too careworn for Darcy's liking.

Putting his arm around his son's shoulder, Darcy drew him to his side.

"Well you mustn't worry yourself any further, Son. As you see I am quite well. My shoulder pains me, but there has been no sign of infection and Pattinson tells me the wound is already beginning to heal. I will be whole and healthy again soon."

"Will you tell me what happened?" James asked, looking up at him. "I have been imagining all sorts of terrible scenarios."

"If you wish it, of course I shall," Darcy responded before he warned, "Though some of the details are not pleasant."

"Whatever you wish to tell me, Father, I am old enough to hear," James replied and Darcy smiled softly.

"Yes, I daresay you are."

&#8286;&#8286;

Elizabeth looked up from the book she had been reading when her husband joined her in the sitting room which connected their chambers.

"Well?" she asked as he came to sit down. "Is all well?"

"Yes," Darcy sighed with a small smile. "We had a good talk - I left him to sleep."

"I'm glad," Elizabeth replied, reaching across and taking his hand. "It must have been so hard for him."

"Yes," Darcy agreed. "But now we can put the entire unhappy episode behind us and move on."

"Yes - at least until we see Ellerslie again," Elizabeth pointed out and Darcy sighed tiredly, rubbing his eyes. "Why do we not have an early night? It has been a long day, and dinner was rather animated."

Darcy gave a snort of laughter at that understatement.

"I pray to God that our every family meal is not like that."

"I enjoyed it," Elizabeth smiled playfully. "I had no idea you Darcys could be so boisterous."

"Neither did I," Darcy teased.

"Oh, so it is my fault?"

"Entirely," Darcy stated with a grin and Elizabeth laughed in spite of herself. "You are far too lively."

"Well come along, then, old man," Elizabeth teased in response, standing and pulling him to his feet. "Let's put you to bed."

"I will teach you to treat me with a bit more respect," Darcy replied with mock severity, the smile tugging at the corners of his mouth spoiling the effect. "Old man, indeed."

"I would like to see you try," Elizabeth challenged with a saucy smile and left him to follow her into her room, stopping in the doorway to offer him a come-hither look.

Darcy laughed quietly to himself, shaking his head and following after his wife, his tiredness all but forgotten.

# Chapter 17

On the morning of her birthday, Catherine Darcy woke early and quickly threw off the covers, scrambling out of bed and pulling on her dressing gown over her nightclothes. With the sound of her bare feet muffled by the thick carpet, she ran down the hallway to her brother's room, knocking excitedly.

"Wake up, James! Wake up!"

Not waiting for him to appear she carried on to her father's room, neglecting to knock at all before she opened the door and hurried inside; she came up short when she saw the empty bed, momentarily puzzled before she realised that her father must be sleeping next door with Elizabeth. With an expectant smile Catherine went through the connecting door of the two chambers, ready to rouse her father and Elizabeth from sleep, but once again was confounded by the sight of an empty bed. A quick glance around the room showed that it was indeed unoccupied and with a slightly puzzled frown Catherine turned away, retracing her steps through her father's room and back to her brother's door.

"James?"

She knocked tentatively and then opened the door a fraction, poking her head inside so that she could see another empty bed! Perhaps they are having breakfast, Catherine thought to herself reasonably and she slowly made her way downstairs, feeling a little left out and disappointed. Even Agatha, who usually slept somewhere in the family wing was missing! Too occupied with her own unhappy thoughts to pay any mind to the sounds coming from behind the closed breakfast door room, Catherine was therefore completely caught off guard when she stepped into the room and was greeted by an enthusiastic chorus of "Happy Birthdays" from her father, Elizabeth and James and Mr and Mrs Hughes.

"I thought you'd forgotten!" She cried and then promptly burst into tears.

"Oh princess," Darcy swept her up in his arms, half laughing, half concerned. "Of course we didn't forget! We just wanted to surprise you! Look here, Mrs Maddison has made all of your favourites for you, and here are your presents which you may open once we've all eaten."

Catherine snuffled and wiped her face on the sleeve of her dressing gown as Elizabeth came forward to press a kiss to her cheek.

"Happy Birthday, sweet. Will you come and sit down? We've saved a special space for the birthday girl."

Catherine nodded and Darcy gently set her down; James stepped forward and offered his hand with a broad grin.

"You silly moppet - forget your birthday indeed!"

Catherine giggled shyly as her brother led her to her seat and the four adults all shared slightly relieved looks, glad that disaster had been averted.

All six sat down together to their meal, Catherine especially delighted by the pineapple which her father and Elizabeth had managed to procure for the occasion, knowing it was a favourite of hers. When they had all eaten their fill and Catherine's impatience was quite palpable, Darcy finally offered her the first of her gifts, a collection of books and a blank manuscript volume in which she could copy out her favourite extracts (Darcy had been assured by the shopkeeper that this was something young ladies enjoyed doing, and Catherine seemed to find the idea pleasing). From James she received a small, delicate brooch and was as equally delighted with it as the collection of ribbons and sashes she received from Elizabeth. From her aunt and uncle there was a new pair of silk slippers and her final gift was a new sampler pattern from Mr and Mrs Hughes whose gifts were always practical. In a complete turnabout of her earlier feelings, Catherine felt herself a very lucky little girl and said as much before she thanked each of them in turn for her gifts.

"You are very welcome, princess," Darcy said after he had received his kiss. "Now run along back upstairs and get dressed - we are all going for a ride in the carriage."

"I will wear one of my new sashes and ribbons," Catherine declared before she rushed away; when she reappeared a moment later to retrieve the aforementioned sashes and ribbons, James and Darcy both stifled smiles and Elizabeth rose to her feet.

"Here, poppet, let me help you."

"Thank you, Lizzy," Catherine said and between them they carried her gifts from the room and went upstairs.

"Well," Darcy sighed once they had gone, allowing his smile to break free. "That went well, I think - with the exception of the start, of course."

"I cannot believe she thought we had forgotten," James laughed. "As if we would - or *could!*"

Darcy just smiled and then turned to address Mr and Mrs Hughes.

"Thank you for your gift, it was very good of you."

"It was our pleasure, Sir," Mr Hughes replied honestly. "And the least we could do."

"Do you have any plans for today?" Darcy asked - the children would have no lessons that day, and so the couple were free to spend it how they wished.

"Yes," Mr Hughes responded. "We thought to walk to Lambton and call upon some friends there; we have been away for some time, after all, and it will be good to see them once again."

"If you do not feel like walking, you are welcome to ride instead. Hanes can see to it."

"Thank you, Sir," Mr Hughes smiled and inclined his head. "That is very kind of you."

Darcy waved away the thanks.

"I think I shall go and check that the carriage is ready. Coming, Son?"

James nodded and stood up with his father.

"We shall see you at dinner," Darcy said to Mr and Mrs Hughes and then he and James left the breakfast room and went out to the stables.

"Is everything in readiness?" Darcy asked the two grooms who were attending to the harnesses.

"Very nearly, Your Grace," one of them replied and Darcy nodded before moving to survey the two matching chestnuts who stood waiting to be off. "You'd think they were twins, wouldn't you James?"

"Yes, Father," James agreed. "Did you find them, or was it Mr Hanes?"

"Hanes," Darcy admitted with a grin. "The man has a gift - I've no idea how he does it."

The horse nearest him pawed the ground and tossed its head impatiently and Darcy ran a soothing hand down its neck, "Shh, there now. Not much longer, then we'll be off. Any sign of them yet, Son?" he asked James who had a clearer view of the house.

"Yes, that looks like them now," James replied and when Darcy moved to his side he saw that Elizabeth and Catherine were walking towards them hand in hand, clearly enjoying their conversation. Smiling at the picture they painted, Darcy waited until they had reached them before opening the door to the open top carriage and bowing low.

"Your carriage awaits, My Lady."

Catherine laughed and looked expectantly at Elizabeth; Elizabeth smiled.

"I think he means you, darling."

"Oh!" Catherine blushed and then stepped forward, accepting her father's hand and carefully climbing up into the carriage. She smiled prettily when Darcy kissed her hand.

"You look lovely, princess." Turning back to his wife, Darcy smiled and offered his hand again. "And now my other lady, who I must say also looks lovely."

"You are all charm today, my dear," Elizabeth noted amusedly as she accepted his help up and took the seat beside Catherine.

"I *know* I look lovely, you don't need to tell me," James quipped cheekily before Darcy had a chance to say anything and he hopped up into the carriage as his father laughed heartily and then climbed up himself.

"Well, is everyone ready?" Darcy asked once they were all settled. "Yes? In that case, drive on!" He called to the groom awaiting that very instruction and their carriage rolled away from the house.

ৎ০৫৪

Two weeks later, Elizabeth and Darcy were trying to enjoy a few moments together whilst the children were at their lessons and there was nothing urgent demanding their attention when their solitude was disturbed by a knock at the door and the appearance of one of the many footmen.

"Yes, what is it now Deacon?"

Elizabeth bit back a smile at her husband's tone before she turned to hear the footman's reply.

"I am sorry to disturb you, Sir, but Sir Benedict Hadlock and Lady Hadlock have come to call."

"Very well," Darcy sighed. "Show them to the yellow parlour and tell them we shall be there shortly."

"Very good, Sir," Deacon bowed and went to do as instructed.

"Well," Elizabeth said brightly after a moment, "we had best go and greet our guests. Is there anything in particular I should know before I meet them?" she asked playfully - this was the latest in a long line of wedding visits and if he had the opportunity her husband had tended to provide her with a brief description of who she was about to meet.

"No - they are quite unremarkable," Darcy replied uncharitably and Elizabeth tutted and scolded him.

"Now, now, my love. You know as well as I that these visits are a matter of course. Would you prefer they did not come?"

"I simply wish," Darcy sighed, "that we had been granted a few more days of privacy before these visits all began."

"As do I," Elizabeth quietly agreed. "But that is not to say that we cannot still enjoy them. I think I shall like some of our neighbours very much."

"Only some?" Darcy asked with an arched brow, smiling when Elizabeth pursed her lips slightly.

"Only some. I am not like Jane, after all."

"No - and I am glad of it," Darcy stated warmly, earning himself a smile. "In truth, I have very little to do with the Carstones or the Leighs, but as you say, their visits were unavoidable."

"And we shall have to return them," Elizabeth pointed out with a frown, thinking of the vulgarity of Mrs Carstone and the ignorance of Lord Leigh.

"At our leisure," Darcy muttered. "Fortunately. But the Hadlocks are good people," he told her, brightening slightly. "I daresay you will like them."

"Then lead on, my love." Elizabeth stood up and accepted the arm he offered her. "And introduce me to yet more of my new neighbours. How many more are left, do you think?" she asked lightly as they walked through the front hall.

"I have not the slightest idea," Darcy admitted with a rueful smile. "My social sphere has been limited to immediate family and close friends for the last ten years at least. I have had very little to do with the neighbourhood at large."

"And now you must pretend that you know who all these people are who are calling upon us," Elizabeth noted with an amused grin. "Poor you."

"It has been quite a hardship," Darcy agreed jokingly. "Though I seem very fortunate in my choice of wife, for you are proving so much more adept at socialising than I."

"So you married me for my social skills?" Elizabeth surmised with a light laugh.

"Amongst other things," Darcy replied with a tender smile just as they reached the yellow parlour and the waiting footman opened the door for them.

Elizabeth had imagined that the Hadlocks would be the same age as Mr and Mrs Bennet and was surprised to find that that was only the case with Sir Benedict, for his wife appeared to be much younger than he. Briefly glancing up at her husband and wondering why he had not mentioned that the Hadlocks' circumstances were similar to their own, Elizabeth smiled her welcome when Darcy greeted the other couple and introduced her to them.

"Well, congratulations to both of you - I hope you are very happy together," Sir Benedict expressed warmly. "And it is a pleasure to meet you at last, Your Grace," he said to Elizabeth with a smile.

"At last, Sir Benedict?" Elizabeth queried with a playful look.

"What my husband means to say," Lady Hadlock stated before Sir Benedict could, shooting her husband an amused look, "is that we are pleased to finally meet you, and would have come sooner had we not only just returned to the country ourselves."

"Yes - and not that we read and heard a lot about you and were wild with curiosity," Sir Benedict added cheekily, quite ruining his wife's attempt at discretion with obvious enjoyment.

Elizabeth laughed lightly at the older gentleman's words and even his wife rolled her eyes with resigned amusement.

"In all seriousness, though," Sir Benedict said. "It is lovely to meet you. After holding out for so long, we knew that you had to be rather special for your husband here to even think of marrying again."

Elizabeth picked up on a particular phrase Sir Benedict had used.

"Holding out?"

"Of course," Sir Benedict began but caught Darcy's look and stopped himself. He smiled knowingly as he stated, "Perhaps a story for another time."

"I see I have some questions I must ask my husband later," Elizabeth noted with a smile as she looked up at Darcy, who quickly changed the subject.

"You say you have only just come into the country - were you in town, or elsewhere?"

"We were in Ireland," Lady Hadlock replied as Darcy gestured for them to sit down and they all found themselves seats. "Our daughter lives there," she added for Elizabeth's benefit. "And has just had her first child."

"A boy," Sir Benedict announced whilst Elizabeth quietly offered Lady Hadlock her congratulations. "A fine, healthy boy. Our son-in-law was very pleased - he has five sisters, and his father was apparently the only boy amongst seven children."

"And do you have any more children?" Elizabeth asked Lady Hadlock.

"Yes, two sons. Our eldest, Henry, is on the continent presently, and our youngest, Daniel, has just recently taken orders."

"Has he found himself a living?" Darcy enquired.

"Yes, in Kent," Lady Hadlock responded. "It is further from home than I would like, of course, but it is a very good situation."

"We shall just have to visit him often," Sir Benedict said, patting his wife's hand and Elizabeth smiled as she watched their interactions, coming to her own conclusions about their relationship.

When the Hadlocks had stayed the required time and taken their leave, Elizabeth turned to her husband and decided to see if she was right.

"They seem a lovely couple," she observed.

"Yes, I have always found them good company," Darcy agreed. "And their two sons are fine fellows."

"Lady Hadlock seems quite a bit younger than her husband," Elizabeth commented lightly.

"Many years," Darcy confirmed.

"I suppose it was all arranged?" Elizabeth guessed and was pleased when Darcy nodded.

"Yes - she was only seventeen, I think. I remember my father telling me about it. Her sister had embarrassed the family and Lady Hadlock was left with very few prospects. Sir Benedict offered and he was respectable and rich enough to satisfy her parents, despite the age difference."

"They seem quite happy together, though," Elizabeth noted and Darcy looked at her curiously.

"To what do all these questions tend, my dear?"

Elizabeth smiled.

"I am merely trying to ascertain whether my impression of our recently departed guests was correct."

"And what have you found?"

"That it was - they seem happy together, but there is no love there. I thought it an arranged match, with little affection to begin with, but one they have both learned to be happy with - and as you say that was very much the case."

"Do you always make such a study of our guests?" Darcy asked with amusement but Elizabeth shook her head.

"Not always, no. I couldn't help wondering, though, when I saw the difference in their ages why you did not mention it, considering the difference in *ours*. I see why now, though."

"Because our circumstances are totally different," Darcy replied in a tone which held notes of defensiveness and Elizabeth reached out and touched his arm.

"Yes, quite, quite different. It was interesting what Sir Benedict said though," she said, changing the subject completely, "about having read about me. I've suspected all along that our story caused quite a stir, but Sir Benedict was the first to confirm it for me."

"It is not every day that an old, lonely Duke marries a beautiful, charming young woman after a whirlwind - and secret - courtship, I suppose," Darcy noted amusedly and Elizabeth laughed at the picture he painted.

"It did not feel quite so romantic at the time," she commented and then seeing her husband's face fall quickly added, "Oh, do not mistake me - falling in love was wonderful, but it is also rather frightening. The doubts, the uncertainty, the insecurities. It is a leap of faith, really, isn't it - falling in love? Trusting that the other person will catch you when you jump."

"I hadn't thought of it like that before," Darcy admitted quietly. "But I daresay you are right."

Elizabeth smiled and then looked around the quiet, empty room. "Do you think we will have any more visitors today?"

"Probably," Darcy predicted regretfully. "Why do you ask?"

"I feel inclined to take advantage of the fact that we are alone once more, and am wondering how long it will last."

Elizabeth had no sooner said this than the door opened and James and Catherine burst in, happily announcing that they had finished their lessons for the day and reminding their father and Elizabeth of their promise to walk outside with them.

"Fortunately, my dear, we have the rest of our lives to take advantage of."

&0C3

"Look, he's going to jump again!"

James, Darcy and Elizabeth all watched as one of the newest additions to the stables galloped up to the fence and cleared it in a graceful jump.

"See how well he jumps already," Darcy noted happily. "He has great form - give him a few more years and some training and he'll be a prized hunter, mark my words."

Elizabeth smiled at her husband's obvious pleasure. She had known before how much he loved horses but had not known how active a role he played in the management of his stables and the training of their occupants. It truly was his passion and his enjoyment was quite infectious.

"Are you going to ride now?" James asked as they turned away from the paddock and back towards the stables; when his father replied in the affirmative he said, "I shall see you later, then."

"Would you like to join us, James?" Elizabeth offered. "Your father has been showing me different parts of the estate and we're going up to the North Ridge today."

"You should come, Son," Darcy seconded Elizabeth's offer. "It has been a while since you last rode, and I'm sure your lessons can be postponed until this afternoon."

It was clear from his smile that James was happy with the invitation, even before he replied.

"Thank you, I will. I will go change."

"Take your time, we will wait for you," Darcy replied to his son's back as James ran back towards the house. "It was good of you to invite him," he said to his wife when they were alone.

"I thought he would enjoy it," Elizabeth replied with an easy smile. "And you know I've always enjoyed his company."

"And because he is my son, I do not begrudge him yours," Darcy teased as they walked slowly back to the stables, obviously referring to the parade of visitors they had had since their marriage. "I do not at all mind sharing you with either of my children - in fact, it brings me great pleasure to see you all together."

"These last few weeks, they have been wonderful," Elizabeth responded softly. "I thought myself fond of the children even before you and I married, but now I see I had not even begun to love them. You are my family, all three of you, and I find I have no need of anyone else."

"I know just what you mean," Darcy assured her warmly and they shared a look of understanding before they were met by two grooms who had their mounts ready and waiting for them.

"I really must sit down and do a drawing of you," Elizabeth said to Fletcher as she sat atop Dot, waiting for Darcy whilst he instructed that James' usual mount be readied for him. "You are far too handsome to overlook."

Dot tossed her head and snorted and Elizabeth laughed lightly as she bent down to stroke her horse's neck.

"Oh, don't be jealous. I already have dozens of pictures of you." Looking up as Darcy walked over to Fletcher's side, Elizabeth smiled as she noted, "Oh dear, you have far too many beautiful horses, my love. Who is this? I am afraid I have quite forgotten."

"This is Piera."

"How old is she?" Elizabeth asked as Dot studied the new arrival with interest.

"Eight," Darcy responded, going to check the straps on Piera's saddle before returning to Fletcher and gaining the saddle with his usual effortless elegance. "I think next year I will see about getting James a new mount - he will be old enough to join the hunt soon, after all, and will need a horse suitable for the task."

"He is already tall enough to manage it, I think," Elizabeth replied and Darcy smiled. "Though I suppose he still lacks the necessary experience."

"Yes, precisely," Darcy nodded. "Haversham keeps a fine pack, and the hunt here is first rate - only the best riders are able to participate."

Elizabeth nodded her understanding and they let the subject drop as they could see James approaching; when he reached them he smiled at them both and then quickly mounted Piera, obviously keen to be off. After a few adjustments to his stirrups he was ready and Darcy led the way out of the yard, steering Fletcher towards the path which would take them up to the North Ridge and then slowing so all three could ride side by side.

"We should make the most of the wide path whilst we can," he said to Elizabeth. "We shall have to go single file later on."

"How steep a climb is it?"

"Not very, and the path is good," Darcy assured her. "And Dot seems very surefooted."

"She is a good girl," Elizabeth noted fondly, patting Dot's neck. "It is so good to be able to ride again - I missed it so much whilst we were in town."

"How long have you been riding, Elizabeth?" James asked and Elizabeth pondered the question for a moment.

"I was eight, I believe, the first time I rode a horse and I fell immediately in love with it."

"And how long have you had Dot?"

"Six years," Elizabeth responded much more confidently. "Seven next month."

"She was a birthday present, then," Darcy surmised and Elizabeth smiled.

"Yes - well remembered."

Darcy smiled enigmatically as he replied.

"I made a point of remembering."

"Oh really?" Elizabeth noted amusedly; then she purposefully changed the subject and asked James, "So, James, can you tell me what I am looking at? That house over there - do you know who's that is?"

"That is Mr Hadlee's house," James replied quietly and Elizabeth immediately regretted her choice of distraction.

"I had a note from him yesterday," Darcy stated after they were all silent for a moment. "I asked him to keep me informed off his wife's welfare and he wrote to say that she is not much improved."

"Oh dear," Elizabeth sighed sadly and James frowned down at the reins in his hands.

"What is wrong with her, Father?" he asked eventually.

"She is traumatised, I think is the word John used," Darcy replied. "Physically there was no lasting damage, but she is still distressed by the recollection of what occurred."

"Has she, is it just her and Mr Hadlee at home?" Elizabeth asked. "Is there anyone else she could talk to?"

"I do not know," Darcy replied with a confused look. "But why, if she has John, would she need anyone else?"

Elizabeth looked at him with patient sympathy.

"That is just what I would expect you to think, being a man. There are certain things, though, that a woman feels more comfortable discussing with another woman, no matter how much she loves her husband. And I imagine in this instance that Mrs Hadlee may be keeping things from her husband as well, for fear of upsetting him. It is what I would do," she concluded softly.

Darcy was silent and thoughtful for some time before he replied.

"Perhaps I could suggest to Hadlee that he write to his sister-in-law. She lives in Scotland, I believe, but I'm sure she would come if her sister needed her to."

Elizabeth agreed that that was a good plan and they rode on in silence for some minutes. Eventually, she forced herself to brighten.

"Come, it is too fine a day for such dark thoughts. Let us speak of other things. What do you think of a trip to the coast, James? Your father and I were discussing the possibility last night."

"I would love to go," James replied with a smile. "But I cannot say the same for Cathy. She does not like to swim."

"Well she would not have to if she did not wish to," Elizabeth responded fairly. "We thought to make a party of it - my sister and her family and the Fitzwilliams could all join us - and I'm sure

Catherine would be quite happy to sit with Jane and Georgiana and Clara."

Agreeing that his sister could have no objections to that arrangement, James pressed both Elizabeth and his father for more details and the three of them continued their discussion until the path narrowed and they were forced to ride single file. When they eventually reached the top of the ridge, the view was utterly breathtaking and more than ample reward for the long ride. Elizabeth, her eyes on the scene in front of her, slid down from her saddle and slowly approached the edge of the ridge, peering down to the forest below.

"Not too close, please, my dear," Darcy said as he came to stand with her and James joined them. "You will make me nervous."

"What do you think, Lizzy?" James asked, smiling up at her.

"Beautiful," Elizabeth sighed. "So beautiful. I have never seen a landscape like this."

"Wait until you see the peaks," Darcy promised. "I plan to take you there one day."

"That sounds wonderful," Elizabeth replied with a smile and then turned back to admire the view once more.

# Chapter 18

Elizabeth smiled as the footman who had escorted them announced their names to the rest of the guests already present.

"I am still not quite used to hearing myself announced as a Duchess!" she confided quietly to her husband.

Their hosts for the evening, Lord and Lady Andrews, came forward to greet them before Darcy had a chance to reply.

"Good evening! I hope you are both well?"

"Very well, thank you, Andrews," Darcy responded with a smile - he had always liked Lord and Lady Andrews and counted them amongst his few friends in the neighbourhood; he was pleased that Elizabeth appeared to like them as well.

"Please allow me to say how lovely you look this evening, Your Grace," Lord Andrews said to Elizabeth, who smiled.

"Why thank you, My Lord. It is lovely to see you both again. I understand from my husband that you and he have been friends for many years, and I hope that we can be friends also - all four of us," she added with a smile for Lady Andrews.

"I am sure we shall," the other woman responded warmly. "And not only because of the friendship that exists between our husbands, for Lady Fitzwilliam tells me that you are something of an artist."

"My new sister exaggerates my talent," Elizabeth demurred. "But I have heard much of yours."

Lady Andrews waved away her words.

"My friends and family are the only ones who have seen my work, and one can hardly trust them to offer an unbiased opinion."

"That is exactly what I think," Elizabeth agreed and beside her her husband chuckled softly.

"I see that besides your artistic talents, you also have modesty in common. I can say without doubt that you are both extremely talented," he stated confidently, somewhat put out when both ladies laughed lightly.

"I think you have just very effectively proved our point, my dear," Elizabeth told him with a playful smile and even Darcy had to laugh as he admitted his mistake.

"Will you relinquish your wife's arm to me, Farleigh?" Lord Andrews asked good-naturedly. "And allow me the honour of escorting her about the room?"

"If your wife will grant me the honour of escorting her, gladly," Darcy replied charmingly and Elizabeth and Lady Andrews smiled as they exchanged places.

"Come along then, my dear," Lord Andrews said to Elizabeth as he led her away from Darcy. "Let us see if we can find someone you have not yet met - I daresay you have been overwhelmed with visits these last few weeks."

"Yes," Elizabeth admitted lightly. "Though they have abated recently - we began returning the visits just yesterday."

"No doubt that will keep you occupied for some time," Lord Andrews predicted. "And you must have enough to occupy your time already, what with learning your way around your new home and acquainting yourself with everyone at Pemberley."

Elizabeth smiled playfully.

"Excuse me for saying so, My Lord, but I cannot imagine you speak from *recent* personal experience. Do you have a daughter recently married, perchance?"

"Yes," Lord Andrews admitted with a chuckle. "Not three months ago. Lady Andrews has received many a letter from her, asking for advice and detailing all that she has had to do since arriving at her new home."

Elizabeth smiled but had no chance to respond; their conversation had taken them over to the small group sat by the large bay windows which consisted of Sir Benedict and Lady Hadlock, Lord and Lady Haversham and a young lady whom Elizabeth did not know and who Lord Haversham introduced as his daughter, Lady Victoria Garville.

"Good evening, Your Grace," Lady Victoria greeted her with an elegant curtsey and Elizabeth, who put the other woman's age at about twenty felt a little uncomfortable with the deference shown to her new rank.

"Good evening, Lady Victoria," she replied with an open and friendly smile. "It is a pleasure to meet you."

"And you, Your Grace," Lady Victoria replied. "I was sorry to have missed the opportunity before now."

"You were in Bath?" Elizabeth queried, looking between Lady Haversham and her daughter, trying to remember what the older woman had told her regarding her daughter. "Staying with relatives? Have I remembered rightly?"

"Yes, with my aunt and uncle," Lady Victoria responded, smiling more openly now. "I returned on Wednesday."

"I have never been to Bath," Elizabeth admitted to the general surprise of her companions. "My father does not travel much, and my aunt and uncle much prefer town. Perhaps I shall persuade my husband to take me," she concluded and Sir Benedict laughed and predicted she wouldn't have much trouble convincing him.

"It might be beneficial for the Duke to take the waters there," Lady Haversham suggested. "To help his shoulder."

"Yes, I heard he'd injured himself," Sir Benedict said, looking over at where Darcy stood speaking with some of the Andrews' other guests. "He looks quite well, though, and I neglected to ask about it when we called on you. What did he do to himself?"

"It was entirely my fault," Elizabeth began with a practised smile and she related the story she and William had agreed upon.

"Ha!" Lord Haversham chortled merrily. "Only a newly married man would be so gallant!"

"Well it is good to know that you would leap to my aid if I needed it, my dear," his wife commented dryly as she smacked her husband's arm with her fan and they all laughed at his faux pas.

"But..." Lord Haversham tried to defend himself but then obviously thought better of it; he smiled ruefully and said, "I shall stop before I make it worse."

"A good idea, I think," Lord Andrews agreed, still chuckling. His attention was caught by the appearance of a footman and he announced, "Ah, dinner is served. Your Grace."

He offered Elizabeth his arm and together they led the rest of the company into dinner. As Lord Andrews directed her to her place, Elizabeth glanced over her shoulder to find her husband, returning the smile he sent her when he caught her eye before taking the seat a footman held out for her.

She was pleased to find that Lady Victoria was seated beside her and set about becoming better acquainted with the young woman. Lady Victoria was quite plain looking, with the same unremarkable features as her father - she had inherited her mother's lustrous blond locks, however, and Elizabeth knew she would not be the last woman to eye them with envy! Their conversation throughout dinner was varied and interesting, and Elizabeth was pleased to find that Lady Victoria seemed to be quite a sensible, well informed woman with an appealing sense of humour. They were halfway through the meal when Elizabeth requested that Lady Victoria address her by her Christian name, for she was sure that they were to become great friends and friends could not stand on such formality.

"Then you must call me Victoria," her new friend replied with a smile. "But please, *never* Vicky. My brother insists on calling me that, and I have always hated it."

"You have my word," Elizabeth replied solemnly. "My family and friends sometimes call me Lizzy, but I have no preference either way."

"I think Elizabeth is more befitting a Duchess," Victoria teased lightly. "Don't you?"

"Oh, undoubtedly," Elizabeth agreed. "But I still have trouble thinking of myself as such. We have not been married long," she added, looking down the table at her husband who caught her eye and smiled.

"You seem happy together," Victoria commented; when Elizabeth looked at her she blushed and added, "I couldn't help noticing."

"We are," Elizabeth replied quietly. "Very. I thoroughly recommend marriage to a good man who loves you, Victoria. It is delightful."

Victoria laughed quietly.

"If only I could find a good man to love me, I daresay I should act on your recommendation forthwith."

Elizabeth smiled but knew that her new friend's marriage prospects, or lack of them, was not a good topic of conversation whilst sat at dinner.

"Once William and I have finished returning all of the wedding visits, you must come to Pemberley. Then we can have a proper talk. Do you ride?"

"Yes," Victoria replied with a smile at the rapid change of subject. "I enjoy it very much. My father, as I'm sure your husband will have told you, is a very keen sportsman and I have ridden all my life."

"Well we simply *have* to be friends now," Elizabeth declared playfully. "For I love to ride as well and I cannot imagine not liking anyone who shares in my passion."

"My father tells me that your husband keeps very fine stables," Victoria commented after allowing herself a light laugh at Elizabeth's teasing. "I have never seen them, but Father says they are known throughout England."

"They are rather impressive," Elizabeth admitted. "And some of the horses are beautiful. Though I must confess that I still love my darling Dot the most."

Victoria admitted that it was much the same with her and her mount, Jingo, and she and Elizabeth fell to discussing the many virtues of their horses and making plans to go riding together as soon as possible.

Darcy, sat some distance from his wife, watched her happily conversing with Lady Victoria with a pleased feeling, glad that the two seemed to be getting along very well. In the back of his mind he had been worried that Elizabeth would miss the companionship of people her own age, knowing that the average age of the majority of their visitors had been nearer that of her aunt and uncle. Her sister and Georgiana were not far away, of course, but still, he had hoped that she would find a friend in Lady Victoria and was happy that that seemed to be the case.

"I must congratulate you again, Farleigh," Lord Andrews said, breaking into Darcy's thoughts. "On finding yourself such a lovely wife."

*She found me*, Darcy thought to himself, watching Elizabeth laugh at something that was said to her, her smile and eyes brightening the whole room for him.

"Thank you," he finally remembered to reply, tearing his eyes away, but it was too late and the damage was done; the men sat near him had all noticed his preoccupation and were suppressing smiles whilst their wives and daughters were all looking at him as though he had said something terribly romantic and sweet.

Darcy cleared his throat awkwardly and kept his eyes fixed on his plate, lest he make himself seem as much a lovesick fool as he privately knew he was.

80C3

After breakfast the following morning, Elizabeth installed herself in the mistress' study and set about writing some letters. She took up a fresh sheet of parchment and began a letter to her aunt and uncle, who were eager to hear how she was getting on, how she liked her new home, how she liked her new neighbours etc, etc, etc. Once that was out of the way, Elizabeth began her reply to Charlotte's missive and enjoyed the task much more, amusing herself for several minutes with the retelling of a number of entertaining incidents which had occurred since her arrival at Pemberley - almost all of them involving Agatha and the children in some way. Next she wrote to both Jane and Georgiana, detailing the tentative plans she and William had made for a trip to the seaside and inviting both of their families to join them. And then there was only one more reply to write before she had to turn her attention to the letters of housekeeping she meant to send to Mrs Carey at Longbourn and Mrs Dawson in London.

Picking up the letter that had arrived last week, Elizabeth felt a smile tugging at her lips even before she began to re-read it.

*My darling Elizabeth,*

*How are you, my dear? Town has been quite dreary since your husband whisked you away to some romantic hideaway on the coast somewhere and I have been utterly desolate without your company to delight me. I have no idea how I shall survive not seeing you for the rest of the summer.*

*There, is my cousin jealous enough now, do you think? I can imagine him reading this over your shoulder with a ferocious glare on his face, itching to snatch the offending missive away and cast it into the fire. Would you let him, or would you clutch it to your breast and defy him? Hmm, it would not do to consider that image too much, I think.*

*I shall endeavour to be serious. I have heard vague whisperings that your husband landed himself in a spot of bother on your brief return to town, so I sincerely hope you are both well. How is married life treating you? I frequently amuse myself by imagining you blissfully happy at Pemberley, a picture of contented domesticity, and it never fails to make me laugh aloud when I attempt to transplant myself into that picture - as though I would ever fit into such a scene. It is a credit to your considerable charms, my dear Elizabeth, that I, even if only for a moment, ever considered the notion.*

*I am leaving town tomorrow, a friend is hosting one of the usual summer house parties and I am availing myself of his hospitality. No doubt it shall be dreary and dull, but it will be better than staying here. And I am told there will be ladies present, so that at least will make things a little more interesting.*

*I wonder whether I shall ever see a reply to this shocking missive?*

*Your friend and utter scoundrel,*
*George Wickham*

As it happened, Elizabeth had *not* let her husband read the letter over her shoulder, though he knew she had received it and did not seem to object to a correspondence between herself and his cousin. Whether he would still be of that opinion had he seen what Mr Wickham had written Elizabeth privately doubted, but she knew that Mr Wickham was only teasing and that there was no harm in it. Pausing for a moment to consider her response, Elizabeth eventually put her pen to paper and wrote,

*Dear Mr Wickham,*

*Thank you for your concern for my husband's welfare - you hid it well, but there was at least a sentence or two in your letter where you genuinely seemed to care about how he fared. I shall neither confirm nor deny whatever you may have heard vaguely whispered and shall only say that he is quite well and almost completely recovered.*

*As you have little or no experience of contented domesticity, I find it amusing to think of your imagining me living in such a state and I wonder what it is exactly that you imagine I am doing? That I am blissfully happy I shall not attempt to deny, no doubt it is practically seeping into the page. I think you would find me rather smug now, Mr Wickham, and not quite so delightful.*

*I hope you enjoy your house party, though you seemed not to be looking forward to it. Though you did not expressly say so, I suppose the ladies you think will make your stay more interesting are of the married, rather than the unmarried, kind? Unless you have decided to change the habit of a lifetime? Or have  taken my advice and are trying to find yourself a wife forthwith?*

*Stranger things have happened, I suppose.*

*Your unoptimistic friend,*
*Elizabeth Darcy*

Satisfied that it was neither too forward nor too discouraging (she enjoyed their playful bantering and suspected if she were too formal with him he would mock her mercilessly), she addressed the letter and put it with the others waiting to be sent. The letter to Mrs Dawson at the house in town was but the work of a moment and then, finally, she had only one more to write to Mrs Carey and she would be finished.

*Dear Mrs Carey,*

*I hope you and everyone else at Longbourn are well. Myself, my husband and the children are all very well and have been enjoying the very fine weather we have been having.*

*I was sorry to hear of Mr Nichols' decision to leave Longbourn, though I cannot claim not to understand his reasons. If he has not already left the neighbourhood and is in need of a reference, please inform him that I would be more than happy to furnish him with one; or, failing that, an application to my uncle for such would be equally as effective.*

*I must own that I was confused by the rest of your letter. I understood that Mr Hounsell was employed by my father as some kind of assistant with his work - but you say that he has replaced Mr Nichols as steward? Is he at all qualified for the position? Mr Nichols worked too hard for Longbourn to be brought to ruin by mismanagement. I am asking for your honest opinion about the man, Mrs Carey, so that I may know how to act. If it should prove necessary I will come to you and set things right once more - I only wait for your opinion on the matter.*

*Please pass on my greetings to everyone and tell them that I hope they are all well. The cook here at Pemberley seems very good, but I daresay I shall be writing to Mrs Braddock at Christmas for her pudding recipe - no one makes it quite like her! And please tell Miss Lewis that I am to visit the school here today and am eager to see whether it meets the high standards she has set with her teaching.*

*Yours,*
*Elizabeth Darcy*
*Duchess of Farleigh*

*P.S. I am certain you have not forgotten, but please remember to send Reverend Baker some of your lovely preserves. He would never ask, but I know how much he enjoys them.*
*E.D*

Reading through what she had written to check that she had left nothing and no-one out, Elizabeth nodded and sealed the missive, affixing it with her new seal. The situation with Mr Nichols was regrettable and the mysterious Mr Hounsell was something of a worry, but Elizabeth had too much to occupy her attention these days to worry about it for long.

Putting it out of her mind, Elizabeth picked up her letters and left her study, handing them over to a nearby footman to put them with the rest of the post waiting to be sent. Glancing at the clock in the hall, she noted that she had a few minutes before she had to meet with Mrs Reynolds and went to her husband's study, knocking lightly. He had also decided to spend the day working and when he called for her to enter she found him sat behind his desk with his steward, Mr Benson, sat opposite him.

"Please, don't get up," she said when both men moved to rise. "I just thought I'd come and see you before I speak with Mrs Reynolds."

"Have you finished writing your letters?" Darcy asked as she came to stand near him, thinking of the one he had received earlier and which he needed to discuss with her later. Benson occupied himself with reading one of the ledgers whilst the couple talked.

"Yes, just now," Elizabeth replied. She smiled and added, "I told Charlotte about the incident with Agatha and Deirdre - I thought it would amuse her."

"Oh, no doubt," Darcy agreed, a suppressed grin twisting his lips. How Agatha, a very large Great Dane, could be so terrified by such a small cat was something he would never understand.

"Do you still plan on going to visit the school after luncheon?" he asked after a moment and Elizabeth nodded. "Will you walk or ride?"

"I thought I would walk," Elizabeth replied.

"Make sure you have someone accompany you - it is a fair way."

"If it pleases you," Elizabeth responded lightly, but Darcy still picked up on the fact that her tone wasn't quite normal and lightly grasped her hand.

"It does. Please?" he added quietly and after a moment Elizabeth sighed and nodded.

She was used to her freedom at Longbourn, but she did recognise that things were different here; different now that she was no longer simply Miss Gardiner. It would just require some adjustment, that was all.

"I shall leave you to your business," she said after the clock on the mantle chimed the hour. "And see you for luncheon."

Darcy pressed a brief kiss to the back of her hand and then released her, watching her go before turning back to Benson.

"Good morning, Ma'am," Mrs Reynolds greeted Elizabeth when she stepped into the small but comfortable room set aside for the housekeeper. "Shall we remove upstairs so that we are more comfortable?"

"Whatever you think best, Mrs Reynolds," Elizabeth replied. "If everything we need to look over is already here, do not trouble yourself to move it all on my account. I will be quite happy to sit here with you, as long as we have some tea," she concluded with a smile which Mrs Reynolds returned.

"That can easily be arranged, Ma'am."

Elizabeth nodded and took a seat.

"In that case, shall we get started?"

ဆာ၈

"Is something troubling you, William?" Elizabeth asked as they walked down to the dining room for dinner later that same day. She looked closely at her husband and could see some tension around his eyes, a sure sign that he was preoccupied by something.

"I had a letter from Ellerslie this morning," Darcy admitted with a sigh.

"Why did you not say?" Elizabeth replied. "How is he? What did he say?"

"He is coming here, Tuesday next," Darcy began before they reached the dining room and put off further conversation until they were both seated and the first course served. "He intends to fulfil his promise to you of one final visit. They sail a week later."

"He has not changed his mind, then," Elizabeth noted sadly and Darcy shook his head, pushing his uneaten food around on his plate. Elizabeth reached over and softly laid her hand over his. "I'm sorry, my love."

"As am I," Darcy replied, turning his hand over and interlacing their fingers. "Sorry for my friend, sorry for Hadlee and his wife, sorry for Frank."

"And yourself?" Elizabeth ventured quietly. "Ellerslie is your oldest friend."

"Yes." Darcy was silent for a long time. "I hope to God that he survives this."

"We shall both of us keep him in our prayers," Elizabeth stated softly and Darcy spared her a small smile and raised her hand to his lips to press a brief kiss upon it.

"You have been thinking about this all day, haven't you?" she guessed after a moment. "I thought you seemed quiet at luncheon."

Darcy nodded and admitted that was the case.

"I wish you had told me earlier," Elizabeth expressed and Darcy pressed her hand.

"I did not wish to trouble you - you seemed so happy and busy."

"No matter how busy I seem, William," Elizabeth stated firmly, "the concerns of you and our family will always take precedence."

"I will bear that in mind in future," Darcy replied and his wife gave a quick nod, satisfied.

"I must confess that I was a little dismayed at the timing of Ellerslie's visit," he commented after a moment. "I had plans for your birthday."

"Plans can easily be changed," Elizabeth replied lightly. "And I do not mind putting them off until after his visit."

Darcy nodded but it was clear that he was still a bit miffed and Elizabeth's curiosity was aroused.

"So what did you have planned, then, my love? And does it involve the children? For they have kept very quiet about it if it does."

Darcy smiled properly for the first time that night.

"I am not saying a word. You shall just have to wait and see."

"And I thought you promised no more surprises," Elizabeth playfully reminded him.

"I believe we agreed that I am allowed to spoil you so long as you are allowed to spoil me," Darcy replied with a grin. "And considering the surprise you all organised for my birthday, I think it is only fair that I be allowed to reply in kind."

"I see I shall never win this argument," Elizabeth commented. "So I shall simply let you have your way this time."

"I promise you will like your surprise," Darcy stated, taking up her hand and kissing it.

"Of that I have no doubt," Elizabeth replied warmly and they shared a smile before turning back to their meal.

"So, did Ellerslie have anything else to say? Besides the details of his travel plans?" Elizabeth asked some time later and Darcy took a sip of his wine before replying.

"Yes - it seems that Frank's problems stem not only from the amount of alcohol he consumes, but from other substances as well."

Elizabeth's brows rose.

"Opium?"

"So it would seem," Darcy responded. "Ellerslie has kept him at home and he is showing signs of withdrawal from whatever he was taking."

"If it is only beginning now, surely the voyage will be terrible for him?" Elizabeth stated, wide eyed.

Darcy nodded grimly.

"I begin to see the wisdom of Ellerslie's plan. Frank will hardly be able to survive the coming months without them having some lasting effect on him."

"Let us hope it is a positive effect," Elizabeth expressed and Darcy added his wholehearted agreement.

"It makes me very thankful, you know," he admitted suddenly after some moments of silence. "That James is and has always been such a good boy. Though I suppose he is still only young, and once he is away from home..."

"William!" Elizabeth stopped him with a slightly amused smile. "The thought of James becoming at all like Frank - it is nonsense. You have raised him too well for that, he is too fine a young man to stray so far from the path you have set him on."

"Yes of course, of course you are right." Darcy smiled ruefully and shook his head. "I worry too much sometimes, don't I?"

"Sometimes," Elizabeth replied fondly, smiling lovingly at her bashful husband who made a show of drinking some more of his wine.

"Come, will you tell me more about you day? How did you find Mr Garret?"

Elizabeth was more than happy to oblige his request and they spent the rest of the meal speaking of the tenants and their families and the plans Elizabeth and Mr Garret had for their welfare.

# Chapter 19

On the morning of her birthday, Elizabeth Darcy was woken very early by the loving attentions of her husband, who gently coaxed her from sleep to wakefulness with soft kisses.

"Mmmm, good morning," Elizabeth purred as she reached up to thread her fingers into her husband's hair, briefly holding his lips against the sensitive skin of her neck.

"Good morning," he murmured deeply beside her ear before catching the lobe between his teeth, "and Happy Birthday."

"Thank you," Elizabeth sighed with a smile and then moaned deep in her throat when one of Darcy's roaming hands found a particularly sensitive spot. She tried to return the gesture but Darcy gently caught hold of her hand, shaking his head.

"We cannot. There is too much of a chance we will be disturbed by two children eager to wish you a happy birthday."

"Well, that would be unfortunate," Elizabeth replied with a sigh and an adorable pout which Darcy was quick to kiss away.

"That is not to say that we cannot still enjoy ourselves," he murmured against her lips, his hands caressing her skin beneath her nightgown.

"But what if they come in?" Elizabeth asked breathlessly as her husband resumed his sensuous attack on her neck.

"It will teach them to knock," Darcy muttered and smiled on hearing her breathy laugh.

"I love you, William," she said, holding his face between her hands.

"And I love you, Elizabeth," Darcy replied tenderly. "Happy Birthday."

Elizabeth smiled and wrapped her arms around his shoulders, drawing him down to her and intending to enjoy their moment of early morning privacy. Outside in the corridor, James managed to catch up with his sister just as she was about to burst into Elizabeth's room unannounced.

"*Cathy!*"

"What?" Catherine asked blankly, surprised by his tone; Agatha, who was with them, sniffed at the gap under the door and pawed the floor impatiently.

"You must knock first," James told her, releasing her arm and gentling his tone.

"Why?" Catherine asked. "We never have before."

"I know, but it is different now Father is married. Trust me," James added when his sister looked about to press him for more information - information he had no intention of sharing with his nine year old sister. "You just need to remember, alright?"

"Alright," Catherine agreed with a little shrug and then proceeded to knock loudly on the heavy oak door.

James rolled his eyes resignedly and waited for a response; when he heard his father call for them to come in, he opened the door for his sister and followed her and Agatha inside.

"Happy Birthday Lizzy!" Catherine announced happily as Agatha leapt up onto the bed and Darcy had to wrestle her away from his face, which she was enthusiastically trying to lick.

"Thank you," Elizabeth replied, laughing at her husband's struggles. She welcomed Catherine up onto the bed with them and returned the little girl's warm embrace, smiling when she was rewarded with an extra kiss.

"Happy Birthday Elizabeth," James added his own good wishes, sitting down at the foot of the bed, next to his father's feet. Agatha, who Darcy had managed to get to lie down, shifted so her head was in his lap and her wagging tail was beating between the two adults. "I'm sorry about Agatha - she insisted on coming with us."

"Oh that's alright," Elizabeth replied before adding with a laugh, "Though she's lucky Deirdre wasn't sleeping in her usual place on that bench!"

"Thank God," Darcy said with a chuckle. "All hell would have broken loose!"

"Speak of the devil," Elizabeth noted with an amused smile and she pointed to the door from her dressing room through which Deirdre had just sauntered. James picked up a discarded pillow and tossed it in Deirdre's direction, missing her entirely but still earning himself a rebuke from both Elizabeth and his father.

"I'm sorry," he said, chastened. "I just, she's a bit mean to Agatha, isn't she?"

"That is no reason to throw things at her, James," Darcy told him and his son nodded.

"You're right. I'm sorry Elizabeth, I won't do it again."

"It's alright James," Elizabeth assured him lightly. She frowned as she admitted, "She is becoming quite mean. Wilson suggested I have her put out in the stables during the day and I think I might have to."

"There are plenty of mice out there for her to eat," James noted and Elizabeth smiled and agreed that Deirdre would probably be quite happy with the arrangement.

"Enough about that wretched creature," Darcy declared, chuckling when his wife pretended offence and smacked his arm. "It is time we were up. Run along and get dressed you two and we shall meet you for breakfast."

"And then we will give Elizabeth her present?" Catherine asked and when Darcy nodded she hopped down from the bed and ran to do as she was told.

"I will see you at breakfast," James said, properly taking his leave of them before following after his sister, calling for Agatha to come and making sure to shut the door behind them.

The sudden silence following the trio's departure seemed very loud and Elizabeth and Darcy grinned at each other before the latter pressed a quick kiss to his wife's lips and swept the covers aside.

"Come, a fine morning awaits us. We must make the most of the day before Ellerslie arrives."

"I am sure it will not be as bad as that," Elizabeth replied hopefully as she too rose from the bed.

"Perhaps not," Darcy admitted. "But I doubt he will be in any mood to celebrate with us. And I fear our visit to Hadlee will be singularly unpleasant and difficult," he concluded with a frown and Elizabeth was quick to soothe his cares away.

"Do not worry about that now," she said quietly as she leant up on her tiptoes to press a soft kiss to his lips.

Darcy cupped her face in both of his hands and deepened the kiss, holding her for several long moments before reluctantly breaking away.

"We will retire early tonight," he stated resolutely and Elizabeth smiled.

"What about our guest?"

"He will be tired from his journey," Darcy replied and Elizabeth chuckled at his tone - Ellerslie, it seemed, had little choice in the matter!

Enticed by his wife's bright smile, Darcy almost allowed himself to kiss her again but stopped himself at the last moment.

"No, I must away."

"Yes, do go - I wish to open my gift, and I cannot get dressed until you leave me," Elizabeth teased, and with one final chaste peck Darcy was gone.

"Just a little further."

Elizabeth clutched her husband's hand tightly as her foot caught on something and disrupted her tentative stride. She resisted the urge to open her eyes, but barely.

"It's alright, I've got you," Darcy assured her. James and Catherine were walking with them and he shared a conspiratorial grin with his two children as they led Elizabeth towards the stables - and her gift. When they had walked around to the side of the main stable block, James went ahead to open the gate to the pen and Catherine took Elizabeth's spare hand.

"This way, Lizzy!"

Elizabeth's keen senses soon told her where they were.

"The stables? But...?"

"You'll see," Darcy said quietly into her ear and Elizabeth smiled and began to run through all the possibilities in her mind. Nodding to James, Darcy watched as his son carefully opened the gate and then led his wife inside. A tiny bark all but gave the game away and Darcy, Catherine and James all quickly looked at Elizabeth who had gone quite still.

"What was that?"

Quickly stepping out of the pen, Darcy pushed the gate shut.

"You can open your eyes now, love."

Elizabeth did as she was bid, gasping with surprise when she saw the gorgeous puppy sat in the grass at her feet, looking up at her with obvious interest. She dropped to her knees, reaching out a hand to stroke the puppy's head, delighted when it barked again and began to playfully nibble on her fingers. Elizabeth turned her delighted smile towards her husband and children.

"Does it have a name?"

"No, not yet," Darcy replied. "We thought you should decide what to call her."

"Her?" Elizabeth repeated and turned to look back at her puppy, considering.

"Do you like her?" Catherine asked eagerly and Elizabeth was surprised to feel tears in her eyes.

"I love her. She is beautiful, and I've always wanted a dog and - oh, dear, look at me, I'm getting a bit emotional."

Elizabeth smiled an embarrassed smile and wiped her eyes, laughing lightly a moment later when her puppy began bouncing around on the grass, chasing a large bumblebee as it meandered past. Opening the gate, Darcy let James and Catherine into the small pen and then stepped in after them, making sure to shut the gate behind him. He assisted Elizabeth to her feet and put his arm around her waist.

"I'm glad you like her," he said quietly and Elizabeth smiled up at him.

"Will you tell me about her?"

"She is an Irish Setter and is, I think, about four months old. We've had her here for about a week,"

"A week!" Elizabeth gave a startled laugh. "However did you manage to hide her for so long?"

"With difficulty," Darcy responded with a grin before going on, "She's been here for a week and so far Agatha seems to get on with her very well - we wanted to be sure there would be no difficultly there. And we let her meet Dot yesterday, just briefly, and Dot seemed quite calm so in future I'm sure you'll be able to take her riding with you. Sir Benedict tells me that the breed is a very active one that appreciates a lot of exercise."

"Oh, of course!" Elizabeth quickly put two and two together. "Lady Hadlock said that they had just returned from Ireland - they brought her back with them, didn't they?"

"Yes, her and two others," Darcy admitted with a smile at her quick mind. "The red coat is quite distinctive to the Irish breed and I thought you would like it."

"It is beautiful," Elizabeth agreed. "So silky."

"Have you decided what you will call her, Lizzy?" Catherine asked and Elizabeth thought for a long moment.

"I think I will call her Poppy."

James laughed

"How fitting."

Poppy, as she was now called, bored with chasing the bee, trundled over to Elizabeth and took a great mouthful of her dress and began tugging on it playfully. Darcy groaned as Elizabeth laughed and bent down to rescue her hem from the puppy's mouth.

"I had forgotten what a menace puppies can be."

"Does Mrs Reynolds know about her?" Elizabeth asked with a playful twinkle, laughing when her husband confessed he had not yet informed their housekeeper about the new addition. "I shall let you be the one to tell her, my love."

"How kind," Darcy replied dryly, then grinned at her teasing.

"You should see her with Agatha," James commented a moment later, laughing lightly. "She runs between her legs and pulls on her tail and tries to bite her ears - though of course she cannot reach!"

Elizabeth laughed and the sound drew a happy bark from Poppy who seemed excited by all the attention.

"Oh, you are adorable," Elizabeth cooed, already in love with the little dog. She gave Poppy a final pat and then stood up, facing her smiling family. "Thank you so much, all of you."

She embraced and kissed both of the children and then turned to her husband, leaning up to briefly kiss his lips.

"You are too good to me."

"Nonsense," Darcy replied warmly and Elizabeth smiled lovingly before briefly kissing him again.

ᏋᏅᏣ

Ellerslie tiredly climbed down from his carriage and smiled for what felt like the first time in weeks when he saw Darcy and Elizabeth standing on the steps, looking happy and healthy and the picture of marital felicity. Despite the problems with which he currently grappled, Ellerslie was genuinely happy for his friend and wished him and Elizabeth well. Greeting their guest, Darcy and Elizabeth brought Ellerslie into the house and soon had him sat down with a warm cup of tea.

"You look tired, my friend," Darcy commented with concern as he took the seat beside Elizabeth and opposite Ellerslie.

"I have had much to do, these past weeks," Ellerslie admitted. "Arrangements, visits, business - I have been well occupied."

"And everything is arranged to your satisfaction?" Darcy asked. "You are ready to depart?"

Ellerslie nodded.

"Yes. I must call on my sister on my journey from here to London, but everything else is in readiness."

"It would be pointless for us to attempt to change your mind, I suppose?" Elizabeth quietly asked and Ellerslie smiled sadly at her.

"Quite pointless, yes."

Elizabeth silently nodded and Ellerslie watched as Darcy gently pressed her hand and looked reassuringly at her.

"Please," he stated, surprising the couple who both turned to look at him. "Do not trouble yourselves about me. Do not make yourselves unhappy, at least," he amended when Darcy opened his mouth to protest. "I do not want my situation to cast a pall over your happiness."

Darcy and Elizabeth exchanged a quick look, relieved that they had decided not to mention to Ellerslie that it was Elizabeth's birthday and that his visit had already made more of an impact than he would have wanted it to.

"Where are the children?" Ellerslie asked after a moment when neither his friend nor Elizabeth offered a protest. "Are they outside enjoying the sunshine?"

"They are upstairs currently," Elizabeth responded. "But if you feel up to a walk we could have them fetched and all go together?"

"That sounds wonderful," Ellerslie agreed, setting aside his empty tea cup. "If you allow me a moment to change out of these dusty things."

"Of course," Elizabeth granted easily and smiled at her husband's friend. "Mrs Reynolds has prepared your usual room for you - I'm sure you know your way?"

"Yes," Ellerslie replied with a chuckle at her teasing, feeling his mood lighten. "I will return shortly."

"There is no rush," Darcy told him and with a nod Ellerslie left the room.

When he returned to the parlour he found the whole family together, their attention focused on a small puppy snuffling around on the floor.

"Hello there," Ellerslie greeted the puppy as it ran over to him and enthusiastically sniffed his boots. "And who is this?"

"Her name is Poppy and she is Lizzy's birthday present," Catherine informed him in a rush to be helpful.

"Indeed? And when was the happy day?" Ellerslie asked lightly, bending to stroke the funny little creature and smiling at his hostess.

"It is today!" Catherine replied before Elizabeth had a chance and her father winced as she added, "Didn't you know?"

"No, I did not," Ellerslie responded as he slowly straightened. He quirked a brow and looked at his friend who simply shrugged and smiled ruefully.

"Oh, well, yes it is Lizzy's birthday today and she is twenty and,"

"That is quite enough, thank you darling," Elizabeth laughingly interrupted Catherine's enthusiastic monologue. "A lady does not like to reveal her age to everyone, you know."

"Oh dear," Catherine apologised with a cheeky smile which Elizabeth couldn't help returning.

"Well, Happy Birthday, Your Grace," Ellerslie intoned. He gave a slight bow and added, "I am sorry to have interrupted on such an important day."

"Thank you," Elizabeth replied quietly. "But please, it is Elizabeth. And the interruption was more than welcome," she added with a warm smile.

"You are too good to say so," Ellerslie responded and Darcy was quick to correct him.

"I assure you, Ellerslie, we are neither of us so hospitable as to make an unwanted guest welcome today. Well," he amended with a laughing glance at his wife. "*I* certainly am not."

"No, I know just how rude you can be when it suits you," Ellerslie agreed with a reluctant smile and Darcy chuckled.

"Come, shall we go for our walk?" Elizabeth spoke up, setting the subject aside in favour of other things. "Luncheon will be waiting for us when we return."

"Can I please hold Poppy's lead, Lizzy?" James asked keenly and Elizabeth smilingly granted him her permission.

"I am relying on you to wear her out, James. Perhaps then she will be too tired to maul any more of the furniture!"

"I wouldn't count on it, my love," Darcy stated, offering his hand to his wife to help her to her feet. "Though I suppose it is worth a try."

"If Agatha joins us," Ellerslie suggested as he followed the family from the room and down to the front hall. "Perhaps she could run around and help keep the puppy occupied."

Darcy laughed and pointed to the front steps, visible through the open front door, and Ellerslie could see Agatha stretched out and fast asleep in the warm midday sun.

"Ah, perhaps not," he commented with a grin and then shared a smile with his two hosts before accepting his things from a waiting footman.

ဆင္သ

John Hadlee's anger as he stood in front of Ellerslie was almost palpable, and Darcy was not surprised to see that his friend looked decidedly uncomfortable.

"What would you like me to tell you, *Your Grace*?" Hadlee asked in response to Ellerslie's tentative enquiry as to the health of Mrs Hadlee. He spoke in a frigid tone, his opinion of the older man obvious in the derisive way he uttered the final two words.

"Well I, that is, what...Nothing." Ellerslie sighed heavily, his shoulders slumping. He looked as though he had aged twenty years since the night of the attack. "Nothing, forgive me, I had no right to ask. I will go." He turned to Darcy and said, "I will meet you outside."

Hadlee shifted uncomfortably from one foot to the other as he watched Ellerslie walk away.

"Wait."

Ellerslie stopped and turned back.

"She is recovering. Her sister is staying here with us and together we are helping her. She will be alright, I think."

Ellerslie nodded and it was clear that he remained silent because he was too close to losing his composure to speak.

"I hope." Hadlee cleared his throat and frowned down at his boots before looking back up at Ellerslie. "I hope you return safely from your travels."

Both Darcy and Ellerslie's brows rose at this statement and Hadlee smiled humourlessly.

"Do not mistake me. I care only because you are Farleigh's friend, and he is one of the best men I know. Your son I would be happy to see perish," he concluded coldly. "But I know your demise would grieve our mutual friend here."

Ellerslie nodded and both men looked at Darcy, who shifted uncomfortably at the attention. Fortunately he was saved from further embarrassment by Ellerslie, who quietly took his leave and left Darcy and Hadlee alone. Darcy studied the younger man thoughtfully, wondering what he was feeling, and after a moment Hadlee smiled ruefully.

"When you initially wrote and requested that you be allowed to bring him here, my first response was to refuse you. But then I thought to myself, no, let him come, and I shall finally have some satisfaction."

Darcy's brows rose at this revelation and Hadlee glanced towards the door through which Ellerslie had just exited and sighed.

"When I saw him, however, I could not bring myself to strike him. I could not summon the necessary anger. I pity him, I think."

"You should," Darcy replied darkly, finally voicing his deepest fears aloud. "I do. I think he will die, and die knowing that he has failed with his son. Either that, or Frank will die first and he will blame himself for the rest of his life."

"Does he not deserve the blame, though?" Hadlee asked quietly. "Or at least a sizeable portion of it?"

"Why? Because he raised his son in the same manner that everyone else does? Because he hired him the best tutors, sent him to the best schools, shared with him all his wealth and privileges? Ellerslie is a good man, and he did his best - the best that he knew how to do. And until a few years ago Frank was - if not as good a man as his father - certainly not the degenerate he is now. He has made his own choices, and the blame should lie with him, but Ellerslie is determined to take it all upon himself. And I think it will kill him in the end, one way or the other."

"Well, I pray it does not come to that," Hadlee quietly stated as Darcy turned away and took refuge at the window, staring out over the grounds of Hadlee's home. "For your sake as much as his."

Darcy nodded his recognition and took a deep, steadying breath. He held it for a few moments and then sighed, releasing his pent up frustration and burgeoning despair.

"I should be going," he said, turning back to Hadlee. "It is my wife's birthday today, and we have a special dinner planned."

"Please give her my best wishes. And please thank her for her suggestion regarding my wife's need for female companionship," Hadlee added earnestly. "Her sister's presence has been of great comfort to her."

Darcy nodded.

"I will. And please tell your wife that whenever she is ready, Elizabeth is looking forward to making her acquaintance."

"I hope it will not be too much longer," Hadlee expressed and he even managed a smile. The two friends shook hands and said goodbye and Darcy went out to join Ellerslie in the carriage waiting patiently in front of the house. He climbed up and took his seat before catching the other man's eye; Ellerslie shook his head, indicating that he did not want to talk, and Darcy let him have his way. They rode back to Pemberley in silence.

ᘒᑕᘔ

"Please take care of yourself, Ellerslie."

Ellerslie managed a smile as Elizabeth briefly embraced him and kissed his cheek.

"I will do my best," he promised and Elizabeth nodded as she stepped back.

"And you must write to us," she added. "Whenever possible. Not only to tell us that you are well, but so that we may hear all about

Antigua and what it is like there. I am sure you will have many interesting stories to tell."

"I promise I will write when I can," Ellerslie assured her and, finally satisfied, Elizabeth nodded and moved slightly away, allowing her husband to come forward and address his friend.

Darcy and Ellerslie looked at one another, neither really sure what to say. They had stayed up very late the night before, sitting together in Darcy's study and drinking and talking until the early hours of the morning. They had said everything that needed to be said, spoken words and expressed sentiments which only the darkness had made them comfortable enough to voice aloud. Their friendship had endured throughout their lives, and both were conscious that it might very soon be at a permanent end, but they had each said their piece and now, faced with Ellerslie's imminent departure, there were few words left to them.

Finally, Darcy offered his hand.

"Good luck Matthew."

Ellerslie took Darcy's hand and held it tightly.

"I wish you every happiness, Fitzwilliam. I could not have asked for a better friend."

"Nor I."

The two friends shook hands and then parted for the last time. Elizabeth approached her husband and he put his arm around her waist, holding her close as he watched his friend climb into his coach. Ellerslie waved from the window and they both returned the gesture as his coach pulled away, watching it roll down the drive and away from the house. Darcy watched until the coach disappeared from sight and was suddenly, depressingly certain that he would never see his friend again.

&#8277;&#8278;

Sir Charles laughed at his son's exuberance as Daniel ran into the parlour where he and Jane and the rest of the party were waiting, announcing the arrival of the Darcy family with excitement.

"I saw their carriage, it is just coming now!" Daniel went on and his father called him over to his side.

"Then we had best be quiet, else we shall spoil the surprise," Sir Charles told his son and shared a smile with Colonel Fitzwilliam who similarly instructed his own two sons to stay quiet.

They could all hear the sounds of the Darcys out in the entrance hall and waited with expectant smiles as their steps approached.

"Happy Birthday!"

Elizabeth jumped, completely caught off guard, and then laughed delightedly.

"Oh, goodness!"

Darcy chuckled as his wife rounded on him and playfully accused him.

"I thought we agreed no more surprises!"

"We did," he replied innocently. "I had absolutely nothing to do with this."

Elizabeth laughed at his audacity.

"A likely story!"

"Happy Birthday Lizzy," Jane said, coming forward to embrace her sister and breaking up the friendly argument between husband and wife.

"Thank you," Elizabeth responded and then enthused, "You look radiant!"

"Oh, thank you," Jane replied demurely, resting a hand over her small bump. "I feel very well."

"I am glad to hear it," Elizabeth said with a smile, thinking it had been too long since she had last seen her sister. Moving further into the room, Elizabeth greeted all of her family members and happily accepted their warm birthday wishes. The plan for the day, she was soon informed, consisted largely of a picnic by the lake and perhaps a few games with the children, if she were happy to play.

"Of course," Elizabeth granted when Daniel eagerly pressed her to play baseball with them. "Same teams as last time? We have a score to settle, don't we, Bradley?"

"Yes!" Bradley proclaimed, turning to his older brother, cousin and friend and informing them, "Me and Lizzy will beat you!"

"That's the spirit, Son," Richard encouraged his youngest with a broad grin. "I think I could be tempted to join you, you know. Can't remember the last time I put bat to ball."

"Oh please, Papa," Joe implored. "That would be fantastic."

"Well, if these two agree to play as well," Richard nodded to Sir Charles and Darcy. "I could hardly say no."

As he had intended, all the boys set about convincing the two men to play with them and neither Sir Charles or Darcy were proof against their persuasion.

"Yes, that is all very well," Jane spoke up, smiling in spite of herself. "But before you can play we must have luncheon, so I suggest we all make our way down to the lake."

Sir Charles was immediately at Jane's side, offering her his arm and assisting her to her feet; Elizabeth smiled at her brother-in-law's solicitude and then accepted her own husband's arm when he offered it.

"This was what you meant, when you said that you had plans for my birthday that had to be changed for Ellerslie's visit," she commented quietly to him and when he nodded admitted, "I forgot you had said that - I thought Poppy was my surprise."

"I rather thought you did," Darcy replied with a grin. "Happy Birthday - again."

"Thank you," Elizabeth replied quietly and they followed the Bingleys from the room and out to the front steps.

Poppy and Agatha, who Darcy had insisted they bring with them for reasons Elizabeth now understood, were waiting outside with a footman and the entire group spent some time fussing over the young puppy, who was delighted with all of the attention. As James took control of Poppy's lead and went on ahead with the other boys, Catherine walked between Elizabeth and Jane, holding the former's hand whilst shooting intrigued looks at the latter's expanding tummy.

"When are you going to have your baby, Lady Jane?" she asked eventually and all six of the adults smiled at her question.

"In about five months," Jane replied. "Perhaps a little less."

"And will it be a boy or a girl?"

"We do not know; it is not possible to tell. But I would dearly love a little girl just like you, princess," Jane admitted and Catherine smiled and blushed prettily at the compliment.

"And what about you, Uncle Charles?" Catherine asked, leaning around so she could see Sir Charles. "What would you like?"

"As long as the babe is healthy, I would be happy with a boy or girl," Sir Charles replied and the adults all smiled and agreed with the sentiment, knowing the trouble the couple had had in the past.

"I think when I have a baby I would like a little girl more," Catherine surprised them all by stating. "Then I could buy her pretty dresses and ribbons."

"I think it is a little too soon to be thinking about that, princess," Elizabeth commented with an amused smile as Darcy ruefully shook his head. "Though I am sure when the time comes that you will be a wonderful mother."

"I hope I am just like you," Catherine replied with disarming honesty and Elizabeth stopped to kiss her cheek.

"I love you Catherine, thank you," she said quietly as she straightened and Catherine smiled up at her.

"I love you too, Mama. Oh look, I can see the picnic! Come on Lizzy!"

Sharing a look with her husband, who seemed just as touched by Catherine's almost casual declaration, Elizabeth allowed Catherine to lead her on ahead of the others. Darcy watched them go, a lump in his throat.

"Oh William," Georgiana sighed happily as Richard smiled his equal pleasure. "They are so sweet together. Elizabeth is so good with her, and with James too. I do not think you could have chosen any better."

"Well of course not!" Sir Charles teased and they all laughed, lightening the moment and sparing Darcy the necessity of formulating a reply.

They soon reached the picnic area and sat down to their meal, chatting and laughing and generally having a fine time of it. Darcy and the other two men fell to discussing the latest developments on the continent and the possibility that Richard would soon be called back to London; James listened with half an ear to their conversation as he sat with the other boys, quite interested in what was happening in Europe and the world outside of England. And Catherine sat with her aunt and young cousin and chatted happily about her own birthday and the presents she had received. The boys, however, could not remain settled for long and were soon up again, eager to begin their game.

"We have not finished our luncheon," Sir Charles noted with a laugh, indicating his plate which was still half full. "Sit down for a bit longer boys."

"Or better yet," Darcy spoke up. "Take the dogs for a walk around the lake. We will have finished by the time you return and then we can have our game."

Though Daniel took some persuading, Joe and Bradley were happy with that plan and James agreed to go with them to keep an eye on the younger boys. Elizabeth watched them all walk away, Agatha trotting along quite happily at James' side and Poppy dashing about in front of them, pulling Joe along with her.

"Did you train Agatha yourself, my love, or have someone do it for you?" she asked her husband, turning to look at him as he replied.

"I had help from one of the grooms. Why, do you think we will need help with Poppy?" Darcy asked with a smile and Elizabeth laughed.

"Yes, I do. I would prefer not to be dragged around the grounds when I walk her, and avoiding another swim would be nice too," she added and Jane and Georgiana both smiled at the remembrance.

"Jane," Elizabeth spoke quietly to her sister some time later. "Have you heard from anyone at Longbourn recently? Only I wrote to Mrs Carey some time ago and have yet to receive any reply, which is most unlike her."

"No, I never write," Jane replied. "I'm sorry."

"It's alright," Elizabeth assured her. "I have written another letter and William is having his post boy deliver it directly. I'm sure my last was simply lost."

"Yes, I'm sure that must be it," Jane agreed casually and they let the subject drop, though questions still nagged at the back of one sister's mind.

"Oh look, here are the boys back," Richard pointed to the small group making their way towards them, Poppy running on ahead and Agatha bringing up the rear. "Time for our game. Will any of you ladies be joining us?" he asked as he got to his feet. "Besides Elizabeth, of course."

"We are quite comfortable here, thank you very much," Georgiana replied with a smile, shooing her husband away. "Go and enjoy your game."

Richard did as he was bid and strolled over to join the boys; Darcy offered Elizabeth a hand up and the two of them, along with Sir Charles, also went over to the boys and joined the debate about how the eight of them should be divided into teams. In the end it was decided that Sir Charles, Richard, Daniel and Joe would form one team, Darcy, Elizabeth, James and Bradley the other. A toss of a coin decided that Darcy's team would bat first, and the game began. There was much laughter and friendly competition as they played, everyone cheering their teammates on and congratulating each other on fine hits and good catches.

When it was Bradley's turn to bat, his father (who was bowling) came a little closer to make it easier for his son and Elizabeth helped Bradley hold the bat firmly. Richard bowled a nice slow ball and Bradley swung for it, catching the ball with the very edge of the bat.

"Go Bradley!" Elizabeth called as the ball flew behind them and Daniel, playing as backstop, ran after it. As Bradley dashed off towards first base, Darcy caught up with Daniel and effortlessly swept him up off the floor, holding the laughing boy under one arm.

"Not so fast, if you please," Darcy teased as Richard and the rest of his team laughed and offered only token protests against Darcy's cheating.

"Go Bradley, keep going!" Elizabeth called, spurring the little boy on as he ran for the next base. "Get to second!"

Darcy finally put Daniel down and allowed him to fetch the ball, throwing it to Richard as Bradley made it to second base and scored half a point.

"Good job, Son!" Richard congratulated Bradley who was grinning from ear to ear, vastly pleased with himself.

Darcy stepped up for his turn to bat and Richard grinned at him.

"We owe you for that."

"Do your worst," Darcy taunted and Elizabeth and James laughed at their bantering.

"Charles, get ready!" Richard called and Sir Charles moved further away from the pitch, ready to field Darcy's hit. "Ready, Joe?"

"Ready," Joe affirmed, marking second base and ready for anything that came his way.

"Get ready to run Bradley," Elizabeth reminded the youngest boy. "As soon as the ball leaves your father's hand, run!"

Richard bowled a fast and straight ball but Darcy nevertheless hit it well and sent it soaring off to the left. He sprinted for first base as Richard yelled for Charles to get the ball and Bradley ran for third base as fast as his legs would carry him. His uncle, however, was too quick and was soon right behind him, about to run him out when he scooped up his young nephew and ran with him the rest of the way. Elizabeth and James cheered loudly as the pair passed the fourth base.

"Christ, I'm getting too old for this," Darcy huffed with a rueful grin as he set Bradley down. He collapsed tiredly onto the grass and tried to get his breath back.

"Too much for you, Darcy?" Richard chortled as Elizabeth stepped up for her turn to bat.

She was caught out, rather brilliantly, by Sir Charles and James was unlucky with his running on his next go. As the two teams swapped over, Richard carelessly tossed the ball to his cousin.

"Let's see what you can do. You used to have a quick arm, if I remember rightly."

"Actually," Darcy replied with a grin as he handed the ball to his wife. "Elizabeth is bowling for us."

Richard looked surprised and then smiled; Elizabeth saw it and laughed.

"I wouldn't jump to conclusions if I were you, Colonel."

Richard held his hands up with a laugh.

"I didn't say anything!"

"You didn't have to," Elizabeth responded with a knowing smile and then walked over to the bowling circle.

Darcy took second base as his son went out deep to field and Bradley stood as backstop. Richard stood behind his youngest son, ready to give Bradley a hand as backstop as Daniel stepped up to bat, followed by Joe. Both boys managed to strike the ball and made it to second base, earning half a point each. Darcy and his team had scored five and a half points and Richard was convinced his team could best that score. He swapped places with Sir Charles and stepped up for his turn to bat, facing Elizabeth expectantly. He had seen her bowl for the two boys and was confident he could get a good hit. Elizabeth smiled at the Colonel and then bowled the first ball - fast and straight - and watched as he swung and missed and Bradley easily fielded it.

"One," Elizabeth said as Richard adjusted his stance slightly and then brandished the bat.

She bowled again, faster, and again Richard swung and missed it.

"Two," Elizabeth said as she caught the ball Bradley threw back to her. "Last chance, Colonel."

Richard glared playfully at her and Elizabeth smiled as she bowled the final ball, which he managed to clip with the bat, getting him as far as second.

Darcy smiled smugly at his cousin as they stood together at second base.

"Did I forget to mention that Elizabeth played baseball quite a lot when she was younger?"

"Yes, you did," Richard grumbled and then playfully poked his cousin in the chest. "You, Fitzwilliam Darcy, are a cheat."

"Now, now cousin," Darcy replied with infuriating good cheer. "Don't be a sore loser."

Richard made an indignant noise but before he could reply they were distracted by Sir Charles, who managed to hit the ball and send it flying between second and third base. Darcy made to run after it but was hampered by the hold Richard had on the back of his waistcoat.

"Richard!" Darcy laughed and the two men wrestled with one another as Sir Charles sprinted past and James had to run in from deep field to get the ball. Richard only let go of his cousin when Sir Charles was past fourth base and patted Darcy on the shoulder.

"Turnabout is fair play, eh Darcy?"

Darcy just laughed and shook his head.

The score was now at two and a half points and though Daniel managed to get another half point, Joe was caught out. Darcy's team only needed to get one more of Richard's team out, and Richard's team only needed two and a half points to draw level; it was a tight game, and even Jane and Georgiana, watching from the picnic blankets, were excited about who would win. Sir Charles scored another point and the pressure was on Richard to score at least half a point and not get caught or stumped out. Elizabeth bowled her fastest ball but Richard still managed to hit it well and, despite brilliant fielding on James' part, still made it safely past fourth base.

"This is it, boys," Richard rallied his team together. "Half a point in it. Daniel, you're next, but no pressure."

Daniel nodded and stepped up to face his aunt, who suppressed a smile at his determined expression. She bowled a nice, arching ball for him and watched as it flew over her head towards third base. Her husband fielded it at a rather leisurely pace and Daniel made it safely to second base, beaming when the rest of his team cheered loudly.

"No pressure now, Charles," Richard said with a grin, clapping the other man on the shoulder. "You can win this for us."

"Thank you, Richard," Sir Charles responded with a grin and bent to pick up the bat. He smiled over at his sister-in-law and teased, "I don't suppose you could bowl me a nice one like you did for Daniel, could you?"

"Not a chance," Elizabeth replied and bowled two fast balls, both of which Charles missed.

Deciding to see if she could catch him off guard, Elizabeth bowled the last ball slower and with a bit of spin, watching as Charles swung and the ball glanced off the edge of the bat, going high into the air and behind him. Sir Charles sprinted off towards first base as Bradley, still playing as backstop, ran forwards, hands out in front of him and neck craned backwards as he watched the ball. Everyone watching seemed to hold their breath as the ball began to descend and then landed securely in Bradley's outstretched hands.

There was a moment of stunned silence before everyone erupted into cheers, Richard the loudest of all of them as he scooped his son up into his arms.

"That's my boy! Brilliant catch, Son, utterly brilliant! Well done!"

The outcome of the game was all but forgotten as all the players came over to offer their own congratulations, marvelling over the great catch.

"Did you see, Mama, did you see?" Bradley ran over to Georgiana who enfolded her little boy in her arms.

"Of course I saw! My clever little boy! Well done you!"

It took a long time for the excitement to die down and attention to finally turn to the outcome of the game. Richard and the rest of his team were happy to tie and playfully argued that if it hadn't been for Bradley they would have won.

"Well we shall simply have to have a rematch," Darcy told his cousin as they walked back to the picnic area to join the others and have some refreshments.

"Fine by me, but I want Bradley on my team next time," Richard teased. "He's the secret weapon, obviously."

Elizabeth handed her husband a glass of lemonade once he'd settled down beside her.

"I think I shall have this, and then play with the dogs for a bit. The poor things were straining to join our game."

Darcy grinned ruefully as he gratefully drank his cool lemonade.

"You will forgive me if I do not join you. I have had enough running around for one day."

"But your stamina is usually so impressive," Elizabeth replied flirtatiously and laughed lightly when her husband almost choked on his drink.

She patted him gently on the back, smiling innocently as Darcy glared playfully at her.

"That was intentional."

"Oh completely," Elizabeth agreed lightly, setting aside her glass and standing. "But what did your cousin say earlier? Turnabout is fair play. You delight in flustering me, my love; I'm only returning the favour."

"Touché," Darcy responded quietly with a rueful grin as he watched his wife walk over to Agatha and Poppy and untie them.

"Here, Elizabeth," Richard offered Elizabeth the ball they had played their game with. "See how Poppy does at a bit of fetch."

"She'll probably just try and eat it," Elizabeth predicted as she tossed the ball away and both dogs bounded after it, Poppy trying her best to keep up with the huge strides of Agatha.

"May I?" Joe asked and Elizabeth gave the ball to him once Agatha had brought it back.

He threw it a little harder than was necessary and they all watched as the ball skidded across the grass and into the water. Agatha, undaunted, chased after it and jumped into the lake, the water level only reaching her shoulders.

"Poppy no!" Elizabeth called, rushing forwards as the eager puppy followed Agatha and jumped heedlessly into the water. "Poppy!"

"Elizabeth wait, let me!" Darcy called after his wife, quickly getting to his feet and jogging over to the water's edge.

Elizabeth dropped to her knees on the bank and reached down, scooping her distressed puppy from the water and into her lap. Agatha clambered out next to them, the ball in her mouth, and proceeded to shake the water from her coat, covering both Elizabeth and Darcy as he arrived at her side.

"What is it about you and water?" Darcy asked with amused exasperation as he crouched down besides his wife. "Is she alright?"

"I think so," Elizabeth replied, stroking Poppy's head. "Just wet and a bit frightened."

"I don't think she'll be doing that again anytime soon," Darcy responded and offered his hand. "Come, we can use one of the picnic blankets to dry her off. And then we had best take you home," he added with a pointed look at Elizabeth's filthy and soaking wet dress.

"Wilson is going to shout at me," Elizabeth predicted with a sigh as she stood up, Poppy still in her arms.

"I'm so sorry," Joe said to them as they walked back to the others. "I didn't mean for the ball to go that far."

"It's alright Joe," Darcy assured his nephew, patting his shoulder. "It wasn't your fault - Poppy just didn't know any better."

"Here, Lizzy, use this," Jane offered, handing Elizabeth a spare blanket which she used to rub Poppy dry, ignoring the weak yelps of protest.

"Do you think we shall ever be able to have a picnic without you ruining your dress, Elizabeth?" Georgiana asked playfully as she watched her sister-in-law at her task.

Elizabeth laughed.

"I do hope so!"

"At least you did not fall in this time," James pointed out with a grin and Darcy chuckled quietly to himself. When Elizabeth turned to look at him he admitted, "I think I shall always remember that day. I knew from your reaction that you were special."

"My reaction?" Elizabeth queried and Darcy smiled as he replied.

"You laughed."

"Well, I thought it was quite funny," Elizabeth responded lightly and Darcy's smile widened.

"And that, my dear, is what was special."

ଞଓଔ

On Thursday morning Darcy had business on the estate with his steward and decided to take his son with him; Elizabeth was to spend the day with her new friend, Lady Victoria, and so he knew neither he nor James would be much missed. He and James left quite early and with Catherine tucked away upstairs with Mrs Hughes, Elizabeth decided to go out to the stables a little early.

"Good morning Dot," she greeted her horse cheerily, entering Dot's stall. "How are you, hmmm? Getting used to all the new faces?"

Dot nuzzled her waist and Elizabeth offered her one of the chunks of carrot, stroking her nose as she ate happily. Hearing someone approach, Elizabeth turned to look over her shoulder and smiled.

"Good morning, Greg."

"Good morning, Ma'am," Greg replied respectfully but Elizabeth could immediately tell that something was troubling him. She silently gestured for him to join her in the stall.

"Is everything alright? Lucy, she is well?"

"Yes, she is quite well," Greg replied, absently stroking a hand over Dot's shoulder.

"But?" Elizabeth prompted. "I can see that something is troubling you Greg. You do not have to tell me, of course, but I hope that if it is something I can help with...?"

She trailed off quietly and waited as Greg hesitated before finally confiding in her.

"There's been a letter sent to Lucy from home, from her sister by the looks of it, but, well, we can't get it, not yet anyway, and Lucy is worried about what's in it. She's worried her mam might be sick, or her pa. We can't think of any other reason for them to write."

"I see," Elizabeth responded with a delicate frown. "That is worrying. And the letter, it is at the inn in Lambton, I suppose?"

Greg nodded mutely and Elizabeth knew what was being left unsaid - that they could not afford to pay the postage on a letter that had come so far.

She touched Greg's arm.

"I understand. Wait here for me, I will return shortly."

"Oh no, Lizzy, I never meant!" Greg objected, reaching out to forestall her and inadvertently catching hold of her hand.

Elizabeth smiled and pressed his hand as she replied.

"I know you didn't, but I still want to help you. Now wait here."

She returned to the house and collected the necessary money for the postage before going back to the stables and handing the coins to Greg.

"Go now and fetch your letter and take it home to your wife. I will tell Mr Hanes I have sent you on an errand, so don't worry about that."

Greg nodded and moved away, though he stopped when Elizabeth called him back.

"I will mostly likely be out riding with Lady Victoria when you return, but if there is anything in the letter which you feel I need to know, come and find me."

"Of course," Greg replied, but he looked puzzled.

"I have not heard from anyone at Longbourn for several weeks," Elizabeth admitted quietly. "I am sure it is nothing, but at the same time I am not easy about it. If there is any news in your letter that you think I need to hear, I would be grateful if you could find me as soon as possible."

"I will," Greg nodded again and left on his errand, leaving Elizabeth feeling a strange sense of foreboding which she decided to try and dispel with a thorough grooming session of Dot. She had just started when she remembered that she had to speak to Mr Hanes and tell him why Greg was not working. The stables were quite quiet at this time of day - it was best to work the horses in the morning before the sun became too strong - and she only passed one groom on her way to Mr Hanes' office. As she approached the door she heard voices from within.

"...and now he's gone off somewhere. I saw him go myself."

"I still do not see why you were watching in the first place, Gordon."

"I told you, Sir, I was just fetchin' a longer rein when I saw them together. Whispering and being all familiar like, touching and holding hands. I seen em' together before, you know, and thought then there was something fishy going on. Imagine them carrying on together, behind his back..."

"What, exactly, are you implying?" Mr Hanes demanded brusquely.

"That is precisely what I would like to know," Elizabeth stated coldly as she pushed open the door to Mr Hanes' office and stepped inside. She could not remember ever being so angry in her life and her voice shook with suppressed fury as she added, "Mr Gordon, is it?"

"Your Grace!"

Both men were shocked by her sudden appearance but Gordon, who Elizabeth recognised as the second in charge, looked particularly aggrieved.

Though she dearly wished to take the man to task for saying such despicable things about her, Elizabeth knew it would be beneath her dignity. Instead she turned and addressed Mr Hanes.

"On second thoughts, I have heard quite enough. I expect you to deal with this, Mr Hanes. Good day to you."

*If Mr Hanes has any sense*, Elizabeth thought furiously as she swept from the room, *he will dismiss that man before my husband comes home!* Her good mood well and truly ruined, Elizabeth found a groom and ordered him to have Dot saddled and ready as soon as may be. Her anger and indignation making her restless, she paced up and down in the yard, paying no heed to her surroundings. She could not *believe* the audacity of the man, to *spy* on her and to leap to such erroneous and insulting conclusions and share them with another person. How *dare* he?

When the groom led Dot out to her, Elizabeth fortunately realised that she was still too angry to ride and would likely do either herself or Dot an injury if she attempted it. Apologising to the groom and requesting that he keep Dot ready for when Lady Victoria arrived, she walked away from the stables, her footsteps taking her across the lawn to the rose garden. Designed by her husband's late mother, the rose garden was intricate and beautiful, a maze of walkways and arches. At this time of year it was in full bloom and a veritable riot of colours and perfumes bombarded Elizabeth's senses as she followed one of the pathways and found herself a bench to sit upon and cool her anger.

Sometime later, hearing the sound of a carriage, Elizabeth looked up and saw that her visitor had arrived and would soon be reaching the front steps. Mentally preparing herself to pretend that everything was perfectly fine, Elizabeth stood up and walked back across the lawn, fixing a smile on her face as Lady Victoria stepped down from the carriage. The two women greeted one another as the groom who had ridden Lady Victoria's horse dismounted and brought Jingo over to his mistress. Elizabeth was full of praise for her friend's fine mount and led them both to the stables where Dot was waiting for them.

"Shall we set off?" Elizabeth asked Victoria after she had given both horses the last few bits of carrot which she still had in her pocket.

"Please, lead the way," Victoria replied and both women gained the saddle.

"We shall be riding up East Hill, and then returning past the waterfall and around the lake," Elizabeth told the groom who was assisting them and then led the way out of the stable yard. Her husband liked for her to inform someone of where she intended to ride before she set off, but Elizabeth was mindful that should Greg have anything to tell her, he would need to know where to look.

Lady Victoria was good and pleasant company and with her as a companion Elizabeth was very nearly able to forget her troubles. Lady Victoria was also a very able horsewoman and as soon as they were clear of the manicured park they gave Dot and Jingo their heads and galloped together across the open fields. When they eventually slowed to a walk to allow the horses a chance to get their breath back, both women were flushed and a little breathless themselves.

"Oh, I am glad it is not just I who enjoys a vigorous gallop!" Lady Victoria enthused, her spirits high. "Mother is constantly telling me it is not ladylike, but now I shall simply tell her that the Duchess of Farleigh enjoys it too."

"And I'm sure your mother will reply," Elizabeth pointed out dryly, "that the Duchess of Farleigh has the advantage of being both married, and a Duchess."

"Alas, you are probably right!" Lady Victoria laughed. "Though it is beastly of you to say so."

"If it is any consolation," Elizabeth commented dryly, thinking of the situation with Mr Gordon, "There are as many rules for a married woman as there are for an unmarried one."

"Yes, I expect there are," Lady Victoria replied. "Though you are so fortunate, married to the Duke. He is such a fine man."

Elizabeth shot her friend an amused look as Lady Victoria blushed slightly and flapped her hand.

"No, no, I did not mean it like that. I simply meant that you are lucky to have married a good man, not that you are lucky to have married the Duke. Mother is determined that I be engaged by the end of the next Season and I doubt I am going to be as fortunate as you."

"You do not know that," Elizabeth replied sensibly. "You do not know who you will meet. I would never have imagined myself in my current position six months ago, let alone almost a year. Wait and see what happens."

"Well whatever happens," Lady Victoria stated with a smile. "I am very glad to have met you, Elizabeth."

"And I you," Elizabeth warmly replied and the two shared a smile.

As they reached the top of East Hill and admired the view, Elizabeth asked Victoria to tell her more about Bath and she, in turn, spoke about the time she had spent on the coast with William and the places they had visited.

They were on their way back to the house when Victoria asked Elizabeth about Longbourn.

"And your home before you married the Duke? What was it like there? Is it far from here?"

"Yes, quite far," Elizabeth admitted quietly, her mood sinking at the mention of Longbourn. "My father's estate is in Hertfordshire - it is about one hundred and thirty miles."

"And you have no other siblings, besides Lady Jane?" Victoria asked and Elizabeth indicated that that was correct. "I should have liked a sister."

"I daresay I would have preferred a brother," Elizabeth admitted with a light laugh. "But Jane is the perfect sister, so I cannot complain."

"She has always seemed a very kind lady to me," Victoria replied and Elizabeth thanked her for the compliment.

"And your brother, what is he like?" she asked, and Victoria rolled her eyes.

"He is quite typical for his set - wealthy, handsome and insufferable. He would be very good company were he not so full of himself."

Elizabeth laughed.

"Well, I will look forward to meeting him."

They were just riding up the drive to the stables when a figure, which Elizabeth quickly recognised as Greg, came running towards them. Her heart was in her mouth as she rode to meet him and quickly dismounted.

"What is it, what has happened?"

"You need to read this," Greg told her and handed her the letter he carried.

# Chapter 20

Elizabeth took the letter with a shaking hand and only managed to read through the first paragraph before her legs almost gave out and Greg had to hold her upright. Neither noticed that they had an audience.

"How?!" Elizabeth gasped uncomprehendingly. "Why wasn't I told? Oh Father."

"Come, Lizzy, let me take you to the house," Greg spoke quietly to her but Elizabeth hardly heard him, still trying to digest the shocking news.

They both jumped when an angry voice spoke from behind them.

"Foster, unhand my wife this instant."

"William," Elizabeth moaned and promptly abandoned Greg for the superior comforts of her husband's arms.

Darcy was momentarily distracted from his anger by his wife's distress.

"Elizabeth, are you unwell?"

"Her father is sick," Greg informed his employer, thinking only to be helpful. At the look Darcy sent him, he fell silent and averted his eyes.

"Go back to work," Darcy brusquely ordered the young man. "And take my wife's horse with you. Lady Victoria, if you will forgive me I will take my wife inside now."

"Of course," Lady Victoria replied quickly, not really understanding what was happening but knowing that her friend was clearly upset. "I will take my leave, unless there is anything I can do..."

"That is kind of you, but my wife just needs to rest," Darcy replied and Lady Victoria silently nodded her acquiescence and slowly rode Jingo towards the stables, leaving the couple alone. "Come, Elizabeth - can you walk?"

"Yes," Elizabeth nodded and tried to pull herself together. "Yes, I am fine. I just, I don't understand..." she murmured distractedly and began to read the letter once more.

Darcy stopped her with a firm hand and firmer command.

"Not now. We need to return to the house."

"But," Elizabeth began to protest, looking up at her husband. She stopped when she saw the tightness of his jaw and compression of his lips. "What is wrong? What has happened?"

Darcy shook his head and only then did Elizabeth see, over his shoulder, the gathering of staff around the stables and the attempts Mr Hansen was making to get them to go back to their work. Eventually they all did as they were told, though with many looks and glances in her and her husband's direction.

"William, " Elizabeth began but Darcy cut her off.

"We can discuss this later - you are clearly unwell. I will take you to your room and you can rest whilst I address the issue."

"I am not unwell and I want to discuss this now," Elizabeth stubbornly replied, her temper flaring at his high-handed manner.

"You have made enough of a spectacle of yourself for one day," Darcy snapped back. "You *will* go to your room, and you *will* wait until I am ready to discuss this with you."

"How dare you?!" Elizabeth gasped, hurt and outraged. "How dare you address me like a child? I am your wife!"

"Then you should bloody well act like it!" Darcy hissed furiously and it felt like he had slapped her. Elizabeth just stared at him, trying to reconcile this man with the husband she knew.

"Let go of my arm," she eventually stated hollowly; when he did not release her she carried on in the same tone. "I will go to my room and stay there - now let go of my arm."

Darcy released his grip on her arm which he had barely been aware of holding at all, and Elizabeth turned and walked away from him, the letter still clutched in one hand. Darcy watched her go, his feelings conflicted.

"*Shit!*" He bit out furiously and turned away from his wife and stalked back towards the stables to try and rescue the situation before it became completely unmanageable.

He had returned from his business to find the stables seemingly deserted and had left James with the horses whilst he went in search of his staff. He had found a group of them all together, talking animatedly amongst themselves until one of them had spotted him and the whole group had fallen abruptly silent. After demanding why they were not at work and receiving no clear answer, he had ordered them back to their jobs and gone in search of Mr Hanes.

The story he had had from his stable master was both infuriating and deeply embarrassing.

"Your Grace," Mr Hanes greeted him anxiously when he reached the stables and Darcy had to remind himself to keep his temper with the man.

"Bring Foster to me, and have everyone assemble in the yard in ten minutes."

"Yes Sir, right away," Hanes replied and hurried away to do his bidding.

Alone for the moment, Darcy sighed tiredly and ran a hand through his hair, giving it a frustrated tug as his mind repeated his argument with Elizabeth back to him, reminding him of his harsh words to her. But what else could he have said? She had shamed him with her behaviour. He knew there was no real impropriety, but there was still the appearance of it and in a situation like this, that was enough. He had warned her before about her familiarity with Foster, and she had not heeded him, and what had been the result? He was left with no choice but to dismiss a good worker and was forced to bear the indignity of dispelling rumours of his wife's supposed infidelity. He may have been harsh with her, but the situation merited it!

Darcy was disturbed from his thoughts by the appearance of Greg, who tentatively knocked on the doorframe to announce his presence.

"Come in and shut the door," Darcy said and Greg promptly did as ordered.

"I want you to tell me what went on here this morning between yourself and my wife," Darcy instructed the young man standing nervously before him and Greg stumbled over his reply.

"N-nothing, Sir! Nothing like what Gordon said, at least. She, your wife that is, she was getting Dot ready to ride and I went over to her and we got talking, like we always do, but she could tell that something weren't quite right with me and..."

Darcy listened to the tale with an impassive face, waiting for Greg to finish.

"That's it? That is the whole truth?"

"Yes Sir, I swear it, Sir!" Greg vowed strongly. He seemed to steel himself for a moment before staunchly adding, "Her Grace would never do nothing wrong, Sir. She is honourable and, and good!"

"I do not need you to tell me about my own wife, Foster," Darcy bit out; angry at the liberty Greg was taking. "This familiarity between you, it ends now. The only reason I have not dismissed you is because it would make this situation worse, but if you ever presume to," Darcy cut off the rest of his sentence, aware that his anger was getting the better of him. He took a deep breath and after a moment went on, "I will not have you, however unknowingly, bring shame upon my good name. From now on you will keep any and all interactions with my wife strictly professional, or you will find yourself without a job. Do I make myself clear?"

"Yes, Sir," Greg murmured, eyes down and Darcy watched him for a moment before brusquely ordering him out.

The unpleasant interview out of the way, Darcy went out to the yard where Hansen and the rest of the stable workers were all assembled. They all fell silent when he appeared and Darcy stood looking at them for so long without saying anything that a number had begun to shift uncomfortably before he finally spoke.

"I will only say this once. Mr Gordon has been dismissed because he made false, unfounded accusations about your mistress. If any of you are heard repeating those accusations, here or elsewhere, you will be similarly dismissed. This incident is to be forgotten and you are to continue treating my wife with the respect that she deserves - I will not accept anything less. Now return to your duties and remember what I have said to you."

Darcy did not stay to see the effect of his words; he turned away and took the side door out of the stables and walked to the house, trying to decide what he should say to his wife. He was somewhat surprised when he reached the second floor to find it a hive of activity and he stopped a passing maid to ask what was happening.

"We are preparing Her Grace's trunks for departure, Sir," the poor girl nervously informed him and scurried away when Darcy dismissed her with a wave of his hand.

Darcy went to his wife's room and entered to find her busily packing a small case and Wilson overseeing the packing of two larger trunks.

"What is the meaning of this?" Darcy demanded and Elizabeth span around to face him as Wilson glared furiously in his direction but otherwise ignored him completely.

"I am leaving," Elizabeth informed him.

"Don't be absurd!" Darcy scoffed but Elizabeth saw the flicker of alarm which passed across his face at her pronouncement; she was in no mood to feel any sympathy, however, and laughed without humour.

"I am not leaving *you* - I am going to Longbourn."

"Not without my permission," Darcy told her imperiously, unprepared for the situation and thus handling it badly.

"I do not need your permission!" Elizabeth shouted at him as she furiously threw down the book she had been holding. "I am not one of your servants! I am leaving as soon as the carriage is ready and if you prevent me from going I will never forgive you."

"There is no need for this," Darcy stated, gesturing to the half packed trunks. "If you would just calm down we could discuss this like,"

"Adults?" Elizabeth finished for him, sounding even angrier than before. "As opposed to? But of course I am just an immature, misbehaving child in your eyes, aren't I?"

"When you behave like this, your immaturity is quite apparent," Darcy retorted coldly, stung by the intimation that he thought her anything less than a grown woman.

Her eyes stinging with unshed tears which she was adamantly refusing to let fall, Elizabeth shook her head sadly.

"So this is how you really see me? Thank you for making it so abundantly clear."

Realisation fell over Darcy like a bucket of cold water and he tried to backtrack.

"Elizabeth, I didn't mean,"

But Elizabeth wouldn't let him go on.

"I need to finish packing - we will leave within the hour."

"I will come with you," Darcy began but his wife shook her head.

"There is no reason. I will not be gone long - I doubt the end is far away."

"The end?" Darcy repeated with a sense of alarm. "Then your father, he is...?"

"Dying? Yes," Elizabeth replied. "And you would have known that had you thought to ask. But you did not, which is why I prefer to go alone. Now if you will excuse me, I must say goodbye to the children."

She walked away from her husband and only burst into tears once she was sure she was out of earshot, tucked away in one of the unused bedrooms down the hallway from her own. Still standing where Elizabeth had left him, Darcy was plagued by indecision and unsure about what he should do. He was startled by a loud bang and looked sharply at Wilson, who had let the lid of one of the trunks fall shut. It was just the two of them in the room and they regarded one another with mutual ire.

"Perhaps you should read the letter," Wilson suggested with a glance at the bedside table where Elizabeth had left the missive, "before you do anymore damage."

"Or you could simply tell me what has happened and spare me the necessity," Darcy responded and Wilson glared at him fiercely before begrudgingly relenting.

"What has Elizabeth told you regarding the staff at Longbourn?"

"I am aware that until recently Mr Nichols was the steward there, and Mrs Carey is the housekeeper, but beyond that..."

"And Mr Hounsell, you have heard mention of him? For he is at the root of all this trouble, it seems."

"What does the letter say?" Darcy asked, worried now by Wilson's dire tone.

"Elizabeth's father is gravely ill and has been confined to his bed for several weeks, though very few people have been allowed to see him in that time. Mr Hounsell, who was initially employed only as an assistant, has gradually gained influence over the Viscount and has so advanced himself that he now effectively controls the whole house and estate at Longbourn. All the servants that were loyal to Elizabeth - Mrs Carey, Mrs Braddock, Mr Nichols, Mr Carey - they have all been dismissed and replaced by associates of Mr Hounsell and the house is almost entirely serviced by those loyal to him, including his wife, who is now housekeeper. The disruption this caused to the routine of the house greatly agitated Elizabeth's father and he was apparently further unsettled by the total incompetence of the new staff Mr Hounsell had hired. The strain upon the Viscount finally became too much when he discovered that some of his work had been disturbed by a careless maid, and he suffered an apoplexy. He has been bedridden ever since, attended by a doctor of Mr Hounsell's choosing. According to Mrs Foster's sister (who wrote the letter), only Mr and Mrs Hounsell and one or two maids are allowed into his room and it was through one of these maids that they were able to learn that the Viscount is gravely ill and near death."

"How could this have happened? Why did no one write before now?"

"There was no one left to write," Wilson replied. "By the time the Viscount was taken ill all the old staff were gone, and before then I am sure Mr Hounsell took steps to prevent any letters being sent and received. Miss Lewis or Reverend Baker could have been relied upon to send word, but the former was also dismissed and the latter is with his sister in Shropshire, whose husband has taken ill. Likely it was assumed by the rest that Elizabeth was aware of the situation and did not care, and it was only when the Viscount took ill and she did not appear that people became suspicious."

"This Mr Hounsell," Darcy asked with a thoughtful frown, "is he dangerous, do you think? He is clearly a devious and cunning man, but do you think he will become violent when my wife arrives and confronts him with his crimes - which I have no doubt she intends to do?"

"Does it matter what I think?" Wilson asked with a knowing look. "You have obviously reached your own conclusion."

Darcy shot the outspoken, infuriating woman a cold look before turning on his heel and striding into his own chamber, calling for Pattinson and instructing that a case be packed for him and loaded onto the carriage waiting outside.

"Before you do that, though," Darcy added, "fetch me a new set of riding clothes."

"Of course, Sir, at once," Pattinson stated, hiding his surprise that his master was going to go on horseback rather than ride in the carriage with the Duchess.

Darcy quickly changed and then sat down to pen some letters to some business associates he was due to meet with the following day and some notes of instruction for his steward and Mrs Reynolds. He heard Elizabeth return to her chamber next door and when he was finished with his task he went in search of the children. They were both sat together in the playroom and Catherine hopped off her seat and ran to him when he appeared in the doorway.

"Oh, Papa, is it not horrible about Lizzy's papa? Is he very sick?"

"I believe so, though we will only know once we have seen him and spoken to the doctor," Darcy replied as he briefly embraced his daughter and then led her back over to where her brother now stood.

"You are going with Lizzy, aren't you, Father?" James questioned and Darcy wondered how much his son understood about the situation.

"I am," Darcy confirmed and James definitely seemed relieved to hear it. "We shall leave as soon as the carriage is loaded. I am sorry it is so sudden."

"It is alright, we will be fine," James responded, putting his arm around his sister's shoulders. "We shall take care of one another, and Mr and Mrs Hughes will take care of us."

"You are a good boy, Son," Darcy complimented sincerely, briefly gripping James' shoulder. "I have no doubt you will look after your sister whilst we are gone. And Poppy and Agatha too," he added with a smile between his two children. "You must take care of them both for us."

"We already promised Lizzy that we would walk Poppy every day," Catherine informed her father and Darcy nodded and smiled.

"Very well then. I must see to more of the arrangements, but when we are ready to leave we will send for you to say goodbye. Go back to your lessons now, and I will see you again in a little while."

Both children did as they were bid and Darcy left them to go downstairs; he found that almost everything was in readiness for his wife's departure and ordered that Fletcher be saddled and brought to him as soon as possible.

The first indication Elizabeth had that she was not going to be travelling alone came when she arrived downstairs to find the children saying goodbye to their father and wishing him a safe journey. Doing her best to hide her reaction to the news, Elizabeth smiled and embraced Catherine as the little girl bid her farewell.

"I hope your papa gets better Lizzy," Catherine said and Elizabeth kissed the top of her head.

"Thank you, princess - so do I."

"I will miss you," Catherine told her with a little sob and Elizabeth held her tighter.

"I will miss you too. I promise I will not be gone long."

Catherine nodded and wiped her eyes, stepping away so that Elizabeth could say goodbye to James.

"I hope you have a safe journey," James expressed and then, a little awkwardly, put his arms around Elizabeth and embraced her. "I will miss you too."

"I will miss you as well," Elizabeth replied tearfully, kissing James' cheek and managing a small smile. "Do take care."

"We will be fine," James assured her with a confident smile and Elizabeth nodded. "I hope *you* will be," he added quietly and Elizabeth patted his cheek in a decidedly maternal manner.

"I will be fine. I shall see you both soon," she said as she stepped away and then turned to enter the carriage.

As she was making herself comfortable she could see Darcy saying one final farewell to the children and watched as he strode over to Fletcher and mounted with his usual easy grace. Once the carriage had rolled away from the house, Elizabeth sat back against the cushions and regarded her maid with a speculating frown.

"You knew about this, I suppose?" she said at last and Wilson nodded.

"I believe your husband decided that it was not safe for you to confront Mr Hounsell alone."

"You might have told me," Elizabeth responded harshly but Wilson just smiled as she picked up her knitting and began counting stitches.

"I happen to agree with him - who knows how Mr Hounsell will react when you suddenly appear?"

Elizabeth opened her mouth to argue but then thought better of it. She stared moodily out of the window, very conscious of the fact that her husband was riding alongside the carriage on the opposite side. There was silence for almost an hour before she eventually broke it.

"Am I wrong to feel it so? Do I take on too much?"

"Take on?" Wilson repeated, setting aside her knitting. "No, for that implies that you are exaggerating your feelings, which I doubt is the case. No, I am sure you are every bit as hurt and upset as you appear to be. Whether you are *right* to be so upset, that is a more difficult question."

"I did not think he would ever speak to me the way he did," Elizabeth confessed and felt tears coming at the thought of what her husband had said to her.

"Perhaps that is only because he has never had occasion to in the past," Wilson replied sensibly. "You have known all along, though, that your husband is a proud man. Not unduly so, and certainly not without reason, but he is proud of his family and his good name. Today you jeopardised that for the first time and are upset because his reaction displayed to you a side of his character you had not seen before."

Elizabeth did not attempt to argue with Wilson's disturbingly accurate assessment of the situation.

"I could forgive his anger quite easily, but I cannot forget his choice of words or his manner of speaking. He made me feel like a foolish child."

"I am certain that was not his intention," Wilson responded firmly. "That being said, however innocent you were of wrongdoing you were nevertheless imprudent and incautious and your husband was, I think, within his rights to remind you that as his wife you should really be neither."

Elizabeth covered her face with her hand.

"I never meant for any of this to happen!"

"I know you didn't, petal," Wilson soothed. "And I am sure your husband does as well. He was just angry and embarrassed—"

"By me!" Elizabeth pointed out, sitting back with a noise of anguish. "Because I have made it seem - because everyone now thinks that I am cuckolding him!"

"I see you understand why your husband reacted the way he did," Wilson noted dryly and Elizabeth glared at her, not quite ready to completely absolve her husband.

"It is all because of that damned letter," Elizabeth muttered to herself some time later. "I wish it had never been sent."

"Do you?" Wilson queried, studying Elizabeth for her reaction. "You would likely have learnt of your father's illness too late had it not been."

"I know," Elizabeth replied with a decidedly dark and unhappy smile. "I would also not have quarrelled with William and likely been very happy in my ignorance of the situation at Longbourn. I think it is a fair indication of the quality of my character that I find that the distinctly more preferable option."

"I think you should refrain from casting judgement upon yourself when the issue in question pertains to your father," Wilson recommended quietly. "You have never been able to be fair to yourself where he is concerned."

Elizabeth stared at her maid and then rapidly blinked to clear away the tears forming in her eyes. She accepted the handkerchief Wilson wordlessly offered her and wiped her cheeks.

"I do not know what I would do without you."

"Neither do I," Wilson responded, not entirely joking, and Elizabeth laughed tearfully.

ೞଔ

When they finally reached the inn at which they were to spend the night, the owner, hearing the arrival of the carriage, came out personally to meet them and welcomed his guests warmly, hiding his surprise that both the Duke and Duchess had arrived when he had been told to only expect the latter.

"I trust my wife's room is ready," Darcy stated with a quick glance at Elizabeth as she came to stand beside him.

"Indeed it is, Your Grace," the owner responded quickly. "Though I am sorry to say I have only the one room prepared for you. I had thought - the lad who came - but perhaps I was mistaken...?"

"No, there was no mistake," Darcy responded after a slight pause, to Elizabeth's silent dismay. "Only a change of plans. If you could have an additional room prepared for me, I would be most grateful."

"Of course, Your Grace," the owner stated with a slight bow. "At once. I am afraid the room will be in a separate part of the building, though," he added tentatively, fearing that his esteemed guests would not be happy with that arrangement.

Darcy shot another quick glance at his wife whose head was bowed before replying.

"That will be fine."

After this pronouncement by her husband, Elizabeth managed to find her voice.

"Perhaps whilst my husband's room is being prepared you could show me to my own, as I am quite tired from our journey and wish to rest a while before dinner?"

"Of course, Your Grace, please follow me."

Elizabeth chanced a glance at her husband and then hurried after the owner before he had a chance to offer any sort of reaction. Darcy watched her disappear inside, wishing that he had said something - wishing that *she* had said something - to indicate that there was a chance for them to reconcile.

Wilson, who had watched the entire exchange from a discreet distance, rolled her eyes at the behaviour of both her mistress and her master and resolved in her mind to bring things to a head before the night was out. It would not do to allow the discord to continue into a new day.

&#8526;&#8475;

Elizabeth was disturbed from her unhappy thoughts when Wilson sighed loudly.

"Oh, those silly grooms, they never do anything right."

"What is the matter?" Elizabeth asked quietly from her seat at the window, from which she had been staring unseeingly out into the night.

"One of your trunks is missing," Wilson replied. "The small one with the brass clasp. I saw them take it from the carriage myself, so they must have put it with your husband's things. I will go and fetch it now."

Elizabeth nodded and then turned back to the window, missing Wilson's smile as she left the room and briskly made her way to the other side of the inn where (she had earlier learnt) the Duke's room was. Knocking firmly on the door, Wilson assumed a neutral expression and waited for Pattinson to answer the summons. He appeared neither surprised nor displeased to see her, but Wilson knew that he was probably both, and too well trained to show it.

"Who is it, Pattinson?" The Duke's voice came from inside the room and Pattinson turned slightly to answer his master.

"It is Wilson, Sir."

Wilson heard the sound of the Duke getting swiftly to his feet and soon he appeared in the doorway.

"Is something amiss with my wife?"

"No, Sir," Wilson replied with uncharacteristic softness, touched by the obvious concern he had for her mistress. "I have come in search of one of her trunks - it does not appear to be in her room, and I know that it was unloaded from the carriage. I thought perhaps it might be in here."

A quick check of the pile of trunks in the corner of Darcy's room ascertained that Elizabeth's trunk was indeed amongst them, and Wilson made all the necessary noises of surprise and satisfaction to find it there.

"I shall require help carrying it back to my mistress' room," she commented quietly to herself. "I shall send for a boy."

"No, no, there is no need," Pattinson interposed as he bent to pick up the trunk. "I can carry it."

Darcy, who had for some time been studying Wilson intently, slowly shook his head.

"No, Pattinson, allow me. I wish to speak to my wife in any case."

"If you are sure, Your Grace," Pattinson replied, handing over the trunk and glancing between his master and Wilson, the latter quickly hiding her satisfied smile.

"Yes," Darcy told his man. "And I can manage by myself for the rest of the night - go and find yourself some dinner and I will see you in the morning."

"Very good, Sir," Pattinson responded with a bow and watched as his master left the room, followed by Wilson.

"Meddling woman," he muttered to himself, a reluctant smile playing about his lips.

"Did you find the trunk, Wilson?" Elizabeth asked when she heard the door to her room opening, not bothering to look away from the window.

"Yes, it was in my room," Darcy replied and watched his wife jump and abruptly turn to face him.

"If you could please put it here with the others, Sir," Wilson directed him and Darcy did as he was bid, glad for the distraction.

"Well, now that that problem is resolved," Wilson stated briskly, looking backwards and forwards between her silent mistress and master. "And if you have no further need of me, Ma'am, I think I shall go and join Mr Pattinson and have a spot of dinner."

"Very well, Wilson, thank you," Elizabeth managed to reply with tolerable composure.

Wilson nodded and Darcy watched as she curtseyed to them both and departed, closing the door behind her with a soft thud. Alone with his wife for the first time since their argument, Darcy was suddenly at a loss for words. Turning slightly to observe the room he noted the small fire burning in the grate.

"I doubt you shall need a fire tonight - it is still rather warm out."

"Yes," Elizabeth agreed quietly and Darcy could have kicked himself for beginning a discussion about the weather simply because he could not think of what else to say to his wife.

"And you are happy with the room?" Darcy asked awkwardly, wishing for a little more encouragement from Elizabeth.

"Yes, it is quite comfortable," Elizabeth responded and then pushed herself to ask, "And your room, you are happy with it?"

Darcy gave a slight shrug, feeling miserable.

"It is adequate. I will simply have to make do."

"You do not have to," Elizabeth murmured and Darcy quickly looked at her. She almost lost her courage but forced herself to go on. "That is, if you do not wish to. If you think you would be more comfortable here then I would be happy for you to stay."

Darcy reached his wife in two quick strides and pulled her into his arms.

"Oh Elizabeth," he sighed, clutching her to him. "Elizabeth, my love, I am so sorry, please forgive me," he implored, his hands moving up to cradle her face. "I should never have said those things, I did not mean them, I was just angry with Gordon and Foster."

"No, no, I am sorry," Elizabeth replied breathlessly, her hands gripping the lapels of his coat. "I'm sorry for being so imprudent, for causing the situation in the first place. You mustn't blame yourself for being angry; it was nothing more than I deserved."

Darcy shook his head.

"I had no business speaking to you the way I did. I forgot myself and I am heartily sorry for it."

"But if I had not," Elizabeth argued but Darcy again cut her off.

"I should still never have - "

Elizabeth placed two fingers against his lips to silence her husband and after a moment he huffed a rueful sigh.

"Perhaps we should not quarrel for the greater share of blame," she suggested quietly, realising that they were both too anxious to exonerate the other. "And simply say that we both were at fault."

"Perhaps that would be best," Darcy responded after a moment. "But I will only agree to it if you tell me that you accept my apology."

"I do," Elizabeth assured him, managing a tearful smile. "But you must tell me that you forgive my imprudence."

"I do," Darcy averred, reaching up and wiping away a stray tear with the pad of his thumb. "I am truly sorry, Elizabeth."

"I know," she whispered and Darcy bent and pressed a whisper-soft kiss to her lips.

"I never meant to hurt you," Darcy murmured as he drew back, unable to excuse his own conduct so easily, but Elizabeth pressed two fingers to his lips again.

"Enough now - it is over with. Let us move on."

Elizabeth's stomach chose that precise moment to rumble rather loudly and Darcy grinned lopsidedly.

"To dinner, perhaps?"

"Later," Elizabeth replied and reached up with both hands to cup his face and draw his lips down to hers, kissing him with an intoxicating combination of longing and promise, to which Darcy could not help responding - as had been her intention.

# Chapter 21

They did eventually go down for dinner, but neither was inclined to linger over the meal for very long. They were anxious to return to the privacy of Elizabeth's room and spend the night in each other's company, laying their argument and the issues it had raised to rest. Wishing to hold one another, they changed into their nightclothes and climbed into the small bed, Elizabeth's head resting on Darcy's shoulder as they both admired the clear starry night's sky through the open window.

"We shall have another fine day tomorrow," Darcy predicted softly and Elizabeth made an amused sound of agreement. "Why do you laugh?"

"Do you always speak of the weather when you are struggling to begin a difficult conversation?" Elizabeth asked in response, tilting her head so her husband could see the playful light in her eyes.

"Apparently so," Darcy replied with a reluctant grin. "Though in truth it is a habit I have only just discovered I have."

"I suppose that is your way of saying that before I came along you did not have difficult conversations with anyone," Elizabeth noted. "I can easily believe it."

"I would say, rather, that I rarely had conversations when I cared so much about the feelings of the other person involved," Darcy countered quietly and Elizabeth was silent for a moment, in recognition of his words.

"I think that that was perhaps the difference, when you spoke to me earlier," she said eventually and Darcy tightened his arms around her just a fraction.

"It undoubtedly was," he admitted with a heavy sigh. "In my anger I did not realise how much my words would injure you. I am so sorry," he expressed again but Elizabeth shook her head and kissed his shoulder.

"So am I, for by the same token I did not realise, in my naivety, how much my actions could injure *you*. I forget sometimes that I am no longer simply Lizzy Gardiner of Longbourn, free to do as I wish. I will try harder in future to act as I should as your wife."

"Please do not try too hard," Darcy requested, gently tilting her chin up so he could see her face. "I love you just as you are, Elizabeth. I would hate to see you lose any part of yourself in a bid to become something you are not. I would not change a thing about you, my love."

"Really?" Elizabeth whispered and Darcy could see that she was sceptical.

"Really," he averred. "If I had wanted a perfect Duchess, I would have married someone else. But I married *you*, because you are wonderful. Because you bring me such joy, just by being yourself. You are *my* perfect Duchess, and I could never be happy with anyone else."

Elizabeth nodded but she was too overwhelmed to speak and knew hardly how to express all that she felt as a result of her husband's words. Seeing this, Darcy drew her atop his chest and held her in his arms, anchoring her and steadying her with his calm, quiet strength. Lying in her husband's arms, any lingering hurt or resentment caused by his earlier words gradually faded away from Elizabeth's mind, leaving nothing but relief and contentment. She knew that she would never *truly* forget what had been said, but only in the sense that she intended to learn from it. Her husband meant the world to her, and she never wanted to place him in such a difficult position again; she did not want for him to ever be ashamed of her, and she did not want to *feel* that he was. She would adjust her behaviour accordingly, secure in the knowledge that he would also learn from the mistakes that had been made that day. She trusted that his apology was sincere - trusted that he had not intended to hurt her - and was too eager for a reconciliation to even consider withholding her forgiveness.

Darcy shifted his position slightly and when his wife asked him if she was too heavy, smiled.

"Hardly. And even if you were, I would never admit it. I have no intention of letting you go for some time yet."

"You are staying here tonight, aren't you?" Elizabeth asked. "The bed is not too small?"

"It is tiny," Darcy responded with a chuckle. "But we will manage."

"And when we leave here tomorrow?" Elizabeth inquired quietly.

"I think I shall ride," Darcy admitted. "I would gladly sit with you in the carriage, but unless your maid is willing to ride Fletcher, I fear we will be a little crowded."

Elizabeth laughed lightly and Darcy smiled at the sound.

"Are you laughing at the thought of Wilson riding my horse, or at the thought of my trying to tell her to do it?"

"The latter, I'm afraid," Elizabeth admitted as she looking up at her husband, her smile infectious. "I can just imagine the look on her face!"

"Hmmm," Darcy grinned in spite of himself. "I must confess I am torn between offering her a raise or giving her notice."

"Why?" Elizabeth asked with wide eyes, torn between laughter and shock. "What has she done?"

"You are not aware that she engineered the entire situation with your "missing" trunk?" Darcy asked, smiling when Elizabeth's mouth formed a surprised "o".

"She didn't?"

"Oh yes, she did," Darcy averred. "She's a crafty one, that maid of yours. She also speaks to me however she damn well pleases," he added with a slight frown, remembering Wilson's manner when they had been discussing the letter from Longbourn.

"If it is any comfort," Elizabeth pointed out, "she speaks to me like that as well. She certainly gave me plenty to think about on our way here."

"What did she say?" Darcy asked and was surprised by what Elizabeth told him of her conversation with her maid. When she spoke about her father and her feelings about the letter, Darcy felt a stab of guilt at the part he had had to play in his wife's unhappiness.

"I am sorry I was not more supportive," he told her as he tucked some of her hair behind her ear. "I was too wrapped up in the situation with Gordon and Foster, which is really no excuse at all. But if I had known,"

"I know," Elizabeth assured him softly and he fell silent and let her speak. "I am just glad that we are reconciled. The situation with my father and Longbourn is terrible enough - I do not think I could have borne it, if you and I were still..."

"Shh," Darcy hushed his wife, whom he could see was becoming upset. "It is alright now - all will be well. I am here for you, whatever you may need."

"Just you," Elizabeth whispered, leaning up and pressing her lips to his. "Only you."

"I am here," Darcy repeated and rolled them both over, pressing his wife into the pillows and telling her without words that she was not, and never would be, alone.

ဆာ

There were signs of neglect all around them as the carriage passed through the gates of Longbourn and followed the drive up to the house, and Elizabeth and Wilson shared a look of consternation to see the grounds and several of the buildings looking uncared for and shabby. When the house itself finally came in to view, Elizabeth gasped in dismay.

"Oh, the tower! Look Wilson, a part of it has crumbled. I told Mr Nichols before I left that it needed repairing."

"Obviously he had no opportunity to carry out your wishes," Wilson replied darkly and Elizabeth, who had had no charitable feelings towards Mr Hounsell, felt positively furious with the conniving scoundrel. The carriage came to a smart stop and Elizabeth let herself out. Darcy dismounted from Fletcher and was quickly at her side.

"How do you wish to proceed?"

"First and foremost, I wish to see my father," Elizabeth replied. "Before I do, however, we must find a lad to fetch Dr Ashwell here to us. He has been my father's physician for many years and I wish for him to take over his treatment."

Darcy nodded and turned to his coachman.

"John? Take the carriage round and have one of the grooms sent for Dr Ashwell - they will know his directions at the stables?" he checked with his wife, who assured him that he was correct. "Tell them that it is at my wife's behest, if you meet with any opposition. Pattinson, go with him and see that our things are unloaded and sent to the appropriate rooms."

"Right away, Sir," both men replied and left Elizabeth, Darcy and Wilson alone at the foot of the front steps.

"The new servants certainly have a thing or two to learn about greeting visitors," Wilson muttered to herself as she peered up at the silent and dull house. "Where are they all?"

"I have no idea," Elizabeth replied, gathering up her skirts. "But it seems as though we shall have to fend for ourselves."

She marched up the stairs, Darcy right behind her and Wilson grumbling to herself as she followed after them both. The front hall was deserted and they passed through it quickly, taking the main staircase up to the second floor.

"Look at this!" Wilson tutted, running a finger along the banister and bringing it away covered in dust. "Filthy! Your mother must be turning in her grave."

"Thank you, Wilson," Elizabeth replied pointedly, glancing over her shoulder at her maid. "I am quite aware how deplorable a state the house is in."

Wilson wisely kept any further comment to herself and followed silently after her mistress as she walked resolutely along the hallway leading to her father's suite of rooms. They had very nearly reached their destination when they heard the sounds of laughter and revelry coming from one of the rooms to their left, and Elizabeth stopped dead in her tracks.

"What is it?" Darcy asked, noticing the way his wife's face drained of all colour and then flushed an angry shade of red.

"Those are my mother's rooms," she replied in a tight voice and then before Darcy could say anything more, threw open the door to the chamber and burst in upon the three very surprised inhabitants. They were all sat around a table, glasses of wine and a deck of cards spread out before them.

"Who the devil are you?" One man demanded angrily, rising from his chair and regarding them with a fierce expression. "What business have you here? How dare you enter this house!"

"I might ask you the same questions!" Elizabeth retorted furiously. "I am Elizabeth Darcy, Duchess of Farleigh and this is my father's house. Now tell me at once who you are and what *your* business is here."

"Your G-grace," the man stammered, falling into a deep and clumsy bow. "Forgive me, I did not realise."

"Your name, Sir," Elizabeth repeated coldly and the man straightened and replied.

"Winstone, Your Grace. I am the butler here, and this is Mrs Hounsell, the housekeeper, and Dr Grant, the Viscount's physician."

"And Mr Hounsell - where is he?" Elizabeth demanded.

"He is speaking with the Viscount currently, Your Grace."

Elizabeth nodded and regarded the three for a moment with a furious glare.

"Your services are no longer required Mr Winstone, Mrs Hounsell, Dr Grant. Kindly collect your things and leave this house."

"You cannot do that!" Mrs Hounsell objected loudly and Darcy spoke up before Elizabeth could reply.

"I beg to differ, Madam. Now do as my wife has bid you, before I send for the magistrate and have you all arrested for the part you have played in my father-in-law's suffering."

"Wilson, if you could perhaps stay and see that they leave with all due haste? And with nothing they should not take with them?"

Elizabeth requested of her maid who stepped forward and responded with obvious relish.

"With pleasure, Ma'am."

Satisfied that Wilson would manage to see the three off (and that they were not foolish enough to try anything untoward), Elizabeth and Darcy went through the connecting door to the Viscount's chambers, in search of their true prey. On their journey down from Pemberley they had discussed at length what they knew of the situation at Longbourn, and had both agreed that Mr Hounsell was the mastermind of the entire scheme and who they really had to concern themselves with. Finally entering her father's room, Elizabeth faltered as the stale, putrid air washed over her and her eyes struggled to adjust to the dim, murky light. She felt her husband clasp her arm in a steadying grip as a voice from the direction of the bed addressed them.

"Your Grace, this is a surprise. I am Mr Hounsell, your father's steward, and it is a pleasure to meet you at last, though of course I wish it were under better circumstances. Your father is, I am afraid to tell you, very ill and..."

"I am aware that my father is ill, you despicable wretch," Elizabeth spat, her anger at his smooth manner and forward address overwhelming her sense of decorum. "It is your own doing! Now get away from him!"

Elizabeth rushed over to her father's beside as Mr Hounsell, standing on the opposite side, began to edge away from them both and towards the door.

Darcy, who was watching him very closely, calmly spoke up.

"I would not try it, if I were you. Unless you wish to find yourself restrained, stay right where you are and do not move until I tell you to do so. Is that clear?"

"Perfectly, Your Grace," Mr Hounsell replied with a short bow which reeked of disdain. "As you wish."

Elizabeth, at her father's side, paid little heed to the conversation between the two men.

"Papa? Papa, can you hear me? It is Lizzy. Papa?"

One side of her father's face had clearly been affected by the attack but one of his eyes still opened and regarded her steadily.

"It is Lizzy, Papa - can you see me?" Elizabeth asked, taking hold of his one good hand and squeezing it gently. "I am here now."

Her father spoke with great difficultly, one side of his face almost completely paralysed, but Elizabeth was still able to distinguish her name and smiled tearfully upon hearing it.

"Yes Papa, it is I."

Darcy stepped closer to his wife and gently pressed her shoulder.

"Elizabeth, I will take Mr Hounsell downstairs and have someone watch him whilst I see if Dr Ashwell has come. I will return shortly."

Elizabeth nodded and was about to ask him to check how Wilson fared when her father tried to speak again; he was looking at Darcy and clearly asking who he was.

"This is my husband, Papa. His name is William. We have come to take care of you."

Her father squeezed her hand and looked between them again.

"...H...happy?"

"Yes," Elizabeth managed to reply before the tears came. "Yes, we are very happy. I love him very much."

"G...g-ood," the Viscount sighed and squeezed her hand again before closing his eyes, too weak to do much more.

Darcy, feeling quite affected by the scene, gave father and daughter some privacy and turned to Mr Hounsell, indicating that the other man go ahead of him out into the hallway. Darcy had just closed the door behind them when Hounsell addressed him.

"I am afraid I am at a loss to understand what Her Grace meant when she implied that I had caused the Viscount's illness, Your Grace. As Dr Grant will attest, my employer suffered an apoplexy as a result of too much stress, brought on by overwork. I am not sure if you are aware how hard the Viscount was wont to work on his scientific studies."

"Cease, Mr Hounsell," Darcy firmly instructed the other man. "I have no interest in hearing you speak."

"Very well, Your Grace," Mr Hounsell replied humbly. "But if you would send for Dr Grant."

"Your 'doctor' friend has been dismissed," Darcy interrupted coldly, stopping their progress and facing the other man. "As have Mr Winstone and your wife. We know what you have been doing here, Mr Hounsell, and you will be held to account for it."

The veneer of civility abruptly fell away from Hounsell's face at Darcy's pronouncement and he regarded Darcy with undisguised loathing and anger. Already on his guard, Darcy straight away perceived the change and had pinned Hounsell against the wall with an arm at his throat before the other man had a chance to do more than take a threatening step towards him.

"Your Grace?" Pattinson came running down the hallway with two grooms in tow.

"Perfect timing," Darcy lightly complimented his man, not taking his eyes off Hounsell. "Take this man downstairs and have him put somewhere he can be watched over until I am ready to deal with him."

"Right away, Sir," Pattinson responded briskly and at his nod the two grooms took a hold of Hounsell and dragged him away. "Are you well, Sir?"

Darcy rubbed his shoulder and nodded.

"Yes, I'm fine. It just niggles me every now and then, when I do too much."

"The lad who we sent for Dr Ashwell has returned - the doctor is not far behind him," Pattinson informed his master and Darcy was pleased with the news.

"Have you seen Wilson anywhere?" he asked Pattinson, surprised when his man stifled a laugh.

"Indeed, Sir - last I saw her she was shouting at some poor woman and evicting her from the house. It was quite a sight."

Darcy allowed himself a quick grin before issuing further instructions.

"Find her and assist her with the task she was given; when it is done, send her back to my wife. I will return to the Viscount's chamber - please send a maid to me there, preferably one who was not hired by Mr Hounsell. And please, Pattinson, make sure that Mr Hounsell is watched at all times. I do not trust him at all."

Pattinson assured him that he would carry out his wishes and Darcy returned to the Viscount's room secure in the knowledge that he could completely rely on his man. He entered to find that Elizabeth had opened the drapes and windows, letting light and fresh air into the room, and was just about to extinguish the fire.

"The air in here is just awful," she complained to him when she heard him return. "It will only have made him feel worse. As soon as we can we must move him to another room and have him washed and bathed and dressed in clean things. And a shave, he must have a shave. Mr Carey used to double as his man but he is gone now, else I would have him do it. I am not sure who to ask in his stead, but I am sure there will be someone. But the doctor, have you heard ought of him? Is he coming?"

"Yes, he will be here shortly," Darcy replied, glad that he could at least address one of the issues Elizabeth had raised. "And I have asked that one of the maids from your time be sent up to us, so that we can begin to make arrangements for your father's care."

As if on cue, there was a knock at the door and it was opened by a petite young maid whom Elizabeth immediately recognised.

"Rosa!"

"Oh, Miss Lizzy!" Rosa rushed into the room, paying no heed to Darcy's presence. "Oh Miss, I knew you would come. I knew something was wrong when you didn't come before - it was that cruel Mr Hounsell, keeping things from you. But I went and told Bertha Hutchins and she wrote to her sister, Lucy, and I knew she would tell you and...well, here you are now, Miss, and I am ever so glad!"

"So it was you, then, who told Bertha about my father's illness," Elizabeth replied. "I should have known it would be you - you always were so good to us."

"Nay, Miss, you were the ones who've been good to me," Rosa responded intently. "Me and my Harry."

"I hope he is well," Elizabeth expressed and Rosa assured her her son was very well indeed. "I am glad of it. But now I need your help, Rosa."

"Of course, Miss, anything you need."

"Dr Ashwell is coming to see my father, and we need to be ready to do whatever he asks. You must go down and gather up all those you think trustworthy and competent and have them prepare hot water and towels and whatever else Dr Ashwell might need. If Dr Ashwell agrees we shall move my father to another chamber which will need to be aired out and prepared for him, and he shall need a bath and a fresh set of clothes. And some food I think would also not go amiss. What have his eating habits been like, Rosa, since his attack?"

"Very bad, Miss, I'm sorry to say," Rosa responded sadly. "Dr Grant ordered he be fed only broth and soup and Mr Hounsell insisted that only he and Dr Grant and Mr Winstone be the ones to feed His Lordship. I've been sneaking him some bits of bread and fruit when I can miss, but Mr Hounsell rarely lets anyone in here alone. I tried to keep him clean and comfortable as well, Miss, but Mr Hounsell says it was bad for him to be disturbed, though I think His Lordship must be miserable trapped in his bed like that."

"You are a good girl, Rosa," Elizabeth stated, surprising the young girl by briefly embracing her. "Thank you for trying to look after my father."

"It was the least that I could do, Miss," Rosa replied and Elizabeth smiled sadly before releasing her.

"Go and fetch the others like I told you, and we can make a start before Dr Ashwell arrives."

Rosa bobbed a quick curtsey and then span away, disappearing through the door that led to the servant's stairwell. Darcy watched her go and then turned to look at his wife, one brow arched.

"What?" Elizabeth asked with a smile, amused in spite of the situation by his expression.

"I cannot remember the last time I was so thoroughly disregarded," Darcy stated dryly and Elizabeth chuckled.

"I suppose you are unused to being overlooked."

"Indeed," Darcy responded. "I can see that everyone here holds you in very high regard - you are their mistress, and they are glad to have you back."

"Well I am glad that *you* are here," Elizabeth replied quietly. "If I had come here without you and had to face all this alone...I would not have handled it at all well."

"I think you would have handled it as well as you are handling it now," Darcy countered firmly, feeling proud of his wife. "You underestimate yourself."

"Perhaps," Elizabeth conceded; she sighed and added, "Though I fear that this is only the beginning."

"We will make it through," Darcy assured her and briefly pressed her hand. "I will stay with you for the doctor's visit, but then if you do not need me there are a few things I must see to. I wish to search Mr Hounsell's rooms before I speak with him - I have a feeling that there is more to this situation than meets the eye - and depending on what I find we may have to send for the magistrate. I will let you know before I do anything, though."

"I trust you to do what you think is right," Elizabeth assured him. "I can better care for my father knowing that you are seeing to the other issues."

"Then leave everything to me," Darcy replied just as the sounds of approaching footsteps reached them and Dr Ashwell finally appeared.

ಬಂಗ

"Well," Dr Ashwell pronounced when he came to find Darcy and Elizabeth sat waiting in the adjoining chamber. "He is both better and worse than I feared."

"In what sense, Doctor?" Elizabeth asked as she got to her feet.

"Well he is very weak and, I am sorry if this distresses you, frankly undernourished. It will take time, especially considering his age, to rebuild his strength and I must say I find it disgusting that he was allowed to deteriorate so far! Whoever this Grant character was, he was certainly no doctor!"

"And the good news?" Darcy asked, placing a supporting hand on his wife's back, seeing that talk of how her father had been neglected was upsetting her.

"From what I have observed during my examination, and what the maid Rosa has told me of her own observations, there has already been quite significant improvement in terms of the severity of His Lordship's paralysis. With time and a programme of appropriate treatment, we may hope for even further improvement. Not recovery, that is very uncommon, but improvement, certainly."

"How bad is it?" Elizabeth asked. "Is his entire right side paralysed?"

"No, not entirely," Dr Ashwell replied positively. "Though he is currently unable to raise his arm or move his leg, there is some movement in his foot and he was able to weakly grasp my hand. According to Rosa he could do neither immediately following the attack, so there is yet hope for further improvement - as I said."

Elizabeth nodded and asked the question that had been plaguing her since she had first seen her father.

"Will he ever walk again?"

"At this point, it is hard to say," Dr Ashwell admitted, removing his spectacles and cleaning them with his handkerchief. "It all depends on the extent of his improvement. I have seen cases similar to this where the individual has been able to walk with the assistance of another, so it is not beyond the realms of possibility that your father may one day be able to walk again."

"And what of his mental state?" Elizabeth asked delicately, knowing that Dr Ashwell, who had been her father's friend of sorts for many years, would understand what she was really asking.

"His faculties seem mostly intact. He is perhaps a little confused, but his physical weakness is likely impacting upon his mental prowess. His speech, as you know, has been greatly affected by the attack, though we may hope for improvement there as well, with time. It is difficult to judge at the moment what other effects the attack may have had; I would suggest waiting until he has recovered some of his strength before making any further assessments."

"Very well," Elizabeth agreed. "Thank you, Doctor, for being so thorough. I know I had many questions."

"It is my duty to answer them to the best of my ability," Dr Ashwell replied with a kindly smile; he sobered to add, "I am only sorry I was not able to examine your father before now. I only received the vaguest report of his attack, and when I attempted to call upon him was told that he was quite well and not receiving visitors. Perhaps I should have insisted."

"Short of physically forcing your way into the house, Doctor, I doubt there was much else you could have done," Elizabeth noted and Dr Ashwell frowned darkly.

"Indeed, you are probably correct. I gather that your presence here means that Mr Hounsell no longer holds sway?"

"I shall be dealing with him shortly," Darcy spoke up, glancing down at his wife and then looking back at the doctor. "Whilst I do, perhaps my wife could assist you with making her father more comfortable. I know she wishes to have him moved to another room, if you think it wise."

"I do," Dr Ashwell affirmed. "Though I do not think it advisable to move him very far. What options do we have, Miss....forgive me - Your Grace?"

"If you will follow me, Doctor," Elizabeth replied, sharing a parting look with her husband before leading Dr Ashwell from the room. "I will show you where I thought we could move him."

Satisfied that he was no longer required, Darcy stepped out into the hallway and directed his steps towards the main hall, intent on locating a servant who could take him to Mr Hounsell's room. He met Pattinson and Wilson coming the other way and his brows rose at the state of the latter, her normally immaculate appearance in complete disarray.

"What on earth happened?" he asked, his surprise evident.

"Mr Winstone and Mrs Hounsell both attempted to abscond with some of His Lordship's property," Wilson replied stiffly, her demeanour not at all altered despite the fact that she was covered in dust and her hair was escaping its pins. "I put a stop to it."

"You were not hurt, I hope," Darcy expressed, mindful of Wilson's age and the rather large bulk of Mr Winstone.

"No, Sir," Wilson replied. "Mrs Hounsell had sent a maid to do her dirty work and I easily dealt with the girl myself, and Mr Pattinson was so kind as to offer me assistance when Mr Winstone expressed his dissatisfaction at being caught red-handed."

One glance at Pattinson's swollen knuckles told Darcy exactly what kind of assistance he had offered and he was forced to suppress a smile.

"Very well - thank you for your diligence. My wife is with the Doctor currently and would welcome your assistance with her task - once you have refreshed yourself, of course. Pattinson, if you would come with me."

"Of course, Sir," Pattinson replied readily, falling into step beside his master as Wilson carried on in the opposite direction. The valet allowed himself one backwards glance before giving Darcy his full attention.

"I intend to search Mr Hounsell's rooms - I doubt he would stoop to petty theft like the other two, but I am certain he will be hiding something. He has gone to a lot of effort to establish himself here, and I cannot help but think there must be more to this situation than at first appears."

"You do not think he simply meant to establish himself here indefinitely, living off His Lordship's wealth?" Pattinson asked thoughtfully and Darcy shook his head.

"If Mr Hounsell had intended to live out his life here, it would make no sense to allow the Viscount to slowly die, which is what he was doing. No, he has some purpose which he has been seeking to accomplish whilst the Viscount is alive but which does not require him to live much longer."

"What do you intend to do with him?" Pattinson asked and from his tone it was clear that he thought whatever punishment richly deserved.

"That depends on what I find," Darcy replied and then called out to a footman passing in the hall below.

He had the footman, Eden, take them to Mr Hounsell's room and then instructed him to have all of the staff not currently assisting Elizabeth or guarding Mr Hounsell assemble in the ballroom in half an hour.

"And when you have done that," Darcy concluded, having decided that the young footman seemed trustworthy. "I want you to go to the housekeeper's room and bring me a ledger with the names of all the servants so that we may conduct a count."

"Yes, Your Grace, at once," Eden replied with a deep bow and hurried off to do Darcy's bidding.

When Eden had left them, Darcy tried the door to Hounsell's room and was not surprised to find it locked. He stepped back but then turned to Pattinson when he felt a hand on his arm.

"Please, allow me, Sir. You do not want to aggravate your shoulder again today."

"You do not suggest we simply go to Mr Hounsell and request he hand us the key?" Darcy asked with significant amusement as he nevertheless moved aside.

"If the gentleman has any sense, he will have disposed of it," Pattinson replied sensibly and then hurled himself at the door, the lock giving way with a satisfying crunch.

"Well done, Pattinson," Darcy complimented as he stepped into the room.

Pattinson patted himself down and rearranged his clothing.

"Thank you, Sir."

"Well, you take that side and I will start over here with the desk. I suspect we are looking for papers of some kind," Darcy said as he approached the small desk in the corner of the room and took a seat.

"Very good, Sir," Pattinson replied and began his search.

They were disturbed about fifteen minutes later by the appearance of Eden, who was so distracted by the broken door that Darcy had to prompt him twice to speak.

"Yes?! Oh, forgive me Sir. I have passed word around the staff to assemble in the ballroom, as you requested."

"And the ledger?"

"I am afraid the door to the housekeeper's room is locked Sir, and we have been unable to locate the key," Eden replied regretfully.

"Then you have my permission to break the door down - you seem a strong enough lad to manage it. Take care not to injure yourself in the process, mind."

"Ummm, yes Sir, right away," Eden replied with a slightly bemused look and left again as quickly as he had come.

Darcy shared an amused grin with his man Pattinson before turning back to the task at hand. It was not much later before he found what he had been looking for.

He had to credit Mr Hounsell for the ingenious hiding place- beneath the wooden window sill - but the inappropriate admiration quickly died a death when Darcy began to read through the papers he had found hidden there.

"Bastard," he breathed and Pattinson quickly turned to him, abandoning his search of the wardrobe.

"What have you found, Sir?"

"Bank drafts," Darcy held one of them up for Pattinson to see as he counted through the rest. "Almost two dozen of them, dated back several months and increasing in value. Look, this last one was signed only yesterday, for £1000. And this one five days ago, for the same amount."

"But why would the Viscount sign it? Unless he did not know what he was signing?"

"I suspect that was probably the case all along," Darcy sighed. "Though even more so now. From what my wife has told me of her father, he has never had much success managing his affairs. Mr Hounsell probably laid these before him with some plausible excuse and the Viscount signed them, not knowing that Mr Hounsell was intending to pocket the funds himself."

"How much is there?" Pattinson asked quietly and Darcy did a few quick calculations and felt a flash of hot anger at the amount that Mr Hounsell had attempted to steal.

"Close to ten thousand."

There was an angry silence which Pattinson eventually broke.

"Shall I send for the magistrate, Sir?"

"Not yet," Darcy replied thoughtfully. "I must consider this, and speak to Mr Hounsell. We need to know what damage has already been done."

"You think he may already have withdrawn some funds?"

"If he is as cunning as he seems, I am certain of it," Darcy replied darkly and gestured to Pattinson to follow him as he left Mr Hounsell's room. "Come, I must address the staff."

When they reached the ballroom, Darcy was surprised by how few servants were gathered there. A glance at the ledger Eden handed to him, however, showed that the number of people present seemed roughly accurate, and that the house was obviously running with only skeleton staff.

"Good day to you all," Darcy greeted the assembled staff. "Thank you for appearing so promptly. This should not take long - I simply wish to ascertain who is here, and how long you have been in the Viscount's employ. My man here will call out your name, and you will raise your hand and state the date when you first came to work here. Is that clear to you all?"

When there was a murmuring of agreement, Darcy nodded to Pattinson and waited as his man ran through the list of names and made a note of when each individual had come to Longbourn. When the last name had been read out, Pattinson quietly informed Darcy that there were four people missing (not including those helping care for the Viscount) and that over half of those present had been employed in the time since Mr Hounsell had arrived. Darcy quietly thanked Pattinson for the information and then turned to address the room once more.

"Thank you for your patience. I just have a few questions for you now, and then you may return to your work." Darcy paused for a moment and then asked, "Now that Mr Hounsell has been dismissed, are all of you still happy to remain working here? I assure you that none of you will be dismissed without good reason, but second-rate service will not be tolerated from now on. If you believe you will be happier working elsewhere, this is your chance to leave with a good reference. Do any of you wish to seek another position in another house?"

There was complete silence, and no one moved at all, until two footmen eventually raised their hands and Darcy nodded.

"Very well - speak to me again later and I will see to your references. As for the rest of you, the Viscount is your master here, but he is currently, as I am sure you are all aware, very ill. My wife and I therefore intend to remain here for the foreseeable future and we have high expectations of you all. At the very least we require you to be hardworking, diligent, capable and honest, and if you do not think you are able to meet those standards, I suggest you take me up on my offer to let you leave with a good reference."

"Now, a word about the situation here and the actions of Mr Hounsell. After I have spoken with you all I intend to have the magistrate summoned to begin criminal proceedings against Mr Hounsell. I have no doubt that some of you are in complete ignorance of his crimes and are thus completely blameless; at the same time, however, I have no doubt that some of you were party to his schemes and as such are just as guilty as he. The problem, of course, is that I have no way of knowing who is guilty and who is not - unless you all help me."

"I need information from you. I am sure you know who amongst your number has done wrong, and I would like for you to tell me. You need not fear any repercussions. I intend to have all of you speak with Pattinson one by one, so that no one need ever know who said what about whom. And I am not interested in petty grievances or disagreements - I simply want to know who may have assisted Mr Hounsell in his schemes. Depending on what I learn, those individuals may also be handed over to the magistrate, but at the very least they will be dismissed without reference." Darcy allowed a moment for his words to sink in before asking, "Now, do any of you wish to reconsider my offer to leave now with a good reference?"

He was not wholly surprised when four more hands went up.

෨⃝෬

Leaving Pattinson to interview the staff and ascertain whatever he could about Mr Hounsell and his schemes, Darcy finally went to speak to the man himself. He felt he had the upper hand and was determined to use this knowledge to his advantage. Nodding to the two grooms who were standing guard outside the room where Mr Hounsell had been placed, Darcy quietly entered and shut the door behind him, turning to face the other man. Mr Hounsell had not risen on his arrival and Darcy knew that it was an intentional slight.

"Are you comfortable, Mr Hounsell?" he asked as he took the seat opposite and settled in for a long conversation.

"Perfectly, Your Grace, thank you for your condescension," Mr Hounsell replied in a tone which easily could have been taken for deferential, had not his eyes given away his utter disdain for his company.

"I would not recommend provoking me, Mr Hounsell," Darcy replied calmly. "Currently, I am inclined to sort this out as quickly and discreetly as possible, but that could easily change."

Mr Hounsell responded to this pronouncement with silence and Darcy went on conversationally.

"Your wife has departed the house - I am told she stated her intention to await you at the inn. She was naturally searched before she left, and her rooms as well, and I am sorry to say was found to be in the possession of a number of items she had no business in attempting to keep. Attempted theft is a serious business, though I suppose it is nothing to the trouble you are in."

"What do you want?" Mr Hounsell interrupted, sounding almost bored.

"*I* want?" Darcy repeated lightly; the man across from him sighed his frustration.

"If you didn't want something from me, you would have simply have sent for the magistrate and handed me over. So, what do you want?"

"I want to know, when did you make the first withdrawal?" Darcy asked quietly and saw Mr Hounsell's surprise before he had a chance to hide it. "Yes, I have been to your room and found what you have been hiding. Now, as I said, I want to know when you made the first withdrawal."

"What makes you think I've made any?" Mr Hounsell asked in response and Darcy sighed.

"Don't insult my intelligence. There was always a risk of your being caught; of course you will have made withdrawals already. Now tell me when, and at which bank? Or banks, I suppose is more likely."

"If I tell you, what happens to me?" Mr Hounsell asked, clearly prevaricating and looking for the best way out of his current predicament.

"What do you think will happen?" Darcy responded coolly. "I am sure you gave this scheme of yours a lot of thought before you embarked upon it; no doubt you considered the repercussions as well. So, tell me, what do you think will happen?"

Mr Hounsell smiled coldly and nodded, sounding impressed as he replied.

"Very clever, Your Grace. I see you have more sense than most of your contemporaries. You won't trick me, however. If I admit to having considered the repercussions of my 'scheme' I am essentially admitting that there was a 'scheme' in the first place - which I do not admit. I admit to no wrongdoing."

"I expected no less," Darcy admitted. "Because of course you are aware that as the situation currently stands, there is little or no proof of wrongdoing on your part. The existence of these bank drafts is undoubtedly suspicious, but unless the money is found it will be very difficult to prove that you have been stealing it. I have no doubt that you have prepared your excuses very well and can account for every pound spent in your time here, and that to discover any discrepancies would take a lot of time and effort."

Mr Hounsell's expression, carefully blank, told Darcy that he was absolutely correct in his assumptions.

"So, as I said, as things currently stand you appear to be in the clear. Your wife, on the other hand." Darcy concluded slowly. "There is the troubling matter of the attempted theft."

"I had nothing to do with that," Mr Hounsell stated without even a moment's hesitation and Darcy smiled, pleased.

"So keen to throw her to the wolves? I confess I'd hoped you would be."

"What?" Mr Hounsell demanded, clearly confused by Darcy's abrupt change in demeanour.

"Well, as I'm sure *your* lack of loyalty is indicative of *hers*, no doubt she will be eager to tell me a few things about you if it means helping herself," Darcy explained helpfully. "I'm sure I can find something that you are guilty of. Of course you could spare me the trouble and simply tell me what I want to know. Or..."

"Or?" Mr Hounsell repeated when Darcy let the word hang.

"I could have you hanged," Darcy stated quietly, suddenly deadly serious. "Easily. Stealing from a Viscount, my father-in-law? You could be sent to the gallows tomorrow, if I ordered it. And I will, if you do not give me what I want. Now *tell me.*"

There was a long silence whilst Mr Hounsell considered his options before he finally relented and gave the names of the two banks where he had made withdrawals and the dates of each visit.

"And how much did you take?" Darcy asked and Mr Hounsell objected.

"You never said..."

Darcy just regarded the other man coldly, challenging him to test him further.

"Three," Mr Hounsell admitted at last and Darcy's brows rose at the amount.

"And how much can you return? And do not say none of it."

"One," Mr Hounsell replied sullenly and when Darcy glared at him quickly added, "No, just listen! I have debts. That is why I took the position here - I needed to disappear for a while. I kept the one for us, but the rest I've paid the men I owe."

"And how much do you still owe?" Darcy asked patiently.

"Enough," Mr Hounsell replied darkly and Darcy sighed and withdrew the stack of bank drafts from his pocket.

"How much of what is here would you have kept for yourself?"

"Three," Mr Hounsell admitted with obvious reluctance and Darcy was unable to help shaking his head at the amount of money the other man owed, to apparently rather unsavoury characters, if he had come into Hertfordshire to hide.

"Well well," Darcy sighed, sitting back in his chair and regarding Mr Hounsell thoughtfully. "You are rather caught between a rock and a hard place, aren't you? Though which I am, I wouldn't like to say."

Mr Hounsell glared at him and Darcy almost smiled.

"I suppose I have a choice, don't I? Either I keep you here and hand you over to the magistrate and let the law deal with you, or I let you go and wait for the men you owe money to catch up with you. Which option do you find preferable?"

"I am dead either way," Mr Hounsell responded and Darcy did not argue the point.

"Not necessarily. I have a proposition for you. Do everything I ask of you, and I will see that rather than being hanged you are deported instead. You don't deserve such mercy, considering what you have done here, but that is my offer."

"What do you ask?" Mr Hounsell queried and Darcy laughed at his audacity.

"You think to quibble over the terms when your choice is between life or death? You can be rather stupid for a clever man, Mr Hounsell."

Looking like he resented being in Darcy's debt as much as he clearly did, Mr Hounsell relented.

"I accept your terms. I will do whatever you ask."

"Then we have a deal," Darcy pronounced briskly, getting up and striding over to the desk on the other side of the room. "Here is some paper and some ink. For your first task, I require any information you may have for the staff you dismissed - beginning with Mr and Mrs Carey and Mr Nichols. If you have the information elsewhere, direct one of the grooms outside to fetch it for you. I will return in half an hour and expect you to have it ready for me."

"That is it?" Mr Hounsell asked, his surprise obvious.

"That is only the beginning, Mr Hounsell," Darcy replied over his shoulder as he went on his way. "Now do as I've asked."

# Chapter 22

Darcy took one look at his wife and went directly to her side.

"Come, Elizabeth, you must sit down - you look exhausted."

"I am," Elizabeth replied tiredly, gratefully sinking into the chair her husband pulled out for her. "There is just so much to do; and you know how little I slept last night."

"How is your father?"

"We have just settled him in his new room; he has had a bath and a shave and been changed into clean clothes. He seems much more comfortable now, though he became quite agitated with all the activity. He had just fallen asleep when I left him and hopefully he will rest for some time."

Darcy nodded.

"I am glad to hear it. Now just sit here for a moment and I will have some tea brought - would you like something to eat? You really should eat something, it is hours since breakfast."

"Yes, I think I could manage something," Elizabeth replied, managing a small smile. "Thank you, William."

"You are welcome," Darcy replied and stepped out for a moment to find a servant to carry his request down to the kitchen. "It should not be long," he assured his wife when he stepped back into the room.

"How is everything here?" Elizabeth asked as he took the seat beside hers. "I have been so busy upstairs; this is the first opportunity I have had to come down."

"Everything is under control," Darcy responded confidently. "Pattinson and I have already weeded out those unfit to remain in your father's employ, and I have spoken to all the rest and impressed upon them the need for good service if they wish to keep their place."

"And how did you 'weed out' those who have been sent on their way?" Elizabeth asked with an intrigued smile, "No doubt you were very clever about it."

"That is not for me to judge," Darcy replied with a suppressed grin - he then told Elizabeth about the speech he had given to the servants and his offer of references to those who opted to leave.

"So they essentially incriminated themselves," Elizabeth surmised with a smile. "How devious of you, my love."

"It was foolish indeed for them to raise their hands - the latter four in particular. I was inclined to give the first two the benefit of the doubt and keep my word, but several of the other servants made it clear that neither of them were to be trusted. I explained to the six of them that they had the choice to leave without references, or leave with the magistrate, and in the end they were all quite happy to go."

"You do not think that they will cause trouble elsewhere?" Elizabeth questioned with a worried frown but Darcy was quick to put her fears to rest.

"I heard nothing of their behaviour to alarm me, and Pattinson and I agreed, when we had both spoken with them, that they were not bad men as such. They simply took advantage of the situation and attempted to benefit from it. There was no real wrongdoing, at least not on their own initiative. I am sure that letting them go will not result in more trouble. I would not have let them leave otherwise."

"Yes, I am sure you are right," Elizabeth replied. "I trust your judgement, of course."

Darcy smiled slightly to show that he did not mind her questioning him.

"I suppose you have spoken to Mr Hounsell?"

Darcy nodded but waited until the footman had left before replying.

"Yes, we had quite an interesting conversation."

Elizabeth handed him a cup of tea and sipped her own before forcing herself to ask what Mr Hounsell had been doing.

"You suspect him as well?" Darcy asked, surprised at her perception, though he knew he really shouldn't be. His wife, after all, was a very clever woman.

"I think he must have spent a lot of time and energy on his attempts to gain control of my father and his household, and I can't imagine he went to so much effort for no purpose."

Darcy nodded and took a moment to decide where to begin.

"Yes, you are unfortunately quite correct."

Elizabeth listened closely as her husband detailed exactly what he had found in Mr Hounsell's room and the conversation he had had with him. She paled slightly at the sheer amount of money Mr Hounsell had attempted to steal, but apart from that she showed no other reaction to what Darcy told her.

"What do you have him doing now?" Elizabeth asked when her husband fell silent after showing her the addresses Mr Hounsell had been able to provide for Mr Nichols and Mr and Mrs Carey.

"He is in your father's study," Darcy admitted. "I tasked him with an assessment of the state of your father's work; it has been neglected in the time since your father's attack, and I thought Mr Hounsell would be best able to judge what can and should be done with the projects your father was working on."

"I had not even thought," Elizabeth sighed, covering her eyes in a defeated gesture. "It is yet another thing for us to worry about. My father has not made mention of it yet, but it is surely only a matter of time, and once he regains his strength he will likely become agitated when he realises that none of it has been seen to."

"Yes, those were my thoughts exactly," Darcy replied. "Hence why I have enlisted Mr Hounsell. He will provide us with an accurate assessment which we can then present to your father; hopefully not all will be lost."

"You should speak to Mr Seymour - or have Mr Hounsell do it. He is the head gardener and will be able to tell us whether the greenhouses and conservatory have been tended to properly since my father's attack. Hopefully, Mr Seymour will have continued his work without my father's direct supervision, but I suppose I cannot take that for granted considering all that has been going on here."

Darcy got to his feet and approached his wife, drawing her from her chair and into his arms.

"You have my word I will do everything I can to set things to rights."

"I do not need your word," Elizabeth replied softly, leaning heavily into him and relying on his strength to hold her up. "I know I can count on you."

"There are others here whom you may also count on," Darcy stated, pulling back slightly and offering an encouraging smile. "Wilson and Pattinson, of course, but several others as well. Many of the existing staff expressed their relief at your return, and I am sure they will do everything they can to assist you. There is much for us to do, I readily admit that, but we do not have to do it all alone."

Elizabeth nodded and managed to return his smile.

"You are right. I am just tired and a little overwhelmed. My father is in better health than I expected to find him, but the situation here is so much more complicated than I had anticipated."

"Hmm," Darcy hummed his agreement. "It is certainly a challenge. But we have time, now that your father is out of danger and Mr Hounsell can do no more damage, we have time to put things right. Starting with this," he concluded, picking up the sheet of paper on which the addresses of the senior staff were written. "We have been fortunate, they have all settled not too far away and within easy distances of each other. I will send a rider out today, and hopefully we should have their replies by tomorrow at the very latest."

"If I were in their place," Elizabeth confessed with a troubled frown, "I do not think I would come back. To be treated in such a manner after so many years of loyal service - I do not think I could stand for it."

"And I think that they will come back for *you*," Darcy replied with an affectionate look, stroking his wife's cheek. "In fact, if you are not busy it would be a good idea I think for you to write the letters," he teased.

"I will if you wish me to," Elizabeth responded but Darcy shook his head with a light laugh.

"No, I was only teasing. Truly, I do not think there is any need. I will write to them and make it clear that you are the one desiring their return. I am sure that will be enough. Hopefully, all three of them will agree to return and we will be some way towards restoring order."

Elizabeth nodded but Darcy could tell her mind was on something else; he caught her eye and patiently waited for her to share her thoughts with him.

"I think I would like to speak with him, Mr Hounsell," she said at last, slowly but with firm conviction.

"Of course, if that is what you want. If you have finished eating, perhaps I could take you to him."

Elizabeth shook her head.

"There is no need, I can go alone. You should stay and write your letters."

Darcy tried not to take the slight personally, but his feelings must have shown on his face for Elizabeth sighed softly.

"It is not that I do not want you there, I just think it will be easier for me to ask certain questions, and hear his answers to them, without feeling too exposed. I will speak with you afterwards, I promise."

"If you are sure," Darcy responded, trying to be supportive but feeling a little worried. He suddenly felt a powerful urge to protect his wife, sure that she would hear nothing good from Mr Hounsell, whatever she intended to ask him about.

"I am," Elizabeth assured him gently. "I will come and find you when I am ready."

She pressed a quick kiss to his lips and turned away, leaving Darcy to watch her go. Sighing heavily and running a hand through his hair in an agitated gesture, he turned his attention to the letters he had to write and focused on the task with single-minded determination, trying not to think about his wife.

&#8270;‘’&#8476;

Upon hearing the door to the study open, Mr Hounsell looked up from the book he had been studying with a neutral expression, hiding his hope for a reprieve. When he saw who had come to see him, he slowly closed the book and set it aside as she instructed the footman who had been watching over him to wait outside the door.

"Have you made much progress, Mr Hounsell?" Elizabeth asked the man watching her closely, determined that she would not give him the satisfaction of seeing her lose her composure for the second time.

"Yes, some," Mr Hounsell replied. "Though I will need to view the greenhouses and the conservatory before I can finish."

"I am sure that can be arranged," Elizabeth responded neutrally. "I wonder - does Mr Seymour still work here, or did you dismiss him as well?"

"No he is still here, and as far as I am aware has been performing all of his usual duties," Mr Hounsell informed her and Elizabeth did not think much of his attempts to be helpful.

"That is something, at least. Though if no one has been making any observations or recording changes, there is little point to any of it."

Mr Hounsell shifted uncomfortably before he replied.

"Some of the projects are lost causes now, yes, but not all of them. There are one or two, for instance, which require fully matured specimens and it will be weeks yet until they are ready. And there are others as well, ready now and just waiting to be completed and recorded."

Elizabeth nodded but did not reply and felt Mr Hounsell watching her anxiously as she moved about the room, noting things both familiar and new and remembering all the time she had once spent here when she was younger.

"You are aware, I suppose, that for all intents and purposes I used to occupy the position my father gave to you when you first came here?"

"His Lordship did mention that you used to help him, yes."

"By all accounts you were better at it than I," Elizabeth mused, stopping before a portrait of her mother which hung above the mantelpiece. "Though that does not surprise me - daughters do not make for good employees."

"I ?" It was clear from his confused expression that Mr Hounsell did not understand and Elizabeth smiled humourlessly.

"Oh, I do not mean to imply that he paid me - certainly not with money at least. I was very young, you see, and desperate for attention; whenever he paid me a moment of notice I treasured it like the rarest diamond, not realising that he valued my *usefulness* more than he valued *me*. I soon realised my mistake," she concluded softly and almost to herself, though Mr Hounsell heard every word.

Elizabeth was silent for a long time before going on.

"I suppose you are wondering why I am confessing these things to you, of all people. I simply wish for you to understand that I am very well acquainted with my father's character, with his capacity for neglect. And I want you to bear that in mind when you answer the questions I am about to put to you, because I will know when you are lying."

Mr Hounsell nodded quickly but Elizabeth did not believe he understood how serious she was.

"I am in earnest. You should think very carefully about how you answer, because despite what my husband may have promised you earlier, *I* will ultimately decide what happens to you, and currently I am not at all inclined to honour his promises."

Again Mr Hounsell nodded and paled slightly swallowing nervously and Elizabeth was satisfied that she had made her point.

"What I would first like to know," she began after a moment of consideration, "is whether you interfered in the correspondence between my father and me?"

"Interfered?" Mr Hounsell repeated slowly but Elizabeth had no patience for his prevaricating.

"Yes, interfered. Did you prevent any letters being sent or received? Did you influence when he wrote to me, or what he said? Did you read the letters I sent to him?"

Mr Hounsell suddenly looked very uncomfortable.

"I doubt you can make me think any less of you than I already do, Mr Hounsell! Now answer me."

"I read the letters you wrote to him," the man across from her admitted. "But I never prevented any of them from reaching your father, or prevented him sending any to you. There was one occasion when I influenced the wording of his letter to you, but it was only that one time."

"And which letter was that?"

"The one he sent when he sent your things to London," Mr Hounsell admitted and almost winced at the furious look in Elizabeth's eyes.

"And whose idea was it to send my things to London?"

"The initial idea was your father's - he thought you would have need of a few items. But I was the one who had everything sent to you."

Mr Hounsell felt miserable after making this confession, as though he had just signed his own death warrant; he had every reason to fear, because Elizabeth was struggling to contain her anger with the man stood across from her.

"Why? Why would you do that?"

"Because I wanted you to stay away," Mr Hounsell replied. "I knew that if you came here the game would be up. Your father intended to put off your visit anyway; he was busy with his work and he had just started a new project that he wanted to be ready before you came, and I decided I could easily make you think that he did not want you to come at all. So I sent all of your things to London, knowing that that, when combined with your father's letter, would be enough to make you stay away."

Elizabeth thought back to the day her father's letter had arrived and realised that Mr Hounsell was right. It was the presence of all of her belongings which had really stung and turned what would have been just a typically insensitive letter from her father into something so much worse. She knew she could not entirely absolve her father, however, and considered what Mr Hounsell had said.

"My father wanted to put off my visit? That was his own idea? And he had no intention of attending the wedding either, I suppose?"

"No, he did not want to leave Longbourn," Mr Hounsell replied and then evidently stopped himself from saying more.

"What else?" Elizabeth asked, noticing his hesitation.

"He had reason enough to not want to leave or for you to come here - he *was* very busy with his work. But there was another reason - a gift, for you, a wedding present. He started it the day he received your uncle's letter announcing your engagement, and he did not want to leave with it unfinished, or for you to come. He was going to say as much in his letter but I persuaded him that any mention of it would make you curious and encourage you to visit sooner," Mr

Hounsell concluded with a sigh, resigned to telling the complete truth.

"What sort of gift?" Elizabeth asked suspiciously, unable to help thinking that Mr Hounsell was lying to her.

"A book - it is here somewhere," Mr Hounsell replied and began rooting around on one of the many bookshelves. "It is, or will be, a book of Gallica roses. Each entry will be accompanied by a brief description, an illustration and a pressed bloom. It was very nearly finished when His Lordship had his attack; we were just waiting for two of the late summer bloomers. Ah, here it is - it is not bound yet, but this should all be in order."

Mr Hounsell transferred a small stack of parchment to her father's desk and Elizabeth cautiously approached, doubt still warring within her.

"And you say he intended this as a wedding gift?"

"Yes - look here," Mr Hounsell flicked through a few pages and carefully drew one from the stack, holding it out to her.

Elizabeth accepted the page and read the short passage, written in her father's hand.

*For my daughter, Elizabeth Hyacinth, on the occasion of her marriage. With a father's love.*

Elizabeth dropped the page onto the desk and turned away from Mr Hounsell, lest he see the tears which overwhelmed her.

"His lordship also had plans for a new rose," Mr Hounsell spoke to her back. "Which he intended to name for you. The details are here somewhere."

"That is quite enough, thank you Mr Hounsell," Elizabeth managed to force out through the lump in her throat. "I quite understand."

There was a long moment of silence during which Mr Hounsell waited uncomfortably for Elizabeth to turn back to him; when he saw her discreetly wiping her eyes, he quickly focused his attention on the desk so that when she did eventually turn around, he was not caught watching her.

"I suppose this must all be abandoned now," Elizabeth stated, her composure restored - she gestured to the stack of papers on the desk. "At least until next year."

"Not necessarily," Mr Hounsell surprised her by reply. "I am sure that the last few roses will still be in bloom, and it would be easy to collect the necessary cuttings and for me to complete the illustrations."

Elizabeth gave him a very cold look.

"Do not try to redeem yourself now Mr Hounsell - it is far, far too late for that. You know, you *must* know how much importance my father places on his work, and yet you have left it all to ruin. Of course, in light of the fact that you have been allowing him to slowly starve to death, your neglect of your other responsibilities shouldn't really surprise me," she added with biting sarcasm and Mr Hounsell visibly paled.

"I have not...I did not mean for him to die," he protested loudly. "I just wanted him to be, to stay...weak..."

"Weak enough for you to control him?" Elizabeth suggested and after a moment Mr Hounsell nodded. "And yet, you controlled him easily enough when he was in full health - enough to take over this house and steal thousands of pounds from him," she pointed out and took grim satisfaction from the increasingly alarmed expression on Mr Hounsell's face.

"I think I have heard enough from you," Elizabeth stated, beginning to turn away. "I thank you for being honest, if not for anything else."

"Wait! What is going to happen to me?" Mr Hounsell asked as she walked towards the door.

Elizabeth halted her progress but did not bother to turn around as she replied.

"You have stolen thousands of pounds from my father; you have disrupted this household and the lives of those who live and work here; you have caused, however indirectly, my father to suffer an attack which has left him paralysed and bedridden for potentially the rest of his life. You almost allowed him to die as a result of intentional neglect and you very nearly destroyed whatever little affection I had left for him because it suited your purpose. What do you *think* is going to happen to you, Mr Hounsell?"

There was a very tense silence that was only broken when Elizabeth wrenched open the door and slammed it behind her, leaving Mr Hounsell alone to consider his fate.

ೞറ

Darcy eventually found his wife sitting on a small bench beside the now empty school house. He had been looking for her for almost an hour - since one of the footmen watching over Mr Hounsell had come and discreetly informed him about her abrupt exit from the house - and he breathed a silent sigh of relief when he spotted her. Approaching slowly, he could tell the moment she registered his presence because she quickly wiped her face and turned to smile up at him.

"Have you been looking for me?"

"Yes," Darcy replied as he regarded her thoughtfully for a moment and then took a seat next to her.

"Not for long, I hope."

"No, not long," Darcy lied and they fell silent. Not wanting to introduce the subject of Mr Hounsell straight away, Darcy looked around himself and noted, "So, this is the school. It seems very respectable."

"Yes, Miss Lewis does a fine job of keeping it nice," Elizabeth replied. "I do hope we can get her back," she sighed heavily and Darcy put his arm around her shoulders and drew her close.

"Do you want to talk about it?"

"Where do I start?" Elizabeth muttered tiredly, resting her cheek against his shoulder. "It is all such a mess."

"What did you speak about with Mr Hounsell?" Darcy asked gently and he immediately felt his wife stiffen.

"I think I hate that man," she replied in a soft tone which was somehow worse than if she'd shouted.

"I daresay you have every reason to," Darcy responded, surprised when Elizabeth laughed darkly.

"Yes, and you do not yet know all."

She told him about her conversation with Mr Hounsell, about the letter and the wedding gift - all of it. She even admitted what her parting words had been, though she was sure her husband would not agree with her. Surprisingly, he did.

"You must be sure, but if you are, then it will be done. I think, on reflection, that deportation *is* too lenient. The alternative is no more or less than he deserves."

Elizabeth was silent as she considered whether she could live with the responsibility of condemning a man to death.

"I think we should send for the magistrate, and leave it up to him to decide," she slowly said at last. "The evidence is all there, he has admitted to wrongdoing and there are many others who will attest to it. Let the magistrate decide what his fate will be - that way my conscience is clear."

"Very well," Darcy agreed, hiding his relief. By no means did he care what became of Mr Hounsell, but it was a heavy burden to bear, sending a man to his death, and he was glad that his wife would be spared that particular hardship.

They fell silent again until Elizabeth eventually found her voice.

"A bad man, a bad father and a bad daughter. We caused this mess, the three of us together."

"You cannot think you bear any of the responsibility for this," Darcy protested and Elizabeth looked up at him.

"Why not? Would this have happened had I paid more attention? Had I sent more letters or bothered to visit? Had I not resented my father or considered him a burden?"

"The responsibility for that lies with him," Darcy argued but Elizabeth shook her head.

"And with me. He is a bad father - has always been a bad father - but I have made it worse by being a bad daughter."

"If *you* are a bad daughter," Darcy interrupted heatedly, "then what does that make your sister? Where is she? Where has she been all this time?"

"Jane has a life and family of her own," Elizabeth defended her sister and Darcy pounced on her words.

"Yes, exactly, and so do you! If you do not blame your sister for leaving and concentrating on her own life, you cannot blame yourself for doing the same."

"I..." Elizabeth began to argue but realised she did not know what to say in response to that.

"Elizabeth," Darcy said softly, taking her hand. "You cannot blame yourself. Your father is, by all accounts, a very difficult man and the fact that you have any affection for him at all is, I think, quite remarkable. You have done so much - I know you have *tried* so hard - but you must realise that no one expects any more of you, *except you.*"

Throughout this short speech Elizabeth felt tears swelling up inside of her and with her husband's final words they burst forth, leaving her sobbing heavily as he wrapped his arms protectively around her and held her tight. She was guilt-ridden, she was worried, she was angry and she was hurt, but most of all, she was sad. Sad all the way down to her bones, sadder than she could ever have imagined a week ago. Sad that her father, who did love her in his way, had never been able to show it, and sad because the little affection he did show her could never be enough. She needed more than her father could give, and knew she always would.

ಶೋಚಿ

Elizabeth spoke hopefully into the darkness.
"William, are you still awake?"

"Hmmm?"

"Never mind, go back to sleep."

"No, it is alright - and I am awake now," Darcy replied, rubbing his face and rolling onto his side so that he could face his wife. "Can you not sleep?"

"No," Elizabeth admitted, tucking herself under his chin and smiling softly when he put his arms around her. "I cannot quiet my mind."

"Is anything in particular troubling you?" Darcy asked, knowing that there was much she had to choose from.

Following their conversation outside the school, they had returned to the house and the various tasks awaiting them. The magistrate had come and taken Mr Hounsell away, and with his departure from the house a cloud seemed to have lifted; the remaining servants went about their duties with much greater ease, and both Darcy and Elizabeth had also felt an easing of the many burdens they had to bear. The magistrate would need to return to speak with them all about the actions of Mr Hounsell, but it was enough to know that the matter was being dealt with and the responsibility was no longer theirs.

After a quiet and simple dinner, Elizabeth had returned to sit with her father whilst Darcy wrote letters to their friends and family. Elizabeth had sent a note to Jane before their departure from Pemberley briefly detailing the situation at Longbourn, and Darcy wrote a much more thorough missive to his friend Sir Charles, making it very clear how things currently stood. He was interested to discover what response his letter would garner.

He wrote several other letters to their neighbours in Derbyshire, explaining their absence and apologising for the necessity of cancelling engagements. To Mrs Reynolds, he addressed a short missive apprising her of the intended length of their absence from Pemberley, trusting that she would pass the message on to his steward and would manage things ably for the duration they remained from home. When these letters were all written and sealed, he began one to his children, struggling for a moment over how much he should say. They would be worried on Elizabeth's behalf, he knew, and in the end he settled for explaining that the Viscount was quite unwell but had every chance of recovery. He briefly described the house and grounds at Longbourn and then dedicated an entire paragraph to enquiries about what they had been doing in the time since he and Elizabeth had left them. He had no doubt that they were being well looked after, but he still wanted to hear that they were happy and content. When he was done, he left a space for Elizabeth to add her own paragraph and went in search of her.

Settled in his new rooms and dressed in clean clothes, clean shaven and with a good meal in his belly, his father-in-law already seemed much improved. He even recognised Darcy as he slowly approached the bed and shakily offered his hand to him when Darcy was close enough. One of the servants had found a tablet and chalk for the Viscount to use and he managed quite well with his good hand; it was certainly easier for him than trying to talk extensively. Elizabeth helped him by holding the tablet still and Darcy watched as the Viscount slowly wrote a message. When Elizabeth held it up for Darcy to read, he looked to her for help deciphering it.

"He says that I have been telling him about you," Elizabeth told him with a smile, looking between the two men. "And Pemberley and the children, too."

"All good things, I hope," Darcy responded lightly, making a point to speak slowly and clearly, pleased when his father-in-law smiled his comprehension.

"Of course," Elizabeth assured him. "I was just telling Papa about the beautiful gardens, and the conservatory."

The Viscount nodded vigorously and, taking back the tablet from his daughter, wrote, *Climate?*

Though Darcy was confused by the question, Elizabeth easily understood the path her father's mind was following.

"You mean how does the climate differ from the one you have here, and how does it affect the growth of the plants?" Her father nodded again. "Well, I am sure William will be able to satisfy your curiosity much better than I. Would you mind?" Elizabeth asked, looking up at her husband.

Darcy could see the sadness in her eyes and shook his head. "No, not at all."

"Then if you will excuse me, I will return in a moment," Elizabeth stated, pressing her father's hand and rising to her feet.

"I have been writing to the children - you will find the letter on the desk in our chamber, if you wish to add to it. I left a space for you to do so," Darcy told his wife quietly and was pleased when she managed a smile for him before turning away and leaving him alone with his father-in-law.

Darcy knew precisely what had upset his wife. All she wanted was for her father to be interested in her new life and family, and the man could not even manage to listen for five minutes! Tamping down on his irritation and reminding himself of his belief (conviction almost) that the Viscount was ill in some way, Darcy took the seat his wife had vacated and regarded his father-in-law with a neutral expression. He expected the Viscount to question him about Pemberley, and was therefore surprised when the elder man took up the tablet again and wrote, *Where is Mr Hounsell?*

Darcy hesitated before replying, not knowing what to say, fearing that if he admitted that Mr Hounsell was gone, his father-in-law would likely become distressed. Before he could decide what to say, the Viscount spoke.

"He isss...gone?"

"Yes," Darcy admitted quietly. "Along with Mrs Hounsell, Dr Grant and Mr Winstone."

"G-ood. Incompe..tent."

Darcy's brows rose at this reply but he remained silent, seeing that the Viscount was now writing on his tablet again, *Others back? Carey?*

"We hope so," Darcy replied. "I have sent letters to them all today - we should know by tomorrow."

The Viscount nodded.

"G-ood. Better."

Darcy suddenly felt a wave of unexpected sympathy for his father-in-law. His mind was evidently quite intact and unaffected by the attack, and yet he was confined to his bed, unable to properly express his thoughts or move without aid. And to spend weeks alone, entirely at the mercy of Mr Hounsell and his cohorts, feeling himself slowly wasting away and powerless to stop it must have been torture! Whatever his faults, no one deserved that.

Realising that he had been silently staring at his father-in-law, Darcy began speaking.

"I am told that Mr Seymour has been taking care of everything in the greenhouses and conservatory, but I am sorry to say that Mr Hounsell has not been carrying out his duties for many weeks. Before he left we had him prepare an assessment of the state of the projects you had been working on, and I shall bring it to you tomorrow. If you would like to speak to Mr Seymour also, I am sure that can be arranged."

"See it...now," the Viscount stated, trying to sit up; Darcy laid a restraining hand on his shoulder.

"Not tonight, no. It is too late and Elizabeth will be cross with me if I let you tire yourself. Tomorrow after breakfast would be better."

His father-in-law made a few sounds of protest but soon collapsed back against the pillows, the effort all but exhausting him. He appeared greatly disgruntled and Darcy awkwardly patted his shoulder before he withdrew his hand.

"I am sure it is frustrating for you, but if you could be patient a little longer we will soon have everything restored to order and you can resume your work once more."

The Viscount picked up his tablet and Darcy waited patiently as he wrote a long message on it.

*Elizabeth stay? Help me? No Hounsell, need her. Much to do. She will stay?*

"Elizabeth and I will stay as long as it takes to restore order here," Darcy replied tightly, his clenched jaw muscles the only outward indication of his annoyance. "But then we will return to our home."

The Viscount frowned and made a noise of obvious irritation and Darcy abruptly stood up, afraid that he was going to lose his temper.

"I will find you a replacement for Mr Hounsell, Sir. You needn't worry."

His father-in-law's expression cleared at once.

"Oh...good."

And with that, any sympathy Darcy had felt for the man died a swift death.

"William, did you hear me?"

Elizabeth's quiet query brought Darcy back to himself and he shook his head and replied.

"No, I'm sorry, I was lost in thought. What did you say?"

"I said that I'm worried about what will happen to my father once we leave."

"I have been thinking about that too," Darcy admitted with a sigh.

The thought had crossed his mind to offer to have the Viscount come and live with them, but he had just as quickly decided that he didn't want his father-in-law anywhere near Pemberley. Not only on account of his own feelings, but because he knew that it would only make Elizabeth miserable and her happiness was of utmost importance to him. He would find another solution which would ensure that the Viscount was taken care of and Elizabeth could live her life free of guilt.

"I don't want to stay here a moment longer than is absolutely necessary," Elizabeth confessed to the darkness. "I know that is terrible -"

"It isn't."

"- but I don't care. I just want to go home. Being around my father, it makes me think of all the things I cannot have and I would much rather go home and enjoy all the things I do have instead."

"All you need do is tell me, and we will leave straight away," Darcy responded, finding her lips in the darkness and sealing his promise with a kiss.

"As much I would like to, however, I cannot just leave my father...unprotected," Elizabeth went on when they separated. "His condition means that he will require constant care, but more than that I need someone here to watch over him, to make sure that nothing like this happens again. I cannot ask Mr Nichols because he already has so much to manage without having to act as my father's minder, but I do not know who else I can trust."

"I might know someone," Darcy commented slowly, the thought just occurring to him. "In fact, he would be ideal."

"Really? Who?" Elizabeth asked curiously.

"Benson's son," Darcy replied. "He has been learning from his father for the past six months and I had been thinking of sending him up to Scotland to learn the estate there, but we could just as easily bring him here. He is a good lad - honest, hardworking and trustworthy. Together he and Mr Nichols could manage things."

"We would still need to find someone to help with my father's work - the illustrations and such," Elizabeth mused thoughtfully and Darcy took her response as acceptance of his suggestion.

"That can easily be arranged - a letter to my solicitor in town would be enough to start the search."

"But do you think Mr Benson's son - I'm sorry, I do not know his name - do you think he would be happy here?"

"Oliver, and yes, I think he would be. When not minding your father he will have the opportunity to learn with Mr Nichols, on a new estate and away from his father's influence; he strikes me as a young man eager to make his own way in the world. I do not anticipate his wanting to remain here indefinitely, but I think he will be happy for at least a year or two. That will give us time to find a more permanent solution."

Elizabeth was silent for a moment as she considered the idea and eventually nodded.

"Very well, it is certainly worth asking at least."

"I will write to him and his father tomorrow," Darcy responded and felt a pleasant sense of satisfaction at having found a possible solution.

Elizabeth evidently felt the same way because he could feel her smiling when she kissed him.

"I have said this so many times already, but I do not know what I would do without you, William."

"You know I only want you to be happy."

"Yes, but how will I ever repay you?" Elizabeth asked teasingly, shifting closer.

"There is no need..." Darcy began to reply but stopped when one of her hands slipped beneath the covers and she murmured against his lips.

"Are you quite sure?"

"Well..." Darcy teased, drawing out the word.

Elizabeth laughed against his lips and Darcy smiled at the sound, pleased to hear its return, before her wandering hands effectively sent his thoughts scattering.

&#8180;–

When Elizabeth woke the next morning she could tell it was very late by the amount of light pouring into the room around the sides of the curtains, and the fact that William was not beside her and his side of the bed was cool. Sitting up and tossing the covers aside, Elizabeth called for her maid, hoping that Wilson was nearby. She was not disappointed and Wilson promptly appeared in the door to the dressing room.

"Good morning, petal. Did you sleep well?"

"Too well, I gather," Elizabeth responded. "Why did you not wake me? It must be very late."

"Your husband ordered that you be left to rest," Wilson replied. "He said something about you not getting much sleep the last few nights."

"That is hardly of consequence," Elizabeth muttered irritably as she pulled on a robe and climbed out of bed. "I have things to do."

"He also said you would say that," Wilson informed her mistress with an amused look. "And to tell you that everything is in hand and there is no need to worry. The servants all have their duties and have been acting according to the timetable you set out yesterday - you needn't worry yourself, petal, most of them well remember how the house used to run."

"And my father? How is he?" Elizabeth asked, beginning to accept that William was perhaps right to insist she get some rest.

"He is well enough," Wilson replied. "Mr Seymour is with him currently and together they are going over the details of your father's work."

"I hope Mr Seymour remembers not to mention our discussion," Elizabeth worried.

Realising that her father would be distressed to discover that the gift he had been preparing remained unfinished, Elizabeth had spoken with Mr Seymour and arranged to complete the final few illustrations, and to present them to her father as Mr Hounsell's work rather than her own.

"I am sure you can rely upon his discretion," Wilson assured her calmly. "Now, whilst we wait for the water for your bath would you like anything to eat? Shall I have them send up a tray?"

"Yes please," Elizabeth replied. "I assume William has eaten already?"

"Yes," Wilson affirmed. "He has been hard at work for hours already."

"Doing what?"

"Making arrangements for the repairs, I believe," Wilson said, referring to the collapsed portion of the tower. "Amongst other things."

Elizabeth closed her eyes tiredly.

"Yet another thing I had forgotten about. Will it never end?"

"Sooner than you think, I'm sure," Wilson replied and Elizabeth opened her eyes and looked at her sharply. Wilson smiled as she revealed, "Mr Nichols has agreed to return - he will be here the day after tomorrow."

"Oh, that is good news!" Elizabeth happily stated. "And the Careys, have they responded yet?"

"Not yet, no," Wilson replied. "But I am sure we will hear from them soon. I spent some time yesterday speaking with the old servants and I gather that Mr and Mrs Carey always hoped to be able to return - hence why they settled so close by."

"If only we could find Miss Lewis, then I would be quite content," Elizabeth admitted. "No one could do a better job than her."

"Leave it to your husband," Wilson told her confidently. "He will manage it."

Elizabeth nodded and then lapsed into a thoughtful silence as she considered the situation as it now stood. Wilson left her to her thoughts and went to order Elizabeth's breakfast and the water for her bath, returning to find her mistress sat at the desk and busily writing.

"I am writing to my uncle," Elizabeth explained when she noticed Wilson's presence. "I cannot believe I have neglected to do so before now! But of course he needs to be made aware of the situation - as does my aunt - and perhaps he will agree to help us. It would make much more sense for him to oversee things here, after all, living so much closer than William and I."

"Mr Bennet should share the responsibility, certainly," Wilson agreed. "As should your sister, but I daresay there is little chance of *that* happening."

"Wilson," Elizabeth cautioned her outspoken maid and Wilson wisely refrained from further comment.

Elizabeth finished and sealed her letter, leaving it on the desk whilst she quickly bathed and dressed. Once she was ready and had finished her breakfast she picked up the letter and took it with her as she went to find her husband, eventually locating him in the library.

Darcy looked up from the letter he had been writing on hearing the door open and smiled when his wife appeared.

"Good morning, my dear," he greeted Elizabeth as she came over to him.

"Good morning," Elizabeth replied, leaning over the desk and kissing his cheek.

"What was that for?" Darcy asked as she straightened.

"For taking such good care of me," Elizabeth responded lightly. "I feel much better having had an extra few hours of sleep."

"I am glad to hear it," Darcy replied, smiling slightly as he watched Elizabeth tilt her head so as to read the address of the letter he was currently working on. "I am writing to my solicitor in London; there are a number of matters I need him to attend to."

"I have just written to my uncle," Elizabeth said, adding her missive to the pile of those he had already written and which were waiting to be sent. "I only thought of him this morning - with everything that has been happening it quite slipped my mind to inform him and my aunt."

"Do you think your aunt will want to come here and see her brother?" Darcy asked, not familiar with the relationship between the Viscount and Mrs Bennet.

"Perhaps," Elizabeth granted thoughtfully. "It is difficult to say, really - I cannot recall the last time my aunt and uncle visited Longbourn, but I suppose the situation does call for it."

"Wilson told you the news about Mr Nichols?"

"Yes, I was very happy to hear it."

"As was I," Darcy admitted. "It will certainly make things easier, not having to look for a new steward. And I shall accomplish things much quicker with the assistance of someone well acquainted with the estate and its business."

"You could ask me, you know," Elizabeth pointed out with a playful smile, though she meant what she said. "I daresay you'd be surprised by how much I know."

Darcy hesitated a moment and then took his wife's advice.

"Who would you recommend I engage for the repairs?"

"The damage is extensive enough to warrant outside help, then?" Elizabeth responded, not having seen for herself the state that the roof and tower were now in. When Darcy nodded she suggested, "Then I would send for Cartwright, over in Biggleswade. He assisted my father in the design of the greenhouses and is well respected in the area for his work. He would be able to survey the damage and decide what work needs to be done, and can be relied upon to act in your stead when dealing with the blacksmith and stonemason."

Darcy smiled.

"I am sorry I did not think of asking for your opinion, it would have saved me time and effort."

"Well now you know," Elizabeth responded lightly. "Is there anything else I can help you with?"

"Not at the moment, no, but if I think of anything I will be sure to consult you," Darcy replied and Elizabeth nodded. "What are your plans for today?" he asked after a moment.

"I have some work to do for my father," Elizabeth began. "But I intend to call upon Bertha Hutchins first; it was her letter which Greg brought to me," she explained and then winced at her slip.

Fortunately Darcy let it pass without comment.

"What work do you have to do?"

"I intend to finish the last few illustrations for the book he was preparing," Elizabeth admitted. "It will not take me long, and it would upset my father if all his hard work went to waste," she added when she saw her husband's frown.

"You are kinder to him than he deserves," Darcy commented and was surprised when Elizabeth laughed.

"Only when it suits me! I am hardly the perfect daughter, but this is an argument we have already had, and one which we are both determined to win, so I shall let the subject lie. Honestly, my love, it is no hardship for me to sit down and draw a few roses - just let me do this for him."

"Very well," Darcy granted with a sigh. "I will not argue when you claim to be such an imperfect daughter, if only because you are a perfect wife whom I love to distraction."

Elizabeth laughed at his teasing and rewarded him with a sweet kiss.

ഈ രു

The following day, Elizabeth and Darcy were both surprised by the arrival of a most unexpected visitor. They were sat together discussing the news that the Careys had agreed to return when they heard the sound of a carriage; waiting for their visitor to be brought to them, they speculated as to whether it could be Mr Nichols come a day early and were thus very surprised when Mr Bennet appeared.

"Uncle!" Elizabeth exclaimed, rising and going forward to meet him. "This is unexpected. Surely you only received my letter today?"

"This very morning, in fact," Mr Bennet replied. "And my wife dispatched me here forthwith. She intends to follow me the day after tomorrow."

"Well, you are both very welcome," Elizabeth expressed and her uncle smiled and then turned to greet her husband.

"It is good to see you again, Your Grace."

"Please, Farleigh will do," Darcy responded. "And it is good to see you as well. You and your wife have both been well since we last saw you?"

"Oh, quite well, quite well, though of course this news is very upsetting," Mr Bennet replied, gesturing about himself. "What a mess! I confess that at first I could scarcely credit the things you wrote in your letter Lizzy, but I suppose everything must be as you say."

"I am sure it was a shock to you, and my aunt as well," Elizabeth replied sympathetically, and Darcy noted she did not say a word about her own shock. "I am sorry I did not inform you sooner of the situation, but there has been much for us to do since arriving."

"I am glad to hear that Mr Hounsell has been dealt with," Mr Bennet stated with a glare. "The sheer villainy, the audacity of the man! I am of half a mind to speak with the magistrate myself to see that the fellow gets the punishment he deserves."

"I am sure that justice will be served," Darcy replied calmly. "My wife and I trust the magistrate in this matter."

Mr Bennet seemed to accept Darcy's words and Elizabeth shot her husband a relieved smile before asking her uncle whether he would like some tea and other refreshment.

"Tea would be just the thing, thank you Lizzy," Mr Bennet replied. "If you would both join me, perhaps we could all sit down and you could explain the situation to me more thoroughly. I am determined to be of use, but first I need to understand the lay of the land."

Both Elizabeth and Darcy assented to the plan and the trio remained shut away together for the better part of an hour as the couple detailed all that had gone on during Mr Hounsell's reign and the steps they had taken towards restoring order since their arrival. Mr Bennet was as pleased as they were by the news that Mr Nichols and the Careys had agreed to return and was highly impressed by all that his niece and her husband had accomplished.

"If the Benson boy does not agree to come here, and I would not blame him if he did not relish the prospect, I have an idea for who else might do. I think you are quite right to look for someone to assist Mr Nichols; it is too much to ask him to mind your father as well as the estate. Finding someone to assist with your father's work will I am sure be more difficult, but I think that is the least pressing of all our concerns."

Darcy was gratified to hear Mr Bennet refer to "our concerns" and could see that his wife also appreciated how sincere her uncle apparently was in his desire to help.

"What puzzles me," Mr Bennet went on, "is how Mr Hounsell came to be here in the first place. It cannot have been a mere coincidence, and yet I do not know how he became aware of your father's need for an assistant."

"We have been wondering the same thing," Elizabeth admitted with a glance at her husband. "I asked my father and he claims not to know; Mr Hounsell simply presented himself one day and my father was happy to take him on."

"Without taking any of the usual precautions I'll wager," Mr Bennet interrupted. "He has himself to thank for his trouble, it seems."

Elizabeth pursed her lips but otherwise did not respond to her uncle's assertion, leaving it to her husband to reply.

"A visit to Mr Hounsell would perhaps provide us with the answers we seek, but then again perhaps not. Now that we have handed him over to the magistrate he has no reason to help us."

"Then, I daresay it will remain a mystery," Mr Bennet predicted and moved the conversation on to another subject.

The "mystery", however, was solved the following day by none other than Mr Nichols.

"Before we say anything more, I have something I must tell you all."

Elizabeth, Darcy and Mr Bennet all exchanged slightly surprised looks and then turned back to Mr Nichols.

"Please, Mr Nichols, go on."

"It was through my actions that Mr Hounsell came to be here," Mr Nichols confessed. "I was aware of His Lordship's need for an assistant with his work and none of the enquiries I made locally were met with any success. I wrote to an associate in London, detailing the requirements of the position and less than a fortnight later Mr Hounsell arrived. I was not present myself when he first came to the house and spoke with His Lordship, and so was unable to interview him as I would have wished before offering him any employment. If I had had the chance; but there is little point in dwelling on what might have been. The responsibility for this entire situation resides with me and I will understand should you wish to reconsider your offer of re-employment. I would have related this all to you in my letter, but I felt it was better that I explain myself in person. I apologise for..."

"May I stop you there, Mr Nichols?" Elizabeth gently interrupted him, smiling gently at the hardworking and honest man whom she had always valued. "You have no reason to apologise and we shall not be rescinding our offer to you to return. Now, I believe my husband has a number of matters to discuss with you so if you could meet him in the library once you have unpacked all of your things, we would greatly appreciate it. As I am sure you can imagine, there is much to do!"

"I am ready now, Your Grace," Mr Nichols responded with a slight bow, his relief evident. "My things can wait."

"In that case," Darcy spoke up. "Come with me - I have been trying to make sense of the accounts but Mr Hounsell has left them in a sorry state indeed. I have only been able to locate..."

Elizabeth smiled as Mr Nichols fell into step beside her husband and they left the room together deep in conversation.

"Well," Mr Bennet breathed, sounding pleased. "That is one less thing to worry about, and the mystery of Mr Hounsell's appearance is solved. What shall we turn our attention to now?"

"I have several household matters I must attend to," Elizabeth responded. "And I promised my father I would help him re-assess the state of his projects."

"Then let me do that," Mr Bennet offered. "You have enough to do already and I am sure I can manage your father for an hour or so. You have earned a break," he concluded softly and Elizabeth smiled her thanks.

"Will my aunt be happy in the chamber besides yours, do you think, or should I put her somewhere else? With the damage to the roof my options are limited but if you do not think the room next to yours appropriate I am sure I could find something better."

"The room next to mine will be fine," Mr Bennet assured her. "And if she has any complaints I will be sure not to let you hear them. Your aunt is coming here to help, not to make a nuisance of herself!" He concluded with a playful grin and Elizabeth smiled at his teasing.

"In fact, once the Careys have arrived I believe your aunt and I will be able to manage things ourselves," Mr Bennet went on thoughtfully. When Elizabeth turned to look at him with obvious surprise he smiled softly and told her, "Yes - manage without you and your husband was what I meant. I think you should consider returning home."

"But there is still so much to do..." Elizabeth began to protest.

"Nothing that we could not manage," Mr Bennet pointed out. "And nothing that you should feel you have to. I am not saying that you should leave immediately, or that I want you to go, but do not feel as though you have to stay. You have a life and family waiting for you at Pemberley, and as soon as you are happy to go - go. With a clear conscience," he added pointedly and Elizabeth could not deny that that was the crux of the matter.

"Please just think about it," Mr Bennet softly told her when they reached the top of the stairs and when Elizabeth nodded he smiled and headed in the direction of her father's chambers, leaving his niece to her thoughts.

ಬಂ

"Hmmm, another long day," Darcy sighed and groaned as he stretched out on the bed, still fully clothed.

Elizabeth smiled at him over her shoulder as she sat at the dressing table, brushing out her hair. They had dismissed Pattinson and Wilson for the night and were enjoying some quiet time alone before going to bed.

"And it shall be another busy day tomorrow, what with your aunt and the Careys all due to arrive. And I have an appointment at the bank in the afternoon as well," he remembered with a groan.

"Perhaps you could send Mr Nichols in your stead?" Elizabeth suggested, laying down the brush and standing up.

"I cannot - I must go myself. There are arrangements to make which must be done in person."

Elizabeth was aware of the fact that her husband, in addition to replacing the money Mr Hounsell had stolen and paying for the repairs, was also using his own funds to replenish Longbourn's coffers. Her father and Mr Hounsell, through a combination of mismanagement and neglect had managed to bring the estate to the very edge of ruin and Elizabeth knew it would take quite a significant investment to restore it to anything approaching prosperity.

"Well, I have something to tell you which should make tomorrow more bearable."

"Oh, and what is that?" Darcy asked absently, his eyes closed as his body began to relax.

"I want to go home on Saturday," Elizabeth quietly stated, watching for his reaction.

Darcy opened his eyes and twisted his head to look at her.

"Are you sure?"

"Quite sure," Elizabeth replied. "I spoke with my uncle this afternoon and he is happy to manage everything in our stead."

"But what about *you?*" Darcy asked, more concerned about her own feelings than those of her uncle. "Would you really be happy to go?"

"Yes," Elizabeth's reply was unequivocal. "I want to go home. I want to see the children. I am satisfied that my father is out of danger and that everything here is now in hand; there is nothing more I can expect from this situation. I – *we* - have done everything we can; now it is time to return home."

"Is this on my account?" Darcy asked quietly.

"Partly, yes. But am I not allowed to make a decision based on your welfare? You do it constantly; you came here because you wanted to support me, because you love and care for me. Well I want to leave, because I love and care for you and I want to do what is right for you. For us," she amended softly and waited for her husband to reply.

"Well, I can hardly argue with your logic," Darcy noted with affection as he brushed some hair away from her face. "Saturday it is."

"Saturday," Elizabeth repeated and they shared a smile of mingled happiness, contentment and relief.

# Chapter 23

"Papa!" Catherine called joyously, rushing down the front steps. Her father met her halfway and she laughed as he swept her up and around in a circle before safely drawing her into his arms.

"What a welcome home!" Darcy declared as James and Elizabeth greeted one another with a little less exuberance, but no less warmth. He kissed his daughter's cheek and then set her down, smiling as Catherine ran to Elizabeth and threw her arms about her waist.

"Hello, Son," Darcy greeted James with a broad smile, patting him on the back and gripping his shoulder. "It is good to see you."

"And you, Father," James replied happily. "I am glad you are home."

"It is good to be back," Darcy admitted with a contented sigh before turning to his wife and daughter, who stood side by side with an arm around each other. "Shall we go in?"

They were all distracted by a loud bark and turned to see Agatha and Poppy bounding up the driveway from the stables to the house, the younger puppy struggling to keep up.

"Ah, I wondered where you'd got to," Darcy noted affectionately as Agatha arrived at his feet and butted his legs for attention. "Hello, old girl. Been taking care of the place for me?"

Elizabeth was just as pleased to see her dog, amazed by the changes in her appearance.

"Look how she has grown! We can only have been gone ten days!"

Poppy yapped and bounced and rushed about between them all, still very much an over-excitable little puppy.

"We have been training her," Catherine informed Elizabeth and her father proudly. "Look, show them James what she can do."

James stepped forward and bent down to Poppy's level, attempting to calm her with soothing words and steady pets. When she was at last paying him attention he held out a hand and made a fist.

"Sit!"

After a moment of hesitation Poppy flopped down and sat with her head tilted to one side, tongue lolling from her mouth, waiting expectantly for her treat. James dug a hand into one of his pockets and retrieved the final piece of biscuit he was carrying and rewarded her with it. Elizabeth was delighted and Darcy very impressed by the trick, congratulating his children on their success - which he did not doubt was the result of a lot of time and effort.

"One of the grooms helped us with her," James explained, stroking Poppy behind the ears. "And Agatha as well. We used her to show Poppy what she was supposed to do."

"What a clever idea," Elizabeth complimented and Darcy patted Agatha's side with affection.

"Well, we had best go in," Elizabeth stated after a moment, offering Catherine her hand. "Your father and I have had a long journey and are in desperate need of some tea!"

"Was your journey pleasant, Father?" James asked Darcy as they followed after the other two, Poppy and Agatha trotting along behind them.

"Quite uneventful, Son," Darcy responded. "We made good time, though it seemed to take forever; we were both eager to be home again."

"And Elizabeth's father? How is he?"

"He is much improved. He is being well looked after."

"I am glad," James replied quietly. "I think Elizabeth would have been very upset had he been very ill."

"Yes, she would have been," Darcy sighed; he smiled down at his son and patted his shoulder. "You are a good boy."

"So you keep saying," James quipped and laughed when his father tugged him to his side and ruffled his hair. "Ah, Father, get off!"

Smiling at the antics of James and her husband, Elizabeth turned back to Catherine.

"So as well as training Poppy, what have you and James been doing whilst we have been away?"

"We have been having our lessons with Mr and Mrs Hughes," Catherine replied just as they reached the parlour where the two people in question were awaiting them. "And we have had visits from Daniel and Aunt and Uncle Fitzwilliam."

"Daniel?" Darcy repeated, having heard his daughter. He looked at his son. "Sir Charles was here?"

"Yes, they came yesterday and last week as well," James replied. "Sir Charles asked that you let him know when you were home, so that he may call upon you."

"I will do that, thank you, Son," Darcy responded lightly, but his thoughts were with his friend.

He had received Sir Charles's reply to his letter the day before he and Elizabeth departed Longbourn and had not been particularly surprised by the contents. A part of him could not blame his friend - Lady Jane was several months pregnant after all, and given the trouble they had had in the past he could understand why Sir Charles was reluctant to leave her - especially for the sake of a man like the Viscount. At the same time, however, he did not and could not like how easily Sir Charles and Lady Jane left the responsibility of caring for the Viscount to others. He supposed that by visiting Pemberley and the children Sir Charles was trying to show that he was willing to help in other ways, but it did not earn him much credit with Darcy. Sir Charles was his dear friend, and he and Lady Jane were good people, but Darcy's opinion of them both would never be as high as it had been before this episode.

Returning his attention to the room and those within it, Darcy greeted Mr and Mrs Hughes and spent a few moments enquiring how his children had behaved during his absence. He was gratified when the couple both expressed their continued pleasure with the behaviour of their charges, though if he were completely honest, he was not too surprised. He knew his children were well-mannered and polite and was very proud of them. Sitting down to a well-deserved cup of tea, Darcy smiled upon perceiving how happily Elizabeth interacted with both Catherine and James. She had not been herself since receiving the letter about her father and had been quiet for most of their journey from Longbourn. He could tell, however, that she was not merely putting on an act for the benefit of the children, but that she was genuinely happy to be in their company. Darcy hoped that her spirits would continue to rise and would soon be completely restored by their return to their home and family.

Feeling that her papa was being left out and not being able to contribute much to the discussion Elizabeth was having with James about his progress with riding, Catherine hopped off the settee she had been sharing with Elizabeth and went to sit beside her father instead. She smiled up at him and was pleased when he transferred his tea cup to his other hand so that he could put his arm around her.

"I missed you very much princess," Darcy softly told his daughter. "Very much indeed."

"I missed you too, Papa," Catherine replied. "But I was happy because Elizabeth went with you and you don't have to go alone anymore when you leave us."

Darcy smiled affectionately at her logic.

"Having Elizabeth for company was lovely, but I still much prefer it when the four of us are all together. Or perhaps I should say the six of us," he teased, nodding to Agatha asleep at his feet and Poppy as she sniffed about by the fireplace.

"Eight, Papa," Catherine corrected him. "You mustn't forget Mr and Mrs Hughes."

"Indeed, you are quite right, how remiss of me," Darcy replied whilst sharing a smile with the couple who had heard Catherine's words.

"Can I tell you a secret Papa?" Catherine asked unexpectedly, and Darcy nodded and bent low to hear it. "I think I like it *best* of all when it is just me and you."

Darcy kissed the top of his daughter's head, noticing as he did so that she was showing signs of becoming as tall as Georgiana one day, if her recent growth spurt was any indication.

"I love you too, princess," he told her affectionately and smiled when he felt Catherine put both her arms around him and squeeze him tight.

ഇരുന്ന

"Good morning Darcy!"

Returning his friend's easy greeting, Darcy gestured for Sir Charles to take a seat and took the one opposite.

"I came as soon as I could," Sir Charles said as he made himself comfortable. "As I mentioned in my letter, the Hursts have been visiting with us the past few days, though they left us yesterday."

"I hope they are both well," Darcy expressed, having some slight acquaintance with his friend's elder sister and her husband.

"Oh, yes, quite well, quite well," Sir Charles responded lightly.

"And your wife? Elizabeth asked me to ask after her - she will not have the opportunity to pay a visit before our trip to the seaside, and wishes to know how her sister is faring."

"You may tell Lizzy that Jane is very well," Sir Charles replied with a pleased and satisfied air. "The doctor sees her regularly, just to be sure, but she continues on very well. I daresay I would not have agreed to take part in your little seaside excursion were she not doing so well."

Darcy nodded and said that he would share Sir Charles's good report with his wife, knowing that Elizabeth would be pleased to hear that her sister was well.

"We are still going ahead then, with our sojourn?" Sir Charles asked after a moment. "I had wondered whether you and Lizzy would still be willing to go, having only just returned home. I also wondered whether you would even be home in time, but here you are!"

"Yes," Darcy responded neutrally. "There was a time when we thought we might have to cancel the trip, but fortunately, Mr and Mrs Bennet were so good as to assume control of everything at Longbourn, allowing Elizabeth and myself to return home. It is admittedly not ideal for us to have to leave again so soon after arriving, but we have all been looking forward to this trip for weeks and would hate to spoil it for everyone else."

"I must say I am looking forward to it myself," Sir Charles admitted with a laugh. "It has been years since I have taken a trip to the sea. I hope you know that I intend to take Daniel swimming, regardless of whether they have any bathing machines where we are going - where *are* we going, by the way? I know you told me the name of the place, but it has quite slipped my mind."

"Theedlethorpe," Darcy replied patiently. "We will travel to Lincoln on Thursday and spend the night at an inn just outside of the city, and then on Friday we will go on to Theedlethorpe and spend the rest of the day and night there before returning to Lincoln on Saturday afternoon and home on Sunday."

"Ah yes, I remember now," Sir Charles nodded. "You have planned it all down to the finest detail, as always!"

"Except that I neglected to select a place where it is guaranteed they will have bathing machines," Darcy pointed out dryly. "In fact, I doubt very much that there will be any at Theedlethorpe. It is a very quiet place, not at all popular."

"All the better," Sir Charles teased. "If I am forced to expose myself I would rather do it to as few people as possible."

"I would rather you not do it at all," Darcy responded flatly and his friend laughed at him.

"Come Darcy, do not be a prude! One can hardly go all that way and not enjoy the pleasure of a dip in the sea!"

"As long as you remain decent," Darcy granted reluctantly. "I suppose I cannot stop you."

"No, you cannot," Sir Charles agreed with a playful grin. "And I daresay the others will all be joining me. You can stay with the ladies and preserve your dignity."

Darcy shot his friend a playful glare and when Sir Charles finally stopped laughing turned the conversation back towards the issue of

Longbourn and their father-in-law, determined to thoroughly apprise his friend of the situation. What Sir Charles chose to do with the information was up to him, but Darcy felt that it needed to be done - only then would he have peace of mind.

"I must say I think it very good of you to go to all that trouble, Darcy," Sir Charles observed lightly when Darcy had finished telling him about everything he and Elizabeth had had to do.

Darcy's brows rose significantly at this response from his friend.

"Yes, well, he is my father-in-law."

"You'd never met him before though, had you," Sir Charles pointed out. "A lot of effort to go to on behalf of a total stranger."

"Any effort I expended was on behalf of my wife," Darcy responded, his tone significantly colder than it had been. "And any effort Elizabeth expended was on behalf of her father who is, after all, still a member of her family, despite his many shortcomings."

Despite *his* many shortcomings, Sir Charles was not a stupid man and he recognised the implicit criticism in Darcy's response. However, though he shifted in his chair and awkwardly looked away, he made no attempt to reply or defend himself. Darcy supposed he should have felt slightly mollified by the proof that Sir Charles was not completely ignorant of his failure in his duty to his family, but in truth he was just further irritated by the lack of response from his friend. In fact, it made him think even less of Sir Charles, knowing that his friend was aware of his failings and neglecting to act, rather than simply ignorant of his wrongdoing.

"And how was the situation when you left it?" Sir Charles asked after an uncomfortable silence and Darcy answered with a sigh.

"Better. Most of the old servants have returned and Mr Bennet has found a man to assist Mr Nichols with the management of the estate and watching over the Viscount. I had offered the job to Benson's son, but he preferred to remain here with his father for a little while longer. We are still trying to locate Miss Lewis, and if she cannot be found then we shall have to see about finding someone else to run the school."

"If I can help at all, let me know," Sir Charles replied and Darcy nodded, deciding to accept the little that his friend was willing to do and be grateful.

"Well, I suppose I had best be on my way," Sir Charles stated, getting to his feet. Darcy stood as well and offered his friend his hand.

"Thank you for calling. And thank you for bringing Daniel to visit with James and Catherine whilst Elizabeth and I were away," he added and returned his friend's smile with a genuine one of his own.

"It was the least that I could do," Sir Charles replied and then looked a little awkward at the realisation of how true that was. "Well, until Thursday then. Give my best to Lizzy and the children."

"And mine to Lady Jane and Daniel," Darcy replied and then walked with his friend to the door of his study and watched him go.

Shaking his head and willing himself to just let it all pass, Darcy stepped back into his study and shut the door behind him, settling down for a few hours of work.

⊱⊰

"Look Lizzy, isn't this one pretty?"

Elizabeth looked up from her embroidery to smile at Catherine as the little girl came over to her, offering the flower she had just picked for Elizabeth to look at.

"Oh yes, very pretty. Add it to the others - how many do you have now?" Elizabeth looked into the small basket on Catherine's arm. "Nearly there - a few more and then we can sit and trim them and make them into bouquets."

Catherine smiled and skipped back to the flower border from which she was carefully selecting her blooms. Elizabeth watched her go and then turned to look at James, returning the smile he sent her. He was sat with his back against a tree trunk, his book propped open on his knee, and Elizabeth was struck by how much he looked like his father. When she told him as much James chuckled.

"Yes, people often say that to me. I cannot say that I mind, and I hope that I resemble him in other ways as well," he admitted and it was obvious how much he admired his father and aspired to be like him.

"You do," Elizabeth honestly assured him. She was delighted with how well she and James got on - with how close they had become since her marriage to his father. She felt sincere affection for him and was proud of the young man he was becoming; proud as an older sister would be at seeing her little brother grow up. "I have always thought that."

James appeared pleased by her words and smiled before returning to his book. The three of them were enjoying a little time outside before luncheon; James and Catherine had spent the morning at their lessons and Elizabeth had been shut away with Mrs

Reynolds, attending to the arrangements for the ball she and William were hosting which was now less than a month away. Tempted outside by the beautiful weather, Elizabeth had gathered up the two children and together they had found a shady place to sit and pick flowers, read and embroider in peace.

"Lizzy look, someone is coming."

Both Elizabeth and James turned to look where Catherine was pointing, seeing two men approaching them from the path which led around the lake.

"That is Mr Garret on the left, but I do not recognise the man with him," James supplied and grinned when Elizabeth complimented him on his good eyesight. "Mr Garret's proportions are quite distinctive."

Smiling at James' tease and silently admitting to herself that Mr Garret's diminutive height did make him rather recognisable, Elizabeth raised a hand and waved to the two men, offering her greetings when they drew closer.

"Good day to you, Your Grace," Mr Garret responded politely. "And to you as well, My Lord, Lady Catherine."

"Might you introduce us to your friend?" Elizabeth replied with a smile and a look towards the other gentleman, who seemed a few years younger than Mr Garret but shared some similarity with him.

"Indeed, with pleasure! This is my brother, Dr Edmund Garret; brother, this is Her Grace, the Duchess of Farleigh, Lord James Darcy, Marquess of Granby, and Lady Catherine Darcy."

Dr Garret bowed and expressed his pleasure at making their acquaintance. He had an easy going, affable manner and Elizabeth liked him immediately.

"I thought I saw some resemblance between you," she admitted as she looked between the two men. "Though of course you are slightly taller than your brother, Dr Garret."

Both men laughed at her thinly veiled teasing.

"Yes, he is - to my everlasting regret."

"I presume you are staying with your brother, Dr Garret?" Elizabeth asked lightly.

"Indeed I am, Your Grace," he replied. He smiled and revealed, "I have only recently returned from several years abroad and have been anxious to see my brother again after so long apart."

"Where did you travel?" James asked, drawing all their attention to him. "If you do not mind my asking," he added quietly.

"Not at all," Dr Garret assured him easily. "And I have just returned from New South Wales. My friend is the governor there and I sailed with him six years ago."

Elizabeth smiled at the expression of keen interest on James' face and invited both men to sit with them.

"It would be cruel to keep you standing when I can see that James has many questions to ask you, Dr Garret."

"We would be happy to join you," Mr Garret replied and settled himself down near Elizabeth whilst his brother sat closer to James and encouraged him to ask him whatever he liked.

Elizabeth attempted to make conversation with Mr Garret but was soon distracted by the fascinating tales which Dr Garret had to tell of his travels to the far side of the world. She was so distracted, in fact, that she completely lost track of time and was surprised when her husband's voice interrupted Dr Garret's latest story.

"Ah, here you are! I see now why you all failed to appear for luncheon - you have company."

Both Mr Garret and his brother rose to their feet to greet Darcy, the former bowing and introducing his brother before apologising for keeping Elizabeth and the children from their luncheon.

"Oh, there is no need to apologise," Darcy assured him easily. "And this is your brother - well, I am very glad to meet you at last, Sir. Your brother has told me about you many times."

"Thank you, Your Grace," Dr Garret replied with a slight bow. "It is a pleasure to meet you. My brother and I were on our way to see you when we came across Her Grace and the children."

"He has been telling us of his travels, Father," James piped up and Darcy could see how much his son had been enjoying the experience - his eyes fairly shone with excitement.

"Yes, I quite lost track of time," Elizabeth admitted, smiling when her husband offered a hand to help her up. "We had best go in for luncheon - will you join us, gentlemen?" she asked the two brothers. "You would be more than welcome."

"Thank you, yes," Mr Garret responded. "That is very kind of you, Your Grace."

Elizabeth waved away his thanks and Darcy spoke to his children.

"Remember to bring everything with you please James, Catherine."

"What about my flowers?" Catherine asked, holding up the basket which she had spent so long filling.

"We shall arrange them after luncheon," Elizabeth assured her. "Mrs Reynolds will make sure they are looked after until then."

Catherine nodded and ran to her father's side, taking his hand and walking with him back to the house. James and Dr Garret fell into step beside one another, and Mr Garret offered his arm to Elizabeth.

"I hope we are not intruding."

"Nonsense," Elizabeth replied. "You know you are always welcome, Mr Garret. And I wish to hear more of your brother's adventures," she added playfully and they shared a smile.

When they reached the house, rather than going inside Darcy led the small party around to the terrace and the table where they were to have luncheon, making the most of the beautiful weather. A footman served them all glasses of cool lemonade and Darcy raised his in a toast.

"To the traveller's safe return."

Both Mr Garret and his brother seemed highly gratified by this attention and were all smiles as they touched glasses with their neighbours at the table. James, who was impatient to hear more from Dr Garret, turned to his father.

"Dr Garret was just telling us when you arrived about the voyage across to New South Wales, and the time the ship almost struck the ice at the pole."

"Indeed?" Darcy responded, brows raised with surprise.

Dr Garret smiled modestly.

"Well, we saw the ice in time and the captain took the necessary steps to avoid a collision; there was no real danger."

"Perhaps you should start from the beginning, Doctor," Darcy suggested with an amused look, noticing that his son *and* his wife seemed to be most eager to hear the tale. "We are all ears."

~✦~

"You were a long while."

Darcy gently shut the door to the music room behind him and wandered over to join his wife where she sat at the pianoforte.

"Yes," he replied. "James was full of Dr Garret's adventures - he will not sleep for hours yet, I'll wager."

"You sound as though you don't approve," Elizabeth observed calmly; she shuffled along the bench to make room for him and when Darcy had sat beside her added, "Surely you did not disapprove of Dr Garret?"

"Certainly not," Darcy responded, idly pressing a few of the keys. "I just hope he hasn't given my son any ideas."

"And if he has?" Elizabeth asked, studying her husband's profile.

Darcy hesitated and then grinned ruefully.

"There is little I can do about it."

Elizabeth smiled and patted his arm.

"I highly doubt that James is going to rush off to the other side of the world. He was telling me just this afternoon how much he wishes to be like you."

"Really?" Darcy asked with a smile and Elizabeth told him what James had said. "Well, that is good to hear," he stated when Elizabeth had finished, trying not to sound too pleased. "Though in truth, I would not stand in his way if he wished for a little adventure - in fact, I intend to encourage him to travel once he is old enough."

"On the condition that he comes back," Elizabeth noted amusedly and Darcy chuckled and admitted she was right.

"I confess I am quite envious," Elizabeth commented a moment later. "You men are allowed to go wherever you please; we ladies have to rely on someone to take us."

"Well you may take comfort in the fact that I am willing to take you anywhere you wish to go," Darcy replied gallantly and laughed when Elizabeth smacked his arm. "I am in earnest! Well...almost. I would take you anywhere within reason."

"That would not include New South Wales then, I take it?" Elizabeth teased. "Dr Garret certainly made it sound fascinating."

"A little too hot for our tastes, I fear," Darcy pointed out and Elizabeth was forced to admit he was probably right. "And there are plenty of other places that are just as exotic - and not all the way around the other side of the world! Africa, for instance, or the Balkans."

"You would take me there?" Elizabeth asked with wide eyes, excited by the prospect.

"One day, perhaps," Darcy replied with a smile. "When the children are grown and it is just the two of us."

"I shall hold you to that, my love," Elizabeth promised, drawing a chuckle from her husband. She smiled and then had to cover her mouth to hide a small yawn. "Oh dear, excuse me. It has been a long day."

"Has it?" Darcy asked and Elizabeth thought for a moment before.

"No, you're right, it hasn't really been long at all. I do not know why I am so tired at the moment - I have been sleeping much better."

"Perhaps it is just the stress of the last two weeks or so," Darcy suggested, raising a hand and rubbing her back in a soothing motion. "You have been under a lot of strain."

"But so have you, and you are fine," Elizabeth pointed out and Darcy only just refrained from saying that was because he was a man, realising that his wife probably would not appreciate it. He settled for making a non-committal noise and then suggesting that they retire early.

"Not yet," Elizabeth replied with a shake of her head. "Let me play for you - I have not done so for so long."

"If you like," Darcy granted. "Shall I play the suitor and turn the pages for you?" he teased and Elizabeth laughed lightly but assured him he need not trouble himself.

She played as well as she usually did, with the same lightness of touch and expressiveness which had always characterised her style and which Darcy had always so enjoyed.

"Lovely," he complimented quietly as the final notes faded away and he leant close to press a soft kiss to the side of her neck, admiring the light blush on her cheeks when he pulled away.

"I really ought to practice more," Elizabeth commented lightly, absently running her fingers over the keys.

"Not tonight, though, I hope," Darcy responded and Elizabeth turned towards him, noting their close proximity.

"Oh? Is there something else you would like for me to do?" she asked and watched as her husband raised a hand; she felt rather than saw him trace the line of her collarbone with a feather light touch, her skin breaking out into goose bumps.

"No," Darcy eventually replied, his concentration focused on her lips. "But there is certainly something I would like for us to do together."

"How intriguing," Elizabeth teased with an enticing smile. "Do tell."

"I would much rather show you," Darcy murmured and finally touched his lips to hers. When Elizabeth leant into him he wrapped an arm around her waist and held her firmly pressed against his chest, deepening the kiss.

They were both slightly startled a moment later by the loud and discordant sound of Elizabeth accidently depressing three or four of the piano keys with her elbow; laughing quietly between themselves, they untangled themselves and stood up, Elizabeth making sure to shut the piano cover before accepting her husband's arm and retiring upstairs for the night.

Darcy couldn't help noticing how pale his wife seemed as he handed her up into their carriage on the morning of their departure, and quietly, so that the children would not hear, asked her if she was feeling well.

"Yes, I'm perfectly fine," Elizabeth replied lightly.

She knew that if she admitted to having felt unwell all morning he would not let her go, and she did not want to spoil their plans. She added a smile to carry her point and was relieved when her husband eventually nodded and stepped back so James could climb up and into the carriage with her and Catherine. They travelled the short distance to the Bingleys' home, meeting the Fitzwilliam family there and collecting Daniel and Sir Charles. Jane came out to see them off, and Elizabeth had a quiet word with her when Jane approached the window of the carriage.

"When we return, may I call on you? I would like to speak with you about Father."

"Very well," Jane granted with obvious reluctance, but she stepped away from the window before Elizabeth had a chance to reply.

Wondering at her sister's manner, Elizabeth absently welcomed Daniel into the carriage and saw him seated comfortably beside James. She heard the Colonel calling to see whether they were all ready to go, and they were soon underway. Though the carriage was well sprung and rocked very little, the motion was still enough to make Elizabeth feel quite unwell again and she was forced to sit with her head back and her eyes closed, taking slow and deep breaths

"Elizabeth, are you alright?" James asked, leaning forward and watching her concernedly. "You do not look well."

"It is just the motion of the carriage, James," Elizabeth replied, opening her eyes and managing a smile. "For some reason it is unsettling me today. I am sure it will pass."

"I shall open the window a little," James said, moving to do just that. "Perhaps a little fresh air will help."

Elizabeth smiled softly as the cool air washed over her and did indeed feel a little better.

"Thank you dear, that does help."

James smiled at the unexpected but not unwelcome endearment. The younger two children seemed curious more than anything else and James distracted them as well as he could, leaving Elizabeth to sit in peace. He was relieved when she eventually regained her usual colour and was able to sit normally and join in their conversation, though he still made a mental note to tell his father about Elizabeth's indisposition. When they stopped to change horses for the second time and have a spot of luncheon, James finally had the opportunity to speak with his father.

Dismounting from Fletcher, Darcy turned and was surprised to find his son standing close and obviously waiting for him.

"Is everything alright, Son?"

James glanced over his shoulder to where Elizabeth was standing and speaking to his aunt before turning back to his father and replying.

"Yes. I just thought you should know that Elizabeth seemed quite unwell when we first left Netherfield, though she seems fine now."

Darcy looked sharply in the direction of his wife, finding her watching him and James with a slight smile on her face, as though she had known that James would speak to him.

"Thank you for telling me James," he told his son. "I shall speak with Elizabeth and make sure everything is alright. Why don't you join the others?"

James nodded and left his father to follow the rest of their party inside the inn.

Elizabeth smiled ruefully as her husband walked over to her.

"I hope he did not make it seem too bad?"

"He only said that you seemed quite unwell," Darcy replied, taking her elbow and leading her away from the busy yard. "When I asked you when we left home if you were feeling well - you lied to me?"

"I was somewhat economical with the truth, yes," Elizabeth responded but seeing that her husband was unimpressed endeavoured to be more serious. "I did not want you to worry - or to jeopardise our plans. Truly, my love, I am quite well. I woke feeling a little nauseous but by the time we were leaving Pemberley I had already begun to feel much better; it was only the motion of the carriage when we left Netherfield which made me feel unwell again, but as I hope James told you I soon recovered and I feel perfectly fine now."

Darcy studied his wife worriedly, wanting to believe her.

"You are not just saying that because...?"

"I promise you, William," Elizabeth interrupted him firmly. "I am quite, quite well. And I give you my word that if I begin to feel unwell again I will tell you straight away."

It took several more such reassurances before Darcy allowed himself to be convinced, and even then he still made a point of having Elizabeth promise not to hide such things from him in future. Elizabeth had just solemnly given him her word when Richard stepped out of the inn and called out to them.

"Will you be joining us anytime soon, do you think?"

Darcy glared in his cousin's direction as his wife bit back a smile and looped her arm through his.

"Come, love, let us have some luncheon. I find I am quite famished."

Darcy allowed himself to be led away, though he resolved to keep a close eye on his wife from here on in. He trusted her to keep her word, but at the same time he did not doubt that they had very different ideas of what was worth worrying about.

They finally joined the rest of their party in a private room which the owner had set aside for them. Before she took her place, Elizabeth stopped behind James' seat and bent to press a quick kiss to his cheek.

"Thank you for taking such good care of me, James."

Blushing deeply, James smiled shyly and mutely nodded and Elizabeth patted his shoulder before moving away and taking her seat.

&#8526;&#8478;

The sickness Elizabeth had experienced did not return again that day, and when she woke the following morning she felt in perfect health; indeed, excited by the prospect of reaching the coast that day, her spirits were rather high and her husband was forced to admit that she seemed perfectly fine and that the trouble of the day before had just been a passing indisposition. They reached the inn at Theedlethorpe just before two o'clock in the afternoon and the children, Daniel and Joseph in particular, were anxious to go directly to the beach. Leaving most of the servants to manage the unloading of the carriages and to see to the horses, the whole party walked the short distance from the inn to the seafront, Darcy leading the way and Agatha bounding on ahead. A friend of his father's had owned an estate two miles outside of Theedlethorpe and he had visited the place as a boy.

Whilst the four boys ran about on the sand, chasing each other and Agatha, Elizabeth and the other adults laid out enough blankets for them all to sit on; Georgiana then gracefully settled herself onto one of the blankets and invited Elizabeth and Catherine to join her. The latter did so, but the former declined the invitation with a smile.

"Are you going into the water?" Georgiana asked, watching as Elizabeth bent to unlace her boots.

"I shall go for a paddle, yes," Elizabeth replied brightly and Sir Charles applauded her decision.

He stripped off his coat and called out to his son as he began to unbutton his waistcoat.

"Fancy a swim, Dan?"

All four boys gave very positive replies to this offer and hurried over to the blankets, carelessly tossing their hastily discarded items of clothing into a messy pile.

"Boys! Boys!" Georgiana objected, taking up the items and brushing the sand off them. "Please take care; here, give everything to me."

Elizabeth stifled a laugh when Colonel Fitzwilliam attempted to hand his wife *his* coat and she tossed it back at him.

"You are perfectly capable of folding your own clothes, my dear."

 Soon all four of the boys were down to just their trousers and the two men their breeches and shirts.

"Are you not joining us Father?" James asked, noticing that Darcy was still practically fully clothed, having only removed his coat on account of the heat.

"Your father is far too fastidious to even think of joining us, James," Sir Charles teased as he carelessly removed his shirt and let it drop on top of his other clothes. "Now - last one to the water is a rotten egg!"

Daniel, James and Joseph all chased off after him and Richard picked up his youngest son and carried him down to the water, not intending to allow Bradley to swim alone. Darcy, Elizabeth, Catherine and Georgiana smiled and watched them go before Elizabeth turned to her companions and asked if any of them would like to join her for a walk in the waves. Catherine and Georgiana were quite happy to just sit and watch the others, but Darcy agreed to accompany her. He removed his boots and rolled up the cuffs of his breeches and then offered his wife his arm. Elizabeth looked at his outstretched arm and then smiled up at him impishly; realising her intent, Darcy grinned and together they raced down to the water. Agatha bounded out of the sea to meet them, soaking a large portion of Elizabeth's dress and almost making her fall.

"Agatha, here, here, fetch this," Darcy coaxed, picking up the nearest piece of jetsam he could find and throwing it down the beach. "Go on, fetch it girl!"

Laughing at the state she was already in, Elizabeth accepted her husband's hand and allowed him to tug her out of reach of the waves. They watched James and the other boys playing in the water, smiling at their antics.

"This was a wonderful idea," Elizabeth said, her cheeks flushed and her eyes dancing with happiness, and Darcy could do nought but agree. He was reminded of their brief honeymoon and was amazed to think how much time had passed, and how much had happened, since then.

Agatha splashed her way back over to them and interrupted the moment, dropping the stick at Elizabeth's feet and barking expectantly. Elizabeth snatched it up with a playful smile and dashed away, Agatha chasing after her through the waves. Darcy stood with a soft smile on his face, admiring the picture his wife presented with her hair escaping its pins and tousled by the sea breeze, her dress half soaked and covered in sand and her face alight with joyous laughter. He could hear the sounds of both of his children's happiness too, and not for the first time was overwhelmed by a sense of his good fortune.

—

Having tucked his two children into bed, Darcy stepped out into the hallway and carefully shut the door to their room behind him. His cousin had just done the same with his two sons and grinned at Darcy.

"They will all sleep like the dead tonight!"

Darcy laughed silently and agreed that he was probably right; the boys had spent most of the afternoon in the sea and even Catherine had been persuaded to join them all when they had set about building a sandcastle. Returning downstairs, Darcy and his cousin re-joined the others, taking the seats nearest their respective wives. Sir Charles handed them fresh glasses of wine and then proposed a toast.

"To a fine day out. And to Darcy, for organising the whole thing with the precision of a military campaign."

"Hardly," Darcy scoffed and then smiled and accepted the thanks of his relations and friend. "It was my pleasure."

They chatted and laughed amiably between themselves for some time until Sir Charles suggested that they play cards; a pack was quickly located when they all agreed to the idea and they played a few rounds of whist until Georgiana declared that it was time for her to retire. Richard rose to accompany her and Sir Charles also agreed that it was getting late; they all turned to Elizabeth and Darcy, expecting them to announce their intention to retire as well.

"Elizabeth and I thought we would go for a walk on the beach before we retired," Darcy admitted.

"How lovely," Georgiana replied and wished them both a good night before going upstairs to bed, followed shortly by her husband. "I will see you both in the morning."

"Good night."

"Shall we?" Darcy asked once they were alone and Elizabeth smiled her acquiescence. "Will you be warm enough as you are, or shall I go up and fetch you a coat?"

"I'm sure I will be fine as I am," Elizabeth responded. "And if not, I shall avail myself of your coat."

Chuckling at her teasing, Darcy led his wife out into the warm night, pleased to discover that the moon was bright and provided enough light to see by.

"Come," he said quietly and together they followed the path they had taken earlier down to the beach.

"It is certainly a different place at night," Elizabeth commented quietly as they looked out over the black sea, watching the silver light dancing on the surface of the water.

Turning to the north, they slowly walked up the beach, speaking softly and quietly. They were so lost in one another that they did not realise how long they had been walking until Darcy happened to glance behind them and realised how far they had come.

"We should turn back, before it becomes very late. We will be tired tomorrow otherwise."

"I care not," Elizabeth replied softly. "Today has been the perfect day and more than worth a little tiredness."

Darcy stopped and put his hands on her waist.

"I am glad you have enjoyed it. It is good to see you smile again, after everything that has happened."

"I have resolved not to think of it," Elizabeth stated quietly as she laid her palms on his chest and looked up at him. "In fact, I have resolved that there is little point in dwelling on that which I cannot change, or that which only makes me miserable. I have too much to live for to allow the past to spoil it."

"I admire your philosophy," Darcy responded and heard his wife laugh quietly.

"Thank you - now let us see if I can adhere to it."

"I will help you," Darcy promised and was rewarded with a soft kiss.

"I suppose we should go back," Elizabeth murmured against his lips when they had exchanged several more kisses, each more lingering than the last.

"We should," Darcy agreed deeply, making no move to do so. A moment later he felt his wife shiver in his arms and it was enough to recall him to their surroundings. "Come, take my coat and let us return."

Elizabeth offered a few protests but her husband was adamant and so she allowed him to drape his coat around her shoulders before they slowly ambled their way back towards the inn, where a warm bed and a good night's sleep awaited them.

# Chapter 24

The following morning Elizabeth again woke to feel a little nauseous, though not as badly as she had felt the morning they had left Pemberley, and was more frustrated than alarmed by the return of her strange malady. Fortunately, with the company of so many others to distract him, her husband did not notice that she was not feeling well and Elizabeth was easily able to justify to herself her decision not to tell him. Indeed, by the time they had all eaten breakfast (she ate only very little as she gingerly sipped her tea) she was feeling much better again and was pleased that she had not worried her husband needlessly.

They were to depart Theedlethorpe after luncheon in order to reach Lincoln by nightfall, but they still had the morning to enjoy and make the most of. The weather continued fine, though a little breezy and perhaps too cold to make swimming enjoyable, and the whole party went down to the beach once more. As Darcy took his daughter to comb for shells, Elizabeth joined Sir Charles and the boys for a boisterous game of tag.

Crouching down to dig out a pretty looking shell from the sand, Darcy rubbed it clean with his fingers and offered it to his daughter.

"Here, princess, look at this one."

Catherine accepted the shell from him and examined it from all angles, noting the different colours running through it. She added it to the small collection they had amassed.

"It is a shame it is broken, though I still think it pretty enough to keep."

Darcy smiled and then straightened, prepared to continue their search. Suddenly, there were shouts from the others and he sharply span around in their direction; the boys were all huddled together in a group and both Georgiana and Richard were hurrying towards them. He could see neither Elizabeth nor Sir Charles.

"Papa, what is it?" Catherine asked, sensing that something was wrong.

Darcy did not reply, he only shook his head and took her hand, hurrying towards the others. As they drew closer to the group Richard turned to him.

"It is alright, we think she has just fainted."

"Mama!" Catherine cried and her uncle quickly scooped her up into his arms to comfort her as Darcy went to his wife's side.

Sir Charles and Georgiana were on their knees beside her and the former moved out of the way so that Darcy could take his place.

"What happened?" he asked as he did so, glancing between his sister and friend and then back down at his still unconscious wife.

"I don't know," Sir Charles replied, sounding perplexed. "One minute she was running around with us and then the next - I tried to catch her, but was too far away. But look, she is coming round!"

Darcy had seen Elizabeth's eyelids flutter and took hold of her hand just as she opened her eyes and blinked up at him.

"What happened?" she asked quietly, looking confusedly between him and Georgiana.

"You fainted, love," Darcy replied calmly. "How are you feeling? Do you think you can sit up?"

"Y-yes, I feel fine," Elizabeth responded; she seemed quite bemused. "Did I really faint?"

"You certainly did, and gave us all quite a shock, I don't mind telling you!" Georgiana teased and was pleased when her sister-in-law smiled.

"Come, let's sit you up," Darcy said, putting his arm around her back. He was relieved when she did not seem adversely affected by the change in orientation and pleased that she even managed to smile at the fact that she was covered in sand again.

"Oh dear," Elizabeth noted weakly when she saw the expressions of her audience. "I have given you all quite a fright, haven't I? I'm so sorry."

"It is not your fault," her husband replied and then slipped his arm under her legs. "Come, I will carry you back and we shall send for the doctor to see you."

"Oh William, I do not need the doctor," Elizabeth protested as her husband stood up and held her securely in his arms. "And it is much too far for you to carry me. Please, you must let me walk."

"I must do no such thing," Darcy responded and began walking in the direction of the inn.

Elizabeth continued to protest against the necessity with such spirit that the others were all much reassured about her well-being. James still followed closely behind his father, though, and Catherine ordered that her uncle follow after all three, not wanting to be left behind but unwilling to surrender the comfort of her uncle's arms. When they reached the inn, Georgiana left her husband and Sir Charles to watch over the children as she followed Darcy and Elizabeth up to their room.

She waited until her brother had gently laid his wife upon the bed before coming forward.

"I will help Elizabeth change her dirty things. You should go down and reassure James and Cathy."

Elizabeth could see that her husband was torn between wanting to stay with her and wanting to comfort his children and smiled reassuringly.

"I am quite well now, my love. Go and speak with James and Catherine and tell them I am alright. Georgiana will take care of me whilst you are gone."

Darcy hesitated for a moment before bending to press a lingering kiss on his wife's forehead and then reluctantly departing. Georgiana watched him go and then turned to her sister-in-law with her hands on her hips and a speculative expression. She then took a seat next to Elizabeth on the bed.

"Tell me something, Elizabeth," she began. "Have you been feeling unwell at all lately? Particularly early in the day?"

Elizabeth looked at Georgiana with surprise.

"Yes, I have. This morning and the day before yesterday."

"And have you been feeling tired as well - perhaps overly so?"

"I...yes, I have. How do you...?"

"Elizabeth, my dear, do you not see?" Georgiana patiently replied, though her smile was becoming larger by the minute. "Do you not know what all these things - the sickness in the morning, the tiredness, the faintness - do you not know what they mean?"

Elizabeth's expression was confused at first, but only for a second. Then her eyes widened and she mutely shook her head.

"Indeed, Elizabeth, I think it the most likely explanation."

"But...but surely it is too soon?" Elizabeth breathed, quite unable to process this unexpected development. "I - we have only been married less than three months!"

"Plenty of time," Georgiana replied cheerfully; she then regarded her sister-in-law closely and asked, "Are you not pleased?"

"I...I do not..." A dreamy expression suddenly appeared on Elizabeth's face and Georgiana laughed to herself even before Elizabeth sighed, "Yes, yes I am very pleased. Do you really think...?"

"I believe so," Georgiana assured her. "Especially if you have missed your courses," she added delicately and smiled when Elizabeth nodded after a thoughtful moment. "The doctor will have to see you and confirm it, of course, though that can wait until you are at home. For now I would suggest we change your gown and then I fetch my brother so that you can share the news with him."

"Yes," Elizabeth agreed, her eyes suddenly bright with tears. "Yes, I must tell him at once. Unless..." she suddenly looked worried. "Do you think I should tell him now, or wait until I am certain? I will not know for sure until I feel the quickening."

"Elizabeth, dear," Georgiana patted her hand and calmly pointed out, "My brother will not rest until he knows the reason for your fainting."

"Yes, I suppose you are right. But I would hate to disappoint him," Elizabeth worried, nibbling her bottom lip.

"There is very little chance of that," Georgiana assured her affectionately. "And my brother would want to know, and I am sure you want to tell him," she added and Elizabeth's smile told her she was right. "Come, let us get you out of these dirty things. Once we have done that I will fetch my brother and then have some food sent up for you, so that you do not faint again."

"Thank you," Elizabeth replied with such a happy, dazed look that Georgiana could not resist briefly embracing the younger woman.

*No, thank you Elizabeth,* she thought to herself as she imagined her brother's joy at the news that he was to be a father again.

ജ‍ന

Darcy entered the room he had been sharing with his wife with a questioning look, unsure how she was faring. Seeing her husband's hesitation, Elizabeth smiled and held a hand out to him, pleased when he immediately strode over to her.

"Should you not be lying down?" Darcy asked with a worried frown when he reached her.

Elizabeth shook her head.

"No, I am quite alright. Georgiana said that she would have some food sent up for me and once I have had that I shall be perfectly fine."

"But what is wrong? Something must be wrong - you have been tired and unwell and now you have fainted."

"William, please," Elizabeth soothed her husband, who she could see was quite upset. She supposed that his experiences with his first wife were making him especially nervous about her health. "There is nothing wrong with me - "

"But you..."

" - I am pregnant," Elizabeth concluded and then smiled brilliantly, having never said the words before. She watched the effect they had on her husband with tender amusement.

Darcy went completely still for a few seconds and then suddenly expelled all of his breath in a rush, gulping in another deep breath as his eyes widened and he looked down at his still smiling wife with amazement and disbelief. A great upsurge of joy then swept over him and he finally found his voice, the words all tumbling from him in a rush.

"My love - is this true? You are in earnest?"

"Yes!" Elizabeth laughed tearfully, profoundly touched by his response. "Of course I am in earnest!"

"Oh Elizabeth, Elizabeth," Darcy murmured, cupping her face and kissing her soundly. "Elizabeth, my darling, my dearest love."

"You are pleased, then, I take it?" Elizabeth asked playfully and Darcy laughed, more at himself than at anything else.

"Yes! I cannot...I am to be a father again; *we* are to have a child! Elizabeth, I hardly know how to describe how this makes me feel," he admitted.

"I know," Elizabeth assured him, touching his face and revelling in his expression of heartfelt joy. "I feel the same way."

Darcy was glad to hear her say so.

"You are not worried because it is so soon?"

"I was shocked at first, I will own," Elizabeth replied. "But all I can think now is how long these next nine months will seem!"

"Did you know...did you have any suspicions?" Darcy asked and Elizabeth blushed and laughed.

"No, I had none. I certainly should have done - as soon as your sister pointed out all of my symptoms, I realised straight away. But I think perhaps I did not consider it because we have only been married such a short time."

"We shall have to have the doctor examine you as soon as we get home," Darcy said. "Then we shall know how far along you are."

Elizabeth nodded and then smiled.

"It certainly explains why I have been so tired lately."

"Yes - and I have been so worried about you!" Darcy replied, shaking his head. "And this is the happy outcome," he added quietly, gently placing his hand over where he could imagine his child growing.

His almost reverential expression brought tears to Elizabeth's eyes and as she placed her hand over his she sent up a silent prayer to whoever was watching over them that she and her baby would be well.

℘☙

After availing herself of the food Georgiana had ordered for her and drinking a few cups of very sweet tea, Elizabeth was much her usual self again. She and Darcy explained to all the children and Sir Charles that she had fainted because she had not eaten a proper breakfast (which was partially true) and seeing how she appeared fully recovered, they were happy to accept the explanation that was given. James would have been inclined to still be a little worried, had not his father's demeanour entirely reassured him - for Darcy could not stop himself from smiling every time he looked at his wife. James reasoned that that would hardly have been the case if something was really wrong with Elizabeth.

Putting the whole episode behind them, the rest of their day continued as planned. They took an early luncheon at Theedlethorpe before departing for Lincoln, the excitement and activity of the last two days catching up with several of the younger children during the journey. Catherine fell asleep with her head in Elizabeth's lap, and even Daniel nodded off with his cheek pressed against the window of the carriage.

"I cannot imagine that is very comfortable!" Elizabeth teased in a whisper and James chuckled quietly and shook his head.

"How are you feeling?" he enquired quietly and Elizabeth smiled as she assured him she was quite well. "The motion is not disturbing you?"

"No, not at all," Elizabeth replied and wished that she could explain the situation to him.

She had agreed with her husband, though, that it was better to wait until they were absolutely certain she was pregnant and had felt the quickening before telling either Catherine or James, lest (heaven forbid) the worst happen and they be upset.

"With the exception of this morning, I enjoyed these last few days very much," James admitted and Elizabeth smiled.

"I am glad. And I hope you enjoy the next few weeks before you leave us," she added and James nodded but did not say anything.

"Are you looking forward to going to school?" Elizabeth asked softly.

James hesitated before replying.

"Yes and no. I am excited by the prospect of going to school, of meeting all my fellow students and furthering my studies, but I will miss you all very much," he concluded, looking at his sleeping sister, Agatha as she lay on the floor at his feet and finally, Elizabeth.

"We will miss you as well," she stated warmly. "Very much. We will write to you very often and send you all manner of nice things."

"I will look forward to it, particularly the nice things," James teased and Elizabeth laughed quietly. Catherine stirred in her sleep and Elizabeth carefully adjusted her position so that the little girl would be more comfortable.

"Will you know anyone at the school?" she asked when Catherine had settled once more.

"No, well, one boy. Do you know my father's friend, Lord Hallam?"

"The name does ring a bell," Elizabeth admitted, trying to recall where she had heard it before. "Oh, yes, I remember now - he is involved with the Royal Academy, is he not?"

"Yes, that is him," James responded. "His youngest son will be in the year above mine."

"Well perhaps the two of you will become friends," Elizabeth suggested. "Though I am sure there will be plenty of other boys happy to befriend you."

"I hope so," James admitted and Elizabeth thought his concern natural for a boy in his situation, faced with the prospect of leaving home for the first time and going to a place where he knew practically no one.

"You will be fine," Elizabeth assured him with an affectionate smile. "And you know that your father and I are always here for you, if you are not."

James nodded and smiled shyly.

"I do, thank you."

The carriage hit a bump in the road and Daniel was rudely knocked awake; Elizabeth could tell that James was perhaps happy for the distraction - he was still shy about showing and receiving affection - and was quite content to sit back and enjoy her own thoughts as the two boys chatted between themselves. The possibility that she could soon be a mother had not quite sunk in yet, and were she of a more fanciful nature she might have thought she had dreamt the whole thing. Though she trusted Georgiana's judgement, a part of her was still conscious of the fact that nothing was certain and would not be for many weeks yet. It was difficult to keep that in mind, however, when her own happiness, which already threatened to overwhelm her, was further augmented by the almost palpable joy of her husband. That he was such a wonderful father to James and Catherine was what had made her fall in love with him in the first place, and the strength of his reaction to her news filled her with such happiness. She had never for a moment doubted her husband's capacity for love, but it was still a comfort to know that her child would be dearly cherished by both of its parents.

୫୦୯୫

Jane greeted her sister as Elizabeth entered the parlour.

"Good morning, Lizzy. You look very well."

"And you look utterly radiant," Elizabeth responded, approaching her sister and giving Jane's bump an affectionate pat. "You are both doing well, I hope."

"Oh yes, I feel quite well," Jane responded as she carefully resumed her seat. "Though I think this baby a good deal larger than Daniel was - I do not recall being quite so round last time!"

"What is it like, Jane? What does it feel like?" Elizabeth couldn't resist asking.

"It is hard to describe, really," Jane replied thoughtfully. "Though I dearly love it; I feel...complete. Why do you ask?" she curiously inquired, aware that her sister had never asked her about pregnancy before.

"Because...oh Jane, because I am pregnant!" Elizabeth confessed with all the joy and excitement that she still felt. The doctor had seen her the day before and had confirmed that she was showing all the usual early signs of pregnancy, and predicted that if all went well the baby would be born in the spring.

"But you have only been married a few weeks!" Jane exclaimed, not particularly kindly.

"Over two months," Elizabeth replied, unable to help the defensive note in her voice.

"Well, yes, but still, it is so soon," Jane pointed out, sounding, if anything, quite irritated.

Elizabeth felt something cold creep into the place where her affection for her sister resided. She knew, of course, the trouble her sister and brother had had trying to have another child, but had assumed that Jane would be happy for her regardless. Apparently she had been mistaken, and on top of everything else it was hard for her to accept Jane's reaction.

"But of course I am very happy for you, Lizzy," Jane went on insincerely, or so it seemed to Elizabeth. "And for your husband, too. He must be delighted! How fortunate you are!"

"Yes, we are very happy," Elizabeth responded woodenly, struggling with how she should feel about Jane's reaction. Was she being too sensitive?

"Have you seen the doctor yet? Do you know when the baby will be born? Have you experienced any of the sickness?"

Jane peppered her with a series of similar questions, apparently happy to share her experiences with her younger sister. Elizabeth did her best to her side of the conversation, but in the end curtailed the discussion of her pregnancy and brought their conversation around to the reason for her visit; their father.

Jane's face lost its happy expression in an instant.

"Yes, Father. Quite a mess he caused, from what I understand. It does not surprise me; he always was incapable of looking after himself."

Elizabeth blinked and then looked at her sister as though seeing her for the first time.

"Have you always thought that?" she asked and Jane gave her a confused look.

"Thought what?"

"That he is incapable of looking after himself," Elizabeth repeated and Jane nodded.

"Of course. I daresay you were too young to remember what he was like, but Mama had to do everything for him. Even when she was sick, she was still managing everything for him - he did not make any allowances for her at all. I'm sure that if he had she might have recovered...but I suppose there is little use in dwelling on it."

"So is that why you were so happy to marry Sir Charles so soon after Mama died?" Elizabeth asked quietly but again Jane just looked confused. "You did not want to have to take her place."

"Of course I didn't," Jane replied, as though it were the most obvious thing in the world. "I daresay Father would have *expected* me to, but Charles and I had already postponed our wedding because of Mama's illness. It was perhaps a little too soon after she passed away, but I'm sure she would have understood."

"Oh yes, I'm sure," Elizabeth muttered. She couldn't decide whether she was more appalled at her sister's selfishness, or the fact that she had not noticed it before now.

"I'm not sure what all this has to do with the situation with Father, though, Lizzy," Jane said.

"Do you not think we should at least discuss what has happened? Do you not wish to hear about his welfare?"

Her sister looked briefly annoyed, and then responded.

"Lizzy, do not be like that. Perhaps I should have done more to help, but I just...I do not care for him, Lizzy. I never have, and neither does Charles. It is alright for you, you were too young, and you do not remember what it was like when Mama was alive. If you could remember how he treated her - like a servant! And you know how he is, Lizzy - so dependant! If only he behaved as a man should, perhaps then I could think well of him, but I simply cannot. I really think him quite pathetic."

"And that excuses you from all responsibility for him?" Elizabeth questioned, realising that that was the harshest speech she had ever heard from Jane.

"Oh I don't know," Jane replied carelessly, waving a hand. "I know I should do more, but I cannot bring myself to feel guilty about doing so little. That makes me a terrible daughter, I suppose."

"A poor sister, at least," Elizabeth quietly stated and could see how little her sister liked the sentiment. "Can you honestly deny it, Jane? After admitting that you did not want to take Mama's place, and yet leaving me to do the same? After saying that you knew how he treated her like a servant but leaving me to be treated the same way? My husband is so angry with you for your failure to help us with Father, Jane, and I have been defending you to him; how can I argue with him now when he says you are selfish, after everything I have just heard you say?"

"Lizzy!" Jane objected sharply, feeling the insults.

"I was eleven, Jane," Elizabeth went on, angry and hurt. "Eleven. You should have taken care of me; you should have made sure I was happy and well, not run off to marry your betrothed practically the moment our mother was laid to rest!"

Jane frowned and shook her head.

"You don't know what it was like."

"Don't I?" Elizabeth retorted, gesticulating angrily. "You speak of how hard it was for *you* to live with Father when Mama was alive, but did you never take a moment to imagine how hard it would be for *me* to live with him *alone*? No, of course you didn't - because you didn't care!"

"That's not true!" Jane objected strongly, but Elizabeth just shook her head and looked away.

"I think it is, Jane," she stated hollowly. "And I think it is still true today. At the very least you should have offered to help me, even if you don't care about Father. I would have done everything I could to help you."

Elizabeth had just uttered these final words when Sir Charles entered the room, his ready and welcoming smile fading to a look of concern when he saw his wife's stormy and piqued expression.

"What is it Jane?" he asked, rushing forward to comfort her. "Is it the babe, do you need the doctor? Shall I send for…?"

"No Charles, I am quite well," Jane assured her husband a little shortly, trying to see past him to her sister.

"I think I should take my leave," Elizabeth said stiffly as she abruptly stood up. "I…say hello to Dan for me. I will see myself out."

She disappeared from the room without hearing any protest from her sister, wondering why she had expected one.

ℰᏇ

Darcy paused in his writing and consulted his watch for what must have been the tenth time, anxiously listening for the sounds of a carriage. He had asked to accompany his wife on her visit to Netherfield, but Elizabeth had laughed him off, teasing him for his solicitude and assuring him that she was sure the journey to Netherfield would not be too taxing. His concern for her physical wellbeing, however, had not been Darcy's only motivation for asking to join her; he was worried about what Jane would say, and how Elizabeth would respond to it. On reflection he had realised that he had perhaps been too vocal in his criticism of his sister-in-law, and was concerned that he had damaged the impression Elizabeth had of her. If that were the case, Darcy was very much worried that a few wrong words from Jane would be enough to spoil the relationship shared by the sisters.

He had just taken up his pen to resume his work when he finally heard the sounds he had been listening for. Going to the window, he saw the carriage rolling up the drive and decided to go out to meet it. Descending the front steps, he was surprised to see the carriage continue directly on to the stables and followed after it in confusion.

"John?" he called to his coachman when he had caught up to the carriage; some grooms were already unharnessing the horses but there was no sign of Elizabeth. "Where is my wife?"

"Her Grace decided she would like to walk, Sir," John replied from his seat atop the carriage. "We dropped her off as we passed the East Wood, Sir."

Darcy wanted to ask whether Elizabeth had seemed upset or distressed, but ultimately refrained. Though he wished to seek out his wife, he trusted her to come to him when she was ready and decided to grant her the solitude she obviously wished for. Half an hour later a footman appeared to tell him that Elizabeth had returned from her walk but that she intended to attend to several household matters, and some more of the preparations for the ball, before going to visit with Mr Garret and his brother. Frowning slightly, Darcy thanked and then dismissed the footman, wondering if his wife was intentionally avoiding him or if he were just imagining things.

Deciding that there was only one way to be certain, he set aside the letter he had been working on and proceeded directly to his wife's study. He was surprised to find Mrs Reynolds sat alone, until his housekeeper explained that Elizabeth was just changing and would be down directly.

"How are the preparations for the ball progressing?" he asked for lack of anything else to say.

"Very well, Sir," Mrs Reynolds replied confidently. "We have only to settle a few more details - everything else is decided. Her Grace is most efficient."

This was high praise from his housekeeper, and Darcy smiled. He heard the sound of footsteps and turned in time to see Elizabeth enter.

"Oh! Hello William," she greeted him; her voice had a brittle quality and Darcy was convinced that she had quarrelled with her sister. "Were you waiting for me? Did you need something?"

"No, not at all," Darcy replied, studying her closely as she walked to her desk and seated herself behind it, her movements agitated. "I simply wished to say hello, and to ask how your visit with your sister was."

"Oh, it was fine," Elizabeth replied lightly, her smile forced.

"And did you discuss what you planned to discuss?" he asked, conscious of the presence of Mrs Reynolds.

"What? Oh, yes, we did," Elizabeth affirmed, not looking at him and shuffling some papers on her desk.

"And?" Darcy pressed.

"And it was a pleasant visit but now I really do have things to do, so if you would excuse us...?"

Darcy's brows rose at this obvious dismissal and he stared at his wife; Elizabeth flushed and looked away as the silence lengthened and Mrs Reynolds looked fixedly down at her hands, trying to be as inconspicuous as possible.

Darcy finally relented.

"Very well. I shall leave you to your business. I shall be in my study when you are ready to talk to me, Elizabeth."

He turned and left the room, leaving Elizabeth in uncomfortable silence with Mrs Reynolds. Fortunately, the elder woman was nothing if not tactful and quickly introduced a new topic of conversation, pretending that nothing was amiss. Burying herself in preparations for the ball, orders for new curtains in the music room and resolving an argument between two of the upstairs maids, Elizabeth was thankful for the distraction from her unhappy thoughts.

&#x204A;&#x2E33;

An hour before dinner, Darcy quietly entered his wife's dressing room to find Wilson sat repairing the hem of one of Elizabeth's dresses. He had not seen his wife since their encounter earlier on and wondered what sort of reception he would receive now.

Wilson obviously sensed his thoughts because she paused in her work.

"My mistress is reading; I was planning on leaving her for another quarter of an hour and then going to speak with her about dinner."

Darcy nodded and thanked her before going through into his wife's room. Elizabeth was sat in the window, watching the fading light of the day. She looked over when Darcy entered and he was relieved to see her smile; he walked towards her and took a seat at the other end of the bench, facing his wife.

"You are well?"

"Yes- I had a slight headache earlier, but I think it was just from too much sun on my walk back from the rectory. I feel much better now," Elizabeth replied quietly.

"Good," Darcy nodded. He fell silent and Elizabeth sighed heavily.

"I don't want to talk about it."

"I know," Darcy murmured softly. "But I think you need to. And I want you to talk to me Elizabeth - please."

Elizabeth shook her head.

"I can't."

"Why not?" Darcy asked, trying not to sound hurt.

"Because I said some things which I am not proud of, and I couldn't bear for you to know them," Elizabeth finally admitted. "You would judge me harshly for it, and I would rather not damage your opinion of me."

"Elizabeth," Darcy sighed, his expression serious. "I sincerely doubt that anything you said could affect my opinion of you. I love you, and I always will."

Elizabeth only shook her head again and he felt the sting of her rejection.

"Will you really not talk to me?"

"I don't have anything to say," Elizabeth replied. He did not reply and she expected him to go; instead he reached out and took her hand, silently cradling it within his own.

"Will?" she questioned tentatively after several moments; he was gently stroking her palm and combined with his continued silence it was quite unnerving.

"I cannot make you talk to me, Elizabeth, but I'm not going anywhere," Darcy replied quietly, holding his wife's gaze. Eventually she nodded and gave his hand an almost imperceptible squeeze. They sat and watched the sun go down together.

&#8526;&#8579;

Darcy slowly came awake the following morning and when he opened his eyes was surprised to find his wife propped up on her elbows watching him.

"I told Jane that I thought she was selfish and that she didn't care about me. She all but admitted that she left me to cope with Father alone because she didn't want to have to, and I told her that was selfish. She was annoyed with me and I think I let my temper get the better of me, but that doesn't make what I said any less true. I was too angry and upset to realise that yesterday, but I see it now. I'm sorry I refused to talk to you about it."

"What made you change your mind?" Darcy asked. "About telling me, I mean."

"I think my emotions were too raw yesterday," Elizabeth admitted. "I have never argued with Jane before, and it was not a pleasant experience. I thought that you would be appalled too, and I didn't want that. But I was thinking about it all night, about what I'd said and what Jane said, and I realised that I hadn't said anything that wasn't true. It was harsh, and would have been better left unsaid, but it was still true. I still feel awful about it, and I've written her a letter apologising, but I don't think I have any reason to be ashamed of myself. At least not with regards to my sister," she amended with a rueful look. "I treated *you* very badly yesterday."

"Perhaps I should not have pushed you to confide in me," Darcy admitted with a sigh, brushing some hair away from her face. "That was my initial resolve, at least - I forgot all about it when I saw how upset you were."

Elizabeth smiled and then yawned sheepishly behind her hand.

"Tired?" Darcy asked amusedly.

"Yes - as I said, I did not sleep very much during the night."

"Then go back to sleep," Darcy advised. "There is nothing pressing awaiting you - take some rest."

"Will you stay with me?" Elizabeth asked as she lay down next to him.

"Of course," Darcy averred and tucked her head under his chin.

They were silent for some time until Elizabeth quietly spoke.

"I do not think Jane and I will ever be as close as we were before. I am sure she will accept my apology, but I doubt she will ever truly forget what I said to her. And I cannot look at her the same way now."

Darcy felt a twinge of guilt.

"I am sorry if by voicing my opinion of your sister I made you think ill of her."

"I think perhaps you just opened my eyes," Elizabeth replied thoughtfully. "And then Jane showed me exactly what you had seen all along."

"Still..." Darcy began to argue but Elizabeth stopped him with a gentle touch of her fingers to his lips.

"It was not your fault. It was not mine either."

Darcy nodded and they lapsed once more into silence; finally he thought to ask whether Elizabeth had shared their happy news with her sister. He felt her negative response in the stiffening of her body even before she replied.

"Yes, I told her. Her reaction is what precipitated our quarrel."

"What do you mean?"

"I think that jealous is perhaps too strong a word, but she certainly thought of herself first. She was amazed that it had happened so soon," Elizabeth elaborated when she saw her husband's confused look. "And only after she had said as much did she remember to offer her congratulations. I confess I was not impressed."

"No, I don't suppose you were," Darcy replied, sounding just as displeased as she had been.

"She recovered well enough, and said all the right things and asked all the right questions, but I don't think I will ever forget that initial reaction. She seemed almost..."

"Go on," Darcy urged when she trailed off.

"She seemed almost annoyed," Elizabeth admitted finally.

"What possible reason could she have to be annoyed?" Darcy questioned.

Elizabeth hesitated again, wondering if she should really voice the suspicion which had been lurking in the back of her mind for several months now. The words, once said, could never be taken back.

"Elizabeth?" Darcy prompted again and Elizabeth made her decision.

"I wonder sometimes whether Jane wishes for more attention for herself. She has waited several years for another child, and my marriage, and now my pregnancy – perhaps she feels I have overshadowed her news with my own. Is it awful of me to think that she feels that way?"

"It is awful of her," Darcy responded without hesitation. "If she does indeed feel that way."

"I'm sure I'm wrong," Elizabeth stated but only silence met her pronouncement and she signed. "However she feels, she is still my sister and I love her. That being said, I will never think as well of her as I once did."

Darcy remembered that he had reached that conclusion less than a week ago, and couldn't decide how he felt now that Elizabeth had done the same. As long as it did not make her unhappy, he supposed it was for the best.

# Chapter 25

Darcy smiled to himself as he noticed his wife's agitation, moving to her side and taking hold of her hand. He could hear the sounds of their visitors in the front hall and knew they would not be alone much longer.

"Are you nervous?"

"No," Elizabeth denied, and then smiled ruefully. "Well, that is perhaps not entirely true. I am nervous on her behalf, rather than my own. I would hate to say anything which would make her uncomfortable."

"I am sure you needn't worry," Darcy assured her affectionately. "You have always seemed to me to know the right thing to say. Just be yourself, and all will be well."

Elizabeth nodded, pressing his hand in thanks. She then turned to face the door with a welcoming smile upon her face as a footman announced their visitors.

"Mr and Mrs John Hadlee to see you, Sir, Ma'am."

"Hadlee," Darcy greeted his friend warmly. "It is good to see you again - and Mrs Hadlee, a pleasure as well. Come, allow me to introduce you to my wife. Elizabeth, this is my good friend John Hadlee, whom you have already met, and his wife. Mrs Hadlee, my wife - Elizabeth."

Elizabeth curtseyed gracefully, pleased that her husband had taken the initiative and handled the introductions so deftly.

"It is a pleasure to meet you at last, Your Grace," Claire Hadlee stated quietly, though with a kind and sincere smile. "I am sorry to have not made your acquaintance before now."

"And I am very pleased to meet you as well, Mrs Hadlee," Elizabeth replied warmly. "And I also regret we have not met before now, though I daresay my husband and I have been kept very busy these past few weeks. The summer has been quite eventful," she concluded with a smile at Darcy, who grinned and shook his head.

"That is certainly one word for it," he quipped and then gestured for their guests to take a seat. "Please, make yourselves comfortable."

"Shall I ring for tea?" Elizabeth asked as John Hadlee saw his wife seated and then took the chair next to hers.

"That would be lovely, thank you, Your Grace," Hadlee replied and so Elizabeth pulled the bell pull and then took her own seat.

"I suppose you must be busy with the preparations for the ball," Hadlee noted and then smiled at his wife, "We received our invitation on Monday, didn't we, my dear?"

"Yes," Claire Hadlee affirmed quietly. "I am looking forward to it very much."

Elizabeth smiled warmly, hoping that her expression was not at all pitying. Knowing what she did of the circumstances surrounding the incident with Frank Ellerslie, Elizabeth admired the other woman her strength but still could see that Claire Hadlee was not comfortable with the thought of attending the ball. It was touching to see how she exerted herself, and how her husband was so discreetly solicitous to her care, and Elizabeth thought that she would very much like to be friends with Claire Hadlee.

"I am glad to hear it. I hope all of our prospective guests share in your feelings, and that you all enjoy yourselves. I have never hosted a ball before," Elizabeth admitted with a disarming smile. "Though, fortunately, I have Mrs Reynolds to guide me. If the evening is at all a success it will be entirely down to her."

"You are too modest, my love," Darcy objected affectionately. "I'd have you know that Mrs Reynolds is as full of praise for you as you are for her."

"Well that is certainly flattering," Elizabeth teased lightly, sharing a smile with both of the Hadlees. "Especially considering how full of praise I am for her."

"My mother always envied you Mrs Reynolds, you know," Hadlee revealed with a grin; he chuckled when Darcy seemed surprised. "Oh yes, she would have poached her away if she could."

"How fortunate for me that she never found a way!" Elizabeth joked and was pleased when both Hadlee and his wife laughed lightly.

"How is your mother, Hadlee?" Darcy asked politely. "She no longer resides with you, I gather."

"No, she lives with my aunt in Kent now," Hadlee replied. "And she seemed well and happy the last time we saw her didn't she, my dear?"

"Yes," Claire Hadlee agreed. "I believe she is very happy in the company of her sister."

"And Kent is such a beautiful county," Elizabeth noted. "William and I spent a few days on the coast near Margate following our wedding and I was most enamoured of the place."

Whilst they all four discussed the delights of Kent and the coastline there, the tea things arrived and Elizabeth set about making her guests and her husband a cup.

"Four sugars for my husband, please," Claire Hadlee requested. "And just one for myself."

Elizabeth tried to hide her smile but could not quite manage it; fortunately the other woman was not offended and, as their husbands were still busy talking, lent forward.

"I have told him time and again that he will spoil his teeth with so much sugar, but he always insists on having four!"

"It is his prerogative I suppose," Elizabeth replied with a glance at the gentleman in question.

"To rot his teeth? Yes, I suppose so," Claire Hadlee granted with a smile. "Though I do hope our daughter does not pick up his bad habit - she has quite a sweet tooth herself already!"

Elizabeth laughed lightly.

"Catherine is the same. She must have chocolate with her breakfast else she is sure to be most put out!"

"Oh, I was the same as a girl," the other woman confessed. "And I insisted on it before bed also. Indeed, I still indulge that habit every once in a while."

"So do I!" Elizabeth whispered and they shared a light laugh.

"What are you two whispering about?" Darcy asked, distracted by their laughter.

"Bad habits," Elizabeth responded with an impertinent grin and her new friend hid her smile behind her tea cup.

"I hope you will bring your daughter with you the next time you visit - or perhaps I could visit you and bring Catherine with me."

"Alicia would certainly like that," Hadlee expressed. "And you are welcome any time."

Elizabeth smiled at the sentiment and then turned to Mrs Hadlee.

"Are you acquainted with Lady Victoria Garville, Mrs Hadlee?"

"Yes," Claire Hadlee replied. "Though the acquaintance is only a slight one. Why do you ask?"

"Victoria and I have a standing arrangement to meet once a week, to walk or ride in the park and take tea together, and if it would please you to join us you are more than welcome," Elizabeth offered warmly and was pleased when the other woman smiled.

"I believe I would like that very much."

"Good! Victoria is to come tomorrow, though I appreciate that may be too short notice for you."

"I have no engagements for tomorrow," Claire Hadlee assured her.

"Wonderful," Elizabeth enthused. "Then you will join us?"

"Yes, I will, thank you."

Elizabeth waved away the thanks.

"Oh, the pleasure is mine, I assure you. And I confess I have an ulterior motive; I am seeking to ensure that I have good company once the hunting begins and my husband abandons me to the thrill of the chase!"

She smiled playfully at Darcy as he and Hadlee both laughed.

"Somehow I find it hard to imagine you languishing away in my absence, my love," Darcy noted with a wry grin.

"Only because I shall have Victoria and Mrs Hadlee to keep me company," Elizabeth teased. "Alone I am sure I would waste away without you."

"Well we cannot have that," Darcy quipped; he smiled at Claire Hadlee. "How have you survived your husband's absences, Mrs Hadlee?"

"Very well," the lady responded with a smile at her husband. "Though perhaps that is only because we have been married longer."

"I certainly hope so!" Hadlee joked and they all laughed.

"I hear that you are an avid horsewoman, Your Grace," Hadlee addressed Elizabeth. "It has long been tradition for the ladies to join their husbands on one of the hunts - I am sure you must intend to do so?"

Darcy glanced at his wife, wondering what she would say; fortunately Elizabeth seemed ready with a response.

"As much as I would love to, I am afraid it will not be possible for me to join you this season. Dot, my horse, has recently sustained an injury and I would not be comfortable attempting such a challenging ride on an unfamiliar mount. Neither would my husband be easy if I attempted it," Elizabeth added, reaching over and pressing Darcy's hand affectionately. "So I shall wait until next year to join you."

"Oh, that is unfortunate," Hadlee commiserated. "Though your decision is most prudent. Some of the hunts here are very demanding and it would be terrible were anything to happen to you."

"My thoughts exactly," Elizabeth agreed with a smile and then deftly moved the conversation along. "When is the first hunt scheduled, do you know?"

Of course Hadlee did know and they fell into a discussion of the hunting calendar, of the routes and those who participated and, finally, the finest mounts which would feature. For her own part, Elizabeth was genuinely engaged in all that was said, though she suspected that Claire Hadlee was just indulging her husband's interest, and thought all the better of the other woman for it.

"Will you be riding Fletcher, or one of your other hunters?" Hadlee asked Darcy at one point, jokingly adding, "You are rather spoiled for choice, after all!"

Darcy smiled and did not attempt to deny it.

"I shall ride Fletcher for the more difficult routes, but I had thought to debut Baltar this season. He is ready, I think."

Hadlee whistled his appreciation, chuckling when his wife tapped his arm in reprimand.

"Forgive me, my dear, but you do not know the horse to which Farleigh is referring. I saw him first - what was it, a year ago? - and he was extremely impressive then. If he has improved even more...well, I eagerly anticipate seeing him in action."

"When you call again I will show Dylan to you," Darcy promised. "He holds, if anything, even more promise."

"If you can improve his temperament," Elizabeth noted with a smile. "Though I cannot deny that he is a fine jumper - the ease with which he hops over the fences certainly attests to that!"

Darcy smiled and expressed his agreement; his friend shook his head and good-naturedly complained.

"You have all the luck, Farleigh. Your hunters are the envy of the entire county, and you took both the Derby and the Oaks this year with your Thoroughbreds!"

"I confess I was surprised that Valeria won, after her poor showing in the thousand Guineas," Darcy admitted, and then added with a grin, "But I knew Barker would come away with it."

"I must say, Your Grace," Claire Hadlee commented with a smile. "I much prefer the names you give your horses to some of the others I have heard."

"Yes, you do hear of some quite ridiculous names, don't you," Elizabeth agreed with a laugh. "What was the one you mentioned to me last week?" she asked her husband.

"Plenipotentiary," Darcy replied and then chuckled lightly when Claire Hadlee rolled her eyes. "The name is often shortened to Plenipo, which is a little better, I think."

"Will your son be joining us for the hunt this season - before he leaves for school?" Hadlee asked and Darcy shook his head.

"Not this season, no. He is still too young."

"I was riding the hunt by his age," Hadlee pointed out fairly.

"Yes, and if I recall correctly you fell and broke your arm on the - what was it, the third hunt?" Darcy responded with a knowing look and his friend smiled ruefully and held up his hands.

"I take your point."

Darcy nodded and smiled and the moment passed. A glance at the clock revealed that the Hadlees had stayed longer than they had originally intended and they reluctantly rose to take their leave.

"Victoria is to arrive at half past eleven," Elizabeth told Claire Hadlee as their husband's said goodbye to one another. "And I promise that *we* shall not spend the entire time discussing horses and hunting."

The other woman looked surprised for a moment and then laughed lightly.

"I thought I had managed to look interested! But I am pleased to know I shall not have to worry about convincing anyone tomorrow."

Elizabeth smiled and they said goodbye to one another; standing with her husband, she watched as their guests were escorted from the room by one of the footmen and then turned to look up at Darcy with a smile.

"Well, wasn't that enjoyable?"

"Very much so," Darcy agreed. "And not at all uncomfortable - you needn't have worried."

"I am looking forward to seeing Mrs Hadlee again tomorrow," Elizabeth stated. "I am sure she and Victoria will get along and we shall all become good friends."

"I am sure you shall," Darcy concurred with a quick kiss. "I like to see you making friends."

"And I like making them," Elizabeth teased and moved away before Darcy could make any response. "I think I shall go and visit Dot - all this talk of horses has reminded me how long it is since I last did so."

"Shall I accompany you?" Darcy offered but Elizabeth shook her head.

"I know Mr Benson is waiting for you. Go and tend to your business, and I will see you later."

Darcy nodded and Elizabeth left him with a smile and a quick wave. She left the house via the kitchens, her pockets full of carrot and apple as she strolled across to the stables, cheerily wishing a good day to those she passed on her way. She found Poppy making a nuisance of herself in the yard whilst Agatha dozed in the shade of one of the carriages and brought the young dog along with her as she went inside to Dot's stall. She was pleasantly surprised to find Greg already there, and as Poppy climbed into the stall Elizabeth greeted her groom.

"Good afternoon, Foster."

"Good afternoon, Your Grace," Greg replied politely; he had strictly adhered to Darcy's edict and only spoke to Elizabeth when spoken to, and even then only briefly.

"I thought I would come and say hello," Elizabeth explained as she entered the stall. She smiled as Dot nuzzled her face and offered a chuck of carrot to the horse.

"I was just giving her a quick brush," Greg responded. "I will come back later."

Elizabeth wanted to tell him he didn't have to go but held herself back; instead she smiled and held out her hand for the brush.

"Let me finish it, I haven't done it for a while."

"As you wish," Greg handed her the brush and bowed his head before stepping out of the stall, nudging Poppy back inside with his foot before shutting the gate.

"I hope you are well, Mr Foster," Elizabeth expressed with a warm look, trying to show that she was still his friend, despite what the situation demanded of them both. "And your wife, also."

"We are," Greg replied with a slight smile. "Thank you again for the things you brought from home - it was very good of you."

"It was the least that I could do," Elizabeth stated and they shared a final smile before Greg walked away.

Sighing resignedly, Elizabeth turned to Dot and offered her a bit of apple and then dropped a bit for Poppy to enjoy too. She lamented that her new status had come at the cost of one of her oldest friendships, though it was the only complaint she had about being married, and she knew that she was very fortunate to be able to say so. She also regretted that it would be many months before she was permitted to ride again, though once again she had no other complaints about the condition which necessitated her giving up one of her favourite past times.

ଧଦ୍ଧ

"What a pity about the weather," Lady Victoria Garville lamented as she strolled alongside Elizabeth and Claire Hadlee, peering up at the cloudy sky. "After all the sun we have been having, it had to be cloudy on the day of our walk."

"Perhaps we should simply be grateful it is not raining," Elizabeth commented with a smile. "Though I for one am not unhappy to have a slight reprieve from the heat - I rather alarmed poor Dr Garret last week when I made myself unwell with too much sun."

"Oh, you poor thing," Lady Victoria lamented. "It really can make you feel quite awful, can't it?"

"Yes, though it was entirely my own fault," Elizabeth replied. She smiled at Claire Hadlee and noted, "I can tell by your lovely fair skin that you are not prone to such a mistake."

"Oh, thank you, Your Grace."

"Please, call me Elizabeth," Elizabeth requested for the third or fourth time. She was determined to make the other woman comfortable and coax her out of her shell. "And as for my skin - I believe my aunt would say that I am positively brown and coarse, but I confess I do not much care."

"As long as your husband has no objections, I suppose," Lady Victoria teased and Elizabeth smiled archly at her friend as she replied.

"Even then, I shouldn't much care either."

"No, I don't suppose you would," Lady Victoria laughed and even Claire smiled.

They walked on a little further until Lady Victoria remembered something which she had wanted to tell Elizabeth.

"My brother is home for a visit - you shall be able to meet him tonight at dinner."

"I look forward to it," Elizabeth responded, her lips twitching with amusement. She turned to her other companion and explained, "Lady Victoria has informed me that her brother is wealthy, handsome and insufferable and so naturally I cannot wait to meet him!"

The other woman stifled a laugh as Lady Victoria objected.

"You weren't supposed to tell anyone else I said that."

"Wasn't I? Do forgive me," Elizabeth teased and laughed when her friend scowled at her. She turned back to Claire Hadlee, "Have you had the pleasure of meeting the gentleman in question?"

"Yes, I have," she confirmed.

"And?" Elizabeth pressed; Lady Victoria smiled when Claire Hadlee glanced quickly at her.

"You needn't worry I will be offended - as Elizabeth has just demonstrated, I abuse my brother quite freely, so you are free to do so as well."

"In truth I do not know His Lordship well," she began slowly. "But I thought him...typical for a man of his age."

Lady Victoria laughed gaily as Elizabeth complimented the smiling Claire Hadlee.

"Oh bravo, very politic."

"I shall have to remember that," Lady Victoria said when she had calmed herself. "It may prove a helpful euphemism."

"What would be mine, do you think?" Elizabeth asked with playful curiosity.

Lady Victoria regarded her for a moment.

"Delightfully quick-witted."

"An impertinent tease, I suppose is what that means," Elizabeth guessed with a laugh.

"Something like that," Lady Victoria responded playfully. "What would be mine?"

"Hmm, what do you think?" Elizabeth asked Claire and they both were silent for a moment.

"Surprisingly verbose?" Claire finally ventured and smiled when Lady Victoria burst out laughing and Elizabeth chuckled quietly.

"I believe we have stumbled upon a new game," she noted with a grin. "Who shall we do next?"

"I cannot think of one for you, Mrs Hadlee," Lady Victoria admitted. "But I have the perfect one for my mother - enjoys being helpful."

Elizabeth smiled in spite of herself.

"That would apply equally as well to my aunt, I think."

"What about Lord Leigh?" Lady Victoria proposed with a wicked grin and Elizabeth shared a look with Claire Hadlee.

"I am beginning to wonder about the wisdom of this game, now that I think about it," she confessed but when Lady Victoria pressed her she sighed and granted, "Oh, very well, just one more. Lord Leigh you say?"

All three of them were quiet until the silence was once again broken by Claire Hadlee.

"An appreciator of good food and wine?"

Elizabeth and Lady Victoria laughed at the very accurate description of Lord Leigh, who tended to drink too much and was terribly overweight.

"You are good at this," Lady Victoria complimented the other woman with a smile. "If only I could think of one for you."

"Well whilst you think on it," Elizabeth stated. "I think it is time we turn back and return to the house."

They accordingly did turn and retraced their steps along the way they had come, Lady Victoria quickly abandoning her attempt to formulate an appropriate euphemism in favour of more conversation. They reached the house and Lady Victoria entered first, Elizabeth pausing for a moment when Claire Hadlee touched her arm.

"Your Grace," the lady began before Elizabeth interrupted her.

"Elizabeth, please."

"Elizabeth," Claire began again. "I just wanted to thank you for inviting me - it has been a very pleasant morning."

"I am glad you could come," Elizabeth replied. "I hope we shall become good friends, Claire - may I call you Claire?"

The other woman nodded.

"I would like that."

"I am glad," Elizabeth replied and they shared another smile before joining Lady Victoria inside for tea.

&#x200d;ℰℭ𝓑

As she stood on her husband's arm and watched Lord Haversham approach with a gentleman whom she knew to be his son, Elizabeth was hard pressed to keep herself from smiling. She steadfastly avoided looking at Lady Victoria for fear of totally losing her composure but her husband still noticed her struggle and bent down to whisper in her ear.

"What is so funny?"

"I will tell you later," Elizabeth whispered back a moment before Lord Haversham and his son reached them.

"Farleigh, Your Grace; so pleased you could join us this evening," Lord Haversham greeted them and then addressed Elizabeth. "I do not believe you have met my son, Your Grace?"

"I have not yet had the pleasure," Elizabeth replied politely, noticing as Lord Haversham handled the introductions that the young Lord Garville was eyeing her with some curiosity.

"It is a pleasure to meet you at last, Your Grace," he stated when they had each bowed and curtseyed to one another. "I gather that you and my sister have become quite close friends, and she has told me much about you."

"And likewise, Victoria has told me much about you," Elizabeth replied with a friendly smile, suppressing the amusement she felt when Lord Garville seemed pleased to hear it. She supposed he was about five or six and twenty and wondered whether he would have seemed so young to her had Victoria not complained to her of his immaturity. Glancing up at her husband and comparing them in her mind, she decided that yes, he would have.

"I offer you my congratulations, Sir," Lord Garville addressed Darcy. "On your wins at the Derby and the Oaks. I was at the Derby myself and had my money on your colt and he had a fine run - a great run."

Darcy smiled and thanked the young man for his congratulations but made no attempt to further the conversation.

"Come, come Son, save this talk for later - we do not want to bore Her Grace."

"Of course, you are right - I'm sorry, Your Grace," Lord Garville apologised and Elizabeth assured him that it was not necessary.

"Will you be staying long with your parents?" she asked to move the conversation along.

"My plans are not yet fixed, but certainly for a few weeks," Lord Garville replied. "I am here to join the hunt; it has been a while since I have taken part and I look forward to riding with them once more."

Elizabeth and her husband shared an amused look at the young man's apparent inability to discuss anything but sport. After indulging Lord Garville for a few minutes with a discussion of the first scheduled hunt, Darcy politely excused them both and led his wife away to another part of the room.

"Will you tell me now what was so funny?" he requested quietly so that he would not be overheard.

"Lady Victoria, Claire and I were amusing ourselves earlier by devising euphemisms to describe people we know," Elizabeth revealed with a confidential smile. "Lord Garville's was 'typical for his age' and I think he has just proved it very apt."

"*Very* apt," Darcy agreed. "What others did you devise?" he asked curiously.

"An appreciator of fine food and wine," Elizabeth replied with a nod in the direction of Lord Leigh, smiling when her husband choked on a laugh. "That was Claire's suggestion - we discovered she was rather good at it, though we could not think of one for her."

"You are on first name terms with one another already, I note."

"Yes," Elizabeth smiled and nodded. "She was quite shy with us at first, but as I said yesterday I think we shall all be good friends."

Darcy smiled but before he could reply they were joined by Sir Benedict and Lady Hadlock, whom they greeted with pleasure. It was not long before dinner was announced and Elizabeth was happy to have Sir Benedict escort her to the dining room, with Darcy following behind with Lady Hadlock.

"You must tell me how you have been getting on with your new addition," Sir Benedict said once he had seen her seated. "Has she been wreaking havoc?"

"Not at all," Elizabeth denied; then she smiled and admitted, "Well, perhaps a little bit. She is very high spirited."

"Yes, that is a characteristic of the breed," Sir Benedict replied with a nod.

"How many do you have at home?" Elizabeth asked curiously, laughing when Sir Benedict told her. "Seven! And I thought Poppy was enough of a handful!"

Sir Benedict chuckled.

"I have a boy whom I employ specifically to care for them and keep them exercised. It probably seems quite odd, but my wife and I are very fond of the breed."

"That does not seem odd to me at all," Elizabeth assured him. "My father is very fond of flowers and employs a man to help him study them, and my husband is very fond of horses and has a least ten men to keep them. Each to his own, I say."

"Hear, hear," Sir Benedict replied and they touched their glasses in a friendly toast.

"You must know a good deal about dogs then, Sir Benedict," Elizabeth commented thoughtfully as she set her glass down.

"Quite a bit, I suppose," Sir Benedict granted. "Why, do you have a problem?"

"My husband and I are a little worried about Agatha," Elizabeth confessed. "We were just discussing the other day how old she is getting. I think the years may be catching up with her."

"It seems likely," Sir Benedict replied gently. "How old is she now? Twelve years?"

"Almost fourteen," Elizabeth replied and Sir Benedict assumed a sorry expression.

"Well, yes, I would say that at that age she cannot have much longer left. When dogs die of old age they usually slow down considerably in the months leading up to it, and will often seek out solitude. When she begins to do that, it would perhaps be best to prepare yourselves, and the children, for the inevitable."

Elizabeth nodded but had to look down at her plate for a moment, caught off guard by a wave of emotion at the thought of Agatha passing away. She managed a smile when Sir Benedict patted her hand with sympathy and looked up at the kindly older gentleman.

"If you think your husband would like another Great Dane sometime in the future, I may know a man who can help."

"I do not think Agatha could ever be replaced," Elizabeth replied. "But I shall certainly keep that in mind, thank you."

"You're welcome my dear," Sir Benedict replied, patting her hand again before turning his attention to his meal to give the young woman beside him a chance to fully regain her composure.

Following the conclusion of the meal and the separation of the sexes, Elizabeth found herself the centre of polite attention as the other ladies all pressed her for details about the upcoming ball and progress of the arrangements. She was happy to answer their queries, though she had found that her mind was more often elsewhere and that it was hard to care as much as she felt she ought to about her first ball as her husband's wife. Her pregnancy was an obvious and happy distraction, but the situation with her father (and the wait between letters from her uncle) also played on her mind. And as the time drew ever nearer, Elizabeth found herself thinking more and more of James' imminent departure for school - an event which would take place but three days after the ball. She knew that she had her priorities right, but suspected that not all of the ladies would agree with her and so pretended to be as engrossed by the arrangements as she was expected to be.

Unsurprisingly, given her feelings, Elizabeth was happy to see the gentlemen when they finally rejoined them and was thankful for the distraction they provided. Lady Haversham had the card tables brought out and most of the guests sat down for a few games of whist, though Elizabeth, Darcy and Lord and Lady Andrews all declined, preferring to sit together and talk. Like Darcy, Lord Andrews was a patron of the Royal Society and he and his wife were full of news about the latest exhibitions and what was planned for the Little Season.

During the conversation with Lord and Lady Andrews, Darcy kept half an eye on his wife, aware that she was quickly tiring. Elizabeth had always been an early riser, but for the past week or so she had been woken even earlier than usual by the sickness, and it was obviously catching up with her. She would not complain and would stay as long as he wished to, he knew, and so he made the decision for them to return home. He knew he had the right of the matter when Elizabeth only offered a few protests and together they said goodnight to their hosts and the rest of the guests, Darcy accepting the blame for their early departure. Once home, Darcy led his wife straight upstairs to their bedroom, opening the door for her and ushering her in ahead of him. Wilson appeared from the direction of Elizabeth's dressing room, a frown furrowing her brow.

"Is something the matter?" she asked, obviously worried by their early return.

"No, everything is fine," Elizabeth assured her. "I am just rather tired, and William kindly decided we should come home early."

"Yes, you do look quite dead on your feet," Wilson agreed and Elizabeth laughed lightly.

"Thank you very much."

"You're quite welcome, petal," Wilson responded teasingly, smiling affectionately as she helped Elizabeth with her shawl and gloves.

Darcy stood back and watched their interaction with a small smile. Despite the occasional disagreement, he had something of a soft spot for Wilson - if only because of the obvious and sincere love she had for his wife. Indeed, since learning of Elizabeth's pregnancy, Wilson had become, if anything, even more affectionate and fussed over her charge like a mother hen. Darcy did not know why he had not realised it before now, but he could at last see that Wilson had filled the void left by Elizabeth's father and mother (and apparently sister) and was likely the reason why Elizabeth had survived alone for so many years.

Leaving his wife to change into her night things, Darcy went through to his own room and changed out of his dining clothes, putting on a nightshirt and donning a dressing gown before returning to his wife's rooms. He found her waiting for him with a hairbrush in hand.

"I thought you would like to do this for me," she said when she saw him and he smiled and came forward.

"Is Wilson gone?" he asked as he sat down and accepted the brush from her.

"Yes," Elizabeth quietly replied as she turned slightly away and her husband began to brush her hair out in slow strokes. She allowed her eyes to slip shut and let out a deep breath. "I am very tired tonight."

"I know you are," Darcy quietly murmured, touching her shoulder. "I shall do this and then we will go to bed and get some sleep. And tomorrow I think you should have a quiet day."

"That would be nice, and I do not have anything planned," Elizabeth noted.

"Speaking of plans," Darcy commented with a smile in his voice. "There was a lot of talk about your ball tonight, wasn't there?"

"Our ball," Elizabeth corrected; she then sighed and admitted, "And yes, there was a lot of talk about it. Far too much in my opinion. I tire of it."

"Do you?" Darcy queried, surprised to hear her say so.

"I know I should not," Elizabeth replied, "but there are more important things for me to think about. Whenever I hear the ball mentioned, my mind simply reminds me that James will be leaving us three days later."

She felt the brush still for a moment before her husband resumed the steady strokes, and wondered what he thought of her opinion.

"Do you think...should I be more concerned about the ball, do you think? I know it is my first as your wife, and it is important..."

"I think," Darcy responded, wrapping his arms around her waist from behind and pressing her back to his chest, "that you are wonderful. James knows how important he is to you - I know how important he is to you - and if everyone else considers a silly little ball more important, then that is their misfortune."

Elizabeth turned her head and rubbed her cheek against his chest.

"I am going to miss him so much when he leaves."

"As am I," Darcy admitted. "Though I am excited by the prospect of what he will become. I think he will be a fine man, though I do say so myself," he added with a chuckle, kissing his wife's temple.

"I think I would like this babe to be a boy," Elizabeth quietly stated, placing her hand on her belly.

"Really?" Darcy responded. "You would not prefer a little girl?"

"I should love a daughter also, but I would like this first to be a boy," Elizabeth replied. She looked up at her husband. "I would like a son just like you."

Her words produced a lump in his throat and Darcy could not articulate a response; seeing this, his wife smiled lovingly and reached up to stroke his cheek as she softly pressed her lips to his. Filled with the desire to show her what her words made him feel, Darcy returned the kiss and then got to his feet, scooping his wife up in his arms and carrying her over to their bed.

# Chapter 26

Careful not to wake his sleeping wife, Darcy attempted to turn the page of his book with just one hand. It was awkward, but he thought it worth the inconvenience; Elizabeth was asleep with her head resting on a pillow in his lap, holding his other hand, and he would not disturb her for the world. Having finally managed to accomplish the deed, Darcy was just settling down for another few minutes of undisturbed reading when there was a quiet knock at the door, followed by the appearance of the butler.

"I am so sorry for disturbing you, Sir," the man began in hushed tones, but he got no further. He was jostled slightly from behind and could only make indignant noises as the unexpected guest bustled into the room without invitation.

"Fitzwilliam, my darling, there you are! I tried to tell this silly man that there was no need to announce *me*, but he would insist. Oh, but I can see I am disturbing you! This must be your new wife! What a pretty little thing! Rather young, isn't she?"

Elizabeth, who had been rudely awakened by the sudden appearance of their guest, sat up and rather blearily rubbed her eyes. Darcy got to his feet and placed himself slightly in front of her, allowing his wife a moment to collect herself whilst he faced the woman who had barged in upon their solitude so audaciously.

"Mrs Montgomery," he began. "This is quite unexpected."

"Oh yes, I'd hoped to give you a nice surprise," Mrs Montgomery replied blithely. "But please, Fitzwilliam, there is no need to be so formal - you really must call me Caroline."

Darcy deftly avoided calling her anything by turning to offer his wife his hand and assisting her to her feet; he shot her an apologetic smile.

"Elizabeth, I have no doubt that you have already been introduced to our guest - Mrs Caroline Montgomery, Sir Charles' sister."

"Yes," Elizabeth replied, wide awake now and ready with a welcoming smile. "Though it has been many years since we last met."

"Oh, decades!" Mrs Montgomery exaggerated with a laugh. "You were still just a child, I'm sure of it. You are still, compared to me," she joked, tossing her head and laughing again. "I feel quite ancient when I look at you. No wonder Fitzwilliam was so quick to snap you up!"

"I feel very fortunate to have secured his regard," Elizabeth responded stiffly, remembering in an instant that on the few occasions in the past when she had met Sir Charles' sister she had not liked her at all.

"And I am sure you have," Mrs Montgomery replied in a tone which only increased Elizabeth's ire. "But I can easily see how you must have caught his eye!"

Disliking the topic of conversation, Darcy deftly steered it in another direction.

"Have you been long in the area, Mrs Montgomery? Your brother did not mention that you were visiting last time I heard from him."

"Oh, it was a last minute thing," the lady replied with a careless wave of her hand; she had advanced further into the room and was looking at the seating arrangement, obviously trying to decide where she would prefer to sit despite having not been invited to do so.

Darcy shared a look with his wife and they sat down together on the sofa as their guest settled herself on one of the large wingback chairs.

"I have spent the summer with a friend of mine in Cumbria - Lady Nathan, do you know her? - and I decided I couldn't possibly travel down to town without stopping to see Charles and dear Jane first," Mrs Montgomery went on. "Isn't she altered? The poor thing - I confess I was quite shocked to see her looking so...substantial."

"I gather it is rather normal for a lady in her condition," Darcy pointed out dryly and Elizabeth was forced to hide a smile at his tone.

"Yes, well, I daresay you know more about it than I, Fitzwilliam dear," Mrs Montgomery granted with a simpering laugh. "And Jane tells me I am to wish you joy as well! I am sure I'd never heard of anyone being blessed so early into their marriage before, though Jane explained that it is one of the many benefits of your youth, my dear," she added crudely, smiling at Elizabeth.

"Indeed," Elizabeth responded tightly, making a mental note to have words with her sister - she had asked Jane to tell no-one but Sir Charles about her condition. "Well, I thank you for your good wishes, Mrs Montgomery, but if you would please be so good as to keep your knowledge to yourself we would both very much appreciate it. It is still very early days yet, you see."

"Of course, I understand perfectly," Mrs Montgomery assured her with a knowing smile, obviously drawing her own conclusions as to why a babe was expected so early. "Your secret is safe with me."

Elizabeth stiffened at the implied insult but felt her husband rest his hand on the small of her back and give it a reassuring rub; once again he changed the subject of conversation before things got out of hand.

"Do you have plans to remain at Netherfield long?"

"I have not decided yet," Mrs Montgomery replied. "Though I would not miss your ball for the world! As a rule I do not like them, but I am certain that yours will be delightful, though it is your first, Eliza. I suppose you are awfully nervous about it," she added with false sympathy, looking at Elizabeth.

"On the contrary," Darcy stated before Elizabeth could respond. "My wife is a charming hostess, and I have no doubt that our guests will enjoy themselves immensely."

"And who could not?" Mrs Montgomery replied. "Indeed, I have often reflected that the balls here at Pemberley are utterly superior to all others!"

"It is fortunate, then, that you do not like them as a rule," Darcy responded. "Because this is the first I have hosted in the last ten years, and it may be as many years again before we host another."

"Surely you jest with me!"

"We prefer the company of those who we are close to," Darcy stated whilst sharing a look with his wife; he turned back to their guest as he concluded, "To those who we are not. It is hard to be selective with ones guests when one has a whole ballroom to fill."

"Sadly true," Mrs Montgomery agreed as Elizabeth put her hand to her lips to cover her grin. "And perhaps it is better this way - a ball at Pemberley would not be so special a thing, after all, if you were to host them often."

Darcy smiled but made no further reply and there was a slightly awkward silence as he and Elizabeth both regarded their guest with the same expectant look, waiting for her to realise that it was time for her to take her leave. Unfortunately, Mrs Montgomery had always cared more about her own desires than anyone else's, and she still had more to say.

"It was such a pity I was not in town for your wedding! I should love to have been there. Charles tells me it was a small, quiet family affair - the very best in my opinion. I have never understood how anyone could countenance having dozens of guests at their wedding, though my own was very large by anybody's standards. My late husband would insist, though, and who was I to deny him?"

She paused in expectation of a response and when none was forthcoming ploughed on again.

"And I suppose your little darlings were guests on the special day, Fitzwilliam? How are they? It has been so many years since I last saw them; they must be almost grown by now! I daresay I should like to see if James is as handsome as his father, and if Charlotte has inherited Anne's beauty!"

"Catherine," Darcy corrected, an idea popping into his head. "My daughter's name is Catherine. But if you wait here one moment, I will fetch the children and bring them to you."

"Oh, that is so good of you, Fitzwilliam - I really do long to see them," Mrs Montgomery enthused.

"It is my pleasure. Now if you will excuse me for a moment."

Elizabeth watched her husband go with a sense of amused irritation, making a mental note to punish him for his abandonment.

"Well," Mrs Montgomery turned on Elizabeth with what struck her as a particularly calculating smile. "I shall always be sorry to see dear Fitzwilliam go, but I cannot say I am not pleased to have the opportunity to speak with you alone, Eliza. You do not mind if I call you Eliza, do you? I always have, haven't I? I remember when I first saw you, you know; how I thought to myself that you were such a sad little thing. I thought the same when I saw poor James after his mother had died; both he and Fitzwilliam were so very forlorn. It quite broke my heart to see them so downcast, though I flatter myself that I helped ease Fitzwilliam's burden a little. It is such a great source of pleasure to me, to know that I am of comfort to my friends, and Fitzwilliam and I have been such close friends for so long. Why, it has been close to twenty years!"

"So long?" Elizabeth affected amazement. "I should have thought you just a child twenty years ago - obviously I was mistaken!"

It was a petty remark, but Elizabeth thought it well earned and derived a certain amount of satisfaction from witnessing the discomfiture it caused the woman sat across from her.

"Yes, well," Mrs Montgomery said with a forced laugh. "I was still very young when Charles first introduced us."

"Of course you were," Elizabeth replied with a smile.

Both ladies looked up when the door opened, expecting Darcy to return with the children in tow. He appeared alone, however, with an apologetic smile.

"I'm terribly sorry, Mrs Montgomery, but the children have apparently gone for a walk with their governess. Such a shame for you to have missed seeing them."

"I would be happy to wait until they return..." Mrs Montgomery began but Darcy was shaking his head regretfully.

"I am afraid that Elizabeth and I have an engagement this afternoon. I have taken the liberty of calling for your carriage, as we really must change and be off ourselves very soon. You do not mind?"

"Of course not," Mrs Montgomery replied graciously, getting to her feet. "I would not presume to keep you. And I shall see you both again very soon, I'm sure."

"Then please allow me to escort you to your carriage," Darcy came forward and offered his arm, acting every bit the gentleman.

Elizabeth bid her guest an admirably cordial farewell, and sat down to await the return of her husband. When he eventually reappeared, she smiled when she saw his grin.

"And what engagement do we have this afternoon that is so pressing?" she asked playfully as Darcy shut the door and came to sit beside her.

"Well I should like to read some more of my book," Darcy teased. "And you could do with more rest, I think."

"After such an encounter, certainly," Elizabeth agreed dryly, shaking her head. "Wasn't it kind of her to visit us, darling *Fitzwilliam.*"

Darcy rolled his eyes and sat back, putting his arm around his wife's shoulders when she leant back against him.

"I do not think kindness had anything to do with it. Hateful woman."

Elizabeth looked at him, surprised by his vehemence, and Darcy sighed.

"I would not say such, except that I have reason to think ill of her. For years she practically threw herself at me in the forlorn hope that I would marry her, and when she failed to snare me in her trap she turned instead to insinuating herself into my life in any way possible. She made false overtures of friendship to Anne and tried to ingratiate herself with Georgiana, though fortunately my sister is too clever to fall for such an obvious ploy. She claims a level of intimacy between us which I would never allow to exist, and her over-familiarity has frequently been an embarrassment, especially when her husbands were still living. It has been impossible for me to avoid her altogether because of Charles, but I see her very rarely and it is always an unpleasant experience."

"I confess that I have never liked her," Elizabeth admitted when he was finished. "She was always very dismissive of me when I was younger; cruel almost."

"She certainly has no love of children," Darcy agreed. He looked down at his wife and stated, "And I have no doubt that I will have even less reason to think well of her after today - I suppose she said some things to you?"

"Nothing of consequence," Elizabeth assured him. "And nothing I gave credence to. I know a jealous woman when I see one, my love," she added.

"You remember when you first met Sir Benedict, and he mentioned my having "held out" so long against marriage? He was referring to Mrs Montgomery, and her obvious...pursuit of me."

"I had wondered about that," Elizabeth replied with a smile which her husband eventually returned. "Something Mrs Montgomery said did intrigue me, though. She said that she had been of comfort to you after Anne died."

Darcy groaned and rolled his eyes.

"An added burden, rather. She came to say goodbye to her 'dear friend', she said, and then insisted on visiting almost every day for a fortnight following the funeral. Eventually, I took Catherine and James up to the estate in Scotland."

Elizabeth covered her mouth with her hand to hide her laugh and her husband protested that it wasn't funny.

"That you felt you had to run away all the way to Scotland? No, I do not see how that is funny at all," Elizabeth responded with playful impertinence, pleased to see the reluctant grin tugging at the corners of her husband's lips.

"She is very beautiful," she mused after a moment, recalling Mrs Montgomery's fine figure and striking features. "And rich as well, obviously. How long ago did her husband die?"

"Which one?" Darcy responded. "Her first husband died about ten years ago, but her second only the year before last. Both were wealthy, aged and childless, and Mrs Montgomery has benefitted accordingly."

His tone made it perfectly clear what he thought of Mrs Montgomery and her marriages, and Elizabeth decided that it was high time they ceased speaking of it.

"Are James and Catherine really out walking?" she asked lightly.

"I haven't the faintest idea," Darcy replied carelessly, smiling when his wife laughed. "I should enjoy a walk though - shall we take them out?"

"That sounds like a lovely idea," Elizabeth agreed and together they went in search of their children.

When they had all donned the appropriate footwear and rounded up Poppy and Agatha, the four of them wandered in the direction of the lake. As they passed one of the small jetties on the lake James turned to his father and made a request.

"Before I leave for school, Father, could we perhaps go out onto the lake again? Perhaps in the sailboat, or in the rowboat if Lizzy and Cathy want to come with us."

"Of course we can James," Darcy replied readily. "I am sure we could make a day of it; we could invite your cousins to join us, and have a picnic out here by the lake."

"Actually Father," James admitted. "I should prefer to spend the day with just you. I would be happy to invite my cousins to join us another day, but I would like to have one day at least with just our family present."

Elizabeth smiled at James for the sweet sentiment as Darcy assured his son that they would do whatever he wished.

"Within reason, of course," he added when James grinned mischievously.

"We will be able to visit James when he is at school, won't we?" Catherine asked from her place beside Elizabeth.

"Yes of course," Elizabeth assured the little girl before adding, "though perhaps not as often as we would like. James will be very much occupied with his studies, you see, though we will see him during his breaks from school."

"So he will be home for Christmas?" Catherine clarified. "And his birthday?" she asked when Elizabeth nodded.

Elizabeth looked at Darcy for a response and he smiled at his daughter.

"We shall visit him for his birthday, and bring all his presents to him."

"I will look forward to it very much," James admitted softly; his birthday was halfway into the school term and he had a feeling that after so many weeks away from home he would be missing his family terribly. He smiled weakly when his father placed a hand on his shoulder.

"What if James does not like school?" Catherine asked with a slight frown, looking between the two adults. "He will be able to come home, won't he?"

"I am happy to go, Cathy," James replied before either Darcy or Elizabeth could. "And am certain I will enjoy it very much."

"But if he does not," Darcy warmly averred. "His home is here with us."

As father and son shared a look, Elizabeth smiled softly to herself and directed Catherine's attention to some ducks swimming close by on the water, giving the pair a moment. Eventually James took his sister for a closer look and Darcy took up his place by Elizabeth's side.

She looked up at her husband, and he obviously felt her look because he smiled sadly and shook his head, silently indicating that he did not know what to say. Taking his hand, Elizabeth gave it a tight squeeze and then turned with him to watch James playing with Catherine and the two dogs. The prospect of change did not make her unhappy, but she still made a point of committing such precious moments to memory - and suspected that her husband did much the same.

80C8

The time remaining before the ball, and James' subsequent departure, passed by too quickly for all four members of the Darcy family. The promised boating day took place, as did many other such excursions and outings, all planned with a view towards making James' last days at Pemberley as enjoyable as could be, and allowing the four of them to spend as much time together as possible. Darcy and Elizabeth declined many an invitation from their neighbours during this time, preferring to remain at home, and cared not what people thought; their friends, though, were not inclined to feel neglected and certainly understood the couple's desire to spend time with James before he left.

Though they were made to suffer through another two visits from Mrs Montgomery, the whole family also enjoyed many visits from family members and close friends who came to say their farewells. The Fitzwilliams were with them very often, and Sir Charles and Daniel were very welcome too. They were not so overwhelmed with visitors that they had no time to themselves, however, and dinner every night was reserved for the four members of the Darcy family alone. It was a happy but bittersweet time, and all too soon the day of the ball was upon them.

&#9753;&#9755;

"I think this must be the finest gown I have ever worn."

Elizabeth smiled at her reflection in the mirror as she softly smoothed her hands over the front of her gown, turning slowly this way and that and admiring the beautiful cut.

"And I think that it would not look half so fine were anyone else wearing it," Wilson replied from behind her as she fussed about with Elizabeth's hair.

Elizabeth laughed in response and was then surprised to hear her husband speak.

"I quite concur, Wilson."

Darcy smiled from his position in the doorway as his wife turned to him.

"How long have you been standing there? Wilson, how long as he been there?"

"I'm sure I don't know," Wilson replied evenly, though she had first noticed the Duke lounging against the doorway about ten minutes ago.

"Can a man not take a moment to admire his wife?" Darcy asked by way of a reply; he pushed himself upright and approached Elizabeth, noting the blush which had suffused her cheeks in response to his words. "Can he not look upon her with thoughts of no more than her beauty?"

"He can," Elizabeth replied quietly. "But he must be prepared for her to be embarrassed by his look."

"Hence why I was hiding in the doorway, knowing you could not see me," Darcy teased in a low voice and chuckled when his wife blushed anew, though at least this time she smiled too.

He drew away from temptation and addressed his wife's maid.

"May I take her away, Wilson?"

"As you wish, Your Grace," Wilson replied. "My mistress is ready."

"But I have no jewellery..." Elizabeth began to point out, but stopped when her husband took her hand.

"I have something for you - come with me."

Shooting Wilson a curious look, Elizabeth allowed herself to be led away by her husband into his room. He let go of her hand and walked over to a chest of drawers, opening one and retrieving a neat wooden box and bringing it over to her.

"This is for you," he said as he offered it to Elizabeth and she took it from him with an intrigued smile.

"Why are you giving me gifts?" she asked before opening it, smiling when her husband laughed ruefully and shook his head.

"I wonder if there will ever be a day when I may do so without your questioning me!" He teased and then urged her to open the box. "It is for tonight; it is our first ball together as husband and wife and I wanted to mark the occasion."

"Well I suppose that is a good enough reason," Elizabeth teased in response.

"I am glad you think so," Darcy responded dryly. "Now please, open it!"

Elizabeth did as he asked, her eyes widening when she saw the beautiful sapphire and diamond necklace contained within.

"Do you like it?" Darcy asked. "It is not new; it belonged to my mother."

"It is lovely," Elizabeth assured him. "Will you help me?"

"Of course."

Darcy accepted the box from her and drew out the necklace; Elizabeth turned her back to him and he lowered the necklace around her neck and carefully fastened it.

"How does it look?" Elizabeth asked as she turned to face him, delicately fingering the precious stones; Darcy smiled and cupped her face in his hands.

"Beautiful," he replied, and then softly kissed her lips.

"It must go well with my gown," Elizabeth commented when they had parted. "Did you speak with Wilson about it?"

"But of course," Darcy responded lightly. "I do not claim to wholly understand all of the intricacies of your wardrobe, my love, but even I know that a lady's jewels must match her gown."

Elizabeth laughed lightly at his teasing and then suddenly caught sight of the clock on the mantelpiece and exclaimed over the time.

"We said that we would check on the children before we go down; we should do so before it gets too late."

Darcy offered her his arm.

"Let us go, then."

They went to Catherine's room first, finding her fast asleep. Carefully so as not to disturb her, Elizabeth adjusted the covers and brushed some hair behind her ear before pressing a light kiss to

Catherine's cheek. Darcy watched from a slight distance, his heart touched by the scene and when Elizabeth moved away he bestowed another kiss upon his daughter before following his wife quietly from the room. When they went to James' room, they found him reading by the dim light of a lone candle, holding his book so close to the flame that Darcy feared for the pages. His son looked a little chagrined to be caught still up, and grinned sheepishly when Darcy plucked the book from his hands and tucked it onto the bookshelf.

"If you do not sleep now, you will be kept awake by the sounds of the ball when it begins," he told his son quietly.

"Yes, Father," James replied and added, "I'm sorry."

Darcy reached down and ruffled his hair.

"Maybe next time you should light another candle, hmm? You'll damage your eyes trying to read in this poor light."

"Yes, Father," James replied again, though this time he was smiling. "Good night."

"Good night, Son," Darcy responded and stepped away as Elizabeth wished James a good night and they left him to get into bed and go to sleep.

"I think he thought you were going to tell him off," Elizabeth commented when they were in the hallway and Darcy had closed the door behind them.

"I probably should have done," Darcy replied as they slowly walked down the hallway together. "But I used to do the same thing when I was a boy; and I see no real harm in it."

They shared a smile and continued downstairs, going to the library where they were to await the arrival of Lady Georgiana and the Colonel, who were due to come a little earlier than the rest of their guests. As Elizabeth took a seat Darcy went to the sideboard and poured them both a glass of wine, handing his wife hers before offering a toast.

"To a successful and enjoyable evening."

ະບເຽ

An hour into the evening, an hour spent standing beside her husband and greeting a seemingly endless stream of guests, Elizabeth received a most unexpected surprise.

"Mr Wickham!"

"Darling Elizabeth," the man before her responded with his usual lazy grin. "I believe I have told you to call me George."

"Yes," Elizabeth replied. "But you did not tell me that you would be gracing us with your presence tonight. I thought you still in Wiltshire?"

"I have come up to Nottinghamshire to visit my mother, and thought I would make good on my threat to attend your ball," Mr Wickham replied, referring to the last letter he had written to her some weeks ago.

"Is Lady Wickham not with you?" Elizabeth asked, seeing that he was alone.

"Unfortunately my mother is not in the best of health - oh, it is nothing serious," Mr Wickham assured her when Elizabeth looked concerned. "But she did not think she was well enough to attend."

"I hope you will give her our best," Elizabeth responded and Mr Wickham bowed lowly.

Darcy, who had until this point been kept occupied by another of their guests, was finally able to turn and greet his cousin.

"Mr Wickham, this is a surprise. Welcome."

"Thank you, cousin," Mr Wickham responded. "Your wife mentioned that you were hosting a ball in her last letter to me, and I could not resist the temptation."

"We are delighted you could join us, I'm sure," Darcy replied amusedly; any slight feelings of possessiveness his cousin's familiarity with his wife might once have inspired were now a thing of the past.

Mr Wickham smiled at Darcy's reply and then turned to his hostess.

"Might I be so bold as to request a set with you, darling Elizabeth?"

"You may," Elizabeth granted before quietly adding, "though I think you perhaps a little too bold for being so familiar in such a setting. Would the third set suit?"

"I should be delighted," Mr Wickham replied with a deep bow, adding with a mock smile when he straightened, *"Your Grace."*

Elizabeth rolled her eyes.

"Until later then."

She and Darcy both watched Mr Wickham stroll away and then turned to look at each other.

"Let us hope he does not cause any trouble tonight," Darcy remarked quietly, but their next guests were already approaching and so Elizabeth had no chance to ask him what he meant.

A quarter of an hour later, Elizabeth smiled brightly when she saw Lady Victoria approaching with her parents and brother. She warmly greeted her friend and admired her gown and hair, quite truthfully teasing that she was jealous of how beautifully the latter was arranged. Lady Victoria laughed and responded that she was jealous of Elizabeth's gown, and the two friends agreed that they were even.

"You missed a fine ride the other day, Farleigh," Lord Haversham was saying to his host as the ladies talked. "You will join us for the next, won't you?"

"Monday, isn't it?" Darcy replied. "Yes, I think I will."

"I hope you bring the hunter Hadlee was telling us about," Lord Garville put in enthusiastically. "I should like to see him in action, as it were."

"Perhaps," Darcy responded neutrally and smiled and nodded as the family moved off and the next set of guests took their place.

It was not much long after Lady Victoria and her family had arrived that Elizabeth and Darcy were finally able to leave the entranceway and enter the bustling ballroom, the latter signalling to the musicians that it was time for the dancing to begin. As he led his wife to the head of the rapidly forming line of dancers, Darcy caught sight of his cousin and couldn't quite stifle a groan of frustration.

"What's wrong?" Elizabeth asked, having heard him.

"My cousin's choice of partner for the set," Darcy replied with a frown. Elizabeth attempted to see down the line of dancers but did not have his advantage of height and so he added, "Mrs Montgomery."

"Oh," Elizabeth replied. Then her eyes widened and she turned to him sharply, "They are not...they have not...?"

"Knowing what you do of them both, are you really surprised?" Darcy responded with one eyebrow arched.

"No," Elizabeth admitted, frowning now as well. "But I did not realise. Is their...association of long standing?"

"As far as I am aware, they have not been linked together since before Mrs Montgomery's latest marriage; though now she is once again a widow..." Darcy replied, letting Elizabeth come to her own conclusions.

"They are not hurting anyone, I suppose," Elizabeth commented, thinking that her friend, for all his faults, really was too good for Mrs Montgomery.

"Indeed. I shall keep an eye on them in any case," Darcy stated. "I care not how they chose to conduct themselves away from here, but I will not allow them to cause a scene; tonight is important for you."

"Perhaps we are getting ahead of ourselves. Perhaps they will simply dance together and that will be the end of it."

"I am too well acquainted with their past history to believe that," Darcy replied. "I pray that they do not become aware of precisely how well suited they are," he muttered to himself, though not quietly enough, for Elizabeth still heard him and asked him what he meant.

"She wishes for a connection to my family, and he needs a rich wife, and with the death of her most recent husband, Mrs Montgomery is even wealthier than before. I am sure my cousin will be hard pushed to resist."

"Does he? Need a rich wife, I mean," Elizabeth asked curiously and Darcy winced inwardly at his blunder.

"We cannot discuss it here," he replied. "But yes, he does."

"There is one way we could easily keep them apart," Elizabeth mused after a moment as the last of the couples were taking their places. "You can distract her, and I can distract him."

"I do not care about it enough to agree to *that*," Darcy stated unequivocally and Elizabeth laughed lightly.

"Because you are unwilling to give up my company for the night, or are unwilling to bear with hers?"

"What do you think?" Darcy responded with a grin, just as the first bars of the set were played.

"I certainly hope the former!" Elizabeth teased as they came together in the dance and as Darcy laughed heartily many of their guests smiled and commented on the obvious enjoyment their hosts had in each other's company.

When the set finally concluded and Darcy was leading his wife to her partner for the next, he kept half an eye on his cousin and was not surprised to see him lead Mrs Montgomery away to a secluded corner of the ballroom. Seeing his distraction, the Colonel followed his gaze and then chuckled.

"Ah, George is in fine form tonight, I see. Who is his latest conquest? He made quick work of it, whoever she is!"

"Richard," Darcy rebuked him quietly. "Do try not to be so coarse when speaking in the presence of our wives."

"I'm sorry, quite right," the Colonel responded and apologised to Georgiana and Elizabeth. Then he turned back to his cousin. "So, who is the lady?"

"Mrs Montgomery," Darcy admitted with a sigh and then glared angrily at his cousin when the Colonel gave a choked laugh. "It is not a laughing matter!"

"I beg to differ," the Colonel countered. "Do you suppose he realises that he is a substitute for you?"

"I doubt he cares," Georgiana responded on behalf of her brother, who she could see was becoming increasingly frustrated with her husband's flippancy.

"Well leave them to it, I say; they know what they are about," the Colonel stated with a shrug and Darcy reluctantly agreed with him.

"Or," Georgiana suggested, "you could tell Sir Charles and let him deal with her."

Elizabeth and Darcy shared a look which spoke volumes about their opinion of whether Sir Charles would exert himself to interfere. Before they could discuss it further, however, the second set began to form up and Elizabeth was obliged to go with the Colonel, leaving Darcy and Georgiana together.

"Go and speak with Sir Charles," Georgiana quietly counselled her brother. "At least make him aware so that he can step in should anything embarrassing be about to occur."

Darcy nodded.

"Yes, I think I will."

He found Sir Charles speaking with a few other gentlemen and after a few minutes of casual conversation drew him apart from the others.

"Is something the matter, Darcy?" Sir Charles asked when he perceived his friend's slight frown.

"Not as such," Darcy began hesitantly; this was awkward in the extreme. "It is just that...you are aware that Mr Wickham is here tonight? He is with your sister currently."

"I am sure that Caroline knows how to conduct herself, Darcy!" Sir Charles responded with a laugh. "She is hardly a debutante that I must watch over."

"Of that I am well aware," Darcy responded dryly. "However, I do not wish for anything to overshadow the success of the evening; Elizabeth went to great effort planning this ball, as I'm sure you can imagine. Nothing must happen to embarrass her," he concluded pointedly.

Sir Charles looked at him keenly, finally getting the point.

"Where are they?" His friend asked and Darcy breathed a sigh of relief. He pointed out the couple. "Very well, I shall keep my eye on them."

Darcy nodded.

"I appreciate that this must be awkward for you Charles," he added with an uncomfortable look. "But I thought it best."

"I have come to the conclusion that you almost always know better than I, Darcy," Sir Charles surprised him by saying and Darcy wasn't quite sure what to say in response.

"Will you join me on Monday for a ride out with Lord Haversham and a few others?" He asked instead.

"I would like that, thank you," Sir Charles replied with a smile and Darcy was happy to return it; he hoped they had taken the first step towards mending their friendship.

Bidding his Sir Charles farewell, Darcy wandered around the ballroom, stopping every now and then to speak with friends. The evening seemed to be going very well so far, and Darcy was pleased for his wife, knowing how much effort she had put into the arrangements. He was speaking with Lord and Lady Andrews when the second set ended and Colonel Fitzwilliam brought Elizabeth over to him. She looked at him in question and he smiled reassuringly.

"I couldn't help noticing that your sister is not present this evening, Your Grace," Lady Andrews said to Elizabeth after she had greeted the couple. "I hope she is not unwell."

"She is quite well, Lady Andrews," Elizabeth assured the older woman. "I believe she is being careful not to over exert herself in her delicate condition."

"When is the happy event due to take place?"

"November," Elizabeth stated with a smile.

"I expect James and Catherine will be happy to have a new cousin," Lord Andrews commented. "Though I daresay they would be even happier with a new sibling. We look forward to an announcement from *you*," he concluded as he looked between the Darcy couple.

As Lady Andrews affectionately chided her husband to not say such things, Elizabeth and Darcy shared an amused look. Though they dearly wished to share their news with their family and friends, they knew they had to wait for the quickening and the certainty it would bring.

"Ah, I think the next set is about to begin," Lord Andrews noted as the musicians played the signal. "We shall let you go - you must have partners awaiting you."

Almost immediately after these words had been uttered, Mr Wickham appeared from out of the crowd; having bowed to Lord and Lady Andrews he turned towards Elizabeth with a smile.

"I believe this dance is mine, Your Grace."

Elizabeth accepted his outstretched hand and said goodbye to her companions before allowing him to lead her away. Darcy watched her go for a moment before reminding himself of his duty and going in search of Lady Victoria, whom he had asked to partner him for the set.

Elizabeth assumed her place in the line of dancers and regarded her partner with a slight smile.

"Does something amuse you, Your Grace?" Mr Wickham asked politely.

"Not at all," Elizabeth replied.

"No?" Mr Wickham queried. "Not even the sudden absence of my last dance partner?"

"I had not noticed whom it was you last danced with."

"Liar," her partner accused with a grin. "Her brother swooped in and took her away from me; quite spoiled my fun, I must say."

"Perhaps Sir Charles was concerned for her welfare," Elizabeth suggested. The dance began and the steps brought them together as Mr Wickham replied.

"I had not realised you all thought me so dangerous."

"I think there was danger on both sides, don't you?" Elizabeth asked pointedly, thinking of what her husband had said regarding the motives of each.

Mr Wickham's expression hardened for a moment and then he smiled sarcastically.

"How good of your husband to reveal the truth of my embarrassed circumstances to you."

"He did not; certainly not before tonight, at least, and even then he gave only the vaguest hint," Elizabeth defended her husband spiritedly. "You have just been more explicit than he was."

Her partner had the grace to appear chagrined and they were silent for some moments. Eventually, as they came together in the dance Mr Wickham spoke again.

"Well, now you know the sorry truth."

"You could have told me yourself, you know," Elizabeth replied. "I wouldn't have thought any less of you."

"I am sure you would have," Mr Wickham countered. "I almost told you once," he suddenly said. "That night when you were angry with me because I had not contradicted the rumours about a possible engagement between us."

"I remember," Elizabeth affirmed.

"And do you remember my saying that there were reasons why I could not offer for you?" her partner asked, and Elizabeth laughed inadvertently.

"Yes, and I also remember telling you that your reasons did not matter," she reminded him. "Because I had no intention of marrying you."

"Because you did not care for me," Mr Wickham stated with a smile.

"And because I happened to be in love with your cousin," Elizabeth pointed out and Mr Wickham grinned.

"Yes, that too."

Elizabeth smiled reluctantly and they continued through a few more of the steps.

"I hope you know that, whatever your faults, you deserve better than a woman like Mrs Montgomery. She is awful."

"Your Grace," Mr Wickham teased. "I'm touched that you should think so."

"I mean it," Elizabeth responded seriously and her partner sobered and smiled affectionately.

"I know you do. I confess that it pleases me to know that you think so much of me - better than I do of myself, certainly."

"I wouldn't be so sure of that," Elizabeth noted dryly and Mr Wickham laughed at her quip.

"No, perhaps not," he admitted with a grin. "I should say rather that you give me more credit than I give myself."

"Because I think you too good for Mrs Montgomery?" Elizabeth asked.

"Yes. She is both beautiful and rich, and that is good enough for me; you think that it is not."

"How can it be?" Elizabeth countered and her partner laughed.

"I believe I told you once not to make the mistake of thinking too well of me, Elizabeth. I am as shallow as I seem."

"I do not believe you," Elizabeth responded with a smile, shaking her head.

"You think that because you are happy with your marriage and your family that everyone must also be happy with the same. Some people are made happy by other things."

"Like Mrs Montgomery?" Elizabeth replied with an expression of disbelief.

"If you had let me enjoy her as I wished to, I daresay she would have made me very happy before the end of the night," Mr Wickham responded with a roguish grin. "Several times, perhaps."

Elizabeth didn't know whether she was more appalled or amused and her companion laughed at her reaction to his scandalous statement.

"You are awful," she accused him with a reluctant grin.

"Not as awful as Mrs Montgomery, I hope," Mr Wickham teased and Elizabeth couldn't help laughing.

"No, not quite that awful," she assured him and they shared a smile and enjoyed the rest of their dance.

When it was over, Elizabeth declined her partner's offer to return her to her husband; she had spotted John and Claire Hadlee in the crowd and directed her footsteps towards them, leaving Mr Wickham to amuse himself however he chose.

Claire and her husband smiled when they saw Elizabeth approaching and when she reached them were quick to offer their compliments about the evening so far.

"You have been enjoying yourself, then?" she asked Claire delicately, knowing that her friend had been a little uneasy about attending after what had happened.

"I have," Claire assured her; she looked up at her husband and smiled softly before turning back to Elizabeth and saying, "John and I have danced twice already, and there are many people here whom I have not seen for several weeks, and whom I am happy to see again."

"I am glad you are having a good time," Elizabeth responded warmly and the two of them shared a smile.

She remained speaking with the couple for a few minutes more before saying farewell and going in search of her husband. As she made her way around the outskirts of the ballroom, heading for the place where she had left Darcy speaking with Lady Andrews, she stopped several times to speak with her guests, pleased to make the better acquaintance of many of them. A few asked her where her husband was, and she laughed and said she had lost him in the crowd, which was not very far from the truth! Just as she sighted his tall figure not too far away, a voice called her name and she turned to see Lady Victoria standing with her brother and mother; she happily went over to join them but before her friend could say a word her brother addressed Elizabeth.

"Did we see you dancing with Mr Wickham just now?" When Elizabeth nodded Lord Garville added, "Yes, I thought it was him. Do you know if he will be in the area long?"

"I am not aware of his plans," Elizabeth replied, smiling curiously. "Why do you ask?"

"I thought I would invite him to ride with us," Lord Garville stated. "I have heard much of his skill - everyone says he is a bold and daring rider. I should like to see it for myself."

"Then go and ask him, instead of standing here and boring us with all your talk of horses!" Lady Victoria snapped irritably and Elizabeth blushed for her friend when Lady Haversham harshly rebuked her.

As her brother strutted away with offended dignity, Lady Victoria apologised to Elizabeth.

"Forgive me, Elizabeth, that was very ill mannered of me."

Elizabeth assured her friend that she need not apologise and Lady Victoria smiled her relief.

"I suspect, my dear, that you would not be so irritated with your brother and all his talk of horses if it had not spoiled your hopes for the evening," Lady Haversham then pointed out, smiling knowingly.

"*Mother!*" Lady Victoria objected, blushing with embarrassment.

Elizabeth, of course, was all curiosity.

"Almost every time a gentleman has approached us - perhaps with the intention of asking Victoria to dance - Peter has managed to engage him in a discussion of some sort, usually involving horses, and the opportunity to dance has been missed," Lady Haversham explained helpfully and Elizabeth did her best to hide her smile.

"I cannot believe you told her that, Mother," Lady Victoria complained to Lady Haversham, and whilst she did so Elizabeth was already busy locating her friend a suitable partner.

"Excuse me a moment," she said quickly and disappeared before either of her two companions could respond. She returned again after a few minutes on the arm of a tall, fair haired gentleman.

"Lady Haversham, Lady Victoria, may I introduce Mr Healy? He is nephew to Sir Benedict Hadlock. Mr Healy, my dear friend Lady Victoria Garville and her mother, Lady Haversham."

Mr Healy bowed low and fortunately missed the glare Lady Victoria threw at Elizabeth as she curtsied to the gentleman.

"I wonder that we have never been introduced, Mr Healy," Lady Haversham politely addressed the young man before her. "I have known Sir Benedict for many years."

"This is the first time I have had the pleasure of visiting my uncle," Mr Healy replied, and his voice was slightly accented. "I have until recently resided with my parents in Ireland and am due to take up a position in town in October. My uncle was kind enough to invite me to stay until then."

"Mr Healy is to begin his training to become a barrister," Elizabeth supplied helpfully and was pleased to see Lady Haversham smile and nod graciously, effectively giving Mr Healy her stamp of approval.

"Which part of Ireland do you come from, Mr Healy?" Lady Victoria asked, making an effort to exert herself. "Are you acquainted with Sir Benedict and Lady Hadlock's daughter, Mrs Maher?"

"Yes, I am," Mr Healy responded with a broad smile, which rendered him rather handsome. "Mrs Maher would oft come and stay with my family before she married, and her husband is a good friend of my oldest brother. But to answer your first question, my family's home is just outside Dublin."

The conversation proceeded from there, and seeing that her presence was no longer required Elizabeth politely excused herself to go and find her husband.

Darcy smiled down at his wife when she finally reached his side.

"I was beginning to wonder where you'd got to."

"I was fulfilling my role as hostess," Elizabeth replied and glanced over her shoulder to see Lady Victoria chatting quite happily with Mr Healy still.

"Have you been matchmaking?" Darcy asked with amusement, following her line of sight.

Elizabeth laughed lightly and turned back to him.

"Certainly not! I simply found Victoria a handsome and agreeable gentleman to ask her to dance - her brother had apparently spoiled her other opportunities."

"Speaking of dancing," Darcy responded. "I believe this next is mine."

"I believe you are right," Elizabeth replied and as her husband led her to join the other dancers she was pleased to see Mr Healy and Lady Victoria taking their places.

She caught her friend's eye and laughed when Lady Victoria first shot her a playful glare, and then rolled her eyes resignedly and mouthed a silent thank you.

*You're welcome*, Elizabeth mouthed back and then they each turned their attention to their respective partners.

After supper, Elizabeth and Georgiana decided to disappoint their husbands and declined to dance the next set, shooing Darcy and the Colonel away so that they could speak privately for a while. Georgiana was one of the very few people who were aware of

Elizabeth's condition, and Elizabeth welcomed the chance to speak with her new sister.

"Have you told anyone else?" Georgiana asked at one point. "Your aunt and uncle?"

"No, not yet," Elizabeth replied. "I told Jane very shortly after I saw the doctor, and she has since informed Mrs Montgomery, but I do not think anyone else has been told."

"Mrs Montgomery?" Georgiana repeated, keeping her voice diplomatically neutral. Elizabeth smiled without humour.

"I did ask that Jane tell only her husband; I am sure she simply forgot."

"I hope you do not mind my asking, Elizabeth," Georgiana began gently. "But are things quite well between you and Jane? When I last spoke with her she implied that you had not seen each other for over a fortnight. She seemed – displeased."

"We quarrelled," Elizabeth admitted. "The situation with my father and Longbourn - it has been a difficult time. I said some things I shouldn't have, and though Jane accepted my apology we have not seen each other since. I confess I do not know what I would say to her," she concluded with a slight frown.

"What do you mean?" Georgiana questioned and after a slight hesitation Elizabeth responded.

"Jane is my very dear sister and always will be," she stated thoughtfully. "But I have an entirely new impression of her, and until I can reconcile myself to the changes, I think it best we avoid each other's company." Elizabeth could see that Georgiana was shocked by her answer and her expression was regretful as she noted, "I'm sorry, I should not have said such to you - I know Jane is your good friend."

"But you are as well," Georgiana countered, briefly touching her arm. "I shall not take sides in your disagreement, but I hope you know that you may always confide in me."

"I do, thank you," Elizabeth assured her with a smile. "And I thank you for all you have done for James these past few weeks; he will have the best memories of home when he leaves on Friday."

Georgiana smiled and waved away her thanks.

"We love to spend time with you all."

"I hope you will continue to visit often even after James has left," Elizabeth expressed. "I think Catherine will feel his absence most keenly."

"I think you and William will as well," Georgiana noted with an affectionate smile and Elizabeth agreed that she was probably right.

"Though, of course, your thoughts may be distracted," Georgiana added with a pointed look at Elizabeth's waist.

"I worry that is what James will think when the time comes for us to tell him," Elizabeth admitted with a troubled look. "That our thoughts have not been with him whilst he is away at school because we care more about the babe."

"I do not believe for a second that James would think that," Georgiana firmly asserted. "Were he less secure in the love of my brother and you, perhaps he would entertain such fears, but James can be in no doubt as to how much you both care for him."

"Yes," Elizabeth nodded. "I'm sure you are right. I am still so new to this," she added with a weak smile. "William makes it seem so easy, but sometimes I feel quite out of my depth."

"We all do, at first," Georgiana assured her. "But whenever you have these doubts, Elizabeth, you need only look to James and Catherine to see that they both love you."

"And I them," Elizabeth averred softly, feeling tears forming. "So dearly."

"There you are then," Georgiana replied softly and discreetly passed her emotional sister a handkerchief. "You had best wipe your eyes; my brother is approaching and he will make a fuss if he sees you."

Elizabeth chuckled and dabbed at her eyes; she tucked the handkerchief away and then turned to face her husband, who did indeed look a little worried.

"I am fine," she assured him before he had the chance to ask. "Just feeling overly sentimental; I daresay you should be used to it by now," she teased and Darcy couldn't help smiling in response.

"Are you finished talking?" he asked, looking between the pair. "May I have my dance now?"

"Are we finished?" Elizabeth asked Georgiana playfully. "I am not certain...?"

"I believe so," Georgiana responded with a smile. "Though I notice that *my* husband has not been so quick to reclaim me," she added with an eye roll.

"My darling, you wound me," Colonel Fitzwilliam exclaimed dramatically as he suddenly appeared out of the crowd. "After I battled my way through the sea of guests to reach your side, only to hear you maligning me...!"

"Come," Darcy said quietly to his wife, drawing her away from his sister and cousin and leaving them to their playful argument. "I am owed a dance."

Elizabeth smiled and was happy to let him lead her away to join the other couples readying themselves to dance.

# Chapter 27

$E$lizabeth slowly came awake to the sound of someone softly saying her name. With her eyes still shut she made a quiet noise of protest and felt the answering chuckle rumbling beneath her ear as she lay in her husband's arms, her cheek resting against his chest.

"It is almost noon, my love," Darcy told his wife softly. "We must get up; else we will sleep away the whole day."

"That is a welcome prospect," Elizabeth replied sleepily, absently rubbing her palm over his torso and shoulder; the scar left by Frank Ellerslie's bullet felt rough and course against her sensitive skin.

"But we promised the children that we would tell them about the ball," Darcy reminded her with a patient smile. In truth he was still tired himself and could understand that his wife was even more so, but a promise was a promise nonetheless.

"So we did," Elizabeth sighed and reluctantly rolled away, rubbing her eyes and turning to look at her smiling husband. "Have you been awake long?"

"Not long, no," Darcy assured her.

Deirdre, who had been curled up in her usual place on the bench at the end of the bed, decided at that moment to test her luck and crept over the covers towards her owner.

"Good morning poppet," Elizabeth greeted her cat; Deirdre purred loudly as she nuzzled Elizabeth's outstretched hand whilst at the same time shooting Darcy an evil look.

"On that note," Darcy remarked with a resigned smile, tossing aside the covers and climbing out of bed. "I shall leave you to wash and dress. Knock when you are done," he added, leaning over to kiss his wife. Deirdre predictably hissed at him. "Oh shut up."

He smiled when Elizabeth stifled a laugh and pulled her cat protectively into her arms, leaving her to it and going through to his bedroom. Agatha, who usually slept in front of the fire in his room, got to her feet and wandered over to greet him.

"Good morning old girl," he said as he patted her side affectionately. "Did you sleep well? You must have been tired after all the excitement last night - so many new people for you to investigate!"

Agatha licked his hand and then followed him over to his dressing room where Pattinson already had everything ready for his bath.

"Don't even think about getting in there," Darcy commanded, pointing his finger at Agatha; she backed away from the bath and lay down in the corner. "Good girl. Good morning, Pattinson," Darcy added after nodding with satisfaction.

"Good morning, Sir," Pattinson replied evenly. "Shall I leave you to bathe?"

"Please," Darcy responded. "If you leave my clothes on the chair I can get dressed myself; I will call you when I am ready to shave."

"Very good," Pattinson nodded and did as instructed.

When he was gone Darcy discarded his robe and stepped into the steaming hot bath water. Agatha watched his every move with pleading eyes and as he leant back against the tub he grinned.

"It is piping hot, girl. You'd be out again in a shot. I'll take you out later," Darcy promised and then shut his eyes with a contented sigh, relaxing further into the water.

Once they were both cleaned and dressed for the day, Elizabeth and Darcy located their two children and the whole family assembled together in one of the ground floor parlours. Whilst Elizabeth and Darcy enjoyed a very late breakfast, James and Catherine peppered them with questions about the ball. When the children's curiosity had finally been assuaged, Elizabeth suggested that they all go out for a walk. They called for the dogs to join them, and when they left the house James and Catherine ran on ahead with Agatha and Poppy as Elizabeth and Darcy followed behind them, walking arm in arm.

"Here, Cathy, throw it to me!" James called to his sister, waving his arms.

They had found a large stick and Catherine was holding it high above her head as both dogs barked and ran around her feet. She tried to throw it to her brother, but wasn't strong enough and the stick landed about ten feet from where James stood.

Darcy and Elizabeth laughed as they watched James and the two dogs all rush towards the stick, waiting to see who would reach it first. James threw himself onto his front, covering his clothes with grass stains in the process, and managed to get a hand to the stick just before Agatha got hold of the other end. They playfully wrestled for it for a few moments, Poppy barking madly as she tried to join in too, but eventually Agatha won out and jumped away with the stick in her mouth.

"Oh no you don't!" James laughed as he scrambled to his feet. "Come on Cathy!"

Agatha was too clever to let herself be caught and turned tail and started running, James chasing after her with Poppy on his heels and Catherine calling for him to slow down as Agatha led them all in circles. Darcy and Elizabeth couldn't help laughing as they watched the two children and two dogs run round and round in circles, shouting and barking.

"You win, I quit!" James announced breathlessly, toppling onto the grass and panting heavily. His sister collapsed on top of him. "Oooff!"

"Sorry," Catherine giggled, laughing when Poppy scrambled onto James' chest and started licking his face.

Darcy was watching his son struggling to dislodge the determined puppy when Elizabeth suddenly grasped his arm in a painful grip.

"Will!"

"What?" he asked sharply, alarmed by the tone of her voice. Elizabeth raised her arm and pointed to the prone figure lying on the grass and Darcy felt his heart drop.

"Agatha!" Catherine cried, suddenly realising that she was missing and seeing the dog lying still a few feet away.

As James and Darcy both rushed to Agatha, Elizabeth caught Catherine in her arms.

"No no, come away, princess. Stay with me."

"But what's wrong with her?" Catherine demanded. "Why isn't she moving?"

Darcy knelt beside his dog and gently laid his hand on her side, feeling for any movement. James was beside him and Poppy was gingerly sniffing Agatha's face, as though expecting her to wake up at any moment.

"Father?" James asked fearfully. "Is she...?"

"Yes," Darcy croaked and had to clear his throat. He slowly ran his hand over Agatha's smooth coat. "Yes, she's gone."

"Will?" Elizabeth called tentatively, holding Catherine as the little girl cried into her dress.

Darcy turned to look over his shoulder and simply shook his head. Elizabeth gasped and then nodded, controlling her emotions with sheer force of will.

"Catherine, sweetheart; we need to say goodbye. Come with me and say goodbye to Agatha." When Catherine simply clutched her tighter, Elizabeth bent and scooped her daughter up into her arms. "Shh, everything is alright, I've got you. Do you want to say goodbye?"

She felt Catherine nod and brought her over to where Agatha lay. Setting the little girl down, Elizabeth went down on her knees and encouraged Catherine to do the same. They were both in tears as they gently patted Agatha for the final time and said their goodbyes.

"I don't understand," James whispered brokenly, touching one of Agatha's paws. "She was fine a minute ago."

"I know," Darcy replied quietly, his voice thick with suppressed emotion. "Her heart must have given out. I do not think she would have felt any pain."

James nodded mutely and continued to stroke Agatha's paw. Darcy heard him swallow thickly and turned to look at his son, who was clearly trying his hardest not to cry. He put his arm around James' shoulders and pulled him close.

"It's alright, Son," he whispered and wrapped his other arm around his son when James turned his face into his chest and began to cry silently.

&#8462;&#8463;

Her husband's face was as sombre as she had ever seen it when Elizabeth found him standing over his daughter, watching Catherine as she slept. She went to his side, the thin stream of light from the partially open door illuminating his features.

"I couldn't sleep," Darcy whispered, leaning down and smoothing the cover over Catherine's shoulders. He had already been to James' room.

Beside him, Elizabeth slid her arms around his waist, silently offering him comfort.

"I feel so terrible," he confided.

"I know you do," Elizabeth replied quietly.

"I will never forget the look on their faces when they realised what had happened - that Agatha was really..."

"Nor I," Elizabeth whispered.

"I know she was old and that her time was coming, but why did it have to be today? And why so suddenly?"

Swallowing over the lump of sorrow in her throat, Elizabeth replied.

"I don't know. I don't know why it had to be today or why it was so sudden, but I am glad that she did not have to suffer, that she was happy before she died."

Realising that he had upset his wife, Darcy reached up and smoothed her tousled hair off her face and pressed a soft kiss against her temple.

"Come to bed, my love," Elizabeth said when she had composed herself. "Let her sleep," she added when Darcy glanced back at Catherine as she drew him firmly towards their bedchamber.

When they were both in bed again and Elizabeth had curled into his arms, Darcy sighed heavily.

"I cannot remember a worse day than this in a long time."

Elizabeth nodded, her soft cheek sliding against his arm, and he tightened his hold, drawing her tighter against him as they both recalled the terrible events of the afternoon which had so upset them and the children.

"I do not know what I should do," Darcy confessed to the darkness after several minutes of unhappy silence. "How can I send James to school now, after what has just happened? But term begins in five days, and if he were to miss it he would be behind the other boys."

"Speak to him," Elizabeth advised. "Tell him that you want him to stay, but leave the choice to him. He is upset, but he is mature enough to decide for himself."

Darcy nodded mutely and they lapsed once more into silence. Eventually Elizabeth fell asleep from pure exhaustion and about an hour later Darcy was finally able to drift off into an uneasy sleep as well.

ऒC3

They were all very subdued the next day. Darcy had made arrangements for Agatha to be buried down by the lake, and he had sent word to the stone mason in Lambton to carve a stone to mark the grave. As he was sitting with his family, eating his breakfast in silence, a footman arrived with a note to say that the stone had been delivered and put into place. Thanking the footman who had delivered the message, Darcy carefully folded up the note and then turned to address his wife and children.

"When we have all finished here, I think we should all go together down to the lake to visit Agatha's grave and say our final goodbyes."

"I would like that," Elizabeth replied, resting her hand over his. "Would you like that?" she asked the two children softly.

Catherine nodded mutely and James cleared his eyes before replying.

"Yes. I wanted...where have you had her buried, Father?"

"Underneath the willow tree," Darcy responded, "where she liked to sleep."

Catherine began to cry softly and Elizabeth put her arm around her; she looked at everyone's breakfast plates in turn and decided.

"I think we have all finished. Let us go now."

Darcy nodded and got to his feet, James following suit. Elizabeth took Catherine's hand and the four of them filed out of the breakfast room, accepting their coats from two waiting footmen and stepping outside into the bright but windy day.

It was only a short walk down to the lake and the place where Agatha had been buried. The wind was strong and surprisingly cold, and when they reached the willow tree the family drew closer together, Elizabeth and Darcy standing behind James and Catherine as they all looked down upon the newly placed stone. It simply read "Agatha", and Elizabeth thought it especially poignant for its simplicity. Catherine unexpectedly dropped to her knees, and Elizabeth was about to help her up when the young girl reached into her pocket and drew out a battered old toy - Agatha's favourite.

"I brought you this," Catherine said as she carefully placed it on top of the stone. "I thought you would want it."

"I wish I had thought of that," James said as he dropped down beside his sister, reaching out to trace the outline of Agatha's name.

"Do you have any biscuits?" Catherine asked, knowing her brother's habit of keeping a spare biscuit or two in the pockets of all his coats.

James dug a hand into his pocket and smiled tremulously as he drew out a few broken pieces. He laid them next to the toy.

"There you are, Agatha. Now you have everything you need."

Standing behind them, Elizabeth's throat was beginning to physically pain her with the effort of holding back tears. Beside her, Darcy had turned his face away, obviously struggling with his composure as well, and it was several moments before he finally turned back and found his voice.

"Come. Let us leave her in peace."

James sniffed and wiped his eyes before getting to his feet and helping his sister to hers. They looked up at their father who surprised them both by bending and drawing them into his arms for a fierce embrace.

"I am so proud of you both," he murmured thickly and kissed the tops of their heads before releasing them. He caught Elizabeth's eye and they shared a look of mutual understanding before taking the two children back to the house.

ဢ03

Darcy sat patiently in the saddle, waiting for James to join him. They had ridden together up to North Ridge, Darcy a little way ahead of his son, and eventually James appeared and directed Piera to stand beside Fletcher. As Elizabeth had suggested, Darcy had spoken to his son and made it clear that, whilst he wished for him to stay, the decision of whether or not to delay his departure for school rested with him. James had owned himself reluctant to go, but had eventually decided to leave as planned.

"I used to come here often when I was a boy," Darcy said, breaking the comfortable silence that had settled between them. "My father first brought me here when I was still just learning to ride, thinking to test me, and I was immediately taken with the place and the view. In the years following I would ride up here when I was troubled or upset, seeking peace and solitude. I came here the day my mother died," he confessed softly, staring out over the rolling hills, lost in thought. "My father came to fetch me himself - I did not realise I had been gone for hours. He was not angry and he did not say anything; he just sat beside me as you are now until I was ready to return."

"Were you...are you very like him?" James asked quietly.

"I have been told that I am," Darcy replied with a slight smile, glancing at his son. "Physically, we were very alike - just as you are very like me. In terms of character...I remember many years ago, when your mother was still living, my aunt, Lady Wickham, came to visit with us. The day before she was due to depart, we were walking together in the garden and she told me that she felt as though if she closed her eyes it would be like speaking to her brother again, rather than me. I knew how highly she thought of my father, so I was proud that she felt that way."

James nodded and then turned to look at the view; Darcy could tell he wanted to say something, and so waited patiently.

"I want to make you proud, Father," James said at last. "I want you to be proud of me as your son, and as a Darcy."

"I already am," Darcy responded. "Surely you know that."

"Yes, but it has not been put to the test," James replied. "Not yet - not properly. When I am at school, I will be representing you and our family. I will not just be James anymore, I will be Lord Granby."

"Yes, I suppose that is true," Darcy patiently stated. "But first and foremost you are my son; you are and always will be 'just James' to me. I love you, and I am proud of you, and I trust you."

"I do not want to disappoint you," James replied quietly and Darcy knew they had likely reached the heart of the matter.

"You never could," he assured his son. "I know you have good principles James, that you are intelligent and honourable and good. As long as you stay true to those values, and to yourself, I know you will never disappointment me."

James nodded and Darcy reached over and grasped his shoulder.

"Are you certain you wish to leave tomorrow?" he asked, and James let out a deep breath and nodded again.

"It is going to be hard to go," his son admitted. "But I want to do it - I need to do it. I see it as a test, and I would be disappointed in myself if I failed it."

Darcy squeezed James' shoulder.

"I understand."

James smiled and Darcy dropped his hand, taking out his pocket watch to check the time.

"We had best return, before we are missed. Elizabeth will already be wondering what has become of us."

"Yes," James smiled his agreement. "I will miss her very much," he admitted, his smile fading. "And Catherine too, of course."

"They will both miss you," Darcy replied. "I will as well. You had best write to us!" He threatened playfully.

"What will you do if I do not?" James asked cheekily and Darcy laughed in spite of himself. "Ride to the school and demand a reason why?"

"Either that, or leave you there for Christmas as punishment," Darcy responded and James laughed.

"Touché!"

Darcy grinned and then turned Fletcher about.

"Come, we should go back. When we get to level ground we can see how Piera does against Fletcher - though only if you think you are up to it, of course."

"Of course!" James declared eagerly and followed his father to the track which would lead them down from the ridge and home again.

The rest of the day passed by too quickly for all of them, and suddenly the day of James' departure was upon them. They breakfasted as a family and then went out to the waiting carriage.

"Are you sure you have packed everything?" Elizabeth asked worriedly. "You have not left anything behind?"

"Yes," James replied patiently, for at least the third time. He shared an amused look with his father before turning back to Elizabeth. "Yes, I am absolutely certain I have everything I need."

Elizabeth realised he was teasing her and laughed at herself.

"I'm sorry, am I mothering you? I am, aren't I?"

"Yes," James stated; then he smiled shyly and admitted, "I don't mind."

"I think I would still do it even if you did," Elizabeth replied and then pulled him close for a tight hug. "Take care, James. I will miss you."

"I will miss you too," James responded quite genuinely. When Elizabeth kissed his cheek he blushed as always and turned to his sister to hide his embarrassment.

Catherine hugged her brother's waist tightly.

"I don't want you to go!"

"I will be back soon," James replied. "And I will write every week."

"Promise?" Catherine asked, looking up at her brother with wide, trusting eyes.

"Promise," James averred, smiling brightly. He was pleased when his sister managed to smile in return.

Leaving Catherine with Elizabeth and his father, James turned to say goodbye to the couple hovering in the background. Mr and Mrs Hughes had been responsible for him in differing ways over the years, and he would miss them both very much. He had been pleased to learn that Mr Hughes had agreed to take up a place at the estate school whilst his wife stayed on as Catherine's governess, and James knew that his father planned to have Mr Hughes tutor Catherine as well when she was a little older. He liked the thought of being able to see and spend time with his tutor during his breaks from school.

At last it was time for them to depart and James said a final goodbye to a tearful Elizabeth and a crying Catherine. He put on a brave face for them both, smiling and trying to tease away their tears, but soon had to take refuge in the carriage for fear of losing his composure as well. Darcy kissed his wife and daughter and climbed into the carriage behind his son. Elizabeth and Catherine waved them away and soon faded out of sight as the carriage rolled away from the house.

"Could we please stop on the hill, Father?" James asked in a choked voice. He cleared his throat before adding, "I would like one last look."

"Of course," Darcy readily agreed and when they reached the point in the road which afforded the best view of the house he tapped the roof of the carriage with his cane.

James opened the door and hopped down, walking a little ways away from the carriage. Darcy decided to allow his son some privacy and waited patiently beside the carriage, chatting with John the coachman.

James looked down into the valley, trying to memorise the scene though in his heart he knew it was already ingrained in his mind. He knew he would be returning in a few months, and had spent many a month away from home before now, but this departure still felt different; momentous, even.

Eventually he tore himself away and wandered back to the carriage and his waiting father, who straightened on seeing his approach.

"Ready?" Darcy asked.

James took a deep breath and nodded.

"Yes, I'm ready."

# Chapter 28

Darcy rode up to the stables and returned the salutations of his host, Lord Haversham.

"Ah, Farleigh, glad you could join us!"

"It was never in doubt, I assure you," Darcy responded and then dismounted from Fletcher, leaving his horse with one of the many grooms.

He spent some time greeting the other gentleman who had been invited by Lord Haversham to join the ride out. He couldn't help noticing, as he was speaking with John Hadlee, that his cousin Mr Wickham was not present, and was surprised to find it so - he had understood that Lord Garville had invited the other man expressly. He mentioned it to his host when the latter passed him.

"Yes," Lord Haversham responded. "He was invited - obviously found something better to do!"

This was said with a slightly laughing look directed over Darcy's shoulder; he turned and was surprised and slightly perturbed to see Sir Charles, amongst others, standing there.

"Mr Wickham's is not the only absence of note," Lord Haversham went on, addressing Darcy with a grin. "Where is that beast of a dog of yours? I thought she never left your side."

Darcy was caught off guard by the offhanded mention of Agatha and felt a sharp stab of pain.

"I am sorry to say that Agatha passed away the day after the ball."

"Oh, I'm sorry old man," Lord Haversham replied, looking like he meant it. John Hadlee added his own regrets and Darcy simply nodded and silently accepted their words.

When it was almost time for them to set off and each man moved to mount his ride, Darcy led Fletcher to Sir Charles' side, quietly greeting his uncharacteristically silent friend and gently enquiring if everything was well with him. After glancing about them to make sure they would not be overheard Sir Charles replied.

"I fear I know only too well why Mr Wickham is not here."

Darcy's brows rose in mute surprise and he waited for his friend to elaborate.

"He has been very often at Netherfield," Sir Charles revealed. "I myself have seen him daily, but I do not doubt that he has visited when I am not present."

Lord Haversham surprised them both when he called for them to hurry up and mount, and the two friends briefly broke off their conversation as they did as asked; allowing the rest of the men to go on ahead of them, they rode side by side and continued to talk.

"I know very well that my sister is a grown woman," Sir Charles went on with an unhappy frown. "That she has been married and is now to all intents and purposes completely independent; but that does not change the fact that she is embarrassing both of us by carrying on with a man like Mr Wickham. And under my own roof!"

"Are you absolutely sure...?" Darcy tried to ask, trying to be diplomatic though he knew his cousin and the lady in question too well to really doubt that they had resumed their old affair.

"Yes," Sir Charles bit out angrily. "I may be a fool sometimes, but I am not blind. It is obvious what is going on."

"Then why do you not just forbid him from coming to the house?" Darcy asked.

"And make her go to him?" Sir Charles replied with a note of incredulity.

"You think she would?"

"I think my sister is determined to have her way, damn the consequences to herself or the rest of us," Sir Charles stated darkly. "If I tried to forbid her from seeing him, I would be as good as pushing her into his arms."

"In which case," Darcy responded evenly, "perhaps you should simply leave her to it. Let her disgrace herself, if that is what she is determined to do. As you said, she is a grown woman and responsible for herself; the shame will be hers, not yours."

Sir Charles sighed.

"I have thought about it; many times it has crossed my mind to just ask her to leave and let her do what she wants. But she is still my sister, however badly she behaves, and I still feel a responsibility towards her."

Needless to say, Darcy was not impressed by his friend's hypocrisy; why, after all, did the same rule not apply to their father-in-law? Why did Sir Charles feel no responsibility towards him, no matter how badly he behaved?

"I have tried to speak to Jane," Sir Charles went on, oblivious to his friend's dissatisfaction. "And have encouraged her not to allow Mr Wickham's visits, or at the very least not to allow he and Caroline to spend time alone, but she has not been well recently and I know I cannot expect her to act as my sister's minder."

"Nothing serious, I hope," Darcy expressed; however little he thought of his sister in law's character, he still wished her well.

Sir Charles shook his head.

"No, nothing serious. She has been rather fatigued; this pregnancy has been quite hard on her, I think. I shall be glad when it is all over, and I have a healthy wife and child. But I am sure you of all people can understand my feelings," he added with a smile which Darcy returned.

In truth, Elizabeth's pregnancy did not have him feeling as anxious as he would have anticipated, considering how he had felt when Anne had been pregnant with James and Catherine. He suspected that was largely due to Elizabeth herself; she was the very picture of health and seemed to take any new development in her stride. It was hard to worry when she was so happy and at ease.

Leaving his friend to his thoughts, Darcy joined the other gentleman and allowed himself to enjoy the ride, giving Fletcher free rein and trusting his horse to perform as ably as always. The route Lord Haversham led them on was varied and challenging, combining differing terrains and testing the skills of both horse and rider. Lord Garville, Darcy noted, was a very eager rider whose skill did not quite match his enthusiasm; he watched with vague feelings of disapproval and alarm as the young man pushed his horse to the very limits on the flat sections of the ride, and then urged it over increasingly difficult jumps. Lord Haversham applauded his son's bravery, but Darcy was more inclined to call it recklessness.

His opinion was vindicated when they approached one of the final jumps they had to complete before they turned towards home. It was a blind jump over a stream, a high hedgerow completely obscuring any view of the stream on the other side. The stream was not quite so wide in places, and the bank not as sharp or firm, and most of the riders chose to make the jump there, reaching the other side in safety. Darcy had just completed the jump and wheeled Fletcher around to watch the others when he saw Lord Garville and his mount galloping towards a section of the hedgerow which concealed a much wider part of the stream, with a high and solid bank. All he could do was watch with a certainty of disaster, averting his eyes when both horse and rider fell.

Lord Garville was thrown over the head of his mount and hit the ground hard, though his neck and back were spared any injury. As Lord Haversham and the other riders all rushed to the injured young man's side, Darcy dismounted and went to the horse which lay where it fell, obviously in a great amount of pain and distress.

Two or three of the grooms who had accompanied the gentleman on the ride were already by its side when Darcy joined them.

"His shoulder is broken," Darcy pronounced grimly after a brief exam - he had seen the injury in the past and knew the signs. "Do you have a pistol?" he asked the groom knelt beside him.

"Yes, Your Grace," the man replied soberly.

"I will do it," Darcy stated, holding out his hand. The groom shot him a surprised look and then placed the pistol in his outstretched hand.

Stroking the stricken horse's neck gently, Darcy spoke to it in a soothing voice as he positioned the pistol.

"Everything will be over soon."

There was a second of silence following the sound of the shot, and then the other horses all began to rear up and whinny with distress. Darcy handed the groom back the pistol and stood up, striding angrily over to Fletcher's side.

John Hadlee, who had watched all the proceedings, rushed over to him as Darcy hoisted himself up into the saddle.

"Is the boy alright?"

"He is just bruised, I think," John Hadlee replied. "No permanent injury."

Darcy sincerely believed that Lord Garville deserved to be hurt but wisely kept that thought to himself. He was furious that the younger man's recklessness and stupidity had resulted in the needless death of a fine horse; it was such a waste.

"Are you leaving?" Hadlee asked softly, noting Darcy's grim expression and taut jaw.

"Yes," Darcy bit out tightly. "Tell Haversham that I will call in a few days to see how his son does."

When Hadlee nodded, Darcy wheeled Fletcher around and set off in the direction of home, wanting to put as much distance between himself and the scene which had just played out.

His expression was still grim when he walked into the library, and coupled with the fact that he was still wearing his muddy riding clothes, Elizabeth knew that something must have happened to upset him.

"What is it?" she asked, laying aside the book she had been reading.

Darcy explained what had happened with Lord Garville, striding to and fro in front of the hearth, gesticulating angrily and heaping recriminations upon himself for not saying anything of his concerns to Lord Haversham about Lord Garville's riding.

"From what you have said," Elizabeth replied reasonably, "I doubt Lord Haversham would have listened to you - it seems like he was encouraging his son."

"Yes, but I still could have said *something*," Darcy replied in frustration. "Perhaps then that horse would still be alive."

Elizabeth got to her feet and forced her husband to stop his pacing; she reached up and used her handkerchief to wipe some spots of mud off his cheek as she calmly told him.

"You did all you could. I know it must have been distressing, but it was not your fault and there was nothing more you could have done."

Darcy sighed resignedly and silently admitted that his wife was right. He smiled down at her as she continued to clean the mud from his face.

"Do I look a fright?"

"I wouldn't say that," Elizabeth responded coyly. "You look rather vigorous and manly."

Darcy snorted with amusement and grinned and Elizabeth smiled playfully up at him.

"That is better."

She continued with her ministrations for a few minutes more until her husband casually mentioned that Sir Charles had been at the ride too.

"Oh yes?"

"Yes - apparently Mr Wickham and Mrs Montgomery have resumed their old affair," Darcy revealed. He frowned as he recalled his annoyance with his friend and his distorted sense of responsibility.

"What is it?" Elizabeth asked, seeing his frown.

"It is nothing," Darcy replied, shaking his head. "I just...Charles said that he cannot leave his sister to disgrace herself because he feels a sense of responsibility towards her, and I...his hypocrisy astounds me, is all. Where is his sense of responsibility towards his father-in-law?"

Elizabeth smiled sadly.

"Blood is thicker than water, my love."

"Is that to be his excuse, then?" Darcy replied with dissatisfaction, not at his wife, but at his friend whom he wished was a better person than he apparently was.

"Perhaps," Elizabeth responded with a slight shrug. "I cannot claim to truly understand the workings of his mind, any more than I can my sister's."

"You sound quite resigned to that fact," Darcy noted, looking down at his wife and noting her serene expression.

"Perhaps I finally am," Elizabeth replied. "Perhaps I have finally realised that I will never truly understand how my sister can be so lovely one minute, and so hurtful the next. What I do understand now, though, is that I am not prepared to waste my time worrying about it. I have better things to think about," she concluded, resting her hand on her tummy. "And so do you."

Darcy rested his hand atop of hers as he replied.

"You are completely right."

"I know," Elizabeth responded impertinently, and her husband laughed.

ळ୦ଔ

The following day, the whole family were delighted to receive a letter from James. Elizabeth sat with Catherine in her lap as Darcy read it to them.

*Dear Father, Elizabeth and Cathy,*

*I have been here for four days, and already more has happened than I will ever have time to write about! We have not yet begun lessons, but have been introduced to all of the teachers and the other members of our houses and the rest of our year. For the first two days it was only I and the rest of my year that were here - the older boys began arriving yesterday, and we shall all begin lessons soon.*

*The headmaster, Mr Cater, formally welcomed us all to the school yesterday during our first assembly. He gave quite a speech (I will not bother you with the details) and then allowed his deputy, Mr Teague, to outline the school rules to us. Some of them seem quite odd, but I shall do my best to remember and adhere to them.*

*The other new boys in my house all seem quite nice; one or two are rather loud and already got themselves into trouble with the warden, but there are a number whom I would like to befriend. I am to share my room with three other boys, and am already getting along famously with one of them. His name is Philip Brown and his family is from Lincoln. He is a very small boy but rather friendly and very clever. We had a brilliant chat about Mr Cox's perpetual motion clock, which he has also seen at the Mechanical Museum. Do you remember the day when we all went? With the spider and the swan swimming on the water?*

*My room is quite small and with all four of us sharing is rather cramped, but I am sure we shall make the best of it - it is quite comfortable despite its small size. And the food is fine; not half as bad as I had feared, though I know I have been spoiled by Mrs Maddison and Mrs Procter all these years! I have no fears I shall starve whilst here, though.*

*Philip and I spent this morning exploring the school grounds; it has thirty acres and there is much to see and do. There is a pond where some of the older boys go to swim, though they are not strictly supposed to do so; there is also a greenhouse rather like the one Elizabeth described to me at her father's house. There are no stables, which is a pity, but I suppose it would hardly be practicable to keep enough horses for all the boys to ride.*

*I look forward to the start of lessons; having met all the teachers and heard which subjects they are to teach us I am certain that history will be my favourite. Mr Seymour is quite young compared to the other teachers, but he seemed very knowledgeable when we met him. I am sure I will enjoy his lessons.*

*I miss you all very much. I hope you are all well. Please kiss and embrace one another on my behalf - especially Cathy. And please could you send my copy of Treasure Island with your reply? I seem to have left it behind, despite Elizabeth asking me four or five times whether I had everything!*

*With all my love, your affectionate son and brother,*
*James*

"Well, isn't that lovely," Elizabeth said after she had kissed Catherine's cheek with exaggerated affection, making the young girl giggle. "He has made a friend already."

"And he did forget something after all," Darcy noted with a warm smile, folding up the letter.

"Can I write my own letter back to him, Papa?" Catherine asked. "I will use my neatest writing."

"Of course you can, princess," Darcy replied, touching her cheek. "I am sure your brother would like that very much."

He looked at Elizabeth and they shared a pleased, relieved smile; they had both worried how James would fare during his first few days at school and were reassured by the contents and tone of his letter.

Another letter arrived in the afternoon of the same day, unanticipated and something of a surprise. Darcy was working in his study when a footman brought it to him and after briefly perusing its contents he went in search of his wife.

"Another letter?" she asked when he appeared in her study holding the missive; she had been going through some of the household accounts.

"Yes, it is from Charles," Darcy revealed after making sure the door was firmly closed. "His sister is gone."

"Gone? Gone where?" Elizabeth asked curiously.

"With Mr Wickham, apparently," Darcy replied as he took a seat and passed the letter over the desk to his wife. "As Charles states, he told Mrs Montgomery that Mr Wickham was no longer welcome at Netherfield and she took her leave the very next day, in company with that gentleman, whilst Charles was away on estate business."

"Well," Elizabeth sighed, setting the letter down. "I cannot say I am wholly surprised, though I am somewhat disappointed."

Darcy scoffed and rolled his eyes.

"It is precisely what I expected of both of them; they are far too opportunistic to not take advantage of each other's circumstances."

"You think they will marry, then," Elizabeth surmised lightly.

"Of course," Darcy replied. "He needs a rich wife who has no objections to his circumstances or reputation, and she has always desired a connection to this family. They are perfect for one another."

Elizabeth frowned dubiously.

"I do not think he will marry her; I have more faith in him than that."

"How can you?" Darcy asked with a combination of amusement and disbelief. "Before we were married and he was paying you so much attention, the only reason I wasn't worried that you'd fall for his charms was because I knew you had taken his measure right from the start and realised immediately what sort of man he was. How can you be so aware of his faults and yet still think well of him?"

"Mr Wickham has many faults," Elizabeth conceded. "But I think some of them greatly exaggerated. I also think that I have known worse men than him; he has never done me any harm, and I am certain he would never hurt anyone wilfully. I find I can excuse his loose morals in light of that fact."

Darcy remained unconvinced and in the end they resolved to await further news to see who would be proved right. When a letter arrived a few days later addressed to Elizabeth from Mr Wickham himself, she shot her husband a significant smile and set the letter aside to be opened when they were alone. Going with her husband to his study after they had finished their breakfast, Elizabeth sat down on one of the wingback chairs and broke the seal on the letter.

*My dearest Elizabeth,*

*Is my usual, familiar address enough to alert you to the fact that my status as a bachelor remains unchanged? I daresay it should be - the lady to whom I am sure many people are imagining me ~~chained~~ connected would likely forbid me from using my usual address, being more inclined to jealousy than your magnanimous and broadminded husband.*

*Never fear, my dear friend, I have escaped her clutches. I will not lie and say that I was never tempted by the thought of a more permanent association between us, but I found that I could not so easily forsake my liberty as a single man. That, of course, is what I will say to anyone who asks - in truth (and if you tell anyone I said this I will be forced to revenge myself on you in some way), I knew all along that I was a substitute for my cousin and the joke, after a time, grew thin.*

*Do not concern yourself that I have left Mrs Montgomery broken-hearted; I certainly do not. Her reaction to my refusal of her proposal was more irked than injured, and I believe she is currently in town with her friends, likely abusing me to anyone who will listen. I have decided to spend the winter on the continent. I have had enough of the climate and, with the exception of your fine self I find the company here dull. Perhaps I can find myself a charming, exotic beauty whilst abroad; someone whom I deserve, perhaps?*

*Before we parted ways Mrs Montgomery was so good as to share your news with me. Never fear, you can trust in my discretion (more than you can in hers, certainly!). Please allow me to offer my congratulations. I am happy for you, Elizabeth.*

*Farewell for now.*

*Your friend,*
*George Wickham.*

Elizabeth smiled a little sadly and then passed the letter to her husband for him to read and judge for himself. She hesitated a moment before she handed it to him, a sudden thought occurring to her.

"I shall only let you read it if you promise not to become too piqued," she told him with a smile. "Some of his language is rather familiar, but that is just our way."

"I know it does not mean anything," Darcy assured her and she handed him the letter. He grinned as he added, "Though I reserve the right to be thoroughly piqued if I find he has confessed his love to you."

Elizabeth laughed lightly and shook her head at his teasing before falling quiet and allowing her husband a moment to read the letter.

"Well," Darcy began slowly as he finished the letter and passed it back to his wife. "Perhaps I should give him more credit, after all."

"Because he did not accept Mrs Montgomery's 'proposal'?" Elizabeth asked.

"Yes," Darcy granted. "And because he obviously listens to you. That shows good sense, at the very least."

"I hope he has enough sense to find himself a good wife," Elizabeth responded as she folded up the letter.

"Better at least than Mrs Montgomery?" Darcy teased.

"That would not be hard," Elizabeth replied dryly and Darcy grinned with reluctant amusement.

"Time will tell," he predicted. "Perhaps he will repay your faith in him after all."

"Perhaps," Elizabeth responded thoughtfully; she hoped that her friend would find happiness in the end, whomever it was with.

# Chapter 29

Elizabeth carefully inspected the handkerchief Catherine held out towards her, lightly fingering the fine stitches.

"Wonderful," she pronounced, returning the young girl's smile. "James will be very pleased with his gift."

"I hope so," Catherine expressed as she took back the handkerchief she was in the process of painstakingly embroidering with her brother's initials and bent to her work once more.

Elizabeth and Mrs Hughes exchanged a smiling look before the former asked how Mr Hughes was settling in to his new place.

"Quite well," Mrs Hughes responded, laying aside her own embroidery. "I believe he sees it as something of a challenge. Certainly his new pupils will require more help than James ever did - he always was such a bright boy," the older woman added and Elizabeth smiled at her obvious affection for James.

"By all accounts he is doing well at school," she noted with a smile. "His letters have certainly been very full."

"Yes," Mrs Hughes agreed - she and her husband had been pleased and grateful when Darcy had shared all of his son's letters with them. "We were very pleased to read that he is so happy and settled."

"As were we all!" Elizabeth stated. "We are very much looking forward to seeing him for his birthday, aren't we princess?" she added, addressing Catherine who smiled brightly and expressed her agreement. "Less than a week to go, now!"

"Hopefully I will have these finished by then," Catherine said, indicating the trio of handkerchiefs she intended to gift to her brother.

"I am sure you shall," Elizabeth assured her and let the little girl get back to work as she re-focused her attention on her own embroidery and Mrs Hughes did the same.

They were all still thus occupied half an hour later when Darcy came to find them.

"Look, Papa, I have done one already and this one is almost finished as well," Catherine stated excitedly, holding out her work for her father to see.

"How lovely," Darcy complimented his daughter sincerely as he bent to examine the detail more closely. "You are a very clever girl."

Catherine blushed prettily at the praise and carefully folded up the finished handkerchief and put it to one side.

"I should very much like a set of these myself," Darcy went on with a smile. "For Christmas, perhaps?"

Catherine appeared delighted by the request, but then frowned delicately and looked between her father and Elizabeth,

"But I thought Mama had made you some already?"

"Yes, she did," Darcy affirmed, sharing a smile with his wife. "But I only have the one set from her. I should be very happy to have one from you as well."

"Very well," Catherine granted happily, now that that problem was solved. "I shall make you some for Christmas."

"I shall look forward to it," Darcy replied and kissed the top of her head before straightening and turning to his wife.

"Are you going?" she asked. There was another hunt scheduled for the afternoon and she knew her husband intended to join John Hadlee before they both rode over to where the hunt was to meet.

"Yes," Darcy replied. "The ground should be firm enough, I think. We were fortunate that the rain has abated the past few days, else I daresay the hunt would have been cancelled."

Elizabeth nodded.

"Take care," she added and Darcy smiled and assured her he would be fine.

"You are riding Fletcher?" she asked, and her smile faded when Darcy shook his head.

"I thought I would give Baltar another try," he replied; seeing his wife's expression he promised, "I will be careful."

"I know," Elizabeth responded; she smiled and admitted, "And I have asked John to look after you."

"How embarrassing," Darcy dryly replied and Elizabeth laughed at his response to her confession. "When did you make this request?"

"Well..." Elizabeth prevaricated; she grinned and confessed, "I didn't so much as ask him; rather, Claire knew I was concerned and took it upon herself to speak to her husband on my behalf."

"Wonderful," Darcy groaned, but his smile was tender and amused.

"If it is any consolation," Elizabeth pointed out, "I would have spoken to you about looking after John, but I was certain that you do that already without my having to say anything."

"Well, you may both rest assured that John and I are very careful, as neither of us have any intention of upsetting our wives, who are very dear to us, respectively," Darcy replied and Elizabeth smiled at his gallantry, knowing that despite his teasing he meant what he said.

"I must be going," Darcy stated and bent to briefly kiss his wife before kissing his daughter on the cheek once more. "Have a nice afternoon, princess."

"You too, Father," Catherine replied and she and Elizabeth watched as Darcy strode from the room. "Do you not like riding anymore, Mama?" Catherine asked when he had gone, turning back to Elizabeth who was surprised by the question.

"On the contrary," she replied. "I still enjoy it very much."

"It is just that you have not been riding for so long, I thought perhaps you did not like it anymore," Catherine explained and Elizabeth could understand why Catherine thought so. She was comfortable telling a small white lie, knowing that she could not tell Catherine the truth.

"I have not been able to ride Dot because she has hurt her leg, and I do not want to ride any other horse because I know it would hurt Dot's feelings."

Catherine smiled a little sadly as she replied.

"Like Agatha, when Papa would play with Poppy."

"Yes, just like Agatha," Elizabeth agreed, her voice soft. Poppy was asleep under the opposite sofa and cut quite a lonely figure; Agatha's presence had, after all, always been so substantial.

"I miss Agatha," Catherine admitted. "And James," she added in a very quiet voice.

Elizabeth put her arm around her daughter and drew her close.

"I miss them, too. But when I feel sad, I remember all of the good times we had together and remind myself that we shall see James again very soon, and that Agatha is happy and at peace where she is now."

Catherine nodded mutely and Elizabeth kissed the top of her head before releasing her. The young girl pulled back and looked up at Elizabeth.

"I am glad you are here. If you had not married Papa it would have been just me and him and I think we would have been very sad."

"I think," Elizabeth replied with tears in her eyes. "That your papa would never be sad as long as he had you, princess. But I am glad I am here as well."

Catherine smiled and then turned back to her embroidery, leaving Elizabeth to recover her composure. She dabbed at her eyes with a handkerchief, returning Mrs Hughes' look with a wobbly smile of reassurance. She could have blamed her emotional reaction to Catherine's words on her pregnancy, but knew it was the sentiment which had touched her so deeply.

𝕖𝕆𝕘

Darcy looked up from the contract he had been reading when he heard his name being called. Rising from his chair, he walked around his desk feeling mildly curious and had just reached the door when it was opened and his wife suddenly appeared.

"Oh!" She exclaimed in surprise when she narrowly avoided colliding with his chest.

"Is something the matter?" Darcy asked, amused by her flustered demeanour.

"Jane has had her baby!" Elizabeth startled him by announcing and it was his turn to be flustered.

"When?! We had no word from Charles that it was her time! And how are they - they are both well?"

"Yes, both well," Elizabeth assured him breathlessly - he only then noticed she was holding a letter. "Apparently her pains began late this morning, and the baby was born before the doctor had even arrived!"

"So quickly!" Darcy exclaimed; his thoughts were with his friend. "Charles must have been worried."

"I gather they were all taken rather by surprise," Elizabeth replied with a smile. "It is a boy," she added, remembering she had yet to mention that detail. "They have named him Henry."

"Charles will be pleased," Darcy smiled, leaving his other thought unsaid; Elizabeth was not so circumspect.

"Jane won't be," she predicted. "She very much wanted a girl this time. Though of course that will not matter now Henry has been born; my sister is nothing if not a good mother. And of course Dan will be pleased to have a little brother to play with," she added with a smile.

"Yes," Darcy agreed. "We should send our congratulations," he said, and went back to his desk to pen a quick note. "Shall I ask if they would welcome a visit tomorrow?"

"Yes," Elizabeth nodded, mindful of the fact that the day after tomorrow they were due to leave to visit James at school for his birthday.

After sharing the news with Catherine, Elizabeth thought no more of the issue until the following day when Charles and Jane's response arrived. Apparently it was not convenient for them to visit that day, though they would expect Elizabeth and Darcy on the next; Darcy frowned as he read out the letter.

"Did you mention that we are leaving tomorrow?"

"I did," Darcy averred.

Elizabeth's brows rose and she shook her head.

"Well we shall just have to tell them that tomorrow is not convenient for *us*, and wait until we return to visit."

"Are you sure…?" Darcy began but Elizabeth cut him off.

"Utterly; we are going to see James. My sister will just have to wait."

Darcy nodded his acquiescence and the matter was decided.

ಬಿ೦ಲ್ಬ

"Papa!"

James hurtled down the steps of his dormitory building and collided forcefully with Darcy, who stumbled back a step and laughingly returned his son's fierce embrace. He was delighted to see his son, and could admit to himself that some of his happiness stemmed from the manner of James' greeting. In the back of his mind he had been worried that his son would be somehow embarrassed to demonstrate affection now that he had been away at school, and he was very pleased to find that that was not the case. If anything, James' greeting had been more effusive than was his usual wont.

"Hello, Son," Darcy said affectionately, ruffling his son's hair and then holding him at arm's length. "Happy Birthday."

"Thank you," James replied and then hurried over to greet his sister and Elizabeth with just as much enthusiasm.

"I am so glad to see you all!" He declared when he released his sister and Elizabeth thought she saw his smile waver for a moment before he recovered and the moment passed.

"Will you come inside? I thought you could meet Phillip before we leave."

"That would be lovely," Elizabeth replied, taking Darcy's arm when Catherine rushed to her brother's side and they went hand in hand up the stairs.

Walking behind his son, Darcy thought that he was looking a little thinner than he remembered and made a mental note to see that James ate a very good meal for dinner. Otherwise his son appeared to be very well and his relief was obvious to Elizabeth when he turned to smile down at her. She patted his arm and they followed James and Catherine as the former led them all to a room on the first floor.

"Here he is," James declared happily, bringing them over to a small, thin boy with white blond hair and very pale skin. "Father, Elizabeth, Cathy, this is my good friend, Philip Brown. Philip, this is my sister Catherine, my father and his wife."

For all his apparent frailty, Philip had a bright smile and did not appear particularly shy as he bowed.

"I am very pleased to meet you; James has told me so much about you all."

"And us about you," Catherine replied, speaking on behalf of them all. "Do you really have five sisters?"

"Catherine," Darcy laughingly chided his daughter as Philip grinned and replied.

"Yes, I do."

"I would dearly love a sister," Catherine admitted with a wistful sigh and James laughed and pretended offence.

"Am I so poor a brother, then?"

"No!" Catherine protested, hugging his arm. "You are the best brother in the entire world!"

"That is more like it," James joked and as the others all laughed he affectionately embraced his sister. "Thank you, Cathy."

When the moment passed Elizabeth looked between James and Philip.

"Would Philip perhaps like to join us on our outing, and for dinner later?"

"Oh no, I would not want to intrude," Philip began but James was more excited by the idea.

"Yes! Oh, you should come Philip - it was your idea in the first place. Say you'll come, at least for the day."

Darcy saw Philip smile at James' enthusiasm before the small boy darted an uncertain glance in his direction; realising that he might be inadvertently intimidating the boy, Darcy smiled and seconded his wife's invitation.

"You are very welcome to join us, young man. And it seems my son is very keen for you to do so," he added with a grin and James blushed slightly at his teasing.

"Come if you want to, Philip," he said to his friend and was pleased when Philip gratefully accepted the invitation.

"Come along then," Darcy said, ushering the three children ahead of he and Elizabeth. "Back to the carriage."

"Did you bring Poppy with you?" James asked as they walked down the stairs; he was trying to talk to his father and kept turning to look behind him and nearly tripped twice.

"Yes - now watch where you are going, please!" Darcy replied and was relieved when his son heeded his advice; his relief was short lived though, as James promptly began to run down the remaining steps, followed closely by Philip and Catherine.

Elizabeth laughed lightly when her husband groaned, patting his arm reassuringly.

"I hope you got plenty of sleep last night, my love. Something tells me we are going to be kept on our toes today."

The sound of youthful laughter and shouting combined with excited barking reached them and Darcy smiled with resigned amusement.

"I think you are probably right."

They joined the children by the carriage and allowed them a few moments to play with Poppy, who was delighted with all of the attention. Eventually Elizabeth and Darcy shepherded them all into the carriage and they set off. Their destination was just over an hour away and James' excitement was obvious.

"Are we really going to be able to see inside the house, Father?" he asked for the second time.

"Yes," Darcy replied patiently. "The family are from home and the housekeeper assured me that it is quite common for them to receive visitors."

"Tell me again what is so special about this house, James," Elizabeth requested and James was more than happy to oblige her.

"It is one of the houses where Charles II took refuge after his defeat by Cromwell at the Battle of Worcester in 1651 -"

"Which was the final battle of the Civil War," Philip put in helpfully and James nodded eagerly.

"Yes, exactly, the final battle. Charles had fled the battle and the house where we are going was one of many he stayed at during his escape from Britain."

"I see," Elizabeth replied. "I presume he was being pursued by Cromwell's forces?"

"Oh yes," James nodded. "They even came to the house whilst he was there, but they did not search it. We have been learning about the Civil War with Mr Seymour all this term, you see," he explained, perhaps after seeing the look Elizabeth and Darcy shared with one another. "It is all quite fascinating."

"If I had known you were so interested, Son, I would have sat you down with the diaries of your great-great-great-great-great grandfather," Darcy remarked with a smile. "The third Earl of Farleigh, to be more precise. He supported the king, and would have been sent to the Tower had he not left the country."

Elizabeth noticed that Philip's eyes widened considerably on hearing this and that he regarded her husband with a certain amount of awe; obviously being in company with a Duke was something of a novelty for the young man.

"I had not realised I was interested, in truth," James admitted with a rueful grin. "But Mr Seymour - he is our history tutor - he makes it all seem so fascinating! I cannot wait to tell him about today; he will be quite jealous of us, won't he?" he added, turning to his friend who readily concurred.

"You seem to like this Mr Seymour very much," Darcy remarked; he had noticed how often his son mentioned his history tutor in his letters.

"I do," James averred. "He knows everything! And he does not...he is nice to us," he concluded rather lamely and both Darcy and Elizabeth wondered what he had left unsaid though they let the moment pass.

Soon they reached their destination, and they all disembarked and began to explore. They enjoyed a fine day out together as a family, and Philip was a very welcome addition to their little party. He and James proved delightfully knowledgeable about the house they were visiting and its important place in history, and they guided the others around most happily. Elizabeth and Darcy were both gratified to see James so at ease and clearly content, and Catherine was happy to spend time with her brother again; she also got on very well with Philip, whose experience with his five sisters stood him in good stead with Catherine.

Eventually, it was time for them to return Philip to school; they then took James with them back to the inn where they were staying and sat down to as fine a dinner as was available. Catherine presented her brother with the handkerchiefs she had embroidered for him, and James was as pleased with them as Elizabeth had predicted. She and Darcy then presented James with three new novels and some paper and ink to replenish his current supply.

"So that you may write to us as often as you have heretofore," Elizabeth explained with a smile and James laughed and thanked them both for his gifts.

"There is also this," Darcy said, pushing a small box towards his son.

James looked curiously at his father and then accepted the box; carefully opening it he smiled when he perceived the two items inside.

"I thought, since you have so many letters to write, it was time you had a proper seal," Darcy explained. "And I thought you would like the ring as well."

James examined the solid gold seal for a moment and then took the signet ring from its cushion.

"I have seen this before," he said, recognising the ring. "Isn't it yours?"

"Yes, it used to be, when I was your age," Darcy replied. "I wear my father's now."

James nodded and then slid the ring onto his finger, trying it on for size. It fit perfectly and Elizabeth smiled at this further proof of the similarities between father and son.

"Thank you, Father," James said, sounding pleased. "I...This means very much to me."

"You are welcome, Son," Darcy replied warmly, feeling very proud.

෫෬

It was very hard for them all when the time came to say goodbye to James. His lessons were to resume the following day, so after dinner they took him back to his school and said their goodbyes outside on the steps to his dormitory. It was already dark, but it was still clear that James was very sorry to see them go. He was openly upset, and Darcy spent several moments speaking quietly to him, offering him words of support and comfort. When it was her turn to say goodbye, Elizabeth held him tightly and told him that she loved him and would miss him dearly. When James replied that he loved her and would miss her too, Elizabeth couldn't hold back the tears.

Catherine, of course, was equally upset to say goodbye and clung to her brother fiercely, alternating between pleading with him to come back home and demanding that they stay. Eventually Darcy managed to coax her away, and she wept against his shoulder as James waved to them all and then disappeared inside. When they returned to the inn, Elizabeth put Catherine to bed whilst Darcy saw to their travel arrangements for the next morning. When he joined

Elizabeth in his daughter's room he found her sat upon the bed, rocking Catherine in her arms and softly singing to their little girl.

Approaching the bed, Darcy carefully sat down and smoothed some of Catherine's hair behind her ear before softly stroking her cheek. Eventually Catherine drifted off to sleep and Elizabeth carefully lay her down and Darcy covered her with the quilt.

"Come," he whispered to Elizabeth when he had straightened and it seemed as though Catherine would remain asleep.

Neither was of a mind to go and sit downstairs, so they instead went to their room, taking a seat beside the fire and falling into a quiet discussion of the day they had had.

"I like Philip very much," Elizabeth stated at one point. "He seemed a lovely boy."

"Yes," Darcy agreed. "Much as James had described in his letters; though I confess I was surprised to see him look so...pale. From what James has told us of their adventures together, I expected him to be rather heartier than he appeared."

"I, too," Elizabeth admitted. "But for all his appearance of frailty, he was lively enough today at the manor. There was a moment when I was sure the housekeeper was going to scold us all for being too boisterous!"

Darcy chuckled warmly at the memory, his eyes crinkling in a smile.

"Yes, she was rather fierce, wasn't she?"

"Quite intimidating," Elizabeth agreed.

"I am glad James has made such a good friend," Darcy admitted after a moment. "It was one of my greatest fears that he would not fit in with the other boys; his as well, I know."

Elizabeth nodded sympathetically and reached out to briefly press her husband's hand. Darcy smiled at her and turned his hand over, catching her fingers and holding them.

"He seemed quite happy, didn't he?" he asked, and Elizabeth knew he was seeking reassurance.

"Yes," she stated confidently.

"He was upset when we left him, though," Darcy pointed out with a slight frown.

"Saying goodbye was hard for us all," Elizabeth reasoned fairly. "And I daresay that will become easier with time. He will need more time to adjust to this change - we all will - but I think he is as happy as we can expect him to be under the circumstances. He will be alright," she assured her husband with an affectionate smile and Darcy returned it with a rueful one of his own.

"It would have pleased me to have been able to make the acquaintance of this Mr Seymour whom I have heard so much about," he commented after a moment.

"Yes," Elizabeth agreed. "I daresay Mr Hughes is beginning to feel quite jealous!"

Darcy smiled and then noticed that Elizabeth had become thoughtful; she was remembering something James had said; or rather, not said.

"Did you...do you think, when James said that Mr Seymour was nice to them, do you think he was intimating that his other tutors beat them?" she asked tentatively, having heard about such things but unable to imagine James being subjected to such treatment.

Darcy's jaw tightened as he stiffly replied.

"I am almost certain that is exactly what he was intimating. Certainly when I was at school, our tutors often beat us. Fortunately, James is a good boy and studious; he will not incur the wrath of his tutors as easily as some other boys inevitably will. His rank will also spare him the worst treatment, as well," Darcy added.

"Really?" Elizabeth asked, surprised.

"Of course," Darcy replied. "To beat the son of a rich gentleman is one thing; to beat the son of a Duke is entirely another."

Elizabeth frowned delicately.

"James had best be a genius when he leaves school, else I am not sure his attending will be at all worth the hardship."

Darcy chuckled in spite of himself. Of course he did not like the thought of his son being treated in such a way - indeed, he rather despised it - but it was just the way of things. He had endured the same, and likely James' sons would endure the same as well.

They spoke for several minutes more until Darcy, noticing Elizabeth struggling to suppress a yawn, glanced at the clock. He then looked back at his wife and suggested that they retire early. Elizabeth welcomed the suggestion and said that she would call for Wilson.

"I am sure we can make do by ourselves," Darcy stated as he offered his wife his hand.

Elizabeth easily recognised his look and smiled softly as she placed her hand in his. Darcy had just assisted her to her feet and was drawing her into his arms when they were both surprised to hear a light knock at the door. Exchanging curious glances, they separated to a more respectable distance and Darcy called out to the person to enter.

Catherine's head appeared in the gap of the door.

"Papa?"

"Princess!" Darcy exclaimed softly, ushering her inside; he glanced outside into the hallway and was relieved to see it empty. He did not like that his daughter had ventured from her room alone. "Why are you out of bed?"

Elizabeth was already wrapping Catherine in her spare dressing gown, conscious of the fact that Catherine was only in her nightgown and likely cold.

"I can't sleep," Catherine replied in a small voice, sounding tearful.

"But you were sleeping so soundly before," Elizabeth replied gently.

"Come, I shall take you back to bed, princess," Darcy said, stepping forward.

Catherine began to cry in earnest and shook her head.

"I don't want to go to bed! I don't want to leave! I want to stay here with James!" She declared tearfully and both Elizabeth and Darcy knew they had reached the crux of the matter.

For once Darcy hesitated before replying, his instincts failing him for a moment. Part of him wished to comfort his daughter, but another part of him wanted to be a little firmer with her now that she was getting older. Fortunately, Elizabeth seemed to know just what to say.

"We do not want to leave either, princess," she softly stated. "Of course we don't. But though it is hard for us, we also want James to be happy and I think that he is happy at school. Didn't he seem happy to you today?"

"He was crying when we left," Catherine stubbornly persisted.

"Because he loves us and wishes not to be apart from us," Elizabeth reasoned. "As we love him and wish not to be apart from him. Saying goodbye is always difficult, and it is only natural to feel sad, but I think that your brother is happy to be at school, to be making friends and learning so much. It is hard, but sometimes we have to set aside our own feelings in favour of those of the people we love. James is growing up, he is becoming a young man, and we have to let him do what makes him happy. And we will see him again soon," Elizabeth concluded with a reassuring smile. "Christmas is not so many weeks away; and in the meantime I am sure he will send us very many letters."

"But..." Catherine began to argue but Darcy gently but firmly interrupted her.

"What your mother says is true, princess; it is time for James to move on with his life. I know it is hard, but we must learn to accept the change and do our best to support him. Now say goodnight, and I will take you back to bed."

Elizabeth smiled and pressed an affectionate kiss to Catherine's cheek, watching as the little girl accepted Darcy's hand and they quietly left the room. Whilst Darcy was gone she changed out of her dress and into her nightgown, and was just turning down the bed when he reappeared.

"She is asleep," he replied to Elizabeth's questioning look. "Let us hope she remains so this time."

"Today must have been very difficult for her," Elizabeth commented as she got into bed. She sat back against the pillows and watched as her husband began to undress. "I remember crying so hard when Jane first left Longbourn, and I was older than Catherine is now."

"But Catherine has us," Darcy responded, the silent implication being that Elizabeth had had no-one.

"It is hardly the same," Elizabeth argued fairly. "I am sure if you asked your sister she would tell you how hard it was for her when *you* left," she pointed out with a smile and Darcy was forced to admit that she was probably right.

# Chapter 30

The day following their return to Pemberley, Darcy and Elizabeth went to see Jane, Sir Charles and baby Henry. They found upon their arrival that they were not the only visitors and were delighted to find Mr and Mrs Bennet in attendance. Whilst Darcy disappeared with the other men to Sir Charles' study (after giving Jane his compliments, of course), Elizabeth sat down with the ladies.

"He is a beautiful baby, Jane," she complimented her sister sincerely, smiling softly down at the baby sleeping soundly and feeling very maternal.

"How could he be otherwise, with two such handsome parents?" Mrs Carstone replied happily and Jane smiled demurely at the compliment. "Such a handsome little boy he is, and he'll be a handsome man, too, I'll wager."

Mrs Carstone was a lady a little younger than Mrs Bennet and wife to one of Sir Charles' business associates, who had enjoyed some success and purchased an estate in the neighbourhood. Elizabeth had tried her hardest to like her, but found the lady vulgar and ill-mannered, though Jane seemed to like her well enough.

Elizabeth wasn't quite sure how anyone could call a baby less than a week old "handsome", but she let the comment pass and turned instead to her aunt, asking when she and Mr Bennet had arrived.

"They came as soon as they could," Jane replied before Mrs Bennet could. "Didn't you, Aunt? You left the very day you received our letter, I'm certain Uncle said. It was so good of you to come straight away, though I know I should not have been surprised - you always have been so attentive."

This was said with all of Jane's usual sweetness, and Mrs Bennet responded as warmly as could be expected; Elizabeth meanwhile felt the underlying criticism in Jane's words and was stung by the intimation. To respond, however, would have seemed quarrelsome; a fact which irritated Elizabeth exceedingly.

Unfortunately, this was the first of many such comments from Jane and Elizabeth soon lost count of the number of barbs which her sister sent her way - though Jane never said anything which could openly be construed as critical or harsh. Elizabeth spent most of the time she was with her sister alternating between wondering whether she was imagining it all and wondering whether her sister was really so mean spirited. She had just resolved to just let it pass regardless when Jane made the mistake of mentioning James.

Mrs Bennet was the one to raise the subject.

"I understand from Sir Charles that you and your husband were from home when little Henry here was born?"

"Oh, no Aunt," Jane responded. "Elizabeth did not leave Pemberley until two days later."

"And you did not make time to visit with your new nephew!" Mrs Carstone put in, smiling an admonition at Elizabeth. "I should have been very put out if you were *my* sister, Your Grace. Lady Bingley, I hope you scolded her for the slight," she added teasingly.

"On the contrary," Elizabeth stated, forcing herself to smile. "My sister was very understanding of the circumstances."

"But of course you had to go and see James, rather than stay and see me and Henry," Jane replied lightly. "What difference does a few days make, after all?"

"Less to a new born baby than James, certainly," Elizabeth snapped, suddenly unable to let the undercurrents go ignored any longer. "I won't apologise for prioritising James over Henry, Jane."

"Apologise, Lizzy?" Jane repeated with bewildered confusion as Mrs Bennet and Mrs Carstone both regarded Elizabeth with expressions of surprise. "Why, I never asked you to."

Elizabeth made a muted sound of frustration and abruptly stood up. With a herculean effort she refrained from saying what she wanted to.

"I beg you will excuse me, I am tired and wish to return home. Aunt, you and Uncle are welcome to visit us at Pemberley. Jane, congratulations, I am happy for you and Charles and I hope Henry continues well. Mrs Carstone, it was nice to see you again. Good day to you, ladies."

She swept from the room without waiting for a response and was grateful when no one followed her; she didn't trust herself to speak to anyone but her husband, whom she sent for at the same time she asked for their carriage to be brought round. Darcy needed only one look to see that something was amiss, and that it had nothing to do with Elizabeth being tired. He silently accepted his coat from the footman and then led his wife outside to the front steps where they could await their carriage in relative privacy.

"Jane?" he asked quietly once they were alone; Elizabeth nodded mutely. "What did she say?"

Elizabeth growled her frustration.

"Nothing, everything; I don't know. It all *seemed* so inconsequential ."

"She must have said something," Darcy pressed gently and Elizabeth looked up at him doubtfully.

"She *did*, but everything she said seemed as nothing, too. Indeed, if asked, I am certain my aunt and Mrs Carstone would report that of the two of us, *I* was the one to speak harshly to Jane."

"Elizabeth, love, you are not making much sense," Darcy replied quietly and Elizabeth smiled at his apologetic look. "I don't understand."

"Here is the carriage," she pointed out, taking his hand. "Let us go now and I will try to explain."

"Very well," Darcy agreed, and allowed his wife to lead him down to the carriage where, once they were underway, she tried to fulfil her promise and explain what had happened with Jane.

Darcy's opinions of Elizabeth and Jane, high and low respectively, meant that he had no difficulty believing that the latter had been criticising her sister, and that the former could not have possibly imagined all of the little barbs which Jane had sent her way. Elizabeth owned that she was both relieved and dismayed by his opinion, if only because of what it said about her sister.

"How long has Jane been this way?" she wondered. "Have I just been fortunate in the past not to incur her displeasure, or is this some new facet to her character? Or was I just too ignorant to perceive what I now do so easily? And does *she* perceive what she is doing?" she asked no one in particular, struck by this new thought. "That is more to the point, I think. Does she know and intend to be so hurtful, or is she unconscious of how her words can be construed? I do not know which is worse."

"Elizabeth," Darcy intoned firmly, taking her hand. "You said you would no longer waste your time thinking about this - about any of this."

"I know!" Elizabeth replied; she sighed heavily. "I know; and I won't. I just need a moment to compose myself. You should be proud of my restraint, my love; how I kept my temper in check I do not know."

"It was more than Jane deserves, certainly," Darcy responded. "But I am glad of it; I do not think it would be good for anyone for there to be a complete breach, or to have others know of any discord between you."

"Oh, I know," Elizabeth assured him. "And there is little danger of that – Daniel, Catherine and James would suffer for it and I would not do that to them. This was our first meeting since our quarrel; I shall simply have to hope that in future Jane and I can be in one another's company without any discord."

"You know I will always be here for you, no matter what happens; and James and Catherine - we are your family too, and we love you. Your father and Jane...I know you cannot just forget about them or completely set them aside, but please just remember that you will always have us."

"William," Elizabeth replied softly, staring up at him tenderly. "I could never forget that. I love you all, and being part of this family makes me happier than I have ever been."

"I assure you, Elizabeth, the feeling is mutual," Darcy responded and was rewarded with a loving kiss.

ℰꙮℭ

"More tea, Claire?" Elizabeth offered as she refilled her own cup and her friend smiled and nodded, offering hers. "Victoria?"

"Please," Lady Victoria replied after quickly finishing the last of the cup she had. "It is nice to be able to have just a normal cup of tea, rather than the exotic blend my mother is currently obsessed with. I told you, did I not, that she had it from her friend, whose son had it from a business associate who had recently received a shipment from India. Apparently *everyone* is desperate to try it, but personally I cannot see what all the fuss is about."

"Everyone is always desperate to try what is new and exotic," Claire pointed out.

"Yes, Mr Healy said as much when I discussed it with him," Lady Victoria admitted. "The poor man - mother made him drink some of the new tea and I could tell he despised it, but he was far too polite to show it!"

"So, Mr Healy has been to call, has he?" Elizabeth asked with a teasing smile, sharing a look with Claire.

"You never told us that before, Victoria," Claire added, catching on quickly.

"No, stop it!" Lady Victoria protested laughingly, realising what they were trying to do; but she blushed ever so slightly and Elizabeth smiled delightedly on perceiving it.

"You're blushing!" She teased her friend. "Just how many times has he been to call on you?"

"Only twice," Lady Victoria responded. "And I am not blushing!"

"You most certainly are," Claire countered decisively.

"Well...well, that is only because you have embarrassed me!" Lady Victoria defended herself.

"Are you sure?" Elizabeth pressed, enjoying teasing her friend.

"Yes. I will not deny that I think Mr Healy rather charming, or that I find him quite handsome, but I am hardly infatuated with him. I have only been in company with him on three occasions; and even if I *were* inclined to think of him in that way, he is far too young for me and his prospects are not at all promising - certainly not promising enough for him to consider marrying the daughter of an earl."

"But if you weren't the daughter of an earl?" Elizabeth asked curiously.

"If I weren't the daughter of an earl? Well, as I said, I think him rather handsome and very charming." Lady Victoria responded with a smile, it now being her turn to tease her friends.

"But as you are, however, the daughter of an earl, we shall not expect to hear any news regarding you and Mr Healy," Claire Hadlee stated with a light laugh. "And we shall try to refrain from teasing you any further."

"Please do," Lady Victoria replied warmly. "I have an infuriating tendency to blush with only the slightest provocation when it comes to such matters!"

"Speaking of news," Elizabeth began after allowing herself a light laugh at Lady Victoria's joke. "I have some that I would like to share with you both."

"Really? Do go on," Claire encouraged, sounding intrigued. Lady Victoria was similarly attentive.

"Yes; in fact, I have wanted to tell you for a long time," Elizabeth admitted with a happy smile, her excitement bubbling up to the surface. "I had thought it best to wait, but I cannot stand to do so any longer."

"You are pregnant!" Claire guessed suddenly and when Elizabeth laughed and nodded both of her friends were very vocal in their excitement as they both threw their arms around her.

"Oh Lizzy, *congratulations!*" Lady Victoria declared breathlessly. "I am so happy for you!"

"But how far along are you?" Claire asked, drawing back and surveying Elizabeth with a critical eye. "Have you felt the quickening yet?"

"No, not yet," Elizabeth admitted. "But I have begun to show already. We expect that I will feel something within the next few weeks, God willing."

"I thought you looked different somehow," Lady Victoria declared. "Oh, and that is why you have not ridden for so long!" She realised suddenly, laughing at the thought that she had not realised before.

"Yes," Elizabeth admitted with a smile. "I wanted to tell you earlier, both of you, but I know it is best to wait until one is more certain."

"Do not concern yourself, we understand," Claire assured her and Lady Victoria nodded her agreement. "Your husband must be delighted," Claire noted.

"He is quite pleased, yes," Elizabeth admitted with a soft smile which spoke volumes.

"And the children, do they know?" Lady Victoria asked.

"Not yet," Elizabeth replied. "It was too early when James left for school, and we wanted to tell them both together. I will hopefully have felt the quickening by the time he returns for Christmas, and we will tell both he and Catherine then."

"They will be happy to have another sibling, I'm sure," Claire stated positively. "But come, you must tell us more. When is the baby expected? And have you begun to make any arrangements? Are you planning to have the baby here, or in London? And do you know who you are going to have with you when the time comes? If you need me, I will happily aid you."

Elizabeth smiled and touched her friend's hand affectionately.

"Thank you Claire, that is a lovely thought. The baby is expected sometime in the spring, and I hope to be able to remain here at Pemberley. As to who I wish to have with me, Wilson will be all the support I need," she stated confidently. "I have yet to decide on a midwife, but as long as Wilson is there I am sure I will be fine. Thank you, though, for offering to be with me," she added.

"No thanks needed," Claire assured her. "And I am content knowing that you will not be alone, though if you are seeking a midwife I would recommend my own to you. She was very competent."

Elizabeth smiled and glanced at Lady Victoria.

"Perhaps we could discuss it further when there are no unmarried ladies present," she teased and was delighted by her friend's reaction.

"Oh Lizzy!" Lady Victoria protested. "You sound like my father."

"I am only trying to preserve your innocence," Elizabeth replied, smiling.

"That is exactly what he says!" Lady Victoria responded and all three friends shared a laugh.

ಐಲ೪

Since James' departure for school, the weeks had passed very quickly and the weather had begun to change from summer to autumn and, lately, from autumn into the beginnings of winter. Indeed, since their return from their visit to James for his birthday, Elizabeth had noticed a decided chill in the air which signalled the inevitable arrival of the colder weather. The passage of weeks had also wrought a change with regards to Catherine, who seemed to have suddenly grown quite a bit taller. These two factors combined necessitated a trip to Lambton to purchase the young girl some new winter garments, and Elizabeth arranged the outing with pleasure - she had fond memories of similar outings with her mother when she was still a girl.

They left Darcy to his estate business and took the carriage to Lambton, Catherine promising that she would bring him something back. Their first port of call was to the shoemakers to purchase Catherine a new pair of half-boots; she had taken to joining Elizabeth on some of her walks and needed more suitable footwear.

"That tickles!" She giggled when the proprietor was measuring the length of her foot; he was a middle-aged man and seemed quite charmed by Catherine.

"I do apologise, My Lady," he said as he turned to her other foot. "Just this one left to do now."

Catherine nodded and sat very still, and Elizabeth smiled when she saw her bite her lip to keep from giggling again when the shoemaker touched the sensitive sole of her foot.

"All done," the shoemaker pronounced, getting to his feet. He turned to his daughter who was hovering in the background. "You may assist Lady Catherine with her shoes now."

"I can manage," Elizabeth assured him lightly as she stepped forwards; before the shoemaker or his daughter could protest she had knelt down and helped Catherine put on her shoes, leaving the young girl to tie them as she got to her feet and faced the shoemaker once more. "Shall we discuss which style my daughter would prefer?"

"Of course, Your Grace," he granted, overcoming his surprise. "When Lady Catherine is ready."

"I'm ready!" Catherine announced and appeared at Elizabeth's side. "I should like some boots just like Mama's."

Elizabeth smiled and helpfully held out her foot so that the shoemaker could see the boots she wore. They were, she explained, simple, comfortable and sturdy and fit for their purpose.

"Mama and I like to walk, don't we, Mama?" Catherine added, looking up at Elizabeth.

"Yes, we do," Elizabeth agreed with a smile. "Catherine already has a very fine pair of boots at home - made by yourself, I believe - so we are seeking a more practical pair for her today," she explained.

The shoemaker nodded and assured her that it would be no trouble at all to make Catherine a pair of boots similar to her own, and that he would have them ready within a week. Elizabeth thanked him for his time, encouraged Catherine to do the same, and then took their leave.

"Well, that is our first task complete," she said once they had stepped outside, smiling down at her daughter. "What was next on our list?"

Catherine eagerly reached into the pocket of her coat and drew out the list they had compiled together.

"A new winter coat," she read out.

"Ah yes," Elizabeth remembered and offered Catherine her hand. "Off we go, then!"

A new winter coat was followed by several new pairs of gloves and two new bonnets. Their last stop was at the dressmakers, where Elizabeth intended to surprise Catherine with a special treat.

"Good day to you, Your Grace," the proprietor, Mrs Kendall, greeted them. "And good day to you, Lady Catherine. It is a pleasure to see you both again."

"Thank you Mrs Kendall," Elizabeth replied with a gracious smile. "It is a pleasure to see you and your daughters again, also."

"Can I offer you some tea?" Mrs Kendall asked as she ushered Elizabeth and Catherine towards the small sitting area and her daughters came forward ready to assist in any way they could.

"Some tea would be lovely, thank you," Elizabeth replied. "The weather is rather unpleasant today."

"Indeed it is," Mrs Kendall agreed and one of her daughters disappeared to make the tea. When she returned Mrs Kendall poured cups for Elizabeth and Catherine and only once this task was complete did she ask, "How may I be of service today, Your Grace?"

"We are here for Catherine today," Elizabeth responded, smiling down at her daughter who was demonstrating what a good little girl she was by sitting perfectly and quietly sipping her tea. "What does our list say, princess?"

Catherine carefully set down her cup and consulted the list once more, "I need...We would like," she corrected herself, "three new day dresses and two new nightdresses, as I have grown out of the ones I have."

"Yes, I can see that you are a little bit taller than you were last time I saw you, Lady Catherine," Mrs Kendall noted and Catherine smiled shyly at the observation.

"There is also one other item I would like to add to that list," Elizabeth put in, hiding her smile with an effort. "My husband and I are hosting our families for Christmas, and I should like Catherine to have a special dress for Christmas Day."

Mrs Kendall smiled as Catherine gasped delightedly.

"Really, Mama?"

"Of course," Elizabeth replied lightly. "It is a special occasion."

"Thank you," Catherine responded sincerely and she reached up and pressed a kiss to Elizabeth's cheek, who was very pleased at the gesture.

"You are welcome, princess. Now," she said, turning her attention back to Mrs Kendall, "We place ourselves entirely in your hands, Mrs Kendall."

"Let us look at some fashion plates first," Mrs Kendall replied and one of her daughter's promptly appeared with them, "and see what is to Lady Catherine's taste."

Catherine needed no further encouragement; she sat forward and eagerly considered each option Mrs Kendall laid before her. Elizabeth made the occasional comment, but for the most part she allowed Catherine to speak for herself, feeling happy and proud in the way that a mother feels happy and proud.

When they eventually returned to Pemberley, Darcy was ready and waiting for them in one of the parlours with warm tea and sandwiches. Catherine was too eager to tell him about their excursion to think of taking any sustenance, but Elizabeth gratefully accepted a cup of tea and sat down to listen to Catherine's excited monologue.

"...and after the shoemakers we went to Mr Ellis for my new coat and gloves - it is a lovely green colour, Papa, and we ordered some gloves to match - and then we went to buy some new bonnets, because my blue one has broken and the green and pink one is looking a little worn. And then," she went on with emphasis, "and then we went to Mrs Kendall's and Mama was so good and surprised me when she told Mrs Kendall that, as well as the day dresses and nightdresses which were on our list, as well as those we would like a dress made especially for me for Christmas Day. And Papa," Catherine concluded with a dreamy smile as Darcy nodded along helplessly, trying to keep up with her rapid flow of words, "it is *beautiful*. Or it will be, once it is finished. The style is similar to my pink dress, the one Lady Matlock gifted to me, though a little different around the collar. I did not think we would find the fabric for it today, but Mrs Kendall said that she had just had some new fabrics delivered and thought she had the very one for my dress - and it was perfect, Papa! It is cream with a lovely embroidered pattern and we found some lace to match for the sleeves and some pale yellow ribbon for the waist. I think I will look very nice in it."

"You will look beautiful," Elizabeth assured her, glancing amusedly at her husband who had yet to say a word.

"Well, it sounds like you had a very nice time," he said at last. "And I shall look forward to seeing your lovely dress at Christmas."

Catherine smiled and then suddenly remembered.

"Oh, we ordered you a new hat to replace the one Deirdre clawed."

Darcy laughed.

"Thank you; that was kind of you. I rather liked that hat," he commiserated playfully, shooting a look at his wife who held up her hands.

"You can hardly blame *me*; I was not the one who left your hat where Deirdre could get to it."

"I could have left it atop the wardrobe," Darcy countered. "She still would have mauled it."

"Probably," Elizabeth admitted with complete unconcern; Darcy huffed when Catherine stifled a giggle.

"I miss James; there are too many females in this household combining against me," he complained good-naturedly, which just made Catherine laugh outright.

ဆါ

Elizabeth looked down at Catherine as the two of them walked together along one of the many pathways which criss-crossed Pemberley's grounds.

"Are your new boots more comfortable now, Catherine?"

Catherine smiled and nodded and bounced along a few steps to demonstrate.

"Yes, much more comfortable."

"They do sometimes take a little time to wear in," Elizabeth replied as they wandered along together. "Luckily the weather has been nicer these last few days else we would not have been able to walk."

"It is a bit muddy, though," Catherine pointed out, indicating her new boots which were now coated in a thick layer of mud.

Elizabeth smiled.

"That is just what boots are for. And you are more fortunate than I," she added, picking up the hem of her dress which was of course much longer than Catherine's. "Look at my petticoat - six inches deep in mud at least!"

Catherine giggled.

"Will Wilson scold you?"

"Probably," Elizabeth admitted with a grin and Catherine laughed.

Poppy, who had chased off after a squirrel, ran back over to them and Catherine picked up a stick and began playing with her; Elizabeth stood by watching their antics, smiling to herself. It was probably only because she was standing so still that she felt the gentle fluttering sensation in her stomach.

"Oh!" She exclaimed softly, her hand flying to her stomach. She felt the fluttering again, ever so gentle, and felt answering tears appearing in her eyes.

"Mama?" Catherine asked, looking at her curiously. "Are you alright?"

"Yes," Elizabeth breathed softly; a delighted smile appeared on her face. "Yes, I am perfectly alright. I have...I've just remembered there was something I needed to tell your papa; would you mind very much if we cut short our walk?"

"No I wouldn't mind," Catherine granted easily and she walked over to Elizabeth's side.

"Thank you," Elizabeth said, offering her hand and, on impulse, kissing Catherine's cheek.

Catherine smiled happily at the unexpected gesture and took Elizabeth's hand as Elizabeth called to Poppy to follow them. She could no longer feel the sensation in her stomach, but once was enough. It was with an effort that she kept her pace leisurely, so eager was she to return to the house and find her husband.

"Is my husband still in his study?" she asked the butler when they got back to the house and they were being helped out of the coats.

"His Grace has had to go out on a matter of business," the butler responded. "He asked that I tell you that he will return in time for dinner, Ma'am."

"Thank you," Elizabeth replied and struggled to hide her disappointment. The butler must have noticed, though, because he went on.

"I believe His Grace has only gone so far as Homerton, if you desire his return."

"No, it is fine," Elizabeth forced herself to smile. "Thank you anyway; I shall wait to see him at dinner."

"Very well Ma'am," the butler responded with a slight bow.

"Do I have to go back to my lessons now, Mama?" Catherine asked her and Elizabeth nodded as she looked down at the young girl.

"Yes, I'm afraid so princess. You know it is important for you to attend to your lessons."

"I know," Catherine sighed.

"And I thought Mrs Hughes meant to tutor you in French this afternoon," Elizabeth reminded her. "You enjoy French, do you not?"

"Yes, I suppose I do," Catherine admitted. "More than arithmetic, at least," she added darkly and Elizabeth hid her smile.

"In that case, go on up to Mrs Hughes and I will see you later for dinner."

Catherine did as she was asked, leaving Elizabeth to herself. Feeling strangely deflated, now that she had no one with whom to share her momentous news, it took Elizabeth a moment to realise that there was someone *very* important who deserved to know.

"Wilson?" she called when she entered her bedroom, not seeing her maid anywhere within the main room. Deirdre, who had been asleep on the bed, made a noise of protest at being awakened so rudely. "I'm sorry, sweet."

"In here," Wilson called from the direction of the dressing room; she was just getting to her feet when Elizabeth entered. "I was just...oh, Elizabeth Hyacinth Darcy, just look at your dress!"

Elizabeth laughed delightedly and thoroughly surprised her maid by rushing forward and throwing both arms around her. Wilson had little choice but to return the gesture, gingerly patting Elizabeth's back.

"Elizabeth?"

"I felt it!" Elizabeth announced joyously, pulling back and turning the full strength of her smile on Wilson. "The quickening; I felt it. It was just here," she explained, placing her hand over her small bump. "I felt it twice."

Part of her expected Wilson to say something sensible about how it was to be expected, but Wilson surprised her by becoming rather emotional.

"You did? Oh Elizabeth, that is wonderful. What did it feel like?" Wilson asked keenly.

"A gentle fluttering," Elizabeth described. "Like bubbles, almost. It was quite strange!" She admitted with a light laugh. "Though wonderful at the same time."

Wilson smiled and then reached into the pocket of her dress, withdrawing a handkerchief and using it to dab her eyes. Elizabeth watched all this with open affection and Wilson felt compelled to defend herself.

"It is not every day that the woman you helped deliver as a baby tells you that she has felt the first movements of her own baby."

"No, I suppose not," Elizabeth replied softly and grasped Wilson's hand.

Wilson returned the gesture and then tried to distract attention away from herself.

"How did your husband react to the news?"

"He has gone out," Elizabeth revealed with a wry smile. "You are the first person I have told," she added softly and Wilson was forced to dab away more tears.

"He will be delighted," Wilson predicted; she chuckled and added, "Even more so than usual."

"It is a pity it is only I who can feel it - though more will come in time, of course."

"I think you should enjoy your peace whilst you have it," Wilson advised her amusedly. "If this baby is anything like you were, you will not have a moment's rest. Your poor mother! You did not stop from morning till night."

"Oh dear," Elizabeth smiled at the picture Wilson painted. "Perhaps this baby has inherited some of its father's quiet nature."

"One can only hope," Wilson replied dryly and smiled at Elizabeth's happy laughter.

ᮝᮤᮌ

Darcy grinned ruefully at his butler as he hurried into the house.

"I know, I know, I am late. Have they started without me?"

"Lady Catherine has already dined, but your wife elected to wait for your return. They are both upstairs presently."

"Thank you," Darcy responded with a nod and left his coat and hat with the butler as he headed for the stairs, briskly ascending to the second floor. A quick word with a passing servant sent him in the direction of Catherine's room, and he knocked softly on the door before entering.

"Papa!" Catherine greeted him with a smile; she and Elizabeth were sat together, the latter reading aloud to the former. "You are back. You missed dinner."

"Yes, I'm sorry," Darcy replied apologetically, looking first at his daughter and then his wife; he was struck by the appearance of the latter and almost missed what Catherine said to him.

"We were just finishing this story; will you stay to hear the rest Papa? It is very good."

"I have a better idea," Elizabeth said, gently extracting herself from her place beside Catherine. "I will leave you both to finish the story whilst I see about some dinner for Papa and I."

"Alright," Catherine granted easily. "Goodnight then," she added and offered her cheek for a kiss, which Elizabeth happily bestowed.

"Good night princess."

Elizabeth got to her feet and faced her husband, who was looking at her expectantly, as though he knew that she had something very important to share with him. Not attempting to deny it, Elizabeth laid her hand on his arm as she passed.

"Later. I shall be in our rooms."

She left father and daughter to enjoy their book, confirming with a footman on her way to her room the arrangements she had made earlier for her and her husband to have their meal served in the sitting room adjoining their chambers. She had a feeling that they would appreciate a more intimate setting this evening. Once she had dismissed Wilson for the night, Elizabeth sat down to await the appearance of her husband, absently stroking Deidre when she climbed up onto her lap. She was not surprised to hear the resolute step of her husband not more than quarter of an hour later, and smiled at the thought that he must have rushed through the final two chapters of Catherine's book.

Darcy entered his wife's room and paused only to close the door behind him before approaching her.

"What is it?" he asked without preamble; there was something about her manner, about her appearance and bearing that left him with a sense of expectation. She appeared to be trying to suppress some emotion, though as soon as he had asked his question she answered him with a glowing smile.

"I felt it," Elizabeth replied as she got to her feet, carelessly dislodging Deirdre.

Darcy knew at once to what she was referring and one of his hands flew to her stomach, the palm pressed gently to the ever growing bump.

"When?"

"This afternoon," Elizabeth replied. "Catherine and I were out walking and I had stopped for a moment when I felt it. It was just like everyone has described to me," she admitted. "A gentle fluttering sensation, like bubbles almost."

"Have you felt it again since?" Darcy asked eagerly; when Elizabeth shook her head he nodded and stated reasonably, "It is still early yet. I am sure you will feel it more often as the baby grows."

"Wilson tells me that I was a very active baby," Elizabeth confessed with a smile. "Apparently I plagued my poor mother constantly."

"I can well believe it," Darcy replied with an affectionate grin. "Though I hope you are not made to endure too much."

"It will be worth it," Elizabeth responded confidently and they shared a smile.

Darcy looked down at his wife for a long moment before gently kissing her, releasing a contented sigh as he drew away.

"Finally. It feels as though we have waited so long for this day."

"I know," Elizabeth nodded her agreement and slipped her hands around her husband's waist, tucking herself under his chin. "I suppose now we may tell everyone," she commented after a moment.

"Yes," Darcy replied. They were both quiet and then almost simultaneously laughed lightly. "I do not wish to tell anyone!"

"Nor I," Elizabeth admitted, tilting her head back and smiling up at Darcy. "Though I suppose we should at least inform my aunt and uncle. I am sure my aunt suspected something when they were here, so she will be pleased to hear that she was right."

"She will be pleased for other reasons as well, I'm sure," Darcy noted amusedly. "I *would* like to tell Hadlee," he admitted after a pause. "And I am sure the Havershams, the Andersons and the

Hadlocks would all appreciate being told before the rest of our acquaintances are made aware."

Elizabeth nodded her agreement and then reminded him.

"Do not forget Lady Matlock; she will be most displeased if we neglect to inform her."

"Heaven forbid," Darcy responded with a wry smile. He smiled much more genuinely as he remarked, "We had best inform the staff as well - though I daresay they may already have their suspicions."

"It would be nice to make it official though, wouldn't it?"

"Yes," Darcy replied. "And we shall have to write to London and let the staff there know as well."

Elizabeth nodded and was a quiet a moment.

"I should write to my father as well, shouldn't I? For good or ill, this baby will be his grandchild."

"It certainly would not hurt to send him a letter," Darcy replied. "Though a lack of response may hurt *you*," he amended with a frown.

"I shall not expect one," Elizabeth replied lightly. "That way if one does not come, I will not be disappointed; and if one does, it will be a pleasant surprise."

Darcy smiled and they lapsed into a comfortable silence for a few minutes.

"Of course, we will have to wait a few weeks yet to tell the two most important people."

"Yes," Elizabeth replied. "Thank goodness James returns home in three weeks! I am not sure I could bear to wait much longer."

"Nor I," Darcy averred. "I cannot wait for their reactions."

"Nor I," Elizabeth agreed and she hoped that the next three weeks would pass by swiftly.

"Well," Darcy said after a moment. "After the news you have just given me I must say I am disinclined to spend the evening in anyone's company but yours, my love. Shall we have dinner served in our sitting room?"

"It is all arranged already," Elizabeth replied.

"Clever woman!" Darcy complimented her with a broad smile and Elizabeth laughed lightly at his enthusiasm.

ೞ೦ಚಿ

"Congratulations, Farleigh. If I were not so happy with my own good fortune, I'm sure I would quite envy yours."

Darcy chuckled lightly and touched his glass to his friend Hadlee's.

"Thank you, John."

"And you tell me that Claire already knows?" Hadlee went on after a moment, shaking his head with a smile. "She certainly kept that quiet! Should I be concerned that my wife is so adept at keeping secrets from me, do you think?"

"I politely refrain from commenting," Darcy replied and Hadlee laughed.

"Fair enough! So tell me, when is the baby expected?"

"In the spring," Darcy stated. He smiled softly as he admitted, "I first met Elizabeth in the spring of this year."

"So in one year you will have married her and had a child together; you've made good use of your time, Farleigh!" Hadlee joked, and then seeing that his friend was not of a mind to enter into the joke sobered and said instead, "As I said, you are very fortunate."

"That I well know," Darcy replied softly and intently. He shook off his reflective mood and smiled at his friend. "Speaking of time; isn't it time you provided your daughter with a sibling?"

"I am working on it," Hadlee responded flippantly and Darcy quirked a brow at him.

"Working?"

"Wrong choice of word," Hadlee admitted with a grin, shaking his head.

Darcy allowed himself a smile at his friend's expense before moving their conversation along.

"We plan to write to the rest of our neighbours and inform them that way, before the dinner the Hadlocks are hosting. I am sure Elizabeth will have plenty of callers once the news begins to spread, but at least this way we will be spared the necessity of visiting everyone individually."

"You could just tell Mrs Carstone and spare yourself the trouble of writing," Hadlee quipped dryly and Darcy rolled his eyes.

"I daresay there will be talk enough," he predicted sagely, "with a baby expected so soon into our marriage."

"Those who matter will not give credence to such gossip," Hadlee stated loyally.

"I know. We are confident that our friends will be nothing but happy for us."

"Good," Hadlee nodded, satisfied. He smiled and asked, "So, which would you like - a boy or a girl?"

"A girl, I think," Darcy admitted.

"Really?" Hadlee asked, surprised. "Not another son?"

"Elizabeth wishes for a son," Darcy replied. "In truth, I have not thought about it much; it does not seem that important."

"Most men can only say that once they have their heir and a spare," Hadlee noted with a smile.

"I dislike that term," Darcy responded with a slight frown. "And if this baby is a boy, he certainly won't be treated any differently than James."

"Will you be in the position to be able to do much for him?" Hadlee asked, referring to Darcy's holdings and the possibility of everything going to James.

"There is an estate from my mother which I am free to pass on as I wish," Darcy replied. "Though why we are discussing this I do not know; it could just as easily be a girl," he pointed out with a smile.

"Well whether a boy or girl, you have my congratulations – again - and I hope you will pass them on to your wife," Hadlee stated and Darcy bowed his head in recognition.

A few days later, he was once again accepting the congratulations of a friend when Sir Benedict proposed a toast.

"To the Duke and his lovely wife! I believe I speak for everyone here when I say congratulations, and good health to you both and your child!"

Darcy smiled down the dinner table at Elizabeth as the rest of their dinner companions joined in their host's toast, offering extra words of congratulations to the smiling couple. When Sir Benedict had re-seated himself, Darcy got to his feet and looked around the table at his neighbours and friends.

"Thank you for your kindness; Elizabeth and I are very grateful. And for myself; I have known many of you here for a long time, and you have been my friends through some...trying times. I am glad that now you will share with me in this happiest of times."

Elizabeth smiled softly at her husband as he sat back down and their friends responded warmly to his honest words. He did not often allude to it, and spoke of it even less, but Elizabeth knew that her husband had been quite a lonely and unhappy man during his first marriage, and she was grateful to all those people who had supported him during that time. She hoped, and liked to believe, that many of his friends were now her friends as well, and felt comforted that she could also rely on their support, should the occasion ever arise.

She was distracted from her thoughts by Lady Anderson, who sat immediately across from her, and Lady Hadlock, who sat at the head of the table on her right.

"We assume, since you have made the announcement that you are expecting, that you must have felt the quickening."

"Yes," Elizabeth admitted in response to Lady Hadlock's quiet query. "Last week was the first time and once again since then."

"Your figure does not seem much altered," Lady Anderson remarked, studying her lightly. "Though perhaps there is a slight change."

"I have begun increasing slightly," Elizabeth replied. "Though not enough to have to worry about purchasing new gowns. I shall have to think about it soon, though, I suppose."

"Oh, certainly," Lady Hadlock replied positively. "You will be amazed, my dear. You go so long with no changes at all, and then suddenly you begin to increase steadily until…"

"Until a little before the end, when you seem to double in size!" Lady Anderson joked and Lady Hadlock laughed her agreement and Elizabeth smiled at their levity.

"Perhaps we had best save further discussion until later," Lady Hadlock noted with a smile when she saw Mr Healy going slightly pink around the ears. "Before we embarrass poor Mr Healy any further."

"It is not just Mr Healy you should worry about," Lord Anderson remarked from beside his wife, though his smile was good-natured.

Lady Anderson introduced a new topic for conversation; or rather a variation on the original theme.

"How are your sister and her new son, Your Grace?"

Whilst Elizabeth spoke with Lady Anderson and Lady Hadlock, further down the table her husband was having an enjoyable conversation with her friend, Lady Victoria. He had always thought well of the young woman, and thought immeasurably more of her now that she and Elizabeth were such good friends.

"Elizabeth mentioned that you and your parents are not at home for Christmas," Darcy ventured once they had finished discussing his and Elizabeth's plans for the festive season. "Are you spending it with family?"

"Of a sort," Lady Victoria replied with a resigned expression. "A distant cousin of my father's is hosting a house party and mother has decided we shall all go."

"You do not welcome the prospect?" Darcy questioned delicately.

"I am sure it would be delightful, were we going because we wish to spend the season with our loved ones and friends," Lady Victoria replied. "But we are only going because of whom else is sure to be there, and thus the whole visit is sure to be a tiresome trial."

Darcy nodded lightly, reaching to take a sip of his wine; he understood that Lady Victoria's frustration stemmed from Lady Haversham's attempts to see her daughter married.

"Perhaps you might enjoy yourself," he pointed out fairly. "One can never know what to expect from a new introduction."

Lady Victoria laughed lightly and when Darcy looked at her with a quizzical smile she explained.

"Elizabeth said much the same thing to me once. It seems your own experience has filled you both with romantic optimism; if you do not mind my saying so," she added softly, wondering if she was supposed to speak so to a Duke, even one married to her dearest friend.

"Not at all; though please keep that intelligence to yourself. I fear I am a little too old to be taken seriously, if I admit to being such a romantic fool."

Lady Victoria laughed at his teasing and promised that his secret was safe with her.

Darcy nodded and turned his attention back to his meal, but a few moments later caught himself wondering whether he knew anyone he thought would suit the young woman beside him.

Romantic fool, indeed, he thought amusedly, shaking his head and smiling.

"Does something amuse you, Your Grace?" Lady Victoria asked from beside him, having seen his smile.

"Nothing I would care to admit to," Darcy responded and left Lady Victoria to wonder what he meant.

# Chapter 31

Hearing the sounds of a carriage, Darcy watched his daughter for her reaction. Catherine did not disappoint him; she tossed aside her book and sprang up from her chair, dashing from the room in a blur of green skirts with Poppy on her heels.

"Let us hope it is James' carriage," Elizabeth laughed lightly as she rose to join her husband and they followed after Catherine.

"Be careful on the steps!" Darcy cautioned his daughter; they had had snow that morning and he knew the steps would still be wet, though the staff would have cleared them and the drive of snow.

"James!" Catherine called excitedly as the carriage approached the house, barely able to stand still. She waved when James' face appeared in the window of the carriage. "Welcome home!"

James leapt down from the carriage the moment it was safe to do so, and delighted his sister by sweeping her round in a circle. It was a very noisy and joyous homecoming, and from his position atop the carriage, John the coachman watched the happy family with an affectionate grin.

"Come inside, come inside," Darcy said, ushering his two children into the house. "Come on ratbag," he added to Poppy, clicking his fingers when she continued to sniff at the wheels of the carriage. Poppy eventually obeyed the command and brushed past Elizabeth on her way into the house, leaving a wet smear on her dress.

"Lovely," Elizabeth said with a smiling grimace. "Oh well, never mind," she sighed resignedly and followed the children inside.

"She is so big!" James exclaimed when they reached the parlour and Poppy jumped up, resting her paws on his waist. "Look how tall she is now."

"You have been away for three months, Son," Darcy pointed out reasonably. "She has had plenty of time to grow."

"Yes, of course - I just never expected she would grow so much," James admitted with a grin. "She will be as big as Agatha if she carries on this way!"

"I sincerely hope not," Elizabeth remarked, shaking a head. "Agatha was such a well behaved, calm dog - her size was not a problem. Can you imagine if Poppy were as big, barrelling around the house like a mad thing?"

James and Catherine laughed at the thought, and even Darcy allowed himself a smile. He commanded Poppy to go and lay down in her spot in front of the fire, and was relieved when she obeyed. Happy now that he could give his son his full attention, Darcy turned to James.

"Well, Son, tell us how you have been. Your last letter was over two weeks ago now."

"Oh, I'm quite well, Father," James replied lightly. "You needn't worry about me. The past few weeks were rather hard, what with all the work we had to complete in time for the holiday, but I managed well enough. And the last three days of term we had no lessons at all, so Philip and I and many of the other boys spent the days in the snow. We had the most ferocious snowball fight, Father!"

"Philip as well?" Elizabeth questioned, remembering how frail James' friend had looked.

"Oh yes," James replied positively, grinning. "He has the best aim of anyone I know - I don't think he missed one single time. We were fighting against some of the older boys, and he hit one right in the face. I was glad Philip was on my team!" He concluded merrily.

"It sounds like you certainly enjoyed yourself," Darcy commented with a smile and James nodded.

"If it is alright with you Father, I told Philip that I would write to him over the holiday. His father's house is only in Lincoln."

"Of course it is alright with me, Son," Darcy assured James warmly. "I am sure that he wishes to spend Christmas with his family, but perhaps you might think about inviting him to spend some time here during your next holiday from school," he suggested.

"I was going to ask you about that," James admitted with a smile.

"Your friend is more than welcome, Son," Darcy replied and his son nodded, looking pleased.

"Will dinner be at the usual time?" James asked Elizabeth; when she replied in the affirmative he nodded, "Oh, good; I'm rather hungry. And I have been looking forward to enjoying Mrs Maddison's cooking again."

"Well I gather she has made special arrangements especially for tonight, so you will have a fine meal to look forward to," Elizabeth replied lightly.

"Will you come and see my room, James?" Catherine asked her brother, eager for his attention. "I have some new furniture, and the schoolroom has been re-arranged too. Come, let me show you."

"Alright," James laughed, allowing his sister to pull him up from the couch. "You do not mind?" he thought to ask Elizabeth and Darcy.

"Run along," Darcy responded with a smile, waving them off. "We will come and find you when it is time for dinner."

James smiled and let Catherine lead him away; Poppy got up and followed after them, leaving Elizabeth and Darcy alone in the sudden quiet.

"It is so good to have him home," Elizabeth said, smiling happily. Her husband readily concurred. "It was so sweet when he spun Catherine around."

"Yes," Darcy agreed. He smiled wistfully and added, "I used to do that with him. I doubt I could manage it these days."

"He does seem to have grown since we last saw him," Elizabeth admitted. "If that is at all possible! Whilst he is here I shall have to see if he requires some new clothes," she mused, making a mental note to ask.

"When would be the best time to tell them, do you think?" Darcy asked after a moment, touching Elizabeth's stomach briefly. "Before dinner?"

"After, I think," Elizabeth replied. "We have no plans tomorrow and so do not have to worry about their being a little late to bed. And if we tell them this evening there is no risk of their hearing it from anyone else."

They had informed their household staff that a baby was expected, and had asked that they be discreet around Catherine and James until they were both told the news, but Elizabeth would rather not tempt fate by delaying any longer than necessary.

"After dinner then," Darcy agreed. He smiled lopsidedly. "I feel a little nervous."

"Why?" Elizabeth asked with an intrigued look.

"I don't know really," Darcy replied. "Perhaps because their reactions are very important to me. I am nervous for them to be happy, though that is not to say that I doubt they will be," he added and Elizabeth leant up and pressed a kiss to his cheek.

"It will all be well," she assured him. "Come, I do not see why we must sit here by ourselves - let us go and join the children."

"Very well," Darcy agreed easily and they went upstairs together, finding James and Catherine in the schoolroom with Mr and Mrs Hughes. The couple were to leave in a few days to spend the festive season with some of Mrs Hughes' relations, but they had delayed their departure until after James' return.

"....and Mr Seymour is my history tutor - I'm sure Father has mentioned him to you - and he is by far my favourite tutor, though Mr Charles who teaches us the sciences is also quite good; though at times I think that he does not know quite as much about it as you do, Mr Hughes."

Darcy and Elizabeth shared a smile at James' honest compliment to his old tutor, who looked pleased to receive the praise. They listened happily to James answering the questions both Mr and Mrs Hughes put to him about his school and schoolwork, pleased that James seemed to be applying himself well.

"Come on James, you haven't seen my room yet," Catherine said, taking her brother's hand. "I want to show you my new writing desk."

"Is that where you sit and write your letters to me?" James asked as he let Catherine draw him away. "They are very good letters, by the way."

"Do you really think so?" The four adults all heard Catherine ask delightedly as the two children disappeared down the hallway, and Elizabeth shared a smile with her husband and Mr and Mrs Hughes.

"It seems James will have many demands upon his attention for the time being," she remarked lightly. "We shall have to take turns."

"It is lovely to see them together again," Mrs Hughes replied with an honest smile as her husband nodded his agreement. "Catherine has missed him very much."

"We all have, I think," Darcy commented quietly and the other couple did not deny it. "Will you be joining us for dinner?" he asked Mr and Mrs Hughes. "You are more than welcome to do so."

"We would be honoured, thank you, Sir," Mr Hughes replied after a silent conference with his wife. "Though only if we are not intruding."

"Nonsense," Darcy waved away their concern. "You are practically family."

"Thank you for saying so, Sir," Mr Hughes responded with a slight bow, sounding quite touched by the sentiment. "And if you are sure it will be no trouble, we will happily join you all for dinner."

"It is no trouble at all," Elizabeth assured them easily. "I am sure that Mrs Maddison will have outdone herself on account of James' return, and she will not be inconvenienced by having two more to serve. I shall go and speak with her directly," she concluded, smiling as she added, "I think we had best resign ourselves to only seeing James and Catherine again at dinner."

"I think you are right," Darcy agreed with a chuckle. "At least we have the rest of the holiday to spend time with him."

Elizabeth smiled and then excused herself to go and speak with the cook about the dinner arrangements. Darcy turned to Mr and Mrs Hughes and spent a few minutes discussing their travel arrangements with the couple before excusing himself as well.

He was walking along the hallway past Catherine's room when he heard his children's voices from within. Quietly drawing closer to the partially open door, he stopped a moment to listen.

"...and this is the special dress I wrote to you about. Mama had it made for me especially for Christmas Day. Don't you think it is the loveliest dress I've ever had?"

"It is very pretty," Darcy heard his son reply, and stifled a chuckle at James' tone, so similar to the one he knew he used when forced to comment on any aspect of a lady's wardrobe. "I'm sure you will look lovely in it, Cathy."

"Thank you. Will you have a special outfit, do you think?"

"Perhaps - I shall see what Father says. I do need some new things - some of my coats are a little short in the sleeve for me now."

"Mama would be happy to take you to Lambton."

"I think I will ask Father; he will know more about what I need, after all."

"He will like that. He has missed you very much."

"Has he?"

"He talks about you a lot, and last week when I needed some paper to write you a letter, I went to his study and I found all your letters in the drawer of his desk."

"I have kept all of his, and yours of course."

"I have yours here too. Look, this was the last one. Poppy tore the corner of it though, I'm sorry about that."

"Did she eat it?"

"Yes - she eats anything that you leave near her! She spoiled one of Mama's drawings last month, and Mama was very cross with her. I have never seen Mama so cross with anyone before."

Darcy quietly drew away from the door, glancing around himself to check that there was no one around to witness his next action as he reached up and wiped his eyes. Leaving his children to their conversation, he softly walked away, content and happy with his family all under one roof.

ॐ

"Have we all finished?"

Elizabeth shot an amused glance at James before replying to her husband.

"I think so; unless your son wishes for yet another portion of pudding."

"I have only had two!" James defended himself with a laugh. "But I could not eat another bite; that was delicious."

"I am glad you enjoyed it," Darcy replied before gesturing for the waiting footmen to come forward and clear their plates. "Please give our sincere compliments to Mrs Maddison for the superb meal," he instructed the footman clearing his plate and the young man nodded and withdrew.

"If we are all ready," Elizabeth said as she laid aside her napkin, "Let us go through to the drawing room."

"Can we have some music tonight please, Mama?" Catherine asked as she hopped down from her chair and went to Elizabeth's side.

"Perhaps later," Darcy responded before Elizabeth could. "There is something your mother and I wish to tell you both, but if you still wish it, we can have some music afterwards."

Catherine immediately asked what they wanted to tell them, but James just looked curiously between his father and Elizabeth, silently questioning.

"My wife and I shall retire now, Sir," Mr Hughes stated as they all left the small dining room together. "She is a little tired tonight."

"Very well," Darcy replied with a grateful smile. He would not have minded the other couple being present when he and Elizabeth shared their news, but he appreciated their excusing themselves nonetheless. "Thank you for joining us for dinner."

"It was our pleasure," Mr Hughes responded and then said a quick goodnight to Catherine and James, the latter of whom asked if Mr Hughes would be available on the morrow to speak with him about some of his schoolwork.

After Mr Hughes had assured James that he had no plans for the following day, the couple disappeared upstairs to their rooms. Alone with the two children, Elizabeth and Darcy ushered them into the drawing room where tea things awaited them and Poppy lay asleep on the carpet in front of the fire.

"Come, sit with us," Darcy said to his children as he and Elizabeth sat at either ends of one of the couches. Catherine hopped up beside him, tucking herself into his side, and James sat down next to Elizabeth, looking expectantly between them.

"What do you have to tell us, Papa?" Catherine asked eagerly. "Is it a surprise?"

"Yes, I suppose you could call it that," Darcy replied slowly. Before going on he glanced at Elizabeth, who nodded encouragingly. They had decided beforehand that he would be the one to first share the news. "You see princess, Son, Elizabeth and I, we...You are going to have a new brother or sister. Elizabeth is going to have a baby."

"A baby!" Catherine cried joyously.

"Yes," Elizabeth laughed, delighted by the young girl's genuine and spontaneous reaction as much as she was by James' broad smile. "A baby - sometime in the spring, we believe."

"A boy or girl?" Catherine asked excitedly, before correcting herself hurriedly, "Oh, no, you do not know, do you? I remember Lady Jane said that. Oh I hope it is a girl!"

Darcy laughed and pulled his daughter into his arms, hugging her tightly and making her laugh. Elizabeth was watching the pair and so was slightly caught off guard when James suddenly put his arms around her and kissed her cheek.

"Congratulations!"

"Thank you James," Elizabeth responded warmly when he pulled away, one hand on his shoulder as the other touched his cheek in an affectionate gesture. He blushed as always, but his broad smile remained in place.

"So, I shall have a new brother or sister in the spring," he said as Darcy and Catherine continued to chatter to each other beside him. "Have you known for very long?" he asked curiously.

"Since our trip to the seaside," Elizabeth admitted with a smile. "Though I only felt the quickening three weeks ago."

James nodded.

"That was why you fainted, and why you seemed so unwell, isn't it?"

"Yes," Elizabeth replied. "We wished to tell you both sooner, but it was too early when you left for school, and we wanted to tell you both together, in person."

James smiled and assured her that he understood.

"I thought when I saw you for the first time today that you looked different," he admitted with a shy grin which made Elizabeth laugh. "Now I know why."

Their little tete-a-tete was interrupted by Catherine, who hopped down from her place beside her father and came to embrace Elizabeth.

"Congratulations Mama!"

"Thank you princess," Elizabeth replied as she drew Catherine up and onto her lap, holding her close. "Are you happy you are going to have a new brother or sister?"

"Of course," Catherine declared. "Though I should be happier with a sister."

"Are brothers so bad?" James asked teasingly, and shared a smile with his father when he felt him chuckle beside him.

"You are not," Catherine replied magnanimously. "But if it is a girl we will be able to play dolls together and share all our things. And boys are bossy and messy and mean," she added with a frown.

"I am not mean!" James objected, sounding a little offended.

"I said not you!" Catherine responded spiritedly. "You are my brother; you're different."

"The baby will also be your brother, if it is a boy," Darcy pointed out fairly, sharing a smile with his wife over their daughter's head. "And he will also be your younger brother, too."

"Yes, so you can be the one to boss him around," James quipped with a grin, laughing lightly when his father playfully cuffed him round the head.

"No one will be bossing anyone around," Darcy declared, before adding playfully, "Except perhaps me."

"Hmmhmm," Elizabeth cleared her throat pointedly and arched a brow at her husband.

"And your mother," he added quickly and glared at his son when James stifled a laugh.

"Do you know the name yet?" Catherine asked eagerly. "Have you thought of one?"

Elizabeth smiled at her husband before replying.

"We thought perhaps Madeline if it is a girl, for my mother. We have not decided on a boy's name yet."

"Madeline is a nice name," Catherine decreed, nodding her approval. "Lady Madeline sounds nice."

"I am glad you think so, princess," Darcy replied teasingly, though his daughter missed the joke.

As Catherine continued to question Elizabeth, Darcy looked at his son. James smiled openly back at him.

"I am happy for you, Father."

"And for yourself, I hope?" Darcy asked lightly, though his eyes were serious.

"I am," James replied with a nod. "For all of us, really. Though most especially for you, I think," he added quietly, smiling affectionately at his father.

"For me?" Darcy questioned, surprised.

"For you," James reiterated, but did not elaborate. He just smiled and then turned to his sister to tease her about the possibility of Elizabeth having twins, and their both being boys, leaving his father to consider his words.

"William?" Elizabeth softly tried to get her husband's attention; when he eventually looked at her she smiled gently and told him, "Catherine would still like some music - shall we go through to the music room?"

"Of course," Darcy granted easily. "Though the pair of you must go up to bed soon," he added as he got to his feet and offered Catherine his hand. "It is getting rather late."

"Please, Papa, just a little longer?" Catherine pleaded prettily. "I promise I will go straight to sleep."

"I highly doubt you will be able to keep that promise, princess," Darcy commented wryly, believing that after all the excitement his daughter would likely be awake for a long time yet. "But we shall have some music, nevertheless."

As Darcy went on ahead with Catherine, James and Elizabeth walked together after them. His curiosity getting the better of him, James studied Elizabeth's figure and concluded that she did indeed look different to how he remembered. Elizabeth noticed his scrutiny and smiled when he blushed slightly at being caught.

"I am starting to show now," she said quietly, flattening down the front of her dress so that her bump was visible. James' eyes widened and then he smiled happily.

"Father must be delighted," he said, looking at Darcy walking ahead of them.

"Even more so now," Elizabeth replied with a nod; when James looked at her quizzically she explained, "He was anxious for your reaction - you and your sister. It was very important to him - to us both - that you and Catherine were happy with the news."

"We are," James averred, reaching out and pressing Elizabeth's hand in a spontaneous gesture. "We spoke about the possibility of siblings when father first proposed to you," he admitted with a smile of remembrance, "and we agreed that the thought was a happy one."

"And you know, don't you, that nothing will change between us, or between you and your father," Elizabeth responded firmly. "We will both continue to love you as much as we do now."

"We know," James assured her quietly and Elizabeth's smile was pleased.

They reached the music room and Darcy offered his wife his hand.

"Come, my love, you shall be the first to delight us."

"Any special requests, James?" she asked over her shoulder as Darcy led her to the pianoforte.

James smiled and asked that she play a particular favourite of his; Elizabeth was happy to oblige and as she sat down at the pianoforte James took the seat beside his sister, putting his arm around her shoulders when she leant into him. Despite her protestations, the lateness of the hour was obviously catching up with the young girl.

Darcy took a seat near them and Elizabeth began to play softly, the lilting melody floating over the three members of her audience. It was a rather lengthy piece, and by the time the final notes faded into silence Catherine eyes were closed and her breathing had deepened and lengthened as she fell asleep against her brother, who was also looking sleepy himself. Smiling tenderly, Darcy quietly got up and went to his wife.

They shared a smile at the picture the Catherine and James made together and then Darcy leant down and kissed the side of his wife's neck.

"You have made us so happy. Thank you."

Before Elizabeth could respond he had moved away, going to the couch and carefully scooping his daughter up into his arms. Catherine shifted in her sleep, resting her head against her father's shoulder and wrapping an arm around his neck.

"Come on princess, time for bed. You too, Son."

James got up from the couch but before following after his father he approached Elizabeth where she still sat at the pianoforte.

"Good night James," she said quietly; she smiled when he put his arms around her for the second time that evening and held him close for a long moment.

"Good night Elizabeth," James said quietly when he pulled away, as though he couldn't find the words for what he really wanted to say.

Elizabeth affectionately brushed some hair off his forehead.

"I shall see you in the morning. It is so good to have you home."

"It is good to be home," James responded warmly and with one final smile he was gone, following his father and sleeping sister from the room.

Elizabeth, left alone in the music room, let out a deep sigh. It had been an emotional evening- day, really, and she had a strange urge to cry. Telling herself that it would be silly to do so, Elizabeth turned back to the pianoforte and absently began to play whilst she waited for her husband to return.

After leaving Catherine in the capable hands of her maid and seeing her tucked into bed, Darcy went along to his son's room. He knocked before entering, and opened the door to find the room looking exactly as it always had and James sat in his favourite chair beside the fire. Darcy couldn't help smiling at the familiar and welcome sight.

"I have missed this chair," James admitted, running his hand along one of the arms. "This one is so comfortable, and I think it has moulded slightly to my shape."

"I am rather fond of the one in my chamber," Darcy admitted as he shut the door and approached his son. James stood up and, with just the two of them alone, embraced his father tightly.

"I have missed you so much, Papa," he admitted, his voice muffled against Darcy's coat.

"I have missed you too, Son," Darcy replied honestly, his voice rough. "I do not know how I shall be able to say goodbye to you again when term resumes."

"I hope it will be easier than last time," James admitted; then he smiled and added, "And you will have Elizabeth and Catherine and the baby to comfort you."

"They are not you," Darcy responded firmly, shaking his head. "There is a place in my heart for each of you, and when you are gone no one else can fill the emptiness that is left in your place."

Darcy saw tears appear in James' eyes a moment before he hid his face against his coat.

"Thank you," James murmured. "I think I needed to hear that."

"And I needed to say it," Darcy replied. "You must not think that we do not think of you, Son. There is not a day that goes by that we do not miss you - all of us. And the new baby will not change that."

James nodded and sniffed loudly; when he raised his head to his father his eyes were dry and his smile had returned.

"I am very happy for you and Elizabeth. And I would love another sibling."

"Another sister?" Darcy asked with a grin, "Or a little brother to get into mischief?"

"I do not know," James admitted with a lopsided grin. "I love Catherine, and I do enjoy being an elder brother to her, but I am sure that once I am older I shall worry about her constantly."

Darcy laughed heartily.

"That is my job, Son!"

"Did you not worry about Aunt Georgiana?" James countered knowingly and Darcy was forced to concede the point.

"You are a good boy," he said, ruffling his son's hair. "Though try not to worry too much just yet."

James nodded and after a moment smiled.

"A little brother would be rather fun, though. And he would help me to carry on our family name," he added thoughtfully and Darcy smiled with a mixture of pride and resignation. His son really was growing up too fast.

The clock on the mantelpiece chimed the hour.

"It is late, you should get to bed. I shall say goodnight now."

"Good night, Father," James said with a final, swift hug.

"Good night, James; I love you," Darcy said before releasing him.

"I love you too, Father," James replied shyly and then laughed when Darcy ruffled his hair again before finally taking his leave.

When Darcy reached the music room, he found Elizabeth playing a slow tune on the pianoforte; when she turned to him he saw that she had been crying.

"They are happy tears. Well...I do not know what they are, but they are not *un*happy tears."

"I know exactly what you mean," Darcy responded warmly and when he reached the pianoforte he drew his wife into his arms and just held her for a long, long time.

# Chapter 32

$P$attinson was just about to begin Darcy's morning shave when they both heard Elizabeth call.

"Will?!"

Removing the razor blade just in time to avoid catching Darcy's chin as he turned his head, Pattinson stepped back as Darcy responded.

"In here; what is it?"

Elizabeth burst into his dressing room, wearing only her flimsy nightdress, and Pattinson promptly turned around and faced the wall, busying himself with something or other.

"Come, quick, give me your hand," Elizabeth said excitedly, grasping Darcy's hand when he offered it and pressing it to her bump. "Can you feel that?"

"What?" Darcy asked blankly, not feeling anything. He cast aside the towel which Pattinson had placed around his neck and got to his feet, moving closer to his wife.

"The baby," Elizabeth explained. "He is moving so much; are you sure you cannot feel it? I was sure I could a moment ago," she said as she placed her hand beside his. "There!" She exclaimed when she felt a tiny amount of movement beneath her palm; she moved her husband's hand into place. "There, right there, can you feel it now?"

"Lizzy," Darcy sighed after a moment of complete stillness; he could feel nothing. "I think it is still too early...I felt it!" He exclaimed suddenly, making Elizabeth jump. "I...yes, just then."

Elizabeth smiled at her husband's enraptured expression as he waited to feel his baby move again. His eyes glistened with tears and she reached up and touched his cheek, chuckling when she got soap on her fingers.

"I have interrupted your morning rituals I see," she commented lightly, glancing over at Pattinson; she smiled to herself when she saw he was still resolutely facing in the opposite direction. "Your poor man obviously does not know where to look," she whispered to her husband, whose attention was finally distracted from his baby.

"Hmm?" Darcy responded, looking over at Pattinson. He frowned slightly and asked bemusedly, "Pattinson, what are you doing?"

"Nothing in particular, Sir," Pattinson replied evenly. He had turned to face Darcy upon being addressed by him, but kept his eyes firmly fixed on the floor. "Though I thought I might go and fetch some fresh water - this will have cooled rather much."

Darcy looked at his valet for a moment before turning back to his wife; it was only then that he realised that she was only wearing her nightdress, and that his poor valet was obviously somewhat flustered by seeing Elizabeth so scantily clad. Elizabeth smiled up at him with obvious amusement.

"As I said, I do not think poor Pattinson knows quite where to look," she whispered.

"Come," Darcy responded, taking her arm with the intention of taking her back to her room. He paused a moment to pick up the towel he had discarded, conscious of the soap that was still on his face.

"Fetch some fresh water, Pattinson; I will return shortly," he directed his relieved valet and then smiled down at his wife, who was grinning impishly. "And you, my little minx, come with me."

"Wilson is still in my room, you know," Elizabeth told him playfully as she allowed him to lead her back to her chambers. "And you are just as scantily clad as I," she pointed out, eyeing his bare chest.

"I have no doubt that Wilson is made of sterner stuff than Pattinson," Darcy replied with a grin as Elizabeth laughed.

"She would take that as a compliment, you know."

"Yes, I do know," Darcy quipped lightly. He had no opportunity to test his theory, however, as Wilson was nowhere to be seen when they entered Elizabeth's room.

"Here, let me," Elizabeth said as she took the towel from him and began to wipe away the soap. "You do look silly."

"Thank you, Madam," Darcy responded dryly; he waited until she had finished her self-appointed task before placing a hand over her bump. "Can you still feel her moving?"

"*He* seems to have quieted down now," Elizabeth replied with a smile and a pointed emphasis on the first word.

Darcy smiled but did not respond; they had only recently begun playfully arguing about whether the baby was a boy or a girl, though both knew that they would be delighted with either.

"I cannot feel anything," he softly said after a moment. When Elizabeth confirmed that she could not feel anything either he nodded but did not remove his hand.

"Will?" Elizabeth ventured softly, trying to catch his eye. He seemed very intent and thoughtful.

"I had never felt that before," Darcy admitted suddenly, his voice low and quiet. "The movement of my child before it has been born," he clarified. "Anne was not...it was not something I was permitted to experience with James or Catherine."

"Oh Will," Elizabeth soothed as Darcy tried to swallow past the lump in his throat, fighting down a wave of emotion.

"Thank you," he tried to say, his voice thick. Elizabeth cupped his face in her hands.

"There is no reason for you to thank me. We created this baby together and you have every right to share in this experience with me."

She reached up and pressed a kiss to his lips, only drawing away when she felt him respond.

"Truly, my love, half of the joy of this experience is knowing that I have you to share it with," she explained tenderly. "Surely my dashing into your dressing room barely clothed and scandalising poor Pattinson is proof enough of that!" She added teasingly and was relieved when Darcy chuckled.

He dipped his head and kissed her tenderly for several long moments before slowly drawing away.

"I still thank you," he murmured softly, touching two fingers to her lips when she was about to protest. "You are the most wonderful wife a man could ask for."

"If I am a wonderful wife," Elizabeth responded. "It is only because you are a wonderful husband."

Darcy was in no mood to argue the point and so contented himself with another long kiss, to which his wife responded as warmly as could be expected.

ೞೞೞ

More excitement was to come that afternoon, with a visit from the Fitzwilliam and Bingley families who all came to welcome James home from school. A fresh layer of snow had fallen the day before, and the slow moving carriages contrasted sharply against the brilliant white grounds as they followed the drive down to the house.

The Fitzwilliam family was the first to arrive, and James greeted his cousins and aunt and uncle with open enthusiasm. Lady Georgiana and the Colonel both exclaimed over how much he seemed to have grown in the last few months, the latter complaining good-naturedly that James was indeed taller than he was now.

"Not quite, Uncle," James replied with a smile, standing next to Richard. "See? Father, I am not taller yet, am I?"

Darcy bit back a smile and told a tiny white lie, to spare his cousin his pride.

"No, not quite yet Son."

"Did I say how very pleased I am to see you, James?" Richard joked and they all laughed lightly at his joke.

"James is certainly not the only one who has grown," Lady Georgiana commented with a smile at Elizabeth. "You are glowing," she complimented her sister-in-law.

"I feel very well," Elizabeth responded with a happy look, touching her bump briefly.

"Isn't it wonderful?" Catherine declared. "Mama is going to have a baby soon."

"It is very wonderful," Lady Georgiana agreed. "Are you excited about having a younger brother or sister?"

Catherine nodded and smiled and it was obvious to everyone that she was very happy at the thought of another sibling.

"And you, James?" Richard asked his nephew. "What do you think? Another sister, or a younger brother? Joseph has one of each, and I'm sure he has his favourite!"

"Richard!" Lady Georgiana laughingly scolded her husband. "What a thing to say!"

Bradley and Clara, meanwhile, were both pressing their older brother to admit that they were his favourite, and Joseph was laughing and protesting that he did not have a favourite.

"Yes, because your brother loves you both very much," Richard stated, in a bid to appease his wife and keep the peace. "As do your mother and I. We do not play favourites."

James shared a laughing look with his father who winked at him and then deftly moved the conversation along by introducing the subject of Christmas, and the family party he and Elizabeth would be hosting over the festive period.

"We have received replies to all of the letters we sent out. There will be seventeen of us in all, including us four," he added, referring to his immediate family.

"Seventeen?" His sister repeated.

"Mr and Mrs Bennet, you five, the Bingleys, Lady Matlock and Lady Wickham. It was Elizabeth's idea to invite her," Darcy explained with a smile at his wife. "George is away on the continent currently and Elizabeth suggested that our aunt would enjoy a visit here. In truth, I have been remiss in not inviting her before now; it really has been too long."

"It will be lovely to see her," Georgiana agreed with a smile. "When is everyone due to arrive?"

"My aunt and uncle plan to arrive on the 21$^{st}$," Elizabeth replied. "And Lady Wickham a day or two before."

"My mother will be with us from the 17$^{th}$," Richard put in with a resigned smile. "But we shall not impose upon your hospitality until the 22$^{nd}$."

"We look forward to all of our guests being with us over Christmas," Elizabeth replied diplomatically, and Richard chuckled at her well worded response.

Whilst their respective parents had been having their discussion, the children had been chatting happily amongst themselves. Catherine and Clara were sat together, the younger girl showing the elder her new doll which she had brought with her, whilst their brothers all discussed James' time away at school, Bradley and Joseph laughing at some of the stories their older cousin had to tell.

They all carried on in this way for another twenty minutes before they heard the sounds of another carriage and the Bingleys were subsequently announced. Everyone rose to welcome the new arrivals, Elizabeth and Darcy moving forward.

"Oh, you brought Henry with you - how lovely," Elizabeth enthused warmly when she saw Henry's nurse follow her sister and brother-in-law into the room. "How is my nephew?"

"He is very well," Sir Charles responded happily after shaking Darcy's hand. "Jane did not wish to leave him at home, so we thought we would bring him along to meet everyone."

"A fine idea," Darcy responded as Jane turned to the nurse and accepted her baby from her. "Please, sit here, Lady Bingley," he said to Jane, indicating the seat he had recently vacated.

"Hello Dan," Elizabeth greeted her other nephew affectionately, giving him a quick hug for good measure. She understood that the young boy might be feeling a little left out, what with all the attention everyone was paying to the new baby. "How are you? Have you been enjoying the snow? James and Catherine and I built an enormous snowman on Saturday; if we go out later, I will show him to you."

"Father took me skating on the pond yesterday," Daniel revealed with an excitable grin. "I am not very good at it yet, but Father said I will get better with practice."

"I was never very good at skating, either," Elizabeth confided and they shared a smile before Joseph and the other boys called Daniel's attention away from her.

"He is very small," Catherine noted as she studied the baby in Lady Jane's arms; she gently touched one of Henry's hands. "Look at his tiny fingers."

"Would you like to hold him?" Sir Charles offered; he smiled at Darcy and Elizabeth. "It will be good practice for when her brother or sister arrives."

"Could I?" Catherine asked uncertainly; she looked between her father and Elizabeth for their permission. "Am I allowed?"

"As long as Lady Bingley is happy for you to hold him," Darcy responded evenly. "And you promise to be very careful."

"Of course you can hold him, sweetheart," Jane consented kindly. "Come and sit next to me."

Catherine sat herself down beside Jane and under the careful direction of Jane and her father, she accepted baby Henry into her arms and sat holding him with a delighted smile. Henry did not seem to mind over much the change of position and soon fell back to sleep.

"Oh dear," Elizabeth noted with a light laugh as she was forced to wipe her eyes; she found the sight of her nephew and daughter together quite touching.

"Do not worry," Richard noted with a grin, nodding at his wife. "You are not the only one."

"They make a sweet picture together," Lady Georgiana defended herself with a rueful smile as she discreetly brushed away a sentimental tear. "May I hold him next?" she asked Jane, causing her husband to chuckle quietly.

"Of course," Jane granted with a smile.

The next hour passed by very agreeably. It was the first time in a long time that the group currently gathered together had been in company with one another, and they had all always gotten on very well in the past. Elizabeth and Darcy, if pressed, would have owned to some reluctance to invite Jane and Sir Charles but they had resolved to set aside their own feelings in favour of James'; he had always been close to the three members of the Bingley family, and was obviously happy to see them.

It seemed, however, that Elizabeth and Darcy needn't have worried, for the Bingleys appeared to be once more as they used to think of them - happy, good-natured and very agreeable company. Though a part of Elizabeth rather cynically suspected that Jane was on her best behaviour because of who else was present, she was still rather relieved. The fractious nature of her relationship with Jane over the past few months had been tiring, emotionally draining, and a source of unhappiness which she could wholly do without. It was, essentially, too much effort to be constantly at odds with her sister, and she was relieved that Jane seemed prepared to pretend as though nothing had happened, and to go back to the way things were. It was not the ideal solution, but it was undoubtedly the easiest, and it suited Elizabeth just fine; she had more important things to think about.

"Telling the snowball fight story again, James?" Elizabeth said teasingly at one point, having overheard some of the boys' conversation.

"Yes," James admitted with a grin.

"It sounds brilliant," Joseph enthused. "More fun than when it is just me and Bradley, certainly."

"Well there are a few more of you today," Elizabeth pointed out. "And there is certainly nothing stopping you from going outside now, as long as you wrap up warm."

"Could we really?" Daniel asked excitedly, as the three other boys all waited hopefully for the verdict of their respective parents.

"Of course," Richard granted easily. "In fact, I think I might join you. Darcy?"

"I am fine where I am, thank you," Darcy responded dryly and Richard clapped him on the shoulder.

"As you like, old man. Elizabeth, can I tempt you to join us?"

"You need not tempt me at all, Colonel," Elizabeth replied lightly. "I fully intend on joining you all. I cannot remember the last time I had a good snowball fight."

"Elizabeth," Darcy cautioned quietly; when his wife turned to look at him he said, "You shouldn't. I do not think it prudent, considering."

"No less prudent than you telling me what I can and cannot do, certainly," Elizabeth responded flippantly. She saw at once that her husband had not taken kindly to her response, and on reflection realised that she probably should not have spoken so in front of their current audience. "Though now that I think on it, I see that you are right. Heaven forbid if I should fall or somehow injure myself. I shall content myself to watching whilst the rest enjoy their game, as I still desire some fresh air."

Though she had not phrased it as such, her tone indicated that she was asking for her husband's approval of her plan and Elizabeth was relieved when Darcy nodded and lightly replied.

"Thank you. I hope you enjoy your walk. Please be careful," he added just because he couldn't help himself, and Elizabeth smiled affectionately at him, knowing that he meant well.

"Right, well, come along then," Richard declared loudly, the slightly awkward moment passing. "Sir Charles, are you joining us as well?"

When Sir Charles declined, Richard and Elizabeth shepherded the four boys out of the room and down to the front hall, where a number of footmen helped them all into the coats and scarves and other essential items of winter clothing.

"I see that you know how to handle my cousin's worrying," Richard commented to Elizabeth at one point, grinning as she blushed slightly. "Oh, do not concern yourself; a little bit of healthy disrespect does a man wonders, every now and then."

"You have learnt that from experience, I presume," Elizabeth responded dryly as she accepted Richard's arm and they descended the front steps together.

"You are good friends with my wife; what do you think?" Richard quipped and Elizabeth laughed lightly at his teasing.

"You need not stay with me," she told him after a moment, when the boys had run on ahead and were already throwing snowballs at each other. "I shall follow the path for a little while; go and join the boys."

"If you are certain." Richard hesitated.

"Yes," Elizabeth gave him a little push. "Go on. You have my word I will be careful," she added when he looked uncertain.

"Very well," he relented finally and jogged over to join the boys, who all promptly hit him with a barrage of snowballs.

Chuckling slightly to herself, Elizabeth wandered along the path before stopping and seating herself upon a bench which one of the ground staff had thoughtfully cleared of snow. It was still a beautiful, clear day and the sun was surprisingly warm on her face as she sat and watched Richard and the boys playing.

James, who had been running away from Joseph in a bid to avoid being hit, suddenly lost his footing and fell to the ground, covering himself in snow. Joseph showed no mercy and threw a snowball down at him before running off, leaving James to brush himself down and get to his feet. Elizabeth, seeing all this, noticed how long it took James to get up and that he did not seem to be moving as freely as he had been before his fall.

"James?" she called out to him; he turned in her direction. "Did you hurt yourself?"

"No, I'm fine," he called back, smiling and shaking his head. "Argh!"

The snowball hit James squarely on the back of the head and Bradley dashed away, laughing merrily as James shook his head to try to clear away the snow in his hair. Elizabeth covered her mouth with her gloved hand to try and disguise her laughter.

"I'm sorry!" She called ruefully to James.

"It's alright," he assured her with a smile and dashed off after his younger cousin, calling, "I am going to get you for that one, Bradley!"

ഈരു

"Oh Elizabeth, look at you! You are utterly gorgeous."

Elizabeth laughed and blushed slightly at this effusive compliment.

"I knew there was a reason I liked you so much, Claire. You shower me with flattery."

"It is not flattery at all," Claire Hadlee replied with a smile. "As I am certain your husband will agree."

"Wholeheartedly," Darcy replied with a warm smile before extending his welcome to both Claire and her husband John. "Merry Christmas."

"How are you feeling?" Claire asked Elizabeth keenly. "You really do look very well; do you feel it?"

"Yes," Elizabeth replied lightly. "I am in perfect health. I am perhaps a little tired, but I daresay that is to be expected considering we are hosting quite a large family party."

"And this party tonight, as well," Claire pointed out. "You are very good; I'm not sure I could have managed it."

Elizabeth smiled but did not reply. In truth, she had had to convince her husband to host this gathering of their friends and neighbours, but Elizabeth had been determined to make the festive season special. Not only because it was her first with her new family, but because she had never had the chance to do so in the past. Her father had never been inclined to socialise, and she had spent the last few Christmases alone with him at Longbourn. This year she had promised herself that she would spend the season surrounded by her friends and loved ones.

After a few more minutes of conversation, the Hadlees moved away to speak with some of the other guests, leaving Elizabeth and Darcy alone for the moment.

"Just the Andrews' now," Darcy remarked, noting the guests who had already arrived and were chatting amiably with one another. "They have had the furthest to come, so it is of no surprise that they are a little late."

"The snow is certainly beautiful," Elizabeth commented with a glance out of the window at the softly falling snow. "But it is something of a bother."

"I am amazed to hear you admit that," Darcy teased. "I thought you loved the snow."

"Oh, I still do," Elizabeth replied lightly. "But I can appreciate the problems it causes as well. Your letter would have arrived several days earlier, for instance, had it not been for that last heavy snowfall," she pointed out with a smile.

"Yes, though what are a few days after months of waiting?" Darcy responded dryly and Elizabeth chuckled lightly at his quip.

Darcy had finally received the long awaited letter from his friend Ellerslie, announcing his safe arrival in Antigua. He had been delighted to hear from his friend, and the news coming just days before Christmas had leant it additional poignancy. He was a little sad to think of his friend so far from home at such a time and knew that Ellerslie would often be in his thoughts over the coming days. The tone of the letter had been happy and optimistic, though, and Darcy prayed for the best for his friend.

"Your aunt seems to be more settled now," Elizabeth commented quietly, drawing Darcy from his thoughts.

"I think it was hard for her at first," Darcy replied just as quietly, glancing over at Lady Wickham. "It has been almost ten years since her last visit, and I think this house must hold many memories for her."

Elizabeth nodded and then smiled as she whispered in his ear.

"George looks so like her! I thought so the moment she arrived, but the more I look upon her the more I see him. I suppose I should not be surprised; you and he also look alike. You all share the Darcy characteristics."

"As my cousin is renowned for setting ladies hearts aflutter, and my aunt was regarded as a great beauty in her day, I believe I shall take that as a compliment," Darcy teased with a playful grin.

Elizabeth laughed lightly.

"Do I not pay you enough? Do not worry, my love, I think you quite the most handsome man of my acquaintance."

"Now I shall definitely take *that* as a compliment," Darcy replied with a smile and pressed a kiss to the back of his wife's gloved hand.

"Darcy, stop monopolising your wife's company," Sir Charles joked at that exact moment, appearing at Darcy's side. "We have had a slight disagreement, and require her help in settling it." He offered his arm to his sister-in-law. "Lizzy?"

"I would be a poor hostess if I did not see to the needs of my guests," Elizabeth stated lightly, accepting Sir Charles arm. "Tell me how I may be of assistance."

Darcy watched with a smile as his friend led his wife away before deciding to speak with his two aunts, who were sat together on one of the settees. They both looked up upon his approach, one with a soft smile and the other with an expectant look.

"Do you wish to speak with us, Fitzwilliam?" Lady Matlock asked, still insisting on using that name.

"I simply thought it would be nice for us to talk awhile. I was just saying to Elizabeth how very long it has been since your last visit here - both of you. Far too long, indeed; the responsibility for which most certainly lies at my door."

"You have had a family to care for, and more recently a wife as well," Lady Wickham replied kindly, smiling over at Elizabeth. "I must say again how lovely I think her, Nephew."

"Thank you, Aunt," Darcy responded quietly. He was somewhat surprised when Lady Matlock nodded her agreement.

"She certainly seems to be a worthy mistress of Pemberley; I do not remember the house looking so well since your mother was still living."

"Thank you, Aunt, it is kind of you to say so," Darcy replied again and Lady Matlock nodded her head but beyond that did not acknowledge that she had just paid Elizabeth a compliment.

"Did you hear, Lizzy, that your friend Charlotte Lucas is engaged to be married?"

"Yes, I did hear," Elizabeth responded to her aunt's query with an indulgent smile; Mrs Bennet was as fond as ever of a good piece of news. "Charlotte wrote to me two weeks ago. She seems very happy."

"Yes, I'm sure she does!" Mrs Bennet replied with a light laugh. "She is a very lucky girl; her future husband is quite a catch for her."

"I think she is happy because she is in love with him, and he with her," Elizabeth responded amusedly. "But it certainly helps that he will be able to keep a roof over their heads."

"More than that, certainly!" Mrs Bennet replied and proceeded to enlighten her niece about the wealth and prospects of her friend's betrothed.

"Well I am very happy for Charlotte," Elizabeth interrupted after a few minutes of listening patiently. "And she has promised not to marry until I can attend the ceremony, which makes me even happier!"

"Does Lady Lucas know you will be there?" Mrs Bennet asked keenly. "I must tell her if she does not; imagine, a Duke and Duchess at the wedding of such a plain looking girl."

"Aunt," Elizabeth said, laughing helplessly. "You are utterly without equal."

"Oh, thank you dear," Mrs Bennet replied with a pleased look; then she frowned suspiciously at her niece, "Unless of course you did not mean it as a compliment."

"A compliment, most assuredly," Elizabeth responded with a wide smile, managing to control her mirth.

"I never know with you, you know," Mrs Bennet admitted.

"I know," Elizabeth replied, patting her arm affectionately.

"Oh, looks like the Andrews' have arrived," Sir Benedict Hadlock announced from his position beside the window. "Seems like they're in one piece."

"Please excuse our tardiness," Lord Andrews said once he and his wife and son had been announced and Elizabeth and Darcy had welcomed them. "The snow had drifted onto one of the roads on the other side of Little Pembroke, and our coachmen had to clear the way."

"They had help, it seems," Elizabeth noted with a smile as she looked pointedly at Lord and Lady Andrews' son's boots, which were still wet.

Mr Julian Andrews was a young man of perhaps seven or eight and twenty, tall, with his mother's hair and his father's eyes and their combined good looks. He was a very handsome man, rendered even more so by his smile as he replied.

"I hopped out and did my bit; we would have been terribly late otherwise, rather than just very."

"Well you are forgiven," Darcy assured the trio genially. "Now come and warm yourself by the fire, you must be chilled after spending so long in your carriage."

"I shall be happy to have the chance to dry off these boots," Mr Andrews joked before following his parents towards the fireplace.

"What are you thinking?" Darcy asked his wife as he saw her studying Mr Andrews rather intently.

"Only that I wish Victoria were here," Elizabeth replied with a playful look in her eyes. "I wonder what they would have made of each other."

Darcy chuckled lightly.

"I noticed earlier that there is no mistletoe hanging anywhere; would it have made an appearance if there were more unmarried persons present?"

"Oh, undoubtedly," Elizabeth replied with a smile. "There is little point to it otherwise, with so many married couples here."

"I would not say that," Darcy responded quietly, and close to her ear.

"I do not think you would have manoeuvred me under it," Elizabeth countered. "Not with all these people here."

"Is that a challenge?" Darcy asked, one brow arched.

"Certainly not," Elizabeth denied primly but Darcy was not fooled.

"Well, as there is no mistletoe, I suppose we will never know," he responded and smiled knowingly when Elizabeth replied with a blushing smile.

"I will make sure to put some up next year."

"Come," Darcy said after a moment, reluctantly drawing himself away from his wife. "We are neglecting our guests a little. We should circulate."

"As you like," Elizabeth responded easily, adding, "I shall circulate in this direction."

And she strolled away without another word, falling into conversation with Lady Georgiana, Lady Hadlock and her sister. Darcy watched her go for a moment before wandering over to his cousin and Hadlee.

"Cheer up, Darcy," Richard chided him playfully. "Anyone would think you did not want us here!"

"Heaven forbid that I should prefer the company of my wife to yours, Richard," Darcy responded dryly and both Hadlee and Richard laughed.

"It is something of a relief to know you haven't entirely changed, Darcy," Richard noted, clapping him on the back. "Now come, tell us more about this new filly of yours. Hadlee and I were just envying you your good fortune."

Darcy smiled and was happy to satisfy their interest.

Whilst her husband was discussing horses, Elizabeth was discussing babies; or more particularly her baby, which Lady Hadlock and Lady Georgiana were particularly interested in hearing about. Even Jane seemed genuinely interested in what Elizabeth had to say, and Elizabeth was pleased that the peace between them was holding.

"And have you thought any more about names?" Lady Georgiana asked. "I know you have decided on Madeline for a girl, but have you decided on a boy's name yet?"

Elizabeth glanced uncertainly at her sister to see how she took this news - she had not discussed using their mother's name with Jane - but Jane's face remained calm and impassive.

"We have been thinking about Robin, if it is a boy," she replied when Jane did not respond. "And Matthew, for William's friend. Robin Matthew."

"Robin Matthew Darcy. Lord Robin Matthew Darcy - what a fine sounding name," Lady Hadlock pronounced with a smile.

"It does have a nice ring to it," Lady Georgiana agreed. "And William and the Duke of Bellamy have always been very close. Why Robin, though?"

"I was re-reading A Midsummer Night's Dream," Elizabeth admitted with a smile. "And the name appealed to me. It also seemed fitting, as the baby is due in the spring."

"Let us hope he does not live to be as mischievous as his namesake," Lady Hadlock teased and Elizabeth rubbed her rounded tummy affectionately.

"He has behaved perfectly so far. My maid, Wilson, tells me tales of when my mother was carrying me; apparently I allowed her not a moment of peace!"

"I remember that time," Jane admitted with a soft smile, surprising Elizabeth and the other two ladies. "Mother would let me feel when you were kicking - you were very strong."

"How are your daughter and her son, Lady Hadlock? He must be almost a year old by now, surely?"

"Not quite; he is close to nine months," Lady Hadlock replied and her three companions happily listened to the latest news from Ireland.

They all enjoyed a lovely evening in good company, warmed by the fire, the fine wine and the lively conversations but eventually, worried about the worsening weather, Elizabeth and Darcy's guests all began to reluctantly take their leave.

"You realise, of course, that we will all be thinking about this now for days," Mr Andrews commented laughingly as he and his parents said their farewells to their hosts for the evening; they had been playing a word game and no one had yet guessed the answer to Darcy's puzzle.

"Well you have until Boxing Day to think about it," Elizabeth teased, referring to the hunt planned for that day which her husband and James were due to attend.

"Thank you for a delightful evening," Lady Andrews said warmly. "I hope you have a lovely Christmas with your family."

"I hope you enjoy your Christmas too," Elizabeth replied. "It was lovely seeing you both again, and meeting your son finally. It has been a pleasure, Mr Andrews."

"The pleasure was all mine, Your Grace, I assure you," Mr Andrews replied charmingly, bowing slightly. His parents smiled at him and then said one final farewell before going on their way.

"We had best be going as well," John Hadlee said regretfully as he and Claire approached Darcy and Elizabeth, "before the snow becomes much thicker. We have had a lovely evening."

"It was lovely to see you both," Darcy commented as he and John shook hands. "Thank you for coming; give our love to your daughter tomorrow."

"We will," Claire assured him. "And please do the same with your children. We shall have to arrange something for them all soon."

"Perhaps before the New Year," Elizabeth suggested, "before the other children leave. They certainly seem to be enjoying spending time all together."

The Hadlees both smiled and promised to write in a few days' time when their plans were more fixed.

Eventually all of their guests took their leave, leaving Darcy and Elizabeth alone with their family. They all sat together conversing quietly with one another for a little while longer before Elizabeth eventually admitted that it was time for her to retire.

"Forgive me, I am being a poor hostess," she said as she slowly got to her feet, feeling very tired all of a sudden. Her husband was by her side in a moment, holding her arm in a gentle grip. "Thank you."

"Oh, Elizabeth, do not worry about us. Of course you should go up to bed, you have been on your feet all day," Lady Georgiana said kindly. "I own I am amazed you have lasted so long, it really is getting very late."

"I daresay I shall regret it in the morning," Elizabeth admitted with a rueful smile. She said goodnight to them all and left her husband to look after their relations.

"Poor dear," Lady Wickham said when the door had closed behind Elizabeth. "I hope she has not overtaxed herself."

"I am sure she will be fine after a good night's sleep," Darcy stated confidently; he had ceased to be amazed by his wife's sheer amount of energy, even whilst carrying their child.

"I think I shall go up as well," Lady Jane said quietly, and her husband rose to accompany her. Their departure seemed to decide the others as well, and soon Darcy found himself alone with just Mr Bennet for company.

"Do not stay on my account, Your Grace," the elder man said. "I am quite happy to finish my wine alone; in fact, if you would not mind overmuch I think I may enjoy another glass in the library. I have a book I would like to finish."

"Only if you are sure," Darcy replied, thinking he really would much rather join his wife than keep her uncle company, however much his opinion of Mr Bennet had improved in light of his assistance with Elizabeth's father.

"Yes, yes, quite sure. I shall see you in the morning."

"Good night, then," Darcy said; he smiled slightly and added, "I believe that may be the last of that particular vintage."

Mr Bennet chuckled.

"Then I had best savour it."

Darcy gave a slight bow and left the elder man to his amusements. Quietly entering the rooms he shared with his wife, he paused when he saw her sleeping soundly already. Going through to his room, he found Pattinson still up and quickly changed out of his evening clothes and donned a dressing gown.

"I shall ring for you in the morning, Pattinson," he said to his man as Pattinson gathered up Darcy's shirt and cravat for washing. Pattinson nodded and wished his master a good night before disappearing through the door to the servant's staircase.

Trying to be as quiet as possible, Darcy re-entered Elizabeth's room and slipped off his dressing gown before sliding into bed beside his wife. She stirred in her sleep and rolled towards him, tucking herself into her usual place with her head resting on his shoulder and one of her legs thrown over his. In this position her rounded tummy also rested against him and Darcy placed his hand over the swell of his child, feeling a few soft movements underneath his palm. He pressed a light kiss to his wife's forehead, smiling when she murmured something in her sleep before finally closing his eyes and drifting off to sleep as well.

ଚଠଓଃ

"James, James, wake up!"

"Alright! Alright! I'm up!" James protested laughingly as his sister bounced onto his bed and practically shook him awake.

"Come on," Catherine hurried him, tugging on his arm. "You need to get up and come with me."

"Come where?" James asked as he tumbled out of bed. He pulled on his dressing gown and almost tripping when he trod on the long tie.

"To Mama and Papa's room," Catherine explained excitedly.

"Catherine," James began to protest, certain that they were not allowed to burst in upon their father and Elizabeth so early, even if it was Christmas morning.

"It is alright James, I asked Papa yesterday if we could and he said yes. Come on, they will be waiting for us."

"Are you sure?" James asked as he followed after his sister as she hurried from his room.

"Yes!" Catherine responded with a laugh and James stopped arguing; he did insist, however, on knocking on the door before they entered when they reached Elizabeth's room.

"Come in," Darcy called out with a smile in his voice. He and Elizabeth were sat side by side on the bed in their dressing gowns. "Merry Christmas!"

"Merry Christmas!" Catherine responded happily as she rushed and jumped up onto the bed, hugging and kissing Elizabeth and then her father.

"Merry Christmas, Son," Darcy said as James came to join them. "Just woken up?" he asked with a grin, eyeing James' hair which was standing up in all directions.

"Yes," James replied with a rueful grin, trying to flatten his hair.

"I think it is a lost cause, James," Elizabeth teased and James took her advice and gave up.

"Well, shall we open some presents?" Darcy suggested lightly.

"Oh, presents!" Catherine exclaimed, jumping off the bed in a flurry of pink and white nightdress. "I will be back in a minute!"

Darcy, James and Elizabeth all watched her go with matching smiles.

"She enjoys Christmas, I see."

"That is an understatement," James replied dryly.

Catherine soon returned, her arms laden with a number of prettily wrapped packages.

"What's all this?" Darcy asked as she deposited them on the bed and climbed up by his knees.

"They are for you," Catherine said, handing two each to Elizabeth and Darcy. "From me and James."

"How lovely; I wasn't expecting this at all. Thank you," Elizabeth said and Darcy expressed his surprise and thanks as well.

"These are for you," Elizabeth said as she gave two presents to Catherine. "And this is for you James."

"These are just little things," Darcy explained. "Your real presents will have to wait until later."

"Can we open them now?" Catherine asked.

"Of course you can. I certainly want to know what I have here."

When he opened his presents, Darcy discovered the set of handkerchiefs Catherine had promised him and a new book about Shakespeare's characters; Elizabeth found a new novel and a pretty pair of slippers.

"Thank you, these are lovely," she said to Catherine and James, admiring the slippers.

"Thank you for this," James responded, indicating the novel Elizabeth and Darcy had gifted him with.

"Do you like your present, princess?" Darcy asked his daughter; they had purchased her some more outfits for her dolls, and another assortment of ribbons.

"I do, thank you," Catherine replied, selecting one of the ribbons. "I shall wear this one today; it will go very well with my dress, don't you think Mama?"

"Yes, I think it will be lovely," Elizabeth agreed with a smile. She turned to her husband and proposed, "Shall we move on to the real presents now?"

"James' at least," Darcy replied. "Catherine's will have to wait until we are all dressed."

"Can I show James his present, please Papa?" Catherine asked excitedly as James looked with a curious smile between the three of them.

"We will show him together," Darcy stated, getting up from the bed and moving around to the other side to help Elizabeth to her feet.

"Won't we be seen?" James asked, looking at them all in their dressing gowns.

548

"I doubt anyone else will be up yet," Elizabeth assured him easily. "And if they are - well, we are all family."

"Come on James," Catherine said impatiently, taking his hand. "We have a surprise for you."

"You have been a good girl to keep it a secret for so long, princess," Darcy complimented his daughter as he and Elizabeth followed behind the two children.

"We're here," Catherine announced suddenly, surprising her brother.

"Where?" he asked blankly; they were stood along the same corridor which housed their father's and Elizabeth's rooms and a number of the larger family rooms.

"Open the door and see," Darcy directed with a smile, nodding to the door on the left.

Realising that his present (whatever it was) was probably hidden inside the room, James unsuspectingly opened the door and was somewhat surprised to find it empty, save for the usual furnishings one found in a bedchamber. He looked between Elizabeth, Catherine and his father with a puzzled frown.

"How do you like your new room, Son?" Darcy asked quietly and James' expression quickly morphed to one of surprise.

"My room?" he repeated, turning to look again. It was only then he noticed that the room was newly decorated. "But...I have my own room already."

"Which you are a little too big for now," Elizabeth pointed out fondly. "This shall be your room now, if it pleases you."

"Of course we will have your things brought over from your other room," Darcy added. "And your desk and bookcase, if you like. It is entirely up to you."

"I...I do not know what to say," James admitted and he slowly walked around the room; he went to the window and smiled at the glorious view. "Thank you."

"You are welcome, Son," Darcy replied fondly. "Merry Christmas."

"Merry Christmas," James replied and went to hug first his father, then Elizabeth and then Catherine.

"Well, we shall leave you to explore your new room," Darcy said a moment later. "I'll have some of your things brought over so you can get dressed. You run along and get dressed as well, princess," he said to Catherine, "and we shall all meet by the front door in shall we say, half an hour?"

"Yes Papa!" Catherine agreed as she turned and disappeared down the hallway, excited no doubt because she knew her turn was next.

Elizabeth and Darcy followed after her at a more sedate pace, leaving James to his own devises in his new room. It was so much larger than his old room, but he liked the colour and the furnishings were all handsome and suited his tastes. He wondered whether his father or Elizabeth had had a greater hand in arranging the decorating, and concluded with a smile that it was probably the latter.

Going to the window, James smiled again as he admired the view over the grounds. His eyes were drawn to a point in the distance where he knew Elizabeth's surprise was awaiting her, and he was pleased at the thought that the present he had helped devise for her was as thoughtful as the one she had helped devise for him.

ಬಂಣ

Half an hour later, all four members of the Darcy family were gathered in the front hall; three of them knew what was to come, whilst one was almost bursting with excitement. When some footmen appeared with their outdoor things, Catherine turned to her father.

"Are we doing Elizabeth's present first? I thought that…"

James tried to shush his sister, but it was too late; Elizabeth's eyes widened and she turned to her husband with a slightly accusing look.

"I thought we said we were only doing presents for the children?"

"We did, but can I help it if they decided that they wanted to give you a present?" Darcy replied, fibbing somewhat. He smiled sheepishly when Elizabeth arched her brow at him. "Merry Christmas?"

"I haven't got you anything," Elizabeth replied quietly; she felt bad for not realising that of course her husband would buy her a present.

"I don't need anything," Darcy assured her with a smile. He drew closer and tenderly added, "Knowing I have made you happy is a priceless gift."

Elizabeth smiled reluctantly and relented; she smiled between the two anxiously waiting children.

550

"I see I shall never be able to trust your papa's word when presents are involved."

James and Catherine both laughed and they all donned their coats and scarves.

"We are going outside to show Elizabeth her present," Darcy said when they were ready. "But we are also going outside to find yours, princess."

"Are we?" Catherine replied, her eyes wide. "But what is it?"

"Come with me and see for yourself," James responded, offering his hand.

He led his sister around the side of the house to the stables; just in front of the stables, on a wide open portion of the driveway, Greg Foster stood beside a small chestnut pony.

"Is that for me?!" Catherine squeaked excitedly as soon as she saw the pony.

"Yes," Darcy responded with a chuckle at her reaction. "You are a little too big for Margot now."

"Oh Papa, he is beautiful," Catherine said as she approached the pony and ran her gloved hand over its neck. "What is he called? Is he a boy or a girl?"

"He is a he," Darcy replied with a smile. "And his name is Merion. He is three years old."

"How many hands is he, Father?" James asked as Catherine eagerly accepted some fruit from Greg and fed it to her pony.

"Thirteen; and he will not grow much more," Darcy noted. "The perfect size for young ladies such as this one," he added, bending and kissing his daughter's cheek. "Would you like to ride him?"

"Can I? Is there time?" Catherine asked.

"Of course," Darcy averred and whilst Greg held Merion still he picked Catherine up and deposited her safely in the saddle. "There, how does that feel?"

"He is bigger than Margot," Catherine noted, looking down a little anxiously.

"Here, I will lead you round a bit," Darcy said, accepting the reins from Greg.

Elizabeth, James and Greg all stood to one side as Darcy took Merion in a wide circle.

"Merry Christmas, Ma'am," Greg said quietly at one point, his cheeks ruddy with the cold.

"Merry Christmas to you too, Foster," Elizabeth replied warmly, smiling happily. "And to your wife as well. We shall not keep you much longer so that you may go home to her."

"I was happy to come up," Greg admitted, nodding in Catherine's direction. "He's a sweet pony, and I've been looking forward to seeing how the young lady likes him."

"Very much, I think," James noted and Elizabeth and Greg both voiced their agreement.

Eventually Darcy led Merion back towards the trio and it was obvious from Catherine's bright smile that she already adored her new pony. She held her arms out for Darcy to help her down from the saddle, and surprised him by holding on for a tight hug.

"Thank you so much, Papa; I promise I will ride him every day and take very good care of him."

"You're welcome, princess," Darcy said, kissing her cheek before setting her down. Catherine then thanked Elizabeth for her present before thanking Greg as well for looking after Merion for her.

"It is my pleasure, Milady," Greg responded with a slight bow before turning expectantly to Darcy.

"Yes, the carriage now please Foster," Darcy said and Greg nodded his head and began to lead Merion back to the stables.

"Are we going somewhere?" Elizabeth asked with an amused smile; she was already wondering what her present was.

"Yes, though fortunately not far," Darcy replied. "That wind is rather bitter. Are you warm enough, all of you?"

Elizabeth and James assured him that they were fine, but Catherine admitted that she was a little cold. James promptly put his arm around her and pulled her to his side, rubbing her arm with his gloved hand.

"Better?"

"Much."

Elizabeth and Darcy shared a smile before being distracted by the sights and sounds of the carriage.

"After you, love," Darcy said, opening the door and offering his wife his hand to help her up. Catherine and James climbed in after her and Darcy hopped up and shut the door with a smart snap. "You know the place, John," he called to the coachman and the carriage slowly began to pull away.

"You really are far too good at this," Elizabeth noted after a moment, smiling at her husband.

"At what?"

"Arranging surprises," Elizabeth stated and Darcy chuckled.

"I can certainly think of worse talents."

"Oh, certainly," Elizabeth agreed, smiling. She turned to the children. "Was he always like this?"

"Yes," they chorused, nodding and grinning at their now blushing father.

Fortunately, he was saved from further comment by John the coachman.

"We are here, Sir."

"That was quick," Elizabeth noted with surprise. "Where have you taken me, Will?"

Darcy climbed out of the carriage and turned to offer his wife his hand.

"To quote James; come with me and see for yourself."

Rolling her eyes, Elizabeth gave him her hand and carefully stepped down from the carriage. She saw at once that they were up on the hillside which looked down over the lake and back towards the house.

"Over here," Darcy said, drawing her attention away from the view. Elizabeth followed him a few steps and then stopped when she saw a number of posts and planks marking out a shape on the ground.

"What is this?" she asked curiously, looking at her husband and then at the children.

"This is going to be a lookout," Darcy explained, turning her back to face the view once more. "We have heard you say more than once that this is your favourite spot on the estate, and that you would like one day to sit here and commit the view to canvas. And we thought that we would mark the spot for you, and have a lookout built so that you can come up here and sit in comfort whilst you work."

"And when the weather is nice we can come here and have tea," Catherine added.

"Or you can ride up here on Dot, when you are allowed to ride again," James pointed out.

"My love?" Darcy asked tenderly, seeing that his wife looked about to cry.

"Mmmhmm," Elizabeth managed; she sniffed and blinked, a few tears escaping. "I don't know what to say, this is lovely. It is such a lovely thought."

"We thought you would like it," Darcy replied fondly as the children both looked on with matching smiles; they were used to Elizabeth becoming weepy now.

"It is too much, though," Elizabeth pointed out, wiping her eyes. "You mustn't keep spoiling me this way."

"I do not see why not," Darcy replied calmly. "What are bricks and mortar compared to all you have given us?"

"I have given you no more than you have given me," Elizabeth argued. "And there are three of you and only one of me."

"Precisely," Darcy replied. "And so you require three times the thanks."

"William," Elizabeth tried to argue, smiling in spite of herself. "That was not what I meant at all."

"I know," Darcy admitted quietly, looking at her with soft eyes.

Elizabeth sighed, smiling resignedly. She turned to the children and held her hands out to them; Catherine and James came to her and she kissed them both on the cheek.

"I love you both, very much. Thank you for my gift, and for making me so happy."

"You're welcome, Mama," Catherine responded artlessly whilst James nodded slightly, understanding much more than his younger sister could.

"And I love you," Elizabeth said as she turned to her husband, taking his face between her gloved hands. "My good, loving and kind husband; my fine man. You can build me a lookout if you want, but I shall always know how much you love me because you show me each and every day."

"Not enough," Darcy countered, holding her close. "Not nearly enough, for what I feel."

Elizabeth smiled again and leant up on her tiptoes to press a quick and playful kiss to her husband's lips.

"Then build me a lookout if you must, you silly man."

Darcy was still chuckling when Elizabeth drew away and beckoned to the two children to walk her through the plans for her lookout, and after sending up a quick prayer of thanks to whoever had seen fit to grant him so many blessings, Darcy happily went to join them.

৪০০জ

Made in the USA
Lexington, KY
14 November 2013